BECCA FITZPATRICK
HUSH, HUSH
PARTS I&II

SIMON & SCHUSTER

First published as an omnibus edition entitled Hush, Hush Parts I and II
by Simon and Schuster UK Ltd, A CBS COMPANY in Great Britain in 2014

Hush, Hush first published in the USA in 2009 by Simon & Schuster BFYR,
an imprint of Simon & Schuster Children's Publishing Division.
First published in Great Britain in 2009 by Simon and Schuster UK Ltd
A CBS COMPANY

Crescendo first published in the USA in 2010 by Simon & Schuster BFYR,
an imprint of Simon & Schuster Children's Publishing Division.
First published in Great Britain in 2010 by Simon and Schuster UK Ltd
A CBS COMPANY

www.beccafitzpatrick.com

1 3 5 7 9 10 8 6 4 2

Simon & Schuster UK Ltd
1st Floor, 222 Gray's Inn Road
London WC1X 8HB

Simon & Schuster Australia, Sydney
Simon & Schuster India, New Delhi

A CIP catalogue record for this book is available from the British Library.

PB ISBN: 978-1-47112-346-7
EB ISBN: 978-1-47112-438-9

Printed and bound by CPI Group (UK) Ltd, Croydon, CR0 4YY

www.simonandschuster.co.uk
www.simonandschuster.com.au

I
HUSH, HUSH

For Heather, Christian, and Michael.
Our childhood was nothing if not imaginative.
And to Justin. Thanks for not choosing
the Japanese cooking class—love you.

... GOD SPARED NOT THE ANGELS
THAT SINNED,
BUT CAST THEM DOWN TO HELL,
AND DELIVERED THEM INTO CHAINS
OF DARKNESS,
TO BE RESERVED UNTO JUDGMENT .
. .

—2 PETER 2:4

PROLOGUE

LOIRE VALLEY, FRANCE
NOVEMBER 1565

HAUNCEY WAS WITH A FARMER'S DAUGHTER ON the grassy banks of the Loire River when the storm rolled in, and having let his gelding wander in the meadow, was left to his own two feet to carry him back to the château. He tore a silver buckle off his shoe, placed it in the girl's palm, and watched her scurry away, mud slinging on her skirts. Then he tugged on his boots and started for home.

Rain sheeted down on the darkening countryside surrounding

the Château de Langeais. Chauncey stepped easily over the sunken graves and humus of the cemetery; even in the thickest fog he could find his way home from here and not fear getting lost. There was no fog tonight, but the darkness and onslaught of rain were deceiving enough.

There was movement along the fringe of Chauncey's vision, and he snapped his head to the left. At first glance what appeared to be a large angel topping a nearby monument rose to full height. Neither stone nor marble, the boy had arms and legs. His torso was naked, his feet were bare, and peasant trousers hung low on his waist. He hopped down from the monument, the ends of his black hair dripping rain. It slid down his face, which was dark as a Spaniard's.

Chauncey's hand crept to the hilt of his sword. "Who goes there?"

The boy's mouth hinted at a smile.

"Do not play games with the Duc de Langeais," Chauncey warned. "I asked for your name. Give it."

"Duc?" The boy leaned against a twisted willow tree. "Or bastard?"

Chauncey unsheathed his sword. "Take it back! My father was the Duc de Langeais. I'm the Duc de Langeais now," he added clumsily, and cursed himself for it.

The boy gave a lazy shake of his head. "Your father wasn't the old Duc."

Chauncey seethed at the outrageous insult. "And your father?"

he demanded, extending the sword. He didn't yet know all his vassals, but he was learning. He would brand the family name of this boy to memory. "I'll ask once more," he said in a low voice, wiping a hand down his face to clear away the rain. "Who are you?"

The boy walked up and pushed the blade aside. He suddenly looked older than Chauncey had presumed, maybe even a year or two older than Chauncey. "One of the Devil's brood," he answered.

Chauncey felt a clench of fear in his stomach. "You're a raving lunatic," he said through his teeth. "Get out of my way."

The ground beneath Chauncey tilted. Bursts of gold and red popped behind his eyes. Hunched with his fingernails grinding into his thighs, he looked up at the boy, blinking and gasping, trying to make sense of what was happening. His mind reeled like it was no longer his to command.

The boy crouched to level their eyes. "Listen carefully. I need something from you. I won't leave until I have it. Do you understand?"

Gritting his teeth, Chauncey shook his head to express his disbelief—his defiance. He tried to spit at the boy, but it trickled down his chin, his tongue refusing to obey him.

The boy clasped his hands around Chauncey's; their heat scorched him and he cried out.

"I need your oath of fealty," the boy said. "Bend on one knee and swear it."

Chauncey commanded his throat to laugh harshly, but his

throat constricted and he choked on the sound. His right knee buckled as if kicked from behind, though no one was there, and he stumbled forward into the mud. He bent sideways and retched.

"Swear it," the boy repeated.

Heat flushed Chauncey's neck; it took all his energy to curl his hands into two weak fists. He laughed at himself, but there was no humor. He had no idea how, but the boy was inflicting the nausea and weakness inside him. It would not lift until he took the oath. He would say what he had to, but he swore in his heart he would destroy the boy for this humiliation.

"Lord, I become your man," Chauncey said venomously.

The boy raised Chauncey to his feet. "Meet me here at the start of the Hebrew month of Cheshvan. During the two weeks between new and full moons, I'll need your service."

"A . . . fortnight?" Chauncey's whole frame trembled under the weight of his rage. "I am the Duc de Langeais!"

"You are a Nephil," the boy said on a sliver of a smile.

Chauncey had a profane retort on the tip of his tongue, but he swallowed it. His next words were spoken with icy venom. "What did you say?"

"You belong to the biblical race of Nephilim. Your real father was an angel who fell from heaven. You're half mortal." The boy's dark eyes lifted, meeting Chauncey's. "Half fallen angel."

Chauncey's tutor's voice drifted up from the recesses of his mind, reading passages from the Bible, telling of a deviant race created when angels cast from heaven mated with mortal women. A fearsome and powerful race. A chill that wasn't entirely revulsion crept through Chauncey. "Who are you?"

The boy turned, walking away, and although Chauncey wanted to go after him, he couldn't command his legs to hold his weight. Kneeling there, blinking up through the rain, he saw two thick scars on the back of the boy's naked torso. They narrowed to form an upside-down V.

"Are you—fallen?" he called out. "Your wings have been stripped, haven't they?"

The boy—angel—whoever he was, did not turn back. Chauncey did not need the confirmation.

"This service I'm to provide," he shouted. "I demand to know what it is!"

The air resonated with the boy's low laughter.

I WALKED INTO BIOLOGY AND MY JAW FELL OPEN. Mysteriously adhered to the chalkboard was a Barbie doll, with Ken at her side. They'd been forced to link arms and were naked except for artificial leaves placed in a few choice locations. Scribbled above their heads in thick pink chalk was the invitation:

WELCOME TO HUMAN REPRODUCTION (SEX)

At my side Vee Sky said, "This is exactly why the school out-laws camera phones. Pictures of this in the eZine would be all the evidence I'd need to get the board of education to ax biology. And then we'd have this hour to do something productive—like receive one-on-one tutoring from cute upperclass guys."

"Why, Vee," I said, "I could've sworn you've been looking forward to this unit all semester."

Vee lowered her lashes and smiled wickedly. "This class isn't going to teach me anything I don't already know."

"Vee? As in virgin?"

"Not so loud." She winked just as the bell rang, sending us both to our seats, which were side by side at our shared table.

Coach McConaughy grabbed the whistle swinging from a chain around his neck and blew it. "Seats, team!" Coach considered teaching tenth-grade biology a side assignment to his job as varsity basketball coach, and we all knew it.

"It may not have occurred to you kids that sex is more than a fifteen-minute trip to the backseat of a car. It's science. And what is science?"

"Boring," some kid in the back of the room called out.

"The only class I'm failing," said another.

Coach's eyes tracked down the front row, stopping at me. "Nora?"

"The study of something," I said.

He walked over and jabbed his index finger on the table in front of me. "What else?"

"Knowledge gained through experimentation and observation." Lovely. I sounded like I was auditioning for the audiobook of our text.

"In your own words."

I touched the tip of my tongue to my upper lip and tried for a synonym. "Science is an investigation." It sounded like a question.

"Science is an investigation," Coach said, sanding his hands together. "Science requires us to transform into spies."

Put that way, science almost sounded fun. But I'd been in Coach's class long enough not to get my hopes up.

"Good sleuthing takes practice," he continued.

"So does sex," came another back-of-the-room comment. We all bit back laughter while Coach pointed a warning finger at the offender.

"That won't be part of tonight's homework." Coach turned his attention back to me. "Nora, you've been sitting beside Vee since the beginning of the year." I nodded but had a bad feeling about where this was going. "Both of you are on the school eZine together." Again I nodded. "I bet you know quite a bit about each other."

Vee kicked my leg under our table. I knew what she was thinking. That he had no idea how much we knew about each other. And I don't just mean the secrets we entomb in our diaries. Vee is my un-twin. She's green-eyed, minky blond, and a few pounds over curvy. I'm a smoky-eyed brunette with volumes of curly hair that holds its own against even the best flatiron. And I'm all legs, like a bar stool. But there is an invisible thread that ties us together; both of us swear that tie began long before birth. Both of us swear it will continue to hold for the rest of our lives.

Coach looked out at the class. "In fact, I'll bet each of you knows the person sitting beside you well enough. You picked the seats you did for a reason, right? Familiarity. Too bad the best sleuths avoid familiarity. It dulls the investigative instinct. Which is why, today, we're creating a new seating chart."

I opened my mouth to protest, but Vee beat me to it. "What the crap? It's April. As in, it's almost the end of the year. You can't pull this kind of stuff now."

Coach hinted at a smile. "I can pull this stuff clear up to the last day of the semester. And if you fail my class, you'll be right back here next year, where I'll be pulling this kind of stuff all over again."

Vee scowled at him. She is famous for that scowl. It's a look that does everything but audibly hiss. Apparently immune to it, Coach brought his whistle to his lips, and we got the idea.

"Every partner sitting on the left-hand side of the table—that's your left—move up one seat. Those in the front row—yes, including you, Vee—move to the back."

Vee shoved her notebook inside her backpack and ripped the zipper shut. I bit my lip and waved a small farewell. Then I turned slightly, checking out the room behind me. I knew the names of all my classmates . . . except one. The transfer. Coach never called on him, and he seemed to prefer it that way. He sat slouched one table back, cool black eyes holding a steady gaze forward. Just like always. I didn't for one moment believe he just sat there, day after day, staring into space. He was thinking something, but instinct told me I probably didn't want to know what.

He set his bio text down on the table and slid into Vee's old chair.

I smiled. "Hi. I'm Nora."

His black eyes sliced into me, and the corners of his mouth tilted up. My heart fumbled a beat and in that pause, a feeling of gloomy darkness seemed to slide like a shadow over me. It vanished in an instant, but I was still staring at him. His smile wasn't friendly. It was a smile that spelled trouble. With a promise.

I focused on the chalkboard. Barbie and Ken stared back with strangely cheerful smiles.

Coach said, "Human reproduction can be a sticky subject—"

"Ewww!" groaned a chorus of students.

"It requires mature handling. And like all science, the best approach is to learn by sleuthing. For the rest of class, practice this technique by finding out as much as you can about your new partner. Tomorrow, bring a write-up of your discoveries, and believe me, I'm going to check for authenticity. This is biology, not English, so don't even think about fictionalizing your answers. I want to see real interaction and teamwork." There was an implied Or else.

I sat perfectly still. The ball was in his court—I'd smiled, and look how well that turned out. I wrinkled my nose, trying to figure out what he smelled like. Not cigarettes. Something richer, fouler.

Cigars.

I found the clock on the wall and tapped my pencil in time to the second hand. I planted my elbow on the table and propped my chin on my fist. I blew out a sigh.

Great. At this rate I would fail.

I had my eyes pinned forward, but I heard the soft glide of his pen. He was writing, and I wanted to know what. Ten minutes of sitting together didn't qualify him to make any assumptions about me. Flitting a look sideways, I saw that his paper was several lines deep and growing.

"What are you writing?" I asked.

"And she speaks English," he said while scrawling it down, each stroke of his hand both smooth and lazy at once.

I leaned as close to him as I dared, trying to read what else he'd written, but he folded the paper in half, concealing the list.

"What did you write?" I demanded.

He reached for my unused paper, sliding it across the table toward him. He crumpled it into a ball. Before I could protest, he tossed it at the trash can beside Coach's desk. The shot dropped in.

I stared at the trash can a moment, locked between disbelief and anger. Then I flipped open my notebook to a clean page. "What is your name?" I asked, pencil poised to write.

I glanced up in time to catch another dark grin. This one seemed to dare me to pry anything out of him.

"Your name?" I repeated, hoping it was my imagination that my voice faltered.

"Call me Patch. I mean it. *Call me*."

He winked when he said it, and I was pretty sure he was making fun of me.

"What do you do in your leisure time?" I asked.

"I don't have free time."

"I'm assuming this assignment is graded, so do me a favor?"

He leaned back in his seat, folding his arms behind his head. "What kind of favor?"

I was pretty sure it was an innuendo, and I grappled for a way to change the subject.

"Free time," he repeated thoughtfully. "I take pictures."

I printed Photography on my paper.

"I wasn't finished," he said. "I've got quite a collection going of an eZine columnist who believes there's truth in eating organic, who writes poetry in secret, and who shudders at the thought of having to choose between Stanford, Yale, and . . . what's that big one with the *H*?"

I stared at him a moment, shaken by how *dead on* he was. I didn't get the feeling it was a lucky guess. He *knew*. And I wanted to know how—right now.

"But you won't end up going to any of them."

"I won't?" I asked without thinking.

He hooked his fingers under the seat of my chair, dragging me closer to him. Not sure if I should scoot away and show fear, or do nothing and feign boredom, I chose the latter.

He said, "Even though you'd thrive at all three schools, you scorn them for being a cliché of achievement. Passing judgment is your third biggest weakness."

"And my second?" I said with quiet rage. Who was this guy? Was this some kind of disturbing joke?

"You don't know how to trust. I take that back. You trust—just all the wrong people."

"And my first?" I demanded.

"You keep life on a short leash."

"What's that supposed to mean?"

"You're scared of what you can't control."

The hair at the nape of my neck stood on end, and the temperature in the room seemed to chill. Ordinarily I would have gone straight to Coach's desk and requested a new seating chart. But I refused to let Patch think he could intimidate or scare me. I felt an irrational need to defend myself and decided right then and there I wouldn't back down until he did.

"Do you sleep naked?" he asked.

My mouth threatened to drop, but I held it in check. "You're hardly the person I'd tell."

"Ever been to a shrink?"

"No," I lied. The truth was, I was in counseling with the school psychologist, Dr. Hendrickson. It wasn't by choice, and it wasn't something I liked to talk about.

"Done anything illegal?"

"No." Occasionally breaking the speed limit wouldn't count. Not with him. "Why don't you ask me something normal? Like . . . my favorite kind of music?"

"I'm not going to ask what I can guess."

"You do not know the type of music I listen to."

"Baroque. With you, it's all about order, control. I bet you play . . . the cello?" He said it like he'd pulled the guess out of thin air.

"Wrong." Another lie, but this one sent a chill rippling along my skin. Who was he really? If he knew I played the cello, what else did he know?

"What's that?" Patch tapped his pen against the inside of my wrist. Instinctively I pulled away.

"A birthmark."

"Looks like a scar. Are you suicidal, Nora?" His eyes connected with mine, and I could feel him laughing. "Parents married or divorced?"

"I live with my mom."

"Where's dad?"

"My dad passed away last year."

"How did he die?"

I flinched. "He was—murdered. This is kind of personal territory, if you don't mind."

There was a count of silence and the edge in Patch's eyes seemed to soften a touch. "That must be hard." He sounded like he meant it.

The bell rang and Patch was on his feet, making his way toward the door.

"Wait," I called out. He didn't turn. "Excuse me!" He was through the door. "Patch! I didn't get anything on you."

He turned back and walked toward me. Taking my hand, he scribbled something on it before I thought to pull away.

I looked down at the seven numbers in red ink on my palm and made a fist around them. I wanted to tell him no way was his phone ringing tonight. I wanted to tell him it was his fault for taking all the time questioning me. I wanted a lot of things, but I just stood there looking like I didn't know how to open my mouth.

At last I said, "I'm busy tonight."

"So am I." He grinned and was gone.

I stood nailed to the spot, digesting what had just happened. Did he eat up all the time questioning me on purpose? So I'd fail? Did he think one flashy grin would redeem him? *Yes*, I thought. *Yes, he did.*

"I won't call!" I called after him. "Not—ever!"

"Have you finished your column for tomorrow's deadline?" It was Vee. She came up beside me, jotting notes on the notepad she carried everywhere. "I'm thinking of writing mine on the injustice of seating charts. I got paired with a girl who said she just finished lice treatment this morning."

"My new partner," I said, pointing into the hallway at the back of Patch. He had an annoyingly confident walk, the kind you find paired with faded T-shirts and a cowboy hat. Patch wore neither. He was a dark-Levi's-dark-henley-dark-boots kind of guy.

"The senior transfer? Guess he didn't study hard enough the first time around. Or the second." She gave me a knowing look. "Third time's a charm."

"He gives me the creeps. He knew my music. Without any hints whatsoever, he said, 'Baroque.'" I did a poor job of mimicking his low voice.

"Lucky guess?"

"He knew . . . other things."

"Like what?"

I let go of a sigh. He knew more than I wanted to comfortably contemplate. "Like how to get under my skin," I said at last. "I'm going to tell Coach he has to switch us back."

"Go for it. I could use a hook for my next eZine article. 'Tenth Grader Fights Back.' Better yet, 'Seating Chart Takes Slap in the Face.' Mmm. I like it."

At the end of the day, I was the one who took a slap in the face. Coach shot down my plea to rethink the seating chart. It appeared I was stuck with Patch.

For now.

CHAPTER

2

MY MOM AND I LIVE IN A DRAFTY EIGHTEENTH-century farmhouse on the outskirts of Coldwater. It's the only house on Hawthorne Lane, and the nearest neighbors are almost a mile away. I sometimes wonder if the original builder realized that out of all the plots of land available, he chose to construct the house in the eye of a mysterious atmospheric inversion that seems to suck all the fog off Maine's coast and transplant it into our yard. The house was at this moment veiled by gloom that resembled escaped and wandering spirits.

I spent the evening planted on a stool in the kitchen in the company of algebra homework and Dorothea, our housekeeper. My mom works for the Hugo Renaldi Auction Company, coordinating estate and antique auctions all along the East Coast. This week she was in upstate New York. Her job required a lot of travel, and she paid Dorothea to cook and clean, but I was pretty sure the fine print on Dorothea's job description included keeping a watchful, parental eye on me.

"How was school?" Dorothea asked with a slight German accent. She stood at the sink, scrubbing overbaked lasagna off a casserole dish.

"I have a new biology partner."

"This is a good thing, or a bad thing?"

"Vee was my old partner."

"Humph." More vigorous scrubbing, and the flesh on Dorothea's upper arm jiggled. "A bad thing, then."

I sighed in agreement.

"Tell me about the new partner. This girl, what is she like?"

"He's tall, dark, and annoying." And eerily closed off. Patch's eyes were black orbs. Taking in everything and giving away nothing. Not that I *wanted* to know more about Patch. Since I hadn't liked what I'd seen on the surface, I doubted I'd like what was lurking deep inside.

Only, this wasn't exactly true. I'd liked *a* lot of what I'd seen.

Long, lean muscles down his arms, broad but relaxed shoulders, and a smile that was part playful, part seductive. I was in an uneasy alliance with myself, trying to ignore what had started to feel irresistible.

At nine o'clock Dorothea finished for the evening and locked up on her way out. I flashed the porch lights twice to say good-bye; they must have penetrated the fog, because she answered with a honk. I was alone.

I took inventory of the feelings playing out inside me. I wasn't hungry. I wasn't tired. I wasn't even all that lonely. But I *was* a little bit restless about my biology assignment. I'd told Patch I wouldn't call, and six hours ago I'd meant it. All I could think now was that I didn't want to fail. Biology was my toughest subject. My grade tottered problematically between A and B. In my mind, that was the difference between a full and half scholarship in my future.

I went to the kitchen and picked up the phone. I looked at what was left of the seven numbers still tattooed on my hand. Secretly I hoped Patch didn't answer my call. If he was unavailable or uncooperative on assignments, it was evidence I could use against him to convince Coach to undo the seating chart. Feeling hopeful, I keyed in his number.

Patch answered on the third ring. "What's up?"

In a matter-of-fact tone I said, "I'm calling to see if we can meet tonight. I know you said you're busy, but—"

"Nora." Patch said my name like it was the punch line to a joke. "Thought you weren't going to call. Ever."

I hated that I was eating my words. I hated Patch for rubbing it in. I hated Coach and his deranged assignments. I opened my mouth, hoping something smart would come out. "Well? Can we meet or not?"

"As it turns out, I can't."

"Can't, or won't?"

"I'm in the middle of a pool game." I heard the smile in his voice. "An important pool game."

From the background noise I heard on his end, I believed he was telling the truth—about the pool game. Whether it was more important than my assignment was up for debate.

"Where are you?" I asked.

"Bo's Arcade. It's not your kind of hangout."

"Then let's do the interview over the phone. I've got a list of questions right—"

He hung up on me.

I stared at the phone in disbelief, then ripped a clean sheet of paper from my notebook. I scribbled *Jerk* on the first line. On the line beneath it I added, *Smokes cigars. Will die of lung cancer. Hopefully soon. Excellent physical shape.*

I immediately scribbled over the last observation until it was illegible.

The microwave clock blinked to 9:05. As I saw it, I had two

choices. Either I fabricated my interview with Patch, or I drove to Bo's Arcade. The first option might have been tempting, if I could just block out Coach's voice warning that he'd check all answers for authenticity. I didn't know enough about Patch to bluff my way through a whole interview. And the second option? Not even remotely tempting.

I delayed making a decision long enough to call my mom. Part of our agreement for her working and traveling so much was that I act responsibly and not be the kind of daughter who required constant supervision. I liked my freedom, and I didn't want to do anything to give my mom a reason to take a pay cut and get a local job to keep an eye on me.

On the fourth ring her voice mail picked up.

"It's me," I said. "Just checking in. I've got some biology homework to finish up, then I'm going to bed. Call me at lunch tomorrow, if you want. Love you."

After I hung up, I found a quarter in the kitchen drawer. Best to leave complicated decisions to fate.

"Heads I go," I told George Washington's profile, "tails I stay." I flipped the quarter in the air, flattened it to the back of my palm, and dared a peek. My heart squeezed out an extra beat, and I told myself I wasn't sure what it meant.

"It's out of my hands now," I said.

Determined to get this over with as quickly as possible, I grabbed a map off the fridge, snagged my keys, and backed my

Fiat Spider down the driveway. The car had probably been cute in 1979, but I wasn't wild about the chocolate brown paint, the rust spreading unchecked across the back fender, or the cracked white leather seats.

Bo's Arcade turned out to be farther away than I would have liked, nestled close to the coast, a thirty-minute drive. With the map flattened to the steering wheel, I pulled the Fiat into a parking lot behind a large cinder-block building with an electric sign flashing BO'S ARCADE, MAD BLACK PAINTBALL & OZZ'S POOL HALL. Graffiti splashed the walls, and cigarette butts dotted the foundation. Clearly Bo's would be filled with future Ivy Leaguers and model citizens. I tried to keep my thoughts lofty and nonchalant, but my stomach felt a little uneasy. Double-checking that I'd locked all the doors, I headed inside.

I stood in line, waiting to get past the ropes. As the group ahead of me paid, I squeezed past, walking toward the maze of blaring sirens and blinking lights.

"Think you deserve a free ride?" hollered a smoke-roughened voice.

I swung around and blinked at the heavily tattooed cashier. I said, "I'm not here to play. I'm looking for someone."

He grunted. "You want past me, you pay." He put his palms on the counter, where a price chart had been duct-taped, showing I owed fifteen dollars. Cash only.

I didn't have cash. And if I had, I wouldn't have wasted it to spend a few minutes interrogating Patch about his personal life. I felt a flush of anger at the seating chart and at having to be here in the first place. I only needed to find Patch, then we could hold the interview outside. I was not going to drive all this way and leave empty-handed.

"If I'm not back in two minutes, I'll pay the fifteen dollars," I said. Before I could exercise better judgment or muster up a tad more patience, I did something completely out of character and ducked under the ropes. I didn't stop there. I hurried through the arcade, keeping my eyes open for Patch. I told myself I couldn't believe I was doing this, but I was like a rolling snowball, gaining speed and momentum. At this point I just wanted to find Patch and get out.

The cashier followed after me, shouting, "Hey!"

Certain Patch was not on the main level, I jogged downstairs, following signs to Ozz's Pool Hall. At the bottom of the stairs, dim track lighting illuminated several poker tables, all in use. Cigar smoke almost as thick as the fog enveloping my house clouded the low ceiling. Nestled between the poker tables and the bar was a row of pool tables. Patch was stretched across the one farthest from me, attempting a difficult bank shot.

"Patch!" I called out.

Just as I spoke, he shot his pool stick, driving it into the table-top. His head whipped up. He stared at me with a mixture of surprise and curiosity.

The cashier clomped down the steps behind me, vising my shoulder with his hand. "Upstairs. Now."

Patch's mouth moved into another barely-there smile. Hard to say if it was mocking or friendly. "She's with me."

This seemed to hold some sway with the cashier, who loosened his grip. Before he could change his mind, I shook off his hand and weaved through the tables toward Patch. I took the first several steps in stride, but found my confidence slipping the closer I got to him.

I was immediately aware of something different about him. I couldn't quite put my finger on it, but I could feel it like electricity. More animosity?

More confidence.

More freedom to be himself. And those black eyes were getting to me. They were like magnets clinging to my every move. I swallowed discreetly and tried to ignore the queasy tap dance in my stomach. I couldn't quite put my finger on it, but something about Patch wasn't right. Something about him wasn't normal. Something wasn't . . . safe.

"Sorry about the hang-up," Patch said, coming beside me. "The reception's not great down here."

Yeah, right.

With a tilt of his head, Patch motioned the others to leave. There was an uneasy silence before anybody moved. The first guy to leave bumped into my shoulder as he walked past. I took a step back to balance myself and looked up just in time to receive cold eyes from the other two players as they departed.

Great. It wasn't *my* fault Patch was my partner.

"Eight ball?" I asked him, raising my eyebrows and trying to sound completely sure of myself, of my surroundings. Maybe he was right and Bo's wasn't my kind of place. That didn't mean I was going to bolt for the doors. "How high are the stakes?"

His smile widened. This time I was pretty sure he was mocking me. "We don't play for money."

I set my handbag on the edge of the table. "Too bad. I was going to bet everything I have against you." I held up my assignment, two lines already filled. "A few quick questions and I'm out of here."

"Jerk?" Patch read out loud, leaning on his pool stick. "Lung cancer? Is that supposed to be prophetic?"

I fanned the assignment through the air. "I'm assuming you contribute to the atmosphere. How many cigars a night? One? Two?"

"I don't smoke." He sounded sincere, but I didn't buy it.

"Mm-hmm," I said, setting the paper down between the eight ball and the solid purple. I accidentally nudged the solid purple while writing *Definitely cigars* on line three.

"You're messing up the game," Patch said, still smiling.

I caught his eye and couldn't help but match his smile—briefly. "Hopefully not in your favor. Biggest dream?" I was proud of this one because I knew it would stump him. It required forethought.

"Kiss you."

"That's not funny," I said, holding his eyes, grateful I didn't stutter.

"No, but it made you blush."

I boosted myself onto the side of the table, trying to look impassive. I crossed my legs, using my knee as a writing board. "Do you work?"

"I bus tables at the Borderline. Best Mexican in town."

"Religion?"

He didn't seem surprised by the question, but he didn't seem overjoyed by it either. "I thought you said a few quick questions. You're already at number four."

"Religion?" I asked more firmly.

Patch dragged a hand thoughtfully along the line of his jaw. "Not religion ... cult."

"You belong to a cult?" I realized too late that while I sounded surprised, I shouldn't have.

"As it turns out, I'm in need of a healthy female sacrifice. I'd planned on luring her into trusting me first, but if you're ready now ..."

Any smile left on my face slid away. "You're not impressing me."

"I haven't started trying yet."

I edged off the table and stood up to him. He was a full head taller. "Vee told me you're a senior. How many times have you failed tenth-grade biology? Once? Twice?"

"Vee isn't my spokesperson."

"Are you denying failing?"

"I'm telling you I didn't go to school last year." His eyes taunted me. It only made me more determined.

"You were truant?"

Patch laid his pool stick across the tabletop and crooked a finger for me to come closer. I didn't. "A secret?" he said in confidential tones. "I've never gone to school before. Another secret? It's not as dull as I expected."

He was lying. Everyone went to school. There were laws. He was lying to get a rise out of me.

"You think I'm lying," he said around a smile.

"You've never been to school, ever? If that's true—and you're right, I don't think it is—what made you decide to come this year?"

"You."

The impulse to feel scared pounded through me, but I told myself that was exactly what Patch wanted. Standing my ground, I tried to act annoyed instead. Still, it took me a moment to find my voice. "That's not a real answer."

He must have taken a step closer, because suddenly our bodies were separated by nothing more than a shallow margin of air. "Your eyes, Nora. Those cold, pale gray eyes are surprisingly irresistible." He tipped his head sideways, as if to study me from a new angle. "And that killer curvy mouth."

Startled not so much by his comment, but that part of me responded positively to it, I stepped back. "That's it. I'm out of here."

But as soon as the words were out of my mouth, I knew they weren't true. I felt the urge to say something more. Picking through the thoughts tangled in my head, I tried to find what it was I felt I had to say. Why was he so derisive, and why did he act like I'd done something to deserve it?

"You seem to know a lot about me," I said, making the understatement of the year. "More than you should. You seem to know exactly what to say to make me uncomfortable."

"You make it easy."

A spark of anger fired through me. "You admit you're doing this on purpose?"

"This?"

"This—provoking me."

"Say 'provoking' again. Your mouth looks provocative when you do."

"We're done. Finish your pool game." I grabbed his pool stick off the table and pushed it at him. He didn't take it.

"I don't like sitting beside you," I said. "I don't like being your partner. I don't like your condescending smile." My jaw twitched—something that typically happened only when I lied. I wondered if I was lying now. If I was, I wanted to kick myself. "I don't like you," I said as convincingly as I could, and thrust the stick against his chest.

"I'm glad Coach put us together," he said. I detected the slightest irony on the word "Coach," but I couldn't figure out any hidden meaning. This time he took the pool stick.

"I'm working to change that," I countered.

Patch thought this was so funny, his teeth showed through his smile. He reached for me, and before I could move away, he untangled something from my hair.

"Piece of paper," he explained, flicking it to the ground. As he reached out, I noticed a marking on the inside of his wrist. At first I assumed it was a tattoo, but a second look revealed a ruddy brown, slightly raised birthmark. It was the shape of a splattered paint drop.

"That's an unfortunate place for a birthmark," I said, more than a little unnerved that it was so similarly positioned to my own scar.

Patch casually but noticeably slid his sleeve down over his wrist. "You'd prefer it someplace more private?"

"I wouldn't prefer it anywhere." I wasn't sure how this sounded and tried again. "I wouldn't care if you didn't have it at all." I tried a third time. "I don't care about your birthmark, period."

"Any more questions?" he asked. "Comments?"

"No."

"Then I'll see you in bio."

I thought about telling him he'd never see me again. But I wasn't going to eat my words twice in one day.

Later that night a *crack!* pulled me out of sleep. With my face mashed into my pillow, I held still, all my senses on high alert. My mom was out of town at least once a month for work, so I was used to sleeping alone, and it had been months since I'd imagined the sound of footsteps creeping down the hall toward my bedroom. The truth was, I never felt completely alone. Right after my dad was shot to death in Portland while buying my mom's birthday gift, a strange presence entered my life. Like someone was orbiting my world, watching from a distance. At first the phantom presence had creeped me out, but when nothing bad came of it, my anxiety lost its edge. I started wondering if there was a cosmic purpose for the way I was feeling. Maybe my dad's spirit was close by. The thought was usually comforting, but tonight was different. The presence felt like ice on the skin.

Turning my head a fraction, I saw a shadowy form stretching across my floor. I flipped around to face the window, the gauzy shaft of moonlight the only light in the room capable of casting a shadow. But nothing was there. I squeezed my pillow against me and told myself it was a cloud passing over the moon. Or a piece of trash blowing in the wind. Still, I spent the next several minutes waiting for my pulse to calm down.

By the time I found the courage to get out of bed, the yard below my window was silent and still. The only noise came from tree branches scraping against the house, and my own heart thrumming under my skin.

CHAPTER

OACH MCCONAUGHY STOOD AT THE CHALK-
board droning on and on about something, but my
mind was far from the complexities of science.

I was busy formulating reasons why Patch and I should no
longer be partners, making a list of them on the back of an old
quiz. As soon as class was over, I would present my argument to
Coach. *Uncooperative on assignments,* I wrote. *Shows little interest
in teamwork.*

But it was the things not listed that bothered me most. I found the location of Patch's birthmark eerie, and I was spooked by the incident at my window last night. I didn't outright suspect Patch of spying on me, but I couldn't ignore the coincidence that I was almost positive I'd seen someone looking in my window just hours after I'd met him.

At the thought of Patch spying on me, I reached inside the front compartment of my backpack and shook two iron pills from a bottle, swallowing them whole. They caught in my throat a moment, then found their way down.

Out of the corner of my eye, I caught Patch's raised eyebrows.

I considered explaining that I was anemic and had to take iron a few times a day, especially when I was under stress, but I thought better. The anemia wasn't life-threatening . . . as long as I took regular doses of iron. I wasn't paranoid to the point that I thought Patch meant me harm, but somehow, my medical condition was a vulnerability that felt better kept secret.

"Nora?"

Coach stood at the front of the room, his hand outstretched in a gesture that showed he was waiting for one thing—my answer. A slow burn made its way up my cheeks.

"Could you repeat the question?" I asked.

The class snickered.

Coach said, with slight irritation, "What qualities are you attracted to in a potential mate?"

"Potential mate?"

"Come on now, we haven't got all afternoon."

I could hear Vee laughing behind me.

My throat seemed to constrict. "You want me to list character-istics of a . . . ?"

"Potential mate, yes, that would be helpful."

Without meaning to, I looked sideways at Patch. He was eased back in his seat, one notch above a slouch, studying me with satis-faction. He flashed his pirate smile and mouthed, We're waiting.

I stacked my hands on the table, hoping I looked more com-posed than I felt. "I've never thought about it before."

"Well, think fast."

"Could you call on someone else first?"

Coach gestured impatiently to my left. "You're up, Patch."

Unlike me, Patch spoke with confidence. He had himself posi-tioned so his body was angled slightly toward mine, our knees mere inches apart.

"Intelligent. Attractive. Vulnerable."

Coach was busy listing the adjectives on the board. "Vulner-able?" he asked. "How so?"

Vee spoke up. "Does this have anything to do with the unit we're studying? Because I can't find anything about desired characteris-tics of a mate anywhere in our text."

Coach stopped writing long enough to look over his shoul-der. "Every animal on the planet attracts mates with the goal of

34

reproduction. Frogs swell their bodies. Male gorillas beat their chests. Have you ever watched a male lobster rise up on the tips of his legs and snap his claws, demanding female attention? Attraction is the first element of all animal reproduction, humans included. Why don't you give us your list, Miss Sky?"

Vee held up five fingers. "Gorgeous, wealthy, indulgent, fiercely protective, and just a little bit dangerous." A finger went down with each description.

Patch laughed under his breath. "The problem with human attraction is not knowing if it will be returned."

"Excellent point," Coach said.

"Humans are vulnerable," Patch continued, "because they're capable of being hurt." At this, Patch's knee knocked against mine. I scooted away, not daring to let myself wonder what he meant by the gesture.

Coach nodded. "The complexity of human attraction—and reproduction—is one of the features that set us apart from other species."

I thought I heard Patch snort at this, but it was a very soft sound, and I couldn't be sure.

Coach continued, "Since the dawn of time, women have been attracted to mates with strong survival skills—like intelligence and physical prowess—because men with these qualities are more likely to bring home dinner at the end of the day." He stuck his thumbs in the air and grinned. "Dinner equals survival, team."

No one laughed.

"Likewise," he continued, "men are attracted to beauty because it indicates health and youth—no point mating with a sickly woman who won't be around to raise the children." Coach pushed his glasses up the bridge of his nose and chuckled.

"That is so sexist," Vee protested. "Tell me something that relates to a woman in the twenty-first century."

"If you approach reproduction with an eye to science, Miss Sky, you'll see that children are the key to the survival of our species. And the more children you have, the greater your contribution to the gene pool."

I practically heard Vee's eyes rolling. "I think we're finally getting close to today's topic. Sex."

"Almost," said Coach, holding up a finger. "Before sex comes attraction, but after attraction comes body language. You have to communicate 'I'm interested' to a potential mate, only not in so many words."

Coach pointed beside me. "All right, Patch. Let's say you're at a party. The room is full of girls of all different shapes and sizes. You see blonds, brunettes, redheads, a few girls with black hair. Some are talkative, while others appear shy. You've found one girl who fits your profile—attractive, intelligent, and vulnerable. How do you let her know you're interested?"

"Single her out. Talk to her."

"Good. Now for the big question—how do you know if she's game or if she wants you to move on?"

"I study her," Patch said. "I figure out what she's thinking and feeling. She's not going to come right out and tell me, which is why I have to pay attention. Does she turn her body toward mine? Does she hold my eyes, then look away? Does she bite her lip and play with her hair, the way Nora is doing right now?"

Laughter rose in the room. I dropped my hands to my lap.

"She's game," said Patch, bumping my leg again. Of all things, I blushed.

"Very good! Very good!" Coach said, his voice charged, smiling broadly at our attentiveness.

"The blood vessels in Nora's face are widening and her skin is warming," Patch said. "She knows she's being evaluated. She likes the attention, but she's not sure how to handle it."

"I am not blushing."

"She's nervous," Patch said. "She's stroking her arm to draw attention away from her face and down to her figure, or maybe her skin. Both are strong selling points."

I nearly choked. He's joking, I told myself. No, he's insane. I had no experience dealing with lunatics, and it showed. I felt like I spent most of our time together staring at Patch, mouth agape. If I had any illusions about keeping up with him, I was going to have to figure out a new approach.

I placed my hands flat against the table, held my chin high, and tried to look as if I still possessed some dignity. "This is ridiculous."

Stretching his arm out to his side with exaggerated slyness, Patch hung it on the back of my chair. I had the strange feeling that this was a threat aimed entirely at me, and that he was unaware and uncaring of how the class received it. They laughed, but he didn't seem to hear it, holding my eyes so singly with his own that I almost believed he'd carved a small, private world for us that no one else could reach.

Vulnerable, he mouthed.

I locked my ankles around the legs of my chair and jerked forward, feeling the weight of his arm drop off the back of the seat. I was not vulnerable.

"And there you have it!" Coach said. "Biology in motion."

"Can we please talk about sex now?" asked Vee.

"Tomorrow. Read chapter seven and be ready for a discussion first thing."

The bell rang, and Patch scraped his chair back. "That was fun. Let's do it again sometime." Before I could come up with something more pithy than No, thanks, he edged behind me and disappeared out the door.

"I'm starting a petition to have Coach fired," Vee said, coming to my table. "What was up with class today? It was watered-down porn. He practically had you and Patch on top of your lab table, horizontal, minus your clothes, doing the Big Deed—"

I nailed her with a look that said, Does it look like I want a replay?

"Yeesh," Vee said, stepping back.

"I need to talk to Coach. I'll meet you at your locker in ten minutes."

"Sure thing."

I made my way up to Coach's desk, where he sat hunched over a book of basketball plays. At first glance all the Xs and Os made it look like he'd been playing tic-tac-toe.

"Hi, Nora," he said without looking up. "What can I do for you?"

"I'm here to tell you the new seating chart and lesson plan is making me uncomfortable."

Coach kicked back in his chair and folded his hands behind his head. "I like the seating chart. Almost as much as I like this new man-to-man play I'm working on for Saturday's game."

I set a copy of the school code of conduct and student rights down on top of it. "By law, no student should feel threatened on school property."

"You feel threatened?"

"I feel uncomfortable. And I'd like to propose a solution." When Coach didn't cut me off, I drew a confident breath. "I will tutor any student from any of your biology classes—if you will seat me beside Vee again."

"Patch could use a tutor."

I resisted gritting my teeth. "That defeats the point."

"Did you see him today? He was involved in the discussion. I haven't heard him say one word all year, but I put him next to you and—bingo. His grade in here is going to improve."

"And Vee's is going to drop."

"That happens when you can't look sideways to get the right answer," he said dryly.

"Vee's problem is lack of dedication. I'll tutor her."

"No can do." Glancing at his watch, he said, "I'm late for a meeting. Are we done here?"

I squeezed my brain for one more argument, but it appeared I was fresh out of inspiration.

"Let's give the seating chart a few more weeks. Oh, and I was serious about tutoring Patch. I'll count you in." Coach didn't wait for my answer; he whistled the tune to Jeopardy and ducked out the door.

By seven o'clock the sky had glowered into an inky blue, and I zipped up my coat for warmth. Vee and I were on our way from the movie theater to the parking lot, having just watched The Sacrifice. It was my job to review movies for the eZine, and since I'd already seen every other movie showing at the theater, we'd resigned ourselves to the latest urban chiller.

"That," Vee said, "was the freakiest movie I have ever seen. As a rule, we are no longer allowed to see anything suggestive of horror."

Fine by me. Take into consideration that someone had been

lurking outside my bedroom window last night and compound it with watching a fully developed stalker movie tonight, and I was starting to feel a little bit paranoid.

"Can you imagine?" Vee said. "Living your whole life never having a clue that the only reason you're being kept alive is to be used as a sacrifice?"

We both shuddered.

"And what was up with that altar?" she continued, annoyingly unaware that I would have rather talked about the life cycle of fungi than about the movie. "Why did the bad guy set the stone on fire before tying her down? When I heard her flesh sizzle—"

"Okay!" I practically shouted. "Where to next?"

"And can I just say if a guy *ever* kisses me like that, I will start dry heaving. Repulsive doesn't begin to describe what was going on with his mouth. That was makeup, right? I mean, nobody actually has a mouth like that in real life—"

"My review is due by midnight," I said, cutting across her.

"Oh. Right. To the library, then?" Vee unlocked the doors to her 1995 purple Dodge Neon. "You're being awfully touchy, you know."

I slid into the passenger seat. "Blame the movie." Blame the Peeping Tom at my window last night.

"I'm not talking about just tonight. I've noticed," she said with a mischievous curve of her mouth, "that you've been unusually crabby for a good half hour at the end of bio the past two days."

"Also easy. Blame Patch."

Vee's eyes flicked to the rearview mirror. She adjusted it for a better look at her teeth. She licked them, giving a practiced smile. "I have to admit, his dark side calls to me."

I had no desire to admit it, but Vee wasn't alone. I felt drawn to Patch in a way I'd never felt drawn to anyone. There was a dark magnetism between us. Around him, I felt lured to the edge of danger. At any moment, it felt like he could push me over the edge.

"Hearing you say that makes me want to—" I paused, trying to think of exactly what our attraction to Patch did make me want to do. Something unpleasant.

"Tell me you don't think he's good-looking," Vee said, "and I promise I'll never bring up his name again."

I reached to turn on the radio. Of all things, there had to be something better to do than ruin our evening by inviting Patch, albeit abstractly, into it. Sitting beside him for one hour every day, five days a week, was plenty more than I could take. I wasn't giving him my evenings, too.

"Well?" Vee pressed.

"He could be good-looking. But I'd be the last to know. I'm a tainted juror on this one, sorry."

"What's that supposed to mean?"

"It means I can't get beyond his personality. No amount of beauty could make up for it."

"Not beauty. He's . . . hard-edged. Sexy."

I rolled my eyes.

Vee honked and tapped her brake as a car pulled in front of her. "What? You disagree, or rough-and-roguish isn't your type?"

"I don't have a type," I said. "I'm not that narrow."

Vee laughed. "You, babe, are more than narrow—you're confined. Cramped. Your spectrum is about as wide as one of Coach's microorganisms. There are very few, if any, boys at school you would fall for."

"That's not true." I said the words automatically. It wasn't until I'd spoken them that I wondered how accurate they were. I had never been seriously interested in anyone. How weird was I? "It isn't about the boys, it's about . . . love. I haven't found it."

"It isn't about love," Vee said. "It's about fun."

I lifted my eyebrows, doubtful. "Kissing a guy I don't know—I don't care about—is fun?"

"Haven't you been paying attention in bio? It's about a lot more than kissing."

"Oh," I said in an enlightened voice. "The gene pool is warped enough without me contributing to it."

"Want to know who I think would be really good?"

"Good?"

"Good," she repeated with an indecent smile.

"Not particularly."

"Your partner."

"Don't call him that," I said. " 'Partner' has a positive connotation."

Vee squeezed into a parking space near the library doors and killed the engine. "Have you ever fantasized about kissing him? Have you ever stolen a peek sideways and imagined flinging yourself at Patch and crushing your mouth to his?"

I stared at her with a look I hoped spoke appalled shock. "Have you?"

Vee grinned.

I tried to imagine what Patch would do if presented with this information. As little as I knew about him, I sensed his aversion to Vee as if it were concrete enough to touch.

"He's not good enough for you," I said.

She moaned. "Careful, you'll only make me want him more."

Inside the library we took a table on the main level, near adult fiction. I opened my laptop and typed: *The Sacrifice, two and a half stars*. Two and a half was probably on the low side. But I had a lot on my mind and wasn't feeling particularly equitable.

Vee opened a bag of dried apple chips. "Want some?"

"I'm good, thanks."

She peered into the bag. "If you're not going to eat them, I'll have to. And I really don't want to."

Vee was on the color-wheel fruit diet. Three red fruits a day, two blue, a handful of green . . .

She held up an apple chip, examining it front to back.

"What color?" I asked.

"Make-me-gag-Granny-Smith-green. I think."

Just then Marcie Millar, the only sophomore to make varsity cheerleading in the history of Coldwater High, took a seat on the edge of our table. Her strawberry blond hair was combed into low pigtails, and like always, her skin was concealed under half a bottle of foundation. I was fairly certain I'd guessed the right amount, since there wasn't a trace of her freckles in sight. I hadn't seen any of Marcie's freckles since seventh grade, the same year she discovered Mary Kay. There was three-quarters of an inch between the hem of her skirt and the start of her underwear . . . if she was even wearing any.

"Hi, Supersize," Marcie said to Vee.

"Hi, Freakshow," Vee said back.

"My mom is looking for models this weekend. The pay is nine dollars an hour. I thought you'd be interested."

Marcie's mom manages the local JCPenney, and on weekends she has Marcie and the rest of the cheerleaders model bikinis in the store's street-facing display windows.

"She's having a really hard time finding plus-size lingerie models," said Marcie.

"You've got food stuck in your teeth," Vee told Marcie. "In the crack between your two front teeth. Looks like chocolate Ex-Lax . . ."

Marcie licked her teeth and slid off the table. As she sashayed off, Vee stuck her finger in her mouth and made gagging gestures at Marcie's back.

"She's lucky we're at the library," Vee told me. "She's lucky we didn't cross paths in a dark alley. Last chance—any chips?"

"Pass."

Vee wandered off to discard the chips. A few minutes later she returned with a romance novel. She took the seat next to me and, displaying the novel's cover, said, "Someday this is going to be us. Ravished by half-dressed cowboys. I wonder what it's like to kiss a pair of sunbaked, mud-crusted lips?"

"Dirty," I murmured, typing away.

"Speaking of dirty." There was an unexpected rise in her voice. "There's our guy."

I stopped typing long enough to peer over my laptop, and my heart skipped a beat. Patch stood across the room in the checkout line. As if he sensed me watching, he turned. Our eyes locked for one, two, three counts. I broke away first, but not before receiving a slow grin.

My heartbeat turned erratic, and I told myself to pull it together. I was not going down this path. Not with Patch. Not unless I was out of my mind.

"Let's go," I told Vee. Shutting my laptop, I zipped it inside its carrying case. I pushed my books inside my backpack, dropping a few on the floor as I did.

Vee said, "I'm trying to read the title he's holding . . . hang on . . . How to Be a Stalker."

"He is not checking out a book with that title." But I wasn't sure.

"It's either that or How to Radiate Sexy Without Trying."

"Shh!" I hissed.

"Calm down, he can't hear. He's talking to the librarian. He's checking out."

Confirming this with a quick glance over, I realized that if we left now, we'd probably meet him at the exit doors. And then I would be expected to say something to him. I ordered myself back into my chair and searched diligently through my pockets for nothing whatsoever while he finished checking out.

"Do you think it's creepy he's here at the same time we are?" Vee asked.

"Do you?"

"I think he's following you."

"I think it's a coincidence." This wasn't entirely true. If I had to make a list of the top ten places I would expect to find Patch on any given night, the public library wouldn't make it. The library wouldn't make the top hundred places. So what was he doing here?

The question was particularly disturbing after what had happened last night. I hadn't mentioned it to Vee because I was hoping it would shrink and shrivel in my memory until it ceased to have happened. Period.

"Patch!" Vee stage-whispered. "Are you stalking Nora?"

I clamped my hand over her mouth. "Stop it. I mean it." I put on a severe face.

"I bet he is following you," said Vee, prying my hand away.

"I bet he has a history of it too. I bet he has restraining orders. We should sneak into the front office. It would all be in his student file."

"We are not sneaking into the front office."

"I could create a diversion. I'm good at diversions. No one would see you go in. We could be like spies."

"We are not spies."

"Do you know his last name?" Vee asked.

"No."

"Do you know anything about him?"

"No. And I'd like to keep it that way."

"Oh, come on. You love a good mystery, and it doesn't get better than this."

"The best mysteries involve a dead body. We don't have a dead body."

Vee squealed. "Not yet!"

Shaking two iron pills from the bottle in my backpack, I swallowed them together.

Vee bounced the Neon into her driveway just after nine thirty. She killed the engine and dangled the keys in front of me.

"You're not going to drive me home?" I asked. A waste of breath, since I knew her answer.

"There's fog."

"Patchy fog."

Vee grinned. "Oh, boy. He is so on your mind. Not that I blame you. Personally, I'm hoping I dream about him tonight."

Ugh.

"And the fog always gets worse near your house," Vee continued. "It freaks me out after dark."

I grabbed the keys. "Thanks a lot."

"Don't blame me. Tell your mom to move closer. Tell her there's this new club called civilization and you guys should join."

"I suppose you expect me to pick you up before school tomorrow?"

"Seven thirty would be nice. Breakfast is on me."

"It better be good."

"Be nice to my baby." She patted the Neon's dash. "But not too nice. Can't have her thinking there's better out there."

On the drive home I allowed my thoughts a brief trip to Patch. Vee was right—something about him was incredibly alluring. And incredibly creepy. The more I thought about it, the more I was convinced something about him was . . . off. The fact that he liked to antagonize me wasn't exactly a news flash, but there was a difference between getting under my skin in class and possibly going as far as following me to the library to accomplish it. Not many people would go to that much trouble . . . unless they had a very good reason.

Halfway home a pattering rain flushed out the wispy clouds of fog hovering above the road. Dividing my attention between the road and the controls on the steering wheel, I tried to locate the windshield wipers.

The streetlights flickered overhead, and I wondered if a heavier storm was blowing in. This close to the ocean the weather changed constantly, and a rainstorm could quickly escalate into a flash flood. I fed the Neon more gas.

The outside lights flickered again. A cold feeling prickled up the back of my neck, and the hairs on my arms tingled. My sixth sense graduated to high alert. I asked myself if I thought I was being followed. There were no headlights in the rearview mirror. No cars ahead, either. I was all alone. It wasn't a very comforting thought. I pushed the car to forty-five.

I found the wipers, but even at top speed they couldn't keep up with the hammering rain. The stoplight ahead turned yellow. I rolled to a stop, checked to see that traffic was clear, then pulled into the intersection.

I heard the impact before I registered the dark silhouette skidding across the hood of the car.

I screamed and stomped on the brake. The silhouette thumped into the windshield with a splintering crack.

On impulse, I jerked the steering wheel a hard right. The back end of the Neon fishtailed, sending me spinning across the intersection. The silhouette rolled and disappeared over the edge of the hood.

I was holding my breath, squeezing the steering wheel between white-knuckled hands. I lifted my feet off the pedals. The car bucked and stalled out.

He was crouched a few feet away, watching me. He didn't look at all . . . injured.

He was dressed in total black and blended with the night, making it hard to tell what he looked like. At first I couldn't distinguish any facial features, and then I realized he was wearing a ski mask.

He rose to his feet, closing the distance between us. He flattened his palms to the driver's-side window. Our eyes connected through the holes in the mask. A lethal smile seemed to rise in his.

He gave another pound, the glass vibrating between us.

I started the car. I tried to synchronize shoving it into first gear, pushing on the gas pedal, and releasing the clutch. The engine revved, but the car bucked again and died.

I turned the engine over once more, but was distracted by an off-key metallic groan. I watched with horror as the door began to bow. He was tearing—it—off.

I rammed the car into first. My shoes slipped over the pedals. The engine roared, the RPM needle on the dash spiking into the red zone.

His fist came through the window in an explosion of glass. His hand fumbled over my shoulder, clamping around my arm. I gave a hoarse cry, stomped the gas pedal, and released the clutch. The Neon screeched into motion. He hung on, grip-

ping my arm, running beside the car several feet before dropping away.

I sped forward with the force of adrenaline. I checked the rearview mirror to make sure he wasn't chasing me, then shoved the
mirror to face away. I had to press my lips together to keep from
sobbing.

F LYING DOWN HAWTHORNE, I DROVE PAST MY house, circled back, cut over to Beech, and headed back toward the center of Coldwater. I speed-dialed Vee. "Something happened—I—he—it—out of nowhere—the Neon   "

"You're breaking up. What?"

I wiped my nose with the back of my hand. I was trembling down to my toes. "He came out of nowhere."

"Who?"

"He—" I tried to net my thoughts and funnel them into words. "He jumped in front of the car!"

"Oh, man. Oh-man-oh-man-oh-man. You hit a deer? Are you okay? What about Bambi?" She half wailed, half groaned. "The Neon?"

I opened my mouth, but Vee cut me off.

"Forget it. I've got insurance. Just tell me there aren't deer parts all over my baby. . . . No deer parts, right?"

Whatever answer I was about to give faded into the background. My mind was two steps ahead. A deer. Maybe I could pass the whole thing off as hitting a deer. I wanted to confide in Vee, but I didn't want to sound crazy, either. How was I going to explain watching the guy I hit rise to his feet and begin tearing off the car door? I stretched my collar down past my shoulder. No red marks where he'd gripped me that I could see . . .

I came to myself with a start. Was I actually considering denying it had happened? I knew what I'd seen. It was not my imagination.

"Holy freak show," Vee said. "You're not answering. The deer is lodged in my headlights, isn't he? You're driving around with him stuck to the front of the car like a snowplow."

"Can I sleep at your place?" I wanted to get off the streets. Out of the dark. With a sudden intake of air, I realized to get to Vee's, I'd have to drive back through the intersection where I'd hit him.

"I'm down in my room," said Vee. "Let yourself in. See you in a few."

With my hands tight on the steering wheel, I pushed the Neon through the rain, praying the light at Hawthorne would be green in my favor. It was, and I floored it through the intersection, keeping my eyes straight ahead, but at the same time, stealing glimpses into the shadows along the side of the road. There was no sign of the guy in the ski mask.

Ten minutes later I parked the Neon in Vee's driveway. The damage to the door was extensive, and I had to put my foot to it and kick my way out. Then I jogged to the front door, bolted myself inside, and hurried down the basement stairs.

Vee was sitting cross-legged on her bed, notebook propped between her knees, earbuds plugged in, iPod turned up all the way. "Do I want to see the damage tonight, or should I wait until I've had at least seven hours of sleep?" she called over the music.

"Maybe option number two."

Vee snapped the notebook shut and tugged out the earbuds. "Let's get it over with."

When we got outside, I stared at the Neon for a long moment. It wasn't a warm night, but the weather wasn't the cause of the goose bumps rippling over my arms. No smashed driver's-side window. No bend in the door.

"Something's not right," I said. But Vee wasn't listening. She was busy inspecting every square inch of the Neon.

I stepped forward and poked the driver's-side window. Solid

glass. I closed my eyes. When I reopened them, the window was still intact.

I walked around the back of the car. I'd completed almost a full circle when I came up short.

A fine crack bisected the windshield.

Vee saw it at the same time. "Are you sure it wasn't a squirrel?"

My mind flashed back to the lethal eyes behind the ski mask. They were so black I couldn't distinguish the pupils from the irises. Black like . . . Patch's.

"Look at me, I'm crying tears of joy," Vee said, sprawling herself across the Neon's hood in a hug. "A teeny-tiny crack. That's it!"

I manufactured a smile, but my stomach soured. Five minutes ago, the window was smashed out and the door was bowed. Looking at the car now, it seemed impossible. No, it seemed crazy. But I *saw* his fist punch through the glass, and I *felt* his fingernails bite into my shoulder.

Hadn't I?

The harder I tried to recall the crash, the more I couldn't. Little blips of missing information cut across my memory. The details were fading. Was he tall? Short? Thin? Bulky? Had he said anything?

I couldn't remember. That was the most frightening part.

Vee and I left her house at seven fifteen the following morning and drove to Enzo's Bistro to grab a breakfast of steamed milk. With my hands wrapped around my china cup, I tried to warm away the

deep chill inside me. I'd showered, pulled on a camisole ̗
gan borrowed from Vee's closet, and swept on some makeup,
hardly remembered doing it.

"Don't look now," Vee said, "but Mr. Green Sweater keeps looking this way, estimating your long legs through your jeans. . . . Oh!
He just saluted me. I am not kidding. A little two-finger military
salute. How adorable."

I wasn't listening. Last night's accident had replayed itself in my
head all night, chasing away any chance of sleep. My thoughts were
in tangles, my eyes were dry and heavy, and I couldn't concentrate.

"Mr. Green Sweater looks normal, but his wingman looks hardcore bad boy," said Vee. "Emits a certain don't-mess-with-me signal.
Tell me he doesn't look like Dracula's spawn. Tell me I'm imagining things."

Lifting my eyes just high enough to get a look at him without appearing that I was, I took in his fine-boned, handsome
face. Blond hair hung at his shoulders. Eyes the color of chrome.
Unshaven. Impeccably dressed in a tailored jacket over his green
sweater and dark designer jeans. I said, "You're imagining things."

"Did you miss the deep-set eyes? The widow's peak? The tall,
lanky build? He might even be tall enough for me."

Vee is closing in on six feet tall, but she has a thing for heels.
High heels. She also has a thing about not dating shorter guys.

"Okay, what's wrong?" Vee asked. "You've gone all incommu-
nicado. This isn't about the crack in my windshield, is it? So what

if you hit an animal? It could happen to anyone. Granted, the chances would be a lot slimmer if your mom relocated out of the wilderness."

I was going to tell Vee the truth about what happened. Soon. I just needed a little time to sort out the details. The problem was, I didn't see how I could. The only details left were spotty, at best. It was as if an eraser had scrubbed my memory blank. Thinking back, I remembered the heavy rain cascading down the Neon's windows, causing everything outside to blur. Had I in fact hit a deer?

"Mmm, check it out," said Vee. "Mr. Green Sweater is getting out of his seat. Now that's a body that hits the gym regularly. He is definitely making his way toward us, his eyes pursuing the real estate, your real estate, that is."

A half beat later we were greeted with a low, pleasant "Hello."

Vee and I looked up at the same time. Mr. Green Sweater stood just back from our table, his thumbs hooked in the pockets of his jeans. He was blue-eyed, with stylishly shaggy blond hair swept across his forehead.

"Hello yourself," Vee said. "I'm Vee. This is Nora Grey."

I frowned at Vee. I did not appreciate her tagging on my last name, feeling that it violated an unspoken contract between girls, let alone best friends, upon meeting unknown boys. I gave a half-hearted wave and brought my cup to my lips, immediately scalding my tongue.

He dragged a chair over from the next table and sat backward on it, his arms resting where his back should have been. Holding a hand out to me, he said, "I'm Elliot Saunders." Feeling way too formal, I shook it. "And this is Jules," he added, jerking his chin toward his friend, whom Vee had grossly underestimated by calling "tall."

Jules lowered all of himself into a seat beside Vee, dwarfing the chair.

She said to him, "I think you might be the tallest guy I've ever seen. Seriously, how tall are you?"

"Six foot ten," Jules muttered, slumping in his seat and crossing his arms.

Elliot cleared his throat. "Can I get you ladies something to eat?"

"I'm fine," I said, raising my cup. "I already ordered."

Vee kicked me under the table. "She'll have a vanilla-cream-filled doughnut. Make it two."

"So much for the diet, huh?" I asked Vee.

"Huh yourself. The vanilla bean is a fruit. A brown fruit."

"It's a legume."

"You sure about that?"

I wasn't.

Jules closed his eyes and pinched the bridge of his nose. Apparently he was as thrilled to be sitting with us as I was to have them here.

As Elliot walked to the front counter, I let my eyes trail after him. He was definitely in high school, but I hadn't seen him at

CHS before. I would remember. He had a charming, outgoing personality that didn't fade into the background. If I wasn't feeling so shaken, I might have actually taken an interest. In friendship, maybe more.

"Do you live around here?" Vee asked Jules.

"Mmm."

"Go to school?"

"Kinghorn Prep." There was a tinge of superiority in the way he said it.

"Never heard of it."

"Private school. Portland. We start at nine." He lifted his sleeve and glanced at his watch.

Vee dipped a finger in the froth of her milk and licked it off. "Is it expensive?"

Jules looked at her directly for the first time. His eyes stretched, showing a little white around the edges.

"Are you rich? I bet you are," she said.

Jules eyed Vee like she'd just killed a fly on his forehead. He scraped his chair back several inches, distancing himself from us.

Elliot returned with a box of a half-dozen doughnuts.

"Two vanilla creams for the ladies," he said, pushing the box toward me, "and four glazed for me. Guess I'd better fill up now, since I don't know what the cafeteria is like at Coldwater High."

Vee nearly spewed her milk. "You go to CHS?"

"As of today. I just transferred from Kinghorn Prep."

"Nora and I go to CHS," Vee said. "I hope you appreciate your good fortune. Anything you need to know—including who you should invite to Spring Fling—just ask. Nora and I don't have dates . . . yet."

I decided it was time to part ways. Jules was obviously bored and irritated, and being in his company wasn't helping my already restless mood. I made a big presentation of looking at the clock on my cell phone and said, "We better get to school, Vee. We have a bio test to study for. Elliot and Jules, it was nice meeting you."

"Our bio test isn't until Friday," said Vee.

On the inside, I cringed. On the outside, I smiled through my teeth. "Right. I meant to say I have an English test. The works of . . . Geoffrey Chaucer." Everyone knew I was lying.

In a remote way my rudeness bothered me, especially since Elliot hadn't done anything to deserve it. But I didn't want to sit here any longer. I wanted to keep moving forward, distancing myself from last night. Maybe the diminishing memory wasn't such a bad thing after all. The sooner I forgot the accident, the sooner my life would resume its normal pace.

"I hope you have a really great first day, and maybe we'll see you at lunch," I told Elliot. Then I dragged Vee up by her elbow and steered her out the door.

The school day was almost over, only biology left, and after a quick stop by my locker to exchange books, I headed to class. Vee and I arrived before Patch; she slid into his empty seat and dug through her backpack, pulling out a box of Hot Tamales.

"One red fruit coming right up," she said, offering me the box.

"Let me guess . . . cinnamon is a fruit?" I pushed the box away.

"You didn't eat lunch, either," Vee said, frowning.

"I'm not hungry."

"Liar. You're always hungry. Is this about Patch? You're not worried he's really stalking you, are you? Because last night, that whole thing at the library, I was joking."

I massaged small circles into my temples. The dull ache that had taken up residence behind my eyes flared at the mention of Patch. "Patch is the least of my worries," I said. It wasn't exactly true.

"My seat, if you don't mind."

Vee and I looked up simultaneously at the sound of Patch's voice.

He sounded pleasant enough, but he kept his eyes trained on Vee as she rose and slung her backpack over her shoulder. It appeared she couldn't move fast enough; he swept his arm toward the aisle, inviting her out of his way.

"Looking good as always," he said to me, taking his chair. He leaned back in it, stretching his legs out in front of him. I'd known all along he was tall, but I'd never put a measurement to it. Looking at the length of his legs now, I guessed him to top out at six feet. Maybe even six-one.

"Thank you," I answered without thinking. Immediately I wanted

62

to take it back. Thank you? Of all the things I could have said, "thank you" was the worst. I didn't want Patch thinking I liked his compliments. Because I didn't . . . for the most part. It didn't take much perception to realize he was trouble, and I had enough trouble in my life already. No need to invite more. Maybe if I ignored him, he'd eventually give up initiating conversation. And then we could sit side by side in silent harmony, like every other partnership in the room.

"You smell good too," said Patch.

"It's called a shower." I was staring straight ahead. When he didn't answer, I turned sideways. "Soap. Shampoo. Hot water."

"Naked. I know the drill."

I opened my mouth to change the subject when the bell cut me off.

"Put your textbooks away," Coach said from behind his desk. "I'm handing out a practice quiz to get you warmed up for this Friday's real one." He stopped in front of me, licking his finger as he tried to separate the quizzes. "I want fifteen minutes of silence while you answer the questions. Then we'll discuss chapter seven. Good luck."

I worked through the first several questions, answering them with a rhythmic outpouring of memorized facts. If nothing else, the quiz stole my concentration, pushing last night's accident and the voice at the back of my mind questioning my sanity to the sidelines. Pausing to shake a cramp out of my writing hand, I felt Patch lean toward me.

"You look tired. Rough night?" he whispered.

"I saw you at the library." I was careful to keep my pencil gliding over my quiz, seemingly hard at work.

"The highlight of my night."

"Were you following me?"

He tipped his head back and laughed softly.

I tried a new angle. "What were you doing there?"

"Getting a book."

I felt Coach's eyes on me and dedicated myself to my quiz. After answering several more questions, I stole a glimpse to my left. I was surprised to find Patch already watching me. He grinned.

My heart did an unexpected flip, startled by his bizarrely attractive smile. To my horror, I was so taken aback, I dropped my pencil. It bounced on the tabletop a few times before rolling over the edge. Patch bent to pick it up. He held it out in the palm of his hand, and I had to focus not to touch his skin as I took it back.

"After the library," I whispered, "where did you go?"

"Why?"

"Did you follow me?" I demanded in an undertone.

"You look a little on edge, Nora. What happened?" His eyebrows lifted in concern. It was all for show, because there was a taunting spark at the center of his black eyes.

"Are you following me?"

"Why would I want to follow you?"

"Answer the question."

"Nora." The warning in Coach's voice pulled me back to my quiz, but I couldn't help speculating about what Patch's answer might have been, and it had me wanting to slide far away from him. Across the room. Across the universe.

Coach chirped his whistle. "Time's up. Pass your quizzes forward. Be expecting similar questions this Friday. Now"—he sanded his hands together, and the dry sound of it made me shiver—"for today's lesson. Miss Sky, want to take a stab at our topic?"

"S-e-x," Vee announced.

Precisely after she did, I tuned out. Was Patch following me? Was he the face behind the ski mask—if there even was a face behind a mask? What did he want? I hugged my elbows, suddenly feeling very cold. I wanted my life to go back to the way it was before Patch barged into it.

At the end of class, I stopped Patch from leaving. "Can we talk?"

He was already standing, so he took a seat on the edge of the table. "What's up?"

"I know you don't want to sit next to me any more than I want to sit next to you. I think Coach might consider changing our seats if you talk to him. If you explain the situation—"

"The situation?"

"We're not—compatible."

He rubbed a hand over his jaw, a calculating gesture I'd grown accustomed to in only a few short days of knowing him. "We're not?"

"I'm not announcing groundbreaking news here."

"When Coach asked for my list of desired characteristics in a mate, I gave him you."

"Take that back."

"Intelligent. Attractive. Vulnerable. You disagree?"

He was doing this for the sole purpose of antagonizing me, and that only flustered me more. "Will you ask Coach to change our seats or not?"

"Pass. You've grown on me."

What was I supposed to say to that? He was obviously aiming to get a reaction out of me. Which wasn't difficult, seeing as how I could never tell when he was joking, and when he was sincere.

I tried to inject a measure of self-composure into my voice. "I think you'd be much better seated with someone else. And I think you know it." I smiled, tense but polite.

"I think I could end up next to Vee." His smile appeared just as polite. "I'm not going to press my luck."

Vee appeared beside our table, glancing between me and Patch. "Interrupting something?"

"No," I said, yanking my backpack shut. "I was asking Patch about tonight's reading. I couldn't remember which pages Coach assigned."

Vee said, "The assignment's on the board, same as always. As if you haven't already read it."

Patch laughed, seemingly sharing a private joke with himself.

Not for the first time, I wished I knew what he was thinking. Because sometimes I was positive these private jokes had everything to do with me. "Anything else, Nora?" he said.

"No," I said. "See you tomorrow."

"Looking forward to it." He winked. Actually winked.

After Patch was out of earshot, Vee gripped my arm. "Good news. Cipriano. That's his last name. I saw it on Coach's class roster."

"And that's something to smile about because . . . ?"

"Everybody knows students are required to register prescription drugs with the nurse's office." She tugged at the front pocket of my backpack, where I kept my iron pills. "Likewise, everybody knows the nurse's office is conveniently located inside the front office, where, as it happens, student files are also kept."

Eyes aglow, Vee locked her arm in mine and pulled me toward the door. "Time to do some real sleuthing."

AN I HELP YOU?"

I forced myself to smile at the front office secretary, hoping I didn't look as dishonest as I felt. "I have a prescription I take daily at school, and my friend—"

My voice caught on the word, and I wondered if after today I would ever feel like calling Vee my friend again.

"—my friend informed me that I'm supposed to register it with the nurse. Do you know if that's correct?" I couldn't believe I was standing here, intending to do something illegal. As of late, I was exhibiting a lot of uncharacteristic behavior. First I'd followed Patch to a disreputable arcade late at night. Now I was on the verge of snooping in his student file. What was the matter with me? No—what was the matter with Patch, that when it came to him, I couldn't seem to stop exercising bad judgment?

"Oh, yes," the secretary said solemnly. "All drugs need to be registered. Nurse's office is back through there, third door on the left, across from student records." She gestured into the hallway behind her. "If the nurse isn't there, you can take a seat on the couch inside her office. She should be back any minute."

I fabricated another smile. I'd really hoped it wouldn't be this easy.

Heading down the hall, I stopped several times to check over my shoulder. Nobody came up behind me. The phone out in the front office was ringing, but it sounded a world apart from the dim corridor where I stood. I was all alone, free to do as I pleased.

I came to a stop at the third door on the left. I sucked in a breath and knocked, but it was obvious from the darkened window that the room was empty. I pushed on the door. It moved with reluctance, creaking open on a compact room with scuffed white tiles. I stood in the entrance a moment, almost wishing the nurse would appear so I'd have no choice but to register my iron pills and leave. A quick glance across the hall revealed a door with a window marked STUDENT RECORDS. It too was dark.

I focused my attention on a nagging thought at the back of my mind. Patch claimed that he hadn't gone to school last year. I was pretty sure he was lying, but if he wasn't, would he even have a student record? He'd have a home address at the very least, I reasoned. And an immunization card, and last semester's grades. Still. Possible suspension seemed like a large price to pay for a peek at Patch's immunization card.

I leaned one shoulder against the wall and checked my watch. Vee had told me to wait for her signal. She said it would be obvious.

Great.

The phone in the front office rang again, and the secretary picked up.

Chewing my lip, I stole a second glimpse at the door labeled STUDENT RECORDS. There was a good chance it was locked. Student files were probably considered high security. It didn't matter what kind of diversion Vee created; if the door was locked, I wasn't getting in.

I shifted my backpack to the opposite shoulder. Another minute ticked down. I told myself maybe I should leave. . . .

On the other hand, what if Vee was right and he was stalking me? As his bio partner, regular contact with him could place me in danger. I had a responsibility to protect myself . . . didn't I?

If the door was unlocked and the files were alphabetized, I would have no trouble locating Patch's quickly. Add another few seconds to skim his file for red flags, and I could probably be in and out of the room in under a minute. Which was so brief it might not feel like I'd entered at all.

Things had grown unusually quiet out in the front office. Suddenly Vee rounded the corner. She edged down the wall toward me, walking in a crouch, dragging her hands along the wall, stealing surreptitious glances over her shoulder. It was the kind of walk spies adopted in old movies.

"Everything is under control," she whispered.

"What happened to the secretary?"

"She had to leave the office for a minute."

"Had to? You didn't incapacitate her, did you?"

"Not this time."

Thank goodness for small mercies.

"I called in a bomb threat from the pay phone outside," Vee said. "The secretary dialed the police, then ran off to find the principal."

"Vee!"

She tapped her wrist. "Clock's ticking. We don't want to be in here when the cops arrive."

Tell me about it.

Vee and I sized up the door to student records.

"Move over," Vee said, giving me her hip.

She drew her sleeve down over her fist and drilled it into the window. Nothing happened.

"That was just for practice," she said. She drew back for another punch and I grabbed her arm.

"It might be unlocked." I turned the knob and the door swung open.

"That wasn't nearly as much fun," said Vee.

A matter of opinion.

"You go in," Vee instructed. "I'm going to keep surveillance. If all goes well, we'll rendezvous in an hour. Meet me at the Mexican restaurant on the corner of Drake and Beech." She crouch-walked back down the hall.

I was left standing half in, half out of the narrow room lined wall-to-wall with filing cabinets. Before my conscience talked me out of it, I stepped inside and shut the door behind me, pressing my back against it.

With a deep breath I slouched off my backpack and hurried forward, dragging my finger along the faces of the cabinets. I found the drawer marked CAR–CUV. With one tug the drawer rattled open. The tabs on the files were labeled by hand, and I wondered if Coldwater High was the last school in the country not computerized.

My eyes brushed over the name "Cipriano."

I wrenched the file from the crammed drawer. I held it in my hands a moment, trying to convince myself there was nothing too wrong with what I was about to do. So what if there was private information inside? As Patch's biology partner, I had a right to know these things.

Outside, voices filled the hall.

I fumbled the file open and immediately flinched. It didn't make any sense.

The voices advanced.

I shoved the file randomly inside the drawer and gave it a push, sending it rattling back into the cabinet. As I turned, I froze. On the other side of the window, the principal stopped midstride, his gaze latching onto me.

Whatever he'd been saying to the group, which probably consisted of every major player on the school's faculty, trailed off. "Excuse me a moment," I heard him say. The group continued hustling forward. He did not.

He opened the door. "This area is off-limits to students."

I tried on a helpless face. "I'm so sorry. I'm trying to find the nurse's office. The secretary said third door on the right, but I think I miscounted. . . . " I threw my hands up. "I'm lost."

Before he could respond, I tugged at the zipper on my backpack. "I'm supposed to register these. Iron pills," I explained. "I'm anemic."

He studied me for a moment, his brow creasing. I thought I could see him weighing his options: stick around and deal with me, or deal with a bomb threat. He jerked his chin out the door. "I need you to exit the building immediately."

He propped the door wide and I ducked out under his arm, my smile collapsing.

An hour later I slid into a corner booth at the Mexican restaurant on the corner of Drake and Beech. A ceramic cactus and a stuffed coyote were mounted on the wall above me. A man wearing a sombrero wider than he was tall sauntered over. Strumming chords on his guitar, he serenaded me while the hostess laid menus on the table. I frowned at the insignia on the front cover. The Borderline. I hadn't eaten here before, yet something about the name sounded vaguely familiar.

Vee came up behind me and flopped into the opposite seat. Our waiter was on her heels.

"Four chimis, extra sour cream, a side of nachos, and a side of black beans," Vee told him without consulting the menu.

"One red burrito," I said.

"Separate bills?" he asked.

"I'm not paying for her," Vee and I said at the same time.

After our waiter left, I said, "Four chimis. I'm looking forward to hearing the fruit connection."

"Don't even start. I'm starving. Haven't eaten since lunch." She paused. "If you don't count the Hot Tamales, which I don't."

Vee is voluptuous, Scandinavian fair, and in an unorthodox way, incredibly sexy. There have been days when our friendship was the only thing standing in the way of my jealousy. Next to Vee, the only thing I have going for me are my legs. And maybe my metabolism. But definitely not my hair.

"He'd better bring chips soon," said Vee. "I'll break out in hives if I don't eat something salty within the next forty-five seconds. And anyway, the first three letters in the word diet should tell you what I want it to do."

"They make salsa with tomatoes," I pointed out. "That's a red. And avocados are a fruit. I think."

Her face brightened. "And we'll order virgin strawberry daiquiris."

Vee was right. This diet was easy.

"Be right back," she said, sliding out of the booth. "That time of the month. After that, I want to get the scoop."

While waiting for her, I found myself concentrating on the busboy some tables away. He was hard at work scrubbing a rag over the top of a table. There was something strangely familiar about the way he moved, about the way his shirt fell over the arch of his well-defined back. Almost as if he suspected he was being watched, he straightened and turned, his eyes fixing on mine at the exact same moment I figured out what was so familiar about this particular busboy.

Patch.

I couldn't believe it. I thought about slapping my forehead when I remembered he'd told me he worked at the Borderline.

Wiping his hands on his apron, he walked over, apparently enjoying my discomfort as I looked around for some way to escape, finding I had nowhere to go but deeper into the booth.

"Well, well," he said. "Five days a week isn't enough of me? Had to give me an evening, too?"

"I apologize for the unfortunate coincidence."

He slid into Vee's seat. When he laid his arms down, they were so long, they crossed into my half of the table. He reached for my glass, twirling it in his hands.

"All the seats here are taken," I said. When he didn't answer, I grabbed my glass back and took a sip of water, accidentally swallowing an ice cube. It burned the whole way down. "Shouldn't you be working instead of fraternizing with customers?" I choked.

He smiled. "What are you doing Sunday night?"

I snorted. By accident. "Are you asking me out?"

"You're getting cocky. I like that, Angel."

"I don't care what you like. I'm not going out with you. Not on a date. Not alone." I wanted to kick myself for experiencing a hot thrill upon speculating what a night alone with Patch might entail. Most likely, he hadn't even meant it. Most likely, he was baiting me for reasons known only to him. "Hang on, did you just call me Angel?" I asked.

"If I did?"

"I don't like it."

He grinned. "It stays. Angel."

He leaned across the table, raised his hand to my face, and brushed his thumb along one corner of my mouth. I pulled away, too late.

He rubbed lip gloss between his thumb and forefinger. "You'd look better without it."

I tried to remember what we'd been talking about, but not nearly as hard as I tried to appear unmoved by his touch. I tossed my hair back over my shoulder, picking up the tail of our previous conversation. "Anyway, I'm not allowed to go out on school nights."

"Too bad. There's a party on the coast. I thought we could go." He actually sounded sincere.

I could not figure him out. At all. The earlier hot thrill still lingered in my blood, and I took a long pull on my straw, trying to cool my feelings with a shot of ice water. Time alone with Patch would be intriguing, and dangerous. I wasn't sure how exactly, but I was trusting my instincts on this one.

I affected a yawn. "Well, like I said, it's a school night." In hopes of convincing myself more than him, I added, "If this party is something you'd be interested in, I can almost guarantee I won't be."

There, I thought. Case closed.

And then, without any warning whatsoever, I said, "Why are you asking me anyway?"

Up until this very moment, I'd been telling myself I didn't care what Patch thought of me. But right now, I knew it was a lie. Even though it would probably come back to haunt me, I was curious enough about Patch to go almost anywhere with him.

"I want to get you alone," Patch said. Just like that, my defenses shot back up.

"Listen, Patch, I don't want to be rude, but—"

"Sure you do."

"Well, you started it!" Lovely. Very mature. "I can't go to the party. End of story."

"Because you can't go out on a school night, or because you're scared of being alone with me?"

"Both." The confession just slipped out.

"Are you scared of all guys . . . or just me?"

I rolled my eyes as if to say I *am not answering such an inane question.*

"I make you uneasy?" His mouth held a neutral line, but I detected a speculative smile trapped behind it.

Yes, actually, he had that effect on me. He also had the tendency to wipe all logical thought from my mind.

"I'm sorry," I said. "What were we talking about?"

"You."

"Me?"

"Your personal life."

I laughed, unsure what other response to give. "If this is about me . . . and the opposite sex . . . Vee already gave me this speech. I don't need to hear it twice."

"And what did wise old Vee say?"

I was playing with my hands, and slid them out of sight. "I can't imagine why you're so interested."

He softly shook his head. "Interested? We're talking about you. I'm fascinated." He smiled, and it was a fantastic smile. The effect was a ratcheted pulse—my ratcheted pulse.

"I think you should get back to work," I said.

"For what it's worth, I like the idea that there's not a guy at school who matches up to your expectations."

"I forgot you're the authority on my so-called expectations," I scoffed.

He studied me in a way that had me feeling transparent. "You're not cagey, Nora. Not shy, either. You just need a very good reason to go out of your way to get to know someone."

"I don't want to talk about me anymore."

"You think you've got everyone all figured out."

"Not true," I said. "For example, well, for instance, I don't know much about . . . you."

"You aren't ready to know me."

There was nothing light about the way he said it. In fact, his expression was razor sharp.

"I looked in your student file."

My words hung in the air a moment before Patch's eyes aligned with mine. "I'm pretty sure that's illegal," he said calmly.

"Your file was empty. Nothing. Not even an immunization record."

He didn't even pretend to look surprised. He eased back in his seat, eyes gleaming obsidian. "And you're telling me this because you're afraid I might cause an outbreak? Measles or mumps?"

"I'm telling you this because I want you to know that I know something about you isn't right. You haven't fooled everybody.

I'm going to find out what you're up to. I'm going to expose you."

"Looking forward to it."

I flushed, catching the innuendo too late. Over the top of Patch's head, I could see Vee weaving her way through the tables.

I said, "Vee's coming. You have to go."

He stayed put, eyeing me, considering.

"Why are you looking at me like that?" I challenged.

He tipped forward, preparing to stand. "Because you're nothing like what I expected."

"Neither are you," I countered. "You're worse."

CHAPTER

6

THE FOLLOWING MORNING I WAS SURPRISED TO SEE Elliot walk into first-hour PE just as the tardy bell sounded. He was dressed in knee-length basketball shorts and a white Nike sweatshirt. His high-tops looked new and expensive. After handing a slip of paper to Miss Sully, he caught my eye. He gave a low wave and joined me in the bleachers.

"I was wondering when we'd bump into each other again," he said. "The front office realized I haven't had PE for the past two years. It's not required in private school. They're debating how they're going to fit four years' worth of PE into the next two. So here I am. I've got PE first and fourth hours."

"I never heard why you transferred here," I said.

"I lost my scholarship and my parents couldn't afford the tuition."

Miss Sully blew her whistle.

"I take it the whistle means something," Elliot said to me.

"Ten laps around the gym, no cutting corners." I pushed up from the bleachers. "Are you an athlete?"

Elliot jumped up, dancing on the balls of his feet. He threw a few hooks and jabs into the air. He finished with an uppercut that stopped just short of my chin. Grinning, he said, "An athlete? To the core."

"Then you're going to love Miss Sully's idea of fun."

Elliot and I jogged the ten laps together, then headed outdoors, where the air was laced with a ghostly fog. It seemed to clog my lungs, choking me. The sky leaked a few raindrops, trying hard to push a storm down on the city of Coldwater. I eyed the building doors but knew it was to no avail; Miss Sully was hardcore.

"I need two captains for softball," she hollered. "Come on, look alive. Let's see some hands in the air! Better volunteer, or I'll pick teams, and I don't always play fair."

Elliot raised his hand.

"All right," Miss Sully said to him. "Up here, by home plate. And how about . . . Marcie Millar as captain of the red team."

Marcie's eyes swept over Elliot. "Bring it on."

"Elliot, go ahead and take first pick," Miss Sully said.

Steepling his fingers at his chin, Elliot examined the class, seemingly sizing up our batting and fielding skills just by the look of us. "Nora," he said.

Marcie tipped her neck back and laughed. "Thanks," she told Elliot, flashing him a toxic smile that, for reasons beyond me, mesmerized the opposite sex.

"For what?" said Elliot.

"For handing us the game." Marcie pointed a finger at me. "There's a hundred reasons why I'm a cheerleader and Nora's not. Coordination tops the list."

I narrowed my eyes at Marcie, then made my way over beside Elliot and tugged a blue jersey over my head.

"Nora and I are friends," Elliot told Marcie calmly, almost coolly. It was an overstatement, but I wasn't about to correct him. Marcie looked like she'd had a bucket of ice water flung at her, and I was enjoying it.

"That's because you haven't met anyone better. Like me." Marcie twisted her hair around her finger. "Marcie Millar. You'll hear all about me soon enough." Either her eye twitched, or she winked at him.

Elliot gave no response whatsoever, and my approval rating of him shot up a few notches. A lesser guy would have dropped to his knees and begged Marcie for any attention she saw fit to toss.

"Do we want to stand out here all morning waiting for the rain to come, or get down to business?" Miss Sully asked.

After divvying up teams, Elliot led ours to the dugout and determined the batting order. Handing me a bat, he pushed a helmet on my head. "You're up first, Grey. All we need is a base hit."

Taking a practice swing, and almost nailing him with it, I said, "But I was in the mood for a home run."

"We'll take one of those, too." He directed me toward home plate. "Step into the pitch and swing all the way through."

I balanced the bat on my shoulder, thinking maybe I should have paid more attention during the World Series. Okay, maybe I should have *watched* the World Series. My helmet slipped low on my eyes, and I pushed it up, trying to size up the infield, which was lost under ghoulish wisps of mist.

Marcie Millar took her place on the pitcher's mound. She held the ball out in front of her, and I noticed her middle finger was raised at me. She flashed another toxic smile and lobbed the softball at me.

I got a piece of it, sending it flying into the dirt on the wrong side of the foul line.

"That's a strike!" Miss Sully called from her position between first and second bases.

Elliot hollered from the dugout, "That had a lot of spin on it— send her a clean one!" It took me a moment to realize he was talking to Marcie and not me.

Again the ball left Marcie's hand, arching through the dismal sky. I swung, a pure miss.

"Strike two," Anthony Amowitz said through the catcher's mask.

I gave him a hard look.

Stepping away from the plate, I took a few more practice swings. I almost missed Elliot coming up behind me. He reached his arms around me and positioned his hands on the bat, flush with mine.

"Let me show you," he said in my ear. "Like this. Feel that? Relax. Now pivot your hips—it's all in the hips."

I could feel my face heat up with the eyes of the entire class on us. "I think I've got it, thanks."

"Get a room!" Marcie called to us. The infield laughed.

"If you'd throw her a decent pitch," Elliot called back, "she'd hit the ball."

"My pitch is on."

"Her swing is on." Elliot dropped his voice, speaking to me alone. "You lose eye contact the minute she lets go of the ball. Her pitches aren't clean, so you're going to have to work to get them."

"We're holding up the game here, people!" Miss Sully called out.

Just then, something in the parking lot beyond the dugout drew my attention. I thought I'd heard my name called. I turned, but even as I did, I knew my name hadn't been said out loud. It had been spoken quietly to my mind.

Nora.

Patch wore a faded blue baseball cap and had his fingers hooked in the chain-link fence, leaning against it. No coat, despite the weather. Just head-to-toe black. His eyes were opaque and inaccessible as he watched me, but I suspected there was a lot going on behind them.

Another string of words crept into my mind.

Batting lessons? Nice . . . touch.

I drew a steadying breath and told myself I'd imagined the words. Because the alternative was considering that Patch held the power to channel thoughts into my mind. Which couldn't be. It just couldn't. Unless I was delusional. That scared me more than the idea that he'd breached normal communication methods and could, at will, speak to me without ever opening his mouth.

"Grey! Head in the game!"

I blinked, jerking to life just in time to see the ball rolling through the air toward me. I started to swing, then heard another trickle of words.

Not . . . yet.

I held back, waiting for the ball to come to me. As it descended, I stepped toward the front of the plate. I swung with everything I had.

A huge crack sounded, and the bat vibrated in my hands. The ball drove at Marcie, who fell flat on her backside. Squeezing between shortstop and second base, the ball bounced in the outfield grass.

"Run!" my team shouted from the dugout. "Run, Nora!"

I ran.

"Drop the bat!" they screamed.

I flung it aside.

"Stay on first base!"

I didn't.

Stepping on a corner of first base, I rounded it, sprinting toward second. Left field had the ball now, in position to throw me out. I put my head down, pumped my arms, and tried to remember how the pros on ESPN slid into base. Feetfirst? Headfirst? Stop, drop, and roll?

The ball sailed toward the second baseman, spinning white somewhere in my peripheral vision. An excited chanting of the word "Slide!" came from the dugout, but I still hadn't made up my mind which was hitting the dirt first—my shoes or my hands.

The second baseman snagged the ball out of the air. I dove head-first, arms outstretched. The glove came out of nowhere, swooping down on me. It collided with my face, smelling strongly of leather. My body crumpled on the dirt, leaving me with a mouthful of grit and sand dissolving under my tongue.

"She's out!" cried Miss Sully.

I tumbled sideways, surveying myself for injuries. My thighs burned a strange mix of hot and cold, and when I raised my sweats, to say it looked like two cats had been set free on my thighs would be an understatement. Limping to the dugout, I collapsed on the bench.

"Cute," Elliot said.

"The stunt I pulled or my torn-up leg?" Tucking my knee against my chest, I gently brushed as much of the dirt away as I could.

Elliot bent sideways and blew on my knee. Several of the larger bits of dirt fell to the ground.

A moment of awkward silence followed.

"Can you walk?" he asked.

Standing, I demonstrated that while my leg was a mess of scratches and dirt, I still had the use of it.

"I can take you the nurse's office if you want. Get you bandaged," he said.

"Really, I'm fine." I glanced at the fence where I'd last seen Patch. He was no longer there.

"Was that your boyfriend standing by the fence?" Elliot asked.

I was surprised that Elliot had noticed Patch. He'd had his back to him. "No," I said. "Just a friend. Actually, not even that. He's my bio partner."

"You're blushing."

"Probably windburn."

Patch's voice still echoed in my head. My heart pumped faster, but if anything, my blood ran colder. Had he talked directly to my thoughts? Was there some inexplicable link between us that allowed it to happen? Or was I losing my mind?

Elliot didn't look fully convinced. "You sure nothing's going on between the two of you? I don't want to chase after an unavailable girl."

"Nothing." Nothing I was going to allow, anyway.

Wait. What did Elliot say?

"Sorry?" I said.

He smiled. "Delphic Seaport reopens Saturday night, and Jules and I are thinking about driving out. Weather's not supposed to be too bad. Maybe you and Vee want to come?"

I took a moment to think over his offer. I was pretty sure that if I turned Elliot down, Vee would kill me. Besides, going out with Elliot seemed like a good way to escape my uncomfortable attraction to Patch.

"Sounds like a plan," I said.

CHAPTER

7

IT WAS SATURDAY NIGHT, AND DOROTHEA AND I WERE IN
the kitchen. She had just popped a casserole into the oven
and was sizing up a list of tasks my mom had hanging from a
magnet on the fridge.

"Your mother called. She won't arrive home until late Sunday
night," Dorothea said as she scrubbed Ajax into our kitchen sink
with a vigor that made my own elbow ache. "She left a message on
the machine. She wants you to give her a call. You've been calling
every night before bed?"

I sat on a stool, eating a buttered bagel. I'd just taken a huge bite, and now Dorothea was looking at me like she wanted an answer. "Mm-hmm," I said, nodding.

"A letter from school came today." She flicked her chin at the stack of mail on the counter. "Maybe you know why?"

I gave my best innocent shrug and said, "No clue." But I had a pretty good idea what this was about. Twelve months ago I'd opened the front door to find the police on the doorstep. *We have some bad news*, they said. My dad's funeral was a week later. Every Monday afternoon since then, I'd shown up at my scheduled time slot with Dr. Hendrickson, school psychologist. I'd missed the last two sessions, and if I didn't make amends this week, I was going to get in trouble. Most likely the letter was a warning.

"You have plans tonight? You and Vee have something up your sleeves? Maybe a movie here at the house?"

"Maybe. Honestly, Dorth, I can clean the sink later. Come sit and . . . have the other half of my bagel."

Dorothea's gray bun was coming undone as she scrubbed. "I am going to a conference tomorrow," she said. "In Portland. Dr. Melissa Sanchez will speak. She says you think your way to a sexier you. Hormones are powerful drugs. Unless we tell them what we want, they backfire. They work against us." Dorothea turned, pointing the Ajax can at me for emphasis. "Now I wake in the morning and take red lipstick to my mirror. 'I am sexy,' I write. 'Men want me. Sixty-five is the new twenty-five.'"

"Do you think it's working?" I asked, trying very hard not to smile.

"It's working," Dorothea said soberly.

I licked butter off my fingers, stalling for a suitable response. "So you're going to spend the weekend reinventing your sexy side."

"Every woman needs to reinvent her sexy side—I like that. My daughter got implants. She said she did it for herself, but what woman gets boobs for herself? They are a burden. She got the boobs for a man. I hope you do not do stupid things for a boy, Nora." She shook her finger at me.

"Trust me, Dorth, there are no boys in my life." Okay, maybe there were two lurking on the fringe, circling from afar, but since I didn't know either very well, and one outright frightened me, it felt safer to close my eyes and pretend they weren't there.

"This is a good thing, and a bad thing," Dorothea said scoldingly. "You find the wrong boy, you ask for trouble. You find the right boy, you find love." Her voice softened reminiscently. "When I was a little girl in Germany, I had to choose between two boys. One was a very wicked boy. The other was my Henry. We are happily married for forty-one years."

It was time to change the subject. "How's, um, your godson . . . Lionel?"

Her eyes stretched. "You have a thing for little Lionel?"

"Noooo."

"I can work something out—"

"No, Dorothea, really. Thank you, but—I'm really concentrating on my grades right now. I want to get into a top-tier college."

"If in the future—"

"I'll let you know."

I finished my bagel to the sounds of Dorothea's monotone chatter, interjecting a few nods or "uh-huh's" whenever she stopped talking long enough to wait for my response. I was preoccupied debating whether or not I really wanted to meet Elliot tonight. At first, meeting up had seemed like a great idea. But the more I thought about it, the more doubt crept in. I'd only known Elliot a couple of days, for one. And I wasn't sure how my mom would feel about the arrangement, for another. It was getting late, and Delphic was at least a half-hour drive. More to the point, on weekends Delphic had a reputation for being wild.

The phone rang, and Vee's number showed on the caller ID.

"Are we doing anything tonight?" she wanted to know.

I opened my mouth, weighing my answer carefully. Once I told Vee about Elliot's offer, there would be no turning back.

Vee shrieked. "Oh, man! Oh-man-oh-man-oh-man. I just spilled nail polish on the sofa. Hang on, I'm going to get some paper towels. Is nail polish water-soluble?" A moment later she returned. "I think I ruined the sofa. We have to go out tonight. I don't want to be here when my latest work of accidental art is discovered."

Dorothea had moved down the hall to the powder room. I had no desire to spend the whole night listening to her grunt over the bathroom fixtures as she cleaned, so I made my decision. "How about Delphic Seaport? Elliot and Jules are going. They want to meet up."

"You buried the lead! Vital information here, Nora. I'll pick you up in fifteen." I was left listening to the dial tone.

I went upstairs and pulled on a snug white cashmere sweater, dark jeans, and navy blue driving moccasins. I shaped the hair framing my face around my finger, the way I'd learned to manage my natural curls, and . . . voilà! Half-decent spirals. I stepped back from the mirror for a twice-over and called myself a cross between carefree and *almost* sexy.

Fifteen minutes later to the dot, Vee bounced the Neon up the driveway and beeped the horn staccato-style. It took me ten minutes to make the drive between our houses, but I usually paid attention to the speed limit. Vee understood the word speed, but limit wasn't part of her vocabulary.

"I'm going to Delphic Seaport with Vee," I called to Dorothea. "If my mom calls, would you mind relaying the message?"

Dorothea waddled out of the powder room. "All the way to Delphic? This late?"

"Have fun at your conference!" I said, escaping out the door before she could protest or get my mom on the phone.

Vee's blond hair was pulled up in a high ponytail, big fat curls spilling down. Gold hoops dangled from her ears. Cherry red lipstick. Black, lengthening mascara.

"How do you do it?" I asked. "You had five minutes to get ready."

"Always prepared." Vee shot me a grin. "I'm a Boy Scout's dream."

She gave me a critical once-over.

"What?" I said.

"We're meeting up with boys tonight."

"Last I checked, yes."

"Boys like girls who look like . . . girls."

I arched my eyebrows. "And what do I look like?"

"Like you stepped out of the shower and decided that alone was enough to pass as presentable. Don't get me wrong. The clothes are good, the hair is okay, but the rest . . . Here." She reached inside her purse. "Being the friend that I am, I'll loan you my lipstick. And my mascara, but only if you swear you don't have a contagious eye disease."

"I do not have an eye disease!"

"Just covering my bases."

"I'll pass."

Vee's mouth dropped, half-playful, half-serious. "You'll feel naked without it!"

"Sounds like just the kind of look you'd go for," I said.

In all honesty, I had mixed feelings about going makeup free.

Not because I did feel a little bit naked, but because Patch had put the no-makeup suggestion in my mind. In an effort to make myself feel better, I told myself my dignity wasn't at stake. Neither was my pride. I'd been given a suggestion, and I was open-minded enough to try it. What I didn't want to acknowledge was I'd specifically chosen a night I knew I wouldn't see Patch to test it out.

A half hour later Vee drove under the gates to Delphic Seaport. We were forced to park at the farthest end of the lot, due to heavy opening-weekend traffic. Nestled right on the coast, Delphic is not known for its mild weather. A low wind had picked up, sweeping popcorn bags and candy wrappers around our ankles as Vee and I walked toward the ticket counter. The trees had long since lost their leaves, and the branches loomed over us like disjointed fingers. Delphic Seaport boomed all summer long with an amusement park, masquerades, fortune-telling booths, gypsy musicians, and a freak show. I could never be sure if the human deformities were real or an illusion.

"One adult, please," I told the woman at the ticket counter. She took my money and slid a wristband under the window. Then she smiled, exposing white plastic vampire teeth, smudged red with lipstick.

"Have a good time," she said in a breathless voice. "And don't forget to try our newly remodeled ride." She tapped her side of the glass, pointing to a stack of park maps and a flier.

I grabbed one of each on my way through the revolving gates. The flier read:

DELPHIC AMUSEMENT PARK'S

NEWEST SENSATION!

THE ARCHANGEL

REMODELED AND RENOVATED!

FALL FROM GRACE ON THIS

ONE-HUNDRED-FOOT VERTICAL DROP.

Vee read the flier over my shoulder. Her nails threatened to puncture the skin on my arm. "We have to do it!" she squealed.

"Last," I promised, hoping if we did all the other rides first, she'd forget about this one. I hadn't been afraid of heights for years, probably because I had conveniently avoided them. I wasn't sure I was ready just yet to find out if time had faded my fear of them.

After we hit the Ferris wheel, the bumper cars, the Magic Carpet ride, and a few of the game booths, Vee and I decided it was time to look for Elliot and Jules.

"Hmm," said Vee, looking both ways down the path looping the park. We shared a thoughtful silence.

"The arcade," I said at last.

"Good call."

We had just walked through the doors to the arcade when I saw him. Not Elliot. Not Jules.

Patch.

He glanced up from his video game. The same baseball cap he'd worn when I saw him during PE shielded most of his face, but I was certain I saw a flicker of a smile. At first glance it appeared friendly, but then I remembered how he'd entered my thoughts, and I went cold to the bone.

If I was lucky, Vee hadn't seen him. I edged her forward through the crowd, letting Patch fall out of sight. The last thing I needed was for her to suggest we go over and strike up a conversation.

"There they are!" Vee said, waving her arm over her head. "Jules! Elliot! Over here!"

"Good evening, ladies," Elliot said, making his way through the crowd. Jules moved in his wake, looking about as enthusiastic as three-day-old meat loaf. "Can I buy you both a Coke?"

"Sounds good," said Vee. She was looking right at Jules. "I'll take a Diet."

Jules muttered an excuse about needing to use the restroom and slipped back into the crowd.

Five minutes later Elliot returned with Cokes. After splitting them between us, he rubbed his hands together and surveyed the floor. "Where should we start?"

"What about Jules?" Vee asked.

"He'll find us."

"Air hockey," I said immediately. Air hockey was on the other side of the arcade. The farther away from Patch, the better. I told myself it was a coincidence he was here, but my instincts disagreed.

"Ooh, look!" Vee interjected. "Foosball!" She was already zigzagging her way toward an open table. "Jules and me against the two of you. Losers buy pizza."

"Fair enough," said Elliot.

Foosball would have been fine, had the table not been a short distance from where Patch stood playing his game. I told myself to ignore him. If I kept my back to him, I'd hardly notice he was there. Maybe Vee wouldn't notice him either.

"Hey, Nora, isn't that Patch?" Vee said.

"Hmm?" I said innocently.

She pointed. "Over there. That's him, isn't it?"

"I doubt it. Are Elliot and I the white team, then?"

"Patch is Nora's bio partner," Vee explained to Elliot. She winked slyly at me but made a face of innocence the moment Elliot gave her his attention. I shook my head subtly but firmly at her, transmitting a silent message—stop.

"He keeps looking this way," Vee said in a lowered voice. She leaned across the foosball table, attempting to make her conversation with me appear private, but she whispered loud enough that Elliot had no choice but to overhear. "He's bound to wonder what you're doing here with—" She bobbed her head at Elliot.

I shut my eyes and envisioned banging my head against the wall.

"Patch has made it very clear he'd like to be more than biology partners with Nora," Vee continued. "Not that anyone can blame him."

"That so?" said Elliot, eyeing me with a look that said he wasn't surprised. He'd suspected it all along. I noticed he took a step closer.

Vee shot me a triumphant smile. *Thank me later*, it said.

"It's not like that," I corrected. "It's—"

"Twice as bad," Vee said. "Nora suspects he's stalking her. The police are on the brink of becoming involved."

"Should we play?" I said loudly. I dropped the foosball in the center of the table. Nobody noticed.

"Do you want me to talk to him?" Elliot asked me. "I'll explain we're not looking for trouble. I'll tell him you're here with me, and if he's got a problem, he can discuss it with me."

This was not the direction I wanted the conversation to go. At all. "What happened to Jules?" I said. "He's been gone for a while."

"Yeah, maybe he fell in the toilet," said Vee.

"Let me talk to Patch," Elliot said.

While I appreciated the concern, I did not like the idea of Elliot going head-to-head with Patch. Patch was an X factor: intangible, scary, and unknown. Who knew what he was capable of? Elliot was far too nice to be sent up against Patch.

"He doesn't scare me," Elliot said, as if to disprove my thoughts.

Obviously this was something Elliot and I disagreed on.

"Bad idea," I said.

"Great idea," Vee said. "Otherwise, Patch might get . . . violent. Remember last time?"

Last time?! I mouthed at her.

I had no idea why Vee was doing this, other than that she had a penchant for making everything as dramatic as possible. Her idea of drama was my idea of morbid humiliation.

"No offense, but this guy sounds like a creep," said Elliot. "Give me two minutes with him." He started to walk over.

"No!" I said, yanking on his sleeve to stop him. "He, uh, might get violent again. Let me handle this." I narrowed a look at Vee.

"You sure?" Elliot said. "I'm more than happy to do it."

"I think it's best coming from me."

I wiped my palms on my jeans, and after taking a mostly steady breath, I started closing the distance between me and Patch, which was only the width of a few game consoles. I had no idea what I was going to say when I reached him. Hopefully just a brief hello. Then I could go back and reassure Elliot and Vee that everything was under control.

Patch was dressed in the usual: black shirt, black jeans, and a thin silver necklace that flashed against his dark complexion. His sleeves were pushed up his forearms, and I could see his muscles working as he punched buttons. He was tall and lean and hard, and I wouldn't have been surprised if under his clothes he bore several scars, souvenirs from street fights and other reckless behavior. Not that I wanted a look under his clothes.

When I got to Patch's console, I tapped a hand against the side of it to get his attention. In the calmest voice I could manage, I said, "Pac-Man? Or is it Donkey Kong?" In truth, it looked a little more violent and military.

A slow grin spread over his face. "Baseball. Think maybe you could stand behind me and give me a few pointers?"

Firebombs erupted on the screen, and screaming bodies sailed through the air. Obviously not baseball.

"What's his name?" Patch asked, directing an almost imperceptible nod at the foosball table.

"Elliot. Listen, I have to keep this short. They're waiting."

"Have I seen him before?"

"He's new. Just transferred."

"First week at school and he's already made friends. Lucky guy." He slid me a look. "Could have a dark and dangerous side we know nothing about."

"Seems to be my specialty."

I waited for him to catch my meaning, but he only said, "Up for a game?" He tilted his head toward the back of the arcade. Through the crowd I could just make out pool tables.

"Nora!" Vee called out. "Get over here. Elliot is cramming defeat down my throat!"

"Can't," I told Patch.

"If I win," he said, as if he had no intention of being refused, "you'll tell Elliot something came up. You'll tell him you're no longer free tonight."

I couldn't help it; he was way too arrogant. I said, "And if *I* win?"

His eyes skimmed me, head to toe. "I don't think we have to worry."

Before I could stop myself, I punched his arm.

"Careful," he said in a low voice. "They might think we're flirting."

I felt like kicking myself, because that's exactly what we were doing. But it wasn't my fault—it was Patch's. In close contact with him, I experienced a confusing polarity of desires. Part of me wanted to run away from him screaming, Fire! A more reckless part was tempted to see how close I could get without . . . combusting.

"One game of pool," he tempted.

"I'm here with someone else."

"Head toward the pool tables. I'll take care of it."

I crossed my arms, hoping to look stern and a little exasperated, but at the same time, I had to bite my lip to keep from showing a slightly more positive reaction. "What are you going to do? Fight Elliot?"

"If it comes to that."

I was almost sure he was joking. Almost.

"A pool table just opened up. Go claim it." I . . . *dare* . . . *you.*

I stiffened. "How did you do that?"

When he didn't immediately deny it, I felt a squeeze of panic. It was real. He knew exactly what he was doing. The palms of my hands touched with sweat.

"How did you do that?" I repeated.

He gave me a sly smile. "Do what?"

"Don't," I warned. "Don't pretend you're not doing it."

He leaned a shoulder against the console and gazed down at me. "Tell me what I'm supposed to be doing."

"My . . . thoughts."

"What about them?"

"Cut it out, Patch."

He glanced around theatrically. "You don't mean—talking to your mind? You know how crazy that sounds, right?"

Swallowing, I said in the calmest voice I could manage, "You scare me, and I'm not sure you're good for me."

"I could change your mind."

"Noooora!" Vee called over the din of voices and electronic beeps.

"Meet me at the Archangel," Patch said.

I took a step back. "No," I said on impulse.

Patch came around behind me, and a chill shimmied up my spine. "I'll be waiting," he said into my ear. Then he slipped out of the arcade.

CHAPTER

I WALKED BACK TO THE FOOSBALL TABLE IN A COLD DAZE. Elliot was bent over it, his face showing competitive concentration. Vee was shrieking and laughing. Jules was still missing.

Vee looked up from the game. "Well? What happened? What'd he say to you?"

"Nothing. I told him not to bother us. He left." My voice sounded flat.

"He didn't look mad when he left," Elliot said. "Whatever you said, it must have worked."

"Too bad," Vee said. "I was hoping for some excitement."

"Are we ready to play?" Elliot asked. "I'm getting hungry for some hard-won pizza."

"Yeah, if Jules would ever come back," said Vee. "I'm starting to think maybe he doesn't like us. He keeps disappearing. I'm starting to think it's a nonverbal cue."

"You kidding me? He loves you guys," Elliot said with too much enthusiasm. "He's just slow to warm up to strangers. I'll go find him. Don't go anywhere."

As soon as Vee and I were alone, I said, "You know I'm going to kill you, right?"

Vee raised her palms and took a step back. "I was doing you a favor. Elliot is wild about you. After you left, I told him you have, like, ten guys calling you every night. You should have seen his face. Barely contained jealousy."

I groaned.

"It's the law of supply and demand," Vee said. "Who would've thought economics would come in useful?"

I looked to the arcade doors. "I need something."

"You need Elliot."

"No, I need sugar. Lots of it. I need cotton candy." What I needed was an eraser big enough to scrub away all evidence of Patch from my life. Particularly the mind-speaking. I shuddered. How was he doing it? And why me? Unless . . . I'd imagined it. Just like I'd imagined hitting someone with the Neon.

"I could use a little sugar myself," Vee said. "I saw a vendor near the park entrance on our way in. I'll stay here so Jules and Elliot don't think we ran off, and you can get the cotton candy."

Outside, I backtracked to the entrance, but when I found the vendor selling cotton candy, I was distracted by a sight farther down the walkway. The Archangel rose up above the treetops. A snake of cars zipped over the lighted tracks and dove out of view. I wondered why Patch wanted to meet. I felt a jab in my stomach and probably should have taken it for an answer, but despite my best intentions, I found myself continuing down the walkway toward the Archangel.

I stayed with the flow of foot traffic, keeping my eyes on the distant track of the Archangel looping through the sky. The wind had changed from chilly to icy, but that wasn't the reason I felt increasingly ill at ease. The feeling was back. That cold, heart-stopping feeling that someone was watching me.

I stole a look to both sides. Nothing abnormal in my peripheral vision. I spun a full 180 degrees. A little ways back, standing in a small courtyard of trees, a hooded figure turned and disappeared into the darkness.

With my heart beating faster, I bypassed a large group of pedestrians, putting distance between me and the clearing. Several strides farther on, I glanced back again. Nobody stood out as following me.

When I faced forward again, I ran smack into someone. "Sorry!" I blurted, trying to regain my balance.

Patch grinned down at me. "I'm hard to resist."

I blinked up at him. "Leave me alone." I tried to sidestep him, but he caught me by the elbow.

"What's wrong? You look ready to throw up."

"You have that effect on me," I snapped.

He laughed. I felt like kicking his shins.

"You could use a drink." He still had me by the elbow, and he tugged me toward a lemonade cart.

I dug in my heels. "You want to help? Stay away from me."

He brushed a curl off my face. "Love the hair. Love when it's out of control. It's like seeing a side of you that needs to come out more often."

I smoothed my hair furiously. As soon as I realized I looked like I was trying to make myself more presentable for him, I said, "I have to go. Vee is waiting." A frazzled pause. "I guess I'll see you in class on Monday."

"Ride the Archangel with me."

I craned my neck, staring up at it. High-pitched screams echoed down as the cars thundered over the tracks.

"Two people to a seat." His smile changed to a slow, daring grin.

"No." No *way*.

"If you keep running from me, you're never going to figure out what's really going on."

That comment right there should have sent me running. But it didn't. It was almost as if Patch knew exactly what to say to pique my curiosity. Exactly what to say, at exactly the right moment.

"What is going on?" I asked.

"Only one way to find out."

"I can't. I'm afraid of heights. Besides, Vee's waiting." Only, suddenly the thought of going up that high in the air didn't scare me. Not anymore. In an absurd way, knowing I'd be with Patch made me feel safe.

"If you ride the whole way through without screaming, I'll tell Coach to switch our seats."

"I already tried. He won't budge."

"I could be more convincing than you."

I took his comment as a personal insult. "I don't scream," I said. "Not for carnival rides." Not for you.

In step with Patch, I made my way to the back of the line leading up to the Archangel. A rush of screams lifted, then faded, far above in the night sky.

"I haven't seen you at Delphic before," Patch said.

"You're here a lot?" I made a mental note not to take any more weekend trips to Delphic.

"I have a history with the place."

We edged up the line as the cars emptied and a new set of thrill seekers boarded the ride.

"Let me guess," I said. "You played hooky here instead of going to school last year."

I was being sarcastic, but Patch said, "Answering that would mean shedding light on my past. And I'd like to keep it in the dark."

"Why? What's wrong with your past?"

"I don't think now is a good time to talk about it. My past might frighten you."

Too *late*, I thought.

He stepped closer and our arms met, a brushed connection that caused the hairs on my arm to rise. "The things I have to confess aren't the kind of things you tell your flippant bio partner," he said.

The frigid wind wrapped around me, and when I breathed in, it filled me with ice. But it didn't compare to the chill Patch's words sent through me.

Patch jerked his chin up the ramp. "Looks like we're up."

I pushed through the revolving gate. By the time we made it to the boarding platform, the only empty cars were at the very front and the very back of the roller coaster. Patch headed toward the former.

The roller coaster's construction didn't inspire my confidence, remodeled or not. It looked more than a century old and was made of wood that had spent a lot of time exposed to Maine's harsh elements. The artwork painted on the sides was even less inspiring.

The car Patch chose had a grouping of four paintings. The first depicted a mob of horned demons ripping the wings off a scream-ing male angel. The next painting showed the wingless angel perched on a headstone, watching children play from a distance. In the third painting, the wingless angel stood close to the children, crooking a finger at one little green-eyed girl. In the final paint-ing, the wingless angel drifted through the girl's body like a ghost. The girl's eyes were black, her smile was gone, and she'd sprouted horns like the demons from the first painting. A slivered moon hung above the paintings.

I averted my eyes and assured myself it was the frigid air mak-ing my legs tremble. I slid into the car beside Patch.

"Your past wouldn't frighten me," I said, buckling my seat belt across my lap. "I'm guessing I'd be more appalled than anything."

"Appalled," he repeated. The tone of his voice led me to believe he'd accepted the accusation. Strange, since Patch never degraded himself.

The cars rolled backward, then lurched forward. Not in a smooth way, we headed away from the platform, climbing steadily uphill. The smell of sweat, rust, and saltwater blowing in from the sea filled the air. Patch sat close enough to smell. I caught the slightest trace of rich mint soap.

"You look pale," he said, leaning in to be heard above the click-ing tracks.

I felt pale, but did not admit it.

At the crest of the hill there was a moment's hesitation. I could see for miles, noting where the dark countryside blended with the sparkle of the suburbs and gradually became the grid of Portland's lights. The wind held its breath, allowing the damp air to settle on my skin.

Without meaning to, I stole a look at Patch. I found a measure of consolation in having him at my side. Then he flashed a grin.

"Scared, Angel?"

I clenched the metal bar drilled into the front of the car as I felt my weight tip forward. A shaky laugh slipped out of me.

Our car flew demonically fast, my hair flapping out behind me. Swerving to the left, then to the right, we clattered over the tracks. Inside, I felt my organs float and fall in response to the ride. I looked down, trying to concentrate on something not moving.

It was then that I noticed my seat belt had come undone.

I tried to shout at Patch, but my voice was swallowed up in the rush of air. I felt my stomach go hollow, and I let go of the metal bar with one hand, trying to secure the seat belt around my waist with the other. The car lunged to the left. I slammed shoulders with Patch, pressing against him so hard it hurt. The car soared up, and I felt it lift from the tracks, not fully riveted to them.

We were plunging. The flashing lights along the tracks blinded me; I couldn't see which way the track turned at the end of the dive.

It was too late. The car swerved to the right. I felt a jolt of panic, and then it happened. My left shoulder slammed against the car door. It flung open, and I was ripped out of the car while the roller coaster sped off without me. I rolled onto the tracks and grappled for something to anchor myself. My hands found nothing, and I tumbled over the edge, plunging straight down through the black air. The ground rushed up at me, and I opened my mouth to scream.

The next thing I knew, the ride screeched to a stop at the unloading platform.

My arms hurt from how tightly Patch held me. "Now that's what I call a scream," he said, grinning at me.

In a daze, I watched him place a hand over his ear as if my scream still echoed there. Not at all certain what had just happened, I stared at the place on his arm where my nails had left semicircles tattooed on his skin. Then my eyes moved to my seat belt. It was secured around my waist.

"My seat belt . . ." I began. "I thought—"

"Thought what?" Patch asked, sounding genuinely interested.

"I thought . . . I flew out of the car. I literally thought . . . I was going to die."

"I think that's the point."

At my sides, my arms trembled. My knees wobbled slightly under the weight of my body.

"Guess we're stuck as partners," said Patch. I suspected a small degree of victory in his voice. I was too stunned to argue.

"The Archangel," I murmured, looking back over my shoulder at the ride, which had started its next ascent.

"It means high-ranking angel." There was a definite smugness to his voice. "The higher up, the harder the fall."

I started to open my mouth, meaning to say again how I was sure I'd left the car for a moment and forces beyond my ability to explain had put me safely back behind my seat belt. Instead I said, "I think I'm more of a guardian angel girl."

Patch smirked again. Guiding me down the walk, he said, "I'll take you back to the arcade."

I CUT THROUGH THE CROWD INSIDE THE ARCADE, PASSING the concession counter and restrooms. When the foosball tables came into view, Vee wasn't at any of them. Neither were Elliot or Jules.

"Looks like they left," Patch said. His eyes might have held a sliver of amusement. Then again, with Patch, it could just as easily have been something entirely different. "Looks like you need a ride."

"Vee wouldn't leave me," I said, standing on my tiptoes to see over the top of the crowd. "They're probably playing table tennis."

I edged sideways through the crowd while Patch followed behind, tipping back a can of soda he'd bought on our way in. He'd offered to buy me one, but in my current state, I wasn't sure I could hold it down.

There was no trace of Vee or Elliot at table tennis.

"Maybe they're at the pinball machines," Patch suggested. He was definitely making fun of me.

I felt myself go a little red in the face. Where *was* Vee?

Patch held out his soda. "Sure you don't want a drink?"

I looked from the can to Patch. Just because my blood warmed at the thought of putting my mouth where his had been didn't mean I had to tell him.

I dug through my purse and pulled out my cell. The screen on my phone was black and refused to turn on. I didn't understand how the battery could be dead when I'd charged it right before I left. I pushed the on button again and again, but nothing happened.

Patch said, "My offer's still on the table."

I thought I'd be safer hitching a ride from a stranger. I was still shaken over what had happened on the Archangel, and no matter how many times I tried to flush it out, the image of falling repeated through my head. I was falling . . . and then the ride was over. Just like that. It was the most terrifying thing I'd ever been through. Almost as terrifying, I was the only one who'd seemed to notice. Not even Patch, who'd been right beside me.

I smacked my palm to my forehead. "Her *car*. She's probably waiting for me in the parking lot."

Thirty minutes later I'd canvassed the entire lot. The Neon was gone. I couldn't believe Vee had left without me. Maybe there'd been an emergency. I had no way of knowing, since I couldn't check the messages on my cell. I tried to hold my emotions in check, but if she *had* left me, I had an ample amount of anger simmering under the surface, ready to spill out.

"Out of options yet?" asked Patch.

I bit my lip, pondering my other options. I had no other options. Unfortunately, I wasn't sure I was ready to take Patch up on his offer. On an ordinary day he exuded danger. Tonight there was a potent mix of danger, threat, and mystery all thrown together.

Finally I blew out a sigh and prayed I wasn't about to make a mistake.

"You'll take me straight home," I said. It sounded more like a question than an order.

"If that's what you want."

I was about to ask Patch if he'd noticed anything strange on the Archangel, when I stopped myself. I was too scared to ask. What if I hadn't fallen? What if I'd imagined the whole thing? What if I was seeing things that weren't really happening? First the guy in the ski mask. Now this. I was pretty sure Patch's mind-speaking was real, but everything else? Not so sure.

Patch walked a few parking spaces over. A shiny black

motorcycle rested on its kickstand. He swung on and tipped his head at the seat behind him. "Hop on."

"Wow. Nice bike," I said. Which was a lie. It looked like a glossy black death trap. I had never been on a motorcycle in my life, ever. I wasn't sure I wanted to change that tonight.

"I like the feel of the wind on my face," I continued, hoping my bravado masked my terror of moving at speeds upward of sixty-five miles an hour with nothing standing between me and the road.

There was one helmet—black with a tinted visor—and he held it out for me.

Taking it, I swung my leg over the bike and realized how insecure I felt with nothing but a narrow strip of seat beneath me. I slid the helmet over my curls and strapped it under my chin.

"Is it hard to drive?" I asked. What I really meant was, *Is it safe?*

"No," Patch said, answering both my spoken and unspoken questions. He laughed softly. "You're tense. Relax."

When he pulled out of the parking space, the explosion of movement startled me; I'd been holding on to his shirt with just enough of the fabric between my fingers to keep my balance. Now I wrapped my arms around him in a backward bear hug.

Patch accelerated onto the highway, and my thighs squeezed around him. I hoped I was the only one who noticed.

When we reached my house, Patch eased the bike up the fog-drenched driveway, killed the engine, and swung off. I removed my helmet, balancing it carefully on the seat in front of me, and opened my mouth to say something along the lines of *Thanks for the ride, I'll see you on Monday.*

The words dissolved as Patch crossed the driveway and headed up the porch steps.

I couldn't begin to speculate what he was doing. Walking me to the door? Highly improbable. Then . . . what?

I climbed the porch after him and found him at the door. I watched, divided between confusion and escalating concern, as he drew a set of familiar keys from his pocket and inserted my house key into the bolt.

I lowered my handbag down my shoulder and unzipped the compartment where I stored my keys. They weren't inside.

"Give me back my keys," I said, disconcerted at not knowing how my keys had come into his possession.

"You dropped them in the arcade when you were hunting for your cell," he said.

"I don't care where I dropped them. Give them back."

Patch held up his hands, claiming innocence, and backed away from the door. He leaned one shoulder against the bricks and watched me step up to the lock. I attempted to turn the key. It wouldn't budge.

"You jammed it," I said, rattling the key. I dropped back a step. "Go ahead. Try it. It's stuck."

With a sharp click, he turned the key. Hand poised on the handle, he arched his eyebrows as if to say *May I?*

I swallowed, burying a surge of mutual fascination and dis-quiet. "Go ahead. You're not going to walk in on anyone. I'm home alone."

"The whole night?"

Immediately, I realized it might not have been the smartest thing to say. "Dorothea will be coming soon." That was a lie. Dorothea was long gone. It was close to midnight.

"Dorothea?"

"Our housekeeper. She's old—but strong. Very strong." I tried to squeeze past him. Unsuccessfully.

"Sounds frightening," he said, retrieving the key from the lock. He held it out for me.

"She can clean a toilet inside and out in under a minute. More like terrifying." Taking the key, I edged around him. I fully intended to shut the door between us, but as I turned about, Patch filled the doorway, his arms braced on either side of the frame.

"You're not going to invite me in?" he asked.

I blinked. Invite him in? To my house? With no one else home?

Patch said, "It's late." His eyes followed mine closely, reflecting a wayward glint. "You must be hungry."

"No. Yes. I mean, yes, but—"

Suddenly he was inside.

I took three steps back; he nudged the door closed with his foot. "You like Mexican?" he asked.

"I—" I'd like to know what you're doing inside my house!

"Tacos?"

"Tacos?" I echoed.

This seemed to amuse him. "Tomatoes, lettuce, cheese."

"I know what a taco is!"

Before I could stop him, he strode past me into the house. At the end of the hall, he steered left. To the kitchen.

He went to the sink and ran the tap while scrubbing soap halfway up his arms. Apparently having made himself at home, he went to the pantry first, then browsed the fridge, bringing out items here and there—salsa, cheese, lettuce, a tomato. Then he dug through the drawers and found a knife.

I suspect I was halfway to panicking at the image of Patch holding a knife when something else caught my eye. I took two steps forward and squinted at my reflection in one of the skillets hanging from the pot rack. My hair! It looked like a giant tumbleweed had rolled on top of my head. I clapped a hand to my mouth.

Patch smiled. "You come by your red hair naturally?"

I stared at him. "I don't have red hair."

"I hate to break it to you, but it's red. I could light it on fire and it wouldn't turn any redder."

"It's brown." So maybe I had the teeniest, tiniest, most infinitesimal amount of auburn in my hair. I was still a brunette. "It's the lighting," I said.

"Yeah, maybe it's the lightbulbs." His smile brought up both sides of his mouth, and a dimple surfaced.

"I'll be right back," I said, hurrying out of the kitchen.

I went upstairs and coaxed my hair into a ponytail. With that out of the way, I pulled my thoughts together. I wasn't entirely comfortable with the idea of Patch roaming freely through my house— armed with a knife. And my mom would kill me if she found out I'd invited Patch inside when Dorothea wasn't here.

"Can I take a rain check?" I asked upon finding him still hard at work in the kitchen two minutes later. I placed a hand on my stomach, signaling that it was bothering me. "Queasy," I said. "I think it was the ride home."

He paused in his chopping and looked up. "I'm almost finished."

I noticed he'd exchanged knives for a bigger—and sharper— blade.

As if he had a window to my thoughts, he held up the knife, examining it. The blade gleamed in the light. My stomach clenched.

"Put the knife down," I instructed quietly.

Patch looked from me to the knife and back again. After a minute he laid it down in front of him. "I'm not going to hurt you, Nora."

"That's . . . reassuring," I managed to say, but my throat was tight and dry.

He spun the knife, handle pointing toward me. "Come here. I'll teach you how to make tacos."

I didn't move. There was a glint to his eye that made me think I should be frightened of him . . . and I was. But that fright was equal part allure. There was something extremely unsettling about being near him. In his presence, I didn't trust myself.

"How about a . . . deal?" His face was bent down, shadowed, and he looked up at me through his lashes. The effect was an impression of trustworthiness. "Help me make tacos, and I'll answer a few of your questions."

"My questions?"

"I think you know what I mean."

I knew exactly what he meant. He was giving me a glimpse into his private world. A world where he could speak to my mind. Again he knew exactly what to say, at exactly the right moment.

Without a word, I moved beside him. He slid the cutting board in front of me.

"First," he said, coming behind me and placing his hands on the counter, just outside of mine, "choose your tomato." He dipped his head so his mouth was at my ear. His breath was warm, tickling my skin. "Good. Now pick up the knife."

"Does the chef always stand this close?" I asked, not sure if I liked or feared the flutter his closeness caused inside me.

"When he's revealing culinary secrets, yes. Hold the knife like you mean it."

"I am."

"Good." Stepping back, he gave me a thorough twice-over,

seemingly scrutinizing any imperfections—his eyes shifted up and down, here and there. For one unnerving moment, I thought I saw a secret smile of approval. "Cooking isn't taught," Patch said. "It's inherent. Either you've got it or you don't. Like chemistry. You think you're ready for chemistry?"

I pressed the knife down through the tomato; it split in two, each half rocking gently on the cutting board. "You tell me. Am I ready for chemistry?"

Patch made a deep sound I couldn't decipher and grinned.

After dinner, Patch carried our plates to the sink. "I'll wash, you dry." Hunting through the drawers to the side of the sink, he found a dish towel and slung it playfully at me.

"I'm ready to ask you those questions," I said. "Starting with that night at the library. Did you follow me . . ."

I trailed off. Patch leaned lazily against the counter. Dark hair flipped out from under his ball cap. A smile tugged at his mouth. My thoughts dissolved and just like that, a new thought broke the surface of my mind.

I wanted to kiss him. Right now.

Patch arched his eyebrows. "What?"

"Uh—nothing. Nothing at all. You wash, I'll dry."

It didn't take long to finish the dishes, and when we had, we found ourselves cramped in the space near the sink. Patch moved to take the dish towel from me, and our bodies touched. Neither of us moved, holding to the fragile link that welded us together.

I stepped back first.

"Scared?" he murmured.

"No."

"Liar."

My pulse edged up a degree. "I'm not scared of you."

"No?"

I spoke without thinking. "Maybe it's just that I'm scared of—" I cursed myself for even beginning the sentence. What was I supposed to say now? I was not about to admit to Patch that everything about him frightened me. It would be giving him permission to provoke me further. "Maybe it's just that I'm scared of . . . of—"

"Liking me?"

Relieved that I didn't have to finish my own sentence, I automatically answered, "Yes." I realized too late what I'd confessed. "I mean, no! Definitely no. That is not what I was trying to say!"

Patch laughed softly.

"The truth is, part of me is definitely not comfortable around you," I said.

"But?"

I gripped the counter behind me for support. "But at the same time I feel a scary attraction to you."

Patch grinned.

"You are way too cocky," I said, using my hand to push him back a step.

He trapped my hand against his chest and yanked my sleeve down past my wrist, covering my hand with it. Just as quickly, he did the same thing with the other sleeve. He held my shirt by the cuffs, my hands captured. My mouth opened in protest.

Reeling me closer, he didn't stop until I was directly in front of him. Suddenly he lifted me onto the counter. My face was level with his. He fixed me with a dark, inviting smile. And that's when I realized this moment had been dancing around the edge of my fantasies for several days now.

"Take off your hat," I said, the words tumbling out before I could stop them.

He slid it around, the brim facing backward.

I scooted to the edge of the counter, my legs dangling one on either side of him. Something inside of me was telling me to stop—but I swept that voice to the far back of my mind.

He spread his hands on the counter, just outside my hips. Tilting his head to one side, he moved closer. His scent, which was all damp dark earth, overwhelmed me.

I inhaled two sharp breaths. No. This wasn't right. Not this, not with Patch. He was frightening. In a good way, yes. But also in a bad way. A very bad way.

"You should go," I breathed. "You should definitely go."

"Go here?" His mouth was on my shoulder. "Or here?" It moved up my neck.

My brain couldn't process one logical thought. Patch's mouth was roaming north, up over my jaw, gently sucking at my skin. . . .

"My legs are falling asleep," I blurted. It wasn't a total lie. I was experiencing tingling sensations all through my body, legs included.

"I could solve that." Patch's hands closed on my hips.

Suddenly my cell phone rang. I jumped at the sound of it and fumbled it out of my pocket.

"Hi, sweetheart," my mom said cheerfully.

"Can I call you back?"

"Sure. What's going on?"

I shut the phone. "You need to leave," I told Patch. "Right now."

He'd slid his baseball cap back around. His mouth was the only feature I could see beneath it, and it curved in a mischievous smile. "You're not wearing makeup."

"I must have forgotten it."

"Sweet dreams tonight."

"Sure. No problem." What had he said?

"About that party tomorrow night . . ."

"I'll think about it," I managed to say.

Patch tucked a piece of paper inside my pocket, his touch sending hot sensations down my legs. "Here's the address. I'll be looking for you. Come alone."

A moment later I heard the front door close behind him. A fiery blush worked its way up my face. Too close, I thought. There was nothing wrong with fire . . . as long as you didn't stand too close. Something to keep in mind.

I leaned back against the cabinets, taking short, shallow breaths.

CHAPTER

10

I WAS YANKED AWAKE BY THE SOUND OF MY PHONE RINGING.
Caught with one foot still in a dream, I tugged my pillow over
my head and tried to block out the noise. But the phone rang.
And rang.

The call went to voicemail. Five seconds later, the ringing
started up again.

I reached an arm over the side of the bed, groped around until
I found my jeans, and wiggled my cell out of the pocket.

"Yes?" I said with a wide yawn, leaving my eyes shut.

Someone was breathing angrily on the other end. "What happened to you? What happened to bringing back cotton candy? And while you're at it, how about telling me where you are so I can come strangle you—barehanded!"

I knocked the heel of my hand against my forehead a few times.

"I thought you'd been kidnapped!" Vee went on. "I thought you'd been abducted! I thought you were *murdered*!"

I tried to find the clock in the dark. I bumped a picture frame on the nightstand, and all the frames behind it played dominoes.

"I was sort of delayed," I said. "By the time I made it back to the arcade, you were gone."

"'Delayed'? What kind of excuse is 'delayed'?"

The red numbers on the clock swam into focus. It was just after two in the morning.

"I drove around the parking lot for an hour," Vee said. "Elliot walked the park flashing the only photo I had of you on my cell phone. I tried your cell a zillion times. Hang on. Are you at home? How did you get home?"

I rubbed the corners of my eyes. "Patch."

"Stalker Patch?"

"Well, I didn't have much of a choice, did I?" I said tersely. "You left without me."

"You sound worked up. Really worked up. No, that's not it. You sound agitated . . . flustered . . . *aroused.*" I could feel her eyes widen. "He kissed you, didn't he?"

No answer.

"He did! I knew it! I've seen the way he looks at you. I knew this was coming. I saw it from a mile away."

I didn't want to think about it.

"What was it like?" Vee pressed. "A peach kiss? A plum kiss? Or maybe an al-fal-fa kiss?"

"What?"

"Was it a peck, did mouths part, or was there tongue? Never mind. You don't have to answer that. Patch isn't the kind of guy to deal with preliminaries. There was tongue involved. Guaranteed."

I covered my face with my hands, hiding behind them. Patch probably thought I didn't have any self-control. I'd fallen apart in his arms. I'd melted like butter. Right before I told him he should go, I was pretty sure I'd made a sound that was a cross between a sigh of sheer bliss and a moan of ecstasy.

That would explain his arrogant grin.

"Can we talk about this later?" I asked, pinching the bridge of my nose.

"No way."

I sighed. "I'm dead tired."

"I can't believe you're thinking about keeping me in suspense."

"I'm hoping you'll forget about it."

"Fat chance."

I tried to envision the muscles along my neck relaxing, forestalling the headache I felt creeping on. "Are we still on for shopping?"

"I'll pick you up at four."

"I thought we weren't meeting until five."

"Circumstances have changed. I'll be there even earlier if I can get out of family time. My mom's having a nervous breakdown. She blames my bad grades on her parenting skills. Apparently spending time together is the solution. Wish me luck."

I snapped my phone shut and slid deep into my bed. I pictured Patch's unprincipled grin and his glittering black eyes. After thrashing around in bed for several minutes, I gave up trying to get comfortable. The truth was, as long as Patch was on my mind, comfort was out of the question.

When I was little, Dorothea's godson Lionel shattered one of the kitchen glasses. He swept up all the shards of glass except one, and he dared me to lick it. I imagined falling for Patch was a little like licking that shard. I knew it was stupid. I knew I'd get cut. After all these years one thing hadn't changed: I was still lured by danger.

Suddenly I sat up straight in bed and reached for my cell. I switched on the lamp.

The battery showed fully charged.

My spine tingled ominously. My cell was supposed to be dead. So how had my mom and Vee gotten through?

Rain battered the colorful awnings of the shops along the pier and spilled to the sidewalk below. The antique gas lamps that were staggered down both sides of the street glowed to life. With our umbrellas bumping together, Vee and I hustled down the sidewalk and under the pink-and-white-striped awning of Victoria's Secret. We shook out our umbrellas in unison and propped them just outside the entrance.

A boom of thunder sent us flying through the doors.

I stamped rain from my shoes and shuddered off the cold. Several oil diffusers burned on a display at the center of the store, surrounding us with an exotic, lusty smell.

A woman in black slacks and a stretchy black tee stepped forward. She had a measuring tape snaked around her neck, and she started to reach for it. "Would you girls like a free measuring—"

"Put the damn measuring tape away," Vee ordered. "I already know my size. I don't need reminding."

I gave the woman a smile that was part apology as I trailed after Vee, who was heading toward the clearance bins at the back.

"A D cup is nothing to be ashamed of," I told Vee. I picked up a blue satin bra and hunted for the price tag.

"Who said anything about being ashamed?" Vee said. "I'm not ashamed. Why would I be ashamed? The only other sixteen-year-olds with boobs as big as mine are suffused with silicone—and everyone knows it. Why would *I* have reason to be ashamed?" She rummaged through a bin. "Think they have any bras in here that can get my babies to lie flat?"

"They're called sports bras, and they have a nasty side effect called the uniboob," I said, my eyes picking out a lacy black bra from the pile.

I shouldn't have been looking at lingerie. It naturally made me think about sexy things. Like kissing. Like Patch.

I closed my eyes and replayed our night together. The touch of Patch's hand on my thigh, his lips tasting my neck . . .

Vee caught me off guard with a pair of turquoise leopard print undies slung at my chest. "These would look nice on you," she said. "All you need is a booty like mine to fill them."

What had I been thinking? I'd come this close to kissing Patch. The same Patch who just might be invading my mind. The same Patch who saved me from plunging to my death on the Archangel—because that's what I was sure had happened, although I had zero logical explanations. I wondered if he had somehow suspended time and caught me during the fall. If he was capable of talking to my thoughts, maybe, just maybe, he was capable of other things.

Or maybe, I thought with a chill, I could no longer trust my mind.

I still had the scrap of paper Patch had tucked inside my pocket, but there was no way I was going to the party tonight. I secretly enjoyed the attraction between us, but the mystery and eeriness outweighed it. From now on, I was going to flush Patch out of my system—and this time, I meant it. It would be like a cleansing diet. The problem was, the only diet I'd ever been on backfired. Once I tried to go an entire month without chocolate. Not one bite. At the end of two weeks, I broke down and binged on more chocolate than I would have eaten in three months.

I hoped my chocolate-free diet didn't foreshadow what would happen if I tried to avoid Patch.

"What are you doing?" I asked, my attention drawn to Vee.

"What does it look like I'm doing? I'm peeling the clearance price stickers off these clearance bras and sticking them on the not on sale bras. That way I can get sexy bras at trashy bra prices."

"You can't do that. She'll scan the bar codes when you checkout. She'll know what you're up to."

"Bar codes? They don't scan bar codes." She didn't sound too sure.

"They do. I swear. Cross my heart." I figured lying was better than watching Vee get hauled off to jail.

"Well, it seemed like a good idea. . . ."

"You have to get these," I told Vee, tossing a scrap of silk at her, hoping to distract her.

She held up the panties. Tiny red crabs embroidered the fabric. "That is the most disgusting thing I've ever seen. I like that black bra you're holding, on the other hand. I think you should get it. You go pay and I'll keep looking."

I paid. Then, thinking it would be easier to forget about Patch if I was looking at something more benign, I wandered over to the wall of lotions. I was sniffing a bottle of Dream Angels when I felt a familiar presence nearby. It was like someone had dropped a scoop of ice cream down the back of my shirt. It was the same shivery jolt I experienced whenever Patch approached.

Vee and I were still the only two customers in the shop, but on the other side of the plate-glass window, I saw a hooded figure step back under a shadowed awning across the street. Freshly unsettled, I stood immobile for a whole minute before I pulled myself together and went to find Vee.

"Time to go," I told her.

She was flipping through a rack of nightgowns. "Wow. Look at this—flannel pajamas, fifty percent off. I need a pair of flannel pj's."

I kept one eye glued to the window. "I think I'm being followed."

Vee's head jerked up. "Patch?"

"No. Look across the street."

Vee squinted. "I don't see anyone."

Neither did I anymore. A car had driven past, interrupting my line of vision. "I think they went inside the shop."

"How do you know they're following you?"

"A bad feeling."

"Did they look like anyone we know? For example . . . a cross between Pippi Longstocking and the Wicked Witch of the West would obviously give us Marcie Millar."

"It wasn't Marcie," I said, eyes still trained across the street. "When I left the arcade last night to buy cotton candy, I saw someone watching me. I think the same person is here now."

"Are you serious? Why are you just telling me this now? Who is it?"

I didn't know. And that scared me more than anything.

I directed my voice at the saleslady. "Is there a back door to the shop?"

She looked up from tidying a drawer. "Employees only."

"Is the person male or female?" Vee wanted to know.

"I can't tell."

"Well, why do you think they're following you? What do they want?"

"To scare me." It seemed reasonable enough.

"Why would they want to scare you?"

Again, I didn't know.

"We need a diversion," I told Vee.

"Exactly what I was thinking," she said. "And we know I'm really good at diversions. Give me your jean jacket."

I stared at her. "No way. We know nothing about this person. I'm not letting you go out there dressed like me. What if they're armed?"

"Sometimes your imagination scares me," Vee said.

I had to admit, the idea that they were armed and out to kill was a little far-fetched. But with all the creepy things happening lately,

I didn't blame myself for feeling on edge and assuming the worst.

"I'll go out first," said Vee. "If they follow me, you follow them. I'll head up the hill toward the cemetery, and then we'll bookend them and get some answers."

A minute later Vee left the store wearing my jean jacket. She picked up my red umbrella, holding it low on her head. Other than the fact that she was a few inches too tall, and a few pounds too voluptuous, she passed as me. From where I crouched behind the rack of nightgowns, I watched the hooded figure step out of the store across the street and follow after Vee. I crept closer to the window. Though the figure's baggy sweatshirt and jeans were meant to look androgynous, the walk was feminine. Definitely feminine.

Vee and the girl turned the corner and disappeared, and I jogged to the door. Outside, the rain had turned into a downpour.

Grabbing Vee's umbrella, I picked up my pace, keeping under the awnings, steering clear of the pelting rain. I could feel the bottoms of my jeans dampening. I wished I'd worn boots.

Behind me the pier extended out to the cement-gray ocean. In front of me, the strip of shops ended at the base of a steep, grassy hill. At the top of the hill, I could just make out the high cast-iron fence of the local cemetery.

I unlocked the Neon, cranked the defroster to high, and set the windshield wipers to full power. I drove out of the lot and turned left, accelerating up the winding hill. The trees of the cemetery loomed ahead, their branches deceptively coming to life through the mad chop of the wipers. The white marble headstones seemed to stab up from the darkness. The gray headstones dissolved into the atmosphere.

Out of nowhere, a red object hurtled into the windshield. It smacked the glass directly in my line of vision, then flew up and over the car. I stomped on the brakes and the Neon skidded to a stop on the shoulder of the road.

I opened the door and got out. I jogged to the back of the car, searching for what had hit me.

There was a moment of confusion as my mind processed what I was seeing. My red umbrella was tangled in the weeds. It was broken; one side was collapsed in the exact way I might expect if it had been hurled with force against another, harder object.

Through the onslaught of rain I heard a choked sob.

"Vee?" I said. I jogged across the road, shielding my eyes from the rain as I swept my gaze over the landscape. A body lay crumpled just ahead. I started running.

"Vee!" I dropped to my knees beside her. She was on her side, her legs drawn up to her chest. She groaned.

"What happened? Are you okay? Can you move?" I threw my head back, blinking rain. Think! I told myself. My cell phone. Back in the car. I had to call 911.

"I'm going to get help," I told Vee.

She moaned and clutched my hand.

I lowered myself down on her, holding her tightly. Tears burned behind my eyes. "What happened? Was it the person who followed you? Did they do this to you? What did they do?"

Vee murmured something unintelligible that might have been "handbag." Sure enough, her handbag was missing.

"You're going to be all right." I worked to hold my voice steady. I had a dark feeling stirring inside me, and I was trying to keep it at bay. I was certain the same person who'd watched me at Delphic and followed me shopping today was responsible, but I blamed myself for putting Vee in harm's way. I ran back to the Neon and punched 911 into my cell.

Trying to keep the hysteria out of my voice, I said, "I need an ambulance. My friend was attacked and robbed."

CHAPTER

11

MONDAY PASSED IN A DAZE. I WENT FROM CLASS TO class waiting for the final bell of the day. I'd called the hospital before school and was told that Vee was heading into the OR. Her left arm had been broken during the attack, and since the bone wasn't aligned, she needed surgery. I wanted to see her but couldn't until later in the afternoon, when the anesthesia wore off and hospital staff moved her to her own room. It was especially important that I hear her version of the attack before she either forgot the details or embellished them. Anything she remembered might fill a hole in the picture and help me figure out who had done this.

As the hours stretched toward afternoon, my focus shifted from Vee to the girl outside Victoria's Secret. Who was she? What did she want? Maybe it was a disturbing coincidence that Vee had been attacked minutes after I'd watched the girl follow after her, but my instincts disagreed. I wished I had a better picture of what she looked like. The bulky hoodie and jeans, compounded with the rain, had done a good job of disguising her. For all I knew it could've been Marcie Millar. But deep inside it didn't feel like the right match.

I swung by my locker to pick up my biology textbook, then headed to my last class. I walked in to find Patch's chair empty. Typically, he arrived at the last possible moment, tying with the tardy bell, but the bell rang and Coach took his place at the chalkboard and started lecturing on equilibrium.

I pondered Patch's empty chair. A tiny voice at the back of my head speculated that his absence might be connected to Vee's attack. It was a little strange that he was missing on the morning after. And I couldn't forget the icy chill I'd felt moments before looking outside Victoria's Secret and realizing I was being watched. Every other time I'd felt that way, it was because Patch was near.

The voice of reason quickly extinguished Patch's involvement. He could have caught a cold. Or he could have run out of gas on the drive to school and was stranded miles away. Or maybe there was a high-bets pool game going on at Bo's Arcade and he figured it was more profitable than an afternoon spent learning the intricacies of the human body.

At the end of class, Coach stopped me on my way out the door.

"Hang on a minute, Nora."

I turned back and hiked my backpack up my shoulder. "Yes?"

He extended a folded piece of paper. "Miss Greene stopped by before class and asked me to give this to you," he said.

I accepted the note. "Miss Greene?" I didn't have any teachers by that name.

"The new school psychologist. She just replaced Dr. Hendrickson."

I unfolded the note and read the message scrawled inside.

Dear Nora,

I'll be taking over Dr. Hendrickson's role as your school psychologist. I noticed you missed your last two appointments with Dr. H. Please come in right away so we can get acquainted. I've mailed a letter to your mother to make her aware of the change.

All best,

Miss Greene

"Thanks," I told Coach, folding the note until it was small enough to tuck inside my pocket.

Out in the hall I merged with the flow of the crowd. No avoiding it now—I had to go. I steered my way through the halls until I could see the closed door to Dr. Hendrickson's office. Sure enough, there was a new name plaque on the door. The polished brass gleamed against the drab oak door: MISS D. GREENE, SCHOOL PSYCHOLOGIST.

I knocked on the door, and a moment later it opened from within. Miss Greene had flawless pale skin, sea blue eyes, a lush mouth, and fine, straight blond hair that tumbled past her elbows. It was parted at the crown of her oval-shaped face. A pair of turquoise cat's-eye glasses sat at the tip of her nose, and she was dressed formally in a gray herringbone pencil skirt and a pink silk blouse. Her figure was willowy but feminine. She couldn't have been more than five years older than me.

"You must be Nora Grey. You look just like the picture in your file," she said, giving my hand a firm pump. Her voice was abrupt, but not rude. Businesslike.

Stepping back, she signaled me to enter the office.

"Can I get you juice, water?" she asked.

"What happened to Dr. Hendrickson?"

"He took early retirement. I've had my eye on this job for a while, so I jumped on the opening. I went to Florida State, but I grew up in Portland, and my parents still live there. It's nice to be close to family again."

I surveyed the small office. It had changed drastically since I'd last been in a few weeks ago. The wall-to-wall bookshelves were now filled with academic but generic-looking hardcovers, all bound in neutral colors with gold lettering. Dr. Hendrickson had used the shelves to display family pictures, but there were no snapshots of Miss Greene's private life. The same fern hung by the window, but under Dr. Hendrickson's care, it had been far more brown than green. A few days with Miss Greene and already it looked pert and alive. There was a pink paisley chair opposite the desk, and several moving boxes stacked in the far corner.

"Friday was my first day," she explained, seeing my eyes fall on the moving boxes. "I'm still unpacking. Have a seat."

I lowered my backpack down my arm and sat on the paisley chair. Nothing in the small room gave me any clues as to Miss Greene's personality. She had a stack of file folders on her desk— not neat, but not messy, either—and a white mug of what looked like tea. There wasn't a trace of perfume or air freshener. Her computer monitor was black.

Miss Greene crouched in front of a file cabinet behind her desk, tugged out a clean manila folder, and printed my name on the tab in black Magic Marker. She placed it on her desk next to my old file, which bore a few of Dr. Hendrickson's coffee-mug stains.

"I spent the whole weekend going through Dr. Hendrickson's files," she said. "Just between the two of us, his handwriting gives me a migraine, so I'm copying over all the files. I was amazed to find he didn't use a computer to type his notes. Who still uses longhand in this day and age?"

She settled back into her swivel chair, crossed her legs, and smiled politely at me. "Well. Why don't you tell me a little bit about the history of your meetings with Dr. Hendrickson? I could barely decipher his notes. It appeared the two of you were discussing how you feel about your mom's new job."

"It's not all that new. She's been working for a year."

"She used to be a stay-at-home mom, correct? And after your dad's passing, she took on a full-time job." She squinted at a sheet of paper in my file. "She works for an auction company, correct? It looks like she coordinates estate auctions all down the coast." She peeked at me over her glasses. "That must require a lot of time away from home."

"We wanted to stay in our farmhouse," I said, my tone touching on the defensive. "We couldn't afford the mortgage if she took a local job." I hadn't exactly loved my sessions with Dr. Hendrickson, but I found myself resenting him for retiring and abandoning me to Miss Greene. I was starting to get a feel for her, and she seemed attentive to detail. I sensed her itching to dig into every dark corner of my life.

"Yes, but you must be very lonely all by yourself at the farmhouse."

"We have a housekeeper who stays with me every afternoon until nine or ten at night."

"But a housekeeper isn't the same thing as a mother."

I eyed the door. I didn't even try to be discreet.

"Do you have a best friend? A boyfriend? Someone you can talk to when your housekeeper doesn't quite . . . fit the bill?" She dunked a tea bag in the mug, then raised it for a sip.

"I have a best friend." I'd made up my mind to say as little as possible. The less I said, the shorter the appointment. The shorter the appointment, the sooner I could visit Vee.

Her eyebrows peaked. "Boyfriend?"

"No."

"You're an attractive girl. I imagine there must be some interest from the opposite sex."

"Here's the thing," I said as patiently as possible. "I really appreciate that you're trying to help me, but I had this exact conversation with Dr. Hendrickson a year ago when my dad died. Rehashing it with you isn't helping. It's like going back in time and reliving it all over again. Yes, it was tragic and horrible, and I'm still dealing with it every day, but what I really need is to move on."

The clock on the wall ticked between us.

"Well," Miss Greene said at last, plastering on a smile. "It's very helpful to know your viewpoint, Nora. Which is what I was trying to understand all along. I'll make a note of your feelings in your file. Anything else you want to talk about?"

"Nope." I smiled to confirm that, really, I was doing fine.

She leafed through a few more pages of my file. I had no idea what observations Dr. Hendrickson had immortalized there, and I didn't want to wait around long enough to find out.

I lifted my backpack off the floor and scooted to the edge of the chair. "I don't mean to cut things short, but I need to be somewhere at four."

"Oh?"

I had no desire to go into Vee's attack with Miss Greene. "Library research," I lied.

"For which class?"

I said the first answer that popped to mind. "Biology."

"Speaking of classes, how are yours going? Any concerns in that department?"

"No."

She flipped a few more pages in my file. "Excellent grades," she observed. "It says here you're tutoring your biology partner, Patch Cipriano." She looked up, apparently wanting my confirmation.

I was surprised my tutoring assignment was important enough to make it into the school psychologist's file. "So far we haven't been able to meet. Conflicting schedules." I gave a *What can you do?* shrug.

She tapped my file on her desk, tidying all the loose sheets of paper into one clean stack, then inserted it into the new file she'd hand-labeled. "To give you fair warning, I'm going to talk with Mr. McConaughy and see about setting some parameters for your tutoring sessions. I'd like all meetings to be held here at school, under the direct supervision of a teacher or other faculty member. I don't want you tutoring Patch off school property. I especially don't want the two of you meeting alone."

A chill tiptoed along my skin. "Why? What's going on?"

"I can't discuss it."

The only reason I could think why she didn't want me alone with Patch was that he was dangerous. *My past might frighten you,* he'd said on the loading platform of the Archangel.

"Thanks for your time. I won't keep you any longer," Miss Greene said. She strode to the door, propping it open with her slender hip. She gave a parting smile, but it looked perfunctory.

After leaving Miss Greene's office, I called the hospital. Vee's surgery was over, but she was still in the recovery room and couldn't have visitors until seven p.m. I consulted the clock on my phone. Three hours. I found the Fiat in the student parking lot and dropped inside, hoping an afternoon spent doing homework at the library would keep my mind off the long wait.

I stayed at the library through the afternoon, and before I realized it, the clock on the wall had passed quietly into evening. My stomach rumbled against the quiet of the library, and my thoughts went to the vending machine just inside the entrance.

The last of my homework could wait until later, but there was still one project that required the help of library resources. I had a vintage IBM computer at home with dial-up Internet service, and I typically tried to save myself a lot of unnecessary shouting and hair pulling by using the library's computer lab. I had a theater review of *Othello* due on the eZine editor's desk by nine p.m., and I made a deal with myself, promising I'd go hunt down food as soon as I finished it.

Packing up my belongings, I walked to the elevators. Inside the cage I pushed the button to close the doors, but didn't immediately request a floor. I pulled out my cell and called the hospital again.

"Hi," I told the answering nurse. "My friend is recovering from surgery, and when I checked in earlier this afternoon, I was told she'd be out tonight. Her name is Vee Sky."

There was a pause and the clicking of computer keys. "Looks like they'll be bringing her to a private room within the hour."

"What time do visiting hours end?"

"Eight."

"Thank you." I disconnected and pressed the third-floor button, sending me up.

On the third floor I followed signs to collections, hoping that if I read several theater reviews in the local newspaper, it would spark my muse.

"Excuse me," I said to the librarian behind the collections desk. "I'm trying to find copies of the *Portland Press Herald* from the past year. Particularly the theater guide."

"We don't keep anything that current in collections," she said, "but if you look online, I believe the *Portland Press Herald* keeps archives on their website. Head straight down the hallway behind you and you'll see the media lab on your left."

Inside the lab I signed onto a computer. I was about to dive into my assignment when an idea struck me. I couldn't believe I hadn't thought of it earlier. After confirming no one was watching over my shoulder, I Googled "Patch Cipriano." Maybe I'd find an article that would shed light on his past. Or maybe he kept a blog.

I frowned at the search results. Nothing. No Facebook, no MySpace, no blog. It was like he didn't exist.

"What's your story, Patch?" I murmured. "Who are you—really?"

Half an hour later, I'd read several reviews and my eyes were glazing over. I spread my online search to all newspapers in Maine. A link to Kinghorn Prep's school paper popped up. A few seconds passed before I placed the familiar name. Elliot had transferred from Kinghorn Prep. On a whim, I decided to check it out. If the school was as elite as Elliot claimed, it probably had a respectable paper.

I clicked on the link, scrolled over the archives page, and randomly chose March 21 of earlier this year. A moment later I had a headline.

STUDENT QUESTIONED IN KINGHORN PREP MURDER

I scooted my chair closer, lured by the idea of reading something more exciting than theater reviews.

A sixteen-year-old Kinghorn Preparatory student who police were questioning in what has
been dubbed "The Kinghorn Hanging" has been
released without charge. After eighteen-year-old
Kjirsten Halverson's body was found hanging from
a tree on the wooded campus of Kinghorn Prep,
police questioned sophomore Elliot Saunders,
who was seen with the victim on the night of her
death.

My mind was slow to process the information. Elliot was questioned as part of a murder investigation?

Halverson worked as a waitress at Blind Joe's.
Police confirm that Halverson and Saunders were
seen walking the campus together late Saturday
night. Halverson's body was discovered Sunday
morning, and Saunders was released Monday
afternoon after a suicide note was discovered in
Halverson's apartment.

"Find anything interesting?"

I jumped at the sound of Elliot's voice behind me. I whirled
around to find him leaning against the doorjamb. His eyes were
narrowed ever so slightly, his mouth set in a line. Something

cold flushed through me, like a blush, only opposite.

I wheeled my chair slightly to the right, trying to position myself in front of the computer's monitor. "I'm—I'm just finishing up homework. How about you? What are you doing? I didn't hear you come in. How long have you been standing there?" My pitch was all over the place.

Elliot pushed away from the doorjamb and walked inside the lab. I groped blindly behind me for the monitor's on/off button.

I said, "I'm attempting to jump-start my inspiration on a theater review I'm supposed to have to my editor by later tonight." I was still speaking much too fast. Where was the button?

Elliot peered around me. "Theater reviews?"

My fingers brushed a button, and I heard the monitor drain to black. "I'm sorry, what did you say you're doing here?"

"I was walking by when I saw you. Something wrong? You seem . . . jumpy."

"Uh—low blood sugar." I swept my papers and books into a pile and shoehorned them inside my backpack. "I haven't eaten since lunch."

Elliot hooked a nearby chair and wheeled it next to mine. He sat backward on it and leaned close, invading my personal space. "Maybe I can help with the review."

I leaned away. "Wow, that's really nice of you, but I'm going to call it quits for now. I need to grab something to eat. It's a good time to break."

"Let me buy you dinner," he said. "Isn't there a diner just around the corner?"

"Thanks, but my mom will be expecting me. She's been out of town all week and gets back tonight." I stood and tried to step around him. He held his cell phone out, and it caught me in the navel.

"Call her."

I lowered my gaze to the phone and scrambled for an excuse. "I'm not allowed to go out on school nights."

"It's called lying, Nora. Tell her homework is taking longer than you expected. Tell her you need another hour at the library. She's not going to know the difference."

Elliot's voice had taken on an edge I'd never heard before. His blue eyes snapped with a newfound coldness, his mouth looked thinner.

"My mom doesn't like me going out with guys she hasn't met," I said.

Elliot smiled, but there was no warmth. "We both know you're not too concerned with your mom's rules, since Saturday night you were with me at Delphic."

I had my backpack slung over one shoulder, and I was clutching the strap. I didn't say anything. I brushed past Elliot and walked out of the lab in a hurry, realizing that if he turned the monitor on, he'd see the article. But there wasn't anything I could do now.

Halfway to the collections desk, I dared a glance over my shoulder. The plate-glass walls showed that the lab was empty. Elliot was nowhere to be seen. I retraced my steps to the computer, keeping my eyes on guard in case he reappeared. I turned on the monitor; the murder investigation article was still up. Sending a copy to the nearest printer, I tucked it inside my binder, logged off, and hurried out.

CHAPTER 12

MY CELL PHONE BUZZED IN MY POCKET, AND after confirming I wasn't being evil-eyed by a librarian, I answered. "Mom?"

"Good news," she said. "The auction wrapped up early. I got on the road an hour ahead of schedule and should be home soon. Where are you?"

"Hi! I wasn't expecting you until later. I'm just leaving the library. How was upstate New York?"

"Upstate New York was . . . long." She laughed, but she sounded drained. "I can't wait to see you."

I looked around for a clock. I wanted to stop by the hospital and see Vee before heading home.

"Here's the deal," I told my mom. "I need to visit Vee. I might be a few minutes late. I'll hurry—I promise."

"Of course." I detected the tiniest disappointment. "Any updates? I got your message this morning about her surgery."

"Surgery is over. They're taking her to a private room any minute now."

"Nora." I heard the swell of emotion in her voice. "I'm so glad it wasn't you. I couldn't live with myself if anything happened to you. Especially since your dad—" She broke off. "I'm just glad we're both safe. Say hi to Vee for me. See you soon. Hugs and kisses."

"Love you, Mom."

Coldwater's Regional Medical Center is a three-story redbrick structure with a covered walkway leading up to the main entrance. I passed through the revolving glass doors and stopped at the main desk to inquire about Vee. I was told she'd been moved to a room half an hour ago, and that visiting hours ended in fifteen minutes. I located the elevators and punched the button to send me up a floor.

At room 207, I pushed on the door. "Vee?" I coaxed a bouquet of balloons inside behind me, crossed the small foyer, and found Vee reclining in bed, her left arm in a cast and slung across her body.

"Hi!" I said when I saw she was awake.

Vee expelled a luxurious sigh. "I love drugs. Really. They're amazing. Even better than an Enzo cappuccino. Hey, that rhymed. Enzo cappuccino. It's a sign. I'm destined to be a poet. Want to hear another poem? I'm good at impromptu."

"Uh—"

A nurse swished in and tinkered around with Vee's IV. "Feeling okay?" she asked Vee.

"Forget being a poet," Vee said. "I'm destined for stand-up comedy. Knock, knock."

"What?" I said.

The nurse rolled her eyes. "Who's there?"

"Crab," said Vee.

"Crab who?"

"Crab your towel, we're going to the beach!"

"Maybe a little less painkillers," I told the nurse.

"Too late. I just gave her another dose. Wait until you see her in ten minutes." She swished back out the door.

"So?" I asked Vee. "What's the verdict?"

"The verdict? My doctor is a lard-arse. Closely resembles an Oompa-Loompa. Don't give me your severe look. Last time he came in, he broke into the Funky Chicken. And he's forever eating chocolate. Mostly chocolate animals. You know the solid chocolate bunnies they're selling for Easter? That's what the Oompa-Loompa ate for dinner. Had a chocolate duck at lunch with a side of yellow Peeps."

"I meant the verdict . . ." I pointed at the medical paraphernalia adorning her.

"Oh. One busted arm, a concussion, and assorted cuts, scrapes, and bruises. Fortunately for my quick reflexes, I jumped out of the way before any major damage was done. When it comes to reflexes, I'm like a cat. I'm Catwoman. I'm invulnerable. The only reason he got a piece of me is because of the rain. Cats don't like water. It impairs us. It's our kryptonite."

"I'm so sorry," I told Vee sincerely. "I should be the one in the hospital bed."

"And get all the drugs? Uh-uh. No way."

"Have the police found any leads?" I asked.

"Nada, zilch, zero."

"No eyewitnesses?"

"We were at a cemetery in the middle of a rainstorm," Vee pointed out. "Most normal people were indoors."

She was right. Most normal people had been indoors. Of course, Vee and I had been out . . . along with the mysterious girl who followed Vee out of Victoria's Secret.

"How did it happen?" I asked.

"I was walking to the cemetery like we planned, when all of a sudden I heard footsteps closing in behind me," Vee explained. "That's when I looked back, and everything came together really fast. There was the flash of a gun, and him lunging for me. Like I told the cops, my brain wasn't exactly transmitting, 'Get a visual

ID.' It was more like, 'Holy freak show, I'm about to go splat!' He growled, whacked me three or four times with the gun, grabbed my handbag, and ran."

I was more confused than ever. "Wait. It was a guy? You saw his face?"

"Of course it was a guy. He had dark eyes . . . charcoal eyes. But that's all I saw. He was wearing a ski mask."

At the mention of the ski mask, my heart skittered through several beats. It was the same guy who'd jumped in front of the Neon, I was sure of it. I hadn't imagined him—Vee was proof. I remembered the way all evidence of the crash had disappeared. Maybe I hadn't imagined that part either. This guy, whoever he was, was real. And he was out there. But if I hadn't imagined the damage to the Neon, what really happened that night? Was my vision, or my memory, somehow . . . being altered?

After a moment, a slew of secondary questions raced to mind. What did he want this time? Was he connected to the girl outside Victoria's Secret? Had he known I'd be shopping at the pier? Wearing a ski mask constituted advance planning, so he must have known beforehand where I'd be. And he didn't want me to recognize his face.

"Who did you tell we were going shopping?" I asked Vee suddenly.

She rammed a pillow behind her neck, trying to get comfortable. "My mom."

"That's it? Nobody else?"

"I might have brought it up to Elliot."

My blood seemed to suddenly stop flowing. "You told Elliot?"

"What's the big deal?"

"There's something I need to tell you," I said soberly. "Remember the night I drove the Neon home and hit a deer?"

"Yeah?" she said, frowning.

"It wasn't a deer. It was a guy. A guy in a ski mask."

"Shut up," she whispered. "You're telling me my attack wasn't random? You're telling me this guy wants something from me? No, wait. He wants something from you. I was wearing your jacket. He thought I was you."

My whole body felt leaden.

After a count of silence, she said, "Are you sure you didn't tell Patch about shopping? Because on further reflection, I'm thinking the guy had Patch's build. Tallish. Leanish. Strongish. Sexyish, aside from the attacking part."

"Patch's eyes aren't charcoal, they're black," I pointed out, but I was uncomfortably aware that I had told Patch we were going shopping at the pier.

Vee raised an indecisive shoulder. "Maybe his eyes were black. I can't remember. It happened really fast. I can be specific about the gun," she said helpfully. "It was aimed at me. Like, right at me."

I pushed a few puzzle pieces around my mind. If Patch had attacked Vee, he must have seen her leave the store wearing my

jacket and thought it was me. When he figured out he was following the wrong girl, he hit Vee with the gun out of anger and
vanished. The only problem was, I couldn't imagine Patch brutal-
izing Vee. It felt off. Besides, he was supposedly at a party on the
coast all night.

"Did your attacker look at all like Elliot?" I asked.

I watched Vee absorb the question. Whatever drug she'd been
given, it seemed to slow her thought process, and I could practically hear each gear in her brain grind into action.

"He was about twenty pounds too light and four inches too tall
to be Elliot."

"This is all my fault," I said. "I never should have let you leave
the store wearing my jacket."

"I know you don't want to hear this," said Vee, looking like she
was fighting a drug-induced yawn. "But the more I think on it, the
more similarities I see between Patch and my attacker. Same build.
Same long-legged stride. Too bad his school file was empty. We
need an address. We need to canvass his neighborhood. We need
to find a gullible little granny neighbor who could be coaxed into
mounting a webcam in her window and aiming it at his house.
Because something about Patch just isn't right."

"You honestly think Patch could have done this to you?" I asked,
still unconvinced.

Vee chewed at her lip. "I think he's hiding something. Something big."

I wasn't going to argue that.

Vee sank deeper in her bed. "My body's tingling. I feel good all over."

"We don't have an address," I said, "but we do know where he works."

"Are you thinking what I'm thinking?" Vee asked, eyes brightening briefly through the haze of chemical sedation.

"Based on past experience, I hope not."

"The truth is, we need to brush up on our sleuthing skills," said Vee. "Use them or lose them, that's what Coach said. We need to find out more about Patch's past. Hey, I bet if we document, Coach will even give us extra credit."

Highly doubtful, given that if Vee was involved, the sleuthing would likely take an illegal turn. Not to mention, this particular sleuthing job had nothing to do with biology. Even remotely.

The slight smile Vee had dragged out of me faded. Fun as it was to be lighthearted about the situation, I was frightened. The guy in the ski mask was out there, planning his next attack. It kind of made sense that Patch might know what was going on. The guy in the ski mask jumped in front of the Neon the day after Patch became my biology partner. Maybe it wasn't a coincidence.

Just then the nurse popped her head inside the door. "It's eight o'clock," she told me, tapping her watch. "Visiting hours are over."

"I'll be right out," I said.

As soon as her footsteps faded down the hall, I shut the door to Vee's room. I wanted privacy before I told her about the murder investigation surrounding Elliot. However, when I got back to Vee's bed, it was apparent that her medication had kicked in.

"Here it comes," she said with an expression of pure bliss. "Drug rush . . . any moment now . . . the surge of warmth . . . byebye, Mr. Pain . . ."

"Vee—"

"Knock, knock."

"This is really important—"

"Knock, knock."

"It's about Elliot—"

"Knock, knooooock," she said in a singsong voice.

I sighed. "Who's there?"

"Boo."

"Boo who?"

"Boo-hoo, somebody's crying, and it's not me!" She broke into hysterical laughter.

Realizing it was pointless to push the issue, I said, "Call me tomorrow after you're discharged." I unzipped my backpack. "Before I forget, I brought your homework. Where do you want me to put it?"

She pointed at the trash can. "Right there will be fine."

I pulled the Fiat into the garage and pocketed the keys. The sky lacked stars on the drive home, and sure enough, a light rain started to fall. I tugged on the garage door, lowering it to the ground and locking it. I let myself into the kitchen. A light was on somewhere upstairs, and a moment later my mom came running down the stairs and threw her arms around me.

My mom has dark wavy hair and green eyes. She's an inch shorter than I am, but we share the same bone structure. She always smells like Love by Ralph Lauren.

"I'm so glad you're safe," she said, squeezing me tight.

Safe-ish, I thought.

13

THE FOLLOWING NIGHT AT SEVEN, THE BORDERLINE'S parking lot was packed. After nearly an hour of begging, Vee and I had convinced her parents that we needed to celebrate her first night out of the hospital over chiles rellenos and virgin strawberry daiquiris. At least, that's what we were claiming. But we had an ulterior motive.

I tucked the Neon into a tight parking space and turned off the engine.

"Ew," said Vee when I passed the keys back and my fingers brushed hers. "Think you could sweat a little more?"

"I'm nervous."

"Gee, I had no clue."

I inadvertently looked at the door.

"I know what you're thinking," Vee said, tightening her lips. "And the answer is no. No as in no *way*."

"You don't know what I'm thinking," I said.

Vee vised my arm. "The heck I don't."

"I wasn't going to run," I said. "Not me."

"Liar."

Tuesday was Patch's night off, and Vee had put it into my head that it would be the perfect time to interrogate his co-workers. I envisioned myself sashaying up to the bar, giving the bartender a coy Marcie Millar look, then segueing to the topic of Patch. I needed his home address. I needed any prior arrests. I needed to know if he had a connection to the guy in the ski mask, no matter how tenuous. And I needed to figure out why the guy in the ski mask and the mysterious girl were in my life.

I peeked inside my handbag, double-checking to make sure the list of interrogation questions I'd prepared were still with me. One side of the list dealt with questions about Patch's personal life. The flip side had flirting prompts. Just in case.

"Whoa, whoa, whoa," Vee said. "What is *that*?"

"Nothing," I said, folding the list.

Vee tried to grab the list, but I was faster and had it crammed deep in my handbag before she could get to it.

"Rule number one," Vee said. "There is no such thing as notes in flirting."

"There's an exception to every rule."

"And you're not it!" She grabbed two plastic 7-Eleven sacks from the backseat and swiveled out of the car. As soon as I stepped out, she used her good arm to hurl the sacks over the top of the Neon at me.

"What's this?" I asked, catching the sacks. The handles were tied and I couldn't see inside, but the unmistakable shaft of a stiletto heel threatened to poke through the plastic.

"Size eight and a half," Vee said. "Sharkskin. It's easier to play the part when you look the part."

"I can't walk in high heels."

"Good thing they're not high, then."

"They look high," I said, eying the protruding stiletto.

"Almost five inches. They left 'high' behind at four."

Lovely. If I didn't break my neck, I just might get to humiliate myself while seducing secrets out of Patch's coworkers.

"Here's the deal," said Vee as we strode down the sidewalk to the front doors. "I sort of invited a couple of people. The more the merrier, right?"

"Who?" I asked, feeling the dark stirrings of foreboding in the pit of my stomach.

"Jules and Elliot."

Before I had time to tell Vee exactly how bad I thought this idea was, she said, "Moment of truth: I've sort of been seeing Jules. On the sly."

"What?"

"You should see his house. Bruce Wayne can't compete. His parents are either South American drug lords or come from serious old money. Since I haven't met them yet, I can't say which."

I was at a loss for words. My mouth opened and shut, but nothing came out. "When did this happen?" I finally managed to ask.

"Pretty much right after that fateful morning at Enzo's."

"Fateful? Vee, you have no idea—"

"I hope they got here first and reserved a table," Vee said, stretching her neck while eying the crowd accumulating around the doors. "I don't want to wait. I am seriously two thin minutes away from death by starvation."

I grabbed Vee by her good elbow, pulling her aside. "There's something I need to tell you—"

"I know, I know," she said. "You think there's a slim chance Elliot attacked me Sunday night. Well, I think you've got Elliot confused with Patch. And after you do some sleuthing tonight, the facts will back me up. Believe me, I want to know who attacked me just as much as you. Probably even more. It's personal now. And while we're handing each other advice, here's mine. Stay away from Patch. Just to be safe."

"I'm glad you've thought this through," I said tersely, "but here's the thing. I found an article—"

The doors to the Borderline opened. A fresh wave of heat, carrying the smell of limes and cilantro, swirled out at us, along with the sound of a mariachi band playing through the speakers.

"Welcome to the Borderline," a hostess greeted us. "Just the two of you tonight?"

Elliot was standing behind her inside the dimmed foyer. We saw each other at the same moment. His mouth smiled but his eyes did not.

"Ladies," he said, sanding his hands together as he walked over. "Looking magnificent, as always."

My skin prickled.

"Where's your partner in crime?" Vee asked, glancing around the foyer. Paper lanterns hung from the ceiling, and a mural of a Mexican pueblo spanned two walls. The waiting benches were filled to capacity. There was no sign of Jules.

"Bad news," said Elliot. "The man is sick. You're going to have to settle for me."

"Sick?" Vee demanded. "How sick? What kind of excuse is sick?"

"Sick as in it's coming out both ends."

Vee scrunched her nose. "Too much information."

I was still having a difficult time grasping the idea that something was going on between Vee and Jules. Jules came across sullen, brooding, and completely disinterested in Vee's company or anyone else's. Not one part of me felt comfortable with the idea of Vee spending time alone with Jules. Not necessarily because of how unpleasant he was or how little I knew about him, but because of the one thing I did know: He was close friends with Elliot.

The hostess plucked three menus out of a slotted cubbyhole and led us to a booth so close to the kitchen I could feel the fire of the ovens coming through the walls. To our left was the salsa bar. To our right glass doors moist with condensation led out to a patio. My poplin blouse was already clinging to my back. My sweat might have had more to do with the news about Vee and Jules than with the heat, however.

"Is this good?" the hostess asked, gesturing at the booth.

"It's great," Elliot said, shrugging out of his bomber jacket. "I love this place. If the room doesn't make you sweat, the food will."

The hostess's smile lit up. "You've been here before. Can I start you with chips and our newest jalapeño salsa? It's our hottest yet."

"I like things hot," said Elliot.

I was pretty sure he was being slimy. I'd been way too generous in thinking he wasn't as low as Marcie. I'd been way too generous about his character, period. Especially now that I knew he had a murder investigation hiding along with who knew how many other skeletons in his closet.

The hostess swept him an appraising once-over. "I'll be right back with chips and salsa. Your waitress will be here shortly to take your orders."

Vee plopped into the booth first. I slid in beside her, and Elliot took the seat across from me. Our eyes connected, and there was a fleck of something dark in his. Very likely resentment. Maybe even hostility. I wondered if he knew I'd seen the article.

"Purple is your color, Nora," he said, nodding at my scarf as I loosened it from my neck and tied it around the handle of my handbag. "Brightens your eyes."

Vee nudged my foot. She actually thought he meant it as a compliment.

"So," I said to Elliot with an artificial smile, "why don't you tell us about Kinghorn Prep?"

"Yeah," Vee chimed in. "Are there secret societies there? Like in the movies?"

"What's to tell?" Elliot said. "Great school. End of story." He picked up his menu and scanned it. "Anyone interested in an appetizer? My treat."

"If it's so great, why did you transfer?" I met his eyes and held them. Ever so slightly, I arched my eyebrows, challenging.

A muscle in Elliot's jaw jumped just before he cracked a smile. "The girls. I heard they were a lot finer around these parts. The rumor proved true." He winked at me, and an ice-cold feeling shot from my head to my toes.

"Why didn't Jules transfer too?" asked Vee. "We could have

been the fabulous four, only with a lot more punch. The phenomenal four."

"Jules's parents are obsessed with his education. Intense doesn't begin to cover it. I swear on my life, he's going all the way to the top. The guy can't be stopped. I mean, I confess, I do okay in school. Better than most. But nobody tops Jules. He's an academic god."

The dreamy look returned to Vee's eyes. "I've never met his parents," she said. "Both times I've gone over, they're either out of town or working."

"They work a lot," Elliot agreed, returning his eyes to the menu, making it hard for me to read anything in them.

"Where do they work?" I asked.

Elliot took a long drink of his water. It seemed to me like he was buying time while he devised an answer. "Diamonds. They spend a lot of time in Africa and Australia."

"I didn't know Australia was big in the diamond business," I said.

"Yeah, neither did I," said Vee.

In fact, I was pretty sure Australia had no diamonds. Period.

"Why are they living in Maine?" I asked. "Why not Africa?"

Elliot studied his menu more intensely. "What are you both having? I'm thinking the steak fajitas look good."

"If Jules's parents are in the diamond business, I bet they know a lot about choosing the perfect engagement ring," Vee said. "I've always wanted an emerald-cut solitaire."

I kicked Vee under the table. She jabbed me with her fork.

"Oww!" I said.

Our waitress paused at the end of the table long enough to ask, "Anything to drink?"

Elliot looked over the top of his menu, first at me, then at Vee.

"Diet Coke," Vee said.

"Water with lime wedges, please," I said.

The waitress returned amazingly quickly with our drinks. Her return was my cue to leave the table and initiate step one of the Plan, and Vee reminded me with a second under-the-table prod from her fork.

"Vee," I said through my teeth, "would you like to accompany me to the ladies' room?" I suddenly didn't want to go through with the Plan. I didn't want to leave Vee alone with Elliot. What I did want was to drag her out, tell her about the murder investigation, then find some way to make both Elliot and Jules disappear from our lives.

"Why don't you go alone?" said Vee. "I think that would be a better plan." She jerked her head at the bar and mouthed Go, while making discreet shooing motions below the table.

"I was planning on going alone, but I'd really like you to join me."

"What is it with girls?" Elliot said, splitting a smile between us. "I swear, I've never known a girl who could go to the bathroom alone." He leaned forward and grinned conspiratorially. "Let me in on the secret. Seriously. I'll pay you five bucks each." He reached for his back pocket. "Ten, if I can come along and see what the big deal is."

Vee flashed a grin. "Pervert. Don't forget these," she told me, stuffing the 7-Eleven sacks into my arms.

Elliot's eyebrows lifted.

"Trash," Vee explained to him with a touch of snark. "Our garbage can is full. My mom asked if I could throw these away since I was going out."

Elliot didn't look like he believed her, and Vee didn't look like she cared. I got up, my arms loaded with costume gear, and swallowed my burning frustration.

Weaving through the tables, I took the hall leading back to the restrooms. The hall was painted terra-cotta and was decorated with maracas, straw hats, and wooden dolls. It was hotter back here, and I wiped my forehead. The Plan now was to get this over with as quickly as possible. As soon as I was back at the table, I'd formulate an excuse about needing to leave, and haul Vee out. With or without her consent.

After peeking below the three stalls in the ladies' room and confirming I was alone, I locked the main door and dumped the contents of the 7-Eleven sacks onto the counter. One platinum blond wig, one purple push-up bra, one black tube top, one sequined miniskirt, hot pink fishnet tights, and one pair of size eight and a half sharkskin stiletto heels.

I stuffed the bra, the tube top and the tights back inside the sacks. After sloughing off my jeans, I pulled on the miniskirt. I tucked my hair under the wig and applied the lipstick. I topped it off with a generous coat of high-shine lip gloss.

"You can do this," I told my reflection, snapping the cap back on the gloss and blotting my lips together. "You can pull a Marcie Millar. Seduce men for secrets. How hard can it be?"

I kicked off my driving mocs, stuffed them into a sack along with my jeans, then pushed the sack under the counter, out of sight. "Besides," I continued, "there's nothing wrong with sacrificing a little pride for the sake of intelligence. If you want to approach this with a morbid outlook, you could even say if you don't get answers, you could wind up dead. Because like it or not, someone out there means you harm."

I dangled the sharkskin heels in my line of vision. They weren't the ugliest things I'd ever seen. In fact, they could be considered sexy. Jaws meets Coldwater, Maine. I strapped myself into them and practiced walking across the bathroom several times.

Two minutes later I eased myself on top of a bar stool at the bar.

The bartender eyed me. "Sixteen?" he guessed. "Seventeen?"

He looked about ten years older than me and had receding brown hair that he wore shaved close. A silver hoop hung from his right earlobe. White T-shirt and Levi's. Not bad looking . . . not great, either.

"I'm not an underage drinker," I called loudly above the music and surrounding conversation. "I'm waiting for a friend. I've got a great view of the doors here." I retrieved the list of questions from my handbag and covertly positioned the paper under a glass salt shaker.

"What's that?" the bartender asked, wiping his hands on a towel and nodding at the list.

I slid the list farther under the salt shaker. "Nothing," I said, all innocence.

He raised an eyebrow.

I decided to be loose with the truth. "It's a . . . shopping list. I have to pick up some groceries for my mom on the way home." *What happened to flirting? I asked myself. What happened to Marcie Millar?*

He gave me a scrutinizing look that I decided wasn't all negative. "After working this job for five years, I'm pretty good at spotting liars."

"I'm not a liar," I said. "Maybe I was lying a moment ago, but it was just one lie. One little lie doesn't make a liar."

"You look like a reporter," he said.

"I work for my high school's eZine." *I wanted to shake myself. Reporters didn't instill trust in people. People were generally suspicious of reporters.* "But I'm not working tonight," I amended quickly. "Strictly pleasure tonight. No business. No underlying agendas. None whatsoever."

After a count of silence I decided the best move was to plow ahead. I cleared my throat and said, "Is the Borderline a popular place of employment for high school students?"

"We get a lot of those, yeah. Hostesses and busboys and the like."

"Really?" I said, feigning surprise. "Maybe I know some of them. Try me."

The bartender angled his eyes toward the ceiling and scratched the stubble on his chin. His blank stare wasn't inspiring my confidence. Not to mention that I didn't have a lot of time. Elliot could be slipping lethal drugs into Vee's Diet Coke.

"How about Patch Cipriano?" I asked. "Does he work here?"

"Patch? Yeah. He works here. A couple nights, and weekends."

"Was he working Sunday night?" I tried not to sound too curious. But I needed to know if it was possible for Patch to have been at the pier. He said he had a party on the coast, but maybe his plans had changed. If someone verified that he was at work Sunday evening, I could rule out his involvement in the attack on Vee.

"Sunday?" More scratching. "The nights blur together. Try the hostesses. One of them will remember. They all giggle and go a little screwy when he's around." He smiled as if I might somehow sympathize with them.

I said, "You wouldn't happen to have access to his job application?" Including his home address.

"That would be a no."

"Just out of curiosity," I said, "do you know if it's possible to get hired here if you have a felony on your record?"

"A felony?" He gave a bark of laughter. "You kidding me?"

"Okay, maybe not a felony, but how about a misdemeanor?"

He spread his palms on the counter and leaned close. "No." His tone had shifted from humoring to insulted.

"That's good. That's really good to know." I repositioned myself on the bar stool, and felt the skin on my thighs peel away from the vinyl. I was sweating. If rule number one of flirting was no lists, I was fairly certain rule number two was no sweating.

I consulted my list.

"Do you know if Patch has ever had any restraining orders? Does he have a history of stalking?" I suspected the bartender was getting a bad vibe from me, and I decided to throw all my questions out in a last-ditch effort before he sent me away from the bar—or worse, had me evicted from the restaurant for harassment and suspicious behavior. "Does he have a girlfriend?" I blurted.

"Go ask him," he said.

I blinked. "He's not working tonight."

At the bartender's grin, my stomach seemed to unravel.

"He's not working tonight . . . is he?" I asked, my voice inching up an octave. "He's supposed to have Tuesdays off!"

"Usually, yeah. But he's covering for Benji. Benji went to the hospital. Ruptured appendix."

"You mean Patch is *here*? Right *now*?" I glanced over my shoulder, brushing the wig to cover my profile while I scanned the dining area for him.

"He walked back to the kitchen a couple minutes ago."

I was already disengaging myself from the bar stool. "I think I left my car running. But it was great talking to you!" I hurried as quickly as I could to the restrooms.

Inside the ladies' room I locked the door behind me, drew a few breaths with my back pressed to the door, then went to the sink and splashed cold water on my face. Patch was going to find out I'd spied on him. My memorable performance guaranteed that. On the surface, this was a bad thing because it was, well, humiliating. But when I thought about it, I had to face the fact that Patch was very secretive. Secretive people didn't like their lives pried into. How would he react when he learned I was holding him under a magnifying glass?

And now I wondered why I'd come here at all, since deep inside, I didn't believe Patch was the guy behind the ski mask. Maybe he had dark, disturbing secrets, but running around in a ski mask wasn't one of them.

I turned off the tap, and when I looked up, Patch's face was reflected in the mirror. I shrieked and swung around.

He wasn't smiling, and he didn't look particularly amused.

"What are you doing here?" I gasped.

"I work here."

"I mean here. Can't you read? The sign on the door—"

"I'm starting to think you're following me. Every time I turn around, there you are."

"I wanted to take Vee out," I explained. "She's been in the hospital." I sounded defensive. I was certain that only made me look more guilty. "I never dreamed I'd run into you. It's supposed to be your night off. And what are you talking about? Every time I turn around, there you are."

Patch's eyes were sharp, intimidating, extracting. They calculated my every word, my every movement.

"Want to explain the tacky hair?" he said.

I yanked off the wig and tossed it on the counter. "Want to explain where you've been? You missed the last two days of school."

I was almost certain Patch wouldn't reveal his whereabouts, but he said, "Playing paintball. What were you doing at the bar?"

"Talking with the bartender. Is that a crime?" Balancing one hand against the counter, I raised my foot to unbuckle a sharkskin heel. I bent over slightly, and as I did, the interrogation list fluttered out of my neckline and onto the floor.

I went down on my knees for it, but Patch was faster. He held it over his head while I jumped for it.

"Give it back!" I said.

"'Does Patch have a restraining order against him?'" he read. "'Is Patch a felon?'"

"Give—me—that!" I hissed furiously.

Patch gave a soft laugh, and I knew he'd seen the next question. "'Does Patch have a girlfriend?'"

Patch put the paper in his back pocket. I was sorely tempted to go after it, despite its location.

He leaned back against the counter and leveled our eyes. "If you're going to dig around for information, I'd prefer that you ask me."

"Those questions"—I waved where he'd hidden them—"were a joke. Vee wrote them," I added in a flash of inspiration. "It's all her fault."

"I know your handwriting, Nora."

"Well, okay, fine," I began, hunting for a smart reply, but I took too long and lost my chance.

"No restraining orders," he said. "No felonies."

I tilted my chin up. "Girlfriend?" I told myself I didn't care how he answered. Either way was fine with me.

"That's none of your business."

"You tried to kiss me," I reminded him. "You made it my business."

The ghost of a pirate smile lurked at his mouth. I got the impression he was recalling every last detail of that near kiss, including my sigh-slash-moan.

"Ex-girlfriend," he said after a moment.

My stomach dropped as a sudden thought popped into my mind. What if the girl from Delphic and Victoria's Secret was

Patch's ex? What if she saw me talking to Patch at the arcade and—mistakenly—assumed there was a lot more to our relationship? If she was still attracted to Patch, it made sense that she might be jealous enough to follow me around. A few puzzle pieces seemed to fall into place....

And then Patch said, "But she's not around."

"What do you mean she's not around?"

"She's gone. She's never coming back."

"You mean . . . she's dead?" I asked.

Patch didn't deny it.

My stomach suddenly felt heavy and twisted. I hadn't expected this. Patch had a girlfriend, and now she was dead.

The door to the ladies' room rattled as someone tried to enter. I'd forgotten I'd locked it. Which made me wonder how Patch got in. Either he had a key, or there was another explanation. An explanation I probably didn't want to think about, such as gliding under the door like air. Like smoke.

"I need to get back to work," Patch said. He gave me a once-over that lingered a bit below the hips. "Killer skirt. Deadly legs."

Before I'd formed a single coherent thought, he was through the door.

The older woman waiting for admittance looked at me, then over her shoulder at Patch, who was vanishing down the hall. "Honey," she told me, "he looks slippery as soap."

"Good description," I mumbled.

She fluffed her short, corkscrew gray hair. "A girl could lather up in soap like that."

After I changed back into my clothes, I returned to the booth and slid in beside Vee. Elliot checked his watch and lifted his eyebrows at me.

"Sorry I was gone so long," I said. "Did I miss anything?"

"Nope," said Vee. "Same old, same old." She bumped my knee, and the question was implied. Well?

Before I could return the bump, Elliot said, "You missed the waitress. I ordered you a red burrito." A creepy smile tugged at the corners of his mouth.

I saw my chance.

"Actually, I'm not sure I'm up to eating." I managed a nauseated face that wasn't altogether contrived. "I think I caught what Jules has."

"Oh, man," Vee said. "Are you okay?"

I shook my head.

"I'll hunt down our waitress and get her to box the food," Vee suggested, digging in her purse for keys.

"What about me?" said Elliot, sounding only half joking.

"Rain check?" Vee said.

Bingo, I thought.

CHAPTER

14

I GOT BACK TO THE FARMHOUSE SHORTLY BEFORE EIGHT. I turned my key in the lock, grabbed the doorknob, and shoved my hip against the door. I'd called my mom a few hours before dinner; she was at the office, tying up a few loose ends, not sure when she'd be home, and I expected to find the house quiet, dark, and cold.

On the third shove, the door gave way, and I hurled my handbag into the darkness, then wrestled with the key still jammed in the lock. Ever since the night Patch came over, the lock had developed a greedy disposition. I wondered if Dorothea had noticed it earlier in the day.

"Give—me—the—dumb—key," I said, jiggling it free.

The grandfather clock in the hall ticked on the hour, and eight loud dongs reverberated through the silence. I was walking into the living room to start a fire in the wood-burning stove when there was the rustle of fabric and a low creak from across the room.

I screamed.

"Nora!" my mom said, throwing off a blanket and scrambling into a sitting position on the sofa. "What in the world's the matter?"

I had one hand splayed across my heart and the other flattened against the wall, supporting me. "You scared me!"

"I fell asleep. If I'd heard you come in, I would have said something." She pushed her hair off her face and blinked owlishly. "What time is it?"

I collapsed into the nearest armchair and tried to recover my normal heart rate. My imagination had conjured up a pair of ruthless eyes behind a ski mask. Now that I was positive he wasn't a figment of my imagination, I had an overwhelming desire to tell my mom everything, from the way he'd jumped on the Neon to his role as Vee's attacker. He was stalking me, and he was violent. We'd get new locks on the doors. And it seemed logical that the police would get involved. I'd feel much safer at night with an officer parked on the curb.

"I was going to wait to bring this up," my mom said, interrupting my thought process, "but I'm not sure the perfect moment is ever going to present itself."

I frowned. "What's going on?"

She gave a long, troubled sigh. "I'm thinking about putting the farmhouse up for sale."

"What? Why?"

"We've been struggling for a year, and I'm not pulling in as much as I'd hoped. I've considered taking a second job, but honestly, I'm not sure there are enough hours in the day." She laughed without any trace of humor. "Dorothea's wages are modest, but it's extra money we don't have. The only other thing I can think of is moving into a smaller house. Or an apartment."

"But this is our house." All my memories were here. The memory of my dad was here. I couldn't believe she didn't feel the same way. I would do whatever it took to stay.

"I'll give it three more months," she said. "But I don't want to get your hopes up."

Right then I knew I couldn't tell my mom about the guy in the ski mask. She'd quit work tomorrow. She'd get a local job, and there'd be absolutely no choice but to sell the farmhouse.

"Let's talk about something brighter," Mom said, pushing her mouth into a smile. "How was dinner?"

"Fine," I said morosely.

"And Vee? How's she recovering?"

"She can go back to school tomorrow."

Mom smiled wryly. "It's a good thing she broke her left arm. Otherwise she wouldn't be able to take notes in class, and I can only imagine how disappointing that would have been for her."

"Ha, ha," I said. "I'm going to make hot chocolate." I stood and pointed over my shoulder into the kitchen. "Want some?"

"That actually sounds perfect. I'll start the fire."

After a quick trip to the kitchen to round up mugs, sugar, and the cocoa canister, I came back to find that Mom had a kettle of water on the wood-burning stove. I perched myself on the arm of the sofa and handed her a mug.

"How did you know you were in love with Dad?" I asked, striving to sound casual. There was always the chance that discussing Dad would bring on a tearfest, something I hoped to avoid.

Mom settled into the sofa and propped her feet up on the coffee table. "I didn't. Not until we'd been married about a year."

It wasn't the answered I'd expected. "Then . . . why did you marry him?"

"Because I thought I was in love. And when you think you're in love, you're willing to stick it out and make it work until it is love."

"Were you scared?"

"To marry him?" She laughed. "That was the exciting part. Shopping for a gown, reserving the chapel, wearing my diamond solitaire."

I pictured Patch's mischievous smile. "Were you ever scared of Dad?"

"Whenever the New England Patriots lost."

Whenever the Patriots lost, my dad went to the garage and revved up his chainsaw. Two autumns ago he hauled the chainsaw to the woods behind our property, felled ten trees, and diced them into firewood. We still have more than half the pile to burn through.

Mom patted the sofa beside her, and I curled up against her, resting my head on her shoulder. "I miss him," I said.

"Me too."

"I'm afraid I'll forget what he looked like. Not in pictures, but hanging around on a Saturday morning in sweats, making scrambled eggs."

Mom laced her fingers through mine. "You've always been so much like him, right from the start."

"Really?" I sat up. "In what way?"

"He was a good student, very clever. He wasn't flashy or outspoken, but people respected him."

"Was Dad ever . . . mysterious?"

Mom seemed to turn this over in her mind. "Mysterious people have a lot of secrets. Your father was very open."

"Was he ever rebellious?"

She gave a short, startled laugh. "Did you see him that way? Harrison Grey, the world's most ethical accountant . . . rebellious?"

She gave a theatrical gasp. "Heaven forbid! He did wear his hair long for a while. It was wavy and blond—like a surfer's. Of course, his horn-rimmed glasses killed the look. So . . . do I dare ask what got us on this subject?"

I had no idea how to explain my conflicting feelings for Patch to my mom. I had no idea how to explain Patch, period. My mom was probably expecting a description that included his parents' names, his GPA, the varsity sports he played, and which colleges he planned on applying to. I didn't want to alarm her by saying I was willing to bet my piggy bank that Patch had a rap sheet. "There's this guy," I said, unable to hold back a smile at the thought of Patch. "We've been hanging out lately. Mostly school stuff."

"Ooh, a boy," she said mysteriously. "Well? Is he in the Chess Club? Student Council? The tennis team?"

"He likes pool," I offered optimistically.

"A swimmer! Is he as cute as Michael Phelps? Of course, I always leaned toward Ryan Lochte when it came to appearances."

I thought about correcting my mom. On second thought, it was probably best not to clarify. Pool, swimming . . . close enough, right?

The phone rang and Mom stretched across the sofa to answer it. Ten seconds into the call she flopped back against the sofa and slapped a hand to her forehead. "No, it's not a problem. I'll run over, pick it up, and bring it by first thing tomorrow morning."

"Hugo?" I asked after she hung up. Hugo was my mom's boss,

and to say he called *all the time* was putting it mildly. Once, he'd called her into work on a Sunday because he couldn't figure out how to operate the copy machine.

"He left some unfinished paperwork in the office and needs me to run over. I have to make copies, but I shouldn't be gone more than an hour. Have you finished your homework?"

"Not yet."

"Then I'll tell myself we couldn't have spent time together even if I was here." She sighed and rose to her feet. "See you in an hour?"

"Tell Hugo he should pay you more."

She laughed. "A lot more."

As soon as I had the house to myself, I cleared the breakfast dishes off the kitchen table and made room for my textbooks. English, world history, biology. Arming myself with a brand-new number two pencil, I flipped open the top book and went to work.

Fifteen minutes later my mind rebelled, refusing to digest another paragraph on European feudal systems. I wondered what Patch was doing after he got off work. Homework? Hard to believe. Eating pizza and watching basketball on TV? Maybe, but it didn't feel right. Placing bets and playing pool at Bo's Arcade? It seemed like a good guess.

I had the unexplainable desire to drive to Bo's and defend my earlier behavior, but the thought was quickly put into perspective by the simple fact that I didn't have time. My mom would be home in less time than it took to make the half-hour drive there. Not to mention, Patch wasn't the kind of guy I could just go hunt down. In the past, our meetings had operated on his schedule, not mine. Always.

I climbed the stairs to change into something comfy. I pushed on my bedroom door and took three steps inside before stopping short. My dresser drawers were yanked out, clothes strewn across the floor. The bed was ripped apart. The closet doors were open, hanging askew by their hinges. Books and picture frames littered the floor.

I saw the reflection of movement in the window across the room and swung around. He stood against the wall behind me, dressed head to toe in black and wearing the ski mask. My brain was in a swirling fog, just beginning to transmit run! to my legs, when he lunged for the window, threw it open, and ducked lithely out.

I took the stairs down three at a time. I flung myself around the banister, flew down the hall to the kitchen, and dialed 911.

Fifteen minutes later a patrol car bumped into the driveway. Shaking, I unbolted the door and let the two officers in. The first officer to step inside was short and thick-waisted with salt-and-pepper hair. The other was tall and lean with hair almost as dark as Patch's, but cropped above his ears. In a strange way, he vaguely resembled Patch. Mediterranean complexion, symmetrical face, eyes with an edge.

They introduced themselves; the dark-haired officer was Detective Basso. His partner was Detective Holstijic.

"Are you Nora Grey?" Detective Holstijic asked.

I nodded.

"Your parents home?"

"My mom left a few minutes before I called 911."

"So you're home alone?"

Another nod.

"Why don't you tell us what happened?" he asked, crossing his arms and planting his feet wide, while Detective Basso walked a few paces inside the house and took a look around.

"I came home at eight and did some homework," I said. "When I went up to my bedroom, I saw him. Everything was a mess. He tore my room apart."

"Did you recognize him?"

"He was wearing a ski mask. And the lights were off."

"Any distinguishing marks? Tattoos?"

"No."

"Height? Weight?"

I delved reluctantly into my short-term memory. I didn't want to relive the moment, but it was important that I recall any clues. "Average weight, but a little on the tall side. About the same size as Detective Basso."

"Did he say anything?"

I shook my head.

Detective Basso reappeared and said, "All clear," to his partner. Then he climbed to the second floor. The floorboards creaked overhead as he moved down the hall, opening and shutting doors.

Detective Holstijic cracked the front door and squatted to examine the deadbolt. "Was the door unlocked or damaged when you came home?"

"No. I used my key to get in. My mom was asleep in the living room."

Detective Basso appeared at the top of the stairs.

"Can you show us what's damaged?" he asked me.

Detective Holstijic and I climbed the stairs together, and I led the way down the hall to where Detective Basso stood just inside my bedroom door with his hands on his hips, surveying my room.

I held perfectly still, a tingle of fear creeping through me. My bed was made. My pajamas were in a heap on my pillow, just the way I'd left them this morning. My dresser drawers were shut, picture frames arranged neatly on top. The trunk at the foot of the bed was closed. The floors were clean. The window drapes hung in long, smooth panels, one on either side of the closed window.

"You said you saw the intruder," said Detective Basso. He was staring down at me with hard eyes that didn't miss a thing. Eyes that were expert at filtering lies.

I stepped inside the room, but it lacked the familiar touch of comfort and safety. There was an underlying note of violation and menace. I pointed across the room at the window, trying to hold my hand steady. "When I walked in, he jumped out the window."

Detective Basso glanced out the window. "Long way to the ground," he observed. He attempted to open the window. "Did you lock it after he left?"

"No. I ran downstairs and called 911."

"Somebody locked it." Detective Basso was still eyeing me with razor eyes, his mouth pressed in a tight line.

"Not sure anybody'd be able to get away after a jump like that," Detective Holstijic said, joining his partner at the window. "They'd be lucky to get off with a broken leg."

"Maybe he didn't jump, maybe he climbed down the tree," I said.

Detective Basso whipped his head around. "Well? Which is it? Did he climb or jump? He could have pushed past you and gone out the front door. That would be the logical option. That's what I'd have done. I'm going to ask once more. Think real careful. Did you really see someone in your room tonight?"

He didn't believe me. He thought I'd invented it. For a moment I was tempted to think similarly. What was wrong with me? Why was my reality convoluted? Why did the truth never match up? For the sake of my sanity, I told myself it wasn't me. It was him. The guy in the ski mask. He was doing this. I didn't know how, but he was to blame.

Detective Holstijic broke the tense silence by saying, "When will your parents be home?"

"I live with my mom. She had to make a quick trip to the office."

"We need to ask you both a few questions," he continued. He pointed for me to take a seat on my bed, but I shook my head numbly. "Have you recently broken up with a boyfriend?"

"No."

"How about drugs? Have you had a problem, now or in the past?"

"No."

"You mentioned that you live with your mom. How about Dad? Where's he?"

"This was a mistake," I said. "I'm sorry. I shouldn't have called."

The two officers exchanged looks. Detective Holstijic shut his eyes and massaged the inner corners. Detective Basso looked like he'd wasted enough time and was ready to blow it off.

"We've got things to do," he said. "Are you going to be all right here alone until your mom gets back?"

I hardly heard him; I couldn't pull my eyes off the window. How was he doing it? Fifteen minutes. He had *fifteen* minutes to find a way back inside and put the room in order before the police arrived. And with me downstairs the whole time. At the realization that we'd been alone in the house together, I shuddered.

Detective Holstijic extended his business card. "Could you have your mom call us when she gets in?"

"We'll see ourselves out," Detective Basso said. He was already halfway down the hall.

CHAPTER

15

"YOU THINK ELLIOT *MURDERED* SOMEONE?"

"Shh!" I hissed at Vee, glancing across the rows of lab tables to make sure no one had overheard.

"No offense, babe, but this is starting to get ridiculous. First he attacked me. Now he's a killer. I'm sorry, but Elliot? A murderer? He's, like, the nicest guy I've ever met. When was the last time he forgot to hold open a door for you? Oh, yeah, that's right ... *never*."

Vee and I were in biology, and Vee was lying faceup on a table.

We were running a lab on blood pressure, and Vee was supposed to be resting silently for five minutes. Normally I would have worked with Patch, but Coach had given us a free day, which meant we were free to choose our own partners. Vee and I were at the back of the room; Patch was working with a jock named Thomas Rookery at the front of the room.

"He was questioned as a suspect in a murder investigation," I whispered, feeling Coach's eyes gravitate toward us. I scribbled a few notes on my lab sheet. *Subject is calm and relaxed. Subject has refrained from speaking for three and a half minutes.* "The police obviously thought he had motive and means."

"Are you sure it's the same Elliot?"

"How many Elliot Saunderses do you think there were at Kinghorn in February?"

Vee strummed her fingers on her stomach. "It just seems really, really hard to believe. And anyway, so what if he was questioned? The important thing is, he was released. They didn't find him guilty."

"Because police found a suicide note written by Halverson."

"Who's Halverson again?"

"Kjirsten Halverson," I said impatiently. "The girl who supposedly hanged herself."

"Maybe she did hang herself. I mean, what if one day she said, 'Hey, life sucks,' and strung herself to a tree? It has happened."

"You don't find it a little too coincidental that her apartment showed evidence of a break-in when they discovered the suicide note?"

"She lived in Portland. Break-ins happen."

"I think someone placed the note. Someone who wanted Elliot off the hook."

"Who would want Elliot off the hook?" Vee asked.

I gave her my best duh look.

Vee propped herself up with her good elbow. "So you're saying Elliot hauled Kjirsten up a tree, tied a rope around her neck, pushed her off the limb, then did a breaking-and-entering job on her apartment and planted evidence pointing to a suicide."

"Why not?"

Vee returned the duh look. "Because the cops already analyzed everything. If they're ruling it a suicide, so am I."

"How about this," I said. "Just weeks after Elliot was released from questioning, he transferred schools. Why would someone leave Kinghorn Prep to come to CHS?"

"You've got a point there."

"I think he's trying to escape his past. I think it became too uncomfortable attending school on the same campus where he killed Kjirsten. He has a guilty conscience." I tapped my pencil against my lip. "I need to drive out to Kinghorn and ask questions. She just died two months ago; everyone will still be buzzing about it."

"I don't know, Nora. I'm getting bad vibes about initiating a spy operation at Kinghorn. I mean, are you going to ask about Elliot specifically? What if he finds out? What's he going to think?"

I looked down at her. "He only has something to worry about if he's guilty."

"And then he'll kill you to silence you." Vee grinned like the Cheshire cat. I didn't. "I want to find out who attacked me just as much as you do," she continued on a more serious note, "but I swear on my life it wasn't Elliot. I've replayed the memory, like, a hundred times. It's not a match. Not even close. Trust me."

"Okay, maybe Elliot didn't attack you," I said, trying to appease Vee but not about to clear Elliot's name. "He still has a lot going against him. He was involved in a murder investigation, for one. And he's almost too nice, for two. It's creepy. And he's friends with Jules, for three."

Vee frowned. "Jules? What's wrong with Jules?"

"Don't you think it's odd that every time we're with them, Jules bails?"

"What's that supposed to mean?"

"The night we went to Delphic, Jules left almost immediately to use the bathroom. Did he ever come back? After I left to buy cotton candy, did Elliot find him?"

"No, but I chalked it up to internal plumbing issues."

"Then, last night, he mysteriously called in sick." I scrubbed my pencil's eraser down the length of my nose, thinking. "He seems to get sick a lot."

"I think you're overanalyzing this. Maybe . . . maybe he has IBS."

"IBS?"

"Irritable bowel syndrome."

I discarded Vee's suggestion in favor of mentally stretching for an idea that floated just out of reach. Kinghorn Prep was easily an hour away by car. If the school was as academically rigorous as Elliot claimed, how did Jules continually have time to make the drive to Coldwater to visit? I saw him nearly every morning on my way to school at Enzo's Bistro with Elliot. Plus, he gave Elliot a ride home after school. It was almost like Elliot had Jules in the palm of his hand.

But that wasn't all of it. I scrubbed the eraser more furiously against my nose. What was I missing?

"Why would Elliot kill Kjirsten?" I wondered out loud. "Maybe she saw him do something illegal, and he killed her to silence her."

Vee let go of a sigh. "This is starting to drift into the land of This Makes Absolutely No Sense."

"There's something else. Something we're not seeing."

Vee looked at me like my logic was vacationing in outer space. "Personally, I think you're seeing too much. This feels a lot like a witch hunt."

And then all of a sudden I knew what I was missing. It had been nagging me all day, calling to me from the back of my mind, but I'd been too overwhelmed with everything else to pay attention. Detective Basso had asked me if anything was missing. It just now hit me that something was. I'd set the article about Elliot on top of my dresser last night. But this morning—I consulted my memory to be sure—it was gone. Definitely gone.

"Omigosh," I said. "Elliot broke into my house last night. It was him! He stole the article." Since the article was in plain sight, it was obvious Elliot had torn apart my room to terrorize me—possibly as punishment for finding the article in the first place.

"Whoa, what?" Vee said.

"What's wrong?" asked Coach, coming to a stop beside me.

"Yeah, what's wrong?" Vee chimed in. She pointed and laughed at me from behind Coach's back.

"Um—the subject doesn't appear to have a pulse," I said, giving Vee's wrist a hard pinch.

While Coach probed for Vee's pulse, she made swooning motions and fanned herself. Coach flicked his eyes to mine, looking at me over the top of his glasses. "Right here, Nora. Beating loud and strong. Are you sure the subject refrained from activity, including talking, for the full five minutes? This pulse isn't as slow as I would have expected."

"The subject struggled with the no-talking step," Vee interjected. "And the subject has a hard time relaxing on a rock-hard biology table. The subject would like to propose switching places so Nora can be the new subject." Vee used her right hand to grab me and pull herself upright.

"Don't make me regret allowing you to choose your own partners," Coach told us.

"Don't make me regret coming to school today," said Vee sweetly.

Coach shot her a warning look, then picked up my lab sheet, eyes skimming the all-but-blank page.

"The subject equates biology labs with overdosing on prescription-strength sedatives," Vee said.

Coach chirped his whistle, and all eyes in the class swung our way.

"Patch?" he said. "Mind taking over here? We seem to have run into a partner problem."

"I was so kidding," Vee said quickly. "Here—I'll do the lab."

"You should have thought of that fifteen minutes ago," Coach said.

"Please forgive me?" she asked, batting her eyelashes angelically.

Coach tucked her notebook under her good arm. "No."

Sorry! Vee mouthed over her shoulder at me as she walked reluctantly to the front of the room.

A moment later Patch took a seat on the table beside me. He clasped his hands loosely between his knees and kept a steady gaze on me.

"What?" I said, feeling unnerved by the weight of his stare.

He smiled. "I was remembering the shark shoes. Last night."

I got the usual Patch-induced flutter in my stomach, and like usual, I couldn't distinguish if it was a good thing or a bad thing.

"How was your night?" I asked, my voice carefully neutral as

I attempted to break the ice. My spying adventures still hung uncomfortably between us.

"Interesting. Yours?"

"Not so much."

"Homework was brutal, huh?"

He was making fun of me. "I didn't do homework."

He had the smile of a fox. "Who did you do?"

I was speechless a moment. I stood there with my mouth slightly open. "Was that an innuendo?"

"Just curious what my competition is."

"Grow up."

His smile stretched. "Loosen up."

"I'm already walking on thin ice with Coach, so do me a favor and let's concentrate on the lab. I'm not in the mood to play test subject, so if you don't mind . . ." I looked pointedly at the table.

"Can't," he said. "I don't have a heart."

I told myself he wasn't being literal.

I lowered myself down on the table and stacked my hands on my stomach. "Tell me when five minutes are up." I shut my eyes, preferring not to watch Patch's black eyes examine me.

A few minutes later I opened one eye a slit.

"Time's up," said Patch.

I held one upturned wrist out so he could take my pulse.

Patch took my hand, and a jolt of heat shot up my arm and ended with a squeeze in my stomach.

"The subject's pulse increased on contact," he said.

"Don't write that." It was supposed to sound indignant. If anything, it sounded like I was repressing a smile.

"Coach wants us to be thorough."

"What do you want?" I asked him.

Patch's eyes connected with mine. On the inside, he was grinning. I could tell.

"Except, you know, *that*," I said.

After school I swung by Miss Greene's office for our scheduled appointment. At the end of the school day, Dr. Hendrickson had always kept his door wide open, a nonverbal invitation for students to stop by. Every time I passed down this stretch of hallway now, Miss Greene had the door closed. All the way. The Do not disturb was implicit.

"Nora," she said, opening the door after my knock, "please come in. Have a seat."

Her office was fully unpacked and decorated today. She'd brought in several more plants, and a panel of framed botanical prints hung in a row on the wall above her desk.

Miss Greene said, "I've been thinking a lot about what you said last week. I came to the obvious conclusion that our relationship needs to be built on trust and respect. We won't discuss your dad again, unless you specify."

"Okay," I said warily. What were we going to talk about?

"I heard some rather disappointing news," she said. Her smile faded and she leaned forward, resting her elbows on the desk. She was holding a pen, and she rolled it between her palms. "I don't mean to pry into your private life, Nora, but I thought I made myself perfectly clear concerning your involvement with Patch."

I wasn't quite sure where she was going with this. "I haven't tutored him." And, really, was it any of her business?

"Saturday night Patch gave you a ride home from Delphic Seaport. And you invited him inside your house."

I fought to hold in a choke of protest. "How do you know about that?"

"Part of my job as your school psychologist is to give you guidance," Miss Greene said. "Please promise me you'll be very, very careful around Patch." She looked at me like she was actually waiting for my oath of promise.

"It's kind of complicated," I said. "My ride left me stranded at Delphic. I didn't have a choice. It's not like I seek out opportunities to spend time with Patch." Well, except for last night at the Borderline. In my defense, I honestly hadn't expected to see Patch. He was supposed to have the night off.

"I'm very glad to hear it," Miss Greene answered, but she didn't sound fully convinced of my innocence. "With that out of the way, is there anything else you'd like to talk about today? Anything weighing on your mind?"

I wasn't about to tell her that Elliot broke into my house. I didn't trust Miss Greene. I couldn't put my finger on it, but something about her bothered me. And I didn't like the way she kept hinting that Patch was dangerous but wouldn't tell me why. It was almost like she had an agenda.

I hoisted my backpack off the ground and opened the door. "No," I said.

CHAPTER

16

VEE WAS LEANING AGAINST MY LOCKER, DOODLING
on her cast with a purple marker.

"Hi," she said when there was nothing of the hallway
left between us. "Where've you been? I checked the eZine lab and
the library."

"I had a meeting with Miss Greene, the new school psych." I
said it very matter-of-factly, but on the inside, I had a hollow,
trembly feeling. I couldn't stop thinking about Elliot breaking into

my house. What was stopping him from doing it again? Or from doing something worse?

"What happened?" Vee asked.

I spun my locker combination and traded out books. "Do you know how much a good alarm system costs?"

"No offense, babe, but nobody's going to steal your car."

I pinned Vee with a black look. "For my house. I want to make sure Elliot can't get inside again."

Vee glanced around and cleared her throat.

"What?" I said.

Vee did a hands-up. "Nothing. Nothing at all. If you're still bent on nailing this to Elliot . . . that's your prerogative. It's a crazy prerogative, but hey, it's yours."

I shoved my locker door closed, and the rattle echoed down the hall. I bit back an accusatory response that she of all people should believe me and instead said, "I'm on my way to the library, and I'm sort of in a hurry." We exited the building and crossed the grounds to the parking lot, and I came up short. I looked around for the Fiat, but that's when I remembered my mom had dropped me off on her way to work this morning. And with Vee's arm broken, she wasn't driving.

"Crap," Vee said, reading my thoughts, "we're carless."

Shielding my eyes from the sun, I squinted down the street. "Guess this means we'll have to walk."

"Not we. You. I'd come with, but once a week is my library limit."

"You haven't been to the library this week," I pointed out.

"Yeah, but I might have to go tomorrow."

"Tomorrow's Thursday. In all your life, have you ever studied on a Thursday?"

Vee tapped a fingernail to her lip and adopted a thoughtful expression. "Have I ever studied on a Wednesday?"

"Not that I recall."

"There you have it. I can't go. It would be anti-tradition."

Thirty minutes later, I hiked up the steps leading to the library's main doors. Once inside, I put homework on the back burner and went directly to the media lab, where I combed the Internet trying to find more information on the "Kinghorn Hanging." I didn't find much. Originally there had been a lot of hype, but after the suicide note was discovered and Elliot was released, the news moved on.

It was time to take a trip to Portland. I wasn't going to learn much more sifting through archived news articles, but maybe I'd have better luck doing legwork there.

I logged off and called my mom.

"Do I need to be home by nine tonight?"

"Yes, why?"

"I was thinking of taking a bus out to Portland."

She gave me one of her *You must think I'm crazy* laughs.

"I need to interview some students at Kinghorn Prep," I said. "It's for a project I've been researching." It wasn't a lie. Not really. Of course, it would have been much easier to justify if I weren't burdened by the guilt of keeping the break-in and ensuing police visit from her. I'd thought about telling her, but every time I opened my mouth to say the words, they slipped away. We were struggling to survive. We needed my mom's income. If I told her about Elliot, she'd quit immediately.

"You can't go to the city alone. It's a school night and it will be dark soon. Besides, by the time you get there, the students will have left."

I heaved a sigh. "Okay, I'll be home soon."

"I know I promised you a ride, but I'm stuck at my office." I heard her shuffling papers in the background, and I imagined she had the phone cradled under her chin and the phone cord wrapped around her body several times. "Is it too much to ask you to walk?"

The weather was just this side of cool, I had my jean jacket, and I had two legs. I could walk. The plan sounded a lot more reasonable in my head, because the thought of walking home left my insides hollow. But aside from spending the night in the library, I didn't see any other choice.

I was almost through the library doors when I heard my name called. Turning around, I found Marcie Millar closing the distance between us.

"I heard about Vee," she said. "It's really sad. I mean, who would attack her? Unless, you know, they couldn't help it. Maybe it was self-defense. I heard it was dark and raining. It would be easy to mistake Vee for a moose. Or a bear, or a buffalo. Really, any hulking animal would do."

"Gosh, it was nice talking to you, but I've got a lot of things I'd rather be doing. Like sticking my hand in the garbage disposal." I continued toward the exit.

"I hope she stayed clear of those hospital meals," Marcie said, keeping at my heels. "I hear they're high in fat. She can't stand to gain a lot of weight."

I spun around. "That's it. One more word, and I'll . . ." We both knew it was an empty threat.

Marcie simpered. "You'll what?"

"Skank," I said.

"Geek."

"Slut."

"Freak."

"Anorexic pig."

"Wow," said Marcie, staggering back melodramatically with a hand pressed to her heart. "Am I supposed to act offended? Try this on for size. Old news. At least I know how to exercise a little self-control."

The security guard standing at the doors cleared his throat. "All right, break it up. Take this outside or I'm going to cart the both of you inside my office and start calling parents."

"Talk to her," Marcie said, pointing a finger at me. "I'm the one who's trying to be nice. She verbally attacked me. I was just offering my condolences to her friend."

"I said outside."

"You look good in uniform," Marcie told him, flashing her trademark toxic smile.

He jerked his head at the doors. "Get out of here." But it didn't sound half so gruff.

Marcie sashayed up to the doors. "Mind getting the door for me? I'm short on hands." She was holding one book. A paperback.

The guard pushed on the handicapped button, and the doors automatically glided open.

"Why, thank you," Marcie said, blowing him a kiss.

I didn't follow her. I wasn't sure what would happen if I did, but I was filled with enough negative emotion that I just might do something I'd regret. Name-calling and fighting were beneath me. Unless I was dealing with Marcie Millar.

I turned around and headed back into the library. At the elevators, I stepped into the metal cage and punched the button for the basement level. I could've waited around a few minutes for Marcie to leave, but I knew another way out and decided to take it. Five years ago the city had approved moving the public library into a historic building smack in the center of Old Town Coldwater. The red brick dated back to the 1850s, and the building was complete with a romantic cupola and a widow's walk to watch for vessels coming in from sea. Unfortunately, the building didn't include a parking lot, so an underground tunnel had been dug to connect the library to the underground parking garage of the courthouse across the street. The garage now served both buildings.

The elevator clanked to a stop and I stepped off. The tunnel was lit with fluorescent lights that flickered pale purple. It took me a moment to force my feet to walk. I was struck by the sudden thought of my dad the night he was killed. I wondered if he'd been on a street as remote and dark as the tunnel ahead.

Pull it together, I told myself. It was a random act of violence. You've spent the last year paranoid about every dark alley, dark room, dark closet. You can't live the rest of your life terrified of having a gun pulled on you.

Determined to prove my fear was all in my head, I headed down the tunnel, hearing the soft tap of my shoes on concrete. Shifting my backpack to my left shoulder, I calculated how long it would take to walk home, and whether or not I was up for taking a short-cut across the railroad tracks now that it was dusk. I hoped that if I kept my thoughts upbeat and busy, I wouldn't have time to concentrate on my growing sense of alarm.

The tunnel ended, and a dark form stood straight ahead.

I stopped midstride, and my heart dropped a few beats. Patch was wearing a black T-shirt, loose jeans, steel-toed boots. His eyes looked like they didn't play by the rules. His smile was a little too cunning for comfort.

"What are you doing here?" I asked, pushing a handful of hair off my face and glancing past him to the car exit leading above ground. I knew it was straight ahead, but several of the overhead fluorescent lights were out of service, making it difficult to see clearly. If rape, murder, or any other miscreant activities were on Patch's mind, he'd cornered me in the perfect place.

As Patch moved toward me, I backed up. I came up short against a car and saw my chance. I scrambled around it, positioning myself opposite Patch, with the car between us.

Patch looked at me over the top of the car. His eyebrows lifted.

"I have questions," I said. "A lot of them."

"About?"

"About everything."

His mouth twitched, and I was pretty sure he was fighting a smile. "And if my answers don't make the cut, you're going to make a break for it?" He gave a nod in the direction of the garage's exit.

That was the plan. More or less. Give or take a few glaring holes, like the fact that Patch was a lot faster than me.

"Let's hear those questions," he said.

"How did you know I'd be at the library tonight?"

"Seemed like a good guess."

I didn't for one moment believe Patch was here on a hunch. There was a side to him that was almost predatory. If the armed forces knew about him, they'd do everything in their power to recruit him.

Patch lunged to his left. I countered his move, scurrying toward the rear of the car. When Patch came up short, I did too. He was at the nose of the car, and I was at the tail.

"Where were you Sunday afternoon?" I asked. "Did you follow

me when I went shopping with Vee?" Patch may not have been the guy in the ski mask, but that didn't mean he hadn't been involved in the chain of recent disturbing events. He was keeping something from me. He'd been keeping something from me since the day we met. Was it a coincidence that the last normal day in my life had been right before that fateful day? I didn't think so.

"No. How did that go, by the way? Buy anything?"

"Maybe," I said, thrown off guard.

"Like?"

I thought back. Vee and I had only made it as far as Victoria's Secret. I'd spent thirty dollars on the lacy black bra, but I wasn't about to go there. Instead I related my evening, starting with sensing I was being followed, and ending with finding Vee on the side of the road, the victim of a brutal mugging.

"Well?" I demanded when I finished. "Do you have anything to say?"

"No."

"You have no idea what happened to Vee?"

"Again, no."

"I don't believe you."

"That's because you have trust issues." He splayed both hands on the car, leaning across the hood. "We've been over this."

I felt my temper spark. Patch had flipped the conversation again. Instead of shining on him, the spotlight was directed back on me. I especially didn't like being reminded that he knew all sorts of things about me. Private things. Like my trust issues.

Patch lunged clockwise. I ran away from him, halting when he did. While we were at a standstill again, his eyes locked on mine, almost as if he was trying to glean my next move from them.

"What happened on the Archangel? Did you save me?" I asked.

"If I'd saved you, we wouldn't be standing here having this conversation."

"You mean if you *hadn't* saved me we wouldn't be here. I'd be dead."

"That's not what I said."

I had no idea what he meant. "Why wouldn't we be standing here?"

"You'd still be here." He paused. "I probably wouldn't."

Before I could figure out what he was talking about, he darted for me again, this time attacking from the right. Momentarily confused, I gave up some of the distance between us. Instead of stopping, Patch skirted around the car. I made a break for it, running down the straightaway of the garage.

I made it three cars before he caught hold of my arm. He spun me around and backed me against a cement beam.

"So much for that plan," he said.

I glared at him. There was a lot of panic behind it, though. He flashed a grin brimming with dark intent, confirming that I had every reason to sweat freely.

"What's going on?" I said, working hard to sound hostile. "How come I swear I can hear your voice in my head? And why did you say you came to school for me?"

"I was tired of admiring your legs from a distance."

"I want the truth." I swallowed hard. "I deserve full disclosure."

"Full disclosure," he repeated with a sly grin. "Does this have anything to do with the promise you made to expose me? What exactly are we talking about here?"

I couldn't remember what we were talking about. All I knew was that Patch's gaze felt especially hot. I had to break eye contact, so I trained my eyes on my hands. They were glistening with sweat, and I slid them behind my back.

"I have to go," I said. "I have homework."

"What happened in there?" He tilted his chin back at the elevators.

"Nothing."

Before I could stop him, he had my palm pressed to his, forming a steeple with our hands. He slid his fingers between mine, locking me to him. "Your knuckles are white," he said, brushing his mouth across them. "And you came out looking worked up."

"Let go. And I'm not worked up. Not really. If you'll excuse me, I have homework—"

"Nora." Patch spoke my name softly, yet with every intention of getting what he wanted.

"I had a fight with Marcie Millar." I had no idea where the confession came from. The last thing I wanted was to give Patch another window inside me. "Okay?" I said, pushing a note of exasperation into my voice. "Satisfied? Will you please let go now?"

"Marcie Millar?"

I tried to unlace my fingers, but Patch had a different idea.

"You don't know Marcie?" I said cynically. "Hard to believe, considering you attend Coldwater High, for one. And you have a Y chromosome, for two."

"Tell me about the fight," he said.

"She called Vee fat."

"And?"

"I called her an anorexic pig."

Patch looked like he was trying not to crack a grin. "That's it? No punches? No biting, clawing, or hair pulling?"

I narrowed a look at him.

"Are we going to have to teach you to fight, Angel?"

"I can fight." I tipped my chin up in spite of the lie.

This time he didn't bother restraining the grin.

"In fact, I've had boxing lessons." Kickboxing. At the gym. Once.

Patch held out his hand as a target. "Give me a shot. Hard as you can."

"I'm—not a fan of senseless violence."

"We're all alone down here." Patch's boots were flush with the toes of my shoes. "A guy like me could take advantage of a girl like you. Better show me what you've got."

I inched backward, and Patch's black motorcycle came into view.

"Let me give you a ride," he offered.

"I'll walk."

"It's late, and dark."

He had a point. Whether or not I liked it.

But inwardly, I was caught in a fierce game of tug-of-war. I'd been idiotic to walk home in the first place, and now I was stuck between two bad decisions: ride with Patch, or risk the chance there was someone worse out there.

"I'm starting to think the only reason you keep offering me a ride is because you know how not fond I am of this thing." I blew out a jittery sigh, scrunched the helmet on, then swung on behind him. It wasn't entirely my fault that I was snuggled up close to him. The seat wasn't exactly spacious.

Patch made a low sound of amusement. "I can think of a couple other reasons."

He sped down the straightaway of the garage, gunning it toward the exit. A red-and-white-striped traffic arm and an automatic ticket machine barred the exit. I was just wondering if Patch would slow long enough to feed money into the machine, when he brought the bike to a smooth stop, jolting me even closer into him. He fed the machine, then floored the bike up onto the street above.

Patch edged his bike up my driveway, and I held on to him to keep my balance while I climbed off. I handed back the helmet.

"Thanks for the ride," I said.

"What are you doing Saturday night?"

A moment's pause. "I have a date with the usual."

This appeared to spark his interest. "The usual?"

"Homework."

"Cancel."

I was feeling a lot more relaxed. Patch was warm and solid, and he smelled fantastic. Like mint and rich, dark earth. Nobody had jumped out at us on the ride home, and all the windows on the lower level of the farmhouse glowed with light. For the first time all day I felt safe.

Except that Patch had cornered me in a dark tunnel and was possibly stalking me. Maybe not so safe.

"I don't go out with strangers," I said.

"Good thing I do. I'll pick you up at five."

CHAPTER

17

THERE WAS COLD RAIN ALL SATURDAY, AND I SAT NEAR the window watching it pepper down on the growing puddles in the lawn. I had a dog-eared copy of *Hamlet* in my lap, a pen tucked behind my ear, and an empty mug of hot chocolate at my feet. The sheet of reading comprehension questions on the side table was just as white as it had been when Mrs. Lemon passed it out two days ago. Always a bad thing.

My mom had left for yoga class almost thirty minutes ago, and while I'd practiced a few different ways of breaking the news of my date with Patch to her, in the end I'd let her walk out the door without vocalizing any of them. I told myself it was no big deal, I was sixteen and could decide when and why I left the house, but the truth was, I should have told her I was going out. Perfect. Now I was going to be carting around my guilt all night.

When the grandfather clock in the hall chimed to announce 4:30, I gladly tossed aside the book and jogged upstairs to my bedroom. I'd burned through most of the day with homework and chores, and that had kept my mind off tonight's date. But now that I was down to the final minutes, nervous anticipation overruled all. Whether or not I wanted to think about it, Patch and I had unfinished business. Our last kiss got cut short. Sooner or later, the kiss would need resolving. I had no doubt I wanted resolution, I just wasn't sure I was ready for it tonight. On top of all this, it didn't help that Vee's warning kept popping up like a red flag at the back of my mind. *Stay away from Patch.*

I positioned myself in front of the bureau mirror and took inventory. Makeup was minimal, reserved to a sweep of mascara. Too much tumbleweed hair, but what else was new? Lips could use some gloss. I licked my bottom lip, giving it a wet shine. That got me thinking more about my almost-kiss with Patch, and I got an involuntary rush of heat. If an almost-kiss could do that, I wondered what a full-on kiss could do. My reflection smiled.

"No big deal," I told myself while trying on earrings. The first pair was big, loopy, and turquoise . . . and tried too hard. I put them aside and tried again with topaz teardrops. Better. I wondered what Patch had in mind. Dinner? A movie? "It's a lot like a biology study date," I told my reflection nonchalantly. "Only . . . without the biology and studying."

I tugged on matchstick jeans and ballet flats. I wrapped a Hally-blue silk scarf around my waist, up over my torso, then tied the ends behind my neck to fashion a halter-style blouse. I fluffed my hair, and there was a knock at the door.

"Coming!" I hollered down the stairs.

I did one final check in the hall mirror, then opened the front door and found two men in dark trench coats standing on the porch.

"Nora Grey," said Detective Basso, holding up his police badge. "We meet again."

It took a moment to find my voice. "What are you doing here?"

He tipped his head sideways. "You remember my partner, Detective Holstijic. Mind if we step inside and ask you a few questions?" It didn't sound like he was asking permission. In fact, it sounded just this side of a threat.

"What's wrong?" I asked, dividing a glance between them.

"Is your mom home?" Detective Basso asked.

"She's at yoga. Why? What's going on?"

They wiped their feet and stepped inside.

"Can you tell us what happened between you and Marcie Millar at the library Wednesday evening?" Detective Holstijic asked, plunking down on the sofa. Detective Basso remained standing, scrutinizing the family pictures arranged on the mantel.

His words took a moment to register. The library. Wednesday evening. Marcie Millar.

"Is Marcie okay?" I asked. It was no secret I didn't hold a warm, affectionate place in my heart for Marcie. But that didn't mean I wanted her in trouble, or worse, in danger. I especially didn't want her in trouble if it appeared to involve me.

Detective Basso put his hands on his hips. "What makes you think she's not okay?"

"I didn't do anything to Marcie."

"What were the two of you arguing about?" Detective Holstijic asked. "Library security told us things were getting heated."

"It wasn't like that."

"What was it like?"

"We called each other a few names," I said, hoping we could leave it at that.

"What kind of names?"

"Stupid names," I said in retrospect.

"I'm going to need to hear those names, Nora."

"I called her an anorexic pig." My cheeks stung and my voice was humiliated. If the situation hadn't been so serious, I might have wished I'd invented something a lot more cruel and demeaning. Not to mention something that made a little more sense.

The detectives exchanged a look.

"Did you threaten her?" asked Detective Holstijic.

"No."

"Where did you go after the library?"

"Home."

"Did you follow Marcie?"

"No. Like I said, I came home. Are you going to tell me what happened to Marcie?"

"Can anyone vouch for that?" Detective Basso asked.

"My biology partner. He saw me at the library and offered me a ride."

I had a shoulder propped against one side of the French doors leading into the room, and Detective Basso walked over and took up a post on the opposite side, across from me. "Let's hear about this biology partner."

"What kind of question is that?"

He spread his hands. "It's a pretty basic question. But if you want me to get more specific, I can. When I was in high school, I only offered rides to girls I was interested in. Let's carry that a step further. What's your relationship with your bio partner . . . outside the classroom?"

"You're joking, right?"

One side of Detective Basso's mouth hitched up. "That's what I thought. Did you have your boyfriend beat up Marcie Millar?"

"Marcie was beat up?"

He pushed up from the doorway and positioned himself directly in front of me, sharp eyes boring into me. "Did you want to show her what happens when girls like her don't keep their mouths shut? Did you think she deserved to get a little roughed up? I knew girls like Marcie when I went to school. They ask for it, don't they? Was Marcie asking for it, Nora? Someone beat her up pretty bad Wednesday night, and I think you know more than you're saying."

I was working hard to suppress my thoughts, afraid they might somehow show on my face. Maybe it was a coincidence that on the same night I complained to Patch about Marcie, she took a beating. Then again, maybe it wasn't.

"We're going to need to talk to your boyfriend," Detective Holstijic said.

"He's not my boyfriend. He's my biology partner."

"Is he on his way here now?"

I knew I should be up-front. But on further reflection, I could not accept that Patch would hurt Marcie. Marcie wasn't the nicest person, and she'd acquired more than a handful of enemies. A few of those enemies might be capable of brutality, but Patch wasn't one of them. Senseless beating wasn't his style. "No," I said.

Detective Basso gave a stiff smile. "All dressed up for a Saturday night in?"

"Something like that," I said in the coldest tone I dared.

Detective Holstijic pulled a small notepad out of his coat pocket, flipped it open, and clicked his pen. "We're going to need his name and number."

Ten minutes after the detectives left, a black Jeep Commander rolled to the curb. Patch jogged through the rain to the porch, wearing dark jeans, boots, and a thermal gray T-shirt.

"New car?" I asked after I opened the door.

He gave me a mysterious smile. "I won it a couple nights ago off a game of pool."

"Someone bet their *car?*"

"He wasn't happy about it. I'm trying to stay clear of dark alleys for the next little while."

"Did you hear about Marcie Millar?" I threw it out there, hoping the question would take him by surprise.

"No. What's up?" His answer came easily, and I decided it probably meant he was telling the truth. Unfortunately, when it came to telling lies, Patch didn't strike me as an amateur.

"Someone beat her up."

"A shame."

"Any idea who might have done it?"

If Patch heard the concern in my voice, he didn't show it. He leaned back against the porch railing and rubbed a hand thoughtfully across his jaw. "Nope."

I asked myself if I thought he was hiding something. But reading lies wasn't a strong point of mine. I didn't have a lot of experience. Typically I hung around people I trusted . . . typically.

Patch parked the Jeep behind Bo's Arcade. When we got to the front of the line, the cashier laid eyes first on Patch, then on me. Back and forth they went, trying to make a connection.

"What's up?" Patch said, and put three tens on the counter.

The cashier trained his watchful stare on me. He'd noticed that I couldn't stop staring at the moldy-green tattoos covering every available inch of skin on his forearms. He moved a wad of gum? tobacco? to the other side of his bottom lip and said, "You looking at something?"

"I like your tat—" I began. He bared pointed dog teeth.

"I don't think he likes me," I whispered to Patch when we were a safe distance away.

"Bo doesn't like anybody."

"That's Bo of Bo's Arcade?"

"That's Bo Junior of Bo's Arcade. Bo Senior died a few years ago."

"How?" I asked.

"Bar brawl. Downstairs."

I felt an overwhelming desire to run back to the Jeep and peel out of the lot.

"Are we safe?" I asked.

Patch slanted a look sideways. "Angel."

"Just asking."

Downstairs, the pool hall looked exactly like it had the first night I'd come. Cinder-block walls painted black. Red felt pool tables at the center of the room. Poker tables scattered around the fringe. Low track lighting curving across the ceiling. The congested smell of cigar smoke clogging the air.

Patch chose the table farthest from the stairs. He retrieved two

7UPs from the bar and popped their caps on the edge of the counter.

"I've never played pool before," I confessed.

"Choose a cue." He motioned to the rack of pool sticks mounted on the wall. I lifted one down and carried it back to the pool table.

Patch wiped a hand down his mouth to erase a smile.

"What?" I said.

"Can't hit a home run in pool."

I nodded. "No home runs. Got it."

His smiled stretched. "You're holding your cue like a bat."

I looked down at my hands. He was right. I *was* holding it like a bat. "It feels comfortable this way."

He moved behind me, put his hands on my hips, and positioned me in front of the table. He slid his arms around me and took hold of the pool stick.

"Like this," he said, repositioning my right hand up several inches. "And . . . this," he went on, taking my left hand and forming a circle with my thumb and index finger. Then he planted my left hand on the pool table, like a tripod. He pushed the tip of the pool stick through the circle and over the knuckle of my middle finger. "Bend at the waist."

I leaned into the pool table, with Patch's breath warming my neck. He pulled back on the pool stick, and it glided through the circle.

"Which ball do you want to hit?" he asked, referring to the

triangle of balls arranged at the far end of the table. "The yellow one in front's a good choice."

"Red's my favorite color."

"Red it is."

Patch drew the stick back and forth through the circle, aiming at the cue ball, practicing my stroke.

I squinted at the cue ball, then at the triangle of balls farther down the table. "You're a tiny bit off," I said.

I felt him smile. "How much you want to bet?"

"Five dollars."

I felt him give a soft shake of his head. "Your jacket."

"You want my jacket?"

"I want it off."

My arm jerked forward, and the pool stick shot through my fingers, ramming the cue ball. In turn, the cue ball shot forward, impacted with the solid red, and shattered the triangle, balls ricocheting in all directions.

"Okay," I said, shucking off my jean jacket, "maybe I'm a little bit impressed."

Patch examined my silk-scarf-slash-halter. His eyes were as black as a midnight ocean, his expression contemplative. "Nice," he said. Then he moved around the table, scrutinizing the layout of balls.

"Five dollars says you can't sink the blue striped one," I said, selecting it purposely; it was shielded from the white cue ball by a mass of colorful balls.

"I don't want your money," Patch said. Our eyes locked, and the tiniest dimple surfaced in his cheek.

My internal temperature rose another degree.

"What do you want?" I asked.

Patch lowered his pool stick to the table, took one practice stroke, and drilled the cue ball. The momentum of the cue ball transferred to the solid green, then to the eight ball, and punched the striped blue into a pocket.

I gave a nervous laugh and tried to cover it up by cracking my knuckles, a bad habit I *never* succumbed to. "Okay, maybe I'm more than a little impressed."

Patch was still bent over the table, and he looked up at me. The look warmed my skin.

"We never agreed on a bet," I said, resisting the urge to shift my weight. The pool stick felt a little slick in my hands, and I discreetly wiped a hand on my thigh.

As if I wasn't already sweating enough, Patch said, "You owe me. Someday I'll come to collect."

I laughed, but it wasn't quite on pitch. "You wish."

Footsteps barreled down the stairs across the room. A tall, stringy guy with a hawk nose and shaggy blue-black hair appeared at the bottom. He looked at Patch first, then shifted his gaze to me. A slow grin appeared, and he strode over and tipped back my 7UP, which I'd left on the rim of the pool table.

"Excuse me, I believe that's—" I began.

"You didn't tell me she was so soft on the eyes," he said to Patch, wiping his mouth with the back of his hand. He spoke with a heavy Irish accent.

"I didn't tell her how hard you are on them either," Patch returned, his mouth at the relaxed stage just before a grin.

The guy backed up against the pool table beside me and stuck his hand out sideways. "The name's Rixon, love," he told me.

I reluctantly slid my hand into his. "Nora."

"Am I interrupting something here?" Rixon said, dividing an inquiring look between me and Patch.

"No," I said at the same time Patch said, "Yes."

Suddenly Rixon lunged playfully at Patch, and the two dropped to the floor, rolling and throwing punches. There was the sound of husky laughter, fists laying into flesh, and fabric tearing, and Patch's bare back came into view. Two thick gashes ran the length of it. They started near his kidneys and ended at his shoulder blades, widening to form an upside-down V. The gashes were so grotesque I almost gasped in horror.

"Aye, get off me!" Rixon bellowed.

Patch swung off him, and as he got to his feet, his torn shirt fluttered open. He sloughed it off and tossed it into the trash can in the corner. "Give me your shirt," he told Rixon.

Rixon directed a wicked wink at me. "What do you think, Nora? Should we give him a shirt?"

Patch made a playful lunge forward, and Rixon's hands flew up to his shoulders.

"Easy now," he said, backing up. He peeled off his sweatshirt and tossed it at Patch, revealing a fitted white tee underneath.

As Patch rolled the sweatshirt down over abs hard enough to put a flutter in my stomach, Rixon turned to me. "He told you how he got his nickname, didn't he?"

"Sorry?"

"Before our good friend Patch here got mixed up in pool, the lad favored Irish bare-knuckle boxing. Wasn't very good at it." Rixon wagged his head. "Truth be told, he was downright pathetic. I spent most nights patching him up, and soon after, everyone started calling him Patch. Told him to give up boxing, but he wouldn't listen."

Patch caught my eye and passed me a gold-medal bar-fight grin. The grin alone was scary enough, but under the rough exterior, it held a note of desire. More than a note, actually. A whole symphony of desire.

Patch tipped his head at the stairs and held his hand out to me. "Let's get out of here," he said.

"Where are we going?" I asked, my stomach tumbling to my knees.

"You'll see."

As we ascended the stairs, Rixon called out to me, "Good luck with that one, love!"

CHAPTER 18

ON THE DRIVE BACK, PATCH TOOK THE TOPSHAM EXIT and parked alongside the historic Topsham paper mill sitting on the bank of the Androscoggin River. At one point, the mill had been used to turn tree pulp into paper. Now a big sign across the side of the building read SEA DOG BREWING CO. The river was wide and choppy, with mature trees shooting up on both sides.

It was still raining hard, and night had settled down around us. I had to beat my mom home. I hadn't told her I was going out because . . . well, the honest truth was, Patch wasn't the kind of guy mothers smiled on. He was the kind of guy they changed the house locks for.

"Can we get takeout?" I asked.

Patch opened the driver's-side door. "Any requests?"

"A turkey sandwich. But no pickles. Oh, and no mayonnaise."

I could tell I'd earned one of his smiles that never quite made it to the surface. I seemed to earn a lot of those. This time, I couldn't figure out what I'd said.

"I'll see what I can do," he said, sliding out.

Patch left the keys in the ignition and the heater pumping. For the first couple of minutes, I replayed our evening so far in my mind. And then it dawned on me that I was alone in Patch's Jeep. His private space.

If I were Patch, and I wanted to hide something highly secretive, I wouldn't hide it in my room, my school locker, or even my backpack, all of which could be confiscated or searched without warning. I'd hide it in my shiny black Jeep with the sophisticated alarm system.

I unbuckled my seat belt and rummaged through the stack of textbooks near my feet, feeling a mysterious smile creep to my mouth at the thought of uncovering one of Patch's secrets. I wasn't expecting to find anything in particular; I would have settled for the combination to his locker or his cell phone number. Toeing around old school assignments cluttering the floor mats, I found a faded pine-scented air freshener, an AC/DC Highway to Hell CD, pencil stubs, and a receipt from the 7-Eleven dated Wednesday at 10:18 p.m. Nothing especially surprising or revealing.

I popped open the glove compartment and sifted through the operating manual and other official documents. There was a gleam of chrome, and my fingertips brushed metal. I pulled out a steel flashlight and turned it on, but nothing happened. I unscrewed the bottom, thinking the flashlight felt a little light, and sure enough, there were no batteries. I wondered why Patch kept a nonworking flashlight stored in his glove compartment. It was the last thought I had before my eyes homed in on the rusty liquid that had dried at one end of the flashlight.

Blood.

Very carefully, I returned the flashlight to the glove compartment and shut it out of sight. I told myself there were lots of things that would leave blood on a flashlight. Like holding it with an injured hand, using it to push a dead animal to the side of the road . . . swinging it with force against a body repeatedly until it broke skin.

With my heart thundering, I jumped on the first conclusion that presented itself. Patch had lied. He'd attacked Marcie. He'd dropped me off Wednesday evening, traded his motorcycle for the Jeep, and gone out looking for her. Or maybe their paths had intersected by chance and he'd acted on impulse. Either way, Marcie was hurt, the police were involved, and Patch was guilty.

Rationally, I knew it was a quick draw and a big leap, but emotionally, the stakes were too high to step back and think it over. Patch had a frightening past and many, many secrets. If brutal and senseless violence was one of them, I wasn't safe riding around alone with him.

A flash of distant lightning brightened the horizon. Patch exited the restaurant and jogged across the parking lot holding a brown bag in one hand and two sodas in the other. He went around to the driver's side and ducked inside the Jeep. He lifted his ball cap and scrubbed rain out of his hair. Dark waves flipped up everywhere. He handed me the brown bag. "One turkey sandwich, hold the mayo and pickles, and something to wash it down."

"Did you attack Marcie Millar?" I asked quietly. "I want the truth—now."

Patch lowered his 7UP from his mouth. His eyes sliced into mine. "What?"

"The flashlight in your glove compartment. Explain it."

"You went through my glove compartment?" He didn't sound annoyed, but he didn't sound pleased, either.

"The flashlight has dried blood on it. The police came to my house earlier. They think I'm involved. Marcie was attacked Wednesday night, right after I told you how much I can't stand her."

Patch gave a curt laugh, minus the humor. "You think I used the flashlight to beat up Marcie."

He reached behind his seat and dragged out a large gun. I screamed.

He leaned over and sealed my mouth with his hand. "Paintball gun," he said. His tone had chilled.

I divided looks between the gun and Patch, feeling a lot of white showing around my eyes.

"I played paintball earlier this week," he said. "I thought we went over this."

"Th-that doesn't explain the blood on the flashlight."

"Not blood," he said, "paint. We were playing Capture the Flag."

My eyes shifted back to the glove compartment storing the flashlight. The flashlight was . . . the flag. A mix of relief, idiocy, and guilt at accusing Patch swam through me. "Oh," I said lamely. "I'm—sorry." But it seemed a little too late for sorry.

Patch stared straight ahead through the windshield, his breathing deep. I wondered if he was using the silence to let go of a little steam. I had just accused him of assault, after all. I felt terrible about it, but my mind was too rattled to come up with the right apology.

"From your description of Marcie, it sounds like she's probably racked up a few enemies," he said.

"I'm pretty sure Vee and I top the list," I said, trying to lighten the mood, but not entirely joking, either.

Patch pulled up to the farmhouse and killed the engine. His ball cap was low over his eyes, but now his mouth held the suggestion of a smile. His lips looked soft and smooth, and I was having a hard time averting my eyes. Most of all, I was grateful he seemed to have forgiven me.

"We're going to have to work on your pool game, Angel," Patch said.

"Speaking of pool." I cleared my throat. "I'd like to know when and how you're going to collect on that . . . thing I owe you."

"Not tonight." His eyes watched mine closely, judging my response. I was caught between an easing of my mind and disappointment. But mostly disappointment.

"I have something for you," Patch said. He reached under his seat and pulled out a white paper bag with red chili peppers printed across it. A to-go bag from the Borderline. He set it between us.

"What's this for?" I asked, peeking inside the bag, having absolutely no idea as to what might be inside.

"Open it."

I pulled a brown cardboard box out of the to-go bag and lifted the lid. Inside was a snow globe with a miniature Delphic Seaport Amusement Park captured inside. Brass wires were bent roughly into a circle for the Ferris wheel and twisting loops for the roller coaster; flat sheets of tarnished metal formed the Magic Carpet ride.

"It's beautiful," I said, a little astonished that Patch had thought of me, let alone gone to the trouble of buying me a present. "Thank you. I mean it. I love it."

He touched the curved glass. "There's the Archangel, before it was remodeled." Behind the Ferris wheel a thin wire ribboned to form the hills and valleys of the Archangel. An angel with broken wings stood at the highest point, bowing his head, gazing down without eyes. "What really happened the night we rode it together?" I asked.

"You don't want to know."

"If you tell me you'll have to kill me?" I half joked.

"We're not alone," Patch answered, looking through the wind-shield.

I glanced up and caught my mom standing in the open door-way. To my horror, she stepped out and walked toward the Jeep.

"Let me do all the talking," I said, stuffing the snow globe back in the box. "Don't say a word—not one word!"

Patch hopped out and came around for my door. We met my mom halfway up the driveway.

"I didn't know you were going out," she told me, smiling, but not in a relaxed way. It was a smile that said, We'll talk later.

"It was sort of last minute," I explained.

"I came home right after yoga," she said. The rest was implied. Lucky for me, not so lucky for you. I'd been counting on her going out for smoothies with her friends after class. Nine times out of ten, she did. She turned her attention to Patch. "It's nice to finally meet you. Apparently my daughter's a big fan."

I opened my mouth to give an extremely concise introduction

and send Patch on his way, but Mom beat me to it. "I'm Nora's mom. Blythe Grey."

"This is Patch," I said, racking my brain for something to say that would bring the pleasantries to an abrupt halt. But the only things I could think of were screaming Fire! or faking a seizure. Somehow, both seemed more humiliating than braving a conversation between Patch and my mom.

"Nora tells me you're a swimmer," Mom said.

I felt Patch shake with laughter beside me. "A swimmer?"

"Are you on the school swim team, or is it a city league?"

"More . . . recreational," said Patch, passing me a questioning glance.

"Well, recreational is good too," Mom said. "Where do you swim? The rec center?"

"I'm more of an outdoor guy. Rivers and lakes."

"Isn't that cold?" asked Mom.

At my side, Patch jerked. I wondered what I'd missed. Nothing about the conversation seemed out of the ordinary. And I had to side with my mom on this one. Maine was not a warm, tropical place. Outdoor swimming was cold, even in the summertime. If Patch really was swimming outdoors, he was either crazy or he had a high pain threshold.

"All right!" I said, taking advantage of the lull. "Patch needs to get going." Go! I mouthed at him.

"That's a very nice Jeep," Mom said. "Did your parents buy it for you?"

"I got it myself."

"You must have quite a job."

"I bus tables at the Borderline."

Patch was saying as little as possible, keeping himself carefully shadowed in mystery. I wondered what his life was like when he wasn't around me. At the way back of my mind, I couldn't stop thinking about his frightening past. Up until now I'd fantasized about discovering his deep, dark secrets because I wanted to prove to myself and to Patch that I was capable of figuring him out. But now I wanted to know his secrets because they were a part of him. And despite the fact that I routinely tried to deny it, I felt something for him. The more time I spent with him, the more I knew the feelings weren't going away.

Mom frowned. "I hope work doesn't get in the way of studying. Personally, I don't believe high school students should work during the school year. You have enough on your plates already."

Patch smiled. "It hasn't been a problem."

"Mind if I ask your GPA?" Mom said. "Is that too rude?"

"Gee, it's getting late—" I began loudly, consulting the watch I didn't wear. I couldn't believe my mom was being so uncool about this. It was a bad sign. It could only mean her first impression of Patch was worse than I'd feared. This wasn't an introduction. It was an interview.

"Two-point-two," Patch said.

My mom stared at him.

"He's joking," I said quickly. I gave Patch a discreet push in the direction of the Jeep. "Patch has things to do. Places to go. Pool to play—" I clamped a hand over my mouth.

"Play?" my mom said, sounding confused.

"Nora's referring to Bo's Arcade," Patch explained. "But that's not where I'm headed. I've got a few errands to run."

"I've never been to Bo's," she said.

"It's not all that exciting," I said. "You're not missing anything."

"Wait," said Mom, sounding a lot like a red flag had just sprung up in her memory. "Is it out on the coast? Close to Delphic Seaport? Wasn't there a shootout at Bo's several years ago?"

"It's tamer than it used to be," Patch said. I narrowed my eyes at him. He'd beaten me to the punch. I'd planned on outright lying about Bo's having any history of violence.

"Would you like to come in for ice cream?" Mom asked, sounding flustered, caught between doing the polite thing and acting on the impulse to drag me inside and bolt the door. "We only have vanilla," she added to sour the deal. "It's a few weeks old."

Patch shook his head. "I've got to get going. Maybe next time. It was nice meeting you, Blythe."

I took the break in conversation as my cue and pulled my mom toward the front door, relieved that the conversation hadn't been as bad as it could have been. Suddenly Mom turned back.

"What did you and Nora do tonight?" she asked Patch.

Patch looked at me and raised his eyebrows ever so slightly.

"We grabbed dinner in Topsham," I answered quickly. "Sandwiches and sodas. Purely harmless night."

The trouble was, my feelings for Patch *weren't* harmless.

I LEFT THE SNOW GLOBE IN ITS BOX AND TUCKED it inside my closet behind a stack of argyle sweaters I'd poached from my dad. When I'd opened the present in front of Patch, Delphic had looked shimmery and beautiful, light swirling rainbows from the wires. But alone in my bedroom, the amusement park looked haunted. A camp ideal for disembodied spirits. And I wasn't entirely sure there wasn't a hidden camera inside.

After changing into a stretchy camisole and floral pj pants, I called Vee.

"Well?" she said. "How'd it go? Obviously he didn't kill you, so that's a good start."

"We played pool."

"You hate pool."

"He gave me a few pointers. Now that I know what I'm doing, it's not so bad."

"I bet he could give you pointers in a few other areas of your life."

"Hmm." Normally, her comment might have incited at least a flush from me, but my mood was too serious. I was hard at work, thinking.

"I know I've said this before, but Patch doesn't instill a deep sense of comfort in me," Vee said. "I still have nightmares about the guy in the ski mask. In one of my nightmares, he ripped off his mask, and guess who was hiding under it? Patch. Personally, I think you should treat him like a loaded gun. Something about him isn't normal."

This was exactly what I wanted to talk about.

"What would cause someone to have a V-shaped scar on their back?" I asked her.

There was a moment of silence.

"Freak," Vee choked. "You saw him naked? Where did it happen? His Jeep? His house? Your bedroom?"

"I did not see him naked! It was sort of an accident."

"Uh-huh, I've heard that excuse before," said Vee.

"He had a huge, upside down V-shaped scar on his back. Isn't that a little weird?"

"Of course it's weird. But this is Patch we're talking about. He has a few screws loose. I'm going to take a wild guess and say . . . gang fight? Prison scars? Skid marks from a hit-and-run?"

One half of my brain was keeping track of my conversation with Vee, but the other, more subconscious half had strayed. My memory went back to the night Patch dared me to ride the Archangel. I recaptured the creepy and bizarre paintings on the side of the cars. I remembered the horned beasts ripping the wings off the angel. I remembered the black upside-down V where the angel's wings used to be.

I almost dropped the phone.

"S-sorry, what?" I asked Vee when I realized she'd carried the conversation further and was waiting for my response.

"What. Happened. Next?" she repeated, enunciating each word. "Earth to Nora. I need details. I'm dying here."

"He got in a fight and his shirt ripped. End of story. There's no what-happened-next."

Vee sucked in a breath. "This is what I'm talking about. The two of you are out together . . . and he gets in a fight? What's his problem? It's like he's more animal than human."

In my mind I switched back and forth between the painting of the angel's scars and Patch's scars. Both scars had healed to the color of black licorice, both ran from the shoulder blades to the kidneys, and both curved out as they traveled the length of the back. I told myself there was a good chance it was merely a very creepy coincidence that the paintings on the Archangel depicted Patch's scars perfectly. I told myself a lot of things could cause scars like Patch's. Gang fight, prison scars, skid marks—just like Vee said. Unfortunately, all the excuses felt like lies. Like the truth was staring me in the face, but I wasn't brave enough to look back.

"Was he an angel?" Vee asked.

I snapped to myself. "What?"

"Was he an angel, or did he live up to his bad-boy image? Because, honestly? I'm not buying this whole he-didn't-try-anything version of the story."

"Vee? I have to go." My voice was strewn with cobwebs.

"I see how it is. You're going to hang up before I get the details on the big shebang."

"Nothing happened on the date, and nothing happened after. My mom met us in the driveway."

"Shut up!"

"I don't think she likes Patch."

"You don't say!" Vee said. "Who'd have guessed?"

"I'll call you tomorrow, okay?"

"Sweet dreams, babe."

Fat chance, I thought.

After I got off the phone with Vee, I walked down the hall to my mom's makeshift home office and booted up our vintage IBM. The room was small, with a pitched roof, more of a gable than a room. One greasy window with faded orange curtains from the 1970s looked out at the side yard. I could stand up to my full height in about 30 percent of the room. In the other 70 percent, the top of my hair brushed the exposed beams of the rafters. A single bare bulb hung there.

Ten minutes later the computer secured a dial-up connection to the Internet, and I typed "angel wing scars" into the Google search bar. I hovered with my finger above the enter key, afraid that if I went through with it, I'd have to admit I was actually considering the possibility that Patch was—well, not . . . human.

I hit enter and mouse-clicked on the first link before I could talk myself out of it.

FALLEN ANGELS: THE FRIGHTENING TRUTH

At the creation of the Garden of Eden, heavenly angels were dispatched to Earth to watch over Adam and Eve. Soon, however, some angels set their sights on the world beyond the garden walls. They saw themselves as future rulers over the Earth's population, lusting after power, money, and even human women.

Together they tempted and convinced Eve to eat the forbidden fruit, opening the gates guarding

Eden. As punishment for this grave sin and for deserting their duties, God stripped the angels' wings and banished them to Earth forever.

I skimmed down a few paragraphs, my heart beating erratically.

Fallen angels are the same evil spirits (or demons) described in the Bible as taking possession of human bodies. Fallen angels roam the Earth looking for human bodies to harass and control. They tempt humans to do evil by communicating thoughts and images directly to their minds. If a fallen angel succeeds in turning a human toward evil, it can enter the human's body and influence his or her personality and actions.

However, the possession of a human body by a fallen angel can take place only during the Hebrew month of Cheshvan. Cheshvan, known as "the bitter month," is the only month without any Jewish holidays or fasts, making it an unholy month. Between new and full moons during Cheshvan, fallen angels invade human bodies in droves.

My stare lingered on the computer monitor a few minutes after I finished reading. I had no thoughts. None. Just a complexity of emotions tangling inside me. Cold, panicky amazement and fore-boding among them.

An involuntary shudder roused me to my senses. I remembered the few times I was certain Patch had breached normal communi-cation methods and whispered directly to my mind, just like the article claimed fallen angels could. Comparing this information with Patch's scars, was it possible . . . could Patch be a fallen angel? Did he want to possess my body?

I browsed quickly through the rest of the article, slowing when I read something even more bizarre.

> Fallen angels who have a sexual relationship
> with a human produce superhuman offspring called
> Nephilim. The Nephilim race is an evil and unnat-
> ural race and was never meant to inhabit Earth.
> Although many believe the Great Flood at the
> time of Noah was intended to cleanse the Earth of
> Nephilim, we have no way of knowing if this hybrid
> race died out and whether or not fallen angels
> have continued to reproduce with humans since that
> time. It seems logical that they would, which means
> the Nephilim race is likely on the Earth today.

I pushed back from the desk. I crammed everything I'd read into a mental folder and filed it away. And stamped SCARY on the outside of the folder. I didn't want to think about it right now. I'd sort through it later. Maybe.

My cell phone buzzed in my pocket and I jumped.

"Did we decide avocados are green or yellow?" Vee asked. "I've already filled all my green fruit slots today, but if you tell me avocados are yellow, I'm in business."

"Do you believe in superheroes?"

"After seeing Tobey Maguire in Spider-Man, yes. And then there's Christian Bale. Older, but killer hot. I'd let him rescue me from sword-wielding ninjas."

"I'm being serious."

"So am I."

"When was the last time you went to church?" I asked.

I heard her pop a gum bubble. "Sunday."

"Do you think the Bible is accurate? I mean, do you think it's real?"

"I think Pastor Calvin is hot. In a fortysomething way. That pretty much sums up my religious conviction."

After I hung up, I went to my room and slid under the covers. I threw on an extra blanket to ward off the sudden chill. Whether the room was cold, or the icy feeling originated inside me, I wasn't sure. Haunting words like "fallen angel," "human possession," and "Nephilim" danced me off to sleep.

CHAPTER 20

I TOSSED ALL NIGHT. THE WIND GUSTED THROUGH THE OPEN fields rimming the farmhouse, spraying debris against the windows. I woke several times, hearing shingles being pulled from the roof and tumbling over the edge. Every small noise from the rattle of the windowpanes to my own creaking bedsprings had me jumping out of sleep.

Around six I gave up, dragged myself out of bed, and padded down the hall for a hot shower. Next I cleaned my room—my closet was looking slim, and sure enough, I filled the hamper with three loads of laundry. I was climbing the stairs with a fresh load when a knock sounded at the front door. I opened it to find Elliot standing on the doorstep.

He wore jeans, a vintage plaid shirt rolled to the elbows, sunglasses, and a Red Sox cap. On the outside, he looked all-American. But I knew better, and a jolt of nervous adrenaline confirmed it.

"Nora Grey," Elliot said in a patronizing voice. He leaned in and grinned, and I caught the sour tang of alcohol on his breath. "You've been causing me a lot of trouble lately."

"What are you doing here?"

He peered behind me into the house. "What's it look like I'm doing? I want to talk. Don't I get to come in?"

"My mom's asleep. I don't want to wake her."

"I've never met your mom." Something about the way he said it made the hairs on the back of my neck stand tall.

"I'm sorry, do you need something?"

His smile was half sloppy, half sneering. "You don't like me, do you, Nora Grey?"

By way of answer, I folded my arms across my chest.

He staggered back a step with his hand pressed to his heart. "Ouch. I'm here, Nora, as a last-ditch effort to convince you that I'm an average guy and you can trust me. Don't let me down."

"Listen, Elliot, I have a few things I need to—"

He drilled his fist into the house, smacking his knuckles against the siding hard enough to shake loose chipped paint. "I'm not finished!" he slurred in a heated voice. Suddenly he tipped his head back and laughed quietly. He bent over and placed his bleeding hand between his knees and groaned. "Ten dollars says I'm going to regret that later."

Elliot's presence made my skin crawl. I remembered back several days, when I actually thought he was good-looking and charming. I wondered why I'd been such an idiot.

I was contemplating closing the door and locking it, when Elliot pulled off his sunglasses, revealing bloodshot eyes. He cleared his throat, his voice coming out straightforward. "I came here because I wanted to tell you Jules is under a lot of stress at school. Exams, student government, scholarship applications, yadda, yadda, yadda. He's not acting like himself. He needs to get away from it all for a few days. The four of us—Jules, me, you, Vee—should go camping for spring break. Leave tomorrow for Powder Horn and come back Tuesday afternoon. It'll give Jules a chance to decompress." Every word that came out of his mouth sounded eerily and carefully rehearsed.

"Sorry, I already have plans."

"Let me change your mind. I'll plan the whole trip. I'll get the tents, the food. I'll show you what a great guy I am. I'll show you a good time."

"I think you should leave."

Elliot leaned his hand on the doorjamb, bending toward me.

"Wrong answer." For a fleeting moment, the glassy stupor in his eyes disappeared, something twisted and sinister eclipsing it. I involuntarily stepped back. I was almost positive Elliot had it in him to kill. I was almost positive Kjirsten's death was on his hands.

"Leave, or I'm calling a cab," I said.

Elliot flung the screen door open so hard it smacked back against the house. He grabbed the front of my bathrobe and yanked me outside. Then he shoved me back against the siding and pinned me there with his body. "You're coming camping whether you want to or not."

"Get off me!" I said, twisting away from him.

"Or what? What are you going to do?" He had me by the shoulders now, and he knocked me back against the house again, rattling my teeth.

"I'll call the police." I had no idea how I said it so bravely. My breathing was rapid and shallow, my hands clammy.

"Are you going to shout for them? They can't hear you. The only way I'm letting you go is if you swear to go camping."

"Nora?"

Elliot and I both turned toward the front door, where my mom's voice carried out. Elliot kept his hands on me a moment longer, then made a disgusted noise and shoved me away. Halfway down the porch steps, he looked over his shoulder. "This isn't over."

I hurried inside and locked the door. My eyes started to burn. I dragged my back down the length of the door and sat on the entry rug, fighting the urge to sob.

My mom appeared at the top of the stairs, cinching her robe at the waist. "Nora? What's wrong? Who was at the door?"

I blinked my eyes dry in a hurry. "A guy from school." I couldn't keep the waver out of my voice. "He—he—" I was already in enough trouble over my date with Patch. I knew my mom was planning to attend a wedding and reception tonight for the daughter of a friend from work, but if I told her Elliot had roughed me up, there was no way she'd go. And that was the last thing I wanted, because I needed to drive to Portland and investigate Elliot. Even a sliver of incriminating evidence might be enough to put him behind bars, and until that happened, I wouldn't feel safe. I sensed a certain violence escalating inside him, and I didn't want to see what would happen if it blew out of control. "He wanted my *Hamlet* notes," I said flatly. "Last week he cheated off my quiz, and apparently he's trying to make a habit of it."

"Oh, honey." She came down beside me, stroking my damp hair, which had chilled since my shower. "I can understand why you're upset. I can call his parents if you'd like."

I shook my head.

"Then I'll make breakfast," Mom said. "Go finish dressing. I'll have everything ready by the time you come down."

I was standing in front of my closet when my cell phone rang.

"Did you hear? The four of us are going c-a-m-p-i-n-g for

spring break!" said Vee, sounding bizarrely cheerful.

"Vee," I said, my voice trembling, "Elliot's planning something. Something scary. The only reason he wants to go camping is so he can get us alone. We're not going."

"What do you mean we're not going? This is a joke, right? I mean, we finally get to do something exciting over spring break, and you're saying no? You know my mom will never let me go alone. I'll do anything. Seriously. I'll do your homework for a week. Come on, Nora. One little word. Say it. It starts with the letter Y. . . ."

The hand holding my cell quivered, and I brought up my other hand to steady it. "Elliot showed up at my house fifteen minutes ago, drunk. He—he physically threatened me."

She was quiet a moment. "What do you mean by 'physically threatened'?"

"He dragged me out the front door and shoved me against the house."

"But he was drunk, right?"

"Does it matter?" I snapped.

"Well, he has a lot going on. I mean, he was wrongly accused of being messed up in some girl's suicide, and he was forced to switch schools. If he hurt you—and I'm not justifying what he did, by the way—maybe he just needs . . . counseling, you know?"

"If he hurt me?"

"He was wasted. Maybe—maybe he didn't know what he was doing. Tomorrow he's going to feel horrible."

I opened my mouth, shut it. I couldn't believe Vee was siding with Elliot. "I have to go," I said curtly. "I'll talk to you later."

"Can I be completely honest, babe? I know you're worried about this guy in the ski mask. Don't hate me, but I think the only reason you're trying so hard to pin it on Elliot is because you don't want it to be Patch. You're rationalizing everything, and it's freaking me out."

I was speechless. "Rationalizing? Patch didn't show up at my door this morning and slam me against my house."

"You know what? I shouldn't have brought it up. Let's just drop it, okay?"

"Fine," I said stiffly.

"So . . . what are you doing today?"

I poked my head out the door, listening for my mom. The sound of a whisk scraping the side of a bowl carried up from the kitchen. Part of me didn't see the point in sharing anything else with Vee, but another part of me felt resentful and confrontational. She wanted to know my plans? Fine by me. It wasn't my problem if she didn't like them. "I'm driving to Portland as soon as my mom leaves for a wedding at Old Orchard Beach." The wedding started at 4 p.m., and with the reception following, my mom wouldn't get home until 9 p.m. at the earliest. Which gave me enough time to spend the evening in Portland, and beat her home. "Actually, I was wondering if maybe I could borrow the Neon. I don't want my mom to see the miles I put on my car."

"Oh, boy. You're going to spy on Elliot, aren't you? You're going to snoop around Kinghorn."

"I'm going to do a little shopping and grab dinner," I said, sliding hangers down the rack in my closet. I pulled out a long-sleeved tissue tee, jeans, and a pink-and-white-striped beanie I reserved for bad-hair days and weekends.

"And would grabbing dinner include stopping by a certain diner located a few blocks from Kinghorn Prep? A diner where Kjirsten what's-her-name used to work?"

"That's not a bad idea," I said. "Maybe I will."

"And are you going to actually eat, or just interrogate the workers?"

"I might ask a few questions. Do I get the Neon or not?"

"Of course you do," she said. "What are best friends for? I'll even come with you on this doomed little tromp. But first you have to promise you'll go camping."

"Never mind. I'll take the bus."

"We'll talk about spring break later!" Vee called into the phone before I was able to disconnect.

I'd been to Portland on several occasions, but I didn't know the city well. I stepped off the bus armed with my cell, a map, and my own inner compass. The buildings were redbrick, tall and slender, blocking the setting sun, which blazed out from below a thick stretch of storm clouds, settling the streets under a canopy of shadow. The storefronts all had verandas and quaint signs extending over the doors. The streets were lit by black witch-hat lamps. After several blocks, the congested streets opened up to a wooded area, and I saw a sign for Kinghorn Prep. A cathedral, steeple, and clock tower peered above the treetops.

I stayed on the sidewalk and rounded the corner onto 32nd Street. The harbor was only a few blocks away, and I caught glimpses of boats passing behind the shops as they came in to dock. Halfway down 32nd Street, I saw a sign for Blind Joe's diner. I pulled my interview questions out and read them over one last time. The plan wasn't to look like I was holding an official interview. I hoped that if I casually broached the subject of Kjirsten with the employees, I could tease out something the handful of reporters before me had somehow missed. Hoping the questions were stored to memory, I underhanded the list into the nearest trash can.

The door chimed when I entered.

The floor was yellow and white tile, and the booths were uphol-stered in nautical blue. Pictures of the harbor hung on the walls. I sat in a booth close to the door and shrugged out of my coat.

A waitress in a stained white apron appeared beside me. "Name's Whitney," she told me in a sour voice. "Welcome to Blind Joe's. Special today is the tuna fish sandwich. Soup of the day's lobster chowder." Her pen was poised to take my order.

"Blind Joe's?" I frowned and tapped my chin. "Why does that name sound so familiar?"

"Don't you read the paper? We were in the news for a week straight last month. Fifteen minutes and all that."

"Oh!" I said with sudden clarity. "Now I remember. There was a murder, right? Didn't the girl work here?"

"That would be Kjirsten Halverson." She clicked her pen impatiently. "Want me to bring out a bowl of that chowder to start?"

I didn't want lobster chowder. In fact, I wasn't remotely hungry. "That must have been hard. Were the two of you friends?"

"Hell, no. You going to order or what? I'll let you in on a little secret. I don't work, I don't get paid. I don't get paid, I don't make rent."

Suddenly I wished the waiter across the room were taking my order. He was short, bald back to his ears, and his body type mimicked the toothpicks in the dispenser at the end of the table. His eyes never reached higher than three feet off the ground. As pathetic as I would have felt after the fact, one friendly smile from me might have been enough to have him spilling Kjirsten's entire life story. "Sorry," I told Whitney. "I just can't stop thinking about the murder. Of course, it's probably old news to you. You must have had reporters in here all the time asking questions."

She gave me a pointed look. "Need a few more minutes to look over the menu?"

"Personally, I find reporters irritating."

She leaned in, bracing a hand on the tabletop. "I find customers who take their own sweet time irritating."

I blew out a silent sigh and flipped open the menu. "What do you recommend?"

"It's all good. Ask my boyfriend." She gave a tight smile. "He's the cook."

"Speaking of boyfriends . . . did Kjirsten have one?" *Nice segue*, I told myself.

"Spill," Whitney demanded. "You a cop? A lawyer? A reporter?"

"Just a concerned citizen." It sounded like a question.

"Yeah, right. Tell you what. Order a milkshake, fries, the Angus burger, a bowl of chowder, and give me a twenty-five-percent tip, and I'll tell you what I told everybody else."

I weighed my options: my allowance or answers. "Done."

"Kjirsten hooked up with that kid, Elliot Saunders. The one in the papers. He was in here all the time. Walked her back to her apartment at the end of her shift."

"Did you ever talk to Elliot?"

"Not me."

"Do you think Kjirsten committed suicide?"

"How should I know?"

"I read in the newspaper that a suicide note was found in Kjirsten's apartment, but that there was also evidence of a break-in."

"And?"

"You don't find that a little . . . odd?"

"If you're asking if I think Elliot could have put the note in her apartment, sure I do. Rich kid like that could get away with anything. Probably hired somebody to plant the note. That's how it works when you got money."

"I don't think Elliot has a lot of money." My impression had always been that Jules was the wealthy one. Vee never stopped raving about his house. "I think he went to Kinghorn Prep on scholarship."

"Scholarship?" she repeated on a snort. "What's in the water you been drinking? If Elliot don't got big-time money, how'd he buy Kjirsten her apartment? Tell me that."

I struggled to hold my surprise in check. "He bought her an apartment?"

"Kjirsten never shut up about it. About drove me insane."

"Why would he buy her an apartment?"

Whitney stared down at me, hands on hips. "Tell me you ain't really that dumb."

Oh. Privacy. Intimacy. Got it.

I said, "Do you know why Elliot transferred out of Kinghorn?"

"Didn't know he did."

I juggled her answers with the questions I still wanted to ask, trying to summon them up from memory. "Did he ever meet friends here? Anyone other than Kjirsten?"

"How'm I supposed to remember that?" She gave a hard eye roll. "I look like I got one of them photographic memories?"

"How about a really tall guy? *Really* tall. Long blond hair, good-looking, tailored clothes."

She ripped a ragged fingernail off with her front teeth and dropped it inside the pocket of her apron. "Yeah, I remember that guy. Hard not to. All moody and quiet. He came in once or twice. Wasn't that long ago. Maybe around the time Kjirsten died. I remember 'cause we were serving corned beef sandwiches for St. Patrick's Day and I couldn't get him to order one. Just glared at me like he would have reached across the table and slit my throat if I'd stuck around reading the daily specials any longer. But I think I remember something. It's not like I'm nosy, but I do got ears. Sometimes I can't help hearing things. Last time the tall guy and Elliot came in, they were hunched over a table, talking about a test."

"A test at school?"

"How should I know? From the sound of it, the tall guy failed a test, and Elliot was none too happy about it. He shoved his chair back and stormed out. Didn't even eat all his sandwich."

"Did they mention Kjirsten?"

"The tall guy came in first, asked if Kjirsten was working. I told him no, she wasn't, and he got on his cell phone. Ten minutes later, Elliot strolls in. Kjirsten always handled Elliot's table, but like I said, she wasn't working, so I got it. If they talked about Kjirsten, I didn't hear. But it looked to me like the tall guy didn't want Kjirsten around."

"Do you remember anything else?"

"Depends. You going to order dessert?"

"I guess I'll have a slice of pie."

"Pie? I give you five minutes of my valuable time, and all you order is pie? I look like I got nothing better to do than chitchat with you?"

I glanced around the diner. It was dead. Other than a man hunched over a paper at the counter, I was the only customer.

"Okay . . ." I scanned the menu.

"You're going to want a raspberry lemonade to wash that pie down." She scribbled it on her pad. "And after-dinner coffee." More scribbling. "I'll be looking forward to an additional twenty-percent tip with that." She pinned me with a smug smile, then tucked her pad into her apron and sashayed back to the kitchen.

CHAPTER

21

OUTSIDE, THE WEATHER HAD SHIFTED TO COLD AND drizzling. The lampposts burned an eerie, sallow color that did little against the thick fog brewing along the streets. I hurried out of Blind Joe's, grateful I'd looked at the weather forecast earlier and brought my umbrella. As I passed storefront windows, I saw crowds gathering in the bars.

I was a few blocks from the bus stop when the now familiar icy feeling kissed the back of my neck. I'd felt it the night I was sure someone looked in my bedroom window, at Delphic, and again right before Vee walked out of Victoria's Secret wearing my jacket. I bent down, pretended to tie my shoelace, and cast a surreptitious glance around. The sidewalks on both sides of the street were empty.

The crosswalk light changed, and I stepped off the curb. Moving faster, I tucked my handbag under my arm and hoped the bus was on time. I cut through an alley behind a bar, slipped past a huddle of smokers, and came out on the next street over. Jogging up a block, I veered down another alley and circled back around the block. Every few seconds I checked behind me.

I heard the rumble of the bus, and a moment later it rounded the corner, materializing out of the fog. It slowed against the curb and I climbed aboard, heading home. I was the only passenger.

Taking a seat several rows behind the driver, I slouched to keep out of sight. He jerked the lever to close the doors, and the bus roared down the street. I was on the verge of offering a sigh of relief when I received a text message from Vee.

WHERE U AT?

PORTLAND, I texted back. YOU?

ME 2. AT A PARTY WITH JULES AND ELLIOT. LET'S MEET UP.

WHY ARE YOU IN PORTLAND?!

I didn't wait for her answer; I dialed her directly. Talking was faster. And this was urgent.

"Well? What say you?" Vee asked. "Are you in the partying mood?"

"Does your mom know you're at a party in Portland with two guys?"

"You're starting to sound neurotic, babe."

"I can't believe you came to Portland with Elliot!" I had a sinking thought. "Does he know you're on the phone with me?"

"So he can come kill you? No, sorry. He and Jules ran to Kinghorn to pick up something, and I'm chilling solo. I could use a wingwoman. Hey!" Vee shouted into the background. "Hands off, okay? O-F-F. Nora? I'm not exactly in the greatest area. Time is of the essence."

"Where are you?"

"Hang on . . . okay, the building across the street says one-seven-two-seven. The street is Highsmith, I'm pretty sure."

"I'll be there as soon as I can. But I'm not staying. I'm going home, and you're coming with me. Stop the bus!" I called to the driver.

He applied the brakes, and I was thrown against the seat in front of me.

"Can you tell me which way to Highsmith?" I asked him once I'd made it to the top of the aisle.

He pointed out the windows paneling the right side of the bus. "West of here. You planning to go on foot?" He surveyed me up and down. "'Cause I should warn you, it's a rough neighborhood."

Great.

I had to walk only a few blocks before I knew the bus driver had been right to warn me. The scenery changed drastically. The quaint storefronts were replaced by buildings spray-painted with gang graffiti. The windows were dark, barred up with iron. The sidewalks were desolate paths stretching into the fog.

A slow, rattling noise drifted through the fog, and a woman pushing a cart of garbage bags wheeled into view. Her eyes were raisins, beady and dark, and they twitched their way over me in almost predatory evaluation.

"What we got here?" she said through a gape of missing teeth.

I drew a discreet step back and clutched my handbag against me.

"Looks like a coat, mittens, and a pretty wool hat," she said. "Always wanted me a pretty wool hat." She pronounced the word prit-ee.

"Hello," I said, clearing my throat and trying to sound friendly. "Can you please tell me how much farther to Highsmith Street?"

She cackled.

"A bus driver pointed me in this direction," I said with less confidence.

"He told you Highsmith is this way?" she said, sounding irritated. "I know the way to Highsmith, and this ain't it."

I waited, but she didn't elaborate. "Do you think you could give me directions?" I asked.

"I got directions." She tapped her head with a finger that

strongly resembled a twisted, knotted twig. "Keep everything up here, I do."

"Which way is Highsmith?" I encouraged.

"But I can't tell you for free," she said in a chiding tone. "That's gonna cost you. A girl has to make a living. Nobody ever tell you ain't nothing in life free?"

"I don't have any money." Not much, anyway. Only enough for a bus fare home.

"You got a nice warm coat."

I looked down at my quilted coat. A chilly wind ruffled my hair, and the thought of peeling my coat off sent a flush of goose bumps down my arms. "I just got this coat for Christmas."

"I'm freezing my derrière off out here," she snapped. "You want directions or not?"

I couldn't believe I was standing here. I couldn't believe I was bartering my coat with a homeless woman. Vee was so far in debt to me she might never get out.

I shucked off my coat and watched her zip into it.

My breath came out like smoke. I hugged myself and stamped my feet, conserving body heat. "Can you please tell me the way to Highsmith now?"

"You want the long way, or the short way?"

"Sh-short," I chattered.

"That's gonna cost you too. Short way's got an additional fee attached. Like I said, always wanted me a pretty wool hat."

I tugged the pink and white beanie off my head. "Highsmith?" I asked, trying to hold on to the friendly tone as I passed it over.

"See that alley?" she said, pointing behind me. I turned. The alley was a half block back. "You take it, you come out on Highsmith on the other side."

"That's it?" I said incredulously. "One block over?"

"Good news is, you got a short walk. Bad news is, ain't no walk feel short in this weather. 'Course, I'm nice and warm now I got me a coat and a pretty hat. Give me those mittens, and I'll walk you there myself."

I looked down at the mittens. At least my hands were warm. "I'll manage."

She shrugged and wheeled her cart to the next corner, where she took up a post against the bricks.

The alley was dark and cluttered with trash bins, water-stained cardboard boxes, and an unrecognizable hump that may have been a discarded water heater. Then again, it just as easily could have been a rug with a body rolled inside. A high chain-link fence spanned the alley halfway down. I could hardly climb a four-foot fence on a good day, let alone a ten-foot one. Brick buildings flanked me on both sides. All the windows were greased over and barred.

Stepping over crates and sacks of trash, I picked my way down the alley. Broken glass crunched beneath my shoes. A flash of white darted between my legs, stealing my breath. A cat. Just a cat, vanishing into the darkness ahead.

I reached for my pocket to text Vee, intending to tell her I was close and to watch for me, when I remembered I'd left my cell phone in my coat pocket. Nice going, I thought. *What are the chances the bag lady will give you back your phone?* Precisely—slim to none.

I decided it was worth a try, and as I turned around, a sleek black sedan sped past the opening to the alley. With a sudden glow of red, the brake lights lit up.

For reasons I couldn't explain beyond intuition, I drew into the shadows.

A car door opened and the crackle of gunfire broke out. Two shots. The car door slammed and the black sedan screeched away. I could hear my heart hammering in my chest, and it blended with the sound of running feet. I realized a moment later that they were *my* feet, and I was running to the mouth of the alley. I rounded the corner and came up short.

The bag lady's body was in a heap on the sidewalk.

I rushed over and fell on my knees beside her. "Are you okay?" I said frantically, rolling her over. Her mouth was agape, her raisin eyes hollow. Dark liquid flowered through the quilted coat I'd been wearing three minutes ago.

I felt the urge to jump back but forced myself to reach inside the coat pockets. I needed to call for help, but my cell phone wasn't there.

There was a phone booth on the corner across the street. I ran to it and dialed 911. While I waited for the operator to pick up, I glanced back at the bag lady's body, and that's when I felt cold adrenaline shoot through me. The body was gone.

With a shaky hand, I hung up. The sound of approaching footsteps tapped in my ears, but whether they were near or far, I couldn't tell.

Clip, clip, clip.

He's here, I thought. The man in the ski mask.

I shoved a few coins into the phone and gripped the receiver with both hands. I tried to remember Patch's cell phone number. Squeezing my eyes shut, I visualized the seven numbers he'd written in red ink on my hand the first day we met. Before I could second-guess my memory, I dialed the numbers.

"What's up?" Patch said.

I almost sobbed at the sound of his voice. I could hear the crack of billiard balls colliding on a pool table in the background, and knew he was at Bo's Arcade. He could be here in fifteen, maybe twenty minutes.

"It's me." I didn't dare push my voice above a whisper.

"Nora?"

"I'm in P-Portland. On the corner of Hempshire and Nantucket. Can you pick me up? It's urgent."

I was huddled in the bottom of the phone booth, counting silently to one hundred, trying to remain calm, when a black

Jeep Commander glided to the curb. Patch slid the door to the phone booth open and crouched in the entrance.

He peeled off his top layer—a long-sleeved black T-shirt—leaving him in a black undershirt. He fit the neckhole of the T-shirt over my head and a moment later had my arms pushed through the sleeves. The shirt dwarfed me, the sleeves hanging down well past my fingertips. It mingled the smells of smoke, saltwater, and mint soap. Something about it filled the hollow places inside me with reassurance.

"Let's get you in the car," Patch said. He pulled me up, and I wrapped my arms around his neck and buried my face into him.

"I think I'm going to be sick," I said. The world tilted, including Patch. "I need my iron pills."

"Shh," he said, holding me against him. "It's going to be all right. I'm here now."

I managed a little nod.

"Let's get out of here."

Another nod. "We need to get Vee," I said. "She's at a party one block over."

While Patch drove the Jeep around the corner, I listened to my chattering teeth echo around inside my head. I'd never been this frightened in my life. Seeing the dead homeless woman conjured up thoughts of my dad. My vision was tinged with red, and hard as I tried, I couldn't flush out the image of blood.

"Were you in the middle of a pool game?" I asked, remembering the sound of billiard balls colliding in the background during our brief phone conversation.

"I was winning a condo."

"A condo?"

"One of those swank ones on the lake. I would have hated the place. This is Highsmith. Do you have an address?"

"I can't remember it," I said, sitting up taller to get a better look out the windows. All of the buildings looked abandoned. There was no trace of a party. There was no trace of life, period.

"Do you have your cell?" I asked Patch.

He slid a Blackberry out of his pocket. "Battery's low. I don't know if it will make a call."

I texted Vee. WHERE ARE YOU?!

CHANGE OF PLANS, she texted back. GUESS J AND E COULDN'T FIND WHAT THEY WERE LOOKING 4. WE'RE GOING HOME.

The screen drained to black.

"It died," I told Patch. "Do you have the charger?"

"Not on me."

"Vee's going back to Coldwater. Do you think you could drop me off at her house?"

Minutes later we were on the coastal highway, driving right along a cliff just above the ocean. I'd been this way before, and when the sun was out, the water was slate blue with patches of dark green where the water reflected the evergreens. It was night, and the ocean was smooth black poison.

"Are you going to tell me what happened?" Patch asked.

The jury was still out on whether or not I should tell Patch anything. I could tell him how after the bag lady tricked me out of my coat, she was shot. I could tell him I thought the bullet was meant for me. Then I could try explaining how the bag lady's body had magically vanished into thin air.

I remembered the crazed look Detective Basso had directed at me when I told him someone had broken into my bedroom. I wasn't in the mood to get eyeballed and laughed at again. Not by Patch. Not right now.

"I got lost, and a bag lady cornered me," I said. "She talked me out of my coat. . . ." I wiped my nose with the back of my hand and sniffled. "She got my beanie, too."

"What were you doing all the way out here?" asked Patch.

"Meeting Vee at a party."

We were halfway between Portland and Coldwater, on a stretch of lush and unpopulated highway, when steam spewed suddenly from the hood of the Jeep. Patch braked, easing the Jeep to the roadside.

"Hang on," he said, swinging out. Lifting the hood of the Jeep, he disappeared out of sight.

A minute later he dropped the hood back in place. Brushing his hands on his pants, he came around to my window, gesturing for me to lower it.

"Bad news," he said. "It's the engine."

I tried to look informed and intelligent, but I had a feeling my expression just looked blank.

Patch raised an eyebrow and said, "May it rest in peace."

"It won't move?"

"Not unless we push it."

Of all the cars, he had to win the lemon.

"Where's your cell?" Patch asked.

"I lost it."

He grinned. "Let me guess. In your coat pocket. The bag lady really cashed in, didn't she?"

He scouted the horizon. "Two choices. We can flag down a ride, or we can walk to the next exit and find a phone."

I stepped out, shutting the door with force behind me. I kicked the Jeep's right front tire. I knew I was using anger to mask my fear of what I'd been through today. As soon as I was all alone, I'd break down crying.

"I think there's a motel at the next exit. I'll go c-c-call a cab," I said, my teeth chattering harder. "Y-y-you wait here with the Jeep."

He cracked a slight smile, but it didn't look amused. "I'm not letting you out of my sight. You're looking a little deranged, Angel. We'll go together."

Crossing my arms, I stood up to him. In tennis shoes, my eyes came level with his shoulders. I was forced to tilt my neck back to meet his eyes. "I'm not going anywhere near a motel with you." Best to sound firm so I was less likely to change my mind.

"You think the two of us and a slummy motel make for a dangerous combination?"

Yes, actually.

Patch leaned back against the Jeep. "We can sit here and argue this." He squinted up at the riotous sky. "But this storm is about to catch its second wind."

As if Mother Nature wanted her say in the verdict, the sky opened and a thick concoction of rain and sleet hailed down.

I sent Patch my coldest look, then blew out an angry sigh.

As usual, he had a point.

22

TWENTY MINUTES LATER PATCH AND I WASHED UP AT
the entrance to a low-budget motel. I had not spoken
one word to him as we'd jogged through the sleeting
rain, and now I was not only soaked, but thoroughly . . . unnerved.
The rain cascaded down, and I didn't think we would be returning
to the Jeep anytime soon. Which left me, Patch, and a motel in the
same equation for an undetermined amount of time.

The door chimed on our way in, and the desk clerk stood

abruptly, dusting Cheetos crumbs off his lap. "What'll it be?" he said, sucking his fingers clean of orange slime. "Just the two of you tonight?"

"We n-n-need to borrow your phone," I chattered, hoping he could make sense of my request.

"No can do. Lines are down. Blame the storm."

"What do y-you mean the l-lines are d-down? Do you have a cell?"

The clerk looked to Patch.

"She wants a nonsmoking room," Patch said.

I swiveled to face Patch. *Are you insane?* I mouthed.

The clerk tapped a few keys at his computer. "Looks like we've got . . . hang on . . . Bingo! A nonsmoking king."

"We'll take it," said Patch. He looked sideways at me, and the edges of his mouth tipped up. I narrowed my eyes.

Just then the lights overhead blinked out, plunging the lobby into darkness. We all stood silent for a moment before the clerk fumbled around and clicked on an industrial-size flashlight.

"I was a Boy Scout," he said. "Back in the day. 'Be prepared.'"

"Then you m-m-must have a cell phone?" I said.

"I did. Until I couldn't pay the bill anymore." He drew his shoulders up. "What can I say, my mom's cheap."

His mom? He had to be forty. Not that it was any of my business. I was far more concerned what my mom would do when she arrived home from the reception and found me gone.

"How do you want to pay?" the desk clerk asked.

"Cash," Patch said.

The desk clerk chuckled, bobbing his head up and down. "It's a popular form of payment here." He leaned close and spoke in confidential tones. "We get a lot of folks who don't want their extracurricular activities traced, if you know what I mean."

The logical half of my brain was telling me I couldn't actually be considering spending the night at a motel with Patch.

"This is crazy," I told Patch in an undertone.

"I'm crazy." He was on the brink of smiling again. "About you. How much for the flashlight?" he asked the clerk.

The clerk reached below the desk. "I've got something even better: survival-size candles," he said, placing two in front of us. Striking a match, he lit one. "They're on the house, no extra charge. Put one in the bathroom and one in the sleeping area and you'll never know the difference. I'll even throw in the matchbook. If nothing else, it'll make a good keepsake."

"Thanks," Patch said, taking my elbow and walking me down the hall.

At room 106, Patch bolted the door behind us. He set the candle on the nightstand, then used it to light the spare. Lifting his baseball cap, he shook the ends of his hair like a wet dog.

"You need a hot shower," he said. Taking a few steps backward, he ducked his head inside the bathroom. "Looks like bar soap and two towels."

I tilted my chin up a fraction. "You can't f-force me to stay here." I'd only agreed to come this far because I didn't want to stand out in the downpour, for one, and I had high hopes of finding a phone, for two.

"That sounded more like a question than a statement," said Patch.

"Then ans-s-swer it."

His rogue smile crept out. "It's hard to concentrate on answers with you looking like that."

I glanced down at Patch's black shirt, wet and clinging to my body. I brushed past him and shut the bathroom door between us.

Cranking the water to full hot, I peeled out of Patch's shirt and my clothes. One long black hair was plastered to the shower wall, and I trapped it in a square of toilet paper before flushing it. Then I stepped behind the shower curtain, watching my skin glow with heat.

Massaging soap into the muscles along my neck and down through my shoulders, I told myself I could handle sleeping in the same room as Patch. It wasn't the smartest or safest arrangement, but I'd personally see to it that nothing happened. Besides, what choice did I have . . . right?

The spontaneous reckless half of my brain laughed at me. I knew what it was thinking. Early on I'd felt drawn to Patch by a mysterious force field. Now I felt drawn to him by something entirely different. Something with a lot of heat involved. A connection tonight was inevitable. On a scale of one to ten, that terrified me about an eight. And excited me about a nine.

I shut off the water, stepped out, and patted my skin dry. One glance at my soaked clothes was all I needed to know I had no desire to put them back on. Maybe there was a coin-operated dryer nearby . . . one that didn't require electricity. I sighed and pulled on my camisole and panties, which had survived the worst of the rain.

"Patch?" I whispered through the door.

"Done?"

"Blow out the candle."

"Done," he whispered back through the door. His laughter, too, sounded so soft it could have been whispered.

Snuffing out the bathroom candle, I stepped out, meeting total blackness. I could hear Patch breathing directly in front of me. I didn't want to think about what he was—or wasn't— wearing, and I shook my head to fragment the picture forming in my mind. "My clothes are soaked. I don't have anything to wear."

I heard the sound of wet fabric sliding like a squeegee over his skin. "Lucky me." His shirt landed in a wet heap at our feet.

"This is really awkward," I told him.

I could feel him smiling. He stood way, way too close.

"You should shower," I said. "Right now."

"I smell that bad?"

Actually, he smelled that good. The smoke was gone, the mint stronger.

Patch disappeared inside the bathroom. He relit the candle and left the door ajar, a sliver of light stretching across the floor and up one wall.

I slid my back down the wall until I was seated on the floor, then tipped my head against the wall. In all honesty, I couldn't stay here tonight. I had to get home. It was wrong to stay here alone with Patch, vow of prudence or not. I had to report the bag lady's body. Or did I? How was I supposed to report a vanished body? Talk about insane—which was the terrifying direction my thoughts were starting to go anyway.

Not wanting to dwell on the insanity idea, I concentrated on my original argument. I couldn't stay here knowing Vee was with Elliot, in danger, when I was safe.

After a moment's consideration I decided I needed to rephrase that thought. Safe was a relative term. As long as Patch was around, I wasn't in harm's way, but that didn't mean I thought he was going to act like my guardian angel, either.

Right away, I wished I could take back the guardian angel thought. Summoning up my powers of persuasion, I banished all thoughts of angels—guardian, fallen, or otherwise—from my head. I told myself I probably *was* going insane. For all I knew, I'd hallucinated seeing the bag lady die. And I'd hallucinated seeing Patch's scars.

The water stopped, and a moment later Patch strolled out wearing only his wet jeans hanging low on his waist. He left the bathroom candle lit and the door wide. Soft color glowed through the room.

One quick look and I could tell Patch clocked several hours a week running and lifting weights. A body that defined didn't come without sweat and work. Suddenly I felt a little self-conscious. Not to mention soft.

"Which side of the bed do you want?" he asked.

"Uh . . ."

A fox smile. "Nervous?"

"No," I said as confidently as possible under the circumstances. And the circumstances were that I was lying through my teeth.

"You're a bad liar," he said, still smiling. "The worst I've seen."

I put my hands on my hips and communicated a silent Excuse me?

"Come here," he said, pulling me to my feet. I felt my earlier promise of resistance melting away. Another ten seconds of standing this close to Patch and my defense would be blown to smithereens.

A mirror hung on the wall behind him, and over his shoulder I saw the upside-down V scars gleaming black on his skin.

My whole body went rigid. I tried to blink the scars away, but they were there for good.

Without thinking, I slid my hands up his chest and around to his back. A fingertip brushed his right scar.

Patch tensed under my touch. I froze, the tip of my finger quivering on his scar. It took me a moment to realize it wasn't actually my finger moving, but me. All of me.

I was sucked into a soft, dark chute and everything went black.

I WAS STANDING IN THE LOWER LEVEL OF BO'S ARCADE WITH
my back to the wall, facing several games of pool. The windows were boarded, and I couldn't tell if it was day or night.
Stevie Nicks was coming through the speakers; the song about the
white-winged dove and being on the edge of seventeen. Nobody
seemed surprised by my sudden appearance out of thin air.

And then I remembered I was wearing nothing but a cami and
panties. I'm not all that vain, but standing in a crowd composed

entirely of the opposite sex, my essentials barely covered, and nobody even looked at me? Something was . . . off.

I pinched myself. Perfectly alive, as far as I could tell.

Waving a hand to clear away the hazy cloud of cigar smoke, I spotted Patch across the room. He was sitting at a poker table, kicked back, holding a hand of cards close to his chest.

I padded barefoot across the room, crossing my arms over my chest, making sure to keep myself covered. "Can we talk?" I hissed in his ear. There was an unnerved quality to my voice. Understandable, since I had no idea how I'd come to find myself at Bo's. One moment I was at the motel, and the next I was here.

Patch pushed a short stack of poker chips into the pile at the center of the table.

"Like maybe *now*?" I said. "It's kind of urgent. . . ." I trailed off when the calendar on the wall caught my eye. It was eight months behind, showing August of last year. Right before I started sophomore year. Months before I met Patch. I told myself it was a mistake, that whoever was in charge of ripping off the old months had fallen behind, but at the same time I briefly and unwillingly considered the possibility that the calendar was right where it was supposed to be. And I was not.

I dragged a chair over from the next table and pulled up beside Patch. "He's holding a five of spades, a nine of spades, the ace of hearts . . ." I stopped when I realized that no one was paying attention. No, it wasn't that. No one could *see* me.

Footsteps lumbered down the stairs across the room, and the same cashier who'd threatened to throw me out the first time I'd come to the arcade appeared at the bottom of the stairwell.

"Someone upstairs wants a word with you," he told Patch.

Patch raised his eyebrows, transmitting a silent question.

"She wouldn't give her name," the cashier said apologetically. "I asked a couple of times. I told her you were in a private game, but she wouldn't leave. I can throw her out if you want."

"No. Send her down."

Patch played out his hand, gathered his chips, and pushed out of his chair. "I'm out." He walked to the pool table closest to the stairs, rested against it, and slid his hands inside his pockets.

I followed him across the room. I snapped my fingers in front of his face. I kicked his boots. I flat-out smacked his chest. He didn't flinch, didn't move.

Light footsteps sounded on the stairs, growing closer, and when Miss Greene stepped out of the darkened stairwell, I experienced a moment of confusion. Her blond hair was down to her waist and toothpick straight. She was wearing painted-on jeans and a pink tank top, and she was barefoot. Dressed this way, she looked even closer to my age. She was sucking on a lollipop.

Patch's face is always a mask, and at any given moment I have no idea what he's thinking. But as soon as he locked eyes on Miss Greene, I knew he was surprised. He recovered quickly, all emotion funneling away as his eyes turned guarded and wary. "Dabria?"

My heart hit a faster cadence. I tried to wrestle my thoughts together, but all I could think was, if I was really eight months in the past, how did Miss Greene and Patch know each other? She didn't have a job at school yet. And why was he calling her by her first name?

"How have you been?" Miss Greene—Dabria—asked with a coy smile, tossing the lollipop in the trash.

"What are you doing here?" Patch's eyes turned even more watchful, as if he didn't think "what you see is what you get" applied to Dabria.

"I sneaked out." Her smile twisted up on one side. "I had to see you again. I've been trying for a long time, but security—well, you know. It's not exactly lax. Your kind and my kind—we aren't supposed to mix. But you know that."

"Coming here was a bad idea."

"I know it's been a while, but I was hoping for a slightly more friendly reaction," she said, pushing her lips out in a pout.

Patch didn't answer.

"I haven't stopped thinking about you." Dabria dimmed her voice to a low, sexy pitch and took a step closer to Patch. "It wasn't easy getting down here. Lucianna is making excuses for why I'm absent. I'm risking her future as well as my own. Don't you want to at least hear what I have to say?"

"Talk." Patch's words didn't hold a shred of trust.

"I haven't given up on you. This whole time—" She broke off

and blinked back a sudden display of tears. When she spoke again, her voice was more composed but still held a wavering note. "I know how you can get your wings back."

She smiled at Patch, but he didn't return the smile.

"As soon as you get your wings back, you can come home," she said, speaking more confidently. "Everything will be like it was before. Nothing has changed. Not *really*."

"What's the catch?"

"There is no catch. You have to save a human life. Very judicious, considering the crime that banished you here in the first place."

"What rank will I be?"

All confidence scattered from Dabria's eyes, and I got the feeling he'd asked the one question she'd hoped to avoid. "I just told you how to get your wings back," she said, sounding a touch condescending. "I think I deserve a *thank-you*—"

"Answer the question." But his grim smile told me he already knew. Or had a very good guess. Whatever Dabria's answer was, he wasn't going to like it.

"Fine. You'll be a guardian, all right?"

Patch tipped his head back and laughed softly.

"What's wrong with being a guardian?" Dabria demanded. "Why isn't it good enough?"

"I have something better in the works."

"Listen to me, Patch. There's *nothing* better. You're kidding yourself. Any other fallen angel would jump at the chance to get their wings back and become a guardian. Why can't you?" Her voice was choked with bewilderment, irritation, rejection.

Patch pushed up from the pool table. "It was good seeing you again, Dabria. Have a nice trip back."

Without warning, she curled her fists into his shirt, yanked him close, and crushed a kiss to his mouth. Very slowly Patch's body turned toward her, his stance softening. His hands came up and skimmed her arms.

I swallowed hard, trying to ignore the stab of jealousy and confusion in my heart. Part of me wanted to turn away and cry, part of me wanted to march over and start shouting. Not that it would do any good. I was invisible. Obviously Miss Greene . . . Dabria . . . whoever she was . . . and Patch had a romantic past together. Were they still together now—in the future? Had she applied for a job at Coldwater High to be closer to Patch? Is that why she was so determined to scare me away from him?

"I should go," said Dabria, pulling free. "I've already stayed too long. I promised Lucianna I'd hurry." She lowered her head against his chest. "I miss you," she whispered. "Save one human life, and you'll have your wings again. Come back to me," she begged. "Come home." She broke away suddenly. "I have to go. None of the others can find out I've been down here. I love you."

As Dabria turned away, the anxiety vanished from her face. An expression of sly confidence replaced it. It was the face of someone who'd bluffed their way through a rough hand of cards.

Without warning, Patch caught her by the wrist.

"Now tell me why you're really here," he said.

I shivered at the dark undercurrent in Patch's tone. To an outsider, he looked perfectly calm. But to anyone who'd known him any length of time, it was obvious. He was giving Dabria a look that said she'd crossed a line and it was in her best interest to hop back across it—now.

Patch steered her toward the bar. He planted her on a bar stool and slid onto the one beside it. I took the one next to Patch, leaning in to hear him above the music.

"What do you mean, what am I here for?" Dabria stammered. "I told you—"

"You're lying."

Her mouth dropped. "I can't believe—you think—"

"Tell me the truth, right now," said Patch.

Dabria hesitated before answering. She gave him a fierce glare, then said, "Fine. I know what you're planning to do."

Patch laughed. It was a laugh that said, *I have a lot of plans. Which one are you referring to?*

"I know you've heard rumors about The Book of Enoch. I also know you think you can do the same thing, but you can't."

Patch folded his arms on the bar. "They sent you here to persuade me to choose a different course, didn't they?" A smile showed in his eyes. "If I'm a threat, the rumors must be true."

"No, they're not. They're *rumors*."

"If it happened once, it can happen again."

"It never happened. Did you even bother to read The Book of Enoch before you fell?" she challenged. "Do you know exactly what it says, word for holy word?"

"Maybe you could loan me your copy."

"That's blasphemous! You're forbidden to read it," she cried. "You betrayed every angel in heaven when you fell."

"How many of them know what I'm after?" he asked. "How big of a threat am I?"

She tossed her head side to side. "I can't tell you that. I've already told you more than I should have."

"Are they going to try to stop me?"

"The avenging angels will."

He looked at her with meaning. "Unless they think you talked me out of it."

"Don't look at me like that." She sounded like she was putting all her courage into sounding firm. "I won't lie to protect you. What you're trying to do is wrong. It's not natural."

"Dabria." Patch spoke her name as a soft threat. He might as well have had her by the arm, twisting it behind her back.

"I can't help you," she said with quiet conviction. "Not that way. Put it out of your mind. Become a guardian angel. Focus on that and forget The Book of Enoch."

Patch planted his elbows on the bar, radiating thought. After a moment he said, "Tell them we talked, and I showed interest in becoming a guardian."

"Interest?" she said, a bit incredulously.

"Interest," he repeated. "Tell them I asked for a name. If I'm going to save a life, I need to know who's at the top of your departing list. I know you're privy to that information as an angel of death."

"That information is sacred and private, and not predictable. The events in this world shift from moment to moment depending on human choices—"

"One name, Dabria."

"Promise me you'll forget about The Book of Enoch first. Give me your word."

"You'd trust my word?"

"No," she said, "I wouldn't."

Patch laughed coolly and, grabbing a toothpick from the dispenser, walked toward the stairs.

"Patch, wait—," she began. She hopped off the bar stool. "Patch, please wait!"

He looked over his shoulder.

"Nora Grey," she said, then immediately clamped her hands over her mouth.

There was a faint crack in Patch's expression—a frown of disbelief mixed with annoyance. Which made no sense since, if the calendar on the wall was correct, we hadn't met yet. My name shouldn't have sparked familiarity. "How is she going to die?" he asked.

"Someone wants to kill her."

"Who?"

"I don't know," she said, covering her ears and shaking her head. "There's so much noise and commotion down here. All the images blur together, they come too fast, I can't see clearly. I need to go home. I need peace and calm."

Patch tucked a strand of Dabria's hair behind her ear and looked at her persuasively. She gave a warm shudder at his touch, then nodded and shut her eyes. "I can't see . . . I don't see anything . . . it's useless."

"Who wants to kill Nora Grey?" Patch urged.

"Wait, I see her," said Dabria. Her voice turned anxious. "There's a shadow behind her. It's him. He's following her. She doesn't see him . . . but he's right there. Why doesn't she see him? Why isn't she running? I can't see his face, it's in shadow. . . ."

Dabria's eyes flew open. She sucked in a quick, sharp breath.

"Who?" Patch said.

Dabria curled her hands against her mouth. She was trembling as she raised her eyes to Patch's.

"You," she whispered.

My finger moved off Patch's scar and the connection broke. It took me a moment to reorient myself, so I wasn't ready for Patch, who wrestled me into the bed in an instant. He pinned my wrists above my head.

"You weren't supposed to do that." There was controlled anger in his face, dark and simmering. "What did you see?"

I got my knee up and clipped him in the ribs. "Get—off—me!"

He slid onto my hips, straddling them, eliminating the use of my legs. With my arms still stretched above my head, I couldn't do more than squirm under his weight.

"Get—off—me—or—I'll—scream!"

"You're already screaming. And it isn't going to cause a stir in this place. It's more of a whorehouse than a motel." He gave a hard smile that was all lethality around the edges. "Last chance, Nora. What did you see?"

I was fighting back tears. My whole body hummed with an emotion so foreign I couldn't even name it. "You make me sick!" I said. "Who are you? Who are you *really*?"

His mouth turned even more grim. "We're getting closer."

"*You want to kill me!*"

Patch's face gave away nothing, but his eyes grew cold.

"The Jeep didn't really die tonight, did it?" I said. "You lied. You brought me here so you could kill me. That's what Dabria said you want to do. Well, what are you waiting for?" I didn't have a clue where I was going with this, and I didn't care. I was spitting words in an attempt to keep my horror at bay. "You've been trying to kill me all along. Right from the start. Are you going to kill me now?" I stared at him, hard and unblinking, trying to keep tears from spilling as I remembered the fateful day he'd walked into my life.

"It's tempting."

I twisted beneath him. I tried to roll to my right, then to my left. I finally figured out I was wasting a lot of energy and stopped. Patch settled his eyes on me. They were blacker than I'd ever seen them.

"I bet you like this," I said.

"That would be a smart bet."

I felt my heart pounding clear down in my toes. "Just do it," I said in a challenging voice.

"Kill you?"

I nodded. "But first I want to know why. Of all the billions of people out there, why me?"

"Bad genes."

"That's it? That's the only explanation I get?"

"For now."

"What's that supposed to mean?" My voice rose again. "I get the rest of the story when you finally break down and kill me?"

"I don't have to break down to kill you. If I'd wanted you dead five minutes ago, you'd have died five minutes ago."

I swallowed at the less-than-cheerful thought.

He brushed his thumb over my birthmark. His touch was deceptively soft, which made it all the more painful to endure.

"What about Dabria?" I asked, still breathing hard. "She's the same thing you are, isn't she? You're both—angels." My voice cracked on the word.

Patch rotated slightly off my hips, but kept his hands at my wrists. "If I ease up, are you going to hear me out?"

If he eased up, I was going to bolt for the door. "What do you care if I run? You'll just drag me back in here."

"Yeah, but that would cause a scene."

"Is Dabria your girlfriend?" I could feel each ragged rise and fall of my chest. I wasn't sure I wanted to hear his answer. Not that it mattered. Now that I knew Patch wanted to kill me, it was ridiculous that I even cared.

"Was. It was a long time ago, before I fell to the dark side." He gave a hard smile, attempting humor. "It was also a mistake." He rocked back on his heels, slowly releasing me, testing to see if I'd fight back. I lay on the mattress, breathing hard, my elbows propping me up. Three counts went by, and I hurled myself at him with all the force I had.

I shoved against his chest, but other than swaying back slightly, he didn't move. I scrambled out from under him and took my fists to him. I hammered his chest until the bottoms of my fists began to throb.

"Done?" he asked.

"No!" I drove my elbow down into his thigh. "What's the matter with you? Don't you feel anything?"

I rose to my feet, found my balance on the mattress, and kicked him as hard as I could in the stomach.

"You've got one more minute," he said. "Get your anger out of your system. Then I take over."

I didn't know what he meant by "take over," and I didn't want to find out. I made a leaping run off the bed, with the door in sight. Patch snagged me midair and backed me against the wall. His legs were flush with mine, front to front down the length of our thighs.

"I want the truth," I said, struggling not to cry. "Did you come to school to kill me? Was that your aim right from the start?"

A muscle in Patch's jaw jumped. "Yes."

I swiped a tear that dared escape. "Are you gloating inside? That's what this is about, isn't it? Getting me to trust you so you could blow it up in my face!" I knew I was being irrationally irate. I should have been terrified and frantic. I should have been doing everything in my power to escape. The most irrational part of all was that I still didn't want to believe he would kill me, and no matter how hard I tried, I couldn't smother that illogical speck of trust.

"I get that you're angry—," said Patch.

"I am ripped apart!" I shouted.

His hands slid up my neck, searing hot. Pressing his thumbs gently into my throat, he tipped my head back. I felt his lips come against mine so hard he stopped whatever name I'd been about to call him from coming out. His hands dropped to my shoulders, skimmed down my arms, and came to rest at the small of my back. Little shivers of panic and pleasure shot through me. He tried to pull me against him, and I bit him on the lip.

He licked his lip with the tip of his tongue. "Did you just bite me?"

"Is everything a joke to you?" I asked.

He dabbed his tongue to his lip again. "Not everything."

"Like what?"

"You."

The whole night felt unbalanced. It was hard to have a show-down with someone as indifferent as Patch. No, not indifferent. Perfectly controlled. Down to the last cell in his body.

I heard a voice in my mind. *Relax. Trust me.*

"Omigosh," I said with a burst of clarity. "You're doing it again, aren't you? Messing with my mind." I remembered the article I'd pulled up when I Googled fallen angels. "You can put more than words in my head, can't you? You can put images—very real images—there."

He didn't deny it.

"The Archangel," I said, finally understanding. "You tried to kill me that night, didn't you? But something went wrong. Then you made me think my cell phone was dead, so I couldn't call Vee. Did you plan to kill me on the ride home? I want to know how you're making me see what you want!"

His face was carefully expressionless. "I put the words and images there, but it's up to you if you believe them. It's a riddle. The images overlap reality, and you have to figure out which is real."

"Is this a special angel power?"

He shook his head. "Fallen angel power. Any other kind of angel wouldn't invade your privacy, even though they can."

Because other angels were good. And Patch was not.

Patch braced his hands against the wall behind me, one on either side of my head. "I put a thought in Coach's mind to redo the seating chart because I needed to get close to you. I made you think you fell off the Archangel because I wanted to kill you, but I couldn't go through with it. I almost did, but I stopped. I settled for scaring you instead. Then I made you think your cell was dead because I wanted to give you a ride home. When I came inside your house, I picked up a knife. I was going to kill you then." His voice softened. "You changed my mind."

I sucked in a deep breath. "I don't understand you. When I told you my dad was murdered, you sounded genuinely sorry. When you met my mom, you were nice."

"Nice," Patch repeated. "Let's keep that between you and me."

My head spun faster, and I could feel my pulse beating in my temples. I'd felt this heart-pounding panic before. I needed my iron pills. Either that, or Patch was making me think I did.

I tilted my chin up and narrowed my eyes. "Get out of my mind. Right now!"

"I'm not in your mind, Nora."

I bent forward, bracing my hands on my knees, sucking air. "Yes, you are. I feel you. So this is how you're going to do it? Suffocate me?"

Soft popping sounds echoed in my ears, and a blurry black framed my vision. I tried to fill my lungs, but it was like the air had disappeared. The world tilted, and Patch slipped sideways in my vision. I flattened my hand to the wall to steady my balance. The deeper I tried to inhale, the tighter my throat constricted.

Patch moved toward me, but I flung my hand out. "Get away!"

He leaned a shoulder on the wall and faced me, his mouth set with concern.

"Get—away—from—me," I gasped.

He didn't.

"I—can't—breathe!" I choked, clawing at the wall with one hand, clutching my throat with the other.

Suddenly Patch scooped me up and carried me to the chair across the room. "Put your head between your knees," he said, guiding my head down.

I had my head down, breathing rapidly, trying to force air inside my lungs. Very slowly I felt the oxygen creep back into my body.

"Better?" Patch asked after a minute.

I nodded, once.

"Do you have iron pills with you?"

I shook my head.

"Keep your head down and take long, deep breaths."

I followed his instructions, feeling a clamp loosen around my chest. "Thank you," I said quietly.

"Still don't trust my motives?"

"If you want me to trust you, let me touch your scars again."

Patch studied me silently for a long moment. "That's not a good idea."

"Why not?"

"I can't control what you see."

"That's kind of the point."

He waited a few counts before answering. His voice was low, emotions untraceable. "You know I'm hiding things." There was a question attached to it.

I knew Patch lived a life of closed doors and harbored secrets. I wasn't presumptuous enough to think even half of them revolved around me. Patch lived a different life outside the one he shared with me. More than once I'd speculated what his other life might be like. I always got the feeling that the less I knew about it, the better.

My lip wobbled. "Give me a reason to trust you."

Patch sat on the corner of the bed, the mattress sinking under his weight. He bent forward, resting his forearms on his knees. His scars were in full view, the candlelight dancing eerie shadows across their surface. The muscles in his back heightened, then relaxed. "Go ahead," he said quietly. "Keep in mind that people change, but the past doesn't."

Suddenly I wasn't so sure I wanted this. On almost every level, Patch terrified me. But deep down, I didn't think he was going to kill me. If that was what he wanted, he would have done it already. I glanced at his gruesome scars. Trusting Patch felt a lot more comfortable than slipping into his past again and having no idea what I might find.

But if I backed out now, Patch would know I was terrified of him. He was opening one of the closed doors just for me and only because I'd asked for it. I couldn't make a request this heavy, then change my mind.

"I won't get trapped in there forever, will I?" I asked.

Patch gave a short laugh. "No."

Summoning my courage, I sat on the bed beside him. For the second time tonight, my finger brushed the peaked ridge of his scar. A hazy gray crowded my vision, working from the edges in. The lights went out.

CHAPTER

24

I WAS ON MY BACK, MY CAMI SPONGING UP MOISTURE beneath me, blades of grass poking the bare skin on my arms. The moon overhead was nothing more than a sliver, a grin tipped on its side. Other than the rumble of distant thunder, all was quiet.

I blinked several times in succession, helping my eyes hurry and adapt to the scant light. When I rolled my head sideways, a symmetrical arrangement of curved twigs poking up from the grass solidified in my vision. Very slowly I pulled myself up. I couldn't tear my eyes away from the two black orbs staring at me from just above the curved twigs. My mind worked to place the familiar image. And then, with a horrific flash of recognition, I knew. I was lying next to a human skeleton.

I crawled backward until I came up against an iron fence. I pushed through the muddled moment and recaptured my last memory. I'd touched Patch's scars. Wherever I was, it was somewhere inside his memory.

A voice, male and vaguely familiar, carried through the darkness, singing a low tune. Turning toward it, I saw a labyrinth of headstones stretching like dominoes into the mist. Patch was crouched on top of one. He wore only Levi's and a navy T-shirt, even though the night wasn't warm.

"Moonlighting with the dead?" called the familiar voice. It was rough, rich, and Irish. Rixon. He slouched against a headstone opposite Patch, watching him. He stroked his thumb across his bottom lip. "Let me guess. You've got it in your mind to possess the dead? I don't know," he said, wagging his head. "Maggots squirming in your eyeholes . . . and your other orifices, might be carrying things a bit too far."

"This is why I keep you around, Rixon. Always seeing things from the bright side."

"Cheshvan starts tonight," Rixon said. "What are you doing arsing around in a graveyard?"

"Thinking."

"Thinking?"

"A process by which I use my brain to make a rational decision."

The corners of Rixon's mouth pulled down. "I'm starting to worry about you. Come on. Time to go. Chauncey Langeais and Barnabas await. The moon turns at midnight. I confess I've got my eye on a betty in town." He gave a catlike purr. "I know you like them red, but I like 'em fair, and once I get into a body, I intend to take care of unfinished business with a blonde who was making eyes at me earlier."

When Patch didn't move, Rixon said, "Are you daft? We've got to go. Chauncey's oath of fealty. Not ringing a bell? How about this. You're a fallen angel. You can't feel a thing. Until tonight, that is. The next two weeks are Chauncey's gift to you. Given unwillingly, mind you," he added on a conspirator's grin.

Patch gave Rixon a sidelong glance. "What do you know about The Book of Enoch?"

"About as much as any fallen angel: slim to none."

"I was told there's a story in The Book of Enoch. About a fallen angel who becomes human."

Rixon doubled over with laughter. "You lost your mind, mate?" He welded the outer edges of his palms together, making an open book with his hands. "The Book of Enoch is a bedtime story. And a good one, by the looks of it. Sent you straight to dreamland."

"I want a human body."

"You'd best be happy with two weeks and a Nephil's body. Half-human is better than nothing. Chauncey can't undo what's been done. He swore an oath, and he has to live up to it. Just like last year. And the year before that—"

"Two weeks isn't enough. I want to be human. Permanently." Patch's eyes cut into Rixon's, daring him to laugh again.

Rixon raked his hands through his hair. "The Book of Enoch is a fairy tale. We're fallen angels, not humans. We never were human, and we never will be. End of story. Now, quit arsing around and help me figure out which is the way to Portland." He craned his neck back and observed the inky sky.

Patch swung down off the headstone. "I'm going to become human."

"Sure, mate, sure you can."

"The Book of Enoch says I have to kill my Nephil vassal. I have to kill Chauncey."

"No, you don't," Rixon said with a note of impatience. "You've got to possess him. A process by which you take his body and use it as your own. Not to put a damper on things, but you can't kill Chauncey. Nephilim can't die. And have you thought of this? If you could kill him, you couldn't possess him."

"If I kill him, I'll become human and I won't need to possess him."

Rixon squeezed the inner corners of his eyes as if he knew his argument was falling on deaf ears and it was giving him a headache.

"If we could kill Nephilim, we would have found a way by now. I'm sorry to tell you, lad, but if I don't get into the arms of that blond betty soon, my brains will bake. And a few other parts of my—"

"Two choices," said Patch.

"Eh?"

"Save a human life and become a guardian angel, or kill your Nephil vassal and become human. Take your pick."

"Is this more Book of Enoch rubbish?"

"Dabria paid me a visit."

Rixon's eyes widened, and he snorted a laugh. "Your psychotic ex? What's she doing down here? Did she fall? Lost her wings, did she?"

"She came down to tell me I can get my wings back if I save a human life."

Rixon's eyes got wider. "If you trust her, I say go for it. Nothing wrong with being a guardian. Spending your days keeping mortals out of danger . . . could be fun, depending on the mortal you're assigned."

"But if you had a choice?" Patch asked.

"Aye, well, my answer depends on one very important distinction. Am I roaring drunk . . . or have I completely lost my mind?" When Patch didn't laugh, Rixon said soberly, "There's no choice. And here's why. I don't believe in The Book of Enoch. If I were you, I'd aim for guardianship. I'm half considering the deal myself. Too bad I don't know any humans on the brink of death."

There was a moment's silence, then Patch seemed to shake off his thoughts. He said, "How much money can we make before midnight?"

"Playing cards or boxing?"

"Cards."

Rixon's eyes sparkled. "What do we have here? A pretty boy? Come here and let me give you a proper clatter." He hooked Patch around the neck, pinning him in the crook of his elbow, but Patch got him around the waist and dragged Rixon to the grass, where they took turns throwing clobbering punches.

"All right, all right!" Rixon bellowed, throwing his hands up in surrender. "Just 'cause I can't feel a bloody lip doesn't mean I want to spend the rest of the night walking around with one." He winked. "Won't increase my chances with the ladies."

"And a black eye will?"

Rixon lifted his fingers to his eyes, probing. "You didn't!" he said, swinging a fist at Patch.

I pulled my finger away from Patch's scars. The skin on the back of my neck prickled, and my heart pumped much too fast. Patch looked at me, a shadow of uncertainty in his eyes.

I was forced to accept that maybe now wasn't the time to rely on the logical half of my brain. Maybe this was one of those times when I needed to step out of bounds. Stop playing by the rules. Accept the impossible.

"Then you're definitely not human," I said. "You really are a fallen angel. A bad guy."

That squeezed a smile out of Patch. "You think I'm a bad guy?"

"You possess other people's . . . bodies."

He accepted the statement with a nod.

"Do you want to possess my body?"

"I want to do a lot of things to your body, but that's not one of them."

"What's wrong with the body you have?"

"My body is a lot like glass. Real, but outward, reflecting the world around me. You see and hear me, and I see and hear you. When you touch me, you feel it. I don't experience you in the same way. I can't feel you. I experience everything through a sheet of glass, and the only way I can cut through that sheet is by possessing a human body."

"Or part-human."

Patch's mouth tightened at the corners. "When you touched my scars, you saw Chauncey?" he guessed.

"I heard you talking to Rixon. He said you possess Chauncey's body for two weeks every year during Cheshvan. He said Chauncey isn't human either. He's Nephilim." The word rolled off my tongue in a whisper.

"Chauncey is a cross between a fallen angel and a human. He's immortal like an angel but has all the mortal senses. A fallen angel who wants to feel human sensations can do it in a Nephil's body."

"If you can't feel, why did you kiss me?"

Patch traced a finger along my collarbone, then headed south, stopping at my heart. I felt it pounding through my skin. "Because I feel it here, in my heart," he said quietly. "I haven't lost the ability to feel emotion." He watched me closely. "Let me put it this way. Our emotional connection isn't lacking."

Don't panic, I thought. But already my breathing was faster, shallower. "You mean you can feel happy or sad or—"

"Desire." A barely-there smile.

Keep moving forward, I told myself. Don't give your own emotions time to catch up. Deal with them later, after you have answers. "Why did you fall?"

Patch's eyes held mine for a couple of counts. "Lust."

I swallowed. "Money lust?"

Patch stroked his jaw. He only did that when he wanted to conceal what he was thinking, the giveaway to his thoughts being his mouth. He was fighting a smile. "And other kinds. I thought if I fell, I'd become human. The angels who'd tempted Eve had been banished to Earth, and there were rumors that they'd lost their wings and become human. When they left heaven, it wasn't this big ceremony we were all invited to. It was private. I didn't know their wings were ripped out, or that they were cursed to roam Earth with a hunger to possess human bodies. Back then, nobody had even heard of fallen angels. So it made sense in my mind, that if I fell, I'd lose my wings and become human. At the time, I was crazy about a human girl, and it seemed worth the risk."

"Dabria said you can get your wings back by saving a human life. She said you'll be a guardian angel. You don't want that?" I was confused why he was so set against it.

"It's not for me. I want to be human. I want it more than I've ever wanted anything."

"What about Dabria? If the two of you aren't together anymore, why is she still here? I thought she was a regular angel. Does she want to be human too?"

Patch went deathly still, all the muscles up his arm going rigid. "Dabria's still on Earth?"

"She got a job at school. She's the new school psychologist, Miss Greene. I've met with her a couple times." My stomach gave a hard twist. "After what I saw in your memory, I thought she took the job to be closer to you."

"What exactly did she tell you when you met with her?"

"To stay away from you. She hinted at your dark and dangerous past." I paused. "Something about this is off, isn't it?" I asked, feeling an ominous prickle make its way down my spine.

"I need to take you home. Then I'm going to the high school to look through her files and see if I can find something useful. I'll feel better when I know what she's planning." Patch stripped the bed bare. "Wrap yourself in these," he said, handing me the bundle of dry sheets.

My mind was working hard to make sense of the fragments of information. Suddenly my mouth went a little dry and sticky. "She still has feelings for you. Maybe she wants me out of the picture."

Our eyes locked. "It crossed my mind," Patch said.

An icy, disturbing thought had been banging around inside my head the past few minutes, trying to get my attention. It practically shouted at me now, telling me Dabria could be the guy in the ski mask. All along I thought the person I hit with the Neon was male, just like Vee thought her attacker was male. At this point, I wouldn't put it past Dabria to deceive us both.

After a quick trip to the bathroom, Patch emerged wearing his wet tee. "I'll go get the Jeep," he said. "I'll pull around to the back exit in twenty. Stay in the motel until then."

CHAPTER 25

AFTER PATCH LEFT, I PUT THE CHAIN ON THE DOOR. I dragged the chair across the room and rammed it under the door handle. I checked to make sure the window locks were in place. I didn't know if locks would work against Dabria—I didn't even know if she *was* after me—but I figured it was better to play it safe. After pacing around the room for a few minutes, I tried the phone on the nightstand. Still no dial tone.

My mom was going to kill me.

I'd sneaked behind her back and gone to Portland. And how was I supposed to explain the whole "I checked into a motel with Patch" situation? I'd be lucky if she didn't ground me through the end of the year. No. I'd be lucky if she didn't quit her job and apply to substitute teach until she found a full-time job locally. We'd have to sell the farmhouse, and I'd lose the only connection to my dad I had left.

Approximately fifteen minutes later I peered through the peephole. Nothing but blackness. I unbarred the door, and just as I was about to tug it open, lights flickered on behind me. I whirled around, half expecting to see Dabria. The room was still and empty, but the electricity was back.

The door opened with a loud click and I stepped into the hall. The carpet was bloodred, worn bald down the center of the hallway, and stained with unidentifiable dark marks. The walls were painted neutral, but the paint job was sloppy and chipping.

Above me, a neon green sign spelled the way to the exit. I followed the arrow down the hall and around the corner. The Jeep rolled to a stop on the other side of the back door, and I dashed out and hopped in on the passenger side.

No lights were on when Patch pulled up to the farmhouse. I experienced a guilty squeeze in my stomach and wondered if my mom was driving around, looking for me. The rain had died, and fog pressed against the siding and hung on the shrubs like Christmas tinsel. The trees dotting the driveway were permanently twisted and misshapen from constant northern winds. All houses look uninviting with the lights off after dark, but the farmhouse with its small slits for windows, bowed roof, caved-in porch, and wild brambles looked haunted.

"I'm going to walk through," Patch said, swinging out.

"Do you think Dabria's inside?"

He shook his head. "But it doesn't hurt to check."

I waited in the Jeep, and a few minutes later Patch walked out the front door. "All clear," he told me. "I'll drive to the high school and come back here as soon as I sweep her office. Maybe she left something useful behind." He didn't sound like he was counting on it.

I unbuckled my seat belt and ordered my legs to carry me quickly up the walk. As I turned the doorknob, I heard Patch back down the driveway. The porch boards creaked under my feet and I suddenly felt very alone.

Keeping the lights off, I crept through the house room by room, starting with the first floor, then working my way upstairs. Patch had already cleared the house, but I didn't think an extra pair of eyes would hurt. After I was sure no one was hiding under the furniture, behind the shower curtains, or in the closets, I tugged on Levi's and a black V-neck sweater. I found the emergency cell phone my mom kept in a first-aid kit under the bathroom sink and dialed her cell.

She picked up on the first ring. "Hello? Nora? Is that you? Where are you? I've been worried sick!"

I drew a deep breath, praying the right words would come to me and help me talk my way out of this.

"Here's the deal—" I began in my most sincere and apologetic voice.

"Cascade Road flooded and they closed it. I had to turn back and get a room in Milliken Mills—that's where I am now. I tried calling home, but apparently the lines are down. I tried your cell, but you didn't pick up."

"Wait. You've been in Milliken Mills this whole time?"

"Where did you think I was?"

I gave an inaudible sigh of relief and lowered myself onto the edge of the bathtub. "I didn't know," I said. "I couldn't get ahold of you, either."

"What number are you calling from?" Mom asked. "I don't recognize this number."

"The emergency cell."

"Where's your phone?"

"I lost it."

"What! Where?"

I came to the rocky conclusion that a lie of omission was the only way to go. I didn't want to alarm her. I also didn't want to be grounded for an interminable length of time. "It's more like I misplaced it. I'm sure it will pop up somewhere." On a dead woman's body.

"I'll call you as soon as they open the roads," she said.

Next I called Vee's cell. After five rings I was sent to voice mail.

"Where are you?" I said. "Call me back at this number ASAP." I snapped the phone shut and tucked it into my pocket, trying to convince myself Vee was fine. But I knew it was a lie. The invisible thread tying us together had been warning me for hours now that she was in danger. If anything, the feeling was heightening with each passing minute.

In the kitchen I saw my bottle of iron pills on the counter, and I immediately went for them, popping the cap and swallowing two with a glass of chocolate milk. I stood in place a moment, letting the iron work into my system, feeling my breathing deepen and slow. I was walking the milk carton back to the fridge when I saw her standing in the doorway between the kitchen and laundry room.

A cold, wet substance pooled at my feet, and I realized I'd dropped the milk. "Dabria?" I said.

She tilted her head to one side, showing mild surprise. "You know my name?" She paused. "Ah, Patch."

I backed up to the sink, putting more distance between us. Dabria didn't look anything like she did at school as Miss Greene. Tonight her hair was tangled, not smooth, and her lips were brighter, a certain hunger reflected there. Her eyes were sharper, a smudge of black ringing them.

"What do you want?" I asked.

She laughed, and it sounded like ice cubes tinkling in a glass. "I want Patch."

"Patch isn't here."

She nodded. "I know. I waited down the street for him to leave before I came in. But that's not what I meant when I said I want Patch."

The blood pounding through my legs circled back to my heart with a dizzying effect. I put one hand on the counter to steady myself. "I know you were spying on me during the counseling sessions."

"Is that all you know about me?" she asked, her eyes searching mine.

I remembered the night I was sure someone had looked in my bedroom window. "You've been spying on me here, too," I said.

"This is the first time I've been to your house." She dragged her finger along the edge of the kitchen island and perched herself on a stool. "Nice place."

"Let me refresh your memory," I said, hoping I sounded brave. "You looked in my bedroom window while I was sleeping."

Her smile curved high. "No, but I did follow you shopping. I attacked your friend and planted little hints in her mind, making her think Patch hurt her. It wasn't a far stretch. He's not exactly harmless to begin with. It was in my best interest to make you as frightened of him as possible."

"So I'd stay away from him."

"But you didn't. You're still standing in our way."

"In your way of what?"

"Come on, Nora. If you know who I am, then you know how this works. I want him to get his wings back. He doesn't belong on Earth. He belongs with me. He made a mistake, and I'm going to correct it." There was absolutely no compromise in her voice. She got off the stool and walked around the island toward me.

I backed along the edge of the outer counter, keeping space between us. Racking my brain, I tried to think of a way to distract her. Or escape. I'd lived in the house sixteen years. I knew the floor plan. I knew every secret crevice and the best hiding places. I commanded my brain to come up with a plan: something spur-of-the-moment and brilliant. My back met with the sideboard.

"As long as you're around, Patch won't return with me," Dabria said.

"I think you're overestimating his feelings for me." It seemed like a good idea to downplay our relationship. Dabria's possessiveness appeared to be the main force driving her to act.

An incredulous smile dawned on her face. "You think he has those feelings for you? All this time you thought—" She broke off, laughing. "He's not staying because he loves you. He wants to kill you."

I shook my head. "He's not going to kill me."

Dabria's smile hardened at the edges. "If that's what you believe, you're just another girl he's seduced to get what he wants. He has a talent for it," she added shrewdly. "He seduced your name right out of me, after all. One soft touch from Patch was all it took. I fell under his spell and told him death was coming for you."

323

I knew what she was talking about. I'd witnessed the exact moment she was referring to inside Patch's memory.

"And now he's doing the same thing to you," she said. "Betrayal hurts, doesn't it?"

I shook my head slowly. "No—"

"He's planning to use you as a sacrifice!" she erupted. "See that mark?" She thrust her finger at my wrist. "It means you're a female descendant of a Nephil. And not just any Nephil, but Chauncey Langeais, Patch's vassal."

I glanced at my scar, and for one heart-stopping moment, I actually believed her. But I knew better than to trust her.

"There's a sacred book, *The Book of Enoch*," she said. "In it, a fallen angel kills his Nephil vassal by sacrificing one of the Nephil's female descendants. You don't think Patch wants to kill you? What's the one thing he wants most? Once he sacrifices you, he'll be human. He'll have everything he wants. And he won't come home with me."

She unsheathed a large knife from the wood block on the counter. "And that's why I have to get rid of you. It appears that one way or another, my premonitions were right. Death is coming for you."

"Patch is coming back," I said, my insides sickening. "Don't you want to talk this over with him?"

"I'll make it quick," she continued. "I'm an angel of death. I carry souls to the afterlife. As soon as I finish, I'll carry your soul through the veil. You have nothing to be afraid of."

I wanted to scream out, but my voice was trapped at the back of my throat. I edged around the sideboard, putting the kitchen table between us. "If you're an angel, where are your wings?"

"No more questions." Her voice had grown impatient, and she began closing the distance between us in earnest.

"How long has it been since you left heaven?" I asked, stalling. "You've been down here for several months, right? Don't you think the other angels have noticed you're missing?"

"Not another step," she snapped, raising the knife, scattering light off the blade.

"You're going to a lot of trouble for Patch," I said, my voice not nearly as devoid of panic as I wanted. "I'm surprised you don't resent him for using you when it suits his purpose. I'm surprised you want him to get his wings back at all. After what he did to you, aren't you happy he's banished here?"

"He left me for a worthless human girl!" she spat, her eyes a fiery blue.

"He didn't leave you. Not really. He fell—"

"He fell because he wanted to be human, like her! He had me—he had me!" She gave a scoffing laugh, but it didn't mask the anger or sorrow. "At first I was hurt and angry, and I did everything in my power to forget about him. Then, when the archangels figured out he was seriously attempting to become human, they sent me down here to change his mind. I told myself I wasn't going to fall for him all over again, but what good did it do?"

"Dabria . . . ," I began softly.

"He didn't even care that the girl was made from the *dust of the earth*! You—all of you—are selfish and slovenly! Your bodies are wild and undisciplined. One moment you're at the peak of joy, the next you're on the brink of despair. It's deplorable! No angel will aspire to it!" She flung her arm in a wild arc across her face, wiping away tears. "Look at me! I can barely control myself! I've been down here too long, submerged in human filth!"

I turned and ran from the kitchen, knocking over a chair and leaving it behind me in Dabria's path. I raced down the hall, knowing I was trapping myself. The house had two exits: the front door, which Dabria could reach before me by cutting through the living room, and the back door off the dining room, which she blocked.

I was shoved hard from behind, and I pitched forward. I skidded down the hall, coming to a stop on my stomach. I rolled over. Dabria hovered a few feet above me—*in the air*—her skin and hair ablaze in blinding white, the knife pointed down at me.

I didn't think. I kicked my leg up with all my strength. I arched into the kick, bracing with my nonkicking leg, and aimed for her lower arm. The knife was knocked out of her hand. As I got my feet under me, Dabria pointed at the lamp on a small entryway table, and with a sharp fling of her finger, sent it flying at me. I rolled away, feeling shards of glass slide under me as the lamp shattered on the floor.

"Move!" Dabria commanded, and the entry bench slid to barricade the front door, blocking my exit.

Scrambling forward, I took the stairs two at a time, using the banister to propel me faster. I heard Dabria laugh behind me, and the next instant the banister broke free, crashing to the hall below. I threw my weight back to keep from falling over the unguarded edge. Catching my balance, I raced up the final stairs. At the top I flung myself into my mom's bedroom and slammed the French doors shut.

Racing to one of the windows flanking the fireplace, I looked down two storeys to the ground. There were three bushes in a rock bed directly below, all their foliage gone since autumn. I didn't know if I'd survive a jump.

"Open!" Dabria commanded from the other side of the French doors. A crack split up the wood as the door strained against the lock. I was out of time.

I ran to the fireplace and ducked under the mantel. I had just pulled my feet up, bracing them against the inside of the flue, when the doors swung open, slamming back against the wall. I heard Dabria stride to the window.

"Nora!" she called in her delicate, chilling voice. "I know you're close! I sense you. You can't run and you can't hide—I'll burn this house down room by room if that's what it takes to find you! And then I'll burn my way through the fields behind. I'm not leaving you alive!"

A glow of bright gold light sizzled to life outside the fireplace, along with the roaring whoosh of fire igniting. The flames sent shadows dancing in the pit below. I heard the snap and crackle of fire eating up fuel—most likely the furniture or wood floors.

I stayed cramped in the flue. My heart throbbed, sweat leaking from my skin. I drew several breaths, exhaling slowly to manage the burn in my tightly contracted leg muscles. Patch had said he was going to the school. How long until he came back?

Not knowing if Dabria was still in the room, but fearing that if I didn't leave now, the fire would trap me in, I lowered one leg into the pit, then the other. I came out from under the mantel. Dabria was nowhere in sight, but the flames were licking up the walls, smoke choking all air from the room.

I hurried down the hall, not daring to go downstairs, thinking Dabria would expect me to try to escape through one of the doors. In my bedroom I opened the window. The tree outside was close enough and sturdy enough to climb. Maybe I could lose Dabria in the fog behind the house. The nearest neighbors were just under a mile away, and running hard, I could be there in seven minutes. I was about to swing my leg out the window when a creak sounded down the hall.

Quietly closing myself inside the closet, I dialed 911.

"There's someone in my house trying to kill me," I whispered to the operator. I had just given my address when the door to my room eased open. I held perfectly still.

Through the slats in the closet door, I watched a shadowy figure enter the room. The lighting was low, my angle was off, and I couldn't see a single distinguishing detail. The figure parted the window blinds, peering out. It fingered the socks and underwear in my open drawer. It picked up the silver comb on my bureau, studied it, then returned it. When the figure turned in the direction of the closet, I knew I was in trouble.

Sliding my hand over the floor, I felt for anything I could use in my defense. My elbow bumped a stack of shoe boxes, toppling them. I mouthed a curse. The footsteps trod closer.

The closet doors opened, and I hurled a shoe out. I grabbed another and threw it.

Patch swore in an undertone, yanked a third shoe out of my hands, and hurled it behind him. Wrestling me out of the closet, he got me on my feet. Before I could register relief at discovering him and not Dabria in front of me, he pulled me against him and wrapped his arms around me.

"Are you okay?" he murmured in my ear.

"Dabria's here," I said, my eyes brimming with tears. My knees trembled, and Patch's hold was the only thing keeping me up. "She's burning down the house."

Patch handed me a set of keys and curled my fingers around them. "My Jeep's parked on the street. Get in, lock the doors, drive to Delphic, and wait for me." He tipped my chin up to face him. He brushed a kiss across my lips and sent a flash of heat through me.

"What are you going to do?" I asked.

"Take care of Dabria."

"How?"

He slid me a look that said, *Do you really want details?*

The sound of sirens wailed in the distance.

Patch looked to the window. "You called the police?"

"I thought you were Dabria."

He was already on his way out the door. "I'll go after Dabria. Drive the Jeep to Delphic and wait for me."

"What about the fire?"

"The police will handle it."

I tightened my grip on the keys. The decision-making part of my brain was split, running in opposite directions. I wanted to get out of the house and away from Dabria, and meet up with Patch later, but there was one nagging thought I couldn't shake free. Dabria had said Patch needed to sacrifice me to become human.

She hadn't said it lightly, or to get under my skin. Or even to harden me against him. Her words had come out cold and serious. Serious enough that she tried to kill me to stop Patch from getting to me first.

I found the Jeep parked on the street, just like Patch had said. I put the keys in the ignition and floored the Jeep down Hawthorne. Figuring it was pointless to try Vee's cell again, I dialed her home phone instead.

"Hi, Mrs. Sky," I said, trying to sound like nothing was out of the ordinary. "Is Vee there?"

"Hi, Nora! She left a few hours ago. Something about a party in Portland. I thought she was with you."

"Um, we got separated," I lied. "Did she say where she was going after the party?"

"She was thinking about seeing a movie. And she isn't answering her cell, so I assume she has it turned off for a show. Is everything okay?"

I didn't want to frighten her, but at the same time, I wasn't about to say everything was okay. Not one bit of it felt okay to me. The last time I'd heard from Vee, she was with Elliot. And now she wasn't answering her cell.

"I don't think so," I said. "I'm going to drive around and look for her. I'll start at the movie theater. Will you search the promenade?"

CHAPTER

26

IT WAS THE SUNDAY NIGHT BEFORE THE START OF SPRING
break, and the movie theater was packed. I got in the ticket
line, continually looking around for signs that I'd been followed. Nothing alarming so far, and the press of bodies offered
good cover. I told myself Patch would take care of Dabria and that
I had nothing to worry about, but it didn't hurt to be vigilant.

Of course, deep inside, I knew Dabria wasn't my biggest worry.
Sooner or later Patch was going to figure out I wasn't at Delphic.

Based on past experience, I didn't have any illusions about being able to hide long-term from him. He would find me. And then I'd be forced to confront him with the question I was dreading. More specifically, I dreaded his answer. Because there was a shadow of doubt at the back of my mind, whispering that Dabria had been telling the truth about what it would take for Patch to get a human body.

I stepped up to the ticket window. The nine-thirty movies were just starting.

"One for The Sacrifice," I said without thinking. Immediately I found the title eerily ironic. Not wanting to reflect further on it, I fished in my pockets and pushed a wad of small bills and coins under the window, praying it was enough.

"Jeez," the teller said, staring at the coins spilling under the window. I recognized her from school. She was a senior, and I was pretty sure her name was Kaylie or Kylie. "Thanks a lot," she said. "It's not like there's a line or anything."

Everyone behind me muttered a collective expletive.

"I cleaned out my piggy bank," I said, attempting sarcasm.

"No kidding. Is it all here?" she asked, expelling a drawn-out sigh as she pushed the coins into groups of quarters, dimes, nickels, and pennies.

"Sure."

"Whatever. I don't get paid enough for this." She swept the money into the cash drawer and slid my ticket under the window. "There are these things called credit cards. . . ."

I grabbed the ticket. "Did you happen to see Vee Sky come in tonight?"

"Bee who?"

"Vee Sky. She's a sophomore. She was with Elliot Saunders."

Kaylie or Kylie's eyes bugged out. "Does it look like a slow night? Does it look like I've just been sitting here, memorizing every face that walks past?"

"Never mind," I breathed, heading for the doors leading inside.

Coldwater's movie theater has two screens, behind doors on either side of a concession counter. As soon as the ticket guy ripped my ticket in half, I tugged on the door to theater number two and ducked inside to darkness. The movie had started.

The theater was almost full, except for a few isolated seats. I walked down the aisle, looking for Vee. At the bottom of the aisle I turned and walked across the front of the theater. It was hard to distinguish faces in the darkness, but I was pretty sure Vee wasn't here.

I exited the theater and walked over to the show next door. It wasn't as crowded. I did another walk-through, but again, I didn't see Vee. Taking a seat near the back, I tried to settle my mind.

This whole night felt like a dark fairy tale I'd strayed into and couldn't find my way back out of. A fairy tale with fallen angels, human hybrids, and sacrificial killings. I rubbed my thumb over my birthmark. I especially didn't want to think about the possibility that I was descended from one of the Nephilim.

I pulled out the emergency cell phone and checked for missed calls. None.

I was tucking the phone in my pocket when a carton of popcorn materialized beside me.

"Hungry?" asked a voice from just over my shoulder. The voice was quiet and not especially happy. I tried to keep my breathing calm. "Stand up and walk out of the theater," Patch said. "I'll be right behind you."

I didn't move.

"Walk out," he repeated. "We need to talk."

"About how you need to sacrifice me to get a human body?" I asked, my tone light, my insides feeling leaden.

"That might be cute if you thought it was true."

"I do think it's true!" Sort of. But the same thought kept returning—if Patch wanted to kill me, why hadn't he already?

"Shh!" said the guy next to me.

Patch said, "Walk out, or I'll carry you out."

I flipped around. "Excuse me?"

"Shh!" the guy beside me hissed again.

"Blame him," I told the guy, pointing at Patch.

The guy craned his neck back. "Listen," he said, facing me again. "If you don't quiet down, I'll get security."

"Fine, go get security. Tell them to take him away," I said, again signaling Patch. "Tell them he wants to kill me."

"*I* want to kill you," hissed the guy's girlfriend, leaning around him to address me.

"Who wants to kill you?" the guy asked. He was still looking over his shoulder, but his expression was puzzled.

"There's nobody *there*," the girlfriend told me.

"You're making them think they can't see you, aren't you?" I said to Patch, awed by his power even as I despised his use of it.

Patch smiled, but it was pinched at the corners.

"Oh, jeez!" said the girlfriend, throwing her hands in the air. She rolled her eyes furiously at her boyfriend and said, "Do something!"

"I need you to stop talking," the guy told me. He gestured at the screen. "Watch the show. Here—have my soda."

I swung into the aisle. I felt Patch move behind me, unsettlingly close, not quite touching. He stayed that way until we were out of the theater.

On the other side of the door, Patch hooked my arm and guided me across the foyer to the ladies' room.

"What is it with you and girls' bathrooms?" I said.

He steered me through the door, locked it, and leaned back against it. His eyes were all over me. And they showed every sign of wanting to rattle me to death.

I was backed up against the counter, my palms digging into the edge. "You're mad because I didn't go to Delphic." I raised one shaky shoulder. "Why Delphic, Patch? It's Sunday night. Delphic will be closing soon. Any special reason you wanted me to drive to a dark, soon-to-be deserted amusement park?"

He walked toward me until he was standing close enough that I could see his black eyes beneath his ball cap.

"Dabria told me you have to sacrifice me to get a human body," I said.

Patch was quiet a moment. "And you think I'd go through with it?"

I swallowed. "Then it's true?"

Our eyes locked. "It has to be an intentional sacrifice. Simply killing you won't do it."

"Are you the only person who can do this to me?"

"No, but I'm probably the only person who knows the end result, and the only person who would attempt it. It's the reason I came to school. I had to get close to you. I needed you. It's the reason I walked into your life."

"Dabria told me you fell for a girl." I hated myself for experiencing irrational pangs of jealousy. This wasn't supposed to be about me. This was supposed to be an interrogation. "What happened?"

I desperately wanted Patch to give away some clue to his thoughts, but his eyes were a cool black, emotions tucked out of sight. "She grew old and died."

"That must have been hard for you," I snapped.

He waited a few counts before answering. His tone was so low, I shivered. "You want me to come clean, I will. I'll tell you everything. Who I am and what I've done. Every last detail. I'll dig it all up, but you have to ask. You have to want it. You can see who I was, or you

337

can see who I am now. I'm not good," he said, piercing me with eyes that absorbed all light but reflected none, "but I was worse."

I ignored the roll in my stomach and said, "Tell me."

"The first time I saw her, I was still an angel. It was an instant, possessive lust. It drove me crazy. I didn't know anything about her, except that I would do whatever it took to get close to her. I watched her for a while, and then I got it in my head that if I went down to Earth and possessed a human body, I would be cast out of heaven and become human. The thing is, I didn't know about Cheshvan. I came down on a night in August, but I couldn't possess the body. On my way back to heaven, a host of avenging angels stopped me and ripped out my wings. They tossed me out of the sky. Right away I knew something was wrong. When I looked at humans, all I could feel was an insatiable craving to be inside their bodies. All my powers were stripped, and I was this weak, pathetic thing. I wasn't human. I was fallen. I'd realized I'd given it all up, just like that. All this time I've hated myself for it. I thought I'd given it up for nothing." His eyes focused singularly on me, leaving me feeling transparent. "But if I hadn't fallen, I wouldn't have met you."

My conflicting emotions weighed so heavily inside my chest, I thought they might suffocate me. Biting back tears, I forged ahead. "Dabria said my birthmark means I'm related to Chauncey. Is that true?"

"Do you want me to answer that?"

I didn't know what I wanted. My whole world felt like a joke, and I was the last one to get the punch line. I wasn't Nora Grey, average girl. I was the descendant of someone who wasn't even human. And my heart was smashing itself to pieces over another nonhuman. A dark angel. "Which side of my family?" I said at last.

"Your dad's."

"Where's Chauncey now?" Even though we were related, I liked the idea of him being far away. Very far away. Far enough that the link between us might not feel as real.

His boots were flush with the toes of my tennis shoes. "I'm not going to kill you, Nora. I don't kill people who are important to me. And you top the list."

My heart did a nervous flip. My hands were pressed against his stomach, which was so hard even his skin didn't give. I was keeping a pointless safeguard between us, since not even a towering electrical fence would make me feel secure from him.

"You're impinging on my private space," I said, inching backward.

Patch gave a barely-there smile. "Impinging? This isn't the SAT, Nora."

I tucked a few stray hairs behind my ears and took one sizable step sideways, skirting the sink. "You're crowding me. I need— room." What I needed were boundaries. I needed willpower. I needed to be caged up, since yet again I was proving I couldn't be trusted in Patch's presence. I should have been bolting for the door, and yet . . . I wasn't. I tried convincing myself I was staying because I needed answers, but that was only part of it. It was the other part I didn't want to think about. The emotional part. The part that was pointless fighting.

"Are you keeping anything else from me?" I wanted to know.

"I'm keeping a lot of things from you."

My insides took a steep dive. "Like?"

"Like the way I feel about being locked up in here with you." Patch braced one hand against the mirror behind me, his weight tipping toward me. "You have no idea what you do to me."

I shook my head. "I don't think so. This isn't a good idea. This isn't right."

"There's all kinds of right," he murmured. "On the spectrum, we're still in the safe zone."

I was pretty sure the self-preserving half of my brain was screaming, *Run for your life!* Unfortunately, blood roared in my ears, and I wasn't hearing straight. Obviously I wasn't thinking straight either.

"Definitely right. Usually right," Patch continued. "Mostly right. Maybe right."

"Maybe not right now." I sucked in some air. Out of the corner of my eye I noticed a fire alarm drilled into the wall. It was ten, maybe fifteen feet away. If I was fast, I could cross the room and pull it before Patch stopped me. Security would come running. I'd be safe. And that's what I wanted . . . wasn't it?

"Not a good idea," Patch said with a soft shake of his head.

I bolted for the fire alarm anyway. My fingers closed on the lever and I pulled down to sound the alarm. Only, the lever didn't budge. As hard as I tried, I couldn't get it to move. And then I recognized Patch's familiar presence in my head, and I knew it was a mind game.

I swiveled around to face him. "Get out of my head." I stormed back and shoved hard against his chest. Patch took a step back, steadying himself.

"What was that for?" he asked.

"For this whole night." For making me crazy about him when I knew it was wrong. He was the worst kind of wrong. He was so wrong it felt right, and that made me feel completely out of control.

I might have been tempted to hit him square in the jaw had he not taken me by the shoulders and pinned me against the wall. There was hardly any space left between us, just a thin boundary of air, but Patch managed to eliminate it.

"Let's be honest, Nora. You've got it bad for me." His eyes held a lot of depth. "And I've got it bad for you." He leaned into me and put his mouth on mine. A lot of him was on me, actually. We touched base at several strategic locations down our bodies, and it took all my willpower to break away.

I pulled back. "I'm not finished. What happened to Dabria?"

"All taken care of."

"What exactly does that mean?"

"She wasn't going to keep her wings after plotting to kill you. The moment she tried to get back into heaven, the avenging angels would have stripped them. She had it coming sooner or later. I just sped things up."

"So you just—tore them off?"

"They were deteriorating; the feathers were broken and thin. If she stayed on Earth much longer, it was a signal to every other fallen angel who saw her that she'd fallen. If I didn't do it, one of them would have."

I dodged another one of his advances. "Is she going to make another unwanted appearance in my life?"

"Hard to say."

Lightning quick, Patch caught hold of the hem of my sweater. He reeled me into him. His knuckles brushed the skin of my navel. Heat and ice shot through me simultaneously. "You could take her, Angel," he said. "I've seen both of you in action, and my bet's on you. You don't need me for that."

"What do I need you for?"

He laughed. Not abruptly, but with a certain low desire. His eyes had lost their edge and were focused wholly on me. His smile was all fox . . . but softer. Something just behind my navel danced, then coiled lower.

"Door's locked," he said. "And we have unfinished business."

My body seemed to have swept aside the logical part of my brain. Smothered it, in fact. I slid my hands up his chest and looped my arms around his neck. Patch lifted me at the hips, and I wrapped my legs around his waist. My pulse pounded, but I didn't mind one little bit. I crushed my mouth to his, soaking up the ecstasy of his mouth on mine, his hands on me, feeling on the verge of bursting out of my skin—

The cell phone in my pocket rang to life. I pulled away from Patch, breathing heavily, and the phone rang a second time.

"Voice mail," Patch said.

Deep in the recesses of my consciousness, I knew answering my phone was important. I couldn't remember why; kissing Patch had made every last harbored worry evaporate. I untangled myself from him, turning away so he wouldn't see how worked up ten seconds of kissing him had made me. Internally I was screaming with joy.

"Hello?" I answered, resisting the urge to wipe my mouth for smeared lip gloss.

"Babe!" Vee said. We had a bad connection, the crackle of static cutting across her voice. "Where are you?"

"Where are you? Are you still with Elliot and Jules?" I flattened a hand against my free ear to hear better.

"I'm at school. We broke in," she said in a voice that was naughty to perfection. "We want to play hide-and-seek but don't have enough people for two teams. So . . . do you know of a fourth person who could come play with us?"

An incoherent voice mumbled in the background.

"Elliot wants me to tell you that if you don't come be his partner—hang on—what?" Vee said into the background.

Elliot's voice came on. "Nora? Come play with us. Otherwise, there's a tree in the common area with Vee's name on it."

Pure ice flowed through me.

"Hello?" I said hoarsely. "Elliot? Vee? Are you there?"

But the connection was dead.

CHAPTER
27

WHO WAS THAT?" PATCH ASKED.

My whole body was ringing. It took me a moment to answer. "Vee broke into the high school with Elliot and Jules. They want me to meet them. I think Elliot's going to hurt Vee if I don't go." I looked up at Patch. "I think he's going to hurt her if I do."

He folded his arms, frowning. "Elliot?"

"Last week at the library I found an article that said he was questioned in a murder investigation at his old school, Kinghorn Prep. He walked into the computer lab and saw me reading it. Ever since that night, I've gotten a bad vibe from him. A really bad vibe. I think he even broke into my bedroom to steal the article back."

"Anything else I should know?"

"The girl who was murdered was Elliot's girlfriend. She was hanged from a tree. Just now on the phone he said, 'If you don't come, there's a tree in the common area with Vee's name on it.'"

"I've seen Elliot. He seems cocky and a little aggressive, but he doesn't strike me as a killer." He dipped into my front pocket and extracted the Jeep's keys. "I'll drive over and check things out. I won't be long."

"I think we should call the police."

He shook his head. "You'll send Vee to juvie for destruction of property and B and E. One more thing. Jules. Who is this guy?"

"Elliot's friend. He was at the arcade the night we saw you."

His frown deepened. "If there was another guy, I would remember."

He opened the door and I followed him out. A janitor wearing black slacks and a work-issue maroon shirt was sweeping bits of popcorn in the lobby. He did a double take at the sight of Patch exiting the ladies' room. I recognized him from school. Brandt Christensen. We had English together. Last semester I'd helped him write a paper.

"Elliot is expecting me, not you," I told Patch. "If I don't show up, who knows what will happen to Vee? That's a risk I'm not going to take."

"If I let you come, you'll listen to my instructions and follow them carefully?"

"Yes."

"If I tell you to jump?"

"I'll jump."

"If I tell you to stay in the car?"

"I'll stay in the car." It was mostly true.

Out in the parking lot of the theater, Patch aimed his key fob at the Jeep, and the headlights blinked. Suddenly he came to a halt and swore under his breath.

"What's wrong?" I said.

"Tires."

I dropped my gaze and sure enough, both tires on the driver's side were flat. "I can't believe it!" I said. "I drove over two nails?"

Patch crouched by the front tire, running his hand around the circumference. "Screwdriver. This was an intentional attack."

For a moment I thought maybe this was another mind trick. Maybe Patch had his reasons for not wanting me to go to the high school. His feelings about Vee were no secret, after all. But something was missing. I couldn't feel Patch anywhere inside my head. If he was altering my thoughts, he'd found a new way to accomplish it, because as far as I could tell, what I was seeing was real.

"Who would do that?"

He rose to his full height. "The list is long."

"Are you trying to tell me you have a lot of enemies?"

"I've upset a few people. A lot of folks place bets they can't win. Then they blame me for walking off with their car, or more."

Patch walked one space over to a coupe, opened the driver's side door, and took a seat behind the steering wheel. Reaching under it, his hand disappeared.

"What are you doing?" I asked, standing in the open doorway. It was a waste of breath since I was well aware of what he was doing.

"Looking for the spare key." Patch's hand reappeared, holding two blue wires. With some skill, he removed the ends of the wires and tapped them together. The engine turned over, and Patch looked out at me. "Seat belt."

"I'm not stealing a car."

He shrugged. "We need it now. They don't."

"It's stealing. It's wrong."

Patch didn't look the least bit troubled. In fact, he looked a little too relaxed in the driver's seat. *This isn't the first time he's done this*, I thought.

"First rule of auto theft," he said on a smile. "Try not to hang around the crime scene longer than necessary."

"Hang on one minute," I said, holding up a finger.

I jogged back to the theater. On my way inside, the glass doors reflected the parking lot behind me, and I saw Patch swing out of the coupe.

"Hi, Brandt," I said to the boy still flicking popcorn into a long-handled dustpan.

Brandt looked up at me, but his attention was quickly drawn over my shoulder. I heard the theater doors open and sensed Patch move behind me. His approach wasn't all that different from a cloud eclipsing the sun, subtly darkening the landscape, hinting of a storm.

"How's it going?" Brandt said uncertainly.

"I'm having car trouble," I said, biting my lip and trying on a sympathetic face. "I know I'm putting you in an awkward position, but since I helped you with that Shakespeare paper last semester . . ."

"You want to borrow my car."

"Actually . . . yes."

"It's a piece of junk. It's no Jeep Commander." He looked right at Patch like he was apologizing.

"Does it run?" I asked.

"If by run you mean do the wheels roll, yeah, it runs. But it's not for loan."

Patch opened his wallet and handed over what looked like three crisp hundred-dollar bills. Reining in my surprise, I decided the best thing to do was play along.

"I changed my mind," Brandt said, eyes wide, pocketing the money. He fished in his pockets and underhanded Patch a pair of keys.

"What's the make and color?" Patch asked, catching the keys.

"Hard to tell. Part Volkswagen, part Chevette. It used to be blue. That was before it corroded to orange. You'll fill the tank up before you return it?" Brandt said, sounding like he had his fingers crossed behind his back, pressing his luck.

Patch peeled out another twenty. "Just in case we forget," he said, stuffing it into the front pocket of Brandt's uniform.

Outside, I told Patch, "I could have talked him into giving me his keys. I just needed a little more time. And by the way, why do you bus tables at the Borderline if you're loaded?"

"I'm not. I won the money off a pool game a couple nights back." He pushed Brandt's key in the lock and opened the passenger-side door for me. "The bank is officially closed."

Patch drove across town on dark, quiet streets. It didn't take long to arrive at the high school. He rolled Brandt's car to a stop on the east side of the building and killed the engine. The campus was wooded, the branches twisted and bleak and holding up nothing but a damp fog. Behind them loomed Coldwater High.

The original part of the building had been constructed in the late nineteenth century, and after sunset it looked very much like a cathedral. Gray and foreboding. Very dark. Very abandoned.

"I just got a really bad feeling," I said, eyeing the school's black voids for windows.

"Stay in the car and keep out of sight," Patch told me, passing over the keys. "If anybody comes out of the building, take off." He got out. He was wearing a fitted black crewneck tee, dark Levi's, and boots. With his black hair and dusky skin, it was hard to distinguish him from the background. He crossed the street and, in a matter of moments, blended completely into the night.

CHAPTER

28

Five minutes came and went. Ten minutes stretched to twenty. I struggled to ignore the hair-raising feeling that I was under surveillance. I peered into the shadows ringing the school.

What was taking Patch so long? I shuffled through a few theories, feeling more uneasy by the moment. What if Patch couldn't find Vee? What would happen when Patch found Elliot? I didn't think Elliot could overpower Patch, but there was always a chance—if Elliot had the element of surprise.

The phone in my pocket rang, and I jumped out of my skin.

"I see you," Elliot said when I answered. "Sitting out there in the car."

"Where are you?"

"Watching you from a second-storey window. We're playing inside."

"I don't want to play."

He ended the call.

With my heart in my throat, I got out of the car. I looked up at the dark windows of the school. I didn't think Elliot knew Patch was inside. His voice came across impatient, not angry or irritated. My only hope was that Patch had a plan and would make sure nothing happened to me or Vee. The moon was clouded over, and under a shadow of fear I walked up to the east door.

I stepped into semidarkness. My eyes took several seconds to make something of the shaft of streetlight falling through the window encased in the top half of the door. The floor tiles reflected a waxy gleam. Lockers were lined up on either side of the hallway like sleeping robotic soldiers. Instead of a peaceful, quiet feeling, the halls radiated hidden menace.

The outside lights illuminated the first several feet into the hall-way, but after that, I could see nothing. Just inside the door was a panel of light switches, and I flipped them on. Nothing happened.

Since the power was working outside, I knew the electricity inside had been shut off by hand. I wondered if this was part of Elliot's plan. I couldn't see him, and I couldn't see Vee. I also couldn't see Patch. I was going to have to feel my way through each room in the school, playing a slow game of elimination until I found him. Together we would find Vee.

Using the wall as my guide, I crept forward. On any given weekday, I passed down this stretch of hall several times, but in the darkness it suddenly seemed foreign. And longer. Much longer.

At the first intersection I mentally assessed my surroundings. Turning left would lead to the band and orchestra rooms and the cafeteria. Turning right would lead to administrative offices, as well as a double staircase. I continued straight, heading deeper into the school, toward the classrooms.

My foot caught on something, and before I could react, I went sprawling to the floor. Hazy gray light filtered through a skylight directly overhead as the moon broke between clouds, illuminating the features of the body I'd tripped on. Jules was on his back, his expression fixed in a blank stare. His long blond hair was tangled over his face, his hands slack at his sides.

I pushed back on my knees and covered my mouth, panting air. My legs trembled with adrenaline. Very slowly, I rested my palm on Jules's chest. He wasn't breathing. He was dead.

I jumped to my feet and choked on a scream. I wanted to call out for Patch, but that would give my location away to Elliot—if he didn't already know it. I realized with a start that he could be standing feet away, watching me as his twisted game unfolded.

The overhead light faded, and I made a frantic survey of the hall. More endless hallway stretched ahead. The library was up a short flight of stairs to my left. Classrooms started on the right. On a split moment's decision, I chose the library, groping through the blackening halls to get away from Jules's body. My nose dripped, and I realized I was crying soundlessly. Why was Jules dead? Who killed him? If Jules was dead, was Vee also?

The library doors were unlocked, and I fumbled my way inside. Past the bookshelves, at the far end of the library, were three small study rooms. They were soundproof; if Elliot wanted to isolate Vee, the rooms were an ideal place to put her.

I was just about to start toward them when a masculine groan carried through the library. I came to a halt.

The lights out in the hall powered to life, illuminating the darkness of the library. Elliot's body lay a few feet away, his mouth parted, his skin ashen. His eyes rolled my way, and he reached an arm out to me.

A piercing scream escaped me. Whirling around, I ran for the library doors, shoving and kicking chairs out of my way. Run! I ordered myself. Get to an exit!

I staggered out the door, and that's when the lights in the hall died, plunging everything once again to black.

"Patch!" I tried to scream. But my voice caught, and I choked on his name.

Jules was dead. Elliot was almost dead. Who had killed them? Who was left? I tried to make sense of what was happening, but all reason had left me.

A shove to my back threw me off balance. Another shove sent me flying sideways. My head smashed against a locker, stunning me.

A narrow beam of light swept across my vision, and a pair of dark eyes behind a ski mask swirled into focus. The light came from a miner's headlamp secured over the mask.

I pushed up and tried to run. One of his arms shot out, cutting off my escape. He brought up his other arm, trapping me against the locker.

"Did you think I was dead?" I could hear the gloating, icy smile in his voice. "I couldn't pass up one last chance to play with you. Humor me. Who did you think the bad guy was? Elliot? Or did it cross your mind that your best friend could do this? I'm getting warm, aren't I? That's the thing about fear. It brings out the worst in us."

"It's you." My voice rattled.

Jules ripped off the headlamp and ski mask. "In the flesh."

"How did you do it?" I asked, my voice still trembling. "I saw you. You weren't breathing. You were dead."

"You're giving me too much credit. It was all you, Nora. If your mind wasn't so weak, I couldn't have done a thing. Am I making you feel bad? Is it discouraging to know that out of all the minds I've invaded, yours tops the list as easiest? And most fun."

I licked my lips. My mouth tasted a strange combination of dry and sticky. I could smell the fear on my breath. "Where's Vee?"

He slapped my cheek. "Don't change the subject. You really should learn to control your fear. Fear undermines logic and opens up all sorts of opportunities for people like me."

This was a side of Jules I'd never seen. He'd always been so quiet, so sullen, radiating a complete lack of interest in everyone around him. He stayed in the background, drawing little attention, little suspicion. Very clever of him, I thought.

He grabbed my arm and jerked me after him.

I clawed at him and twisted away, and he drove his fist into my stomach. I stumbled backward, gasping for air that did not come. My shoulder dragged down a locker until I sat crumpled on the floor. A ribbon of air slipped down my throat, and I choked on it.

Jules touched the tracks my nails had carved in his forearm. "That's going to cost you."

"Why did you bring me here? What do you want?" I couldn't keep the hysteria from my voice.

He yanked me up by my arm and dragged me farther down the hall. Kicking a door open, he thrust me inside and I went down, my palms colliding with the hard floor. The door slammed behind me. The only light came from the headlamp, which Jules held.

The air held the familiar odors of chalk dust and stale chemicals. Posters of the human body and cross-sections of human cells decorated the walls. A long black granite counter with a sink stood at the front of the room. It faced rows of matching granite lab tables. We were inside Coach McConaughy's biology room.

A flash of metal caught my eye. A scalpel lay on the floor, tucked against the wastebasket. It must have been overlooked by both Coach and the janitor. I slid it into the waistband of my jeans just as Jules hauled me to my feet.

"I had to cut the electricity," he said, setting the headlamp on the nearest table. "You can't play hide-and-seek in the light."

Scraping two chairs across the floor, he positioned them facing each other. "Have a seat." It didn't sound like an invitation.

My eyes darted to the panel of windows spanning the far wall. I wondered if I could crank one open and escape before Jules caught me. Amid a thousand other self-preserving thoughts, I told myself not to appear frightened. Somewhere in the back of my mind I remembered that advice from a self-defense class I'd taken with Mom after my dad died. Make eye contact . . . look confident . . . use common sense . . . all easier said than done.

Jules pushed down on my shoulders, forcing me into a chair. The cold metal seeped through my jeans.

"Give me your cell phone," he ordered, hand held out for it.

"I left it in the car."

He breathed a laugh. "Do you really want to play games with me? I've got your best friend locked somewhere in the building. If you play games with me, she's going to feel left out. I'll have to think up an extra-special game to make it up to her."

I dug out the phone and passed it over.

With superhuman strength, he bent it in half. "Now it's just the two of us." He sank into the chair facing mine and stretched his legs out luxuriously. One arm dangled off the seat back. "Let's talk, Nora."

I bolted from the chair. Jules hooked me around the waist before I'd made it four steps and shoved me back into the chair.

"I used to own horses," he said. "A long time ago in France, I had a stable of beautiful horses. The Spanish horses were my favorite. They were caught wild and brought directly to me. Within weeks I had them subdued. But there was always the rare horse that refused to be broken. Do you know what I did with a horse that refused to be broken?"

I shuddered for an answer.

"Cooperate, and you have nothing to fear," he said.

I didn't for one moment believe him. The gleam in his eyes wasn't sincere.

"I saw Elliot in the library." I was surprised by the waver in my voice. I didn't like or trust Elliot, but he didn't deserve to die slowly and in pain. "Did you hurt him?"

He scooted closer, as if to share a secret. "If you're going to commit a crime, never leave evidence. Elliot's been an integral part of everything. He knows too much."

"Is that why I'm here? Because of the article I found about Kjirsten Halverson?"

Jules smiled. "Elliot failed to mention that you know about Kjirsten."

"Did Elliot kill her . . . or did you?" I asked on a cold snap of inspiration.

"I had to test Elliot's loyalty. I took away what was most important. Elliot was at Kinghorn on scholarship, and nobody let him forget it. Until me. I was his benefactor. In the end, it came down to choosing me or Kjirsten. More succinctly, choosing money or love. Apparently there's no pleasure in being a pauper among princes. I bought him off, and that's when I knew I could rely on him when it came time to dealing with you."

"Why me?"

"You haven't figured it out yet?" The light highlighted the ruthlessness in his face and created the illusion that his eyes had turned the color of molten silver. "I've been toying with you. Dangling you by a string. Using you as a proxy, because the person I really want to harm can't be harmed. Do you know who that person is?"

All the knots in my body seemed to come undone. My eyes moved out of focus. Jules's face was like an Impressionist painting—blurred around the edges, lacking detail. Blood drained from my head, and I felt myself start to slip off the chair. I'd felt this way enough times before to know I needed iron. Soon.

He slapped my cheek again. "Focus. Who am I talking about?"

"I don't know." I couldn't push my voice above a whisper.

"Do you know why he can't be hurt? Because he doesn't have

a human body. His body lacks physical sensation. If I locked him up and tortured him, it wouldn't do any good. He can't feel. Not an ounce of pain. Surely you've got a guess by now? You've been spending a lot of time with this person. Why so silent, Nora? Can't figure it out?"

A trickle of sweat crept down my back.

"Every year at the start of the Hebrew month of Cheshvan, he takes control of my body. Two whole weeks. That's how long I forfeit control. No freedom, no choice. I don't get the luxury of escaping during those two weeks, loaning my body out, then coming back when it's all over. Then I might be able to convince myself it wasn't really happening. No. I'm still in there, a prisoner inside my own body, living every moment of it," he said in a grinding tone. "Do you know what that feels like? Do you?" he shouted.

I kept my mouth shut, knowing that to talk would be dangerous. Jules laughed, a rush of air through his teeth. It sounded more sinister than anything I'd ever heard.

He said, "I swore an oath allowing him to take possession of my body during Cheshvan. I was sixteen years old." He shrugged, but it was a rigid movement. "He tricked me into the oath by torturing me. After, he told me I wasn't human. Can you believe it? Not human. He told me my mother, a human, slept with a fallen angel." He grinned odiously, sweat sprinkling his forehead. "Did I mention I inherited a few traits from my father? Just like him, I'm a deceiver. I make you see lies. I make you hear voices."

Just like this. Can you hear me, Nora? Are you frightened yet?

He tapped my forehead. "What's going on in there, Nora? Awfully quiet."

Jules was Chauncey. He was Nephilim. I remembered my birthmark, and what Dabria had told me. Jules and I shared the same blood. In my veins was the blood of a monster. I shut my eyes, and a tear slid out.

"Remember the night we first met? I jumped in front of the car you were driving. It was dark and there was fog. You were already on edge, which made it that much easier to deceive you. I enjoyed scaring you. That first night gave me a taste for it."

"I would have noticed it was you," I whispered. "There aren't many people as tall as you."

"You're not listening. I can make you see whatever I want. Do you really think I'd overlook a detail as condemning as my height? You saw what I wanted you to see. You saw a nondescript man in a black ski mask."

I sat there, feeling a tiny crack in my terror. I wasn't crazy. Jules was behind all of it. He was the crazy one. He could create mind games because his father was a fallen angel and he'd inherited the power. "You didn't really ransack my bedroom," I said. " You just made me think you did. That's why it was still in order when the police arrived."

He applauded slowly and deliberately. "Do you want to know the best part? You could have blocked me out. I couldn't have

362

touched your mind without your permission. I reached in, and you never resisted. You were weak. You were easy."

It all made sense, and instead of feeling a brief moment of relief, I realized how susceptible I was. I was stripped wide open. There was nothing stopping Jules from sucking me into his mind games, unless I learned to block him out.

"Imagine yourself in my place," said Jules. "Your body violated year after year. Imagine a hatred so hard, nothing but revenge will cure it. Imagine expending large sums of energy and resources to keep a close eye on the object of your revenge, waiting patiently for the moment when fate presented you an opportunity not just to get even, but to tip the scales in your favor." His eyes locked on mine. "You're that opportunity. If I hurt you, I hurt Patch."

"You're overestimating my value to Patch," I said, cold sweat breaking out along my hairline.

"I've been keeping a close eye on Patch for centuries. Last summer he made his first trip to your house, though you didn't notice. He followed you shopping a few times. Every now and then, he made a special trip out of his way to find you. Then he enrolled at your school. I couldn't help but ask myself, what was so special about you? I made an effort to find out. I've been watching you for a while now."

Nothing short of dread gripped me. Right then, I knew it was never my dad's presence I'd felt, following me like a phantom guardian. It was Jules. I felt the same ice-cold, unearthly presence now, only amplified a hundred times.

"I didn't want to draw Patch's suspicion and backed off," he continued. "That's when Elliot stepped forward, and it didn't take him long to tell me what I'd already guessed. Patch is in love with you."

It all clicked into place. Jules hadn't been sick the night he disappeared into the men's room at Delphic. And he hadn't been sick the night we went to the Borderline. All along it was the simple fact that he had to remain invisible to Patch. The moment Patch saw him, it would all be over. Patch would know Jules—Chauncey—was up to something. Elliot was Jules's eyes and ears, feeding information back to him.

"The plan was to kill you on the camping trip, but Elliot failed to convince you to come," Jules said. "Earlier today, I followed you out of Blind Joe's and shot you. Imagine my surprise when I found I'd killed a bag lady dressed in your coat. But it all worked out." His tone relaxed. "Here we are."

I shifted in my seat, and the scalpel slid deeper into my jeans. If I wasn't careful, it would slip out of reach. If Jules forced me to stand, it might slide all the way down my trouser leg. And that would be the end of that.

"Let me guess what you're thinking," said Jules, rising to his feet and sauntering to the front of the room. "You're starting to wish you'd never met Patch. You wish he'd never fallen in love with you.

Go on. Laugh at the position he's put you in. Laugh at your own bad choice."

Hearing Jules talk about Patch's love filled me with irrational hope.

I fumbled the scalpel out of my jeans and jumped from my seat. "Don't come near me! I'll stab you. I swear I will!"

Jules made a guttural sound and flung his arm across the counter at the front of the room. Glass beakers shattered against the chalkboard, papers fluttering down. He strode toward me. In a panic, I brought the scalpel up as hard as I could. It met his palm, slicing through skin.

Jules hissed and drew back.

Not waiting, I plunged the scalpel down into his thigh.

Jules gaped at the metal protruding from his leg. He jerked it out using both hands, his face contorting in pain. He opened his hands, and the scalpel fell with a clatter.

He took a faltering step toward me.

I shrieked and dodged away, but my hip clipped the edge of a table; I lost my footing and tumbled down. The scalpel lay several feet away.

Jules flipped me on my stomach and straddled me from behind He pressed my face into the floor, crushing my nose and muffling my screams.

"Valiant attempt," he grunted. "But that won't kill me. I'm Nephilim. I'm immortal."

I grabbed for the scalpel, digging my toes into the floor to stretch those last, vital inches. My fingers fumbled over it. I was so close, and then Jules was dragging me back.

I brought my heel up hard between his legs; he groaned and went limp off to one side. I scrambled to my feet, but Jules rolled to the door, kneeling between me and it.

His hair hung in his eyes. Beads of sweat trickled down his face. His mouth was lopsided, one half curled up in pain.

Every muscle in my body was coiled, ready to spring into action.

"Good luck trying to escape," he said with a cynical smile that seemed to require a lot of effort. "You'll see what I mean." Then he sank to the ground.

I HAD NO IDEA WHERE VEE WAS. THE OBVIOUS THOUGHT came to me to think like Jules—where would I hold Vee hostage if I were him?

He wants to make it hard to escape and hard to be found, I reasoned.

I brought up a mental blueprint of the building, narrowing my attention to the upper levels. Chances were, Vee was on the third floor, the highest in the school—except for a small fourth floor, which was more of an attic than anything else. A narrow staircase accessible only from the third floor led up to it. There were two bungalow-style classrooms at the top: AP Spanish and the eZine lab.

Vee was in the eZine lab. Just like that, I knew it.

Moving as quickly as I could through the darkness, I felt my way up two flights of stairs. After some trial and error, I found the narrow staircase leading to the eZine lab. At the top, I pushed on the door.

"Vee?" I called softly.

She let out a small moan.

"It's me," I said, taking each step with care as I maneuvered up an aisle of desks, not wanting to knock over a chair and alert Jules to my location. "Are you hurt? We need to get out of here." I found her huddled at the front of the room, hugging her knees to her chest.

"Jules hit me over the head," she said, her voice rising. "I think I passed out. Now I can't see. I can't see anything!"

"Listen to me. Jules cut the electricity and the shades are drawn. It's just the darkness. Hold my hand. We have to get downstairs right now."

"I think he damaged something. My head is throbbing. I really think I'm blind!"

"You're not blind," I whispered, giving her a small shake. "I can't see either. We have to feel our way downstairs. We're going to leave through the exit by the athletics office."

"He's got chains on all the doors."

A moment of rigid silence dropped between us. I remembered Jules wishing me luck escaping, and now I knew why. A perceptible chill rippled from my heart through the rest of my body. "Not the door I came in," I said at last. "The far east door is unlocked."

"It must be the only one. I was with him when he chained the others. He said that way nobody would be tempted to go outside while we played hide-and-seek. He said outside was out-of-bounds."

"If the east door is the only one left unlocked, he'll try to block it. He'll wait for us to come to him. But we're not going to. We're going out a window," I said, devising a plan off the top of my head. "On the opposite end of the building—this end. Do you have your cell?"

"Jules took it."

"When we get outside, we have to split up. If Jules chases us, he'll have to choose one of us to follow. The other will get help." I already knew who he'd choose. Jules had no use for Vee, except to lure me here tonight. "Run as hard as you can and get to a phone. Call the police. Tell them Elliot is in the library."

"Alive?" Vee asked, her voice trembling.

"I don't know."

We stood huddled together, and I felt her pull her shirt up and wipe her eyes. "This is all my fault."

"This is Jules's fault."

"I'm scared."

"We're going to be fine," I said, attempting to sound optimistic. "I stabbed Jules in the leg with a scalpel. He's bleeding heavily. Maybe he'll give up chasing us and go get medical attention."

A sob escaped Vee. We both knew I was lying. Jules's desire for revenge outweighed his wound. It outweighed everything.

Vee and I crept down the stairs, keeping tight to the walls, until we were back on the main floor.

"This way," I whispered in her ear, holding her hand as we speed-walked down the hall, heading farther west.

We hadn't walked very far when a guttural sound, not quite laughter, rolled out of the tunnel of darkness ahead.

"Well, well, what do we have here?" Jules said. There was no face attached to his voice.

"Run," I told Vee, squeezing her hand. "He wants me. Call the police. Run!"

Vee dropped my hand and ran. Her footsteps faded depressingly fast. I wondered briefly if Patch was still in the building, but it was more of a side thought. Most of my concentration went into not passing out. Because once again, I found myself all alone with Jules.

"It will take the police at least twenty minutes to respond," Jules told me, the tap of his shoes drawing closer. "I don't need twenty minutes."

I turned and ran. Jules broke into a run behind me.

Fumbling my hands over the walls, I turned right at the first intersection and raced down a perpendicular hall. Forced to rely on the walls to guide me, my hands slapped over the sharp edges of lockers and doorjambs, nicking my skin. I made another right, running as fast as I could for the double doors of the gymnasium.

The only thought pounding through my head was that if I could get to my gym locker in time, I could lock myself inside it. The girls' locker room was wall-to-wall and floor-to-ceiling with oversize lockers. It would take Jules time to break into each one individually. If I was lucky, the police would arrive before he found me.

I flung myself into the gym and ran for the attached girls' locker room. As soon as I pushed on the door handle, I felt a spike of cold terror. The door was locked. I rattled the handle again, but it didn't give. Spinning around, I searched frantically for another exit, but I was trapped in the gym. I fell back against the door, squeezed my eyes shut to stave off fainting, and listened to my breath hitch up.

When I reopened my eyes, Jules was walking into the haze of moonlight trickling through the skylights. He'd knotted his shirt around his thigh; a stain of blood seeped through the fabric. He was left in a white undershirt and chinos. A gun was tucked into the waistband of his pants.

"Please let me go," I whispered.

"Vee told me something interesting about you. You're afraid of heights." He lifted his gaze to the rafters high above the gym. A smile split his face.

The stagnant air was sodden with the smells of sweat and wood varnish. The heat had been turned off for spring break and the temperature was icy. Shadows stretched back and forth across the polished floor as the moonlight broke through the clouds. Jules stood with his back to the bleachers, and I saw Patch move behind him.

"Did you attack Marcie Millar?" I asked Jules, ordering myself not to react and give Patch away.

"Elliot told me there's bad blood between the two of you. I didn't like the idea of someone else having the pleasure of tormenting my girl."

"And my bedroom window? Did you spy on me while I was sleeping?"

"Nothing personal."

Jules stiffened. He stepped forward suddenly and jerked on my wrist, spinning me around in front of him. I felt what I feared was the gun press into the nape of my neck. "Take off your hat," Jules ordered Patch. "I want to see the expression on your face when I kill her. You're helpless to save her. As helpless as I was to do anything about the oath I swore to you."

Patch took a couple of steps closer. He moved easily, but I sensed his tightly reined caution. The gun probed deeper, and I winced.

"Take another step and this will be her last breath," Jules warned.

Patch glanced at the distance between us, calculating how quickly he could cover it. Jules saw it too.

"Don't try it," he said.

"You're not going to shoot her, Chauncey."

"No?" Jules squeezed the trigger. The gun clicked, and I opened my mouth to scream, but all that came out was a tremulous sob.

"Revolver," Jules explained. "The other five chambers are loaded."

Ready to use those boxing moves you're always bragging about? Patch said to my mind.

My pulse was all over the place, my legs barely holding me up. "W-what?" I stammered.

Without warning, a rush of power coursed into me. The foreign force expanded to fill me. My body was completely vulnerable to Patch, all my strength and freedom forfeited as he took possession of me.

Before I had time to realize just how much this loss of control terrified me, a crushing pain spiked through my hand, and I realized Patch was using my fist to punch Jules. The gun was knocked loose; it skidded across the gym floor out of reach.

Patch commanded my hands to slam Jules backward against the bleachers. Jules tripped, falling into them.

The next thing I knew, my hands were closing on Jules's throat, flinging his head back against the bleachers with a loud crack! I held him there, pressing my fingers into his neck. His eyes widened, then bulged. He was trying to speak, moving his lips unintelligibly, but Patch didn't let up.

I won't be able to stay inside you much longer, Patch spoke to my thoughts. *It's not Cheshvan and I'm not allowed. As soon as I'm cast out, run. Do you understand? Run as fast as you can. Chauncey will be too weak and stunned to get inside your head. Run and don't stop.*

A high humming sound whined through me, and I felt my body peeling away from Patch's.

The vessels in Jules's neck jumped out and his head drooped to one side. *Come on,* I heard Patch urge him. *Pass out ... pass out ...*

But it was too late. Patch vanished from inside me. He was gone so suddenly, I was left dizzy.

My hands were in my control again, and they sprang away from Jules's neck on impulse. He gasped for air and blinked up at me. Patch was on the floor a few feet away, unmoving.

I remembered what Patch had said and sprinted across the gym. I flung myself against the door, expecting to sail into the hall. Instead it was like hitting a wall. I shoved the push bar, knowing the door was unlocked. Five minutes ago I'd come through it. I hurled all my weight against the door. It didn't open.

I turned around, the adrenaline letdown causing my knees to shake. "Get out of my mind!" I screamed at Jules.

Pulling himself up to sit on the lowest rise of the bleachers, Jules massaged his throat. "No," he said.

I tried the door again. I got my foot up and kicked the push bar.

I smacked my palms against the door's slit of a window. "Help! Can anyone hear me? Help!"

Looking over my shoulder, I found Jules limping toward me, his injured leg buckling under each step. I squeezed my eyes shut, trying to focus my mind. The door would open as soon as I found his voice and swept it out. I searched every corner of my mind but couldn't find him. He was somewhere deep, hiding from me. I opened my eyes. Jules was much closer. I was going to have to find another way out.

Drilled into the wall above the bleachers was an iron ladder. It reached to the grid of rafters at the top of the gym. At the far end of the rafters, on the opposite wall, almost directly above where I stood, was an air shaft. If I could get to it, I could climb in and find another way down.

I broke into a dead sprint past Jules and up the bleachers. My shoes slapped the wood, echoing through the empty space, making it impossible to hear whether Jules was following me. I got my footing on the first ladder rung and hoisted myself up. I climbed one rung, then another. Out of the corner of my eye, I saw the drinking fountain far below. It was small, which meant I was high. Very high.

Don't look down, I ordered myself. Concentrate on what's above. I tentatively climbed one more rung. The ladder rattled, not properly welded to the wall.

Jules's laughter carried up to me, and my concentration slipped.

Images of falling flashed in my mind. Logically, I knew he was planting them. Then my brain tilted, and I couldn't remember which way was up or down. I couldn't decipher which thoughts were mine and which belonged to Jules.

My fear was so thick it blurred my vision. I didn't know where on the ladder I stood. Were my feet centered? Was I close to slipping? Clenching the rung with both hands, I pressed my forehead against my knuckles. Breathe, I told myself. Breathe!

And then I heard it.

The slow, agonizing sound of metal creaking. I closed my eyes to suppress a dizzy spell.

The metal brackets securing the top of the ladder to the wall popped free. The metallic groan changed to a high-pitched whine as the next set of brackets down tore from the wall. I watched with a scream trapped in my throat as the entire top half of the ladder broke free. Locking my arms and legs around the ladder, I braced myself for the backward fall. The ladder wavered a moment in air, patiently succumbing to gravity.

And then it all happened quickly. The rafters and skylights faded away into a dizzying blur. I flew down until, suddenly, the ladder slammed to a stop. It bounced up and down, perpendicular to the wall, thirty feet above ground. The impact jerked my legs loose, my hands my only attachment to the ladder.

"Help!" I screamed, my legs bicycling through air.

The ladder lurched, dropping several more feet. One of my

shoes slid down my foot, caught on my toe, then dropped. Far too long later, it hit the gym floor.

I bit down on my tongue as the pain in my arms deepened. They were tearing out of their sockets.

And then, through the fear and panic, I heard Patch's voice. *Block him out. Keep climbing. The ladder's intact.*

"I can't," I sobbed. "I'll fall!"

Block him out. Close your eyes. Listen to my voice.

Swallowing, I forced my eyes shut. I clung to Patch's voice and felt a sturdy surface take shape beneath me. My feet were no longer hanging in air. I felt one of the ladder rungs digging into the balls of my feet. Focusing with resolve on Patch's voice, I waited until the world crept back into place. Patch was right. I was on the ladder. It was upright, secured to the wall. I regained a measure of determination and continued climbing.

At the top I eased myself precariously onto the closest rafter. I got my arms around it, then swung my right leg up and over. I was facing the wall, with my back to the air shaft, but there was nothing I could do now. Very carefully, I rose up on my knees. Using all my concentration, I starting inching backward across the expanse of the gym.

But it was too late.

Jules had climbed quickly, and was now less than fifteen feet away from me. He climbed onto the rafter. Hand over hand, he dragged himself toward me. A dark slash on the inside of his wrist caught my eye. It intersected his veins at a ninety-degree angle and was nearly black in color. To anyone else, it might have looked like a scar. To me, it meant so much more. The family connection was obvious. We shared the same blood, and it showed in our identical marks.

We were both straddling the rafter, sitting face-to-face, ten feet apart.

"Any last words?" Jules said.

I looked down, even though it made me dizzy. Patch was far below on the gym floor, still as death. Right then, I wanted to go back in time and relive every moment with him. One more secret smile, one more shared laugh. One more electric kiss. Finding him was like finding someone I didn't know I was searching for. He'd come into my life too late, and now was leaving too soon. I remembered him telling me he'd give up everything for me. He already had. He'd given up a human body of his own so I could live.

I wobbled accidentally, and instinctively dropped lower to balance myself.

Jules's laughter carried like a cold whisper. "It makes no difference to me whether I shoot you or you fall to your death."

"It does make a difference," I said, my voice small but confident. "You and I share the same blood." I lifted my hand precariously, showing him my birthmark. "I'm your descendant. If I sacrifice my blood, Patch will become human and you'll die. It's written in The Book of Enoch."

Jules's eyes were devoid of light. They were trained on me, absorbing every word I spoke. I could tell by his expression that he was weighing my words. A flush rose in his face, and I knew he believed me. "You—" he sputtered.

He slid toward me with frantic speed, simultaneously reaching into his waistband to draw the gun.

Tears stung my eyes. With no time for second thoughts, I threw myself off the rafter.

A DOOR OPENED AND CLOSED. I WAITED TO HEAR footsteps approach, but the only sound came from the ticking of a clock: a rhythmic, steady pounding through the silence.

The sound began to fade, winding down. I wondered if I would hear it stop completely. I suddenly feared that moment, unsure of what came after.

A much more vibrant sound eclipsed the clock. It was a

reassuring, ethereal sound, a melodic dance on air. Wings, I thought. Coming to take me away.

I held my breath, waiting, waiting, waiting. And then the clock began to go in reverse. Instead of slowing, the beat became more certain. A spiral-like liquid formed inside me, coiling deeper and deeper. I felt myself pulled into the current. I was sliding down through myself, into a dark, warm place.

My eyes flickered open to familiar oak paneling on the sloped ceiling above me. My bedroom. A sense of reassurance flooded over me, and then I remembered where I'd been. In the gym with Jules.

A shiver slid over my skin.

"Patch?" I said, my voice hoarse from disuse. I tried to sit up, then gave a muffled cry. Something was wrong with my body. Every muscle, bone, cell was sore. I felt like one giant bruise.

There was movement near the doorway. Patch leaned against the doorjamb. His mouth was pressed tight and lacked its usual twinge of humor. His eyes held more depth than I'd ever seen before. They were sharpened by a protective edge.

"That was a good fight back in the gym," he said. "But I think you could benefit from a few more boxing lessons."

On a wave, everything came back to me. Tears rolled up from deep inside me. "What happened? Where is Jules? How did I get here?" My voice cracked with panic. "I threw myself off the rafter."

"That took a lot of courage." Patch's voice turned husky, and he stepped all the way inside my bedroom. He closed the door behind him, and I knew it was his way of trying to lock out all the bad. He was putting a divide between me and everything that had happened.

He walked over and sat on the bed beside me. "What else do you remember?"

I tried to piece my memories together, working backward. I remembered the beating wings I'd heard shortly after I flung myself off the rafter. Without any doubt, I knew I'd died. I knew an angel had come to carry my soul away.

"I'm dead, aren't I?" I said quietly, reeling with fright. "Am I a ghost?"

"When you jumped, the sacrifice killed Jules. Technically, when you came back, he should have too. But since he didn't have a soul, he had nothing to revive his body."

"I came back?" I said, hoping I wasn't filling myself with false hope.

"I didn't accept your sacrifice. I turned it down."

I felt a small Oh form at my mouth, but it never quite made it past my lips. "Are you saying you gave up getting a human body for me?"

He lifted my bandaged hand. Underneath all the gauze, my knuckles throbbed from punching Jules. Patch kissed each finger, taking his time, keeping his eyes glued to mine. "What good is a body if I can't have you?"

Heavier teardrops rolled down my cheeks, and Patch pulled me to him, tucking my head against his chest. Very slowly the panic edged away, and I knew it was all over. I was going to be all right.

Suddenly I pulled away. If Patch had turned down the sacrifice, then—

"You saved my life. Turn around," I ordered solemnly.

Patch gave a sly smile and indulged my request. I rucked his T-shirt up to his shoulders. His back was smooth, defined muscle. The scars were gone.

"You can't see my wings," he said. "They're made of spiritual matter."

"You're a guardian angel now." I was still too much in awe to wrap my mind around it, but at the same time I felt amazement, curiosity . . . happiness.

"I'm your guardian angel," he said.

"I get my very own guardian angel? What, exactly, is your job description?"

"Guard your body." His smile tipped higher. "I take my job seriously, which means I'm going to need to get acquainted with the subject matter on a personal level."

My stomach went all fluttery. "Does this mean you can feel now?"

Patch watched me in silence for a moment. "No, but it does mean I'm not blacklisted."

Downstairs, I heard the quiet rumble of the garage door gliding open.

"My mom!" I gasped. I found the clock on the nightstand. It was just after two in the morning. "They must have opened the bridge. How does this whole guardian angel business work? Am I the only person who can see you? I mean, are you invisible to everyone else?"

Patch stared at me like he hoped I wasn't serious.

"You're not invisible?" I squeaked. "You have to get out of here!" I made a movement to push Patch off the bed but was cut short by a searing jab in my ribs. "She'll kill me if she finds you in here. Can you climb trees? Tell me you can climb a tree!"

Patch grinned. "I can fly."

Oh. Right. Well, okay.

"The police and fire department were here earlier," Patch said. "The master bedroom will need to be gutted, but they stopped the fire from spreading. The police will be back. They're going to have a few questions. If I had to guess, they already tried reaching you on the cell you called 911 on."

"Jules took it."

He nodded. "I figured. I don't care what you tell the police, but I'd appreciate it if you left me out of it." He slid my bedroom window open. "Last thing. Vee got to the police in time. Paramedics saved Elliot. He's in the hospital, but he'll be all right."

Down the hall, at the bottom of the stairs, I heard the house door shut. My mom was inside.

"Nora?" she called. She tossed her purse and keys on the entry table. Her high heels clicked across the wood floors, almost at a running pace. "Nora! There's police tape on the front door! What is going on?"

I looked to the window. Patch was gone, but a single black feather was pressed to the outer pane, held in place by last night's rain. Or angel magic.

Downstairs, my mom flicked on the hall light, a faint ray of it stretching all the way under the crack at the bottom of my door. I held my breath and counted seconds, assuming I had about two more before—

She shrieked. "Nora! What happened to the banister!"

Good thing she hadn't seen her bedroom yet.

The sky was a perfect, rinsed blue. The sun was just starting to fan out across the horizon. It was Monday, a brand-new day, the horrors of the past twenty-four hours far behind. I had five hours of sleep under my belt, and other than the all-over body pain that came from being sucked into death, then spat back out, I felt remarkably refreshed. I didn't want to hang a black cloud over the moment by reminding myself that the police were expected to arrive any minute to take my statement on the night's events. I still hadn't made up my mind what I was going to tell them.

I padded to the bathroom in my nightshirt—mentally blocking the question of how I'd changed into it, since I'd presumably been wearing clothes when Patch brought me home—and sped through my morning routine. I splashed cold water on my face, scrubbed my teeth, and tamed my hair back into a rubber band. In my bedroom, I pulled on a clean shirt, clean jeans.

I called Vee.

"How are you doing?" I asked.

"Good. How are you?"

"Good."

Silence.

"Okay," Vee said in a rush, "I am still totally freaked out. You?"

"Totally."

"Patch called me in the middle of the night. He said Jules roughed you up pretty bad, but that you were okay."

"Really? Patch called you?"

"He called from the Jeep. He said you were asleep in the backseat and he was driving you home. He said he just happened to be driving past the high school when he heard a scream. He said he found you in the gym, but that you'd fainted from pain. The next thing he knew, he looked up and saw Jules jump off the rafter. He said Jules must have snapped, a side effect from all the burdensome guilt he felt over terrorizing you."

I didn't realize I was holding my breath until I let go of it. Obviously, Patch had manipulated a few details.

"You know I'm not buying it," Vee continued. "You know I think Patch killed Jules."

In Vee's position, I'd probably think similarly. I said, "What do the police think?"

"Turn on the TV. There's live coverage right now, Channel Five. They're saying Jules broke into the school and jumped. They're ruling it a tragic teen suicide. They're asking people with information to call the hotline listed at the bottom of the screen."

"What did you tell the police when you first called it in?"

"I was scared. I didn't want to get busted for B and E. So I called in anonymously from a pay phone."

"Well," I said at last, "if the police are ruling it a suicide, I guess that's what happened. After all, this is modern-day America. We have the benefit of forensics."

"You're keeping something from me," said Vee. "What really happened after I left?"

This is where it got sticky. Vee was my best friend, and we lived by the motto No Secrets. But some things are just impossible to explain. The fact that Patch was a fallen-turned-guardian angel topped the list. Directly below it was the fact that I'd jumped off a rafter and died, but was still alive today.

"I remember Jules cornering me in the gym," I said. "He told me all the pain and fear he was going to inflict. After that, the details get hazy."

"Is it too late to apologize?" Vee said, sounding more sincere than she had in our whole friendship. "You were right about Jules and Elliot."

"Apology accepted."

"We should go to the mall," she said. "I feel this overwhelming need to buy shoes. Lots of them. What we need is some good old-fashioned shoe-shopping therapy."

The doorbell rang, and I glanced at the clock. "I have to give the police my statement about what happened last night, but I'll call you after that."

"Last night?" Vee's tone shot up with panic. "They know you were at the school? You didn't give them my name, did you?"

"Actually, something happened earlier in the night." Something named Dabria. "I'll call you soon," I said, hanging up before I had to lie my way through another explanation.

Limping down the hall, I'd made it as far as the top of the stairs when I saw who my mom had invited inside.

Detectives Basso and Holstijic.

She led them into the living room, and although Detective Holstijic collapsed onto the sofa, Detective Basso remained standing. He had his back to me, but a step creaked halfway through my descent, and he turned around.

"Nora Grey," he said in his tough cop voice. "We meet again."

My mom blinked. "You've met before?"

"Your daughter has an exciting life. Seems like we're here every week."

My mom aimed a questioning glance at me and I shrugged, clueless, as if to guess, Cop humor?

"Why don't you have a seat, Nora, and tell us what happened," Detective Holstijic said.

I lowered myself into one of the plush armchairs opposite the sofa. "Just before nine last night I was in the kitchen drinking a glass of chocolate milk when Miss Greene, my school psychologist, appeared."

"She just walked into your house?" Detective Basso asked.

"She told me I had something she wanted, and that's when I ran upstairs and locked myself in the master bedroom."

"Back up," said Detective Basso. "What was this thing she wanted?"

"She didn't say. But she did mention she's not a real psychologist. She said she was using the job to spy on students." I divided a glance among everyone. "She's crazy, right?"

The detectives shared a look.

"I'll run her name, see what I can find," Detective Holstijic said, pulling himself back to his feet.

"Let me get this straight," Detective Basso said to me. "She accused you of stealing something that belonged to her, but she never said what?"

Another sticky question. "She was hysterical. I only understood half of what she was saying. I ran and locked myself inside the master bedroom, but she broke down the door. I was hiding inside the flue of the fireplace, and she said she'd burn the house down room by room to find me. Then she started a fire. Right there in the middle of the room."

"How did she start the fire?" my mom asked.

"I couldn't see. I was in the flue."

"This is crazy," Detective Basso said, shaking his head. "I've never seen anything like this."

"Is she going to come back?" my mom asked the detectives, coming over to stand behind me and placing her hands protectively on my shoulders. "Is Nora safe?"

"Might want to see about getting a security system installed." Detective Basso opened his wallet and held out a card to Mom. "I vouch for these guys. Tell them I sent you, and they'll give you a discount."

A few hours after the detectives left, the doorbell rang again.

"That must be the alarm system company," Mom said, meeting me in the hall. "I called, and they said they'd send a guy out today. I can't stand the thought of sleeping here without some kind of protection until they find Miss Greene and lock her away. Didn't the school even bother to check her references?" She opened the door, and Patch stood on the porch. He wore faded Levi's and a snug white T-shirt, and he held a toolbox in his left hand.

"Good afternoon, Mrs. Grey."

"Patch." I couldn't quite nail my mom's tone. Surprise mixed with discomfiture. "Are you here to see Nora?"

Patch smiled. "I'm here to spec your house for a new alarm system."

"I thought you had a different job," said Mom. "I thought you bussed tables at the Borderline."

"I got a new job." Patch locked eyes with me, and I warmed in a lot of places. In fact, I was dangerously close to feverish. "Outside?" he asked me.

I followed him out to his motorcycle.

"We still have a lot to talk about," I said.

"Talk?" He shook his head, his eyes full of desire. Kiss, he whispered to my thoughts.

It wasn't a question, but a warning. He grinned when I didn't protest, and lowered his mouth toward mine. The first touch was just that—a touch. A teasing, tempting softness. I licked my lips and Patch's grin deepened.

"More?" he asked.

I curled my hands into his hair, pulling him closer. "More."

II
CRESCENDO

To Jenn Martin and Rebecca Sutton,
for your friendship superpowers!
Thanks also to T. J. Fritsche,
for suggesting the character
name Ecanus.

PROLOGUE

THE FINGERS OF THE THORN-APPLE TREE CLAWED at the windowpane behind Harrison Grey, and he dog-eared his page, no longer able to read through the racket. A furious spring wind had hurled itself against the farmhouse all night, howling and whistling, causing the shutters to slam against the clapboards with a repetitive bang! bang! bang! The calendar may have been turned to March, but Harrison knew better than to think spring was on its way. With a storm blowing in, he wouldn't be surprised to find the countryside frozen in icy whiteness by morning.

To drown out the wind's piercing cry, Harrison punched the remote, turning up Bononcini's "Ombra mai fu." Then he set another log on the fire, asking himself, not for the first time, if he would have bought the farmhouse had he known how much fuel it took to warm one little room, let alone all nine.

The phone shrilled.

Harrison picked it up halfway through the second ring, expecting to hear the voice of his daughter's best friend, who had the annoying habit of calling at the latest possible hour the night before homework was due.

Shallow, rapid breathing sounded in his ear before a voice broke the static. "We need to meet. How soon can you be here?"

The voice floated through Harrison, a ghost from his past, leaving him bone cold. It had been a long time since he'd heard the voice, and hearing it now could only mean something had gone wrong. Terribly wrong. He realized the phone in his hand was slick with sweat, his posture rigid.

"An hour," he answered flatly.

He was slow to replace the handset. He shut his eyes, his mind unwillingly traveling back. There had been a time, fifteen years ago, when he froze at the sound of the phone ringing, the seconds pounding out like drums as he waited for the voice on the other end to speak. Over time, as one peaceful year replaced another, he'd eventually convinced himself he was a man who'd outrun the secrets of his past. He was a man living a normal life, a man with a beautiful family. A man with nothing to fear.

In the kitchen, standing over the sink, Harrison poured himself a glass of water and tossed it back. It was full dark outside, and his waxen reflection stared back from the window straight ahead. Harrison nodded, as if to tell himself everything would be all right. But his eyes were heavy with lies.

He loosened his tie to relieve the tightness within him that seemed to stretch his skin, and poured a second glass. The water swam uneasily inside him, threatening to come back up. Setting the glass in the basin of the sink, he reached for the car keys on the counter, hesitating once as if to change his mind.

Harrison eased the car to the curb and killed the headlights. Sitting in darkness, breath smoking, he took in the ramshackle brick row houses in a seedy section of Portland. It had been years— fifteen to be exact—since he had set foot in the neighborhood, and relying on his rusty memory, he wasn't sure he was in the right place. He popped open the glove box and retrieved a time-yellowed scrap of paper. 1565 Monroe. He was about to swing out of the car, but the silence on the streets bothered him. Reaching beneath his seat, he pulled out a loaded Smith & Wesson and tucked it into the waistband of his trousers at the small of his back. He hadn't aimed a gun since college, and never outside a shooting range. The only clear thought in his throbbing head was that he hoped he could still say as much an hour from now.

The tap of Harrison's shoes sounded loud on the deserted pavement, but he ignored the rhythm, choosing instead to focus his attention on the shadows cast by the silver moon. Hunkering deeper into his coat, he passed cramped dirt yards boxed in by chain-link fences, the houses beyond them dark and eerily quiet. Twice he felt as if he was being followed, but when he glanced back, there was no one.

At 1565 Monroe, he let himself through the gate and circled around to the back of the house. He knocked once and saw a shadow move behind the lace curtains.

The door cracked.

"It's me," Harrison said, keeping his voice low.

The door opened just wide enough to admit him.

"Were you followed?" he was asked.

"No."

"She's in trouble."

Harrison's heart quickened. "What kind of trouble?"

"Once she turns sixteen, he'll come for her. You need to take her far away. Someplace where he'll never find her."

Harrison shook his head. "I don't understand—"

He was cut off by a menacing glare. "When we made this agreement, I told you there would be things you couldn't understand. Sixteen is a cursed age in—in my world. That's all you need to know," he finished brusquely.

The two men watched each other, until at last Harrison gave a wary nod.

"You have to cover your tracks," he was told. "Wherever you go, you have to start over. No one can know you came from Maine. No one. He'll never stop looking for her. Do you understand?"

"I understand." But *would his wife? Would Nora?*

Harrison's vision was adapting to the darkness, and he noted with curious disbelief that the man standing before him appeared not to have aged a day since their last meeting. In fact, he hadn't aged a day since college, when they'd met as roommates and become fast friends. *A trick of the shadows?* Harrison wondered. There was nothing else to attribute it to. One thing had changed, though. There was a small scar at the base of his friend's throat. Harrison took a closer look at the disfigurement and flinched. A burn mark, raised and shiny, hardly larger than a quarter. It was in the shape of a clenched fist. To his shock and horror, Harrison realized his friend had been branded. Like cattle.

His friend sensed the direction of Harrison's gaze, and his eyes turned steely, defensive. "There are people who want to destroy me. Who want to demoralize and dehumanize me. Together with a trusted friend, I've formed a society. More members are being initiated all the time." He stopped mid-breath, as if unsure how much more he should say, then finished hastily, "We organized the society to give us protection, and I've sworn allegiance to it. If you know me as well as you once did, you know I'll do whatever it takes to protect my interests." He paused and added almost absently, "And my future."

"They branded you," Harrison said, hoping his friend didn't detect the repulsion that shuddered through him.

His friend merely looked at him.

After a moment, Harrison nodded, signaling he understood, even if he didn't accept it. The less he knew, the better. His friend had made that clear too many times to count. "Is there anything else I can do?"

"Just keep her safe."

Harrison pushed his glasses up the bridge of his nose. He began awkwardly, "I thought you might like to know she's grown up healthy and strong. We named her Nor—"

"I don't want to be reminded of her name," his friend interrupted harshly. "I've done everything in my power to stamp it out from my mind. I don't want to know anything about her. I want my mind washed of any trace of her, so I've got nothing to give that bastard." He turned his back, and Harrison took the gesture to mean the conversation was over. Harrison stood a moment, so many questions at the tip of his tongue, but at the same time, knowing nothing good would come from pressing. Stifling his need to make sense of this dark world his daughter had done nothing to deserve, he let himself out.

He'd only made it a half block when a gunshot ripped through the night. Instinctively Harrison dropped low and whirled around.

His friend. A second shot was fired, and without thinking, he ran in a dead sprint back toward the house. He shoved through the gate and cut around the side yard. He had almost rounded the final corner when arguing voices caused him to stop. Despite the cold, he was sweating. The backyard was shrouded in darkness, and he inched along the garden wall, careful to avoid kicking loose stones that would give him away, until the back door came into sight.

"Last chance," said a smooth, calm voice Harrison didn't recognize.

"Go to hell," his friend spat.

A third gunshot. His friend bellowed in pain, and the shooter called over him, "Where is she?"

Heart hammering, Harrison knew he had to act. Another five seconds and it could be too late. He slid his hand to his lower back and drew the gun. Two-handing it to steady his grip, he moved toward the doorway, approaching the dark-haired shooter from behind. Harrison saw his friend beyond the shooter, but when he made eye contact, his friend's expression filled with alarm.

Go!

Harrison heard his friend's order as loud as a bell, and for a moment believed it had been shouted out loud. But when the shooter didn't spin around in surprise, Harrison realized with cold confusion that his friend's voice had sounded inside his head.

No, Harrison thought back with a silent shake of his head, his sense of loyalty outweighing what he couldn't comprehend. This was the man he'd spent four of the best years of his life with. The man who'd introduced him to his wife. He wasn't going to leave him here at the hands of a killer.

Harrison pulled the trigger. He heard the earsplitting shot and waited for the shooter to crumple. Harrison shot another time. And another.

The dark-haired young man turned slowly. For the first time in his life, Harrison found himself truly afraid. Afraid of the young man standing before him, gun in hand. Afraid of death. Afraid of what would become of his family.

He felt the shots rip through him with a searing fire that seemed to shatter him into a thousand pieces. He dropped to his knees. He saw his wife's face blur across his vision, followed by his daughter's. He opened his mouth, their names at his lips, and tried to find a way to say how much he loved them before it was too late.

The young man had his hands on Harrison now, dragging him into the alley at the rear of the house. Harrison could feel consciousness leaving him as he struggled without success to get his feet under him. He couldn't fail his daughter. There would be no one to protect her. This black-haired shooter would find her and, if his friend was right, kill her.

"Who are you?" Harrison asked, the words causing fire to spread through his chest. He clung to the hope that there was still time. Maybe he could warn Nora from the next world—a world that was closing in on him like a thousand falling feathers painted black.

The young man watched Harrison for a moment before the faintest of smiles broke his ice-hard expression. "You thought wrong. It's definitely too late."

Harrison looked up sharply, startled that the killer had guessed his thoughts, and couldn't help but wonder how many times the young man had stood in this same position before to guess a dying man's final thoughts. Not a few.

As if to prove just how practiced he was, the young man aimed the gun without a single beat of hesitation, and Harrison found himself staring into the barrel of the weapon. The light of the fired shot flared, and it was the last image he saw.

CHAPTER

DELPHIC BEACH, MAINE
PRESENT DAY

PATCH WAS STANDING BEHIND ME, HIS HANDS on my hips, his body relaxed. He stood two inches over six feet tall and had a lean, athletic build that even loose-fit jeans and a T-shirt couldn't conceal. The color of his hair gave midnight a run for its money, with eyes to match. His smile was sexy and warned of trouble, but I'd made up my mind that not all trouble was bad.

Overhead, fireworks lit up the night sky, raining streams of color into the Atlantic. The crowd oohed and aahed. It was late June, and Maine was jumping into summer with both feet, celebrating the beginning of two months of sun, sand, and tourists with deep pockets. I was celebrating two months of sun, sand, and plenty of exclusive time with Patch. I'd enrolled in one summer school course—chemistry—and had every intention of letting Patch monopolize the rest of my free time.

The fire department was setting off the fireworks on a dock that couldn't have been more than two hundred yards down the beach from where we stood, and I felt the boom of each one vibrate in the sand under my feet. Waves crashed into the beach just down the hill, and carnival music tinkled at top volume. The smell of cotton candy, popcorn, and sizzling meat hung thick in the air, and my stomach reminded me I hadn't eaten since lunch.

"I'm going to grab a cheeseburger," I told Patch. "Want anything?"

"Nothing on the menu."

I smiled. "Why, Patch, are you flirting with me?"

He kissed the crown of my head. "Not yet. I'll grab your cheeseburger. Enjoy the last of the fireworks."

I snagged one of his belt loops to stop him. "Thanks, but I'm ordering. I can't take the guilt."

He raised his eyebrows in inquiry.

"When was the last time the girl at the hamburger stand let you pay for food?"

"It's been a while."

"It's been *never*. Stay here. If she sees you, I'll spend the rest of the night with a guilty conscience."

Patch opened his wallet and pulled out a twenty. "Leave her a nice tip."

It was my turn to raise my eyebrows. "Trying to redeem yourself for all those times you took free food?"

"Last time I paid, she chased me down and shoved the money in my pocket. I'm trying to avoid another groping."

It sounded made up, but knowing Patch, it was probably true.

I hunted down the end of a long line that wrapped around the hamburger stand, finding it near the entrance to the indoor carousel. Judging by the size of the line, I estimated a fifteen-minute wait just to place my order. One hamburger stand on the entire beach. It felt un-American.

After a few minutes of restless waiting, I was taking what must have been my tenth bored look around when I spotted Marcie Millar standing two spots back. Marcie and I had gone to school together since kindergarten, and in the eleven years since, I'd seen more of her than I cared to remember. Because of her, the whole school had seen more of my underwear than necessary. In junior high, Marcie's usual MO was stealing my bra from my gym locker and pinning it to the bulletin board outside the main offices, but occasionally she got creative and used it as a centerpiece in the cafeteria—both my A cups filled with vanilla pudding and topped with maraschino cherries. Classy, I know. Marcie's skirts were two sizes too small and five inches too short. Her hair was strawberry blond, and she had the shape of a Popsicle stick—turn her sideways and she practically disappeared. If there was a scoreboard keeping track of wins and losses between us, I was pretty sure Marcie had double my score.

"Hey," I said, unintentionally catching her eye and not seeing any way around a bare-minimum greeting.

"Hey," she returned in what scraped by as a civil tone.

Seeing Marcie at Delphic Beach tonight was like playing What's Wrong with This Picture? Marcie's dad owned the Toyota dealership in Coldwater, her family lived in an upscale hillside neighborhood, and the Millars took pride in being the only citizens of Coldwater welcomed into the prestigious Harraseeket Yacht Club. At this very minute, Marcie's parents were probably in Freeport, racing sailboats and ordering salmon.

By contrast, Delphic was a slum beach. The thought of a yacht club was laughable. The sole restaurant came in the form of a whitewashed hamburger stand with your choice of ketchup or mustard. On a good day, fries were offered in the mix. The entertainment slanted toward loud arcades and bumper cars, and after dark, the parking lot was known to sell more drugs than a pharmacy.

Not the kind of atmosphere Mr. and Mrs. Millar would have their daughter polluting herself in.

"Could we move any slower, people?" Marcie called up the line. "Some of us are starving to death back here."

"There's only one person working the counter," I told her.

"So? They should hire more people. Supply and demand."

Given her GPA, Marcie was the last person who should be spouting economics.

Ten minutes later, I'd made progress, and stood close enough to the hamburger stand to read the word MUSTARD scribbled in black Magic Marker on the communal yellow squirt bottle. Behind me, Marcie did the whole shifting-weight-between-hips-and-sighing thing.

"Starving with a capital S," she complained.

The guy in line ahead of me paid and carried off his food.

"A cheeseburger and a Coke," I told the girl working the stand.

While she stood over the grill making my order, I turned back to Marcie. "So. Who are you here with?" I didn't particularly care who she'd come with, especially since we didn't share any of the same friends, but my sense of courtesy got the better of me. Besides, Marcie hadn't done anything overtly rude to me in weeks. And we'd stood in relative peace the past fifteen minutes. Maybe it was the beginning of a truce. Bygones and all that.

She yawned, as if talking to me was more boring than waiting in line and staring at the backs of people's heads. "No offense, but I'm not in a chatty mood. I've been in line for what feels like five hours, waiting on an incompetent girl who obviously can't cook two hamburgers at once."

The girl behind the counter had her head ducked low, concentrating on peeling premade hamburger patties from the wax paper, but I knew she'd heard. She probably hated her job. She probably secretly spat on the hamburger patties when she turned her back. I wouldn't be surprised if at the end of her shift, she went out to her car and wept.

"Doesn't your dad mind that you're hanging out at Delphic Beach?" I asked Marcie, narrowing my eyes ever so slightly. "Might tarnish the estimable Millar family reputation. Especially now that your dad's been accepted into the Harraseeket Yacht Club."

Marcie's expression cooled. "I'm surprised your dad doesn't mind you're here. Oh, wait. That's right. He's dead."

My initial reaction was shock. My second was indignation at her cruelty. A knot of anger swelled in my throat.

"What?" she argued with a one-shoulder shrug. "He's dead. It's a fact. Do you want me to lie about the facts?"

"What did I ever do to you?"

"You were born."

Her complete lack of sensitivity yanked me inside out—so much so that I didn't even have a comeback. I snatched my cheeseburger and Coke off the counter, leaving the twenty in its place. I wanted badly to hurry back to Patch, but this was between me and Marcie. If I showed up now, one look at my face would tell Patch something was wrong. I didn't need to drag him into the middle. Taking a moment alone to collect myself, I found a bench within sight of the hamburger stand and sat down as gracefully as

I could, not wanting to give Marcie the power to ruin my night. The only thing that could make this moment worse was knowing she was watching, satisfied she'd stuffed me into a little black hole of self-pity. I took a bite of cheeseburger, but it left a bad taste in my mouth. All I could think of was dead meat. Dead cows. My own dead father.

I threw the cheeseburger into the trash and kept walking, feeling tears slip down the back of my throat.

Hugging my arms tightly at the elbows, I hurried toward the shack of bathrooms at the edge of the parking lot, hoping to make it behind a stall door before the tears started falling. There was a steady line trickling out of the women's room, but I edged my way through the doorway and positioned myself in front of one of the grime-coated mirrors. Even under the low-watt bulb, I could tell my eyes were red and glassy. I wet a paper towel and pressed it to my eyes. What was Marcie's problem? What had I ever done to her that was cruel enough to deserve this?

Drawing a few stabilizing breaths, I squared my shoulders and constructed a brick wall in my mind, placing Marcie on the far side of it. What did I care what she said? I didn't even like her. Her opinion meant nothing. She was rude and self-centered and attacked below the belt. She didn't know me, and she definitely didn't know my dad. Crying over a single word that fell from her mouth was a waste.

Get over it, I told myself.

I waited until the red rimming my eyes faded before leaving the restroom. I roamed the crowd, looking for Patch, and found him at one of the ball toss games, his back to me. Rixon was at his side, probably wagering money on Patch's inability to knock over a single weighted bowling pin. Rixon was a fallen angel who had a long history with Patch, and their ties ran deep to the point of brotherhood. Patch didn't let many people into his life, and trusted even fewer, but if there was one person who knew all his secrets, it was Rixon.

Up until two months ago, Patch had also been a fallen angel. Then he saved my life, earned his wings back, and became my guardian angel. He was supposed to play for the good guys now, but I secretly sensed that his connection to Rixon, and the world of fallen angels, meant more to him. And even though I didn't want to admit it, I sensed that he regretted the archangels' decision to make him my guardian. After all, it wasn't what he wanted.

He wanted to become human.

My cell phone rang, jarring me from my thoughts. It was my best friend Vee's ringtone, but I let voice mail take her call. With a squeeze of guilt, I vaguely noted it was the second call of hers I'd avoided today. I justified my guilt with the thought that I'd see her first thing tomorrow. Patch, on the other hand, I wouldn't see again until tomorrow evening. I planned to enjoy every minute I had with him.

I watched him pitch the ball at a table neatly lined with six bowling pins, my stomach giving a little flutter when his T-shirt crept up in the back, revealing a stripe of skin. I knew from experience that every inch of him was hard, defined muscle. His back was smooth and perfect too, the scars from when he'd fallen once again replaced with wings—wings I, and every other human, couldn't see.

"Five dollars says you can't do it again," I said, coming up behind him.

Patch looked back and grinned. "I don't want your money, Angel."

"Hey now, kids, let's keep this discussion PG-rated," Rixon said.

"All three remaining pins," I challenged Patch.

"What kind of prize are we talking about?" he asked.

"Bloody hell," Rixon said. "Can't this wait until you're alone?"

Patch gave me a secret smile, then shifted his weight back, cradling the ball into his chest. He dropped his right shoulder, brought his arm around, and sent the ball flying forward as hard as he could. There was a loud *crack!* and the remaining three pins scattered off the table.

"Aye, now you're in trouble, lass," Rixon shouted at me over the commotion caused by a pocket of onlookers, who were clapping and whistling for Patch.

Patch leaned back against the booth and arched his eyebrows at me. The gesture said it all: *Pay up.*

"You got lucky," I said.

"I'm about to get lucky."

"Choose a prize," the old man running the booth barked at Patch, bending to pick up the fallen pins.

"The purple bear," Patch said, and accepted a hideous-looking teddy bear with matted purple fur. He held it out to me.

"For me?" I said, pressing a hand to my heart.

"You like the rejects. At the grocery store, you always take the dented cans. I've been paying attention." He hooked his finger in the waistband of my jeans and pulled me close. "Let's get out of here."

"What did you have in mind?" But I was all warm and fluttery inside, because I knew exactly what he had in mind.

"Your place."

I shook my head. "Not going to happen. My mom's home. We could go to your place," I hinted.

We'd been together two months, and I still didn't know where Patch lived. And not for lack of trying. Two weeks into a relationship seemed long enough to be invited over, especially since Patch lived alone. Two months felt like overkill. I was trying to be patient, but my curiosity kept getting in the way. I knew nothing about the private, intimate details of Patch's life, like the color of paint on his walls. If his can opener was electric or manual. The brand of soap he showered with. If his sheets were cotton or silk.

"Let me guess," I said. "You live in a secret compound buried in the underbelly of the city."

"Angel."

"Are there dishes in the sink? Dirty underwear on the floor? It's a lot more private than my place."

"True, but the answer's still no."

"Has Rixon seen your place?"

"Rixon is need-to-know."

"I'm not need-to-know?"

His mouth twitched. "There's a dark side to need-to-know."

"If you showed me, you'd have to kill me?" I guessed.

He wrapped his arms around me and kissed my forehead. "Close enough. What time's curfew?"

"Ten. Summer school starts tomorrow." That, and my mom had practically taken a part-time job finding opportunities to drop the knife between me and Patch. If I'd been out with Vee, I could say with absolute certainty that my curfew would have stretched to ten thirty. I couldn't blame my mom for not trusting Patch—there was a point in my life when I'd felt similarly—but it would have been extremely convenient if every now and then she relaxed her vigilance.

Like, say, tonight. Besides, nothing was going to happen. Not with my guardian angel standing inches away.

Patch looked at his watch. "Time to roll."

At 10:04, Patch flipped a U-turn in front of the farmhouse and parked by the mailbox. He cut the engine and the headlights, leaving us alone in the dark countryside. We sat that way for several moments before he said, "Why so quiet, Angel?"

I instantly snapped to attention. "Am I being quiet? Just lost in thought."

A barely-there smile curved Patch's mouth. "Liar. What's wrong?"

"You're good," I said.

His smile widened a fraction. "Really good."

"I ran into Marcie Millar at the hamburger stand," I admitted. So much for keeping my troubles to myself. Obviously they were still smoldering under the surface. On the other hand, if I couldn't talk to Patch, who could I talk to? Two months ago our relationship involved a lot of spontaneous kissing inside our cars, outside our cars, under the bleachers, and on top of the kitchen table. It also involved a lot of wandering hands, tousled hair, and smudged lip gloss. But it was so much more than that now. I felt connected to Patch emotionally. His friendship meant more to me than a hundred casual acquaintances. When my dad died, he'd left a huge hollowness inside me that threatened to eat me from the inside out. The emptiness was still there, but the ache didn't cut half as deep. I didn't see the point in staying frozen in the past, when I had everything I wanted right now. And I had Patch to thank for that. "She was thoughtful enough to remind me my dad is dead."

"Want me to talk to her?"

"That sounds a bit The Godfather."

"What started the war between the two of you?"

"That's the thing. I don't even know. It used to be over who got the last chocolate milk in the lunch crate. Then one day in junior high, Marcie marched into school and spray-painted 'whore' on my locker. She didn't even try to be sneaky about it. The whole school was looking on."

"She went postal just like that? No reason?"

"Yup." No reason I was aware of, anyway.

He tucked one of my curls behind my ear. "Who's winning the war?"

"Marcie, but not by much."

His smile grew. "Go get her, Tiger."

"And here's another thing. Whore? In junior high, I hadn't even kissed anyone. Marcie should have spray-painted her own locker."

"Starting to sound like you've got a hang-up, Angel." He slid his finger under the strap of my tank top, his touch sending electricity humming along my skin. "I bet I can take your mind off Marcie."

A few lights were burning in the upper level of the farmhouse, but since I didn't see my mom's face pressed up against any of the windows, I figured we had some time. I unlatched my seat belt and bent across the console, finding Patch's mouth in the darkness. I kissed him slowly, savoring the taste of sea salt on his skin. He'd shaved this morning, but now his stubble rasped my chin. His mouth skimmed my throat and I felt a touch of tongue, causing my heart to bump against my ribs.

His kiss moved to my bare shoulder. He nudged the strap of my tank top down and brushed his mouth lower along my arm.

Right then, I wanted to be as close to him as I could. I never wanted him to go. I needed him in my life right now, and tomorrow, and the day after. I needed him like I'd never needed anyone.

I crawled over the console, straddling his lap. I slid my hands up his chest, grasped him behind the neck, and pulled him in. His arms circled my waist, locking me against him, and I snuggled in deeper.

Caught up in the moment, I ran my hands under his shirt, thinking only of how I loved the feel of his body heat spreading into my hands. As soon as my fingers brushed the place on his back where his wing scars used to be, a distant light exploded at the back of my mind. Perfect darkness, ruptured by one burst of blinding light. It was like watching a cosmic phenomenon in space from millions of miles away. I felt my mind being sucked inside Patch's, into all the thousands of private memories stored there, when suddenly he took my hand and slid it lower, away from the place where his wings joined with his back, and everything spun sharply back to normal.

"Nice try," he murmured, his lips brushing mine as he spoke.

I nibbled his lower lip. "If you could see into my past just by touching my back, you'd have a hard time resisting the temptation too."

"I have a hard time keeping my hands off you without that added bonus."

I laughed, but my expression quickly turned serious. Even with considerable concentration, I could hardly remember what life had been like without Patch. At night, when I lay in bed, I could remember with perfect clarity the low timbre of his laugh, the way his smile curved slightly higher on the right, the touch of his hands—hot, smooth, and delicious on my skin. But it was only with serious effort that I could pick up memories from the previous sixteen years. Maybe because those memories paled in comparison to Patch. Or maybe because there was nothing good there at all.

"Don't ever leave me," I told Patch, hooking a finger in the collar of his shirt and pulling him close.

"You're mine, Angel," he murmured, brushing the words across my jawbone as I arched my neck higher, inviting him to kiss everywhere. "You have me forever."

"Show me you mean it," I said solemnly.

He studied me a moment, then reached behind his neck and unclasped the plain silver chain he'd worn since the day I met him. I had no idea where the chain had come from, or the significance behind it, but I sensed it was important to him. It was the only piece of jewelry he wore, and he kept it tucked under his shirt, next to his skin. I'd never seen him take it off.

His hands slid to the nape of my neck, where he fastened the chain. The metal fell on my skin, still warm from him.

"I was given this when I was an archangel," he said. "To help me discern truth from deception."

I fingered it gently, in awe of its importance. "Does it still work?"

"Not for me." He interlaced our fingers and turned my hand over to kiss my knuckles. "Your turn."

I twisted a small copper ring off the middle finger of my left hand and held it out to him. A heart was hand-carved into the smooth underside of the ring.

Patch held the ring between his fingers, silently examining it.

"My dad gave it to me the week before he was killed," I said.

Patch's eyes flicked up. "I can't take this."

"It's the most important thing in the world to me. I want you to have it." I bent his fingers, folding them around the ring.

"Nora." He hesitated. "I can't take this."

"Promise me you'll keep it. Promise me nothing will ever come between us." I held his eyes, refusing to let him turn away. "I don't want to be without you. I don't want this to ever end."

Patch's eyes were slate black, darker than a million secrets stacked on top of each other. He dropped his gaze to the ring in his hand, turning it over slowly.

"Swear you'll never stop loving me," I whispered.

Ever so slightly, he nodded.

I gripped his collar and pulled him against me, kissing him more fervently, sealing the promise between us. I locked my fingers between his, the sharp edge of the ring biting into our palms. Nothing I did seemed to bring me close enough to him, no amount of him was enough. The ring ground deeper into my hand, until I was certain it had broken skin. A blood promise.

When I thought my chest might collapse without air, I pulled away, resting my forehead against his. My eyes were shut, my breathing causing my shoulders to rise and fall. "I love you," I murmured. "More than I think I should."

I waited for him to answer, but instead his hold on me tightened, almost protectively. He turned his head toward the woods across the road.

"What's wrong?" I asked.

"I heard something."

"That was me saying I love you," I said, smiling as I traced his mouth with my finger.

I expected him to return the smile, but his eyes were still fixed on the trees, which cast shifting shadows as their branches nodded in the breeze.

"What's out there?" I asked, following his gaze. "A coyote?"

"Something isn't right."

My blood chilled, and I slid off his lap. "You're starting to scare me. Is it a bear?" We hadn't seen bears in years, but the farmhouse was pushed out on the very edge of town, and bears were known to wander closer to town after hibernation, when they were hungry and searching for food.

"Turn the headlights on and honk the horn," I said. Training my eyes on the woods, I watched for movement. My heart edged up a little, remembering the time my parents and I had watched from the farmhouse windows as a bear rocked our car, smelling food inside.

Behind me, the porch lights flashed. I didn't need to turn back to know my mom was standing in the doorway, frowning and tapping her foot.

"What is it?" I asked Patch once more. "My mom's coming out. Is she safe?"

He turned on the engine and put the Jeep in drive. "Go inside. There's something I need to do."

"Go inside? Are you kidding? What's going on?"

"Nora!" my mom called, coming down the steps, her tone aggravated. She stopped five feet from the Jeep and motioned for me to lower the window.

"Patch?" I tried again.

"I'll call you later."

My mom hauled the door open. "Patch," she acknowledged curtly.

"Blythe." He gave a distracted nod.

She turned to me. "You're four minutes late."

"I was four minutes early yesterday."

"Rollover minutes don't work with curfews. Inside. Now."

Not wanting to leave until Patch answered me, but not seeing much of a choice, I told him, "Call me."

He nodded once, but the singular focus to his eyes told me his thoughts were elsewhere. As soon as I was out of the car and on solid ground, the Jeep revved forward, not wasting time accelerating. Wherever Patch was going, it was in a hurry.

"When I give you a curfew, I expect you to keep it," Mom said.

"Four minutes late," I said, my tone suggesting she might be overreacting.

That earned me a stare that had disapproval stamped all over it. "Last year your dad was killed. A couple months ago, you had your own brush with death. I think I've earned the right to be over-protective." She walked stiffly back to the house, arms clamped over her chest.

Okay, I was an unfeeling, insensitive daughter. Point taken.

I turned my attention to the row of trees at the edge of the road opposite. Nothing looked out of the ordinary. I waited for a chill to warn me there was something back there, something I couldn't see, but nothing felt off. A warm summer breeze rustled past, the sound of cicadas filling the air. If anything, the woods looked peaceful under the silver glow of moonlight.

Patch hadn't seen anything in the woods. He'd turned away because I'd said three very big, very stupid words, which had gushed out before I could stop them. What had I been thinking? No. What was Patch thinking now? Had he driven off to escape respond-ing? I was pretty sure I knew the answer. And I was pretty sure it explained why I was left staring at the back of his Jeep.

CHAPTER

FOR THE LAST ELEVEN SECONDS, I'D BEEN
flying facedown, hugging my pillow over my head, trying
to shut out Chuck Delaney's traffic report from downtown Portland, which was coming through my alarm clock loud
and clear. Likewise, I was trying to shut out the logical part of my
brain, which shouted for me to get dressed, promising repercus-
sions if I didn't. But the pleasure-seeking part of my brain won
out. It clung to my dream—or rather, the subject of my dream. He

had wavy black hair and a killer smile. At this moment, he was sitting backward on his motorcycle and I was sitting facing forward, our knees touching. I curled my fingers into his shirt and pulled him in for a kiss.

In my dream, Patch felt it when I kissed him. Not only on an emotional level, but a real, physical touch. In my dream, he became more human than angel. Angels can't feel physical sensation—I knew this—but in my dream, I wanted Patch to feel the soft, silky pressure of our lips connecting. I wanted him to feel my fingers pushing through his hair. I needed him to feel the thrilling and undeniable magnetic field pulling every molecule in his body toward mine.

Just like I did.

Patch ran his finger under the silver chain at my neck, his touch sending a shiver of pleasure rippling through me. "I love you," he murmured.

Bracing my fingertips on his hard stomach, I leaned in, stopping just short of a kiss. I love you more, I said, brushing his mouth as I spoke.

Only, the words didn't come out. They stayed caught in my throat.

While Patch waited for me to respond, his smile faltered.

I love you, I tried again. Once again, the words stayed clamped inside.

Patch's expression turned anxious. "I love you, Nora," he repeated.

I nodded frantically, but he'd turned away. He swung off the motorcycle and left without looking back.

I love you! I yelled after him. I love you, I love you!

But it was as if quicksand had been poured down my throat; the harder I tried to wrestle the words out, the faster they were towed under.

Patch was slipping away in a crowd. Night had fallen down around us in a snap, and I could barely distinguish his black T-shirt from the hundreds of other dark shirts in the masses. I ran to catch up, but when I grabbed his arm, it was someone else who turned around. A girl. It was too dark to get a good read on her features, but I could tell she was beautiful.

"I love Patch," she told me, smiling through shocking red lipstick. "And I'm not afraid to say it."

"I did say it!" I argued. "Last night I told him!"

I pushed past her, eyes scanning the crowd until I caught a glimpse of Patch's trademark blue ball cap. I shoved my way frantically over to him and reached out to catch his hand.

He turned back, but he'd changed into the same beautiful girl. "You're too late," she said. "I love Patch now."

"Over to Angie with weather," Chuck Delaney yapped cheerfully in my ear.

My eyes sprang open at the word "weather." I lay in bed a moment, trying to shake off what was nothing more than a bad dream, and get my bearings. The weather was announced at twenty before the hour, and there was no possible way I was hearing the weather, unless . . .

Summer school! I'd overslept!

Kicking back the covers, I fled to the closet. Shoving my feet into the same jeans I'd discarded at the bottom of the closet last night, I stretched a white tee over my head and layered it with a lavender cardigan. I speed-dialed Patch but three rings later was sent to voice mail. "Call me!" I said, pausing a half second to wonder if he was avoiding me after last night's big confession. I'd made up my mind to pretend it had never happened until it blew over and things returned to normal, but after this morning's dream, I was beginning to doubt I'd let go of it that easily. Maybe Patch was having just as hard a time dropping it. Either way, there wasn't a lot I could do about it right now. Even though I could have sworn he'd promised me a ride . . .

I pushed a headband into my hair in lieu of a hairstyle, snatched my backpack off the kitchen counter, and rushed out the door.

I paused in the driveway long enough to give a scream of exasperation at the eight-by-ten-foot slab of cement where my 1979 Fiat Spider used to sit. My mom had sold the Spider to pay off a three-months-delinquent electricity bill, and to stock our fridge with enough groceries to keep us fed through the end of the month. She'd even dismissed our housekeeper, Dorothea, a.k.a. my surrogate parent, to trim expenses. Sending a hateful thought in the direction of Circumstance, I slung my backpack over my shoulder and started jogging. Most people might consider the rural Maine farmhouse my mom and I live in quaint, but the truth is, there's nothing quaint about the mile-long jog to the nearest neighbors. And unless quaint is synonymous with eighteenth-century drafty money pit situated in the eye of an atmospheric inversion that sucks in all the fog from here to the coast, I beg to differ.

At the corner of Hawthorne and Beech, I saw signs of life as cars zipped along on their morning commute. I used one hand to stick my thumb in the air and the other to unwrap a piece of breath-freshening, toothpaste-replacing gum.

A red Toyota 4Runner braked at the curb, and the passenger window lowered with an automated hum. Marcie Millar sat behind the wheel. "Car trouble?" she asked.

Car trouble as in no car. Not that I was about to admit it to Marcie.

"Need a ride?" she rephrased impatiently when I failed to answer.

I couldn't believe out of all the cars passing down this stretch of road, Marcie's had to be the one to stop. Did I want to ride with Marcie? No. Was I still worked up over what she'd said about my dad? Yes. Was I about to forgive her? Absolutely not. I would have gestured for her to keep driving, but there was one small snag. Rumor had it that the only thing Mr. Loucks liked more than the periodic table of the elements was handing out detention slips to tardy students.

"Thanks," I accepted reluctantly. "I'm on my way to school."

"Guess your fat friend couldn't give you a ride?"

I froze with my hand on the door handle. Vee and I had long ago given up educating small-minded people that "fat" and "curvy" are not the same thing, but that didn't mean we tolerated the ignorance. And I would have gladly called Vee for a ride, but she'd been invited to attend a training meeting for hopeful editors of the school's eZine and was already at school.

"On second thought, I'll walk." I gave Marcie's door a shove, locking it back in position.

Marcie tried on a confused face. "Are you offended I called her fat? Because it's true. What is it with you? I feel like everything I say has to be censored. First your dad, now this. What happened to freedom of speech?"

For a split moment I thought it would be nice and convenient if I still had the Spider. Not only would I not be stranded without a ride, but I might get the pleasure of plowing Marcie over. The school parking lot was chaotic after school. Accidents happened.

Since I couldn't bounce Marcie off my front fender, I did the next best thing. "If my dad owned the Toyota dealership, I think I'd be environmentally minded enough to ask for a hybrid."

"Well, your dad doesn't own the Toyota dealership."

"That's right. My dad's dead."

She raised one shoulder. "You said it, not me."

"From now on, I think it's better if we stay out of each other's way."

She examined her manicure. "Fine."

"Good."

"Just trying to be nice, and look where it got me," she said under her breath.

"Nice? You called Vee fat."

"I also offered you a ride." She floored the gas, her tires spitting up road dust that wafted in my direction.

I hadn't woken up this morning looking for another reason to hate Marcie Millar, but there you go.

Coldwater High had been erected in the late nineteenth century, and the construction was an eclectic mix of Gothic and Victorian that looked more cathedral than academic. The windows were narrow and arched, the glass leaded. The stone was multicolored, but mostly gray. In the summer, ivy crawled up the exterior and gave the school a certain New England charm. In the winter, the ivy resembled long skeletal fingers choking the building.

I was half speed-walking, half jogging down the hall to chemistry when my cell phone rang in my pocket.

"Mom?" I answered, not slowing my pace. "Can I call you ba—"

"You'll never guess who I ran into last night! Lynn Parnell. You remember the Parnells. Scott's mom."

I peeked at the clock on my cell. I'd been fortunate enough to hitch a ride to school with a complete stranger—a woman on her way to kickboxing at the gym—but I was still cutting it short. Less than two minutes to the tardy bell. "Mom? School is about to start. Can I call you at lunch?"

"You and Scott were such good friends."

She'd triggered a faint memory. "When we were *five*," I said. "Didn't he always wet his pants?"

"I had drinks with Lynn last night. She just finalized her divorce, and she and Scott are moving back to Coldwater."

"That's great. I'll call you—"

"I invited them over for dinner tonight."

As I passed the principal's office, the minute hand on the clock above her door ticked to the next notch. From where I stood, it looked caught between 7:59 and eight sharp. I aimed a threatening look at it that said *Don't you dare ring early*. "Tonight's not good, Mom. Patch and I—"

"Don't be silly!" Mom cut across me. "Scott is one of your oldest friends in the world. You knew him long before Patch."

"Scott used to force me to eat roly-polies," I said, my memory starting to come around.

"And you never forced him to play Barbies?"

"Totally different!"

"Tonight, seven o'clock," Mom said in a voice that shut out all argument.

I hurried into chemistry with seconds to spare and slid onto a metal stool behind a black granite lab table on the front row. Seating was two to a table, and I had my fingers crossed that I'd get paired with someone whose understanding of science surpassed my own, which, given my standard, wasn't hard to beat. I tended to be more of a romantic than a realist, and chose blind faith over cold logic. Which put science and me at odds right from the start.

Marcie Millar strolled into the room wearing heels, jeans, and a silk top from Banana Republic that I had on my back-to-school wish list. By Labor Day, the shirt would be on the clearance rack and in my price range. I was in the process of mentally wiping the shirt off the list when Marcie settled onto the stool beside me.

"What's up with your hair?" she said. "Ran out of mousse? Patience?" A smile lifted one side of her mouth. "Or is it because you had to run four miles to get here on time?"

"What happened to staying out of each other's way?" I gave a pointed look at her stool, then mine, communicating that twenty-four inches wasn't staying out of the way.

"I need something from you."

I exhaled silently, stabilizing my blood pressure. I should have known. "Here's the thing, Marcie," I said. "We both know this class is going to be insanely hard. Let me do you a favor and warn you that science is my worst subject. The only reason I'm doing summer school is because I heard chemistry is easier this term. You don't want me as a partner. This won't be an easy A."

"Do I look like I'm sitting beside you for the health of my GPA?" she said with an impatient flip of her wrist. "I need you for something else. Last week I got a job."

Marcie? A job?

She smirked, and I could only imagine she'd pulled my thoughts directly off my expression. "I file in the front office. One of my dad's salesmen is married to the front office secretary. Never hurts to have connections. Not that you'd know anything about it."

I'd known Marcie's dad was influential in Coldwater. In fact, he was such a large booster club donor, he had a say in every coaching position at the high school, but this was ridiculous.

"Once in a while, a file falls open and I can't help but see things," Marcie said.

Yeah, right.

"For example, I know you're still not over your dad's death. You've been in counseling with the school psych. In fact, I know everything about everyone. Except Patch. Last week I noticed his file is empty. I want to know why. I want to know what he's hiding."

"Why do you care?"

"He was standing in my driveway last night, staring at my bedroom window."

I blinked. "Patch was standing in your driveway?"

"Unless you know some other guy who drives a Jeep Commander, dresses in all black, and is superhot."

I frowned. "Did he say anything?"

"He saw me watching from the window and left. Should I be thinking about a restraining order? Is this typical behavior for him? I know he's off, but just how off are we talking?"

I ignored her, too absorbed with turning over this information. Patch? At Marcie's? It had to have been after he left my place. After I said, "I love you," and he bailed.

"No problem," Marcie said, straightening up. "There are other ways to get information, like administration. I'm guessing they'd be all over an empty school file. I wasn't going to say anything, but for my own safety . . ."

I wasn't worried about Marcie going to administration. Patch could handle himself. I *was* worried about last night. Patch had left abruptly, claiming he had something he needed to do, but I was having a hard time believing that something was hanging out in Marcie's driveway. It was a lot easier to accept that he'd left because of what I'd said.

"Or the police," Marcie added, tapping her fingertip to her lip. "An empty school file almost sounds illegal. How did Patch get into school? You look upset, Nora. Am I onto something?" A smile of surprised pleasure dawned on her face. "I am, aren't I? There's more to the story."

I settled cool eyes on her. "For someone who's made it clear that her life is superior to every other student's at this school, you sure make it a habit of pursuing every facet of our boring, worthless lives."

Marcie's smile vanished. "I wouldn't have to if you all would stay out of my way."

"Your way? This isn't your school."

"Don't talk to me that way," Marcie said with a disbelieving, almost involuntary tic of her head. "In fact, don't talk to me at all."

I flipped my palms up. "No problem."

"And while you're at it, *move*."

I glanced down at my stool, thinking surely she couldn't mean— "I was here first."

Mimicking me, Marcie flipped her palms up. "Not my problem."

"I'm not moving."

"I'm not sitting by you."

"I'm happy to hear it."

"*Move*," Marcie commanded.

"No."

The bell cut across us, and when the shrill sound of it died, both Marcie and I seemed to have realized the room had grown quiet. We glanced around, and it hit me with a souring to my stomach that every other seat in the room was taken.

Mr. Loucks positioned himself in the aisle to my right, waving a sheet of paper.

"I'm holding a blank seating chart," he said. "Each of the rectangles corresponds to a desk in the room. Write your name in the appropriate rectangle and pass it on." He slapped the chart down in front of me. "Hope you like your partners," he told us. "You've got eight weeks with them."

At noon, when class ended, I caught a ride with Vee to Enzo's Bistro, our favorite place to grab iced mochas or steamed milk, depending on the season. I felt the sun bake my face as we crossed the parking lot, and that's when I saw it. A white convertible Volkswagen Cabriolet with a sale sign taped in the window: $1,000 OBO.

"You're drooling," Vee said, using her finger to tip my chin closed.

"You don't happen to have a thousand dollars I can borrow?"

"I don't have five you can borrow. My piggy bank is officially anorexic."

I gave a sigh of longing in the direction of the Cabriolet. "I need money. I need a job." I shut my eyes, envisioning myself behind the wheel of the Cabriolet, the top down, the wind swishing my curly hair. With the Cabriolet, I'd never have to bum a ride again. I'd be free to go where I wanted, when I pleased.

"Yeah, but getting a job means you actually have to work. I mean, are you sure you want to blow the entire summer laboring away at minimum wage? You might, I don't know, break a sweat or something."

I dug through my backpack for a scrap of paper and scribbled down the number listed on the sign. Maybe I could talk the owner down a couple hundred. In the meantime, I added browsing the classifieds for part-time employment to my afternoon to-do list. A job meant time away from Patch, but it also meant private transportation. Much as I loved Patch, he always seemed to be busy . . . doing

435

something. Which made him unreliable when it came to rides.

Inside Enzo's, Vee and I placed orders for iced mochas and spicy pecan salads, and plopped down with our food at a table. Over the past several weeks, Enzo's had undergone extensive remodeling to bring it up to speed with the twenty-first century, and Coldwater now had its very first Internet lounge. Given the fact that my home computer was six years old, I was actually excited about this.

"I don't know about you, but I'm ready for vacation," Vee said, pushing her sunglasses to the top of her head. "Eight more weeks of Spanish. That's more days than I want to think about. What we need is a distraction. We need something that will take our minds off this endless stretch of quality education spread out before us. We need to go shopping. Portland, here we come. Macy's is having a big sale. I need shoes, I need dresses, and I need a new fragrance."

"You just bought new clothes. Two hundred dollars' worth. Your mom is going to hemorrhage when she gets her MasterCard statement."

"Yeah, but I need a boyfriend. And to get a boyfriend, you have to look good. Doesn't hurt to smell good too."

I bit a diced pear off my fork. "Have anybody in mind?"

"As a matter of fact, I do."

"Just promise me it's not Scott Parnell."

"Scott who?"

I smiled. "See? Now I'm happy."

"I don't know about any Scott Parnells, but the guy I've got my eye on happens to be hot. Off-the-charts hot. Hotter-than-Patch hot." She paused. "Well, maybe not that hot. Nobody's *that* hot. Seriously, the rest of my day is a wash. Portland or bust, I say."

I opened my mouth, but Vee was faster.

"Uh-oh," she said. "I know that look. You're going to tell me you already have plans."

"Rewind to Scott Parnell. He used to live here when we were five."

Vee looked like she was searching her long-term memory.

"He wet his pants a lot," I offered helpfully.

Vee's eyes lit up. "Scotty the Potty?"

"He's moving back to Coldwater. My mom invited him over for dinner tonight."

"I see where this is going," Vee said, nodding sagely. "This is what's called the 'meet cute.' This is when the lives of two potential romantic partners intersect. Remember when Desi accidentally walked into the men's room and caught Ernesto at the urinal?"

I stopped with my fork halfway between my plate and my mouth. "What?"

"On Corazón, the Spanish soap. No? Never mind. Your mom wants to hook you and Scotty the Potty up. Pronto."

"No, she doesn't. She knows I'm with Patch."

"Just because she knows, doesn't mean she's happy about it. Your mom is going to spend a lot of time and energy turning this equation from Nora plus Patch equals love, to Nora plus Scotty the Potty equals love. And what about this? Maybe Scotty the Potty turned into Scotty the Hottie. Have you thought about that?"

I hadn't, and I wasn't going to either. I had Patch, and I was perfectly happy to keep it that way.

"Can we talk about something slightly more urgent?" I asked, thinking it was time to change the subject before our current one gave Vee even more wild ideas. "Like the fact that my new chemistry partner is Marcie Millar?"

"The ho."

"Apparently she's filing for the front office, and she looked in Patch's file."

"Is it still empty?"

"It looks that way, since she wants me to tell her everything I know about him." Including why he was hanging out in her driveway last night, gazing at her bedroom window. I'd once heard a rumor that Marcie propped a tennis racket in her window when she was open to payment for certain "services," but I wasn't going to think about that. Weren't rumors 90 percent fiction, anyway?

Vee leaned in closer. "What do you know?"

Our conversation lapsed into an uncomfortable silence. I didn't believe in secrets between best friends. But there are secrets . . . and there are hard truths. Scary truths. Unimaginable truths. Having a boyfriend who's a fallen-turned-guardian angel fits into all of the above.

"You're keeping something from me," said Vee.

"Am not."

"Are too."

Thick silence.

"I told Patch I loved him."

Vee covered her mouth, but I couldn't tell if she was stifling a gasp or laughter. Which only made me feel more insecure. Was it that funny? Had I done something even stupider than I already thought?

"What did he say?" Vee asked.

I merely looked at her.

"That bad?" she asked.

I cleared my voice. "Tell me about this guy you're after. I mean, is this a lust-from-afar thing, or have you actually talked to him?"

Vee took the hint. "Talked to him? I had hot dogs at Skippy's with him yesterday for lunch. It was one of those blind date things, and it turned out better than expected. Much better. FYI, you'd know all this stuff if you returned my calls instead of making out with your boyfriend nonstop."

"Vee, I'm your only friend, and it wasn't me who hooked you up."

"I know. Your boyfriend did."

I choked on a Gorgonzola cheese ball. "Patch set you up on a blind date?"

"Yeah, so?" Vee said, her tone edging toward defensive.

I smiled. "I thought you didn't trust Patch."

"I don't."

"But?"

"I tried calling you to vet my date first, but to repeat, you never return my calls anymore."

"Mission accomplished. I feel like the worst friend ever." I gave her a conspirator's smile. "Now tell me the rest."

Vee's resistant tone dropped away, and she mirrored my smile. "His name is Rixon, and he's Irish. His brogue or whatever it's called kills me. Sexy to the max. He's a little on the skinny side considering I'm big-boned, but I'm planning on losing twenty pounds this summer, so everything should even out by August."

"Rixon? No way! I love Rixon!" As a standard rule, I didn't trust fallen angels, but Rixon was an exception. Like Patch, his moral boundaries were drawn in the gray area between black and white. He wasn't perfect, but he wasn't all bad, either.

I grinned, pointing my fork at Vee. "I can't believe you went out with him. I mean, he's Patch's best friend. You hate Patch."

Vee gave me her black-cat look, her hair practically bristling. "Best friends doesn't mean anything. Look at you and me. We're nothing alike."

"This is great. The four of us can hang out all summer."

"Uh-uh. No way. I'm not hanging out with that whack-job boyfriend of yours. I don't care what you told me, I still think he had something to do with Jules's mysterious death in the gym."

A dark cloud fell on the conversation. There had been only

three people in the gym the night Jules died, and I was one of them. I'd never told Vee everything that happened, just enough to get her to stop pressing, and for her own safety, I planned on keeping it that way.

Vee and I spent the day driving around, picking up employment applications from local fast-food joints, and it was nearly six thirty when I got home. I dropped my keys on the sideboard and checked the answering machine for messages. There was one from my mom. She was at Michaud's Market picking up garlic bread, deli lasagna, and cheap wine, and swore on her grave she would beat the Parnells to the house.

I deleted the message and climbed upstairs to my bedroom. Since I'd missed my morning shower, and my hair had frizzed to maximum height during the day, I figured I'd change into clean clothes by way of damage control. Every single memory I had of Scott Parnell was unpleasant, but company was company. I had my cardigan halfway unbuttoned when there was a rap at the front door.

I found Patch on the other side of it, hands in his pockets.

Normally I would have greeted him by bounding straight into his arms. Today I held back. Last night I'd said I loved him, and he'd bolted and allegedly headed straight for Marcie's house. My mood fell somewhere between injured pride, anger, and insecurity. I hoped my reserved silence sent him a message that something

441

was off, and would be until he made a move to correct it, either by apology or explanation.

"Hey," I said, assuming casualness. "You forgot to call last night. Where did you end up going?"

"Around. You going to invite me in?"

I didn't. "I'm glad to hear Marcie's house is just, you know, around."

A momentary flick of surprise in his eyes confirmed what I didn't want to believe: Marcie had been telling the truth.

"Want to tell me what's going on?" I said in a slightly more hostile tone. "Want to tell me what you were doing at her place last night?"

"You sound jealous, Angel." There might have been a note of teasing behind it, but unlike usual, there was nothing affectionate or playful about it.

"Maybe I wouldn't be jealous if you didn't give me a reason to be," I shot back. "What were you doing at her house?"

"Taking care of business."

I swept my eyebrows up. "I didn't realize you and Marcie had business."

"We do, but it's just that. Business."

"Care to elaborate?" There was a heavy dose of allegation crammed between my actual words.

"Are you accusing me of something?"

"Should I be?"

Patch was usually expert at hiding his emotions, but the line of his mouth tightened. "No."

"If being at her house last night was so innocent, why are you having such a hard time explaining what you were doing there?"

"I'm not having a hard time," he said, each word carefully measured. "I'm not telling you, because what I was doing at Marcie's has nothing to do with us."

How could he think this didn't have anything to do with us? Marcie was the one person who took every opportunity to attack and belittle me. Over the past eleven years, she'd teased me, spread horrible rumors about me, and humiliated me publicly. How could he think this wasn't personal? How could he think I'd just accept this, no questions asked? Above all, couldn't he see I was terrified that Marcie would use him to hurt me? If she suspected he was even remotely interested, she'd do everything in her power to steal him for herself. I couldn't stand the thought of losing Patch, but it would kill me if I lost him to her.

Overwhelmed by that sudden fear, I said, "Don't come back until you're ready to tell me what you were doing at her place."

Patch impatiently pushed his way inside and closed the door behind him. "I didn't come here to argue. I wanted to let you know Marcie ran into some trouble this afternoon."

Marcie again? Did he think he hadn't dug a deep enough hole already? I tried to stay calm long enough to hear him out, but I wanted to yell across him. "Oh?" I said coolly.

"She was caught in the crossfire when a group of fallen angels tried to force a Nephil to swear fealty inside the men's room at Bo's Arcade. The Nephil wasn't sixteen, so they couldn't force him, but they had fun trying. They cut him up pretty bad, and broke a few ribs. Enter Marcie. She'd had too much to drink and walked into the wrong restroom. The fallen angel standing guard pulled a knife on her. She's at the hospital, but they'll release her soon. Flesh wound."

My pulse jumped, and I knew I was upset that Marcie had been knifed, but that was the last thing I wanted to reveal to Patch. I crossed my arms stiffly. "Gee, is the Nephil okay?" I vaguely remembered Patch explaining, some time ago, that fallen angels can't force Nephilim to swear fealty until they're sixteen. Likewise, he couldn't sacrifice me to get a human body of his own until I turned sixteen. Sixteen was a darkly magical, even crucial age in the world of angels and Nephilim.

Patch gave me a look that held the tiniest glare of disgust. "Marcie may have been drunk, but chances are she remembers what she saw. Obviously you know fallen angels and Nephilim try to stay under the radar, and someone like Marcie, with a big mouth, can threaten their secrecy. The last thing they want is for her to announce to the world what she saw. Our world operates a lot more smoothly when humans are ignorant of it. I know the fallen angels involved." His jaw tensed. "They'll do whatever it takes to keep Marcie quiet."

I felt a shiver of fear for Marcie but flushed it away. Since when did Patch care one way or the other what happened to Marcie? Since when was he more worried about her than me? "I'm trying to feel bad," I said, "but it sounds like you're concerned enough for the both of us." I jerked on the doorknob and held the door wide. "Maybe you should go check on Marcie, see if her flesh wound is healing properly."

Patch pried my hand loose and shut the door with his foot. "Bigger things than you, me, and Marcie are going on." He hesitated, as if he had more to say, but closed his mouth at the last moment.

"You, me, and Marcie? Since when did you start putting the three of us in the same sentence? Since when does she mean anything to you?" I snapped.

He cupped a hand over the back of his neck, looking very much like he knew he should choose his words carefully before answering.

"Just tell me what you're thinking!" I blurted. "Spit it out! It's bad enough that I have no idea what you're feeling, let alone what you're thinking!"

Patch looked around, as if he was wondering whether I was talking to someone else. "Spit it out?" he said, his tone darkly incredulous. Maybe even annoyed. "What does it look like I'm trying to do? If you'd calm down, I could. Right now you're going to turn hysterical, regardless of what I say."

I felt my eyes narrow. "I have a right to be angry. You won't tell me what you were doing at Marcie's last night."

Patch threw his hands up. *Here we go again,* the gesture said.

"Two months ago," I began, trying to inject pride into my voice to hide the quaver in it, "Vee, my mom—*everyone*—warned me that you were the kind of guy who sees girls as conquests. They said I was just another notch on your belt, another stupid girl you'd seduce for your own satisfaction. They said the *moment* I fell in love with you was the moment you'd leave." I swallowed hard. "I need to know they weren't right."

Even though I didn't want to recall it, the memory of last night resurfaced with perfect clarity. I remembered the whole humiliating scene in vivid detail. I'd said I loved him, and he'd left me hanging. There were a hundred different ways to analyze his silence, none of them good.

Patch wagged his head in disbelief. "You want me to tell you they're wrong? Because I get the feeling you aren't going to believe me, no matter what I say." He glared at me.

"Are you as committed to this relationship as I am?" I couldn't *not* ask it. Not after watching everything come tumbling down since last night. I suddenly realized I had no idea how Patch really felt about me. I thought I meant everything to him, but what if I'd only seen what I wanted? What if I'd grossly exaggerated his feelings? I held his eyes, not about to make this easy on him, not about to give him a second chance to skirt the issue. I needed to know. "Do you love me?"

I can't answer that, he said, startling me by speaking to my thoughts. It was a gift all angels possessed, but I didn't understand why he was choosing now to use it. "I'll stop by tomorrow. Sleep well," he added curtly, heading for the door.

"When we kiss, are you faking it?"

He stopped short. Another disbelieving shake of his head. "Faking it?"

"When I touch you, do you feel anything? How far does your desire go? Do you feel anything close to what I feel for you?"

Patch watched me in silence. "Nora—," he began.

"I want a straight answer."

After a moment, he said, "Emotionally, yes."

"But physically no, right? How am I supposed to be in a relationship, when I have no idea how much it even means to you? Am I experiencing things on a whole different level? Because that's what it feels like. And I hate it," I added. "I don't want you to kiss me because you have to. I don't want you to pretend it means something, when it's really just an act."

"Just an act? Are you listening to yourself?" He tipped his head back against the wall and gave another, darker laugh. He cut me a sideways glance. "Are you done with the accusations?"

"You think this is funny?" I said, hit by a fresh wave of anger.

"Just the opposite." Before I could say more, he turned toward the door. "Call me when you're ready to talk rationally."

"What's that supposed to mean?"

"It means you're crazy. You're impossible."

"I'm crazy?"

He tipped my chin up and planted a quick, rough kiss on my mouth. "And I must be crazy for putting up with it."

I pulled free and rubbed my chin resentfully. "You gave up becoming human for me, and this is what I get? A boyfriend who hangs out at Marcie's, but won't tell me why. A boyfriend who walks out at the first hint of a fight. Try this on for size: You're a—jerk!"

Jerk? he spoke to my thoughts, his voice cold and cutting. I'm trying to follow the rules. I'm not supposed to fall in love with you. We both know this isn't about Marcie. This is about how I feel about you. I have to hold back. I'm walking a dangerous line. Falling in love is what got me in trouble in the first place. I can't be with you the way I want.

"Why did you give up becoming human for me if you knew you couldn't be with me?" I asked, my voice wobbling slightly, sweat prickling the palms of my hands. "What did you even expect from a relationship with me? What's the point of"—my voice caught and I swallowed without meaning to—"us?"

What had I expected from a relationship with Patch? At some point, I must have thought about where our relationship was headed, and what would happen. Of course I had. But I'd been so frightened by what I saw coming that I'd pretended the inevitable away. I'd pretended a relationship with Patch could work, because deep inside, any time with Patch had seemed better than nothing at all.

Angel.

I looked up when Patch spoke my name in my thoughts.

Being close to you on any level is better than nothing. I'm not going to lose you. He paused, and for the first time since I'd known him, I saw a flicker of worry in his eyes. *But I already fell once. If I give the archangels cause to think I'm even remotely in love with you, they'll send me to hell. Forever.*

The news hit me like a blow to the stomach. "What?"

I'm a guardian angel, or at least so I've been told, but the archangels don't trust me. I have no privileges, no privacy. Two of them cornered me last night for a talk, and I walked away with the feeling that they want me to slip up again. For whatever reason, they're choosing now to crack down on me. They're looking for any excuse to get rid of me. I'm on probation, and if I screw this up, my story doesn't have a happy ending.

I stared at him, thinking he had to be exaggerating, thinking it couldn't possibly be that bad, but one look at his face told me he'd never been more serious.

"What happens now?" I wondered out loud.

Instead of answering, Patch sighed with frustration. The truth of the matter was, this was going to end badly. No matter how much we backpedaled, stalled, or looked the other way, one day all too soon, our lives would be ripped apart. What would happen when I graduated and went off to college? What would happen when I followed my dream job to the other side of the country? What would happen when it came time for me to marry or have kids? I wasn't doing anyone a favor by falling in love with Patch more every day.

Did I really want to stay on this road longer, knowing it was only going to end with devastation?

For one fleeting moment, I thought I had the answer—I'd give up my dreams. It was as simple as that. I shut my eyes and let go of my dreams like they were balloons on long, thin ribbons. I didn't need those dreams. I couldn't even be sure they'd come true. And even if they did, I didn't want to spend the rest of my life alone and tortured by the knowledge that everything I'd done meant nothing without Patch.

And then it hit me in a terrible way that neither of us could give up everything. My life would continue marching into the future, and I didn't have the power to stop it. Patch would stay an angel forever; he would continue the path he'd been on since he fell.

"Isn't there anything we can do?" I asked.

"I'm working on it."

In other words, he had nothing. We were trapped on both sides—the archangels applying pressure from one direction, and two futures headed in vastly different directions from the other.

"I want out," I said quietly. I knew I wasn't being fair—I was protecting myself. What other option did I have? I couldn't give Patch a chance to talk me out of it. I had to do what was best for both of us. I couldn't stand here, hanging on, when the very thing I held disappeared more with each passing day. I couldn't show how much I cared when it was only going to make things impossibly hard in the end. Most of all, I didn't want to be the reason Patch lost everything he'd worked for. If the archangels were looking for an excuse to banish him forever, I was only making it easy.

Patch stared at me like he couldn't tell if I was serious. "That's it? You want out? You got your turn to explain yourself, which I don't buy, by the way, but now that it's my turn, I'm supposed to just swallow your decision and walk out?"

I hugged my elbows and turned away. "You can't force me to stay in a relationship I don't want."

"Can we talk about this?"

"If you want to talk, tell me what you were doing at Marcie's last night." But Patch was right. This wasn't about Marcie. This was because I was scared and upset with the deal that fate and circumstance had cut both of us.

I turned back to see Patch drag his hands down his face. He gave a short, unamused laugh.

"If I'd been at Rixon's last night, you'd wonder what was going on!" I flung back.

"No," he said, his voice dangerously low. "I trust you."

Afraid I'd lose my resolve if I didn't act immediately, I smacked the heels of my hands against his chest, knocking him back a step. "Go," I said, tears making my voice rough. "I have other things I want to do with my life. Things that don't involve you. I have college and future jobs. I'm not going to throw it all away on something that was never meant to be."

Patch flinched. "Is this what you really want?"

"When I kiss my boyfriend, I want to know he feels it!"

As soon as I said it, I regretted it. I didn't want to hurt him—I just wanted to get this moment over with as quickly as possible before I unraveled and broke down sobbing. But I'd gone too far. I saw him stiffen. We stood face-to-face, both of us breathing hard.

Then he strode out, yanking the door shut behind him.

Once the door was closed, I collapsed against it. Tears burned at the back of my eyes, but not a single drop fell. I had too much frustration and anger clashing around inside me to feel much of anything else, but I suspected in a way that caused a sob to catch in my throat, that five minutes from now, when everything else had dropped away and I realized the full impact of what I'd done, I'd feel my heart breaking.

I LOWERED MYSELF ONTO THE CORNER OF MY bed, staring into space. The anger was beginning to wear off, but I almost wished I could stay caught up in its fever forever. The emptiness it left behind ached more than the sharp, fiery pain I'd felt when Patch walked out. I tried to make sense of what had just happened, but my thoughts were a disjointed mess. Our shouted words rang in my ears, but they echoed helter-skelter, like I was recalling a bad dream rather than an actual conversation.

Had I really broken up with him? Had I really meant for it to be permanent? Was there no way around fate or, more immediately, the archangels' threats? By way of an answer, my stomach twisted, threatening to be sick.

I hurried to the bathroom and knelt over the toilet, my ears clanging and my breathing coming out shallow and choppy. What had I done? Nothing permanent, definitely nothing permanent. Tomorrow we'd see each other again and everything would go back to the way it had been. This was just a fight. A stupid fight. This wasn't the end. Tomorrow we'd realize how petty we'd been and apologize. We'd put this behind us. We'd make up.

I dragged myself to my feet and turned on the sink faucet. Wetting a washcloth, I pressed it to my face. My mind still felt like it was unraveling faster than a spool of thread, and I squeezed my eyes closed to make the motion stop. *But what about the archangels?* I asked myself again. How could Patch and I have a normal relationship when they were constantly watching us? I froze. They could be watching me right now. They could be watching Patch. Trying to tell if he'd crossed the line. Looking for any excuse to send him to hell, and away from me, forever.

I felt my anger reignite. Why couldn't they leave us alone? Why were they so bent on destroying Patch? Patch had told me he was the first fallen angel to get his wings back and become a guardian angel. Were the archangels angry over that? Did they feel Patch had somehow tricked them? Or that he'd cheated his way back up from the bottom? Did they want to put him in his place? Or did they merely not trust him?

I closed my eyes, feeling a tear travel down the side of my nose. I *take it all back*, I thought. I desperately wanted to call Patch but didn't know whether I'd be putting him at some kind of risk. Could the archangels listen in on phone conversations? How were Patch and I supposed to have an honest talk if they were eavesdropping?

I also couldn't let go of my pride that quickly. Didn't he realize he was just as much in the wrong? The whole reason we'd fought in the first place was because he'd refused to tell me what he was doing at Marcie's house last night. I wasn't the jealous type, but he knew my history with Marcie. He knew this was the one time when I had to know.

There was something else causing my insides to sicken. Patch said Marcie had been attacked in the men's room at Bo's Arcade. What was Marcie doing at Bo's? As far as I knew, nobody at Coldwater High hung out at Bo's. In fact, prior to meeting Patch, I'd never heard of the place. Was it a coincidence that the day after Patch was gazing at Marcie's bedroom window, she'd wandered through Bo's front doors? Patch had insisted there was nothing but business between them, but what did that even mean? And Marcie was many things, among them seductive and persuasive. Not only did she not take no for an answer, she didn't accept any answer that wasn't exactly what she wanted.

What if, this time, she wanted . . . Patch?

A loud rap at the front door brought me out of my reverie.

I curled up in the heaps of pillows on my bed, closed my eyes, and dialed my mom. "The Parnells are here."

"Ack! I'm at the light on Walnut. I'll be there in two minutes. Invite them in."

"I barely remember Scott, and I don't remember his mom at all. I'll invite them in, but I'm not making small talk. I'll hang out in my room until you get back." I tried to convey in my tone that something was wrong, but it wasn't like I could confide in my mom. She hated Patch. She wouldn't sympathize. I couldn't take hearing the happiness and relief in her voice. Not now.

"Nora."

"Fine! I'll talk to them." I snapped my phone shut and threw it across the room.

I took my time walking to the front door and flipped the lock back. The guy standing on the doormat was tall and well built— I could tell, since his T-shirt fit on the snug side and blatantly advertised PLATINUM GYM, PORTLAND. A silver hoop ran through his right earlobe, and his Levi's hung dangerously low on the hips. He wore a pink Hawaiian-print ball cap that looked fresh off a thrift store shelf and had to be an inside joke, and his sunglasses reminded me of Hulk Hogan. Despite all this, he had a certain boyish charm.

The corners of his mouth turned up. "You must be Nora."

"You must be Scott."

He stepped inside and pulled off his sunglasses. His eyes scanned the hall leading back to the kitchen and family room. "Where's your mom?"

"On her way home with dinner."

"What are we having?"

I didn't like his use of the word "we." There was no "we." There was the Grey family, and the Parnell family. Two separate entities that happened to be sharing the same dinner table for one night.

When I didn't answer, he pushed on. "Coldwater's a little smaller than I'm used to."

I folded my arms over my chest. "It's also a little colder than Portland."

He gave me a head-to-toe, then smiled ever so slightly. "So I noticed." He sidestepped me on his way to the kitchen and tugged on the fridge door. "Got any beer?"

"What? No."

The front door was still open, and voices carried in from outside. My mom stepped over the threshold, carrying two brown paper grocery bags. A round woman with a bad pixie-style haircut and heavy pink makeup followed her in.

"Nora, this is Lynn Parnell," my mom said. "Lynn, this is Nora."

"My, my," Mrs. Parnell said, clasping her hands together. "She looks just like you, doesn't she, Blythe? And look at those legs! Longer than the Vegas strip."

I spoke up. "I know this is bad timing, but I'm not feeling well, so I'm going to go lie down—"

I broke off at the black look my mom shot in my direction. I aimed my most unjust look back.

"Scott has really grown up, hasn't he, Nora?" she said.

"Very observant."

Mom set the bags on the counter and addressed Scott. "Nora and I were a little nostalgic this morning, remembering all the things the two of you used to do. Nora told me you used to try to get her to eat roly-polies."

Before Scott could defend himself, I said, "He used to fry them alive under a magnifying glass, and he didn't try to get me to eat them. He sat on top of me and pinched my nose until I ran out of air and had to open my mouth. Then he flicked them inside."

Mom and Mrs. Parnell shared a quick look.

"Scott was always very persuasive," Mrs. Parnell said quickly. "He can talk people into doing things they'd never dream of. He has a knack for it. He talked me into buying him a 1966 Ford Mustang, mint condition. Of course, he hit me at a good time, I was so guilt-ridden over the divorce. Well. As I was saying, Scott probably made the best fried roly-polies on the whole block."

Everyone looked to me for confirmation.

I couldn't believe we were discussing this as if it was a perfectly normal topic of conversation.

"So," Scott piped up, scratching his chest. His bicep flexed when he did, but he probably knew that. "What's for dinner?"

"Lasagna, garlic bread, and a Jell-O salad," said Mom with a smile. "Nora made the salad."

This was news to me. "I did?"

"You bought the Jell-O boxes," she reminded me.

"That doesn't really count."

"Nora made the salad," Mom assured Scott. "I think everything is ready. Why don't we eat?"

Once seated, we joined hands and Mom blessed the food.

"Tell me about apartments in the neighborhood," Mrs. Parnell said, cutting the lasagna and sliding the first piece onto Scott's plate. "How much can I expect to pay for two bedrooms, two baths?"

"Depends how remodeled you want," Mom answered. "Almost everything on this side of town was built pre-1900, and it shows. When we were first married, Harrison and I looked at several inexpensive two-bedroom apartments, but there was always something wrong—holes in the walls, cockroach problems, or they weren't within walking distance of a park. Since I was pregnant, we decided we needed a bigger place. This house had been on the market for eighteen months, and we were able to get a deal we considered almost too good to be true." She looked around. "Harrison and I had planned on fully restoring it eventually, but . . . well, and then . . . as you know . . ." She bowed her head.

Scott cleared his throat. "Sorry about your dad, Nora. I still remember my dad calling me the night it happened. I was working a few blocks away at a convenience store. I hope they catch whoever killed him."

I tried to say thank you, but the words had broken to pieces in my throat. I didn't want to talk about my dad. The raw feelings from my breakup with Patch were enough to deal with. Where was he right now? Was regret eating at him? Did he understand how much I wanted to take back everything I'd said? I suddenly wondered if he'd texted me, and wished I'd brought my phone down to the dinner table. But how much could he even say? Could the archangels read his texts? How much could they see? Were they everywhere? I wondered, feeling very vulnerable.

"Tell us, Nora," Mrs. Parnell said. "What's Coldwater High like? Scott wrestled back in Portland. His team won State the last three years. Is the wrestling team here any good? I was sure we'd faced off against Coldwater before, but then Scott reminded me Coldwater is Class C."

I was slow to pull myself out of the fog of my thoughts. Did we even have a wrestling team?

"I don't know about wrestling," I said flatly, "but the basketball team went to State once."

Mrs. Parnell choked on her wine. "Once?" Her eyes cut between me and my mom, demanding an explanation.

"There's a team picture across from the front office," I said. "From the look of the picture, it was over sixty years ago."

Mrs. Parnell's eyes stretched. "Sixty years ago?" She dabbed her mouth with her napkin. "Is there something wrong with the school? The coach? The athletic director?"

"No biggie," Scott said. "I'm taking the year off."

Mrs. Parnell set down her fork with a loud chink. "But you love wrestling."

Scott shoveled in another bite of lasagna and raised an indifferent shoulder.

"And it's your senior year."

"So?" Scott said around his food.

Mrs. Parnell planted her elbows on the table and leaned in. "So you're not getting into college on your grades, mister. Your only hope this late in the game is that a community college picks you up."

"I've got other stuff I want to do."

Her eyebrows shot up. "Oh? Like repeat last year?" As soon as she said it, I saw a spark of fear in her eyes.

Scott chewed twice more, then swallowed hard. "Pass the salad, Blythe?"

My mom handed the bowl of Jell-O to Mrs. Parnell, who set it down in front of Scott a little too carefully.

"What happened last year?" my mom asked, filling the tense silence.

Mrs. Parnell waved a dismissive hand. "Oh, you know how it is. Scott got into a bit of trouble, usual stuff. Nothing every mother of a teenage boy hasn't seen before." She laughed, but her pitch was off.

"Mom," Scott said in a tone that sounded a lot like a warning.

"You know how boys are," Mrs. Parnell prattled on, gesturing with her fork. "They don't think. They live in the moment. They're reckless. Be glad you have a daughter, Blythe. Oh, my. That garlic bread is making my mouth water—pass a slice?"

"I shouldn't have said anything," my mom murmured, passing the bread. "I can't say enough how delighted we are to have you back in Coldwater."

Mrs. Parnell nodded vigorously. "We're just glad to be back, and all in one piece."

I'd paused eating, dividing glances between Scott and Mrs. Parnell, trying to figure out what was going on. Boys will be boys, that much I could buy. What I wasn't buying was Mrs. Parnell's anxious insistence that her son's trouble fell into the category of typical. And Scott's close supervision of every word that fell from her mouth wasn't helping to change my mind.

Thinking there was more to the story than they were saying, I pressed a hand to my heart and said, "Why, Scott, you didn't go around at night stealing road signs to hang in your bedroom, did you?"

Mrs. Parnell erupted into genuine, almost relieved, laughter. Bingo. Whatever trouble Scott had wormed his way into, it wasn't something as harmless as stealing road signs. I didn't have fifty dollars, but if I did, I would have bet it all on the hunch that Scott's trouble was anything but the usual stuff.

"Well," my mom said, her smile pinched at the corners, "I'm sure whatever happened is in the past. Coldwater is a great place for a fresh start. Have you registered for classes yet, Scott? Some of them fill up quickly, especially the advanced placement classes."

"Advanced placement," Scott repeated with an amused snort. "As in AP? No offense, but I'm not aiming that high. As my mom"— he reached sideways and shook her shoulder in a way that was just a little too rough to be friendly— "so kindly pointed out, if I go to college, it won't be for grades."

Not wanting to give anyone at the table a chance to pull us further away from the topic of Scott's former troubles, I said, "Oh, come on, Scott. You're killing me. What's so bad about your past? It can't be so horrible that you're not willing to tell old friends."

"Nora—," my mom started.

"Get a few DUIs? Steal a car? Joyride?"

Under the table, I felt my mom's foot come to rest on top of mine. She directed a sharp look at me that said, *What's gotten into you?*

Scott's chair scraped back against the floor, and he got to his feet. "Bathroom?" he asked my mom. He stretched his collar. "Indigestion."

"At the top of the stairs." Her voice was apologetic. She was actually apologizing for my behavior, when she was the one who'd set the whole ridiculous evening up. Anyone with a shred of perceptiveness could see that the point of this dinner wasn't to share a meal with old family friends. Vee was right—this was a meet cute. Well, I had news for my mom. Scott and me? Not happening.

After Scott excused himself, Mrs. Parnell smiled wide, as if to erase the past five minutes and start fresh. "So tell me," she said a little too brightly, "does Nora have a boyfriend?"

"No," I said at the same time Mom said, "Sort of."

"That's confusing," Mrs. Parnell said, chewing a forkful of lasagna and looking between Mom and me.

"His name is Patch," Mom said.

"Odd name," mused Mrs. Parnell. "What were his parents thinking?"

"It's a nickname," Mom explained. "Patch gets in a lot of fights. He's always needing to be *patched* up."

Suddenly I regretted ever explaining to her that Patch was his nickname.

Mrs. Parnell shook her head. "I think it's a gang name. All the gangs use nicknames. Slasher, Slayer, Maimer, Mauler, Reaper. Patch."

I rolled my eyes. "Patch is not in a gang."

"That's what you think," Mrs. Parnell said. "Gangs are for inner-city criminals, right? They're roaches that only come out at night." She grew silent, and I thought I saw her eyes flick to Scott's empty chair. "Times are changing. A couple weeks ago I watched a *Law & Order* about a new breed of wealthy suburban gangs. They called them secret societies, or blood societies, or some such nonsense, but it all boils down to the same thing. I thought it was your typical sensationalized Hollywood garbage, but Scott's dad said he's seeing more of this stuff all the time. He would know—him being a cop and all."

"Your husband is a cop?" I asked.

"Ex-husband, rot his soul."

That's enough. Scott's voice drifted out of the shadowy hall, and I jumped. I was on the verge of wondering if he'd gone to the bathroom at all, or if he'd stood just outside the dining room, eavesdropping, when it dawned on me that I didn't think he'd spoken out loud. In fact—

I was pretty sure he'd spoken to my . . . thoughts. No. Not my thoughts. His mother's. And somehow I'd overheard.

Mrs. Parnell flipped her palms up. "All I said was rot his soul—I'm not taking that back, it's exactly how I feel."

"I said stop talking." Scott's voice was quiet, eerie.

My mom spun around, as if just now noticing that Scott had entered the room. I blinked in dazed disbelief. I couldn't really have overheard him speaking to his mom's thoughts. I mean, Scott was human . . . wasn't he?

"Is that how you talk to your own mother?" Mrs. Parnell said, shaking her finger at him. But I could tell it was more for our benefit than for any purpose of putting Scott in his place.

His cold stare stayed fixed on her a moment longer, then he retreated to the front door and yanked it shut at his back.

Mrs. Parnell wiped her mouth, pink lipstick staining her napkin. "The nasty side of divorce." She let go of a long, troubled sigh. "Scott never used to have a temper. Of course, it could be that he's growing up to be his father's son. Well. It's an unpleasant topic and not appropriate for dinner. Does Patch wrestle, Nora? I bet Scott could teach him a few things."

"He plays pool," I said, my voice uninspired; I had no desire to talk about Patch. Not here, not now. Not when the subject of his name had caused a rock to swell in my throat. More than ever, I wished I'd brought my cell phone to the table. I wasn't feeling half so angry, which meant Patch had probably cooled off too. Had he forgiven me enough to send a text or call? Everything was a tangled mess, but there had to be a way around it. This wasn't as bad as it seemed. We'd find a way to work it out.

Mrs. Parnell nodded. "Polo. Now there's a true Maine sport."

"Pool as in pool halls," Mom corrected, sounding a little pale.

Mrs. Parnell cocked her head like she wasn't sure she'd heard right. "Hotbeds of gang activity," she finally said. "The Law & Order I saw? Wealthy, upper-class young men were running their neighborhood pool halls like Las Vegas casinos. Best keep a close eye on that Patch of yours, Nora. Could have a side to him he's keeping from you. A side he's keeping in the dark."

"He's not in a gang," I repeated for what felt like the millionth time, straining to hang on to a courteous tone.

But as soon as I said it, I realized I had no way of knowing for certain that Patch had *never* been in a gang. Did a group of fallen angels count as a gang? I didn't know much about his past, particularly before he met me . . .

"We'll see," Mrs. Parnell said, doubtful. "We'll see."

An hour later, the food was gone, the dishes were washed, Mrs. Parnell had finally left to hunt down Scott, and I retreated to my room. My cell was faceup on the floor, showing that I had no new texts, no new messages, and no missed calls.

My lip quivered, and I dug the heels of my hands into my eyes to stop the tears beginning to blur my vision. To keep from dwelling on all the awful things I'd said to Patch, I tried to work out in my mind a way to repair everything. The archangels couldn't forbid us from talking or seeing each other—not when Patch was my guardian angel. He had to stay in my life. We'd keep doing what we'd always done. In a couple of days, after we'd shaken off our first real fight, things would go back to normal. And who cared about my future? I could work everything out later. It wasn't like I had to have my whole life planned right this moment.

But there was one thing that just wasn't adding up. Patch and I had spent the past two months displaying our affection openly, with no reservations whatsoever. So why was he just now showing concern over the archangels?

My mom poked her head inside my room. "I'm going to pick

up a few toiletries for my trip tomorrow. I should be back soon. Need anything while I'm out?"

I noticed she didn't bring up Scott as potential boyfriend material. Apparently his uncertain past had withered her matchmaking urges. "I'm good, but thanks anyway."

She started to pull the door shut, then stopped. "We sort of have a problem. I let it slip to Lynn that you don't have a car. She volunteered Scott to drive you to summer school. I told her that really wouldn't be necessary, but I think she thought I was only saying no because I was worried we'd be putting Scott out. She said you could pay him back for his time by giving him a tour of Coldwater tomorrow."

"Vee gives me a ride to school."

"I made that clear, but she's not taking no for an answer. It might be better if you explain things to Scott directly. Thank him for the offer, but tell him you already have a ride."

Just what I wanted. More interaction with Scott.

"I'd like you to keep riding with Vee," she added slowly. "In fact, if Scott stops by while I'm out of town this week, maybe it's best to keep your distance."

"You don't trust him?"

"We don't know him very well," she said carefully.

"But Scott and I used to be best friends, remember?"

She looked at me emphatically. "That was a long time ago. Things change."

My point exactly.

"I would just like to know a bit more about Scott before you go spending too much time with him," she continued. "When I get back, I'll see what I can find out."

Well, this was an unexpected turn of events. "You're going to dig up dirt on him?"

"Lynn and I are good friends. She's under a lot of stress. She may need someone to confide in." She took a step toward my dresser, pumped a dot of my hand lotion into her palm, and rubbed her hands together. "If she mentions Scott, well, I'm not going to not listen."

"If it helps build your case that he's still up to no good, I thought he acted really weird at dinner."

"His parents are coming off a divorce," she said in that same carefully neutral tone. "I'm sure he's going through a lot of turmoil. It's hard losing a parent."

Tell me about it.

"The auction ends Wednesday afternoon, and I should be home by dinner. Vee's staying over tomorrow night, right?"

"Right," I said, just now remembering I still needed to discuss this with Vee, but I couldn't imagine there'd be a problem. "By the way, I'm thinking about getting a job." Better to toss it out in the open, especially since with any luck, I hoped to have employment before she returned home.

Mom blinked. "Where did this come from?"

"I need a car."

"I thought Vee was fine with giving you rides."

"I feel like a parasite." I couldn't even run to the store for emergency tampons without calling Vee. Worse, I'd come this close to having to hitch a ride to school today with Marcie Millar. I didn't want to make unnecessary demands on my mom, especially when money was so tight, but I didn't want a repeat of this morning, either. I'd been longing for a car ever since my mom sold the Fiat, and seeing the Cabriolet this afternoon had pushed me to action. Paying for the car myself seemed like a good compromise.

"You don't think a job will interfere with school?" Mom asked, her tone telling me she wasn't wild about the idea. Not that I'd expected her to be.

"I'm only taking one class."

"Yes, but it's chemistry."

"No offense, but I think I can handle two things at once."

At that, she sat on the edge of my bed. "Is something the matter? You're awfully snappy tonight."

I took an extra second to answer, coming very close to telling the truth. "No. I'm fine."

"You seem stressed."

"Long day. Oh, and did I mention Marcie Millar is my chem partner?"

I could tell by her expression that she knew just how deeply this cut. After all, it was my mom I'd run home to for most of the past eleven years after Marcie had had her way with me. And it was my mom who'd picked up the pieces, put me back together, and sent me back to school stronger and wiser and armed with a few tricks of my own.

"I'm stuck with her for eight weeks."

"Tell you what, if you survive all eight weeks without killing her, we can talk about getting you a car."

"You drive a hard bargain, Mom."

She kissed my forehead. "I'll expect a full report on the first couple of days when I get back from my trip. No wild parties while I'm gone."

"I make no promises."

Five minutes later, my mom steered her Taurus down the driveway. I let the curtain drop back in place, curled into the sofa, and stared at my cell phone.

But no calls came in.

I reached for Patch's necklace, still fastened around my neck, and squeezed it harder than I expected. I was struck by the horrible thought that it might be all I had left of him.

THE DREAM CAME IN THREE COLORS: BLACK, WHITE, and a wan gray.

It was a cold night. I stood barefoot on the dirt road, sludge and rain quickly filling the potholes pockmarking it. Rocks and skeletal weeds sprang up intermittently. Darkness consumed the countryside, except for one bright spot: A few hundred yards off the road sat a stone-and-wood tavern. Candles guttered in the windows, and I was just about to head toward the tavern for shelter when I heard the distant jangle of bells.

As the sound of the bells grew louder, I moved a safe distance off the road. I watched as a horse-drawn coach rattled out of the darkness and came to a halt where I'd been standing moments before. As soon as the wheels stopped rolling, the driver flung himself off the coach, splattering mud halfway up his boots. He tugged on the door and stepped back.

A dark form emerged. A man. A cape hung from his shoulders, flapping open in the wind, but the hood was drawn to cover his face.

"Wait here," he told the driver.

"My lord, it's raining heavily—"

The man in the cape gave a nod in the direction of the tavern. "I have business. I shan't be long. Keep the horses ready."

The driver's eyes shifted to the tavern. "But m'lord . . . it's thieves and vagabonds that keep company there. And there's bad air tonight. I feel it in my bones." He rubbed his arms briskly, as if to fight off a chill. "M'lord might be better to hurry back home to the lady and little 'uns."

"Speak nothing of this to my wife." The man in the cape flexed and opened his gloved hands while fixing his gaze on the tavern. "She has enough to worry about," he murmured.

I turned my attention to the tavern, and the ominous candlelight flickering in its small, slanted windows. The roof was crooked too, tilting slightly to the right, as if the tools used to construct it had been far from exact. Weeds choked the exterior, and every now and then a rowdy yell or the sound of shattered glass traveled out from its walls.

The driver dragged the sleeve of his coat under his nose. "My own son died of the plague not two years past. A terrible thing, what you and the lady are sufferin' through."

In the stiff silence that followed, the horses stamped impatiently, their coats steaming. Little puffs of frost rose from their nostrils. The picture was so authentic, it suddenly scared me. Never before had any of my dreams felt this real.

The man in the cape had started across the cobblestone walkway leading to the tavern. The edges of the dream vanished behind him, and after a moment's hesitation I started after him, afraid I'd disappear too, if I didn't stay close. I slipped through the tavern door behind him.

Halfway down the back wall was a giant oven with a brick chimney. Various wooden bowls, tin cups, and utensils flanked the walls to either side of the oven, hanging in place on large nails. Three barrels had been rolled into the corner. A mangy dog was curled up in a sleeping ball in front of them. Overturned stools and a haphazard arrangement of dirty dishes and mugs cluttered the floor, which was hardly a floor at all. It was dirt, tamped smooth and sprinkled with what looked like sawdust, and the moment I stepped on it, the mud already caked on my heels sponged up the dusty earth. I was just wishing for a hot shower, when the appearance of the ten or so customers sitting at various tables around the tavern penetrated my awareness.

Most of the men had shoulder-length hair with odd, pointed beards. Their trousers were baggy and tucked into tall boots, and their sleeves billowed. They wore broad-brimmed hats that reminded me of pilgrims.

I was definitely dreaming of a time far back in history, and since the detail of the dream was so vivid, I should have had at least some idea of what time period I'd dreamed myself into. But I was at a loss. Most likely England, but anywhere from the fifteenth to the eighteenth century. I'd gotten an A in world history this year, but period clothing hadn't been on any of our tests. Nothing in the scene before me had.

"I'm looking for a man," the man in the cape said to the bartender, who was positioned behind a waist-high table that I assumed served as the bar. "I was told to meet him here tonight, but I'm afraid I don't know his name."

The bartender, a short man, bald except for a few wiry hairs standing on end at the top of his head, eyed the man in the cape. "Something to drink?" he asked, spreading his lips to show jagged black stumps for teeth.

I swallowed the nausea that rolled through my stomach at the sight of his teeth and stepped back.

The man in the cape didn't show my same revulsion. He merely shook his head. "I need to find this man as quickly as possible. I was told you'd be able to help."

The bartender's rotted smile faded back behind his lips. "Aye,

I can help you find him, m'lord. But trust an old man and have a drink or two first. Something to warm your blood on a cold night." He pushed a small glass at the man.

Behind the hood, the man shook his head again. "I'm afraid I'm in a bit of a hurry. Tell me where I can find him." He pushed a few warped tokens across the table.

The bartender pocketed the tokens. Jerking his head at the back door, he said, "He keeps to the forest yonder. But m'lord? Be careful. Some say the forest is haunted. Some say the man who goes into the forest is the man who never comes back out."

The man in the cape leaned on the table dividing the two and lowered his voice. "I wish to ask a personal question. Does the Jewish month of Cheshvan mean anything to you?"

"I am not a Jew," the bartender said flatly, but something in his eyes told me this wasn't the first time he'd been asked the question.

"The man I've come to see tonight told me to meet him here on the first night of Cheshvan. He said he needed me to provide a service for him, for the duration of an entire fortnight."

The bartender stroked his chin. "A fortnight is a long time."

"Too long. I wouldn't have come, but I was afraid of what the man might do if I didn't. He mentioned my family by name. He *knew* them. I have a beautiful wife and four sons. I don't want them harmed."

The bartender dropped his voice, as if to share a piece of scandalous gossip. "The man you've come to see is . . ." He trailed off, casting a suspicious look around the tavern.

"He's unusually powerful," the man in the cape said. "I've seen his strength before, and he is a mighty man. I've come to reason with him. Surely he can't expect me to abandon my duties and family for such a length of time. The man will be reasonable."

"I know nothing of this man's reason," the bartender said.

"My youngest son has contracted the plague," the man in the cape explained, his voice taking on a quiver of desperation. "The doctors do not think he'll live long. My family needs me. My son needs me."

"Have a drink," the bartender said quietly. He nudged the glass forward a second time.

The man in the cape turned abruptly from the table and strode toward the back door. I followed.

Outside, I sloshed barefoot through the icy mud after him. The rain continued to pour down, and I had to walk carefully to avoid slipping. I wiped my eyes and saw the man's cape disappear into the line of trees at the edge of the forest.

I stumbled after him, hesitating at the tree line. Cupping my hands to hold back my wet hair, I peered into the deep shadow ahead.

There was a flash of movement and suddenly the man in the cape was running back toward me. He tripped and fell. The branches snagged his cape; in a frenzy, he struggled to untie it from his neck. He gave a high shriek of terror. His arms flailed wildly, his whole body twisting and jerking convulsively.

I shoved my way toward him, twigs scraping my arms, rocks stabbing at my bare feet. I dropped to my knees beside him. His hood was still mostly drawn, but I could see that his mouth was slightly open, paralyzed in a scream.

"Roll over!" I ordered him, yanking to free the fabric trapped beneath him.

But he couldn't hear me. For the first time, the dream took on a familiar edge. Just like every other nightmare I'd ever been trapped in, the harder I struggled, the more the very thing I wanted slipped out of reach.

I grabbed his shoulders and shook him. "Roll over! I can get you out of here, but you have to help."

"I'm Barnabas Underwood," he slurred. "Do you know the way to the tavern? That's a good girl," he said, patting the air as if he was patting an imaginary cheek.

I stiffened. There was no way he could see me. He was hallucinating about another girl. He had to be. How could he see me if he couldn't hear me?

"Run back and tell the barkeep to send help," he continued. "Tell him there is no man. Tell him it is one of the devil's angels, come to possess my body and cast away my soul. Tell him to send for a priest, holy water, and roses."

At the mention of the devil's angels, the hairs on my arms rose.

He snapped his head back toward the forest, straining his neck. "The angel!" he whispered in a panic. "The angel is coming!"

His mouth twisted into distorted shapes, and it looked like he was fighting for control of his own body. He arched back violently, and his hood was flung all the way off.

I was still clutching the cape, but I felt my hands reflexively slacken. I stared at the man with a gasp of surprise caught in my throat. He wasn't Barnabas Underwood.

He was Hank Millar.

Marcie's dad.

I blinked my eyes awake.

Rays of light blazed through my bedroom window. The pane was cracked, and a lazy breeze rustled the first breath of morning across my skin. My heart was still working in double time from the nightmare, but I sucked in a deep breath and reassured myself it wasn't real. Truth be told, now that my feet were planted firmly in my own world, I was more disturbed over the fact that I'd been dreaming about Marcie's dad than anything else. In a hurry to forget it, I shoved the dream aside.

I dragged my cell phone out from under my pillow and checked for messages. Patch hadn't called. Drawing the pillow against me, I curled into it and tried to ignore the hollow sensation inside me. How many hours had it been since Patch walked out? Twelve. How many more until I saw him again? I didn't know. That was what really worried me. The more time passed, the more I felt the wall of ice between us thicken.

Just get through today, I told myself, swallowing the pebble in my throat. The strange distance between us couldn't go on forever. Nothing was going to get resolved if I hid out in bed all day. I would see Patch again. He might even stop by after school. Either that, or I could call him. I kept on with these ridiculous thoughts, refusing to let myself think about the archangels. About hell. About how scared I was that Patch and I were facing a problem neither of us was strong enough to solve.

I rolled out of bed and found a yellow Post-it note stuck to the bathroom mirror.

The good news: I convinced Lynn not to send Scott over this morning to pick you up. The bad news: Lynn is set on the tour of town. At this point I'm not sure saying no is going to work. Would you mind taking him around after class? Keep it short. Really short. I left his number on the kitchen counter.

XOXO—Mom

P.S. I'll call you tonight from my hotel.

I groaned and lowered my forehead to the counter. I didn't want to spend ten more minutes with Scott, let alone a couple of hours.

Forty minutes later, I'd showered, dressed, and consumed a bowl of strawberry oatmeal. There was a knock at the front door, and I opened it to find Vee smiling. "Ready for another fun-filled day of summer school?" she asked.

I grabbed my backpack off a hook in the coat closet. "Let's just get this day over with, okay?"

"Whoa. Who peed in your Cheerios?"

"Scott Parnell." *Patch.*

"I see the incontinence problem didn't go away over time."

"I'm supposed to give him a tour of town after class."

"One-on-one time with a boy. What's to hate?"

"You should have been here last night. Dinner was bizarre. Scott's mom started to tell us about his troubled past, but Scott cut her off. Not only that, but it almost seemed like he was threatening her. Then he excused himself to use the bathroom, but ended up eavesdropping on us from the hall." *And then spoke to his mom's thoughts. Maybe.*

"Sounds like he's trying to keep his life private. Sounds like we might have to do something to change that."

I was two steps ahead of Vee, leading the way out, and I came up short. I'd just experienced a flash of inspiration. "I have a great idea," I said, turning around. "Why don't you give Scott the tour? No, seriously, Vee. You'll love him. He has that reckless, anti-rules, bad-boy attitude. He even asked if we had beer—scandalous, right? I think he's right up your alley."

"No can do. I've got a lunch date with Rixon."

I felt an unexpected stab in the vicinity of my heart. Patch and I had lunch plans today too, but somehow I doubted they were happening. What had I done? I had to call him. I had to find a way to talk to him. I wasn't going to end things like this. It was absurd. But a small voice that I despised questioned why he hadn't called first. He had just as much to apologize for as I did.

"I'll pay you eight dollars and thirty-two cents to take Scott around, final offer," I said.

"Tempting, but no. And here's another thing. Patch probably isn't going to be a happy camper if you and Scott make a habit of this exclusive time. Don't get me wrong. I couldn't care less what Patch thinks, and if you want to drive him crazy, more power to you. Still, I thought I'd raise the point."

I was halfway down the front porch steps, and my footing slipped at the mention of Patch. I thought about telling Vee that I'd called things off, but I wasn't ready to say it out loud. I felt my cell phone, with Patch's picture saved on it, burning in my pocket. Part of me wanted to hurl the phone into the trees on the far side of the road. Part of me couldn't lose him that quickly. Besides, if I told Vee, she'd inevitably point out that a breakup made us free to date other people, which was the wrong conclusion. I wasn't looking elsewhere, and neither was Patch. I hoped. This was just a snag. Our first real fight. The breakup wasn't permanent. Caught up in the moment, we'd both said things we didn't mean.

"If I were you, I'd bail," Vee said, her four-inch heels stabbing down the steps behind me. "That's what I do whenever I find myself in a jam. Call Scott and tell him your cat's coughing up mice intestines, and you have to take it to the vet after school."

"He was over here last night. He knows I don't have a cat."

"Then unless he's got overcooked spaghetti for brains, he'll figure out you're not interested."

I considered this. If I got out of giving Scott a tour of town, maybe I could borrow Vee's car and follow him. Try as I might to rationalize what I'd heard last night, I couldn't ignore the nagging suspicion that Scott had spoken to his mom's thoughts. One year ago I would have brushed the idea off as ridiculous. But things were different now. Patch had spoken to my thoughts numerous times. So had Chauncey (a.k.a. Jules), a Nephil from my past. Since fallen angels didn't age, and I'd known Scott since he was five, I'd already ruled that out. But even if Scott wasn't a fallen angel, he could still be Nephilim.

But if he was Nephilim, what was he doing in Coldwater? What was he doing living an ordinary teen life? Did he know he was Nephilim? Did Lynn? Had Scott sworn fealty to a fallen angel yet? If he hadn't, was it my responsibility to warn him about what lay ahead? I hadn't instantly hit it off with Scott, but that didn't mean I thought he deserved to give up his body for two weeks every year.

Of course, maybe he wasn't Nephilim at all. Maybe I was getting carried away with the imagined belief that I'd overheard him speak to his mom's thoughts.

After chemistry I swung by my locker, traded out my textbook for my backpack and cell, then walked to the side doors offering a clear view of the student parking lot. Scott was sitting on the hood of his silver-blue Mustang. He was still wearing the Hawaiian hat, and it dawned on me that if he kept this up, I wouldn't recognize him without it. Case in point: I didn't even know his hair color. I pulled the Post-it note my mom had left for me out of my pocket and dialed his number.

"This must be Nora Grey," he answered. "I hope you're not ditching me."

"Bad news. My cat's sick. The vet squeezed me in for a twelve thirty appointment. I'm going to have to take a rain check on the tour. Sorry," I finished, not expecting to feel quite this guilty. After all, it was just a little lie. And not one part of me honestly believed that Scott wanted a tour of Coldwater. At least, that's what I was telling myself to ease my conscience.

"Right," Scott said, and broke the connection.

I'd only just closed my cell phone when Vee came up behind me. "Let him down easy, that's my girl."

"Do you mind if I borrow the Neon for the afternoon?" I asked, watching Scott slide off the Mustang and place a call on his cell.

"What's the occasion?"

"I want to tail Scott."

"What for? This morning you made it pretty clear you think he's a bottom-feeder."

"Something about him is . . . off."

"Yeah, it's called his sunglasses. Hulk Hogan, anyone? Either way, no can do. I have my lunch date with Rixon."

"Yeah, but Rixon could give you a ride so I can have the Neon," I said, shooting a glance through the window to confirm that Scott hadn't hopped inside the Mustang yet. I didn't want him leaving before I convinced Vee to hand over the Neon's keys.

"Of course he can. But then I'd look needy. Guys today want a strong, independent woman."

"If you let me take the Neon, I'll fill up the tank."

Vee's expression softened just a tad. "All the way?"

"All the way." Or as much as eight dollars and thirty-two cents would buy.

Vee chewed her lip. "Okay," she said slowly. "But maybe I should come along and keep you company, make sure nothing bad happens."

"What about Rixon?"

"Just because I've gone and snagged myself a hot boyfriend doesn't mean I'm going to leave my best friend high and dry. Besides, I have a feeling you're going to need my help."

"Nothing bad is going to happen. I'm tailing him. He's not going to know I'm there." But I appreciated the offer. The past few months had changed me. I wasn't as naive and heedless as I'd once been, and taking Vee along appealed to me on more than one level. Especially if Scott was Nephilim. The only other Nephil I'd known had tried to kill me.

After Vee called Rixon and canceled, we waited until Scott had angled himself behind the steering wheel and backed out of his parking space before we exited the building. He turned left out of the parking lot, and Vee and I raced for her 1995 purple Dodge Neon. "You drive," Vee said, tossing me the keys. A handful of minutes later, we caught up to the Mustang, and I hung three cars back. Scott got on the highway, heading east toward the coast, and I followed.

A half hour later, Scott exited at the pier and steered into a parking lot at the edge of the strip of shops leading out to the ocean. I drove slower, allowing him time to lock the doors and walk away, then parked two rows over.

"Looks like Scotty the Potty is going shopping," Vee said. "Speaking of shopping, you don't mind if I have a look around while you run amateur-hour surveillance? Rixon said he likes it when girls accessorize with scarves, and my wardrobe is clean out of scarves."

"Go for it."

Staying a half block behind Scott, I watched him walk into a trendy clothing store and exit less than fifteen minutes later with a shopping bag. He went into another store and came out ten minutes later. Nothing out of the ordinary, and nothing that made me think he could be Nephilim. After a third store, Scott's attention was drawn toward a group of college-age girls eating lunch across the street. They sat at an umbrella table on the restaurant's outdoor terrace, wearing cutoffs and bikini tops. Scott pulled out his camera phone and clicked a few candid pictures.

I turned to grimace in the plate-glass window of the coffee shop beside me, and that was when I saw him sitting at a booth inside. He was dressed in khakis, a blue button-down, and an ivory linen blazer. His wavy blond hair was longer now, pulled back into a low ponytail. He was reading the paper.

My dad.

He folded the paper and walked toward the back of the shop.

I ran down the sidewalk to the coffee shop's entrance and pushed my way inside. My dad had disappeared in the crowd. I jogged to the back of the shop, frantically looking around. The black-and-white tiled hallway ended with the men's room on the left, the women's on the right. There was no other exit, which meant my dad had to be in the men's room.

"What are you doing?" Scott asked from directly over my shoulder.

I whirled around. "How—what—*what are you doing here?*"

"I was just about to ask you the same thing. I know you followed me. Don't look so surprised. It's called a rearview mirror. Are you stalking me for a specific reason?"

My thoughts were too jumbled to care what he was saying. "Go inside the men's room and tell me if there's a man in a blue shirt in there."

Scott tapped my forehead. "Drugs? Behavioral disorder? You're acting schizo."

"Just do it."

Scott gave the door a kick, sending it flying open. I heard the swinging of stall doors, and a moment later he returned.

"Nada."

"I saw a man in a blue shirt walk back here. There's no other way out." I turned my attention to the door across the hall—the only other door. I stepped inside the ladies' room and nudged each stall open one at a time, my heart up in my throat. All three were empty.

I realized I was holding my breath, and let it out. I had several emotions strung tight inside me, disappointment and fear at the top of the list. I'd thought I'd seen my dad alive. But it had turned out to be a cruel trick of my imagination. My dad was gone. He was never coming back, and I needed to figure out a way to accept it. I crouched down with my back to the wall and felt my whole body shake with tears.

SCOTT STOOD IN THE ENTRANCE, ARMS FOLDED. "SO this is what the inside of a women's restroom looks like. Got to say, it's a lot cleaner."

I kept my head bowed and wiped my nose with the back of my hand. "Do you mind?"

"I'm not leaving until you tell me why you followed me. I know I'm a fascinating guy, but this is starting to feel like an unhealthy obsession."

I pushed myself to my feet and splashed cold water on my face. Avoiding Scott's reflection in the mirror, I grabbed a paper towel and dried off.

"You're also going to tell me who you were looking for in the men's room," said Scott.

"I thought I saw my dad," I shot back, summoning up all the anger I could to mask the stabbing pain deep inside. "There. Satisfied?" I wadded up the towel and flung it in the trash. I was heading for the exit when Scott let the door drop closed and leaned against it, blocking me.

"Once they find the guy who did it and send him away for life, you'll feel better."

"Thanks for the worst advice I've received yet," I said bitterly, thinking that what would make me feel better was having my dad back.

"Trust me. My dad's a cop. He lives for telling surviving family members that he found the killer. They're going to find the guy who destroyed your family and make him pay. A life for a life. That's when you get your peace. Let's get out of here. I feel like a creep standing in the girls' room." He waited. "That was supposed to make you laugh."

"Not in the mood."

He laced his fingers together on top of his head and shrugged, looking uncomfortable, like he hated awkward moments, let alone knew how to resolve them. "Listen, I'm playing pool at this dive in Springvale tonight. You wanna?"

"Pass." I wasn't in the mood to play pool. All it would accomplish was to fill my head with unwanted memories of Patch. I remembered that very first night when I chased him down to finish a bio assignment and found him playing pool in the basement of Bo's. I remembered when he taught me to play pool. I remembered the way he stood behind me, so close I felt electricity.

Even more, I remembered the way he had always shown up when I needed him. But I needed him now. Where was he? Was he thinking of me?

I stood on the front porch rifling through my handbag for keys. My rain-soaked shoes squeaked against the boards, and my wet jeans rubbed a rash on the inside of my thighs. After tailing Scott, Vee had dragged me into several boutiques to get my opinion on scarves, and while I was giving her my thoughts on a violet silk versus a folksy hand-painted one in neutrals, a storm had blown in from the sea. By the time we'd sprinted to the parking lot and flung ourselves inside the Neon, we'd gone from dry to drenched. We'd blasted the heat the whole drive home, but my teeth were chattering, my clothes felt like ice painted on my skin, and I was still shaken from believing I'd seen my dad.

I shoved my shoulder against the humidity-swelled door, then patted the inside wall until my fingers fumbled the light switch. In the upstairs bathroom, I peeled out of my clothes and hung them over the shower rod to dry. On the other side of the window, lightning pitchforked down through the sky and thunder clamored like it was stomping on the roof.

I'd been alone in the farmhouse through numerous storms before, but all the experience hadn't made me any more accustomed to them. This afternoon's storm was no exception. Vee was supposed to be here now, sleeping over, but she'd decided to meet up with Rixon for a few hours since she'd canceled on him earlier. I wished I could travel back in time and tell her I'd tail Scott by myself, if she'd make sure to keep me company at the farmhouse this evening.

The bathroom lights flickered twice. That was all the warning I got before they drained, leaving me standing in shadowy darkness. Rain threw itself against the window, streaming down it in rivers. I stood in place a moment, waiting to see if the electricity would be restored. The rain turned to hail, striking the windowpanes hard enough that I feared the glass would crack.

I called Vee. "My electricity just went out."

"Yeah, the streetlights just died on me. Slackers."

"Want to drive back and keep me company?"

"Let's see. Not especially."

"You promised you'd sleep over."

"I also promised Rixon I'd meet him at Taco Bell. I'm not going to cancel on him twice in one day. Give me a few hours, then I'm all yours. I'll call you when I'm done. I'll definitely be there before midnight."

I hung up and squeezed my memory, trying to remember where I'd last seen the matches. It wasn't dark enough that I needed candles to see, but I liked the idea of lighting up the place as much as possible, especially since I was alone. Light had a way of keeping the monsters of my imagination at bay.

There were candlesticks on the dining room table, I recalled, wrapping myself in a towel and taking the stairs down to the main level. And pillar candles in the cabinets. But where were the matches?

A shadow moved in the fields behind the house, and I snapped my head toward the kitchen windows. The sheeting rain spilled down the panes, distorting the world outside, and I stepped closer for a better look. Whatever I'd seen was gone.

A coyote, I told myself, feeling a sudden rush of adrenaline. Just a coyote.

The kitchen phone shrilled, and I grabbed for it, half because I was startled and half because I wanted to hear a human voice. I prayed it was Vee calling to say she'd changed her mind.

"Hello?"

I waited.

"Hello?"

Static crackled in my ear.

"Vee? Mom?" At the edge of my vision, I saw another shadow slink through the fields. Sucking in a steadying breath, I reminded myself there was no possible way that I was in any true danger.

Patch might not be my boyfriend, but he was still my guardian angel. If there was trouble, he'd be here. But even as I thought it, I wondered if I could count on Patch for anything anymore.

He must hate me, I thought. He must want nothing to do with me. He must still be furious, and that's why he'd made no effort to contact me.

The trouble with that train of thought was that it only made me angry again. Here I was, worrying about him, but chances were, wherever he was, he wasn't worrying about me. He'd said he wasn't going to just swallow my decision to break up, but that's exactly what he'd done. He hadn't texted or called. He hadn't *anything*. And it wasn't like he didn't have a reason. He could knock on my door right this very minute and tell me what he'd been doing at Marcie's two nights ago. He could tell me why he'd driven off when I told him I loved him.

Yes, I was angry. Only this time, I was going to do something about it.

I slammed the home phone down and scrolled through my cell phone, looking for Scott's number. I was going to throw caution to the wind and take him up on his offer. Even though I knew it was for all the wrong reasons, I wanted to go out with Scott. I wanted to give Patch the finger. If he thought I was going to sit home and cry over him, he was wrong. We'd broken up; I was free to go out with other guys. And while I was at it, I was going to test Patch's ability to keep me safe. Maybe Scott really was Nephilim. Maybe he was even trouble. Maybe he was exactly the kind of guy I should stay away from. I felt a hard smile cross my face as I realized it didn't matter what I did, or what Scott might do; Patch had to protect me.

"Have you left for Springvale yet?" I asked Scott, after keying in his number.

"Hanging with me isn't so bad after all?"

"If you're going to rub it in, I'm not going."

I heard him smile. "Easy, Grey, I'm just playing with you."

I'd promised my mom I'd keep my distance from Scott, but I wasn't worried. If Scott messed with me, Patch would have to step in.

"Well?" I said. "Are you going to pick me up or what?"

"I'll swing by after seven."

Springvale is a small fishing town, and most of it is crammed onto Main Street: the post office, a few fish-and-chips diners, tackle shops, and the Z Pool Hall.

The Z stood one story high, with a plate-glass window offering a view inside to the pool hall and bar. Trash and weeds decorated the exterior. Two men with shaved heads and goatees were smoking on the sidewalk just outside the doors; they ground out their cigarettes and disappeared inside.

Scott parked in an angled slot near the doors. "I'm going to run down a couple blocks and find an ATM," he said, killing the engine.

I studied the storefront sign hanging above the window. THE Z POOL HALL. The name tickled my memory.

"Why does this place sound familiar?" I asked.

"Couple weeks back a guy bled out on one of the tables. Bar brawl. It was all over the news."

Oh.

"I'll come with you," I offered quickly.

He swung out, and I followed suit. "Nah," he called over the rain. "You'll get soaked. Wait inside. I'll be back in ten." Without giving me another chance to tag along, he hunched his shoulders against the rain, shoved his hands in his pockets, and jogged down the sidewalk.

Slicking rain off my face, I tucked myself under the building's overhang and summed up my options. I could go inside alone, or I could wait here for Scott. I hadn't waited five seconds before my skin started to itch. While the sidewalk held little foot traffic, it wasn't completely desolate. Those who were out in the weather wore flannel shirts and work boots. They looked bigger, tougher, meaner than the men who loitered around Main Street in Coldwater. A few gave me eyes as they passed.

I looked down the sidewalk in the direction Scott had taken off and saw him round the building and disappear down the side alley. My first thought was that he was going to have a hard time finding an ATM in the alley next to the Z. My second thought was that maybe he'd lied to me. Maybe he wasn't going in search of an ATM after all. But then what was he doing in an alley, out in the rain? I wanted to follow him but didn't know how I was going to stay out of sight. The last thing I needed was for him to catch me spying on him again. It certainly wouldn't promote trust between us.

Thinking maybe I could figure out what he was doing by watching through one of the windows inside the Z, I tugged on the door handle.

The air inside was cool and coated with smoke and male perspiration. The ceiling was low, the walls concrete. A few posters of muscle cars, a *Sports Illustrated* calendar, and a Budweiser mirror offered the only decoration. No windows paneled the wall dividing me from Scott. I strolled down the center aisle, wading deeper into the shadowy hall, and kept my breathing shallow, trying to filter my intake of carcinogens. When I got to the back of the Z, I fixed my eyes on the exit leading into the rear alley. Not quite as convenient as a window, but it would have to do. If Scott caught me watching him, I could always feign innocence and claim I'd stepped out for fresh air. After making sure no one was watching, I opened the door and stuck my head out.

Hands grabbed the collar of my jean jacket, yanked me out, and backed me against the brick exterior.

"What are you doing here?" Patch demanded. Rain hissed down behind him, spilling off the metal awning.

"Playing pool," I stammered, my heart still frozen from the surprise of being ripped off my feet.

"Playing pool," he repeated, not sounding even close to buying it.

"I'm here with a friend. Scott Parnell."

His expression hardened.

"Do you have a problem with that?" I shot back. "We broke up, remember? I can go out with other guys if I want." I was angry—at the archangels, at fate, at consequences. I was angry for being here with Scott, not Patch. And I was angry at Patch for not pulling me into his arms and telling me he wanted to put everything that had happened to us in the past twenty-four hours behind him. Everything dividing us was washed away, and it was just me and him from now on.

Patch dropped his gaze to the ground and pinched the bridge of his nose. I could tell he was summoning patience from deep within. "Scott's Nephilim. A first-generation purebred. Just like Chauncey was."

I blinked. It was true, then. "Thanks for the info, but I already suspected."

He made a disgusted gesture. "Quit with the bravery act. He's Nephilim."

"Every Nephil isn't Chauncey Langeais," I said testily. "Every Nephil isn't evil. If you'd give Scott a chance, you'd see he's actually quite—"

"Scott isn't any old Nephil," Patch said, cutting me off. "He belongs to a Nephilim blood society that has been growing in power. The society wants to free Nephilim from bondage to fallen angels during Cheshvan. They're recruiting members like crazy to fight back against fallen angels, and a turf war is brewing between the two sides. If the society becomes powerful enough, fallen angels will back off . . . and start relying on humans as their vassals instead."

I bit my lip and looked up at him uneasily. Without wanting to, I remembered last night's dream. Cheshvan. Nephilim. Fallen angels. I couldn't escape any of it.

"Why don't fallen angels usually possess humans?" I asked. "Why do they choose Nephilim?"

"Human bodies aren't as strong or resilient as Nephilim bodies," Patch replied. "A two-week-long possession will kill them. Tens of thousands of humans would die every Cheshvan.

"And it's a lot harder to possess a human," he continued. "Fallen angels can't force humans to swear fealty, they have to convince them to turn over their bodies. That takes time and persuasion. Human bodies also deteriorate faster. Not many fallen angels want to go to the trouble of possessing a human body if it could be dead in a week."

A shiver of foreboding crept through me, but I said, "That's a sad story, but it's hard to blame Scott or any Nephilim, for that matter. I wouldn't want a fallen angel taking control of my body two weeks out of every year either. This doesn't sound like a Nephilim problem. It sounds like a fallen angel problem."

A muscle in his jaw jumped. "The Z isn't your kind of place. Go home."

"I just got here."

"Bo's is mild compared to this place."

"Thanks for the tip, but I'm not really in the mood to hang out at home all night feeling sorry for myself."

Patch folded his arms and studied me. "You're putting yourself in danger to get back at me?" he guessed. "In case you forgot, I'm not the one who called things off."

"Don't flatter yourself. This isn't about you."

Patch dug in his pocket for his keys. "I'm taking you home." His tone told me I was a huge inconvenience, and that if he saw any way around it, he'd gladly opt out.

"I don't want a ride. I don't need your help."

He laughed, but the sound lacked humor. "You're getting in the Jeep, even if I have to drag you inside, because you're not staying here. It's too dangerous."

"You can't order me around."

He merely looked at me. "And while you're at it, you're going to stop hanging out with Scott."

I felt my anger bubbling up. How dare he assume I was weak and helpless. How dare he try to control me by telling me where I could and couldn't go, and who I could spend time with. How dare he act like I'd meant nothing to him.

I sent him a look of cool defiance. "Don't do me any more

favors. I never asked. And I don't want you as my guardian angel anymore."

Patch stood over me, and a drop of rain slid from his hair, landing like ice on my collarbone. I felt it slide along my skin, disappearing beneath the neckline of my shirt. His eyes followed the raindrop, and I began to quiver on the inside. I wanted to tell him I was sorry for everything I'd said. I wanted to tell him I didn't care about Marcie, or what the archangels thought. I cared about us. But the cold hard truth was, nothing I said or did could realign the stars. I couldn't care about us. Not if I wanted to keep Patch close. Not if I didn't want him banished to hell. The more we fought, the easier it was to get swallowed up in hatred and convince myself that he meant nothing to me, and that I could move on without him.

"Take it back," Patch said, his voice low.

I couldn't bring myself to look at him, and I couldn't bring myself to take it back. I tipped my chin up and pinned my eyes on the blur of rain over his shoulder. Damn my pride, and damn his, too.

"Take it back, Nora," Patch repeated more firmly.

"I can't do the right thing with you in my life," I said, hating myself for allowing my chin to tremble. "This will be easier on everyone if we just—I want a clean break. I've thought this through." I hadn't. I hadn't thought this through at all. I hadn't meant to say these words. But a small, horrible, and despicable part of me wanted Patch to hurt as much as I was hurt. "I want you out of my life. All the way."

After a heavy beat of silence, Patch reached around me and shoved something deep into the back pocket of my jeans. I couldn't tell whether I'd imagined that his hand had stayed there a half beat longer than necessary.

"Cash," he explained. "You're going to need it."

I dug the money out. "I don't want your money." When he didn't take the outstretched wad of cash, I slapped it against his chest, meaning to brush past him as I did, but Patch caught my hand, trapping it against his body.

"Take it." The tone of his voice told me I knew nothing. I didn't understand him, or his world. I was a stranger, and I'd never fit in. "Half the guys in there are carrying some form of weapon. If anything happens, throw the money on the table and head for the doors. Nobody's going to follow you with a pile of cash up for grabs."

I remembered Marcie. Was he suggesting that someone might try to knife me? I nearly laughed. Did he honestly think that would scare me? Whether I wanted him as my guardian angel was irrelevant. The fact of the matter was, nothing I said or did would change his duty. He had to keep me safe. The fact that he was here right now proved it.

He released my hand and tugged on the door handle, the muscles along his arm rigid. The door closed behind him, quaking on its hinges.

CHAPTER 6

I FOUND SCOTT LEANING ON HIS POOL STICK AT A TABLE near the front. He was studying a spread of billiard balls when I walked up.

"Find an ATM?" I asked, tossing my damp jean jacket on a metal folding chair pushed up against the wall.

"Yeah, but not before I swallowed ten gallons of rain." He lifted the Hawaiian hat and shook out the water for emphasis. Maybe he'd found an ATM—but not until after he'd finished whatever it was he'd been doing in the side alley. And as much as I would have liked to know what that was, I probably wasn't going to find out any time soon. I'd missed my chance when Patch had pulled me away to tell me I was in over my head here at the Z and should run along home.

I spread my hands on the lip of the pool table and leaned in casually, hoping I looked completely in my element, but the truth was, my heart rate was high. Not only had I just come off a confrontation with Patch, but no one in the near vicinity looked remotely friendly. And try as I might, I couldn't sweep away the memory that someone had bled out on one of the tables. Was it this one? I pushed up from the table and brushed my hands clean.

"We're just about to start a game," Scott said. "Fifty dollars and you're in. Grab a cue."

I wasn't in the mood to play and would have preferred watching, but a quick scan of the room revealed that Patch was seated at a poker table in the back. Even though his body wasn't directly facing mine, I knew he was watching me. He was watching everyone in the room. He never went anywhere without making a careful and detailed assessment of his surroundings.

Knowing this, I tried on the most dazzling smile I had inside me at the moment. "I'd love to." I didn't want Patch to know how upset I was, how much I was hurting. I didn't want him to think I wasn't having a good time with Scott.

But before I could head over to the rack, a short man in wire glasses and a sweater vest came up beside Scott. Everything about him looked out of place—he was groomed, his trousers were pressed, and his loafers were polished. He asked Scott in a voice almost too muted to hear, "How much?"

"Fifty," Scott answered with a touch of annoyance. "Same as always."

"The game has a hundred minimum."

"Since when?"

"Let me rephrase. For you it has a hundred minimum."

Scott went red in the face, reached for his drink on the table's edge, and tipped it back. Then he retrieved his wallet and crammed a wad of cash into the front pocket of the man's shirt. "There's fifty. I'll pay the other half after the game. Now get your bad breath out of my face so I can concentrate."

The short man tapped a pencil against his bottom lip. "You're going to have to settle your account with Dew first. He's getting impatient. He's been generous with you, and you haven't returned the favor."

"Tell him I'll have the money by the end of the night."

"That line wore out its welcome a week ago."

Scott stepped closer, crowding the man's space. "I'm not the only guy here who owes Dew a little."

"But you're the one he's worried won't pay him back." The short man pulled out the cash Scott had tucked in his pocket and let the bills flutter to the ground. "Like I said, Dew's getting restless." He gave Scott a meaningful raise of his eyebrows and walked off.

"How much do you owe Dew?" I asked Scott.

He glared at me.

Okay, next question. "What's the competition like?" I spoke in hushed tones as I eyed the other players scattered around the various pool tables. Two out of every three were smoking. Three out of every three had tattoos of knives, guns, and various other weaponry climbing their arms. Any other night and I might have been scared, or at the very least uncomfortable, but Patch was still in the corner. As long as he was here, I knew I was safe.

Scott snorted. "These guys are amateurs. I could beat them on my worst day. My real competition is in there." He shifted his gaze toward a corridor that branched off from the main area. The corridor was narrow and dim, and led to a room that glowed a luminous orange. A curtain of beads hung across the doorway. One intricately carved pool table sat just back from the entrance.

"That's where the big money plays?" I guessed.

"Back there, I could make in one game what I make in fifteen out here."

Out of the corner of my eye, I saw Patch's gaze flick to me. Pretending not to notice, I reached into my back pocket and took a step closer to Scott. "You need a hundred total for the next game, right? Here's . . . fifty," I said, quickly counting the two twenties and ten Patch had given me. I wasn't a big fan of gambling, but I wanted to prove to Patch that the Z wasn't going to eat me alive and spit me out. I could fit in. Or at least not get pushed around. And if it looked like I was flirting with Scott in the process, so be it. *Screw you,* I thought across the room, even though I knew Patch couldn't hear me.

Scott looked between me and the money in my hand. "Is this a joke?"

"If you win, we'll split the profit."

Scott considered the money with a lust that caught me off guard. He *needed* the money. He wasn't at the Z tonight for entertainment. Gambling was an addiction.

He swiped the money and jogged over to the short man in the sweater vest, whose pencil was furiously but meticulously scribbling numbers and balances for the other players. I stole a glance at Patch, to see his reaction to what I'd just done, but his eyes were on the poker game, his expression undecipherable.

The man in the sweater vest counted Scott's money, skillfully lining up the bills so they all faced the same direction. When he finished, he gave Scott a tight-lipped smile. It looked like we were in.

Scott returned, chalking his pool stick. "You know what they say about good luck. Got to kiss my cue." He stuck it in my face.

I took a step back. "I'm not kissing your pool stick."

Scott flapped his arms and playfully made chicken noises.

I glanced to the back of the hall, hoping to confirm that Patch wasn't watching the humiliating scene unfolding, and that was when I saw Marcie Millar saunter up behind him, lean in, and cross her arms around his neck.

My heart dropped to my knees.

Scott was speaking, tapping the pool stick against my forehead, but the words went right past. I fought to recapture my breath and focused on the blur of concrete straight ahead to ground my complete shock and sense of betrayal. So this was what he meant when he said things with Marcie were strictly business? Because it sure didn't look that way to me! And what was she doing here after having just been knifed at Bo's? Did she feel safe because she was with Patch? On a split-second thought, I wondered if he was doing this to make me jealous. But if that were the case, he would have to have known I'd be at the Z tonight. Which he couldn't have, unless he'd been spying on me. Had he been around more the past twenty-four hours than I'd originally believed?

I dug my fingernails into the palms of my hands, struggling to focus on the pain there, and not the choked, humiliated feeling rising inside me. I stood that way, numb and holding in the threat of tears, before my attention was pulled to the doorway leading into the corridor. A guy in a red muscle tee leaned on the frame. Something was wrong with a patch of skin at the base of his throat—it almost looked deformed. Before I could take a closer look, I was paralyzed by a flash of déjà vu. Something about him was startlingly familiar, even though I knew we'd never met. I had a strong urge to run, but at the same time was overwhelmed by the need to place him.

He picked up the white cue ball from the table closest to him and tossed it lazily a few times in the air.

"Come on," Scott said, waving the pool stick back and forth across my line of vision. The other guys surrounding the table laughed. "Do it, Nora," Scott said. "Just a little peck. For luck."

He slipped the pool stick under the hem of my shirt and lifted it.

I slapped the pool stick away. "Knock it off."

I saw movement from the guy in the red muscle tee. It happened so fast it took two beats of my heart to realize what was about to happen. He cranked his arm and hurled the cue ball across the room. An instant later, the mirror hanging on the far wall shattered, shards of glass raining to the floor.

The room fell silent except for the classic rock playing through the speakers.

"You," the guy in the red muscle tee said. He aimed a handgun at the man in the sweater vest. "Give me the money." He motioned him closer with a flick of the gun. "Keep your hands where I can see them."

Beside me, Scott pushed forward to the front of the crowd. "No way, man. That's our money." A few shouts of agreement rose up from the room.

The guy in the red tee kept the gun trained on the man in the sweater vest, but his eyes roved sideways to Scott. He grinned, baring teeth. "Not anymore."

"If you take that money, I'll kill you." There was a calm fury to

Scott's voice. He sounded like he meant it. I stood frozen in place, barely breathing, terrified of what might happen next, because not one part of me doubted that the gun was loaded.

The gunman's smile grew. "That so?"

"Nobody in here is going to let you leave with our money," Scott said. "Do yourself a favor and put the gun down."

Another murmur of agreement circled the room.

Despite the fact that the temperature in the room seemed to be rising, the guy in the red muscle tee lazily scratched his neck with the barrel of the gun. He didn't appear the least bit worried. "No." Switching the gun to aim at Scott, he ordered, "Get on the table."

"Get lost."

"*Get on the table!*"

The guy in the red tee was two-handing the gun, aiming at Scott's chest. Very slowly, Scott raised his hands level with his shoulders and scooted backward onto the pool table. "You won't leave alive. You're outnumbered thirty to one."

The guy in the red tee crossed to Scott in three strides. He stood directly in front of Scott for a moment, his finger poised on the trigger. A bead of sweat trickled down the side of Scott's face. I couldn't believe he didn't wrench the gun away. Didn't he know he couldn't die? Didn't he know he was Nephilim? But Patch had said he belonged to a Nephilim blood society—how could he not know?

"You're making a big mistake," Scott said, his voice still cool, but spilling the first drop of panic.

I wondered why nobody made a move to help him. As Scott had pointed out, the crowd had the guy in the red tee outnumbered by a landslide. But there was something vicious and frighteningly powerful about him. Something . . . otherworldly. I wondered if they were just as spooked by him as I was.

I also wondered if the queasy and uncomfortably familiar feeling inside me meant he was a fallen angel. Or Nephilim.

Out of all the faces in the crowd, I suddenly found myself locking eyes with Marcie. She stood across the crowd, with something I could only describe as bewildered fascination written all over her expression. I knew, right then, that she had no idea what was about to happen. She didn't realize Scott was Nephilim and had more strength in one of his hands than a human had in his whole body. She hadn't seen Chauncey, the first Nephil I'd ever met, mangle my cell phone in the palm of his hand. She hadn't been there the night he'd chased me through the halls of the high school. And the guy in the red muscle tee? Whether Nephilim or fallen angel, he was likely just as powerful. Whatever was about to happen, it wasn't a mere fistfight.

She should have learned her lesson at Bo's and stayed home. And so should have I.

The guy in the red tee shoved Scott with the gun, and he flew back on the tabletop. Out of surprise or fear, Scott fumbled his pool stick, and the guy in the red tee snatched it up. Without pausing, he leaped onto the table and held the pool stick pointed down at

Scott's face. He drilled the stick into the table an inch from Scott's ear. The pool stick went down with such force, it smashed through the felt surface. Twelve inches of it were visible beneath the table.

I swallowed a scream.

Scott's Adam's apple quivered. "You're crazy, man," he said.

Suddenly a bar stool flew through the air, knocking the guy in the red tee sideways. He caught his balance but had to jump off the table to keep it.

"Get him!" someone in the crowd shouted.

Something like a war cry went up, and more people grabbed for bar stools. I went down on my hands and knees and looked through the forest of legs for the nearest exit. A few bodies away there was a guy with a gun holstered in an ankle strap. He reached for it, and a moment later the splintering sound of shots rang out. What followed was not silence, but more mayhem: swearing, shouting, and fists hammering into flesh. I got to my feet and ran in a crouch toward the back door.

I'd just slipped through the exit when someone hooked the waistband of my jeans and hauled me upright. Patch.

"Take the Jeep," he ordered, shoving his car keys into my hand. A hasty pause. "What are you waiting for?"

My eyes teared up, but I angrily blinked them away. "Quit acting like I'm a huge inconvenience! I never asked for your help!"

"I told you not to come tonight. You wouldn't be an inconvenience if you'd listened. This isn't your world—it's mine. You're so bent on proving you can handle it that you're going to do something stupid and get yourself killed."

I resented that, and opened my mouth to say so.

"The guy in the red shirt is Nephilim," Patch said, cutting me out of the conversation. "The branding mark means he's in deep with the blood society I told you about earlier. He's sworn allegiance to them."

"Branding mark?"

"Near his collarbone."

The deformity was from a branding? I shifted my eyes to the small window set in the door. Inside, bodies swarmed over the pool tables, punches being thrown in every direction. I didn't see the guy in the red tee anymore, but now I understood why I'd recognized him. He was Nephilim. He'd reminded me of Chauncey in a way Scott hadn't even come close to. I wondered if this could somehow mean that, like Chauncey, he was evil. And Scott was not.

A loud noise seemed to rupture my eardrums, and Patch yanked me to the ground. Fragments of glass hailed down around us. The window in the back door had been shot out.

"Get out of here," Patch said, pushing me in the direction of the street.

I turned back. "Where are you going?"

"Marcie's still inside. I'll get a ride with her."

My lungs seemed to lock, no air going in or out. "What about me? You're my guardian angel."

Patch sliced his eyes into mine. "Not anymore, Angel." Before I could argue back, he slipped through the door, vanishing into the mayhem.

Out on the street, I unlocked the Jeep, jerked the seat forward, and floored it out of the parking space. He wasn't my guardian angel anymore? Was he serious? All because I'd told him that's how I wanted it? Or had he said it to scare me? To make me regret saying I didn't want him? Well, if he wasn't my guardian, it was because I was trying to do the right thing! I was trying to make this easier on both of us. I was trying to keep him safe from the archangels. I'd told him exactly why I'd done it, and he was hanging it over my head, as if this whole mess was somehow my fault. As if this was what I wanted! This was more his fault than mine. I had the urge to run back and tell him I wasn't helpless. I wasn't a pawn in his big, bad world. And I wasn't blind. I could see well enough to know something was going on between him and Marcie. In fact, I was now all but certain something was. Forget it. I was better off without him. He was slime. A jerk. An untrustworthy jerk. I didn't need him—for anything.

I rolled the Jeep to a stop in front of the farmhouse. My legs were still trembling, and my breath rattled a little when I exhaled. I was acutely aware of the quiet all around. The Jeep had always been a place of refuge; tonight it felt foreign and isolated, and far too big for just one person. I lowered my head onto the steering wheel and cried. I didn't think about Patch driving Marcie home in her car—I just let the hot air from the vents rush over my skin and breathed in the scent of Patch.

I sat that way, hunched and sobbing, until the needle on the gas gauge dropped half a bar. I dabbed my eyes dry and let go of a long, troubled sigh. I was just about to shut off the engine when I saw Patch standing on the porch, leaning on one of the support beams.

For a moment I thought he'd come to check on me, and tears of relief sprang to my eyes. But I was driving his Jeep. He'd most likely come to take it back. After the way he'd treated me tonight, I couldn't believe there was any other reason.

He walked down the driveway and opened the driver's-side door. "You okay?"

I nodded stiffly. I would have said yes, but my voice was still hiding out in the vicinity of my stomach. The cold-eyed Nephil was fresh in my thoughts, and I couldn't stop wondering what had happened after I left the Z. Had Scott gotten out? Had Marcie?

Of course she had. Patch had seemed bent on making sure of it.

"Why did the Nephil in the red shirt want money?" I asked, climbing sideways into the passenger seat. It was still sprinkling, and even though I knew Patch couldn't feel the damp chill of the rain, it felt somehow wrong to leave him standing in it.

After a count, he got behind the wheel, closing us into the Jeep together. Two nights ago the gesture would have felt intimate. Now it just felt tense and awkward. "He was fund-raising for the

Nephilim blood society. I wish I had a better idea of what they're planning. If they need money, it's most likely for resources. Either that, or to buy off fallen angels. But how, who, and why, I don't know." He shook his head. "I need someone on the inside. For the first time, being an angel puts me at a disadvantage. They're not going to let me within a mile of the operation."

For a split second it occurred to me that he could be asking for my help, but I was hardly Nephilim. I had an infinitesimal amount of Nephilim blood running through my veins that could be traced back over four hundred years to my Nephilim ancestor, Chauncey Langeais. For all intents and purposes, I was human. I wasn't getting on the inside any faster than Patch.

I said, "You said Scott and the Nephil in the red shirt are both part of the blood society, but they didn't seem to know each other. Are you sure Scott's involved?"

"He's involved."

"Then how could they not know each other?"

"My best guess right now is that whoever's running the society is separating the individual members to keep them in the dark. Without solidarity, the chances of a coup are low. More than that, if they don't know how strong they are, the Nephilim can't leak that information to the enemy. Fallen angels can't get information if the society members themselves know nothing."

Digesting this, I wasn't sure whose side I was on. Part of me abhorred the idea of fallen angels possessing the bodies of

Nephilim every Cheshvan. A less noble part of me was grateful they were targeting Nephilim and not humans. Not me. Not anyone I loved.

"And Marcie?" I said, trying to keep my voice neutral.

"She likes poker," Patch said noncommittally. He put the Jeep in reverse. "I should be going. You going to be okay tonight? Is your mom gone?"

I turned in the seat to face him. "Marcie had her arms around you."

"Marcie's sense of personal space is nonexistent."

"So you're an expert on Marcie now?"

His eyes darkened, and I knew I wasn't supposed to go there, but I didn't care. I was so going there. "What's going on between the two of you? What I saw didn't look like business."

"I was in the middle of a game when she came up behind me. It's not the first time a girl has done that, and it probably won't be the last."

"You could have pushed her away."

"She had her arms around me one moment, and the next moment the Nephil threw the cue ball. I wasn't thinking about Marcie. I ran outside to check the perimeter in case he wasn't alone."

"You went back for her."

"I wasn't going to leave her there."

I stayed in my seat a moment, the knot in my stomach so tight it hurt. What was I supposed to think? Had he gone back for Marcie out of courtesy? A sense of duty? Or something entirely different, and much more worrisome?

"I had a dream about Marcie's dad last night." I wasn't even sure why I'd said it. Possibly to communicate to Patch that my pain was so raw it had even entered my dreams. I'd once read that dreams are a way of reconciling what's happening in our lives, and if that was true, my dream was definitely telling me I hadn't come to terms with whatever was going on between Patch and Marcie. Not if I was dreaming about fallen angels and Cheshvan. Not if I was dreaming about Marcie's father.

"You dreamed about Marcie's dad?" Patch's voice was as calm as ever, but something in the way he looked sharply at me made me think he was surprised by this news. Maybe even disconcerted.

"I think I was in England. A long time ago. Marcie's dad was being chased through a forest. Only he couldn't get away, because his cape got tangled in the trees. He kept saying a fallen angel was trying to possess him."

Patch pondered this a moment. Once again, his silence told me I'd said something that interested him. But I couldn't guess what.

He glanced at his watch. "Need me to walk through the house?"

I gazed up at the dark, vacant windows of the farmhouse. The combination of nightfall and drizzling rain cast a gloomy, uninviting feeling all around. I couldn't tell which was less appealing:

going inside alone, or sitting out here with Patch, scared he might be moving on. To Marcie Millar.

"I'm hesitating because I don't want to get wet. Besides, you obviously have somewhere to be." I pushed on the door and swung one leg out. "That, and our relationship is over. You don't owe me any favors."

We locked eyes.

I'd said it to hurt him, but I was the one with the lump in my throat. Before I could say something that would slice deeper, I dashed for the porch, holding my arms over my head to shield my hair from the rain.

Inside, I leaned against the front door and listened to Patch drive away. My vision smeared with tears, and I closed my eyes. I wished Patch would come back. I wanted him here. I wanted him to pull me against him and kiss away the cold, empty feeling slowly freezing me from the inside out. But the sound of tires skimming over the wet road outside never came.

Without warning, the unbidden memory of our last night together before everything collapsed drifted up from my memory. I automatically started to block it. The trouble was, I *wanted* to remember. I needed some way to still have Patch close. Dropping my guard, I let myself feel his mouth on mine. Light at first, then more serious. I felt his body, warm and solid, against mine. His hands were at the nape of my neck, fastening his silver chain. He promised to love me forever. . . .

I turned the deadbolt, dissolving the memory with a click. Screw.
Him. I'd keep saying the words as many times as it took.

In the kitchen, the lights answered at the flip of a switch, and I
was relieved to find the electricity up and running. The phone was
blinking red, and I played the messages.

"Nora," my mom's voice said, "we're getting tons of rain here in
Boston, and they've decided to reschedule the rest of the auctions.
I'm headed home and should be there by eleven. You can send Vee
home if you'd like. Love you and see you soon."

I checked the clock. It was a few minutes before ten. I had only
one more hour alone.

CHAPTER

7

THE FOLLOWING MORNING, I DRAGGED MYSELF OUT
of bed, and after a quick stint in the bathroom that
included dabbing on under-eye concealer and spritz-
ing my hair with curl revitalizer, I moseyed into the kitchen to
find my mom already seated at the table. She had a mug of herbal
tea between her hands, and her hair had a tousled, slept-on look,
which was a nice way of saying she looked like a porcupine. Glancing at me over the top of her mug, she smiled. "Morning."

I slid into the seat opposite and shook shredded wheat into a bowl. My mom had set out strawberries and a small pitcher of milk, and I added both to the cereal. I tried to be conscientious about what I ate, but it always seemed much easier when my mom was home, making sure meals amounted to more than whatever I could grab in ten seconds.

"Sleep well?" she asked.

I nodded, having just eaten a spoonful of cereal.

"I forgot to ask last night," Mom said. "Did you end up taking Scott on a tour of town?"

"I canceled." Probably best to leave it at that. I wasn't sure how she'd react if she found out I'd tailed him to the pier, then spent the evening with him at a dive of a pool hall in Springvale.

Mom's nose wrinkled. "Is that . . . smoke I smell?"

Oh shoot.

"I lit some candles in my room this morning," I said, regretting that I hadn't taken the time to shower. I was sure the Z lingered in my clothes, my sheets, my hair.

She frowned. "That's definitely smoke I smell." Her chair scraped back, and she started to stand, on her way over to investigate.

No use stalling now. I scratched my eyebrow nervously. "I sort of went to a pool hall last night."

"Patch?" We'd settled on a rule not too long ago that I was absolutely not, under any circumstances, allowed to go out with Patch while my mom was away.

"He was there, yes."

"And?"

"I didn't go with Patch. I went with Scott." By the look on her face, I was pretty sure this was worse. "But before you blow up," I rushed on, "I just want to say that my curiosity is killing me. I'm having a really hard time ignoring the fact that the Parnells are doing everything possible to keep Scott's past in the dark. Why is it that every time Mrs. Parnell opens her mouth, Scott is two inches away, watching her like a hawk? What could he have done that was so bad?"

I expected my mom to jump to her feet and tell me that starting the minute I got home from school this afternoon, I was grounded until the Fourth of July, but she said, "I noticed that too."

"Is it just me, or does she seem scared of him?" I continued, relieved that she appeared more interested in discussing Scott than my punishment for spending the evening at a sketchy pool hall.

"What kind of mother is scared of her own son?" Mom wondered aloud.

"I think she knows his secret. She knows what he did. And he knows that she knows." Maybe Scott's secret was simply that he was Nephilim, but I didn't think so. Based on his reaction last night when he'd been attacked by the red-shirted Nephil, I was beginning to suspect he didn't know the truth about who he was, or what he was capable of. He might have noticed his incredible strength or his ability to speak to people's thoughts, but he probably didn't know how to explain it. But if Scott and his mom weren't trying to hide his Nephilim heritage, what were they trying to hide? What had he done that needed so much covering up?

Thirty minutes later, I strolled into chemistry to find Marcie already at our desk, talking on her cell phone, completely ignoring the sign on the whiteboard that read NO CELL PHONES, NO EXCEPTIONS. When she saw me, she gave me her back and cupped a hand over her mouth, clearly wanting privacy. Like I cared. By the time I made it to our desk, the only part of the conversation I picked up was a seductive, "Love you, too."

She slipped her cell inside a pouch at the front of her backpack and smiled at me. "My boyfriend. He doesn't go to high school."

I immediately had a moment of self-doubt and wondered if Patch was on the other end of the line, but he had sworn that what happened between him and Marcie last night meant nothing. I could either stir myself into a jealous frenzy, or I could believe him. I nodded sympathetically. "Must be hard dating a dropout."

"Ha, ha. Just so you know, I'm sending out a text after class to everyone who's invited to my annual summer party Tuesday night. You're on the list," she said casually. "Missing my party is the surest way to sabotage your social life ... not that you have to worry about sabotaging something you don't have."

"Annual summer party? Never heard of it."

She retrieved a makeup compact, which had worn a circle into the back pocket of her jeans, and dabbed pressed powder on her nose. "That's because you've never been invited before."

Okay, hold on. Why was Marcie inviting me? Even though my IQ was double hers, she had to have noticed the frost between us. That, and we didn't share any common friends. Or interests, for that matter. "Wow, Marcie. That's really nice of you to invite me. A little unexpected, but still nice. I'll definitely try to make it." But not very hard.

Marcie bent toward me. "I saw you last night."

My heart beat slightly faster, but I managed to hold my voice level. Noncommittal, even. "Yeah, I saw you, too."

"That was kind of . . . crazy." She left her statement open-ended, as if she wanted me to elaborate for her.

"I guess."

"You guess? Did you see the pool stick? I've never seen anyone do that before. He shoved it through the pool table. Aren't those things made of slate?"

"I was at the back of the crowd. I couldn't see much. Sorry." I wasn't trying to be unhelpful on purpose; this was just one discussion I didn't want to have. And was this why she was inviting me to her party? To instill a sense of trust and friendship into our relationship, so that I'd tell her what, if anything, I knew about what happened last night?

"You didn't see anything?" Marcie repeated, a line of doubt creasing her forehead.

"No. Did you study for today's test? I have most of the periodic table memorized, but the bottom row keeps tripping me up."

"Did Patch ever take you to play pool there? Did you ever see anything like that before?"

Ignoring her, I flipped open my textbook.

"I heard you and Patch broke up," she said, trying a new angle.

I sucked in some air, but a little too late, since my face already felt hot.

"Who called things off?" Marcie asked.

"Does it matter?"

Marcie scowled. "You know what? If you're not going to talk, you can forget coming to my party."

"I wasn't going anyway."

She rolled her eyes. "Are you mad because I was with Patch at the Z last night? Because he doesn't mean anything to me. We're just having fun. It's nothing serious."

"Yeah, it *really* looked that way," I said, letting just enough cynicism seep into my tone.

"Don't be jealous, Nora. Patch and I are just really, really good friends. But in case you're interested, my mom knows a really good relationship therapist. Let me know if you need a referral. On second thought, she's pretty pricey. I mean, I know your mom has this stellar job and all—"

"Question for you, Marcie." My voice was a cool warning, but my hands were shaking in my lap. "What would you do if you woke up tomorrow to find your dad had been murdered? Do you think your mom's part-time job at JC Penney would pay the bills? Next time, before you bring up my family situation, put yourself in my shoes for a minute. One teeny tiny minute."

She held my gaze a long moment, but her expression was so impassive I doubted I'd made her think twice. The only person Marcie could ever empathize with was herself.

After class, I found Vee in the parking lot. She was splayed across the bonnet of the Neon, sleeves rolled above her shoulders, tanning. "We need to talk," she said as I approached. She pulled herself up to sitting and lowered her sunglasses down her nose far enough to make eye contact. "You and Patch are Splitsville, aren't you?"

I climbed onto the bonnet beside her. "Who told?"

"Rixon. For the record, that hurt. I'm your best friend, and I shouldn't have to find these things out through the friend of a friend. Or through the friend of an ex-boyfriend," she added, after thinking it all through. She laid a hand on my shoulder and squeezed. "How are you holding up?"

Not especially well. But it was one of those things I was trying to bury at the bottom of my heart, and I couldn't keep it buried if I talked about it. I eased back against the windshield, raising my notebook to shield the sun. "You know what the worst part is?"

"That I was right all along and now you have to suffer through hearing me say, 'I told you so'?"

"Funny."

"It's no secret Patch is trouble. He's got the whole bad-boy-in-need-of-redemption thing going on, but the catch is, most bad boys don't want redemption. They like being bad. They like the power they get from striking fear and panic into the hearts of mothers everywhere."

"That was . . . insightful."

"Anytime, babe. And what's more—"

"Vee."

She flapped her arms. "Hear me out. I'm saving the best for last. I think this is the time to rethink your priorities when it comes to guys. What we need is to find you a nice Boy Scout who'll make you appreciate the value of having a good man in your life. Take Rixon, for example."

I nailed her with a *You've got to be kidding* look.

"I resent that look," Vee said. "Rixon happens to be a really decent guy."

We stared at each other for three more counts.

"Okay, so maybe Boy Scout is stretching it," Vee said. "But the point of all this is that you could benefit from a nice guy, a guy whose closet isn't solely black. What's up with that, anyway? Does Patch think he's a commando?"

"I saw Marcie and Patch together last night," I said on a sigh. There. It was out.

Vee blinked a few times, digesting this. "What?" she said, her jaw going slack.

I nodded. "I saw them. She had her arms wrapped around him. They were together at a pool hall in Springvale."

"You followed them?"

I wanted to say, *Give me some credit*, but managed only a flat, "Scott invited me to play pool. I went with him, and we ran into them there." I wanted to tell Vee everything that had happened after that moment, but as with Marcie, there were some things I couldn't explain to her. How was I supposed to tell her about the Nephil in the red shirt, or how he'd rammed a pool stick through the table?

Vee looked like she was scrambling for a response. "Well. Like I was saying, once you see the light, you'll never turn back. Maybe Rixon has a friend. Other than Patch, that is . . ." She trailed off awkwardly.

"I don't need a boyfriend. I need a job."

Vee did a full-on grimace. "More job talk, ugh. I just don't get the allure."

"I need a car, and in order to get one, I need money. Hence the job." I had a running list of reasons to buy the Volkswagen Cabriolet lined up in my mind: The car was small, and therefore easy to park, and it was fuel efficient—a bonus, considering I wasn't going to have much money for gas after forking out over a thousand dollars for the car itself. And while I knew it was ridiculous to feel a connection to something as inanimate and practical as a car, I was beginning to view it as a metaphor of change in my life. Freedom to go wherever I wanted, whenever. Freedom to start fresh. Freedom from Patch, and all the memories we shared that I hadn't yet figured out how to slam the door on.

"My mom is friends with one of the night managers at Enzo's, and they're looking for baristas," Vee suggested.

"I don't know anything about being a barista."

Vee shrugged. "You make coffee. You pour it. You carry it to the eager little customers. How hard could it be?"

Forty-five minutes later, Vee and I were at the shore, walking the boardwalk, putting off our homework and noncommittally glancing in storefront windows. Since neither of us had a job, and consequently no money, we were brushing up on our window-shopping skills. We reached the end of the walk and our eyes fell on a bakery. I could practically hear Vee's mouth watering as she pressed her face to the glass and gazed in at the doughnut case.

"I think it's been a whole hour since I last ate," she said. "Glazed doughnuts, here we come, my treat." She was four steps ahead, tugging on the doors.

"I thought you were trying to lose weight for swimsuit season. I thought you were big-boned and wanted to even things out with Rixon."

"You sure know how to ruin the mood. Anyway, how's one little doughnut going to hurt?"

I had never seen Vee eat just one doughnut, but I kept my mouth shut.

We placed an order for a half-dozen glazed and had just taken a seat at a table near the windows, when I saw Scott on the other side of the glass. He had his forehead mashed against the window and he was smiling. At me. Startled, I jumped an inch. He crooked a finger, beckoning me outside.

"I'll be right back," I told Vee.

She followed my gaze. "Isn't that Scotty the Hottie?"

"Stop calling him that. What happened to Scotty the Potty?"

"He grew up. What does he want to talk to you for?" Something of a revelation crossed her face. "Oh, no you don't. You are not allowed to play rebound with him. He's trouble—you said so yourself. We're going to find you a nice Boy Scout, remember?"

I hooked my handbag over my shoulder. "I'm not playing rebound. What?" I said in response to the look she was giving me. "You expect me to just sit here and ignore him?"

She flipped her palms up. "Just hurry up or your doughnut is going to make the endangered species list."

Outside, I rounded the corner and walked back to where I'd last seen Scott. He was lounging against the seat back of a sidewalk bench, thumbs slung in his pockets. "You survive last night?" he asked.

"I'm still here, aren't I?"

He smiled. "A little more excitement than you're used to?"

I didn't remind him that he was the one who'd been stretched out on the pool table with a pool stick drilled one inch from his ear.

"Sorry I left you hanging," Scott said. "Looks like you found your own ride home?"

"Don't worry about it," I said testily, not going to the trouble of hiding my annoyance. "It just taught me never to go out with you again."

"I'll make it up to you. Got time for a quick bite?" He hitched his thumb toward a touristy restaurant down the boardwalk. Alfeo's. I'd eaten there years ago with my dad and remembered the menu as pricey. The only thing I was going to get for under five dollars was water. A Coke if I was lucky. Taking into consideration the exorbitant prices and the company—after all, my last memory of Scott was of him trying to tease my shirt up with a pool stick—I wanted nothing more than to go finish my doughnut.

"Can't. I'm here with Vee," I told Scott. "What happened at the Z last night? After I left."

"I got my money back." Something about the way he said it left me thinking it hadn't been quite that simple.

"Our money," I corrected.

"I've got your half at home," he said vaguely. "I'll drop it by tonight."

Yeah, right. I had a feeling he'd already blown all the money, and then some.

"And the guy in the red shirt?" I asked.

"He got away."

"He seemed really strong. Did he seem that way to you? Something about him was . . . different."

I was testing him, trying to figure out how much he knew, but his only comment was a distracted, "Yeah, I guess. So, my mom keeps harping on me to get out there and make new friends. No offense, Grey, but you're not one of the guys. Sooner or later I'm going to have to branch out. Aw, don't cry. Just remember all the happy moments we've shared together, and I'm sure you'll be comforted."

"You dragged me out here to break off our friendship? How did I get so lucky?"

Scott laughed. "I thought I'd start with your boyfriend. He got a name? I'm beginning to think he's your imaginary friend. I mean, I never see the two of you together."

"We broke up."

Something that resembled a twisted smile crept over his face. "Yeah, that's what I heard, but I wanted to see if you'd cop to it."

"You heard about me and Patch?"

"Some hot chick named Marcie told me. I ran into her at the gas station, and she made sure to come over and introduce herself. By the way, she said you're a loser."

"Marcie told you about me and Patch?" My spine stiffened.

"Want some advice? Some genuine guy-to-girl advice? Forget Patch. Move on. Find some guy who's into the same stuff you are. Studying, chess, collecting and classifying dead bugs . . . and give some serious thought to dying your hair."

"Excuse me?"

Scott coughed into his fist, but I didn't miss that it was to cover up a smile. "Let's be honest. Redheads are a liability."

I narrowed my eyes. "I don't have red hair."

He was full-on grinning. "Could be worse. Could be orange. Wicked-witch orange."

"Are you this big of a jerk to everyone? Because this is why you don't have friends."

"A little rough around the edges is all."

I pushed my sunglasses to the top of my head and made direct eye contact. "For the record, I don't play chess and I don't collect insects."

"But you study. I know you do. I *know* the type. The hallmark of your entire persona is defined by two words. Anal retentive. You're just another standard OCD case."

My mouth fell open. "Okay, so maybe I study a little. But I'm not boring—not *that* boring." At least, I hoped not. "Obviously you don't know me at all."

"Riiiiight."

"Fine," I said defensively. "What's something you're interested in that you think I'd never go for? Stop laughing. I'm serious. Name one thing."

Scott scratched his ear. "Ever gone to battle of the bands? Loud, unrehearsed music. Loud, unruly crowds. Lots of scandalous sex in the bathrooms. Ten times more adrenaline than the Z."

"No," I said a little hesitantly.

"I'll pick you up Sunday night. Bring fake ID." His eyebrows arched, and he graced me with an egotistical, mocking smile.

"No problem," I said, trying to keep my expression ho-hum. Technically, I'd be eating my words if I went out with Scott again, but I wasn't going to stand here and let him call me boring. And I definitely wasn't going to let him call me a redhead. "What should I wear?"

"As little as legally allowable."

I nearly choked. "I didn't know you were big into bands," I said, once I'd recovered my breath.

"I played bass back in Portland for a band called Geezer. I'm hoping to get picked up by someone local. The plan is to scout talent Sunday night."

"Sounds like fun," I lied. "Count me in." I could always back out later. A quick text would take care of it. All I cared about currently was not allowing Scott to call me an anal-retentive wimp to my face.

Scott and I parted ways, and I found Vee waiting at our table, half my doughnut eaten.

"Don't say I didn't warn you," she said, watching my eyes travel to my doughnut. "What did Scotty want?"

"He invited me to battle of the bands."

"Oh boy."

"For the last time, I'm not on the rebound."

"Whatever you say."

"Nora Grey?"

Vee and I looked up to find one of the bakery employees standing over our table. Her work uniform consisted of a lavender polo and a matching lavender name tag that read MADELINE. "Excuse me, are you Nora Grey?" she asked me a second time.

"Yes," I said, trying to figure out how she knew my name.

She was clutching a manila envelope to her chest, and now she held it out to me. "This is for you."

"What is it?" I asked, accepting the envelope.

She shrugged. "A guy just came in and asked me to give it to you."

"What guy?" Vee asked, craning her neck around the bakery.

"He already left. He said it was important that Nora get the envelope. I thought maybe he was your boyfriend. One time a guy had flowers delivered here and told us to give them to his girlfriend. She was at the table in the back corner." She pointed and smiled. "I still remember."

I slid my finger under the seal and glanced inside. There was a sheet of paper, along with a large ring. Nothing else.

I looked up at Madeline, who had a dusting of flour smeared across her cheek. "Are you sure this is for me?"

"The guy pointed right at you and said, 'Give this to Nora Grey.' You're Nora Grey, aren't you?"

I started to reach inside the envelope, but Vee put her hand on mine. "No offense," she told Madeline, "but we'd like a little privacy."

"Who do you think it's from?" I asked Vee, once Madeline was out of earshot.

"I don't know, but I got goose bumps when she gave it to you."

At Vee's words, cold fingers walked down my spine too. "Do you think it was Scott?"

"I don't know. What's inside the envelope?" She slid into the chair directly beside mine for a closer look.

I pulled the ring out, and we inspected it in silence. I could tell just by looking at it that it would be loose on my thumb—definitely a man's ring. It was made of iron, and the crown of the ring, where the stone typically sat, had a raised stamp of a hand. The hand was squeezed into a tight, menacing fist. The crown of the ring was charred black and appeared to have been lit on fire at some point.

"What the—," Vee began.

She stopped when I pulled out the paper. Scrawled in black Sharpie was a note:

THIS RING BELONGS TO THE BLACK HAND. HE KILLED YOUR DAD.

CHAPTER

8

VEE WAS OUT OF HER CHAIR FIRST.

I chased her to the bakery doors, where we rushed out to blinding sunshine. Shielding our eyes, we looked both ways down the boardwalk. We jogged down to the sand and did the same thing. People were scattered all over the beach, but I didn't see one familiar face.

My heart was pounding, and I asked Vee, "Do you think it was a joke?"

"I'm not laughing."

"Was it Scott?"

"Maybe. He was just here, after all."

"Or Marcie?" Marcie was the only other person I could think of who might be thoughtless enough to carry this out.

Vee looked sharply at me. "As a prank? Maybe."

But was Marcie that cruel? And would she even go to the trouble? This was a lot more involved than a hurtful comment in passing. The note, the ring—even the delivery. That took planning. Marcie seemed like the kind of person who got bored after five minutes of planning.

"Let's get to the bottom of this," Vee said, walking back toward the bakery doors. Once inside, she singled out Madeline. "We need to talk. What did the guy look like? Short? Tall? Brown hair? Blond?"

"He was wearing a hat and sunglasses," Madeline answered, casting furtive glances at the other bakery workers, who were beginning to pay Vee some attention. "Why? What was in the envelope?"

"You're going to have to do better than that," Vee said. "What *exactly* was he wearing? Was there a team logo on his hat? Did he have facial hair?"

"I don't remember," Madeline stammered. "A black hat. Or maybe brown. I think he was wearing jeans."

"You *think*?"

"Come on," I said, tugging Vee's arm. "She doesn't remember." I flicked my eyes to Madeline's. "Thanks for your help."

"Help?" Vee said. "She wasn't helpful. She can't go accepting envelopes from strange guys and not remember what they look like!"

"She thought he was my boyfriend," I said.

Madeline nodded vigorously. "I did! I'm so sorry! I thought it was a present! Was something bad in the envelope? Do you want me to call the police?"

"We want you to remember what the psychopath looked like," Vee shot back.

"Black jeans!" Madeline blurted suddenly. "I remember he was wearing black jeans. I mean, I'm almost positive he was."

"Almost positive?" Vee said.

I hauled her outside and down the boardwalk. After she'd had enough time to cool down, she said, "Babe, I'm so sorry about that. I should have looked in the envelope first. People are stupid. And whoever gave you that envelope is the stupidest of all. I'd happily ninja-star them, if I could."

I knew she was trying to lighten the mood, but my thoughts were five steps ahead. I wasn't thinking about my dad's death anymore. We'd come to a narrow divide between shops, and I pulled her off the walk, wedging us between buildings. "Listen, I need to talk to you. Yesterday I thought I saw my dad. Here, at the pier."

Vee stared at me, but said nothing.

"It was him, Vee. It was him."

"Babe—," she began skeptically.

"I think he's still alive." My dad's funeral had been closed casket. Maybe there'd been a mistake, a misunderstanding, and it wasn't my dad who'd died that night. Maybe he was suffering from amnesia, and that's why he hadn't come home. Maybe something else was preventing him. Or someone . . .

"I don't know how to say this," Vee said, looking up, down, everywhere but at me. "But he's not coming back."

"Then how do you explain what I saw?" I said defensively, hurt that she of all people didn't believe me. Tears stung my eyes, and I quickly brushed them away.

"It was somebody else. Some other guy who looks like your dad."

"You weren't there. I saw him!" I didn't mean to snap. But I wasn't going to resign myself to the facts. Not after everything I'd been through. Two months ago I'd flung myself off the gym rafters at school. I knew I'd died. I couldn't deny what I remembered about that night. And yet.

And yet I was alive today.

There was a chance my dad was alive too. Yesterday I'd seen him. I had. Maybe he was trying to communicate with me, send me a message. He wanted me to know he was still alive. He didn't want me to give up on him.

Vee shook her head. "Don't do this."

"I'm not giving up on him. Not until I know the truth. I have to find out what happened that night."

"No, you don't," Vee said firmly. "Lay your dad's ghost to rest. Digging this up isn't going to change the past—it's going to make you relive it."

Lay my dad's ghost to rest? What about me? How was I supposed to rest until I knew the truth? Vee didn't understand. She wasn't the one whose father had been unexplainably and violently ripped away. Her family wasn't shattered. She still had everything.

The only thing I had left was hope.

I spent Sunday afternoon at Enzo's Bistro in the company of the periodic table of the elements, throwing all my concentration into homework, attempting to crowd out any thought of my dad or the envelope I'd received telling me the Black Hand was responsible for his death. It had to be a prank. The envelope, the ring, the note—it was all someone's idea of a cruel joke. Maybe Scott, maybe Marcie. But in all honesty, I didn't think it was either of them. Scott had sounded sincere when he'd offered his condolences to me and my mom. And Marcie's cruelty was almost always immature and spontaneous.

Since I was seated at a computer and already logged in, I ran an Internet search for the Black Hand. I wanted to prove to myself there was no validity in the note. Probably someone had found the ring at a secondhand store, come up with the clever name of the Black Hand, followed me to the boardwalk, and asked Madeline to hand the envelope to me. Looking back, it didn't even matter that

Madeline couldn't remember what the guy looked like, because mostly likely, he wasn't the person behind the prank. That person had probably stopped a random guy on the boardwalk and paid him a few dollars to deliver the envelope. That's what I would have done. If I were a sick, twisted person who got off on hurting other people.

A page of links for the Black Hand popped up on the monitor. The first link was for a secret society that had reportedly assassinated Archduke Franz Ferdinand of Austria in 1914, catapulting the world into World War I. The next link was for a rock band. The Black Hand was also the name of a group of vampires in a role-playing game. Finally, in the early 1900s, an Italian gang dubbed the Black Hand took New York by storm. Not one link mentioned Maine. Not one image showed an iron ring stamped with a fist.

See? I told myself. A prank.

Realizing I'd strayed to the very topic I wasn't supposed to be thinking about, I pinned my eyes back on the homework spread out before me. I needed to get a grip on chemical formulas and calculating atomic mass. My first chemistry lab was coming up, and with Marcie as my partner, I was preparing for the worst by putting in extra hours outside of school to drag along her dead weight. I punched a few numbers into my calculator, then carefully transcribed my answer onto the open page of my notebook, repeating the answer loudly in my head, to block out thoughts of the Black Hand.

At five, I called my mom, who was in New Hampshire. "Checking in," I said. "How's work going?"

"Same old. You?"

"I'm at Enzo's trying to study, but the mango smoothie keeps calling to me."

"Now you're making me hungry."

"Hungry enough to come home?"

She gave one of those "it's out of my control" sighs. "I wish I could. We'll make waffles and smoothies for brunch on Saturday."

At six, Vee called and talked me into meeting her for spinning at the gym. At seven thirty, she dropped me off at the farmhouse. I had just finished showering and was standing in front of the fridge, hunting down the leftover stir-fry my mom had stored there yesterday before leaving, when there was a loud knock at the front door.

I squinted into the peephole. On the other side of the door, Scott Parnell made the peace sign.

"Battle of the bands!" I said aloud, smacking my palm to my forehead. I'd completely forgotten to cancel. I looked down at my pj pants and groaned.

After a failed attempt at fluffing my wet hair, I turned the bolt and opened the door.

Scott checked out my jammies. "You forgot."

"Are you kidding? I've been looking forward to this all day, I'm just running a little late." I pointed over my shoulder at the staircase. "I'll get dressed. Why don't you . . . reheat some stir-fry? It's in a blue Tupperware in the fridge."

I took the stairs up two at a time, shut my bedroom door, and called Vee.

"I need you to come over *now*," I said. "I'm on my way to battle of the bands with Scott."

"Is the point of this call to make me jealous?"

I put my ear to the door. It sounded like Scott was opening and closing cabinets in the kitchen. For all I knew, he was hunting for prescription drugs or beer. He was going to be disappointed on both counts, unless he had unrealistic hopes of getting high on my iron pills. "I'm not trying to make you jealous. I don't want to go alone."

"So tell him you can't go."

"The thing is . . . I kind of want to go." I had no idea where this sudden desire had come from. All I knew was that I didn't want to spend the night alone. I'd put in a full day of homework, followed by spinning, and the last thing I wanted was to stay home tonight and check off my list of weekend chores. I'd been good all day. Make that good my whole life. I deserved to have some fun. Scott wasn't the best date in the world, but he wasn't dead last, either. "Are you coming or not?"

"I have to admit, it sounds a lot better than conjugating Spanish verbs in my room all night. I'll call Rixon and see if he wants to come too."

I hung up and did a quick inventory of my closet. I decided on a pale silk cami, a miniskirt, opaque tights, and ballet flats. I sprayed perfume in the air and walked through it for a light, grapefruity scent. In the back of my mind, I wondered why I was spending the time to clean up for Scott. He was going nowhere in life, we had nothing in common, and most of our brief conversations included flipping insults at each other. Not only that, but Patch had told me to stay away from him. And that's when it hit me. Chances were, I was drawn to Scott because of some deep-rooted psychological reason involving defiance and revenge. And it all pointed back to Patch.

As I saw it, I could do one of two things: sit home and let Patch dictate my life, or ditch my Sunday-school-good-girl self and have a little fun. And even though I wasn't ready to admit it, I hoped Patch found out I'd gone to battle of the bands with Scott. I hoped the thought of me with another guy drove him crazy.

Mind made up, I flipped my head over, dried my hair just enough to give my curls definition, and breezed into the kitchen.

"Ready," I told Scott.

He gave me the second full-body scan of the night, but this time I felt a lot more self-conscious. "Looks good, Grey," he said.

"Right back at you." I smiled, going for chummy, but I felt nervous. Which was ridiculous, since this was Scott we were talking about. We were friends. Not even friends. Acquaintances.

"Cover charge is ten bucks."

I stood there a moment. "Oh. Right. I knew that. Can we stop by an ATM on the way?" I had fifty dollars' worth of birthday money sitting in my checking account. I'd already allocated the money to go toward the Cabriolet, but it wasn't like withdrawing ten was going to kill the deal. At the rate I was saving, I wouldn't be able to buy the Cabriolet before my twenty-fifth birthday anyway.

Scott tossed a Maine driver's license on the counter, with my yearbook photo copied onto it. "Ready, Marlene?"

Marlene?

"I wasn't joking about the fake ID. Not thinking of backing out, are you?" He grinned like he knew exactly how many points my blood pressure had shot up at the thought of using illegal ID, and he'd bet all his money that I'd back out in five seconds. Four, three, two . . .

I swiped the ID off the counter. "Ready."

Scott drove the Mustang through the center of Coldwater to the opposite side of town, down a few winding back roads and across the railroad tracks. He pulled up in front of a four-story brick warehouse overrun with weeds that twined up the exterior. A long line of people waited outside the doors. From what I could tell, the windows had been covered from the inside with black paper, but through the cracks between tape jobs, I saw the slice of a strobe light. A neon blue sign above the door glowed with the words THE DEVIL'S HANDBAG.

I'd been to this section of town once before, in the fourth grade, when my parents drove me and Vee to a haunted house staged for Halloween. I'd never been to the Devil's Handbag, but I was certain just by looking at it that my mom would have rather I kept it that way. Scott's description of the place bounced up from my memory. Loud, unrehearsed music. Loud, unruly crowds. Lots of scandalous sex in the bathrooms.

Oh boy.

"I'll let you out here," Scott said, steering to the curb. "Find us good seats. Close to the stage, in the center."

I climbed out and walked to the back of the line. In all honesty, I'd never been to a club that required a cover charge before. I'd never been to a club, period. My nightlife consisted of movies and Baskin-Robbins with Vee.

My cell sang out Vee's ringtone.

"I hear warm-up music, but all I see are train tracks and some abandoned boxcars."

"You're a couple blocks away. Are you in the Neon, or on foot?"

"In the Neon."

"I'll come find you."

I pulled out of the line, which was growing by the minute. At the end of the block, I rounded the corner, heading toward the tracks Scott had driven the Mustang across to get here. The sidewalk was cracked and uneven from years of disrepair, and with the streetlights placed few and far between, I had to watch my step to keep from snagging my toe and tripping. The warehouses down the block were dark, their windows vacant eyes. The warehouses gave way to abandoned brick townhouses splashed with graffiti. Over a hundred years ago, this had probably been the hub of Coldwater. Not so anymore. The moon cast an eerie, translucent light on the graveyard of buildings.

I folded my arms close to my body and walked faster. Two blocks away, a form materialized out of the smoggy darkness.

"Vee?" I called ahead.

The figure continued toward me, head down, hands pocketed. Not Vee, but a man, tall and slender, with broad shoulders and a vaguely familiar gait. I didn't feel especially comfortable passing by a man alone on this stretch of sidewalk and reached for my cell in my pocket. I was just about to call Vee and get her exact location, when the man passed under a cone of streetlight. He was wearing my dad's leather bomber jacket.

I stopped short.

Completely unaware of me, he climbed a set of steps to his right and disappeared inside one of the abandoned townhouses.

The hairs on my neck rose. "Dad?"

I broke into an automatic jog. I crossed the street without bothering to look for traffic, knowing there was none. When I made it to the townhouse I was sure he'd entered, I tried the tall double doors. Locked. I shook the handles, rattling the doors, but they didn't give. Cupping my hands around my eyes, I peered through one of the windows flanking the door. The lights were off, but I could make out lumps of furniture covered in pale sheets. My heart was beating all over the place. Was my dad *alive*? All this time—had he been living here?

"Dad!" I called through the glass. "It's me—Nora!"

At the top of the staircase inside the townhouse, his shoes vanished down the hall. "Dad!" I yelled, pounding the glass. "I'm out here!"

I backed away, head tilted up, looking at the second-story windows, watching for his shadow to pass by.

The back entrance.

The thought floated to the surface of my mind, and I immediately acted on it. I jogged down the steps, slipping into the narrow passageway cutting between this townhouse and the next. Of course. The back door. If it was unlocked, I could get inside to my dad—

Ice kissed the back of my neck. The chill tiptoed down my spine, momentarily paralyzing me. I stood at the end of the passageway, eyes fastened on the backyard. Bushes swayed docilely in the breeze. The open gate creaked on its hinges. Very slowly I backed away, not about to trust the stillness. Not about to believe I wasn't alone. I'd felt this way before, and it had always signaled danger.

Nora, we're not alone. Someone else is here. Go back!

"Dad?" I whispered, my mind darting.

Go find Vee. You need to leave! I'll find you again. Hurry!

I didn't care what he said—I wasn't leaving. Not until I knew what was going on. Not until I saw him. How could he expect me to leave? He was here. A flutter of relief and nervous excitement bubbled up inside me, eclipsing any fear I felt.

"Dad? Where are you?"

Nothing.

"Dad?" I tried again. "I'm not leaving."

This time there was an answer.

The back door is unlocked.

I touched my head, feeling his words echo there. Something was different about his voice this time, but not noticeably enough to place a finger on it. Slightly colder, maybe? Sharper? "Dad?" I whispered at the faintest volume.

I'm inside.

His voice was louder now, a real sound. Not just in my head this time, but in my ears, too. I turned toward the house, certain he'd spoken through the window. Stepping off the flagstone path, I tentatively laid my palm on the windowpane. I desperately wanted it to be him, but at the same time, the goose bumps popping up all over my skin warned me it could be a trick. A trap.

"Dad?" My voice wavered. "I'm scared."

On the other side of the glass, a hand mirrored mine, five fingertips aligning with my own. My dad's gold wedding band was on the ring finger of his left hand. My blood pumped so hard I felt dizzy. It was him. My dad was inches away. Alive.

Come inside. I won't hurt you. Come, Nora.

The urgency in his words frightened me. I clawed at the window, trying to locate the latch, desperately needing to throw my arms around him and stop him from leaving again. Tears streamed down my cheeks. I thought about running around to the back door, but I couldn't bring myself to leave him, even for a few seconds. I couldn't lose him again.

I splayed my hand on the window, harder this time. "I'm right here, Dad!"

This time, the glass frosted at my touch. Tiny fibers of ice branched across the glass with a brittle, crackling noise. I jerked away at the sudden cold that shot up my arm, but my skin was stuck to the glass. Frozen. Crying out, I tried to free myself using my other hand. My dad's hand melted through the windowpane and closed around mine, holding me so I couldn't run. He jerked me roughly forward, the bricks snagging my clothes, my arm impossibly vanishing into the window. My terrified reflection stared back, my mouth open in a startled scream. The only thought pounding through my head was that this couldn't be my dad.

"Help!" I yelled. "Vee! Can you hear me? Help!"

Thrashing my body side to side, I tried to use my weight to break free. A piercing pain sliced into the forearm he held captive, and an image of a knife burst into my mind with such intensity that I thought my head had split in two. Fire licked my forearm—*he was cutting me open.*

"Stop!" I shrieked. "You're hurting me!"

I felt his presence flex across my mind, his own sight eclipsing mine. There was blood everywhere. Black and slippery . . . and mine. Bile rose in my throat.

"Patch!" I screamed into the night with nothing short of terror and absolute desperation.

The hand dissolved from around mine, and I dropped backward to the ground. Instinctively I clutched my wounded arm against my shirt to stop the bleeding, but to my amazement, there was no blood. No cut.

Gulping air, I stared up at the window. Perfectly intact, it reflected the tree behind me, which swung back and forth in the night air. I scurried to my feet and stumbled out to the sidewalk. I ran in the direction of the Devil's Handbag, turning to glance over my shoulder every few steps. I expected to see my dad—or his doppelgänger—appear from one of the townhouses, holding a knife, but the sidewalk stayed empty.

I faced forward to cross the street and saw the person a half blink before I slammed into her.

"There you are," Vee said, reaching out to steady me as I choked back a scream. "I think we missed each other. I made it to the Devil's Handbag and backtracked to find you. Are you okay? You look ready to throw up."

I didn't want to stand on the street corner any longer. Reflecting on what had just happened at the townhouse, I couldn't help but be reminded of the time I'd hit Chauncey with the Neon. Moments later, the car had returned to normal, leaving no evidence of an accident. But this time it was personal. This time it was my dad. My eyes burned, and my jaw quivered as I spoke. "I—I thought I saw my dad again."

Vee folded her arms around me. "Babe."

"I know. It wasn't real. It wasn't real," I repeated, trying to reassure myself. I blinked several times in succession, tears staining my vision. But it had felt real. So very real . . .

"Do you want to talk about it?"

What was there to talk about? I was being haunted. Someone was messing with my mind. Toying with me. A fallen angel? A Nephil? My dad's ghost? Or was it my own mind betraying me? It wasn't like this was the first time I'd imagined seeing my dad. I'd thought he was trying to communicate with me, but maybe this was a self-defense mechanism. Maybe my mind was making me see things I refused to accept were gone forever. It was filling the void, because that was easier than letting go.

Whatever had happened back there, it wasn't real. It wasn't my dad. He would never hurt me. He loved me.

"Let's go back to the Devil's Handbag," I said, exhaling shakily. I wanted to distance myself from the townhouse as quickly as possible. Once more I told myself that whoever I'd seen back there, he wasn't my dad.

The echoing clash, clang, and whine of drums and guitars

warming up for the show grew louder, and while my panic was slow to subside, I felt my heartbeat slowing down. There was something reassuring about the idea of losing myself inside the swarm of hundreds of bodies packed inside the warehouse. Despite what had happened, I didn't want to go home, and I didn't want to be alone; I wanted to slip into the center of the crowd. There was strength in numbers.

Vee grabbed my wrist and brought me to a halt. "Is that who I think it is?"

Half a block up, Marcie Millar was climbing into a car. Her body looked poured into a little black scrap of fabric that was short enough to show off her black lace thigh-highs and garter belt. Tall, over-the-knee black boots and a black fedora completed the outfit. But it wasn't her outfit that had caught my attention. It was the car. A shiny black Jeep Commander. The engine caught, and the Jeep pulled around the corner and out of sight.

CHAPTER

OLY FREAK SHOW," VEE WHISPERED. "DID I JUST SEE that? Did I really just see Marcie climb into Patch's Jeep?"

I opened my mouth to say something, but it felt like someone had stuffed nails down my throat.

"Was it just me," Vee said, "or could you see her red thong peeking out from under her dress?"

"That wasn't a dress," I said, leaning back against a building for support.

"I was trying to be optimistic, but you're right. That wasn't a dress. That was a tube top stretched down around her bony booty. The only thing keeping it from springing up around her waist is gravity."

"I think I'm going to be sick," I said, the nails-in-the-throat sensation spreading to my stomach.

Vee pushed down on my shoulders, forcing me to sit on a square of sidewalk. "Deep breaths."

"He's going out with Marcie." It was almost too horrific to believe.

"Marcie puts out," said Vee. "That's the only reason. She's a pig. A rat."

"He told me there was nothing going on between them."

"Patch is a lot of things, but honest isn't one of them."

I blinked down the street where the Jeep had vanished. I felt the unexplainable urge to storm after them and do something I hoped I'd regret—like choke Marcie with her stupid red thong.

"This is not your fault," Vee said. "He's the jerk who took advantage of you."

"I need to go home," I said, my voice numb.

Just then a police cruiser came to a stop near the club's entrance. A tall, lean cop in black slacks and a dress shirt angled out. The street was heavily shadowed, but I recognized him immediately. Detective Basso. I'd fallen under the jurisdiction of his job once before, and I had no desire for a repeat performance. Especially since I was fairly certain I wasn't on his list of favorite people.

Detective Basso shouldered his way to the front of the line, flashed his badge at the bouncer, and walked inside without slowing.

"Whoa," Vee said. "Was that a cop?"

"Yes, and he's too old, so don't even think about it. I want to go home. Where did you park?"

"He doesn't look much over thirty. Since when is thirty too old?"

"His name is Detective Basso. He questioned me after the incident with Jules at school." I loved how I kept referring to it as the incident, instead of what it really was. Attempted murder.

"Basso. I like that. Short and sexy, just like my name. Did he frisk you?"

I gave her a sideways look, but she was still gazing at the door he'd gone through. "No. He questioned me."

"I wouldn't mind being handcuffed by him. Just don't tell Rixon."

"Let's go. If the police are here, something bad is going to happen."

"Bad is my middle name," she said, linking her arm through mine and drawing me toward the warehouse entrance.

"Vee—"

"There are probably two hundred people inside. It's dark. He's not going to pick you out of the crowd, if he even remembers you at all. Probably he's forgotten you. Besides, he's not going to arrest you—you're not doing anything illegal. Well, aside from the whole fake ID business, but everybody does that. And if he really wanted to bust the whole place, he'd have brought backup. One cop isn't going to take down this crowd."

"How do you know I have fake ID?"

She gave me an "I'm not as dumb as I look" glance. "You're here, aren't you?"

"How are you planning to get in?"

"Same as you."

"You have fake ID?" I couldn't believe it. "Since when?"

Vee winked. "Rixon is good for more than just kissing. Come on, let's go. Being the good friend you are, you wouldn't even think about asking me to break out of my house and violate the terms of my grounding for nothing. Especially since I already called Rixon, and he's on his way."

I groaned. But this wasn't Vee's fault. I was the one who'd thought coming here tonight was a good idea. "Five minutes, but that's it."

The line was moving fast, pouring into the building, and against my better judgment, I paid the cover charge and followed Vee into the dark, sticky, deafening warehouse. In a way, it felt strangely good to be surrounded by darkness and noise; the music was too loud to think, which meant even if I'd wanted to, I couldn't concentrate on Patch, and what he was doing with Marcie at this precise moment.

There was a bar at the back, painted black, with metal bar stools and pendant lights that hung from the ceiling, and Vee and I slid onto the last two available stools.

"ID?" the guy behind the bar asked.

Vee shook her head. "Just a Diet Coke, please."

"I'll take a cherry Coke," I added.

Vee poked my ribs and leaned sideways. "Did you see that? He asked to see our ID. How awesome is that? I bet he wanted our names but was too shy to ask."

The bartender filled two glasses and slid them down the counter, where they stopped directly in front of us.

"That's a cool trick," Vee shouted at him over the music.

He gave her the finger and moved down the bar to the next customer.

"He was too short for me anyway," she said.

"Have you seen Scott?" I asked, sitting tall on my stool to try to see over the crowd. He should have had plenty of time to park by now, but I didn't see him. Maybe he hadn't wanted to use metered parking and had driven farther out to find free parking. Still. Unless he'd parked two miles away, and that seemed highly unlikely, he should have been here.

"Uh-oh. Guess who just walked in?" Vee's eyes were fixed over my shoulder, and her expression darkened to a scowl. "Marcie Millar, that's who."

"I thought she left!" A jolt of anger fired through me. "Is Patch with her?"

"Negative."

I squared my shoulders and sat even higher. "I'm calm. I can handle it. Most likely, she won't see us. Even if she does, she's not going to come over to talk." And even though not one part of me believed it, I added, "There's probably some twisted explanation for why she got into his Jeep."

"Just like there's a twisted explanation for why she's wearing his hat?"

I flattened my hands on the bar and swung around. Sure enough, Marcie was elbowing her way into the crowd, her strawberry-blond ponytail streaming out the back of Patch's ball cap. If that wasn't evidence they were together, I didn't know what was.

"I'm going to kill her," I said to Vee, turning back to face the bar, gripping my cherry Coke, heat rising in my cheeks.

"Of course you are. And here's your chance. She's beelining this way."

A moment later, Marcie ordered the guy beside me out of his seat and perched herself on top of it. She took off Patch's cap and shook out her hair, then pressed the cap to her face, inhaling deeply. "Doesn't he smell *amazing*?"

"Hey, Nora," Vee said, "didn't Patch have lice last week?"

"What is it?" Marcie asked rhetorically. "Fresh-cut grass? An exotic spice? Or maybe . . . mint?"

I set my glass down a little too hard, and some of the cherry Coke sloshed onto the bar.

"That's really eco-friendly of you," Vee told Marcie. "Recycling Nora's old trash."

"Hot trash is better than fat trash," Marcie said.

"Fat this," Vee said, and she picked up my cherry Coke and underhanded it at Marcie. But someone in the crowd bumped Vee from behind, so instead of sailing straight at Marcie, the Coke spread out and splattered all three of us.

"Look what you did!" Marcie said, jumping off her bar stool so hard she knocked it over. She swiped at the Coke in her lap. "This dress is Bebe! Do you know how much it cost? Two hundred dollars."

"It's not worth that much anymore," Vee said. "And I don't know what you're complaining about. I bet you shoplifted it."

"Yeah? So? What's your point?"

"With you, what you see is what you get. And I see cheap. Nothing says cheap like shoplifting."

"Nothing says fat like a double chin."

Vee's eyes went slitty. "You're dead. You hear me? Dead."

Marcie shifted her eyes in my direction. "By the way, Nora, I thought you'd like to know. Patch told me he broke up with you because you weren't enough of a slut."

Vee smacked Marcie upside the head with her handbag.

"What was that for?" Marcie shrieked, clutching her head.

Vee smacked her other ear. Marcie staggered backward, eyes dazed but quickly narrowing. "You little—," she began.

"Stop!" I shouted, wedging myself between them and holding my arms out. We'd drawn the attention of the crowd, and people were shuffling closer, their interest piqued by the prospect of a cat fight. I didn't care what happened to Marcie, but Vee was a different matter. Chances were, if she got in a fight, Detective Basso would haul her down to the station. Combined with sneaking out of the house, I didn't think jail time would go over well with her parents. "Let's all just back away. Vee, go get the Neon. I'll meet you outside."

"She called me fat. She deserves to die. You said so yourself." Vee's breathing was ragged.

"How do you plan on killing me?" Marcie sneered. "By sitting on me?"

And that was when everything broke loose. Vee snatched her own Coke off the bar and raised her arm, aiming to throw. Marcie turned to run, but in her hurry, tripped backward over her fallen bar stool and toppled to the floor. I swiveled to Vee, hoping to defuse any further violence, when my knee was kicked out from behind. I went down, and the next thing I knew, Marcie was on top, straddling me.

"This is for stealing Tod Bérot from me in fifth grade," she said, punching me in the eye.

I yowled and grabbed my eye. "Tod Bérot?" I shouted. "What are you talking about? That was the *fifth grade!*"

"And this is for sticking that picture of me with a giant zit on my chin on the front page of the eZine last year!"

"That wasn't me!"

Okay, maybe I'd had a little say in the photo selection, but it wasn't like I was the only one. And anyway, Marcie was holding *that* over my head? Wasn't a year a little long to be clinging to a grudge?

Marcie shouted, "And this is for your whore of a—"

"You're crazy!" This time I blocked the hit and managed to grab the leg of the nearest bar stool and overturn it on her.

Marcie shoved the bar stool away. Before I could get my feet under me, she swiped a drink from a passerby and doused me with it.

"An eye for an eye," she said. "You humiliate me, I humiliate you."

I wiped Coke out of my eyes. My right eye flowered with pain where Marcie had punched me. I felt the bruise spreading under my skin, tattooing me blue and purple. My hair was dripping Coke, my best camisole was torn, and I felt demoralized, beaten . . . and rejected. Patch had moved on to Marcie Millar. And Marcie had just punctuated the fact.

My feelings were no excuse for what I did next, but they were definitely a catalyst. I had no clue how to fight, but I closed my hands into fists and clipped Marcie in the jaw. For a moment her expression was frozen in surprise. She scooted off me, two-handing her jaw, gaping at me. Buoyed by my small victory, I lunged for her, but came up short because someone had me under the armpits, hauling me upright.

"Get out of here now," Patch said in my ear, dragging me toward the doors.

"I'm going to kill her!" I said, fighting to get around him.

A gathering crowd enveloped us, chanting, "Fight! fight! fight!" Patch brushed them out of the way and dragged me through. Behind Patch, Marcie got to her feet and flipped me her middle finger. Her grin was smug, her eyebrows high. The message was clear: Bring it on.

Patch handed me off to Vee, then went back and clamped a hand around Marcie's upper arm. Before I could see where he took her, Vee wrestled me toward the nearest exit. We came out in the alley.

"Fun as seeing you fight Marcie was, I figured it probably wasn't worth the cost of you spending the night in jail," Vee said.

"I hate her!" My voice still sounded hysterical.

"Detective Basso was plowing through the crowd when Patch lifted you off her. I figured that was my cue to step in."

"Where did he take Marcie? I saw Patch grab her."

"Does it matter? Hopefully they both get hauled downtown."

Our shoes crunched through the gravel as we ran down the alley toward where Vee had parked. The blue and red lights of a patrol car sliced past the opening of the alley, and Vee and I pressed back against the warehouse.

"Well, that was exciting," Vee said, once we were locked inside the Neon.

"Oh, yeah, sure," I said through my teeth.

Vee licked my arm. "You taste pretty good. You're making me thirsty, smelling like cherry Coke and all."

"This is all your fault!" I said. "You're the one who threw my

Coke at Marcie! If it weren't for you, I wouldn't have gotten in a fight."

"Fight? You laid there and took it. You should have had Patch teach you some moves before you broke up with him."

My cell phone was ringing, and I yanked it out of my bag. "What?" I snapped. When no one answered, I realized I was so worked up that I'd confused the text message chirp with an actual call.

One unread message was waiting for me from an unknown number. STAY HOME TONIGHT.

"That's scary," Vee said, bending sideways to read. "Who have you been giving your number to?"

"It's probably a mistype. It's probably meant for someone else." Of course, I was thinking about the townhouse, my dad, and the vision I'd had of him cutting open my arm.

I tossed the cell into my open bag at my feet and bowed my head into my hands. My eye throbbed. I was scared, alone, confused, and on the verge of crying uncontrollably.

"Maybe it's from Patch," Vee said.

"His number has never shown up as unknown before. It's a prank." If only I could force myself to believe it. "Can we go? I need Tylenol."

"I think we should call Detective Basso. Police love this kind of scary stalker crap."

"You just want to call him so you can flirt with him."

Vee put the Neon in gear. "Just trying to be helpful."

"Maybe you should have tried being helpful ten minutes ago when you threw my drink on Marcie."

"At least I had the guts to."

I turned in my seat, giving her the full weight of my stare. "Are you accusing me of not standing up to Marcie?"

"She stole your boyfriend, didn't she? Granted, he scares the candy out of me, but if Marcie stole my boyfriend, there'd be hell to pay."

I pointed a stiff finger at the street. "Drive!"

"You know what? You really need a new boyfriend. You need a good old-fashioned make-out session to mellow you out."

Why did everyone think I needed a new boyfriend? I didn't need a new boyfriend. I'd had enough of boyfriends to last a lifetime. The only thing a boyfriend was good for was a shattered heart.

CHAPTER

10

AN HOUR LATER, I'D FIXED AND EATEN A LATE SNACK of cream cheese frosting spread on graham crackers, tidied up the kitchen, and watched a little TV. In a shadowy corner of my mind, I hadn't managed to forget the text message warning me to stay home. It had been easier to brush off as a miscall or prank when I was safe and sound inside Vee's car, but now that I was alone, I wasn't feeling anywhere near as confident. I considered turning on some Chopin to break the silence, but I didn't want to handicap my hearing. The last thing I needed was someone sneaking up behind me. . . .

Pull it together! I ordered myself. *Nobody's sneaking up on you.*

After a while, when nothing good was left on TV, I climbed upstairs to my bedroom. My room was, for all intents and purposes, clean, so I color-coded my closet, trying to keep myself busy so I wouldn't be tempted to fall asleep. Nothing would make me as vulnerable as dozing off, and I wanted to delay it as long as possible. I dusted the top of the bureau, then alphabetized my hardcovers. I reassured myself that nothing bad was going to happen. Most likely, I'd wake tomorrow realizing how ridiculously paranoid I'd been.

Then again, maybe the text was from someone who wanted to slit my throat while I slept. On an eerie night like this, nothing was too far-fetched to believe.

Sometime later, I woke in the dark. The drapes on the far side of the room billowed as the electric fan oscillated toward them. The air temperature was overly warm, and my stretchy tank and boy briefs clung to my skin, but I was too caught up in envisioning worst-case scenarios to even think about cracking the window. Looking sideways, I blinked at the numbers on my clock. Just shy of three.

An angry pounding reverberated through the right side of my skull, and my eye was swollen shut. Turning on every light in the house, I padded barefoot to the freezer and assembled an ice pack out of ice cubes and a Ziploc bag. I braved a look in the bathroom mirror and groaned. A violent purple and red bruise flowered from my eyebrow down to my cheekbone.

"How could you have let this happen?" I asked my reflection. "How could you have let Marcie beat you up?"

I shook the last two Tylenol gelcaps out of the bottle in the mirrored cabinet, swallowed them, then curled into bed. The ice stung the skin around my eye and sent a shiver through me. While I waited for the Tylenol to kick in, I wrestled with the mental picture of Marcie climbing inside Patch's Jeep. The image played, rewound, and replayed. I tossed and turned, and even folded my pillow over my head to smother the image, but it danced just out of reach, taunting me.

What must have been an hour later, my brain wore itself out thinking of all the inventive ways I'd like to kill both Marcie and Patch, and I slipped back into sleep.

I woke to the sound of a lock rolling over.

I opened my eyes, but found my vision muddled by the same poor-quality black and white as when I'd dreamed my way into England, hundreds of years ago. I tried to blink it away and bring my normal vision back, but my world stayed the color of smoke and ice.

Downstairs, the front door eased open with a low-pitched creak.

I wasn't expecting my mom home until Saturday morning, which meant it was someone else. Someone who didn't belong inside.

I stole a look around the room for something I could use as a weapon. A few small picture frames were arranged on the night-stand, along with a cheap drugstore lamp.

Footsteps trod softly over the hardwood floors of the foyer. Seconds later, they were on the stairs. The intruder didn't pause, listening for signs that they'd been heard. They knew exactly where they were going. Rolling silently out of bed, I snatched my discarded tights off the floor. I tightened them between my hands and pressed my back to the wall just inside my bedroom door, a clammy sweat beading my skin. It was so quiet I could hear myself breathe.

He stepped through the doorway, and I roped a leg of the tights around his neck, tugging back with all my strength. There was a moment of struggle before my weight jerked forward and I found myself face-to-face with Patch.

He looked from the tights he'd confiscated to me. "Want to explain?"

"What are you doing here?" I demanded, my breathing elevated. I put two and two together. "Was that your text earlier? The one telling me to stay put tonight? Since when do you have an unlisted number?"

"I had to get a new line. Something more secure."

I didn't want to know. What kind of person needed all that secrecy? Who was Patch afraid would be eavesdropping on his calls? The archangels?

"Did it ever occur to you to knock?" I said, my pulse still hammering. "I thought you were someone else."

"Expecting someone else?"

"As a matter of fact, yes!" A psychopath who sent anonymous text messages telling me to make myself accessible.

"It's after three," Patch said. "Whoever you're waiting for can't be that exciting—you fell asleep." He smiled. "You're still sleeping." As he said it, he looked satisfied. Maybe even reassured, as if something he'd been puzzling over had finally worked itself out.

I blinked. Still sleeping? What was he talking about? Wait. Of course. That explained why all color was drained, and I was still seeing in black and white. Patch wasn't really in my bedroom—he was in my *dream.*

But was I dreaming *about* him, or did he actually know he was here? Were we sharing the same dream?

"For your information, I fell asleep waiting for—Scott." I had no idea why I'd said it, other than my mouth got in the way of my brain.

"Scott," he repeated.

"Don't start. I saw Marcie climb inside your Jeep."

"She needed a ride."

I adopted a hands-on-hips pose. "What kind of ride?"

"Not that kind of ride," he said slowly.

"Oh, sure! What color was her thong?" It was a test, and I really hoped he failed.

He didn't answer, but one look at his eyes told me he hadn't failed.

I marched to the bed, grabbed a pillow, and hurled it at him. He sidestepped, and it flopped against the wall. "You lied to me," I said. "You told me there was nothing going on between you and Marcie, but when two people have nothing between them, they don't swap wardrobes, and they don't get inside each other's cars late at night dressed in what could pass as lingerie!" I was suddenly aware of my own clothes, or lack thereof. I stood feet away from Patch in nothing more than a spaghetti-strap tank and boy briefs. Well, there wasn't a lot I could do about it now, was there?

"Swap wardrobes?"

"She was wearing your hat!"

"She was having a bad hair day."

My jaw dropped. "Is that what she told you? And you fell for it?"

"She's not as bad as you're making her out to be."

He did not just say that.

I thrust a finger at my eye. "Not that bad? See this? She gave it to me! What are you doing here?" I demanded again, my rage boiling to an all-time high.

Patch leaned back against the bureau and folded his arms. "I came by to see how you're doing."

"Again, I have a black eye, thanks for asking," I snapped.

"Need ice?"

"I need you to get out of my dream!" I ripped a second pillow off the bed and heaved it violently at him. This time he caught it.

"The Devil's Handbag, black eye. Comes with the territory." He

573

shoved the pillow back at me, as if to punctuate his opinion.

"Are you *defending* Marcie?"

He shook his head. "I don't need to. She handled herself. You, on the other hand . . ."

I pointed at the door. "Out."

When he didn't move, I marched within range and whipped the pillow against him. "I said get out of my dream, you lying, traitorous—"

He wrestled the pillow out of my grasp and walked me backward until I came up against the wall, his motorcycle boots flush against my toes. I was drawing breath to finish my sentence and call him the worst name I could think up, when Patch tugged on the waistband of my underpants and pulled me even closer. His eyes were liquid black, his breathing slow and deep. I stood that way, suspended between him and the wall, my pulse stepping up as I became more aware of his body and the masculine scent of leather and mint lingering on his skin. I felt my resistance start to ebb away.

Suddenly, and without heeding anything but my own desire, I curled my fingers into his shirt and pulled him the rest of the way against me. It felt so good to have him close again. I'd missed him so much, but I hadn't realized just how much until this moment.

"Don't make me regret this," I said, breathless.

"You haven't regretted me once." He kissed me, and I answered so hungrily I thought my lips would bruise. I pushed my fingers up through his hair, clutching him closer. My mouth was all over his, chaotic and wild and starved. All the messy and complicated emotions I'd gone through since we broke up dropped away as I drowned myself in the crazed and compulsive need to be with him.

His hands were under my tank, expertly sliding to the small of my back to hold me against him. I was trapped between the wall and his body, fumbling at the buttons on his shirt, my knuckles brushing solid muscle beneath.

I rucked his shirt down off his shoulders, slamming the door on my brain, which warned that I was making a huge mistake. I didn't want to hear myself out, afraid of what I'd find on the other side. I knew I was setting myself up for more pain, but I couldn't resist him. All I could think was that if Patch really was in my dream, this whole night could be our secret. The archangels couldn't see us. Here, all their rules went up in smoke. We could do whatever we wanted, and they would never find out. No one would.

Patch met me halfway, pulling his arms free from the sleeves and tossing the shirt aside. I slid my hands along perfectly sculpted muscle that sent a ripple of mania through me. I knew he couldn't feel any of this physically, but I told myself love was driving him now. His love for me. I didn't allow myself to think about his inability to feel my touch, or how much or little this encounter really meant to him. I simply wanted him. Now.

He lifted me up, and I wrapped my legs around his waist. I saw his gaze cut to the dresser, then the bed, and my heart flip-flopped with desire. Rational thought had abandoned me. All I knew was that I would do whatever it took to hang on to this unhinged high. Everything was happening way too fast, but the wild certainty of where we were headed was a balm to the cold, destructive anger I'd felt simmering under the surface the past week.

It was the last thought I registered before my fingertip brushed the place where his wings connected to his back.

Before I could stop it, I was sucked inside his memory in a snap.

The smell of leather, and the smooth, slippery feel of it against the underside of my thighs, told me I was in Patch's Jeep even before my eyes had fully adapted to the darkness. I was in the backseat, with Patch behind the wheel and Marcie in the passenger seat. She was wearing the same slinky dress and tall boots I'd seen her in less than three hours ago.

Tonight, then. Patch's memory had whisked me only a few hours back.

"She ruined my dress," Marcie said, picking at the fabric clinging to her thighs. "Now I'm freezing. And I reek of cherry Coke."

"You want my jacket?" Patch asked, eyes on the road.

"Where is it?"

"Backseat."

Marcie unlocked her seat belt, got a knee up on the console, and grabbed Patch's leather jacket off the seat beside me. When she was facing forward again, she tugged the dress up over her head and dropped it on the floor at her feet. Other than her underwear, she was completely naked.

I made a little choked sound in my throat.

She threaded her arms into Patch's jacket and zipped it up. "Take the next left," she instructed.

"I know the way to your house," Patch said, steering the Jeep right.

"I don't want to go home. In two blocks, turn left."

But after two blocks, Patch continued straight.

"Well, you're no fun," Marcie said with a jaded pout. "Aren't you just a little bit curious where I was going to take us?"

"It's late."

"Are you turning me down?" she asked coyly.

"I'm dropping you off, then I'm going back to my place."

"Why can't I come?"

"Maybe someday," Patch said.

Oh, really? I wanted to snap at Patch. *That's more than I ever got!*

"That's not very specific," Marcie smirked, kicking her heels up on the dash, showing off inches of leg.

Patch said nothing.

"Tomorrow night, then," Marcie said. She paused and continued in a velvety voice, "It's not like you have somewhere else to be. I know Nora broke up with you."

Patch's hands tightened on the steering wheel.

"I heard she's with Scott Parnell now. You know, the new guy. He's cute, but she traded down."

"I don't really want to talk about Nora."

"Good, because neither do I. I want to talk about us."

"I thought you had a boyfriend."

"The key word in that sentence is *had*."

Patch took a short right, bouncing the Jeep into Marcie's driveway. He didn't cut the engine. "Good night, Marcie."

She stayed in her seat a moment, then laughed. "You're not going to walk me to the door?"

"You're a strong, capable girl."

"If my daddy's watching, he won't be happy," she said, reaching over to straighten Patch's collar, her hand lingering longer than was appropriate.

"He's not watching."

"How do you know?"

"Trust me."

Marcie lowered her voice further, sultry and smooth. "You know, I really admire your willpower. You keep me guessing, and I like that. But let me make one thing perfectly clear. I'm not looking for a relationship. I don't like messy, complicated things. I don't want hurt feelings, confusing signals, or jealousy—I just want fun. I'm looking for a good time. Think about it."

For the first time, Patch turned to face Marcie. "I'll keep that in mind," he said at last.

From her profile, I saw Marcie smile. She leaned across the console and gave Patch a slow, hot kiss. He started to pull back, then stopped. At any moment, he could have broken the kiss off, but he didn't.

"Tomorrow night," Marcie murmured, pulling away at last. "Your place."

"Your dress," he told her, gesturing at the damp heap on the floor.

"Wash it and give it back to me tomorrow night." She pushed her way out of the Jeep and ran up to her front door, where she slipped inside.

My arms went slack around Patch's neck. I felt too slapped by what I'd seen to form a single word. It was as if he'd thrown a bucket of ice water on me. My lips were swollen from the roughness of his kiss, my heart just as inflamed.

Patch was in my dream. We were sharing it together. Somehow it was real. The whole idea was eerily surreal, bordering on impossible, but it had to be true. If he wasn't here, if he hadn't injected himself quietly and stealthily into my dream, I couldn't have touched his scars and been catapulted into his memory.

But I had. The memory was living, valid, and all too real.

Patch could tell by my reaction that whatever I'd seen wasn't good. His arms bracketed my shoulders, and he tipped his head back to stare at the ceiling. "What did you see?" he asked quietly.

The sound of my heart pounded between us.

"You kissed Marcie," I said, biting my lip hard to stall the tears welling up.

He dragged his hands down his face, then squeezed the bridge of his nose.

"Tell me it's a mind game. Tell me it's a trick. Tell me she has some kind of power over you, that you don't have any choice when it comes to being with her."

"It's complicated."

"No," I said with a fierce shake of my head. "Don't tell me it's complicated. Nothing is complicated anymore—not after everything we've been through. What do you even hope to get out of a relationship with her?"

His eyes flicked to mine. "Not love."

A certain emptiness gnawed its way inside me. All the pieces came together, and I suddenly understood. Being with Marcie was about cheap satisfaction. Self-satisfaction. He really did see us as conquests. He was a player. Every girl was a new challenge, a short-term hookup to broaden his horizons. He found success in the art of seduction. He didn't care about the middle or end of a story—only the beginning. And just like all the other girls, I'd made the huge mistake of falling in love with him. The moment I did, he ran. Well, he'd never have to worry about Marcie confessing her love. The only person she loved was herself.

"You make me sick," I said, my voice trembling with accusation.

Patch crouched down, elbows on his knees, face buried in his hands. "I didn't come here to hurt you."

"Why did you come? To fool around behind the archangels'

backs? To hurt me more than you already have?" I didn't wait for an answer. Reaching for my neck, I yanked at the silver chain he'd given me days ago. It snapped free at the back of my neck hard enough that I should have winced, but I was in too much pain to notice a little more. I should have made him take the chain back the day I called it quits between us, but I realized a little late that up until this moment, I hadn't given up hope. I'd still believed in us. I'd clung to the belief that there was still a way to cut a deal with the stars that would bring Patch back to me. What an utter waste.

I flung the chain at him. "And I want my ring back."

His dark eyes stayed settled on me a moment longer, then he bent and scooped up his shirt. "No."

"What do you mean no? I want it back!"

"You gave it to me," he said quietly, but not gently.

"Well, I changed my mind!" My face was flushed, my whole body hot with rage. He was keeping the ring because he knew how much it meant to me. He was keeping it, because despite his rise in stature to guardian angel, his soul was just as black as it had been the day I met him. And the biggest mistake I'd ever made was fooling myself into believing otherwise. "I gave it to you when I was stupid enough to think I loved you!" I thrust out my hand. "Give it back. Now." I couldn't stand the thought of losing my dad's ring to Patch. He didn't deserve it. He didn't deserve to keep the one tangible reminder I had of real love.

Ignoring my request, Patch walked out.

I opened my eyes.

I clicked on the lamp, my vision returning to full color. I sat up, a hot flash of adrenaline warming my skin. Reaching for my neck, I felt for Patch's silver chain, but it wasn't there. I swept my hand across the wrinkled sheets, thinking it had fallen off while I slept.

But the chain was gone.

The dream was real.

Patch had discovered a way to visit me while I slept.

CHAPTER

11

ONDAY AFTER SCHOOL, VEE DROPPED ME off at the library. I took a moment outside the entrance to call my mom for our daily check-in. As usual, she told me work was keeping her busy, and I told her school was doing the same thing for me.

Inside, I took the elevator to the media lab on the third floor, checked my e-mail, browsed Facebook, and scanned Perez Hilton. Just to torture myself, I Googled the Black Hand again. The same links popped up. I hadn't really expected anything new, had I? Finally, with nowhere left to procrastinate, I flipped open my chemistry text and resigned myself to studying.

It was late by the time I called it quits to go hunt down a vending machine. Out the library's west-facing windows, the sun was tucked deep in the horizon, and night was closing in fast. I bypassed the elevator in favor of the stairs, feeling the need for a little exercise. I'd been sitting so long, my legs were beginning to tingle with sleep.

In the lobby, I fed a few dollars to the vending machine and carried pretzels and a can of cranberry juice back to the third floor. When I returned to the media lab, Vee was sitting on my desk, her glossy yellow high heels propped on my chair. Her expression was a mix of smug amusement and annoyance. She held a small black envelope in the air, caught between two of her fingers.

"This is for you," she said, tossing the envelope on the desk. "And so's this." She held out a paper bakery bag, rolled at the neck. "Thought you might be hungry."

Judging by the disdain in Vee's expression, I had a bad feeling about the card, and took the opportunity to give my attention to what was inside the bag. "Cupcakes!"

Vee grinned. "The bakery lady told me they're organic. Not sure how you make an organic cupcake, and not sure why they cost extra, but there you go."

"You're my hero."

"How much longer do you think you'll be?"

"Thiry minutes, tops."

She laid the keys to the Neon next to my backpack. "Rixon and I are going to grab something to eat, so you'll have to be your own chauffeur tonight. I parked the Neon in the underground garage. Row B. I only have a fourth of a tank left, so don't go crazy."

I took the keys, trying to ignore the unpleasant sting in my heart that I instantly recognized as jealousy. I was jealous of Vee's new relationship with Rixon. Jealous of her dinner plans. Jealous that she was now closer to Patch than I was, because even though Vee had never mentioned it, I was sure she bumped into Patch when she was with Rixon. For all I knew, the three of them watched movies together at night. The three of them, lounging on Rixon's sofa, while I sat in the farmhouse alone. I desperately wanted to ask Vee about Patch, but the truth of the matter was, I couldn't. I'd broken up with him. I'd made my bed, and it was time to lie in it.

Then again, how was one little inquiry going to hurt?

"Hey, Vee?"

She turned back at the door. "Yeah?"

I opened my mouth, and that was when I remembered my pride. Vee was my best friend, but she also had a big mouth. If I asked about Patch, I risked him hearing about it secondhand. He'd find out just how hard a time I was having getting over him.

I pulled on a smile. "Thanks for the cupcakes."

"Anything for you, babe."

After Vee left, I peeled back the paper wrapping on one of the cupcakes and ate alone in the quiet mechanical hum of the lab.

I did another half hour of homework, and ate two more cupcakes, before I finally dared a look at the black envelope sitting at the edge of my vision. I knew I couldn't avoid it all night.

Breaking the seal, I shook out a black card with a small heart embossed at the center. The word sorry was scripted across it. The card was scented with a bittersweet perfume. I raised the card to my nose and breathed deeply, trying to the place the strangely intoxicating scent. The smell of burned fruit and chemical spices stung all the way down the back of my throat. I opened the card.

I was a jerk last night. Forgive me?

Automatically I slid the card an arm's length away. Patch. I didn't know what to make of his apology, but I didn't like the commotion it caused inside me. Yes, he'd been a jerk. And did he think a card from the drugstore could negate it? If so, he was underestimating the damage he'd caused. He'd kissed Marcie. Kissed her! And not only that, but he'd invaded my dreams. I had no idea how he'd done it, but when I woke in the morning, I knew he'd been there. It was more than a little unnerving. If he could invade the privacy of my dreams, what else could he do?

"Ten minutes until closing," a librarian whispered from the doorway.

I sent my three-paragraph essay on amino acids to the printer, then scooped up my books and wedged them inside my backpack. I picked up Patch's card, hesitated once, then ripped it multiple times and tossed the scraps into the trash can. If he wanted to say sorry, he could do it in person. Not through Vee, and not in my dreams.

Halfway down the aisle to pick up my print job, I reached out to steady myself on the nearest desk. The right side of my body felt heavier than the left, and my balance wavered. I took another step, and my right leg crumpled, as if made of paper. I crouched down, gripping the desk with both hands, tucking my head between my elbows to get blood flowing to my brain again. A warm, drowsy feeling swirled through my veins.

Straightening my legs, I came to a wobbly stand, but something was wrong with the walls. They were stretched abnormally long and narrow, as if I was looking at them through a mirror at a fun house. I blinked hard several times, attempting to bring my vision to a focal point.

My bones filled with iron, refusing to move, and my eyelids sank against the stark fluorescent lights. In a panic, I ordered them open, but my body overruled all. I felt warm fingers curl around my mind, threatening to drag it off to sleep.

The perfume, I thought vaguely. In Patch's card.

I was on my hands and knees now. Strange rectangles wavered all around, spinning before me. Doors. The room was lined with open doors. But the faster I crawled toward them, the faster they jumped back. Off in the distance, I heard a somber tick-tock. I moved away from the sound, lucid enough to know that the clock was at the back of the room, opposite the door.

Moments later, I realized that my arms and legs were no longer moving, the sensation of crawling nothing more than an illusion in my head. Scratchy, industrial-grade carpet cushioned my cheek. I fought once more to push myself up, then shut my eyes, all light spiraling away.

I woke in the dark.

Artificially cool air tingled my skin, and the quiet hum of machines whispered all around. I got my hands under me, but when I tried to raise myself up, dots of purple and black danced across my vision. I swallowed the texture of cotton thick in my mouth and rolled onto my back.

That was when I remembered I was still in the library. At least, I was pretty sure that's where I was. I didn't remember leaving. But what was I doing on the floor? I tried to remember how I got here.

Patch's card. I'd breathed in the tangy, bitter perfume. Shortly after, I'd collapsed on the floor.

Had I been drugged?

Had Patch drugged me?

I lay there, heart thumping, eyes blinking so rapidly the blinks came one on top of the other. I tried to get up a second time, but it felt as if someone had a steel boot planted in the center of my chest. With a second, more determined heave, I pulled myself to sitting. Clinging to a desk, I dragged myself all the way to standing. My brain protested the vertigo, but my eyes located the blurry green exit sign above the media lab door. I tottered over.

I turned the handle. The door opened an inch, then caught. I was about to tug harder, when something on the other side of the window set in the door caught my eye. I frowned. That's weird. Someone had tied one end of a length of rope to the outer door handle, and the other end to the handle of the door one room down.

I smacked my hand against the glass. "Hello?" I shouted groggily. "Can anyone hear me?"

I tried the door again, pulling with all my might, which wasn't much, since my muscles seemed to melt like hot butter the minute I tried to exert them. The rope was strung so tight between the two handles, I could only bring the lab door roughly five inches out of the frame. Not nearly enough to squeeze through.

"Is anyone there?" I shouted through the door crack. "I'm trapped on the third floor!"

The library answered with silence.

My eyes were fully adapted to the darkness now, and I found the clock on the wall. Eleven? Could that be right? Had I really slept more than two hours?

I pulled out my cell, but there was no signal. I tried to log on to the Internet but was repeatedly informed that there were no available networks.

Looking frantically around the media lab, I combed my eyes over every object, searching for something I could use to get out. Computers, swivel chairs, filing cabinets ... nothing jumped out at me. I knelt down beside the floor vent and shouted, "Can anyone hear me? I'm trapped in the media lab on the third floor!" I waited, praying to hear a response. My one hope was that there was still a librarian around, finishing up last-minute work before heading out. But it was an hour shy of midnight, and I knew the odds were stacked against me.

Out in the main library, gears clanked into motion as the cage elevator at the end of the hall rose up from the ground level. I jerked my head toward the sound.

Once, when I was four or five, my dad took me to the park to teach me how to ride my bike without training wheels. By the end of the afternoon, I could ride all the way around the quarter-mile loop without help. My dad gave me a big hug and told me it was time to go home and show my mom. I begged for two more loops, and we compromised on one. Halfway around the loop, I lost my balance and tipped over. As I was righting my bike, I saw a big brown dog not far off. It was staring at me. In that moment, as we stood watching each other, I heard a voice whisper, *Don't move*. I gulped a breath and held it, even though my legs wanted to run as fast as they could to the safety of my dad.

The dog's ears pricked and he started toward me in an aggressive lope. I shivered with fear but kept my feet rooted. The closer the dog came, the more I wanted to run, but I knew the moment I moved, the dog's animal instinct to chase would kick in. Halfway to me, the dog lost interest in my statuelike body and took off in a new direction. I asked my dad if he'd heard the same voice telling me to hold still, and he said it was instinct. If I listened to it, nine times out of ten I'd make the best move.

Instinct was speaking now. Get out.

I grabbed a monitor off the closest desk and threw it against the window. The glass smashed, leaving a huge hole in the center. I snatched the three-hole punch off the community work desk just inside the door and used it to knock out the remaining glass. Then I dragged a chair over, climbed up, braced my shoe on the window frame, and jumped out to the hall.

The elevator hissed and vibrated higher, passing the second level.

I covered the hall in a sprint. I pumped my arms harder, knowing I had to reach the stairwell, adjacent to the elevator, before the elevator rose much higher and whoever was inside saw me. I tugged on the stairwell door, expending several precious seconds as I took the time to close it noiselessly behind me. On the far side of the door, the elevator ground to a halt. The retractable door rattled open and someone stepped out. I used the railing to propel myself faster, keeping my shoes light on the stairs. I was halfway down the second flight when the stairwell door opened above me.

I stopped mid-stride, not wanting to alert whoever was up there to my location.

Nora?

My hand slipped on the railing. It was my dad's voice.

Nora? Are you there?

I swallowed, wanting to cry out to him. Then I remembered the townhouse.

Quit hiding. You can trust me. Let me help you. Come out where I can see you.

His tone was strange and demanding. At the townhouse, when my dad's voice had first spoken to me, it was soft and gentle. That same voice had told me we weren't alone and I needed to leave. When he spoke again, his voice was different. It sounded forceful and deceiving. What if my dad had tried to contact me? What if he'd been chased away, and the second, strange voice was someone pretending to be him? I was struck by the thought that someone could be impersonating my dad to lure me close.

Heavy footsteps descended the stairs at a run, jerking me out of my speculations. He was coming after me.

I clattered down the stairs, no longer worrying about keeping quiet. *Faster!* I screamed to myself. *Run faster!*

He was gaining ground, barely more than a flight away. When my shoes hit the ground level, I shoved through the stairwell door, crossed the lobby, and flung myself out the front doors and into the night.

The air was warm and quiet. I was running for the cement steps leading down to the street, when I made a split-second change of plans. I climbed the handrail to the left of the doors, dropping ten or so feet to a small grassy courtyard below. Above me, the library doors opened. I pressed back against the cement wall, my feet stirring trash and tumbleweeds.

The minute I heard the slow tap of shoes descending the cement steps, I raced down the block. The library didn't have its own parking; it shared an underground garage with the courthouse. I ran down the parking ramp, ducked under the parking arm, and swept the garage for the Neon. Where had Vee said she'd parked?

Row B . . .

I ran one aisle over and saw the tail end of the Neon sticking out of a space. I rammed the key into the door, dropped behind the wheel, and cranked the engine. I'd just steered the Neon up the exit ramp when a dark SUV swung around the corner. The driver gunned the engine, heading straight for me.

I thrust the Neon into second gear and stepped on the gas, pulling out in front of the SUV seconds before it would have blocked the exit and boxed me inside the garage.

My mind was too frazzled to think clearly about where I was going. I floored it down another two blocks, ran a stop sign, then veered onto Walnut. The SUV accelerated onto Walnut behind me, holding my tail. The speed limit jumped to forty-five, and the lanes doubled to two. I pushed the Neon to fifty, switching my eyes between the road and the rearview mirror.

Without signaling, I yanked the steering wheel, cutting onto a side street. The SUV razed the curb, following me. I took two more right turns, circled the block, and got back on Walnut. I swerved in front of a white two-door coupe, boxing it between me and the SUV. The traffic light ahead turned yellow, and I accelerated into the intersection as the light flashed red. With my eyes glued to the rearview mirror, I watched the white car roll to a stop. Behind it, the SUV came to a screeching halt.

I took several sharp breaths. My pulse throbbed in my arms, and my hands were clamped tightly around the steering wheel.

I took Walnut uphill, but as soon as I was on the back side of the hill, I crossed oncoming traffic and turned left. I bounced over the railroad tracks, weaving my way through a dark, dilapidated neighborhood of single-story brick houses. I knew where I was: Slaughterville. The neighborhood had earned its nickname over a decade ago when three teens gunned one another down at a playground.

I slowed as a house set far back from the street caught my attention. No lights. An open, empty detached garage stood at the far back of the property. I reversed the Neon up the driveway and into the garage. After triple-checking that the door locks were engaged, I killed the headlights. I waited, fearing that at any moment the SUV's headlights would swing down the street.

Rummaging through my bag, I dug out my cell.

"Hey," Vee answered.

"Who else touched the card from Patch?" I demanded, the words rattling.

"Huh?"

"Did Patch give you the card directly? Did Rixon? Who else touched it?"

"Want to tell me what this is about?"

"I think I was drugged."

Silence.

"You think the card was drugged?" Vee repeated doubtfully at last.

"The paper was laced with perfume," I explained impatiently. "Tell me who gave it to you. Tell me exactly how you got it."

"On my way to the library to drop off the cupcakes, Rixon called to see where I was," she recounted slowly. "We met up at the library, and Patch was riding shotgun in Rixon's truck. Patch gave me the card and asked if I'd give it to you. I took the card, the cupcakes, and the Neon's keys inside to you, then went back out to meet Rixon."

"Nobody else touched the card?"

"Nobody."

"Less than a half hour after smelling the card, I collapsed on the library floor. I didn't wake up for two hours."

Vee didn't answer right away, and I could practically hear her thinking everything through, trying to digest it. At last she said,

"Are you sure it wasn't fatigue? You were in the library a long time. I couldn't work that long on homework without needing a nap."

"When I woke up," I pushed on, "someone was in the library with me. I think it was the same person who drugged me. They chased me through the library. I got out, but they followed me down Walnut."

Another baffled pause. "As much as I don't like Patch, I've got to tell you, I can't see him drugging you. He's a whack job, but he does have boundaries."

"Then who?" My voice was a little shrill.

"I don't know. Where are you now?"

"Slaughterville."

"What? Get out of there before you get mugged! Come over. Stay the night here. We'll work this out. We'll figure out what happened." But the words felt like an empty consolation. Vee was just as perplexed as I was.

I stayed hidden in the garage for what must have been another twenty minutes before I felt brave enough to go back on the streets. My nerves were frayed, my mind reeling. I opted against taking Walnut, thinking the SUV might be cruising up and down it right now, waiting to pick up my tail. Sticking to side streets, I ignored the speed limit and drove in a reckless hurry to Vee's.

I wasn't far from her house when I noticed blue and red lights in the rearview mirror.

Stopping the Neon at the side of the road, I planted my head against the steering wheel. I knew I'd been speeding, and I was frustrated at myself for doing it, but of all the nights to get pulled over.

A moment later, knuckles rapped the window. I pushed the button to lower it.

"Well, well," Detective Basso said. "Long time no see."

Any other cop, I thought. Any other.

He flashed his ticket pad. "License and registration, you know the drill."

Since I knew there was no talking my way around a ticket, not with Detective Basso, I didn't see the point in putting on any pretense of contrition. "I didn't know detective work included filling out speeding tickets."

He gave a razor-thin smile. "Where's the fire?"

"Can I just get my ticket and go home?"

"Any alcohol in the car?"

"Have a look around," I said, spreading my hands.

He opened the door for me. "Get out."

"Why?"

"Get out" —he pointed at the dashed line bisecting the road— "and walk the line."

"You think I'm drunk?"

"I think you're crazy, but I'm checking your sobriety while I've got you here."

I swung out and slammed the door shut behind me. "How far?"

"Until I tell you to stop."

I concentrated on planting my feet on the line, but every time I looked down, my vision slanted. I could still feel the effects of the drug pecking away at my coordination, and the harder I concentrated on keeping my feet on the line, the more I felt myself swaying off into the road. "Can't you just give me the ticket, slap my wrist, and send me home?" My tone was insubordinate, but I'd gone cold on the inside. If I couldn't walk the line, Detective Basso might throw me in jail. I was already shaken, and I didn't think I could handle a night behind bars. What if the man from the library came after me again?

"A lot of small-town cops would let you off the hook like that, sure. Some would even take a bribe. I'm not one of them."

"Does it matter that I was drugged?"

He laughed darkly. "Drugged."

"My ex-boyfriend gave me a card laced with perfume earlier tonight. I opened the card, and the next thing I knew, I passed out."

When Detective Basso didn't interrupt me, I pressed forward. "I slept for more than two hours. When I woke up, the library was closed. I was locked in the media lab. Someone had tied the doorknob. . . ." I trailed off, closing my mouth.

He gestured for more. "Come on, now. Don't leave me at that cliffhanger."

I realized a moment too late that I'd just incriminated myself.

I'd put myself at the library, tonight, in the media lab. First thing tomorrow, when the library opened, they were going to report the broken window to the police. And I had no doubt who Detective Basso would come looking for first.

"You were in the media lab," he prompted. "What happened next?"

Too late to back out now. I'd have to finish and hope for the best. Maybe something I said would convince Detective Basso it wasn't my fault—that everything I'd done was justified. "Someone had tied the door to the media lab shut. I threw a computer through the window to get out."

He tipped his head back and laughed. "There's a name for girls like you, Nora Grey. Crazy makers. You're like the fly that nobody can shoo away." He walked back to his patrol car and stretched the radio out the open driver's-side door. Radioing dispatch, he said, "I need someone to swing by the library and check out the media lab. Let me know what you find."

He leaned back against his car, eyes flicking to his watch. "How many minutes do you think it'll take for them to get back to me? I've got your confession, Nora. I could book you for trespassing and vandalism."

"Trespassing would imply I wasn't tied inside the library against my will." I sounded nervous.

"If someone drugged you and trapped you in the lab, what are you doing here now, roaring down Hickory at fifty-five miles an hour?"

"I wasn't supposed to get away. I broke out of the room while he was coming up the elevator to get me."

"He? You saw him? Let's have a description."

"I didn't see him, but it was a guy. His footsteps were heavy when he came down the stairwell after me. Too heavy for a girl."

"You're stammering. Usually that means you're lying."

"I'm not lying. I was tied in the lab, and someone was coming up the elevator to get me."

"Right."

"Who else would have been in the building that late?" I snapped.

"A janitor?" he offered easily.

"He wasn't dressed like a janitor. When I looked up in the stairwell, I saw dark trousers and dark tennis shoes."

"So when I take you to court, you're going to tell the judge you're an expert on janitorial apparel?"

"The guy followed me out of the library, got into his car, and chased me. A janitor wouldn't do that."

The radio popped with static, and Detective Basso leaned inside for the receiver.

"Finished walking through the library," a man's voice crackled through the radio. "Nothing."

Detective Basso cut cool, suspicious eyes to me. "Nothing? You sure?"

"I repeat: nothing."

Nothing? Instead of relief, I felt panic. I'd smashed the lab window. I *had*. It was real. It wasn't my imagination. It—wasn't.

Calm down! I ordered myself. This had happened before. It wasn't new. In the past, it was always a mind game. It was someone working behind the scenes, trying to manipulate my mind. Was it happening all over again? But . . . *why?* I needed to think this through. I shook my head, ridiculously wishing the gesture would shake out an answer.

Detective Basso ripped the top sheet off his ticket pad and slapped it into my hand.

My eyes brushed over the balance at the bottom. "Two hundred and twenty nine dollars?!"

"You were going thirty over and driving a car that doesn't belong to you. Pay the fine, or I'll see you in court."

"I—I don't have this kind of money."

"Get a job. Maybe it'll keep you out of trouble."

"Please don't do this," I said, injecting all the pleading that I possessed into my voice.

Detective Basso studied me. "Two months ago a kid with no ID, no family, and no traceable past wound up dead in the high school gym."

"Jules's death was ruled a suicide," I said automatically, but sweat tingled the back of my neck. What did this have to do with my ticket?

"The same night he disappeared, the high school counselor lit your house on fire, then did her own disappearing act. There's a link between these two bizarre incidents." His dark brown eyes pinned me in place. "You."

"What are you saying?"

"Tell me what really happened that night, and I can make your ticket go away."

"I don't know what happened," I lied, because there was no alternative. Telling the truth would leave me worse off than having to pay the ticket. I couldn't tell Detective Basso about fallen angels and Nephilim. He'd never believe my story if I confessed that Dabria was an angel of death. Or that Jules was a descendant of a fallen angel.

"Your call," Detective Basso said, flicking his business card at me before folding himself inside his car. "If you change your mind, you know how to reach me."

I glanced at the card as he roared off. DETECTIVE ECANUS BASSO. 207-555-3333.

The ticket felt heavy in my hand. Heavy, and hot. How was I going to come up with two hundred dollars? I couldn't borrow the money from my mom—she could barely afford groceries. Patch had the money, but I'd told him I could take care of myself. I'd told him to get out of my life. What did it say about me if I ran back to him the moment I hit trouble? It was admitting he'd been right all along.

It was admitting I needed him.

CHAPTER

12

TUESDAY AFTER CLASS, I WAS ON MY WAY OUT OF
the building to meet Vee, who'd skipped class to hang
out with Rixon but promised to swing back by school
at noon to chauffeur me home, when my cell phone chirped. I
opened the text message just as Vee hollered my name from the
street.

"Yo, babe! Over here!"

I walked to where she was parallel parked at the curb and folded my arms on the open window frame. "Well? Was it worth it?"

"Skipping class? Heck, yeah. Rixon and I spent the morning playing Xbox at his place. Halo Two." She reached over and unlatched the passenger door.

"Sounds romantic," I said, climbing in.

"Don't knock it till you've tried it. Violence really puts guys in the mood."

"In the mood? Is there something I should know about?"

Vee flashed a hundred-watt grin. "We kissed. Oh man, it was good. It started out all slow and gentle, and then Rixon really started getting into it—"

"Okay!" I cut in loudly. Had I been this sappy when Patch and I were together and Vee was odd man out? I prayed not. "Where to now?"

She scooted back into traffic. "I'm tired of studying. I need to inject a little excitement into my life, and that ain't gonna happen with my nose in a book."

"What did you have in mind?"

"Old Orchard Beach. I'm in the mood for some sun and sand. Plus, my tan could use a base coat."

Old Orchard Beach sounded perfect. It had a long pier that stretched out over the water, an on-the-beach amusement park, and fireworks and dancing after dark. Unfortunately, the beach would have to wait.

I jiggled my cell phone. "We already have plans tonight."

Vee leaned sideways to read the text message and grimaced. "Marcie's party reminder? For real? I didn't realize you guys were new BFFs."

"I was told that missing her party is the surest way to sabotage my social life."

"She's such a ho. Missing her party is the surest way to make my life complete."

"Might want to rethink your attitude, because I'm going—and you're coming with me."

Vee pressed back against her seat, her arms going rigid on the steering wheel. "What's her angle, anyway? Why'd she invite you?"

"We're chemistry partners."

"Seems to me like you're forgiving her for that black eye awfully fast."

"I owe it to her to at least show up for an hour. As her chemistry partner," I added.

"So you're saying the reason we're dragging ourselves to Marcie's party tonight is because you sit beside her every morning in chemistry." Vee gave me the look of someone who knows better.

I knew it was a lame excuse, but not as lame as the truth. I needed to make absolutely certain Patch had moved on to Marcie. When I'd touched his scars two nights ago and been transported into his memory, he'd seemed reserved with Marcie. Up until their kiss, he'd even been short with her. I hadn't made up my mind how he felt about her. But if he'd moved on, it would make it that much easier for me to do likewise. A confirmed relationship between Patch and Marcie would make it easy to hate him. And I wanted to hate him. For both our sakes.

"Your breath smells like liar, liar pants on fire," Vee said. "This isn't about you and Marcie. This is about Patch and Marcie. You want to find out what's going on between them."

I tossed my hands in the air. "Fine! Is that so wrong?"

"Man," she said, wagging her head, "you really are a glutton for punishment."

"I thought maybe we could look in her bedroom. See if we find anything that proves they're together."

"Like used condoms?"

Suddenly my breakfast was rising up my esophagus. I hadn't thought of that. Were they sleeping together? No. I didn't believe it. Patch wouldn't do that to me. Not with Marcie.

"I know!" Vee said. "We could steal her diary!"

"The one she's been carrying around since freshman year?"

"The one she swears would make the National Enquirer look tame," she said, sounding strangely gleeful. "If something is going on between her and Patch, it'll be in the diary."

"I don't know."

"Oh, come on. We'll give it back after we're done. No harm, no foul."

"How? Toss it on her porch and run? She'll kill us if she finds out we took it."

"Sure. Toss it on her porch, or take it during the party, read it somewhere, and put it back before we leave."

"It just seems wrong."

"We won't tell anyone what we read. It'll be our secret. It's not wrong if nobody gets hurt."

I wasn't sold on stealing Marcie's diary, but I could tell Vee wasn't going to let it drop. The most important thing was getting her to agree to come to the party with me. I wasn't sure I was courageous enough to go on my own. Especially since I couldn't count on having a single friend there. So I said, "You'll pick me up tonight, then?"

"Count on it. Hey, can we light her bedroom on fire before we leave?"

"No. She can't know we were snooping in it."

"Yeah, but subtle really isn't my style."

I looked sideways, eyebrows peaked. "No kidding?"

It was just after nine when Vee and I climbed the hill leading up to Marcie's neighborhood. Coldwater's socioeconomic map is easily determined by a simple test: Drop a marble on any street in town. If the marble rolls downhill, you're upper class. If the marble doesn't roll at all, you're middle class. And if you lose the marble in a vapor of fog before you have a chance to find out if it rolls, you're ... well, you live in my neighborhood. The backwoods.

Vee pushed the Neon uphill. Marcie's neighborhood was

older, with mature trees that spilled above the street, blocking all moonlight. The homes had professionally landscaped yards and half circles for driveways. The architecture was Georgian colonial; every house was white with black trim. Vee had the Neon's windows rolled down, and in the distance, we heard the steady pulse of blaring hip-hop.

"What's her address again?" Vee asked, squinting through the windshield. "These houses are so far off the road I can't read the numbers over the garages."

"Twelve-twenty Brenchley Street."

We came to an intersection and Vee turned onto Brenchley. The music intensified as we cruised down the block, and I assumed it meant we were headed in the right direction. Cars were parked bumper-to-bumper down both sides of the street. As we passed an elegantly remodeled carriage house, the music reached an all-time high, vibrating the car. Flocks of people were cutting across the lawn, streaming inside the house. Marcie's house. One look at it, and I had to wonder why she shoplifted. For the thrill of it? To escape her parents' carefully and perfectly crafted image?

I didn't dwell on it longer. A deep ache swirled in my stomach. Parked in the driveway was Patch's black Jeep Commander. Obviously he'd been one of the first to arrive. He'd probably been inside alone with Marcie hours before the party started. Doing what, I didn't want to know. I sucked in a deep breath and I told myself I could handle this. And wasn't this the evidence I'd come looking for?

"What are you thinking?" Vee asked, her gaze also glued to the Commander as we rolled past.

"That I want to throw up."

"All over Marcie's foyer would be nice. But seriously. Are you okay with Patch being here?"

I set my jaw, tilting my chin up slightly. "Marcie invited me tonight. I have the same right to be here as Patch. I'm not going to let him dictate where I go and what I do." Funny, because that's *exactly* what I was doing.

Marcie's front door was open, leading into a dark marble hall crammed with bodies gyrating to Jay-Z. The foyer merged into a large sitting room with a high ceiling and dark Victorian furniture. All of the furniture, including the coffee table, was being used for seating. Vee hesitated in the doorway.

"Just taking a moment to mentally prepare for this," she called to me over the music. "I mean, the place is going to be infested with Marcie. Marcie portraits, Marcie furniture, Marcie odors. Speaking of portraits, we should try to find some old family pictures. I'd like to see what Marcie's dad looked like ten years ago. When his dealership commercials come on TV, I can't decide if it's plastic surgery that makes him look so young, or just massive amounts of makeup."

I gripped her elbow and yanked her flush against me. "You are not ditching me now."

Vee peered inside, frowning. "All right, but I'm warning you, if

I see a single pair of panties, I'm out of here. Same goes for used condoms."

I opened my mouth, then snapped it shut. The chances of seeing both were fairly high, and it was in my best interest not to officially accept her terms.

I was saved from further discussion by Marcie, who sashayed out of the darkness holding a punch bowl. She divided a critical glance between us. "I invited you," she told me, "but I didn't invite her."

"Good to see you, too," Vee said.

Marcie scrutinized Vee slowly, head to toe. "Didn't you used to be on some stupid color diet? Looks to me like you gave up before you even started." She turned her attention to me. "And you. Nice black eye."

"Did you hear something, Nora?" Vee asked. "I thought I heard something."

"You definitely heard something," I agreed.

"Could that be . . . a dog fart I heard?" Vee asked me.

I nodded. "I think so."

Marcie's eyes thinned to slits. "Ha, ha."

"There it went again," Vee said. "Apparently this dog has real bad gas. Maybe we should feed it Tums."

Marcie thrust the punch bowl at us. "Donation. Nobody gets inside without one."

"What?" Vee and I said at the same time.

"Do-nay-shun. You didn't really think I invited you here without an agenda, did you? I need your cash. Pure and simple."

Vee and I eyed the bowl, which was swimming with dollar bills.

"What's the money for?" I asked.

"New cheerleading uniforms. The squad wants ones with bare midriffs, but the school's too cheap to spring for new ones, so I'm fund-raising."

"This should be interesting," Vee said. "The term Slut Squad will take on a whole new meaning."

"That does it!" said Marcie, her face darkening with blood. "You want in? You'd better have a twenty. If you make another comment, I'll boost the cover charge to forty."

Vee poked me in the arm. "I didn't sign up for this. You pay."

"Ten each?" I offered.

"No way. This was your idea. You pick up the tab."

I faced Marcie and pulled on a smile. "Twenty dollars is a lot," I reasoned.

"Yeah, but think how amazing I'll look in that uniform," she said. "I have to do five hundred crunches every night so I can trim my waist from twenty-five to twenty-four inches before school starts. I can't have an inch of fat if I'm going to wear a bare midriff."

I didn't dare pollute my mind with a mental image of Marcie in a promiscuous cheerleading uniform, and instead said, "How about fifteen?"

Marcie cupped a hand on her hip and looked ready to slam the door.

"Okay, calm down, we'll pay," said Vee, reaching into her back pocket. She stuffed a wad of cash into the bowl, but it was dark and I couldn't tell how much. "You owe me big-time," she told me.

"You're supposed to let me count the money first," Marcie said, digging through the bowl, trying to recapture Vee's donation.

"I just assumed twenty was too high for you to count," Vee said. "My apologies."

Marcie's eyes went slitty again, then she turned on her heel and carted the bowl back into the house.

"How much did you give her?" I asked Vee.

"I didn't. I tossed in a condom."

I lifted my eyebrows. "Since when do you carry condoms?"

"I picked one up off the lawn on our way up the walk. Who knows, maybe Marcie'll use it. Then I'll have done my part to keep her genetic material out of the gene pool."

Vee and I stepped all the way inside and put our backs to the wall. On a velvet chaise in the sitting room, several couples were tangled together like a pile of paper clips. The center of the room was filled with dancing bodies. Off the sitting room, an arched entryway led to the kitchen, where people were drinking and laughing. Nobody paid Vee or me any attention, and I tried to rally my spirits at the realization that getting inside Marcie's bedroom unnoticed wasn't going to be as hard as I'd thought. Trouble was, I was beginning to think I hadn't come here tonight to snoop through Marcie's bedroom and find evidence that she was with Patch. In fact, I was dangerously close to thinking I'd come because I knew Patch would be here. And I wanted to see him.

It looked like I was going to get my chance. Patch appeared in the entrance to Marcie's kitchen, dressed in a black polo shirt and dark jeans. I wasn't used to studying him from a distance. His eyes were the color of night and his hair curling under his ears looked like it was six weeks past needing a cut. He had a body that instantly attracted the opposite sex, but his stance said I'm not open to conversation. His hat was still missing, which meant it was probably in Marcie's possession. No big deal, I reminded myself. It was no longer my business. Patch could give his ball cap to whoever he wanted. Just because he'd never loaned it to me didn't hurt my feelings.

Jenn Martin, a girl I'd had math with freshman year, was talking to Patch, but he looked distracted. His eyes circled the sitting room, watchful, as if he wasn't about to trust a single soul there. His posture was relaxed but attentive, almost like he expected something to happen at any moment.

Before his eyes made it around to me, I shifted my gaze. Best not to be caught staring with regret and longing.

Anthony Amowitz smiled and waved at me from across the room. I automatically smiled back. We'd had PE together this year, and while I'd hardly said more than ten words to him, it was nice to think somebody was excited to see me and Vee here.

"Why is Anthony Amowitz using his pimp smile on you?" Vee asked.

I rolled my eyes. "You're only calling him a pimp because he's here. At Marcie's."

"Yeah, so?"

"He's being nice." I elbowed her. "Smile back."

"Being nice? He's being horny."

Anthony raised his red plastic cup to me and shouted something, but it was too hard to hear over the music.

"What?" I called back.

"You look great!" A goofy smile was plastered on his face.

"Oh boy," Vee said. "Not just a pimp, but a smashed pimp."

"So maybe he's a little drunk."

"Drunk and hoping to corner you alone in a bedroom upstairs."

Ugh.

Five minutes later, we were still holding our position just inside the front door. I'd had half a can of beer accidentally sloshed on my shoes, but luckily, there'd been no vomit. I was about to suggest to Vee that we move away from the open door—the direction everyone seemed to run moments before spilling the contents of their stomach—when Brenna Dubois came up and held a red plastic cup out to me.

"This is for you, compliments of the guy across the room."

"Told you," Vee whispered sideways.

I stole a quick glance at Anthony, who winked.

"Uh, thanks, but I'm not interested," I told Brenna. I wasn't very experienced when it came to parties, but I knew not to accept drinks of questionable origin. For all I knew, it was tainted with GHB. "Tell Anthony I don't drink from anything but a sealed can." Wow. I sounded even dumber than I felt.

"Anthony?" Her face twisted with confusion.

"Yeah, Anthony Pimp-o-witz," Vee said. "The guy who's making you play delivery girl."

"You thought Anthony gave me the cup?" She shook her head. "Try the guy on the other side of the room." She turned to where Patch had been standing only minutes ago. "Well, he was over there. I guess he left. He was hot and wearing a black shirt, if that helps."

"Oh boy," Vee said again, this time under her breath.

"Thanks," I told Brenna, seeing no choice but to take the cup. She faded back into the crowd, and I set the cup of what smelled like cherry Coke on the entry table behind me. Was Patch trying to send a message? Reminding me of my flop of a fight at the Devil's Handbag when Marcie had doused me with cherry Coke?

Vee pushed something into my hand.

"What's this?" I asked.

"A walkie-talkie. I borrowed them from my brother. I'll sit on the stairs and keep watch. If anybody comes up, I'll radio."

"You want me to snoop in Marcie's bedroom now?"

"I want you to steal the diary."

"Yeah, about that. I'm sort of having a change of heart."

"Are you kidding me?" Vee said. "You can't chicken out now.

Imagine what's in that diary. This is your one big chance to find out what's going on with Marcie and Patch. You can't pass that up."

"But it's wrong."

"It won't feel wrong if you steal it so fast that the guilt doesn't have time to soak in."

I gave her a pointed look.

"Self-talk helps too," Vee added. "Tell yourself this isn't wrong enough times, and you'll start to believe it."

"I'm not taking the diary. I just want to . . . look around. And steal Patch's hat back."

"I'll pay you the eZine's entire annual budget if you deliver the diary to me in the next thirty minutes," Vee said, beginning to sound desperate.

"That's why you want the diary? To publish it in the eZine?"

"Think about it. It could make my career."

"No," I said firmly. "And what's more, bad Vee."

She heaved a sigh. "Well, it was worth a try."

I looked at the walkie-talkie in my hand. "Why can't we just text?"

"Spies don't text."

"How do you know?"

"How do you know they *do*?"

Figuring it wasn't worth an argument, I tucked the walkie-talkie into the waistband of my jeans. "Are you sure Marcie's bedroom is on the second floor?"

"One of her ex-boyfriends sits behind me in Spanish. He told me every night at ten sharp Marcie undresses with the lights on. Sometimes when he and his friends are bored, they drive over to watch the show. He said Marcie never rushes, and by the time she finishes, he has a cramp in his neck from staring up. He also said there was this one time—"

I clapped my hands over my ears. "Stop!"

"Hey, if my brain has to be polluted with these kind of details, I figure yours should too. The whole reason I know all this vomit-inducing information is because I was trying to help you."

I flicked my eyes toward the stairs. My stomach seemed to weigh twice as much as it had three minutes ago. I hadn't done anything, and I was already sick with guilt. When had I become low enough to snoop in Marcie's bedroom? When had I let Patch twist and tangle me up this way? "I guess I'm going up," I said unconvincingly. "You've got my back?"

"Roger that."

I climbed the stairs. There was a bathroom with tile floors and crown molding at the top. I moved down the hall to my left, passing what looked to be a guest bedroom, and an exercise room equipped with a treadmill and elliptical. I backtracked, this time taking the hall to the right. The first door was cracked, and I peeked inside. The room's color scheme was a frothy pink—pink walls, pink drapes, and a pink duvet with pink throw pillows. The closet had spewed itself onto the bed, floor, and other furniture surfaces. Several photographs, blown to poster size, were tacked to the walls, and all were of Marcie posing seductively in her Razorbills cheerleading uniform. I experienced a mild rush of nausea, then saw Patch's ball cap on the dresser. Shutting myself in the room, I rolled the bill of the cap into a narrow cone and crammed it into my back pocket. Beneath the ball cap, lying on the dresser, was a single car key. It was a spare, but it had a Jeep tag. Patch had given Marcie a spare to his Jeep.

Swiping the key off the dresser, I shoved it deep into my other back pocket. While I was at it, I figured I might as well look for anything else belonging to him.

I opened and closed a few dresser drawers. I looked under the bed, in the hope chest, and on the top shelf of Marcie's closet. Finally I slipped my hand between the mattress and box spring. I pulled out the diary. Marcie's small blue diary, rumored to contain more scandal than a tabloid. Holding it between my hands, I felt the overwhelming temptation to open it. What had she written about Patch? What secret things were hiding in the pages?

My walkie-talkie crackled.

"Oh, crap," Vee said through it.

I fumbled it out of my waistband and pushed the talk button. "What's the matter?"

"Dog. Big dog. It just lumbered into the living room, or whatever you call this humongous open space. It's staring at me. Like, staring right at me."

"What kind of dog?"

"I'm not up-to-date on my dog species, but I think it's a Doberman pinscher. Pointed, snarling face. It resembles Marcie a little too much, if that helps. Uh-oh. Its ears just went up. It's coming toward me. I think it's one of those psychic dogs. It knows I'm not just sitting here minding my own business."

"Stay calm—"

"Shoo, dog, I said shoo!"

The unmistakable growl of a big dog came through the walkie-talkie.

"Um, Nora? We have a problem," Vee said a moment later.

"The dog didn't leave?"

"Worse. It just bounded upstairs."

Just then there was a snapping bark at the door. The barking didn't stop—it grew louder and more snarling.

"Vee!" I hissed into the walkie-talkie. "Get rid of the dog!"

She said something in response, but I couldn't hear over the dog's growls. I flattened my hand to my ear. "What?"

"Marcie's coming! Get out of there!"

I started to shove the diary back under the mattress, but fumbled it. Handfuls of notes and pictures spilled from the pages. In a panic, I raked the notes and pictures into a pile and tossed them back inside the diary. Then I rammed the diary, which was quite small considering how many secrets it was rumored to hold, and my walkie-talkie into the waistband of my jeans and flipped the light switch off. I'd deal with putting the diary back later. Right now, I had to get out.

I raised the window, expecting to have to remove the screen, but it was already done for me. Probably Marcie had removed it long ago to avoid the nuisance when she was sneaking out. That thought gave me a small measure of hope. If Marcie had climbed out before, I could too. It wasn't like I was going to fall and kill myself. Of course, Marcie was a cheerleader and a lot more flexible and coordinated.

Poking my head out the open window, I looked down. The front door was directly below, under a portico supported by four pillars. Swinging one leg out, I found traction on the shingles. After I was sure I wasn't going to slide off the sloped portico, I brought my other leg out. Balancing my weight, I lowered the window back in place. I'd just ducked below the window line when the glass filled with light. The dog's nails clicked against the glass, and it uttered a round of furious barks. Dropping to my stomach, I squeezed as close to the house as I could and prayed Marcie didn't open the window and look down.

"What is it?" Marcie's muffled voice carried through the window-pane. "What's the matter, Boomer?"

A trickle of sweat fell down my spine. Marcie was going to look down, and she was going to see me. I shut my eyes and tried to forget that her house was filled with people I had to attend school with for the next two years. How was I going to explain snooping in Marcie's bedroom? How was I going to explain holding her diary? The thought was too humiliating to bear.

"Shut up, Boomer!" Marcie shouted. "Would somebody hold my dog while I open the window? If you don't hold him, he's stupid enough to jump out. You—in the hall. Yes, you. Grab my dog's collar and don't let go. Just do it."

Hoping the dog's barking would mask any sounds I made, I rolled over and planted my back against the shingles. I swallowed the knot of fright in my throat. I had kind of a phobia about heights, and the thought of all that air between me and the ground had sweat leaking from my skin.

Digging my heels into the roof to push my weight as far away from the ledge as possible, I wrestled the walkie-talkie out of my jeans. "Vee?" I whispered.

"Where are you?" she said through the music blaring in the background.

"Think you could get rid of the dog any day now?"

"How?"

"Be creative."

"Like feed it poison?"

I wiped sweat off my forehead with the back of my hand. "I was thinking more like lock it in a closet."

"You mean touch it?"

"Vee!"

"Okay, okay, I'll think of something."

Thirty seconds ticked by before I heard Vee's voice float through Marcie's bedroom window.

"Hey, Marcie?" she called over the barking. "Not to interfere, but the police are at the front door. They said they're responding to a noise complaint. Do you want me to invite them in?"

"What?" Marcie shrilled directly above me. "I don't see any police cars."

"They probably had to park a couple blocks over. Anyway, as I was saying, I noticed illegal substances in the hands of a few guests."

"So?" she snapped. "It's a party."

"Alcohol is illegal under the age of twenty-one."

"Great!" Marcie shouted. "What am I going to do?" She paused, then raised her voice again. "You probably called them!"

"Who, me?" Vee said. "And lose the free food? No way."

A moment later, Boomer's frantic barking faded into the house, and the bedroom light blinked out.

I held perfectly still a moment longer, listening. When I was positive Marcie's bedroom was empty, I flipped to my stomach and belly-crawled up to the window. The dog was gone, Marcie was gone, and if I could just—

I pressed my palms to the window to force it up, but it didn't budge. Leveraging my hands lower on the pane, I put all my strength into it. Nothing happened.

Okay, I thought. *No big deal.* Marcie must have locked the window. All I had to do was hang out here another five hours until the party ended, then get Vee to come back with a ladder.

I heard footsteps on the walk below and craned my neck to see if by some stroke of luck Vee had come to my rescue. To my horror, Patch had his back to me, walking toward the Jeep. He punched a number into his cell and raised it to his ear. Two seconds later, my cell phone sang out in my pocket. Before I could hurl the cell into the bushes at the edge of the property, Patch came to a stop.

He looked over his shoulder, his eyes traveling up. His gaze fell on me, and I thought it would have been better if Boomer had shredded me alive.

"And here I thought they were called Peeping Toms." I didn't need to see him to know he wore a smile.

"Stop laughing," I said, my cheeks hot with humiliation. "Get me down."

"Jump."

"What?"

"I'll catch you."

"Are you crazy? Go inside and open the window. Or get a ladder."

"I don't need a ladder. Jump. I'm not going to drop you."

"Oh, sure! Like I believe that!"

"You want my help or not?"

"You call this help?" I hissed furiously. "This isn't help!"

He spun his key chain around his finger, then started to walk away.

"You are such a jerk! Get back here!"

"Jerk?" he repeated. "You're the one spying in windows."

"I wasn't spying. I was—I was—" *Think of something!*

Patch's eyes flicked to the window above me, and I watched as understanding dawned on his face. He tilted his head back and gave a bark of laughter. "You were searching Marcie's bedroom."

"No." I rolled my eyes like it was the most absurd suggestion.

"What were you looking for?"

"Nothing." I yanked Patch's ball cap out of my back pocket and flung it at him. "And here's your stupid hat back, by the way!"

"You went in for my hat?"

"A big waste, obviously!"

He fit the hat to his head. "Are you going to jump?"

I took an uneasy look over the edge of the portico, and the ground seemed to drop another twenty feet out of reach. Side-stepping an answer, I asked, "Why did you call?"

"I lost sight of you inside. I wanted to make sure you were okay."

He sounded sincere, but he was a smooth liar. "And the cherry Coke?"

"Peace offering. You going to jump or what?"

Seeing no alternative, I scooted cautiously to the edge of the portico. My stomach flipped circles. "If you drop me . . . ," I warned.

Patch had his arms raised. Squeezing my eyes shut, I slid off the ledge. I felt air break around my body and then I was in Patch's arms, anchored against him. I stayed there a moment, heart hammering from both the adrenaline of falling and from standing so close to Patch. He felt warm and familiar. He felt solid and safe. I wanted to cling to his shirt, bury my face into the warm curve of his neck, and never let go.

Patch tucked a stray curl behind my ear. "Do you want to go back to the party?" he murmured.

I shook my head no.

"I'll drive you home." He used his chin to gesture at the Jeep, because he still hadn't unfolded his arms from around me.

"I came with Vee," I said. "I should catch a ride with her."

"Vee's not going to pick up Chinese takeout on the way home."

Chinese takeout. That would involve Patch coming inside the farmhouse to eat. My mom wasn't home, which meant we would be all alone. . . .

I let my guard slide a little further. Probably we were safe. Probably the archangels were nowhere close. Patch didn't seem worried, so neither should I. And it was just dinner. I'd had a long, unsatisfying day at school, and I was famished from an hour at the gym. Takeout with Patch sounded perfect. How was a casual dinner together going to hurt? People ate dinner together all the time and never carried it further. "Just dinner," I said, more to convince myself than Patch.

He gave the Boy Scout salute, but his smile was up to no good. A bad boy's smile. The wicked, charming smile of a guy who'd kissed Marcie a mere two nights ago . . . and was offering to have dinner with me tonight, most likely with the hope that dinner would lead to something else entirely. He thought one heart-melting smile was all it would take to erase my hurt. To make me forget he'd kissed Marcie.

All my inner turmoil scattered as I was jerked to the present. My speculations died, replaced by a sudden, strong feeling of unease that had nothing to do with Patch, or Sunday night. Goose bumps prickled my skin. I studied the shadows ringing the lawn.

"Mmm?" Patch murmured, detecting my concern, tightening his arms protectively around me.

And then I felt it again. A change in the air. An invisible fog, strangely warm, hanging low, pressing all around, zigzagging closer like a hundred stealthy snakes in the air. The sensation was so disruptive, I had a hard time believing Patch hadn't at least noticed something was off, even if he couldn't feel it directly.

"What is it, Angel?" His voice was low, questioning.

"Are we safe?"

"Does it matter?"

I shifted my eyes around the yard. I wasn't sure why, but I kept thinking, *The archangels. They're here.* "I mean . . . the archangels," I said, so quietly I barely heard my own voice. "Aren't they watching?"

"Yes."

I tried to step back, but Patch refused to let me. "I don't care what they see. I'm tired of the charade." He'd stopped nuzzling my neck, and I saw a certain tormented defiance in his eyes.

I struggled harder to pull away. "Let go."

"You don't want me?" His smile was all fox.

"That's not the issue. I don't want to be responsible for anything happening to you. Let go." How could he be so casual about this? They were hunting for an excuse to get rid of him. He couldn't be seen holding me.

He caressed the sides of my arms, but as I tried to take the opportunity to break away, he caught my hands. His voice broke into my mind. *I could go rogue. I could walk away right now, and we could stop playing by the archangels' rules.* He said it so decidedly, so easily, I knew this wasn't the first time he'd thought it. This was a plan he'd secretly fantasized about many, many times.

My heart was beating wildly. Walk away? Stop playing by the rules? "What are you talking about?"

I'd live on the move, constantly hiding, hoping the archangels don't find me.

"If they did?"

I'd go to trial. I'd be found guilty, but it would give us a few weeks alone, while they deliberated.

I could feel the stricken look on my face. "And then?"

They'd send me to hell. He paused, then added with quiet conviction, *I'm not afraid of hell. I deserve what's coming. I've lied, cheated, deceived. I've hurt innocent people. I've made more mistakes than I can remember. One way or another, I've been paying for them most of my existence. Hell won't be any different.* His mouth quirked into a brief, wry

627

smile. But I'm sure the archangels have a few cards up their sleeves. His smile faded, and he looked at me with stripped honesty. *Being with you never felt wrong. It's the one thing I did right. You're the one thing I did right. I don't care about the archangels. Tell me what you want me to do. Say the word. I'll do whatever you want. We can leave right now.*

It took a moment for his words to settle in. I looked to the Jeep. The wall of ice between us fell away. The wall was only there because of the archangels. Without them, everything Patch and I had been fighting over meant nothing. They were the problem. I wanted to leave them, and everything else, behind and race off with Patch. I wanted to be reckless; thinking only of right here, right now. We could make each other forget about consequences. We'd laugh at rules, boundaries, and most of all, tomorrow. There would only be me and Patch, and nothing else would matter.

Nothing but the promise of what would happen when those weeks drew to a close.

I had two choices, but the answer was clear. The only way I could keep Patch was by letting him go. By having nothing to do with him.

I didn't realize I was crying until Patch ran his thumbs under my eyes. "Shh," he murmured. "It's going to be okay. I want you. I can't keep doing what I'm doing now, living halfway."

"But they'll send you to hell," I stammered, unable to control the quiver in my lower lip.

"I've had a long time to come to terms with it."

I was determined not to show Patch how hard this was for me, but I choked on the tears running down my throat. My eyes were damp and swollen, and my chest ached. This was all my fault. If it weren't for me, he wouldn't be a guardian angel. If it weren't for me, the archangels wouldn't be bent on destroying him. I was responsible for driving him to this point.

"I need one favor," I finally said in a small voice that sounded more like a stranger's than my own. "Tell Vee I walked home. I need to be alone."

"Angel?" Patch reached for my hand, but I pulled free. I felt my feet walking away, one step in front of the other. Farther and farther from Patch they took me, as if my mind had gone numb and turned all action over to my body.

13

THE FOLLOWING AFTERNOON VEE DROPPED ME OFF near the front door to Enzo's. I was dressed in a yellow printed sundress that walked the line between flirty and professional and was far more optimistic than anything I felt on the inside. I stopped in front of the windows to shake out my hair, which had relaxed into waves after being slept on all night, but the gesture felt wooden. I forced a smile. It was the one I'd been practicing all morning. It felt tight at the edges and brittle everywhere in between. In the window, it looked false and hollow. But for a morning following a night spent crying, it was the best I could manage.

After walking home from Marcie's last night, I'd curled into bed, but I hadn't slept. I'd spent the night tormented by self-destructive thoughts. The longer I stayed awake, the more my thoughts took a dizzying departure from reality. I wanted to make a statement, and I was hurting enough not to care how drastic it was. A thought came to me, the kind of thought I never would have entertained in my life before. If I ended my life, the archangels would see it. I wanted them to feel remorse. I wanted them to doubt their archaic laws. I wanted them to be held accountable for ripping my life apart, then ripping it away completely.

My mind swirled and tottered with these kinds of thoughts all night. My emotions shifted through heartbreaking loss, denial, anger. At one point, I regretted not running away with Patch. Any happiness, no matter how brief, seemed better than the long, simmering torture of waking up day after day, knowing I could never have him.

But as the sun began to crack across the sky this morning, I came to a decision. I had to move on. It was either that, or slip into a frozen depression. I forced myself through the motions of showering and dressing, and went to school with fixed determination that no one would see below skin-deep. A pins-and-needles sensation enveloped my body, but I refused to display a single outward sign of self-pity. I wasn't going to let the archangels win. I was going to pull myself back on my feet, get a job, pay off my speeding ticket, finish summer school with the top grade, and keep myself so occupied that only at night, when I was alone with my thoughts and it couldn't be helped, would I think of Patch.

Inside Enzo's, two semicircular balconies spread out to my left and right, with a set of wide stairs leading down into the main eating area and front counter. The balconies reminded me of curved catwalks overlooking a pit. The tables on the balcony were filled, but only a few stragglers drinking coffee and reading the morning paper remained in the pit.

With the help of a deep breath, I took the stairs down and approached the front counter.

"Excuse me, I heard you're hiring baristas," I told the woman at the register. My voice sounded flat in my ears, but I didn't have the energy to try to correct it. The woman, a middle-aged redhead with a name tag that read ROBERTA, looked up. "I'd like to fill out an application." I managed a half smile, but somehow, I feared it wasn't anywhere close to believable.

Roberta wiped her freckled hands on a rag and came around the counter. "Baristas? Not anymore."

I stared at her, holding my breath, feeling all hope deflate inside me. My plan was everything. I hadn't considered what I would do if even one step of it was yanked out from under me. I needed a plan. I needed this job. I needed a carefully controlled life where every minute was planned, and every emotion compartmentalized.

"But I'm still looking for a reliable counter attendant, night shift only, six to ten," Roberta added.

I blinked, my lip quivering slightly in surprise. "Oh," I said. "That's . . . good."

"At night we dim the lights, bring out the baristas, play a little jazz, and try for a more sophisticated feel. It used to be dead in here after five, but we're hoping to lure crowds. Tough economy," she explained. "You'd be in charge of greeting customers and writing down orders, then calling them in to the kitchen. When the food's ready, you'd carry it out to the tables."

I tried to nod eagerly, determined to show her how much I wanted this job, feeling all the tiny cracks in my lips split as I smiled. "That—sounds perfect," I managed in a husky voice.

"Do you have any work experience?"

I didn't. But Vee and I came to Enzo's at least three times a week. "I know the menu by heart," I said, beginning to feel more solid, more real. A job. Everything depended on it. I was going to build a new life.

"That's what I like to hear," Roberta said. "When can you start?"

"Tonight?" I could hardly believe she was offering me the job. Here I was, unable to summon up even a sincere smile, but she was overlooking it. She was giving me a chance. I put my hand forward to shake hers, then noticed a half beat too late that it was trembling.

She ignored my outstretched hand, eying me with her head

cocked to one side in a way that only made me feel more exposed and self-conscious. "Is everything okay?"

I sucked in a silent breath and held it. "Yes—I'm fine."

She gave a brisk nod. "Get here at a quarter to six and I'll issue you a uniform before your shift."

"Thank you so much—," I began, my voice still in shock, but she was already scooting back behind the counter.

As I stepped outside to a blinding sun, I ran calculations in my head. Assuming I was going to make minimum wage, if I worked every night for the next two weeks, I just might be able to pay off my speeding ticket. And if I worked every night for two months, that was sixty nights that I'd be too drowned in work to dwell on Patch. Sixty nights closer to the end of summer vacation, when I could once again throw all my energy into school. I'd already decided to pack my schedule with demanding classes. I could handle homework in every shape and form, but heartbreak was entirely different.

"Well?" Vee asked, coasting up beside me in the Neon. "How'd it go?"

I climbed into the passenger seat. "I got the job."

"Nice. You seemed really nervous going in, almost like you were going to lose it, but no reason to worry now. You're officially a hard-working member of society. Proud of you, babe. When do you start?"

I checked the readout on the dash. "Four hours."

"I'll stop by tonight and request to be seated in your area."

"Better leave a tip," I said, my attempt at humor nearly bringing me to tears.

"I'm your chauffeur. That's better than a tip."

Six and a half hours later, Enzo's was jammed to the walls. My work uniform consisted of a white pintuck shirt, gray tweed slacks with a matching vest, and a newsboy cap. The newsboy cap wasn't doing a very good job of holding up my hair, which refused to stay tucked out of sight. At this moment, I could feel stray curls plastered to the sides of my face with sweat. Despite the fact that I was completely overwhelmed, it felt strangely relieving to be in over my head. There was no time to shift my thoughts, even fleetingly, to Patch.

"New girl!" One of the cooks—Fernando—was shouting at me. He stood behind a short wall that separated the ovens from the rest of the kitchen, flapping a spatula. "Your order is up!"

I grabbed the three sandwich plates, carefully stacked them up my arm in a row, and backed out of the swinging doors. On my way across the pit, I caught the eye of one of the hostesses. She jerked her chin at a newly seated table up on the balcony. I answered with a quick nod. Be there in a minute.

"One prime rib sandwich, one salami, and one roasted turkey," I said, setting the plates down in front of a party of three business-men in suits. "Enjoy your meal."

I jogged up the steps leading out of the pit, pulling my meal order pad out of my back pocket. Halfway down the catwalk, my stride caught. Marcie Millar was directly ahead, seated at my newest table. I also recognized Addyson Hales, Oakley Williams, and Ethan Tyler, all from school. I thought about making an about-face and telling the hostess to give someone else—anyone else—my table, when Marcie glanced up and I knew I was trapped.

A granite-hard smile touched her mouth.

My breathing faltered. Was there any possible way she could know I'd taken her diary? It wasn't until I'd walked home and crawled into bed last night that I remembered I still had it. I would have returned it right then, but it had been the last thing on my mind. The diary had seemed insignificant next to the raw turmoil scraping me both inside and out. As of this moment, it was sitting untouched on my bedroom floor, right beside last night's discarded clothes.

"Isn't your outfit the cutest thing ever?" Marcie said over the prerecorded jazz. "Ethan, didn't you wear a vest just like that to prom last year? I think Nora raided your closet."

While they laughed, I held my pen poised on the order pad. "Can I get you something to drink? The special tonight is our coconut lime smoothie." Could everyone hear the scratch of guilt in my voice? I swallowed, hoping that when I spoke again, the jittery quality would be gone.

"Last time I was in here, it was my mom's birthday," Marcie said. "Our waitress sang 'Happy Birthday' to her."

It took me a whole three seconds to catch on. "Oh. No. I mean—no. I'm not a waitress. I'm a counter attendant."

"I don't care what you are. I want you to sing 'Happy Birthday' to me."

I stood paralyzed, my mind frantically groping for an escape. I couldn't believe Marcie was asking me to humiliate myself this way. Wait. Of course she was asking me to humiliate myself. For the past eleven years, I'd kept a secret scorecard between us, but now I was certain she was keeping her own scorecard. She lived for the chance to one-up me. Worse, she knew her score doubled mine and she was still running up the points. Which made her not only a bully, but a bad sport.

I held out my hand. "Let me see your ID."

Marcie lifted an uncaring shoulder. "I forgot it."

We both knew she hadn't forgotten her driver's license, and we both knew it wasn't her birthday.

"We're really busy tonight," I said, feigning apology. "My manager wouldn't want me to take time away from the other customers."

"Your manager would want you to keep your customers happy. Now sing."

"And while you're at it," Ethan chimed in, "bring out one of those free chocolate cakes."

"We're only supposed to give out one slice, not a whole cake," I said.

"We're only supposed to give out one slice," Addyson mimicked, and the table erupted with laughter.

Marcie reached into her handbag and pulled out a Flip camera. The red power button blinked on, and she aimed the lens at me. "I can't wait to spam this video to the entire school. Good thing I have access to everyone's e-mail. Who would've thought being an office aide would be so useful?"

She knew about the diary. She had to. And this was payback. Fifty points to me for stealing her diary. Twice that many to her for sending a video of me singing "Happy Birthday, Marcie" to all of Coldwater High.

I pointed over my shoulder at the kitchen and slowly backed up. "Listen, my orders are piling up—"

"Ethan, go tell that lovely hostess over there that we demand to speak to the manager. Tell her our *counter attendant* is being cranky," Marcie said.

I couldn't believe it. Less than three hours on the job, and Marcie was going to get me fired. How was I going to pay off my ticket? And good-bye, Volkswagen Cabriolet. Most importantly, I needed the job to distract myself from the useless struggle of finding a way to deal with the blistering truth: Patch was out of my life. For good.

"Time's up," Marcie said. "Ethan, ask for the manager."

"Wait," I said. "I'll do it."

Marcie squealed and clapped her hands. "Good thing I charged my battery."

Subconsciously, I tugged the newsboy cap lower, shielding my face. I opened my mouth. "Happy birthday to you—"

"Louder!" they all shouted.

"Happy birthday to you," I sang louder, too embarrassed to tell if my tone was perilously flat. "Happy birthday, dear Marcie. Happy birthday to you."

Nobody said a word. Marcie stowed the Flip back inside her handbag. "Well, that was boring."

"That sounded . . . normal," Ethan said.

Some of the blood drained from my face. I gave a brief, flustered, triumphant smile. Five hundred points. My solo was worth at least that. So much for Marcie blowing me to smithereens. I had officially taken the lead. "Drinks, anyone?" I asked, sounding surprisingly cheerful.

After scribbling down their orders, I turned to head back to the kitchen, when Marcie called out, "Oh, and Nora?"

I stopped in my tracks. I sucked in a sharp breath, wondering what hoops she thought she could make me jump through next. Oh, no. Unless . . . she was going to out me. Right now. In front of all these people. She was going to tell the world I stole her diary, so they could see just how low and despicable I really was.

"Could you rush our order?" Marcie finished. "We have a party to get to."

"Rush your order?" I repeated stupidly. Did this mean she didn't know about the diary?

"Patch is meeting us at Delphic Beach, and I don't want to be late." Marcie instantly covered her mouth. "I'm so sorry. I wasn't even thinking. I shouldn't have mentioned Patch. It's got to be hard seeing him with someone else."

Any smile I was clinging to slipped. I felt heat creep up my neck. My heart beat so fast it made my head light. The room slanted inward, and Marcie's cutthroat smile was at the center of everything, laughing at me. So everything was back to normal, then. Patch had gone back to Marcie. After I'd walked away last night, he'd resigned himself to the deal fate had handed us. If he couldn't have me, he'd settle for Marcie. How come *they* were allowed to have a relationship? Where were the archangels when it came to keeping tabs on Patch and Marcie? What about *their* kiss? Were the archangels going to let it slide because they knew it meant nothing to either of them? I wanted to scream at the unfairness of it all. Marcie could be with Patch when she didn't love him, but I couldn't, because I did and the archangels knew it. Why was it so *wrong* for us to be in love? Were angels and humans really that different?

"It's fine, I've moved on," I said, injecting a note of cool civility into my tone.

"Good for you," Marcie said, nibbling seductively on her straw, not one part of her looking like she believed me.

Back in the kitchen, I sent Marcie's table's order in to the cooks. I left the "special cooking instructions" space blank. Marcie was in a hurry to see Patch at Delphic Beach? Too bad.

I picked up my waiting order and carried the tray out of the kitchen. To my surprise, I saw Scott standing near the front doors, talking to the hostesses. He was dressed comfortably in loose-fitting Levi's and a snug T-shirt, and given the body language of the two black-clad hostesses, they were flirting with him. He caught my eye and gave a low wave of recognition. I dropped off table fifteen's order, then hiked the stairs.

"Hey," I told Scott, pulling off the newsboy cap to fan my face. "Vee told me I'd find you here."

"You called Vee?"

"Yeah, after you didn't return any of my messages."

I wiped my arm across my forehead, sweeping a few loose hairs back into place. "My cell is in the back. I haven't had a chance to check it since I clocked in. What do you need?"

"What time are you off?"

"Ten. Why?"

"There's a party at Delphic Beach. I'm looking for some poor sucker to drag along."

"Every time we hang out, something bad happens." The light didn't go on in his eyes. "The fight at the Z," I reminded him. "At the Devil's Handbag. Both times I had to scrounge a ride home."

"Third time's a charm." He smiled, and I realized for the first time that it was a very nice smile. Boyish even. It softened his personality, making me wonder if there was another side to him, a side I hadn't seen yet.

Chances were, this was the same party Marcie was headed to. The same party Patch was supposed to be at. And the same beach

I'd been at with him just a week and a half ago, when I'd spoken too early by declaring I was living the perfect life. I never could have guessed how fast it would tailspin.

I did a quick inventory of my feelings, but I needed more than a handful of seconds to figure out how I was feeling. I wanted to see Patch—I would always want to—but that wasn't the question. I needed to determine if I was up to seeing him. Could I handle seeing him with Marcie? Especially after everything he'd told me last night?

"I'll think about it," I told Scott, realizing I was taking too long to answer.

"Need me to swing by at ten and pick you up?"

"No. If I go, Vee can give me a ride." I pointed toward the kitchen doors. "Listen, I need to get back to work."

"Hope to see you," he said, shooting me one final grin before departing.

At closing, I found Vee idling in the parking lot. "Thanks for the pickup," I told her, dropping into shotgun. My legs ached from all the standing, and my ears still rang with the conversation and loud laughter of a packed restaurant—not to mention all the times the cooks and waitresses had shouted corrections at me. I'd carried out at least two wrong orders, and more than once, I'd entered the kitchen through the wrong door. Both times, I'd nearly knocked over a waitress up to her arms in plates. The good news was, I had thirty dollars in tips folded inside my pocket. After I'd paid off my ticket, all my tips would go toward the Cabriolet. I longed for the day when I wouldn't have to rely on Vee to haul me around.

But not quite as much as I longed for the day when I'd have forgotten Patch.

Vee grinned. "This ain't no free service. All these rides are actually IOUs that will come back to haunt you."

"I'm serious, Vee. You're the best friend in the whole world. The bestest."

"Aw, maybe we should commemorate this Hallmark moment and swing by Skippy's for ice cream. I could use some ice cream. Actually, I could really use some MSG. Nothing makes me happy quite like a boatload of freshly fried fast food, smothered in good old-fashioned MSG."

"Rain check?" I asked. "I got invited to hang out at Delphic Beach tonight. You're more than welcome to come," I added quickly. I wasn't at all sure I'd made the best decision when I'd made up my mind to go tonight. Why was I putting myself through the torture of seeing Patch again? I knew it was because I wanted him close, even if close wasn't close enough. A stronger, braver person would cut all ties and walk away. A stronger person wouldn't beat her fists against fate's door. Patch was out of my life for good. I knew I needed to accept it, but there was a big difference between knowing and doing.

"Who all's going?" Vee asked.

"Scott and a few other people from school." No need to mention

Marcie and get an instant veto. I had a feeling I could use Vee's support tonight.

"Think I'll curl up with Rixon and watch a movie instead. I can ask if he's got any other friends he can hook you up with. We could do a double-date thing. Eat popcorn, tell jokes, make out."

"Pass." I didn't want someone else. I wanted Patch.

By the time Vee rolled into Delphic Beach's parking lot, the sky was tar black. High-power lights that reminded me of those on CHS's football field beamed down on the whitewashed wood structures housing the carousel, arcade, and mini golf, causing a halo to hover over the spot. There was no electricity farther down the beach, or in the surrounding fields, making it the one bright spot on the coast for miles. By this time of night I didn't expect to find anyone buying hamburgers or playing air hockey, and I signaled for Vee to pull over near the path of railroad ties cutting down to the water.

I swung out of the car and mouthed a good-bye. Vee waved in response, her cell pressed to her ear as she and Rixon worked out the details of where they'd meet up.

The air still held the earlier heat of the sun and was filled with the sounds of everything from the distant music carrying down from Delphic Seaport Amusement Park high on the cliffs, to surf drumming the sand. I parted the ridge of sea grass that ran parallel to the coast like a fence, jogged down the slope, and walked the thin ribbon of dry sand that was just out of reach of high tide.

I passed small groups of people still playing in the water, jumping waves and hurling driftwood into the darkness of the ocean, even though the lifeguards were long gone. I kept my eyes out for Patch, Scott, Marcie, or anyone else I recognized. Up ahead, the orange flames of a bonfire winked and flitted in the darkness. I pulled out my cell and dialed Scott.

"Yo."

"I made it," I said. "Where are you?"

"Just south of the bonfire. You?"

"Just north of it."

"I'll find you."

Two minutes later, Scott plopped down in the sand beside me. "You going to hang out on the fringe all night?" he asked me. His breath held the tang of alcohol.

"I'm not a big fan of ninety percent of the people at this party."

He nodded, understanding, and held out a steel thermos. "I don't have germs, scout's honor. Have as much as you like."

I leaned over just far enough to smell the contents of the thermos. Immediately I drew back, feeling fumes burn down the back of my throat. "What is it?" I choked. "Motor oil?"

"My secret recipe. If I told you, I'd have to kill you."

"No need. I'm pretty sure taking a drink would get the same result."

Scott eased back, elbows in the sand. He'd changed into a Metallica T-shirt with the sleeves ripped off, khaki shorts, and flip-flops. I was wearing my work uniform, minus the newsboy cap, vest, and pintuck shirt. Luckily, I'd slipped a camisole on before heading out to work, but I had nothing to replace the tweed slacks.

"So tell me, Grey. What are you doing here? I gotta tell you, I thought you'd turn me down for next week's homework."

I leaned back in the sand beside him and slanted a look in his direction. "The jerk act is starting to get old. So I'm lame. So what?"

He grinned. "I like lame. Lame is going to help me pass my junior year. Particularly English."

Oh boy. "If that was a question, the answer is no, I will not write your English papers."

"That's what you think. I haven't started working the Scott Charm yet."

I snorted laughter, and his grin deepened. He said, "What? Don't believe me?"

"I don't believe you and the word 'charm' belong in the same sentence."

"No girl can resist the Charm. I'm telling you, they go wild for it. Here are the basics: I'm drunk twenty-four/seven, I can't hold a job, can't pass basic math, and I spend my days playing video games and passing out."

I flung my head back, feeling my shoulders shake as I laughed. I was beginning to think I liked the drunk version of Scott better than the sober one. Who would have figured Scott for self-deprecating?

"Quit drooling," Scott said, playfully tipping my chin up. "It's going to go to my head."

I gave him a relaxed smile. "You drive a Mustang. That should give you ten points at least."

"Awesome. Ten points. All I need is another two hundred to get out of the red zone."

"Why don't you quit drinking?" I suggested.

"Quit? You kidding? My life sucks when I'm only half-aware of it. If I quit drinking and saw what it's really like, I'd probably jump off a bridge."

We were quiet a moment.

"When I'm wasted, I can almost forget who I am," he said, his smile fading slightly. "I know I'm still there, but only barely. It's a good place to be." He tipped back the thermos, eyes on the dark sea straight ahead.

"Yeah, well, my life isn't so great either."

"Your dad?" he guessed, wiping his upper lip with the back of his hand. "That wasn't your fault."

"Which almost makes it worse."

"How so?"

"If it were my fault, that would imply I messed up. I'd blame myself for a long time, but maybe eventually I could move on. Right now I'm stuck, facing down the same question: Why *my* dad?"

"Fair enough," Scott said.

A soft rain started to fall. Summer rain, with big warm drops splattering everywhere.

"What the hell?" I heard Marcie demand from farther down the beach, near the bonfire. I studied the outlines of bodies as people began shuffling to their feet. Patch wasn't among them.

"My apartment, everyone!" Scott hollered out, jumping to his feet with a flourish. He staggered sideways, barely hanging on to his balance. "Seventy-two Deacon Road, apartment thirty-two. Doors are unlocked. Plenty of beer in the fridge. Oh, and did I mention my mom's at Bunco all night?"

A cheer went up, and everyone grabbed their shoes and other discarded clothing items and hiked up the sand toward the parking lot.

Scott nudged my thigh with his flip-flop. "Need a ride? C'mon, I'll even let you drive."

"Thanks for the offer, but I think I'm done." Patch wasn't here. He was the sole reason I'd come, and suddenly the night felt not only like a letdown, but a waste as well. I should have been relieved at not having to see Patch and Marcie together, but I mostly felt disappointed, lonely, and full of regret. And exhausted. The only thing on my mind was crawling into bed and putting an end to this day as soon as possible.

"Friends don't let friends drive drunk," Scott coaxed.

"Are you trying to appeal to my conscience?"

He dangled the keys in front of me. "How can you turn down a once-in-a-lifetime chance to drive the 'Stang?"

I got to my feet and brushed sand off the seat of my pants. "How about you sell me the 'Stang for thirty dollars? I can even pay cash."

He laughed, slinging his arm around my shoulders. "Drunk, but not that drunk, Grey."

CHAPTER

14

ONCE BACK INSIDE COLDWATER'S CITY LIMITS,
I drove the Mustang across town and took Beech
to Deacon. The rain continued to patter down in
a somber drizzle. The road was narrow and winding, evergreen
trees crowding right up to the edge of the pavement. Around
the next bend, Scott pointed to a complex of Cape Cod–style
apartments with tiny balconies and gray shingles. There was a
run-down tennis court on the small lawn out front. The whole

place looked like it could use a fresh coat of paint.

I angled the Mustang into a parking space.

"Thanks for the ride," Scott said, draping his arm on the back of my seat. His eyes were glassy, his smile hitched up lazily on one side.

"Can you make it inside?" I asked.

"I don't want to go inside," he slurred. "The carpet smells like dog urine and the bathroom ceiling has mold. I want to stay out here, with you."

Because you're drunk. "I have to get home. It's late, and I still haven't called my mom today. She's going to freak out if I don't check in soon." I reached across him and pushed open the passenger door.

As I did, he coiled a lock of my hair around his finger. "Pretty."

I unwound the curl. "This isn't going to happen. You're drunk."

He grinned. "Just a little."

"You're not going to remember this tomorrow."

"I thought we had a bonding moment back at the beach."

"We did. And that's as far as our bond is going. I'm serious. I'm kicking you out. Go inside."

"What about my car?"

"I'll take it home tonight, then bring it by tomorrow afternoon."

Scott exhaled contentedly and relaxed deeper into his seat. "I want to go inside and chill solo with Jimi Hendrix. Would you tell everyone the party's over?"

I rolled my eyes. "You just invited sixty people over. I'm not going to go in and tell them it's called off."

Scott bent sideways out the door and threw up.

Ugh.

I grabbed the back of his shirt, lugged him inside the car, and gave the Mustang enough gas to roll it forward two feet. Then I engaged the foot brake and swung out. I walked around to Scott's side and dragged him out of the car by his arms, being careful to avoid planting my foot in the contents of his emptied stomach. He flung his arm over my shoulder, and it was all I could do to keep from collapsing under his weight. "Which apartment?" I asked.

"Thirty-two. Top right."

The top floor. Of course. Why should I expect to catch a break now?

I dragged Scott up both flights of stairs, panting hard, and staggered through the open door of his apartment, which was alive with the chaos of bodies pulsing and grinding to rap turned up so loud I could feel pieces of my brain shaking loose.

"Bedroom's at the back," Scott murmured in my ear.

I pushed him forward through the crowd, opened the door at the end of the hall, and dumped Scott on the bottom mattress of the bunk bed in the corner. There was a small desk in the adjacent corner, a collapsible cloth hamper, a guitar stand, and a few free weights. The walls were aged white and sparsely decorated with a movie poster for The Godfather Part III and a New England Patriots pennant.

"My room," Scott said, catching me taking in the surroundings. He patted the mattress beside him. "Make yourself comfortable."

"Good night, Scott."

I started to pull the door shut when he said, "Can you get me a drink? Water. I got to wash this taste out of my mouth."

I was antsy to get out of the place but couldn't help feeling an aggravating tug of sympathy for Scott. If I left now, he'd probably wake tomorrow in a pool of his own vomit. I might as well clean him up and get him some ibuprofen.

The apartment's tiny U-shaped kitchen looked out on the living-room-turned-dance floor, and after squeezing through the packed-in bodies blocking the kitchen's entrance, I opened and closed cabinets, hunting for a glass. I found a stack of white plastic cups above the sink, flipped on the tap, and held a cup under the faucet. As I was turning to carry the water back to Scott, my heart jumped. Patch stood several feet away, leaning against the cupboards opposite the refrigerator. He'd separated himself from the crowd, and his ball cap was pulled low, signaling he wasn't interested in soliciting conversation. His stance was impatient. He glanced at his watch.

Seeing no way to avoid him, aside from climbing over the counter directly into the living room, and feeling I owed him civility—plus, weren't we both old enough to handle this maturely?—I moistened my lips, which suddenly felt dry as sand, and walked over. "Having fun?"

The hard lines of his face softened into a smile. "I can think of at least one thing I'd rather be doing."

If that was an innuendo, I was going to ignore it. I boosted myself onto the kitchen counter, legs dangling over the edge. "Staying the whole night?"

"If I have to stay the whole night, shoot me now."

I spread my hands. "No gun, sorry."

His smile was bad-boy perfection. "That's all that's stopping you?"

"Shooting you wouldn't kill you," I pointed out. "One of the downsides of being immortal."

He nodded, a fierce smile creeping out beneath the shadow of his ball cap. "But you would if you could?"

I hesitated before answering. "I don't hate you, Patch. Yet."

"Hate's not strong enough?" he guessed. "Something deeper?"

I smiled, but not enough to show teeth.

We both seemed to sense that nothing good would come of this conversation, especially not here, and Patch rescued both of us by tipping his head toward the crowd behind us. "And you? Staying long?"

I hopped down off the counter. "Nope. I'm delivering water to Scott, and mouthwash if I can find it, then I'm out of here."

He caught my elbow. "You'd shoot me, but you're on your way to nurse Scott's hangover?"

"Scott didn't break my heart."

A couple of beats of silence fell between us, then Patch said in a low voice, "Let's go." The way he looked at me told me exactly what he meant. He wanted me to run away with him. To defy the archangels. To ignore that they'd eventually find Patch.

I couldn't think about what they'd do to him without feeling trapped in ice, cold with fear, and frozen by the sheer horror of it. Patch had never told me what hell would be like. But he knew. And the fact that he wasn't telling me painted a very vivid, very bleak picture.

I kept my eyes nailed to the living room. "I promised Scott a glass of water."

"You're spending a lot of time with a guy I'd call dark, and given my standard, that's a hard-won title."

"Takes a dark prince to know one?"

"Glad you've hung on to your sense of humor, but I'm serious. Be careful."

I nodded. "I appreciate your concern, but I know what I'm doing." I sidestepped Patch and edged through the gyrating bodies in the living room. I had to get away. It was too much standing close to him, feeling that wall of ice so thick and impenetrable. Knowing we both wanted something we couldn't have, even though what we wanted stood an arm's reach away.

I'd made it about halfway through the crowd when someone snagged the strap of my cami from behind. I turned back, expecting to find Patch ready to give me more of his opinion, or maybe, more terrifying, throwing caution to the wind to kiss me, but it was Scott, grinning lazily down at me. He brushed my hair off my face and leaned in, sealing my mouth with his. He tasted like mint mouthwash and freshly scrubbed teeth. I started to draw back, then realized, what did I care if Patch saw? I wasn't doing anything he hadn't already. I had just as much right to move on as he did. He was using Marcie to fill the void in his heart, and now it was my turn, with Scott.

I slid my hands up Scott's chest and laced them behind his neck. He took the cue and pulled me in tighter, tracing his hands down the contour of my spine. So this was what it felt like to kiss someone else. While Patch was slow and practiced and took his time, Scott was playfully eager and a little sloppy. It was completely different and new . . . and not altogether bad.

"My room," Scott whispered in my ear, lacing his fingers between mine and pulling me toward the hall.

I flicked my gaze to where I'd last seen Patch. Our eyes met. His hand was stiff, cupped at the back of his neck, as if he'd been lost in deep thought and had frozen at the sight of me kissing Scott.

This is what it feels like, I thought at him.

Only, I didn't feel any better after thinking it. I felt sad and low and dissatisfied. I wasn't the kind of person who played games or relied on dirty tricks to console myself or boost my self-esteem. But there was still a certain raw pain burning inside me, and because of it, I let Scott guide me down the hall.

Using his foot, Scott nudged open the bedroom door. He killed the lights, and soft shadows settled around us. I glanced at the small twin mattress on the bottom bunk, then at the window. The window was cracked. In a panic-induced moment, I actually imagined myself slipping through the crack and disappearing into the night. Probably a sign that what I was about to do was a huge mistake. Was I really going through with this just to make a point? Was this how I wanted to show Patch the magnitude of my anger and hurt? What did it say about me?

Scott took me by the shoulders and kissed me harder. I mentally flipped through my options. I could tell Scott I was feeling sick. I could tell him I'd changed my mind. I could simply tell him no. . . .

Scott shucked off his shirt and tossed it aside.

"Uh—," I began. I looked around once more for an escape, noting that the bedroom door must have opened, because a shadow blotted out the light spilling in from the hall. The shadow stepped inside and closed the door, and I felt my jaw go slack.

Patch tossed Scott's shirt at him, catching him in the face.

"What the—," Scott demanded, yanking the shirt over his head and rolling it down to cover himself.

"Fly's down," Patch told him.

Scott yanked on his zipper. "What are you doing? You can't come in here. I'm busy. And this is my room!"

"Are you insane?" I told Patch, blood rising in my cheeks.

Patch sliced his eyes toward me. "You don't want to be here. Not with him."

"You don't get to make that call!"

Scott brushed past me. "Let me take care of him."

He made it another two feet before Patch shoved his fist into Scott's jaw with a sickening crunch.

"What are you doing?" I yelled at Patch. "Did you break his jaw?"

"Unnuh!" Scott moaned, clutching the lower half of his face.

"I didn't break his jaw, but if he lays a hand on you, it will be the first of many things to break," Patch said.

"Out!" I ordered Patch, thrusting a finger at the door.

"I'm going to kill you," Scott growled at Patch, opening and closing his jaw, making sure it still worked.

But instead of taking the cue to leave, Patch crossed to Scott in three steps. He flung him around to face the wall. Scott tried to get his bearings, but Patch slammed him against the wall again, disorienting him further. "Touch her," he said in Scott's ear, his voice low and threatening, "and it'll be the biggest regret of your life."

Before leaving, Patch flicked his eyes once in my direction. "He's not worth it." He paused. "And neither am I."

I opened my mouth but didn't have an argument. I wasn't here because I wanted to be. I was here to shove it in Patch's face. I knew it, and he knew it.

Scott rolled around, slouching against the wall. "I could've taken him if I wasn't wasted," he said, massaging the lower half of his face. "Who the hell does he think he is? I don't even know him. You know him?"

Scott obviously didn't recognize Patch from the Z, but there had been a lot of people there that night. I couldn't expect Scott to remember every face. "I'm sorry about that," I said, gesturing at the door Patch had just exited through. "Are you okay?"

He smiled slowly. "Never been better." That said with a welt-like bruise blooming across his jaw.

"He was out of control."

"Best way to be," he drawled, using the back of his hand to wipe a ribbon of blood from the crack of his mouth.

"I should go," I said. "I'll bring the Mustang back after school tomorrow." I wondered how I was supposed to walk out of here, past Patch, and maintain any level of self-dignity. I might as well stroll up to him and admit he was right: I'd only followed Scott back here to hurt him.

Scott crooked his finger under my shirt, holding me in place. "Don't go, Nora. Not yet."

I unhooked his finger. "Scott—"

"Tell me if I'm going too far," he said, tugging his shirt up over his head for the second time. His pale skin glowed in the dark. He'd clearly been spending a lot of time in the weight room, and it showed in the lines of muscle branching down his arms.

"You're going too far," I said.

"That didn't sound convincing." He swept my hair off my neck and nuzzled his face in the curve.

"I'm not interested in you this way," I said, putting my hands between us. I was tired, and a headache was buzzing between my ears. I was ashamed of myself and wanted to go home and sleep and sleep until I forgot this night.

"How do you know? You've never tried me this way."

I flipped on the light switch, flooding the room with light. Scott threw a hand over his eyes and staggered back a step.

"I'm leaving—," I began, then broke off as my eyes fixed on a patch of skin high on Scott's chest, halfway between his nipple and collarbone. The skin was warped and shiny. Somewhere deep in my brain, I made the connection that this must be the branding mark Scott had been given when he swore allegiance to the Nephilim blood society, but it felt like a hazy afterthought, dull in comparison to what had really arrested my attention. The brand was in the shape of a clenched fist. It was identical, down to the exact shape and size, to the raised stamp on the iron ring from the envelope.

With a hand still flung over his eyes, Scott groaned and reached for the bedpost to steady himself.

"What's that mark on your skin?" I asked, my mouth gone dry.

Scott looked momentarily startled, then slid his hand down to cover the mark. "Some friends and I were horsing around one night. It's nothing serious. It's only a scar."

He had the audacity to lie about it? "You gave me the envelope." When he didn't answer, I added more fiercely, "The boardwalk. The bakery. The envelope with the iron ring." The room felt eerily isolated, detached from the throbbing bass out in the living room. In an instant, I no longer felt safe trapped back here with Scott.

Scott's eyes narrowed and he squinted at me through the light, which still seemed to hurt his eyes. "What are you talking about?" His tone was wary, hostile, muddled.

"You think this act is funny? I know you gave me the ring."

"The—ring?"

"The ring that made that mark on your chest!"

He shook his head once, hard, as if to shake off his stupor. Then his arm lashed out, shoving me up against the wall. "How do you know about the ring?"

"You're hurting me," I said with venom, but I was shivering with fear. I realized that Scott wasn't pretending. Unless he was a much better actor than I imagined, he genuinely didn't know about the envelope. But he did know about the ring.

"What did he look like?" He fisted my camisole and shook me. "The guy who gave you the ring—what did he look like?"

"Get your hands off me," I ordered, pushing back. But Scott weighed a lot more than me, and his feet stayed planted, his body trapping me against the wall. "I didn't see him. He had it delivered."

"Does he know where I am? Does he know I'm in Coldwater?"

"He?" I snapped back. "Who is *he*? What's going on?"

"Why did he give you the ring?"

"I don't know! I don't know anything about him! Why don't *you* tell *me*?"

He shuddered hard against the raging panic that seemed to grip him. "*What do you know?*"

I kept my eyes nailed to Scott's, but my throat was clenched so hard it hurt to breathe. "The ring was in the envelope with a note that said the Black Hand killed my dad. And that the ring belonged to him." I licked my lips. "Are you the Black Hand?"

Scott's expression still held deep distrust; his eyes darted back and forth, judging whether or not he believed me. "Forget we had this conversation, if you know what's good for you."

I tried to yank my arm free, but he was still holding on.

"Get out," he said. "And stay away from me." This time he let go, giving me a shove in the direction of the door.

I stopped at the door. I wiped my sweaty palms on my trousers. "Not until you tell me about the Black Hand."

I thought Scott might throw an even more violent rage, but he merely nailed me with a look he might give a dog if he caught it squatting on his lawn. He scooped up his T-shirt and made like he was going to stretch it back over his frame, then his mouth curled into a threatening smile. He threw the shirt on the bed. He loosened his belt, yanked down his zipper, and stepped out of his shorts, leaving him standing in nothing but fitted cotton boxers. He was going for the shock factor, clearly trying to intimidate me into leaving. He'd done a pretty good job of convincing me, but I wasn't going to let him get rid of me that easily.

I said, "You have the Black Hand's ring branded on your skin. Don't expect me to believe you know nothing about it, including how it got there."

He didn't answer.

"The minute I walk out of here, I'm calling the police. If you won't talk to me, maybe you'd like to talk to them. Maybe they've seen the branding before. I can tell just by looking at it that it isn't good." My voice was calm, but my underarms were damp. What a stupid and risky thing to say. What if Scott didn't allow me to leave? I obviously knew enough about the Black Hand to upset him. Did he think I knew too much? What if he killed me, then threw my body in a Dumpster? My mom didn't know where I was, and everyone who'd seen me enter Scott's apartment was wasted. Would anyone remember having seen me tomorrow?

I was so busy panicking, I hadn't noticed Scott had taken a seat on his bed. His face was bent into his hands. His back was quivering, and I realized he was crying silently, great, convulsive sobs. At first I thought he was faking, that this was some kind of trap, but the choked sounds low in his chest were real. He was drunk, emotionally unhinged, and I didn't know how stable that made him. I held still, afraid one slight movement might cause him to snap.

"I racked up a lot of gambling debt in Portland," he said, his voice scratchy with desperation and exhaustion. "The manager at the pool hall was breathing down my neck, demanding the money, and I had to watch my back anytime I left the house. I was living in fear, knowing one day he'd find me, and I'd be lucky to get off with broken kneecaps.

"One night on my way home from work, I was jumped from behind, dragged into a warehouse, and tied to a folding table. It was too dark to see the guy, but I figured the manager had sent him. I told him I'd pay him whatever he wanted if he'd let me go, but he laughed and said he wasn't after my money—in fact, he'd already settled my debts. Before I could figure out if it was his idea of a joke, he said he was the Black Hand, and the last thing he needed was more money.

"He had a Zippo, and he held the flame against the ring on his left hand, heating it. I was sweating bullets. I told him I'd do whatever he wanted—just get me off the table. He ripped open my shirt and ground the ring into my chest. My skin was on fire, and I was yelling at the top of my lungs. He snapped my finger, broke the bone, and told me if I didn't shut up, he'd move down the line until he broke all ten. He told me he'd given me his mark." Scott's voice had dropped to a rasp. "I wet my pants. Right there on the table. He scared the hell out of me. I'll do whatever it takes to never see him again. That's why we moved back to Coldwater. I'd stopped going to school and was hiding out at the gym all day, bulking up in case he came looking for me. If he found me, this time I was going to be ready." Cutting off there, he wiped his nose with the back of his hand.

I didn't know if I could trust him. Patch had made it clear he didn't, but Scott was shaking. His complexion was pasty, misted with sweat, and he plowed his hands through his hair, letting go of a long, wavering breath. Could he make up a story like that? All the details meshed with everything I already knew about Scott. He had a gambling addiction. He'd worked nights in Portland at a convenience store. He'd moved back to Coldwater to escape his past. He had the branding mark on his chest, proof someone had put it there. Could he sit two feet away and lie to me about what he'd gone through?

"What did he look like?" I asked. "The Black Hand."

He shook his head. "It was dark. He was tall, that's all I remember."

I groped for some way to connect Scott and my dad—both of whom were linked to the Black Hand. Scott had been tracked down by the Black Hand after running up debt. In exchange for paying off Scott's debt, the Black Hand had branded him. Had my dad gone through the same thing? Had his murder not been as random as the police originally guessed? Had the Black Hand paid off a debt my dad owed, then killed him when my dad refused to be branded? No. I wasn't buying it. My dad didn't gamble, and he didn't rack up debt. He was an accountant. He knew the value of money. Nothing about his situation tied him to Scott. There had to be something else.

"Did the Black Hand say anything else?" I asked.

"I try not to remember anything about that night." He reached under his mattress and pulled out a plastic ashtray and a pack of cigarettes. He lit up, exhaling smoke slowly, and closed his eyes.

My mind kept rebounding to the same three questions. Had the Black Hand really killed my dad? Who was he? Where could I find him?

And then a new question. Was the Black Hand the leader of the Nephilim blood society? If he was the one branding Nephilim, it made sense. Only a leader, or someone with a lot of authority, would be in charge of actively recruiting members to fight back against fallen angels.

"Did he say why he gave you his mark?" I asked. Clearly the branding was to mark members of the blood society, but maybe there was more. Something only its Nephilim members knew.

Scott shook his head, taking another drag.

"He didn't give you any reason?"

"No," Scott snapped.

"Has he come looking for you since that night?"

"No." I could tell by the wild look in his eyes that he was scared he wouldn't always be able to say as much.

I thought back to the Z. To the red-shirted Nephil. Did he have the same brand as Scott? I was almost certain he did. It only made sense that all members had the same mark. Which meant there were others like Scott and the Nephil at the Z. Members everywhere, recruited by force, but disjointed from any real strength or purpose because they were kept in the dark. What was the Black Hand waiting for? Why was he holding off uniting his members? To keep fallen angels from finding out what he was up to?

Was this why my dad was murdered? Because of something that had to do with the blood society?

"Have you ever seen the Black Hand's brand on anyone else?" I knew I was in danger of pushing too hard, but I needed to determine just how much Scott knew.

Scott didn't answer. He was crumpled on the bed, passed out. His mouth was agape, and his breath smelled strongly of alcohol and smoke.

I shook him gently. "Scott? What can you tell me about the society?" I slapped his cheeks gently. "Scott, wake up. Did the Black Hand tell you that you're Nephilim? Did he tell you what it means?"

But he had crashed into a deep, inebriated sleep.

I ground out his cigarette, pulled a sheet up to his shoulders, and let myself out.

CHAPTER

15

I WAS DEEP IN A DREAM WHEN THE PHONE SHRILLED. I stuck an arm out sideways, swept my hand over the nightstand, and located my cell phone. "Hello?" I said, wiping drool from the rim of my mouth.

"Have you checked the Weather Channel yet?" Vee asked.

"What?" I mumbled. I tried to blink my eyes open, but they were still rolled back in the dream. "What time is it?"

"Blue skies, sizzling temps, zero wind. We are so going to Old

Orchard Beach after class. I'm packing boogie boards in the Neon right now." She belted out the first stanza to "Summer Nights" from *Grease*. I cringed and pulled the phone away from my ear.

I rubbed sleep out of my eyes and watched the numbers on the clock seesaw into focus. That couldn't possibly be a six at the front . . . could it?

"Should I wear a hot pink bandeau, or a metallic gold bikini? The thing about the bikini is, I probably need a tan before I wear it. Gold will make my skin look even more washed out. Maybe I'll wear pink this time, get a base tan, and—"

"Why does my clock say six twenty-five?" I demanded, trying to wade through the haze of sleep long enough to push some volume into my voice.

"Is this a trick question?"

"Vee!"

"Yeesh. Angry much?"

I slammed the phone down and snuggled deeper under the covers. The home phone started ringing downstairs in the kitchen. I folded my pillow over my head. The answering machine picked up, but Vee wasn't that easy to get rid of. She redialed. Again and again.

I speed-dialed her cell. "What?"

"Gold or pink? I wouldn't ask if it wasn't important. It's just . . . Rixon's going to be there, and this is the first time he'll see me in a swimsuit."

"Back up. The plan is for all three of us to go together? I'm not going all the way out to Old Orchard Beach to be the third wheel!"

"And I'm not going to let you sit home all afternoon with your sour face on."

"I don't have a sour face."

"Yes, you do. And you're wearing it right now."

"This is my annoyed face. You woke me up at six in the morning!"

The sky was summer blue from horizon to horizon. The Neon's windows were rolled down, a hot wind ripped through Vee's and my hair, and the heady smell of salt water filled the air. Vee exited off the highway and drove down Old Orchard Street, eyes peeled for parking. The lanes on both sides of the street were backed up with slow-moving cars that rolled along well under the speed limit, hoping for a spot to open up on the street before they slipped past and lost their chance.

"This place is packed," Vee complained. "Where am I supposed to park?" She steered down an alley and slowed to a stop behind a bookstore. "This looks good. Lots of parking back here."

"The sign says employee parking only."

"How are they going to know we aren't employees? The Neon blends right in. All these cars speak low class."

"The sign says violators will be towed."

"They just say that to scare people like you and me away. It's an empty threat. Nothing to worry about."

She wedged the Neon into a space and cranked the parking brake. We grabbed an umbrella and a tote filled with bottled water, snacks, sunscreen, and towels out of the trunk, then hiked down Old Orchard Street until it dead-ended at the beach. The sand was dotted with colorful umbrellas, the frothy waves rolling under the twiggy legs of the pier. I recognized a group of soon-to-be senior guys from school playing Ultimate Frisbee just ahead.

"Normally I'd say we should go check out those guys," Vee said, "but Rixon is so hot, I'm not even tempted."

"When is Rixon supposed to get here, anyway?"

"Hey now. That didn't sound very cheerful. In fact, it sounded just a little bit cynical."

Shielding my eyes, I squinted at the coastline, looking for an ideal place to pitch the umbrella. "I already told you: I hate being the third wheel." The last thing I needed or wanted was to sit under a hot sun all afternoon, watching Vee and Rixon make out.

"For your information, Rixon had a few errands to run, but he promised to be here by three."

"What kind of errands?"

"Who knows? Probably Patch roped him into doing a favor. Patch always has something he needs Rixon to run off and take care of. You'd think Patch could just do it himself. Or at least pay Rixon, so he's not taking advantage of him. Do you think I should wear sunscreen? I'm going to be really mad if I go to all this trouble and don't get a tan."

"Rixon doesn't seem like the kind of guy who lets people take advantage of him."

"People? No. Patch? Yes. It's like Rixon worships him. It's so lame. It makes my stomach heave. Patch is not the kind of guy I want my boyfriend aspiring to be."

"They have a long history together."

"So I've heard. Blah, blah, blah. Probably Patch is a drug dealer. No. Probably he's an arms dealer and has Rixon out playing the sacrificial mule, gunrunning for free and risking his neck."

Behind my knockoff Ray-Bans, I rolled my eyes. "Does Rixon have a problem with their relationship?"

"No," she said, all huffy.

"Then leave it at that."

But Vee wasn't about to let it go. "If Patch isn't dealing in arms, how's he get all his cash?"

"You know where he gets his money."

"Tell me," she said, folding her arms stubbornly across her chest. "Tell me out loud where he gets his money."

"The same place Rixon gets his."

"Uh-huh. Just as I thought. You're ashamed to say it."

I gave her a pointed look. "Please. That's the dumbest thing ever."

"Oh yeah?" Vee marched up to a woman not far away who was building a sand castle with two small children. "Excuse me, ma'am? Sorry to interrupt your quality beach time with the little ones, but my friend here would like to tell you what her ex does for a living."

I clamped my hand around Vee's arm and dragged her away.

"See?" Vee said. "You're ashamed. You can't say it out loud and not feel your insides start to rot."

"Poker. Pool. There. I said it and I didn't shrivel up and die. Satisfied? I don't know what the big deal is. Rixon earns his living the very same way."

Vee shook her head. "You're so in the dark, girl. You don't buy the kind of clothes Patch wears by winning bets at Bo's Arcade."

"What are you talking about? Patch wears jeans and T-shirts."

She put a hand on her hip. "You know how much jeans like that run?"

"No," I said, confused.

"Let's just say you can't buy jeans like that in Coldwater. He probably ships them up from New York. Four hundred dollars a pair."

"You lie."

"Cross my heart, hope to die. Last week, he was wearing a Rolling Stones concert T-shirt with Mick Jagger's autograph. Rixon said it's the real thing. Patch isn't paying off his MasterCard in poker chips. Back before you and Patch were Splitsville, did you ever ask where he really gets his money? Or how he got that nice shiny Jeep?"

"Patch won his Jeep off a poker game," I argued. "If he won a Jeep, I'm sure he could win enough to buy a pair of four-hundred-dollar jeans. Maybe he's just really good at poker."

"Patch told you he won the Jeep. Rixon has a different story."

I flipped my hair off my shoulders, trying to pretend like I couldn't care less about the direction our conversation was headed, because I wasn't buying it. "Oh yeah? What's that?"

"I don't know. Rixon won't say. All he said was, 'Patch would like you to think he won the Jeep. But he got his hands dirty getting that car.'"

"Maybe you heard wrong."

"Yeah, maybe," Vee repeated cynically. "Or maybe Patch is a damn lunatic running an illegal business."

I handed her a tube of sunscreen, maybe just a little too hard. "Put this on my back, and don't miss any areas."

"I think I'm going straight to oil," Vee said, slapping sunscreen across my back. "A little burn is better than spending a whole day at the beach and leaving it as white as when you came."

I craned my neck over my shoulder but couldn't tell how thorough Vee's job was. "Make sure you get under my straps."

"Think they'd arrest me if I take off my top? I really hate tan lines."

I spread my towel under the umbrella and curled up beneath its shade, rechecking to make sure my feet weren't hanging out in the sun. Vee shook her towel out a few feet away and lathered her legs with baby oil. In the back of my mind, I conjured up images of skin cancer I'd seen at the doctor's office.

"Speaking of Patch," Vee said, "what's the latest? Is he still hooked up with Marcie?"

"Last I heard," I said stiffly, thinking the only reason she'd raised the question was to goad me further.

"Well, you know my opinion."

I did, but I was going to hear it again, whether I wanted to or not.

"The two of them deserve each other," Vee said, spraying Sun-In through her hair, misting the air with chemical lemon. "Of course, I don't think it will last. Patch will get bored and move on. Just like he did with—"

"Can we talk about something other than Patch?" I cut in, pinching my eyes closed and massaging the muscles at the back of my neck.

"You sure you don't want to talk? Looks like you've got a lot on your mind."

I rolled out a sigh. No use hiding it. Obnoxious or not, Vee was my best friend and deserved the truth, when I could give it. "He kissed me the other night. After the Devil's Handbag."

"He *what?*"

I pressed the heels of my hands into my eyes. "In my bedroom." I didn't think I could explain to Vee that he'd kissed me inside my dream. The point was, he had. Location was irrelevant. That, and I didn't want to even think about what it meant that he now seemed capable of inserting himself into my dreams.

"You let him *inside?*"

"Not exactly, but he came in anyway."

"Okay," Vee said, looking like she was struggling to come up with a decent response to my idiocy. "Here's what we'll do. We're going to swear a blood oath. Don't give me that look, I'm serious. If we swear a blood oath, you'll have to keep it or something really bad will happen—like rats might gnaw off your feet while you're sleeping. And when you wake up, all that will be left are bloody stumps. Do you have a pocketknife? We'll find a pocketknife, and then we'll both cut our palms and press them together. You'll swear never to be alone with Patch again. That way, if temptation strikes, you'll have something to fall back on."

I wondered if I should tell her that being alone with Patch wasn't always my choice. He moved like vapor. If he wanted alone time with me, he was going to get it. And though I hated to admit it, I didn't always mind.

"I need something a little more effective than a blood oath," I said.

"Babe, get a clue. This is serious stuff. I hope you're a believer, because I am. I'll go hunt down a knife," she said, starting to rise to her feet.

I pulled her back down. "I have Marcie's diary."

"Wh-what?!" Vee sputtered.

"I took it, but I haven't read it."

"Why am I just now hearing about this? And what is taking you so long to crack that baby open? Forget Rixon—let's drive home right now and read it! You know Marcie's talked about Patch in it."

"I know."

"Then why the delay? Are you scared about what it might reveal? Because I could read it first, filter out the bad stuff, and just give you answers, straight up."

"If I read it, I might never speak to Patch again."

"That's a good thing!"

I looked sideways at Vee. "I don't know if it's what I want."

"Oh, babe. Don't do this to yourself. It's killing me. Read the stupid diary and allow yourself closure. There are other guys out there. Just so you know. There will never be a shortage of guys."

"I know," I said, but it felt like a cheap lie. There had never been a guy before Patch. How could I tell myself there'd be one after? "I'm not going to read the diary. I'm going to give it back. Marcie and I have had this ridiculous feud for years, and it's getting old. I just want to move on."

Vee's jaw dropped, and she sputtered a little more. "Can't moving on wait until after you've read the diary? Or at least given me a quick peek? Five minutes, that's all I ask."

"I'm taking the higher road."

Vee rolled out her own sigh. "You're not going to budge, are you?"

"No."

A shadow fell over our towels.

"Mind if I join you lovely ladies?"

We looked up to find Rixon standing over us in swim trunks and a tank, with a towel thrown over his shoulder. He had a gangly build that appeared surprisingly tough and resilient, a hawk nose, and a shag of inky hair that fell across his forehead. A pair of black angel wings was tattooed on his left shoulder, and combined with a heavy five o'clock shadow, he looked like he was employed by the mob. Charming, playful, and up to no good.

"You made it!" Vee said, her smile lighting up her whole face.

Rixon collapsed on the sand in front of us, elbow down, cheek propped on his fist. "What'd I miss?"

"Vee wants me to swear a blood oath," I said.

He cocked an eyebrow. "Sounds serious."

"She thinks it will keep Patch out of my life."

Rixon tilted his head back and laughed. "Good luck with that."

"Hey now," Vee said. "Blood oaths are serious stuff."

Rixon laid his hand intimately on her thigh and grinned affectionately at her, and I felt my chest ache with envy. Weeks ago, Patch would have touched me the same way. The irony was, weeks ago, Vee had probably felt the same way I did now whenever she was forced to hang out with Patch and me. Knowing this should have made swallowing my jealousy a little bit easier, but the pain cut deep. Responding to Rixon, Vee bent forward, placing a kiss on his mouth. I averted my eyes, but it didn't dilute the envy that seemed to hang like a rock in my throat.

Rixon cleared his voice. "Why don't I go buy us some Cokes?" he asked, having the sensitivity to notice that he and Vee were making me uncomfortable.

"Allow me," Vee said, standing and dusting sand off her bottom.

"I think Nora wants to talk to you, Rixon." She made air quotes around the word "talk." "I'd stay, but I'm not a big fan of the subject matter."

"Uh—," I began uncomfortably, not sure what Vee was hinting at, but acutely aware that I wasn't going to like it.

Rixon smiled at me expectantly.

"Patch," Vee said, clarifying things, only to make the air seem ten times heavier than it already was. With that out of the way, she marched off.

Rixon rubbed his chin. "You want to talk about Patch?"

"Not really. But you know Vee. Always there to make an uncomfortable situation ten times worse," I muttered under my breath.

Rixon laughed. "Good thing I'm not easily humiliated."

"I wish I could say the same thing right now."

"How are things?" he asked, trying to break the ice.

"With Patch, or in general?"

"Both."

"They've been better." Realizing there was a good chance Rixon would pass anything I said along to Patch, I quickly added, "I'm on the upswing. But can I ask a personal question? It's about Patch, but if you don't feel comfortable answering, I'm seriously okay with it."

"Shoot."

"Is he still my guardian angel? A while back, after a fight, I told him I didn't want him to be. But I'm not sure where we stand. Is he no longer my guardian simply because I said that's what I wanted?"

"He's still assigned to you."

"How come he's never around anymore?"

Rixon's eyes glinted. "You broke up with him, remember? It's awkward for him. Most guys don't relish the idea of hanging around an ex any longer than they have to. That, and I know he said the archangels are breathing down his neck. He's bending over backward to keep things strictly professional."

"So he's still protecting me?"

"Sure. Just from behind the scenes."

"Who was in charge of matching him to me?"

Rixon shrugged. "The archangels."

"Is there any way to let them know I'd like to be reassigned? It's not working out very well. Not since the breakup, anyway." Not working out? It was *tearing me up* inside. All this touch and go, seeing him, but not being able to have him, was devastating.

He ran his thumb along his lip. "I can tell you what I know, but there's a good chance the information's dated. It's been a while since I was in the loop. Ironically—you ready for this?—you have to swear a blood oath."

"Is this a joke?"

"You cut your palm and shake a few drops of blood into the dust of the earth. Not carpet or concrete—dirt. Then you swear the oath, acknowledging to heaven that you're not afraid to shed your own blood. From dust you came, and to dust you go. In saying the oath, you give up your right to a guardian angel and announce that you accept your fate—without heaven's help. Keep in mind, I'm not advocating it. They gave you a guardian, and for good reason. Someone upstairs thinks you're in danger. I'm going with my gut on this one, but I think it's more than a paranoid hunch."

Not exactly a news flash—I could feel something dark pressing against my world, threatening to eclipse it. The phantom behind my father's reappearing ghost, most notably. I was struck by a thought. "What if the person who's after me is also my guardian angel?" I asked slowly.

Rixon gave a yap of laughter. "Patch?" He didn't sound like it was even a possibility. No surprise there. Rixon had been through everything with Patch. Even if Patch was guilty, Rixon would stand by his side. Blind loyalty above all else.

"If he was trying to hurt me, would someone know?" I asked. "The archangels? The angels of death? Dabria knew when people were close to death. Could another angel of death stop Patch before it's too late?"

"If you're doubting Patch, you've got the wrong guy." His tone had cooled. "I know him better than you. He takes his job as guardian seriously."

But if Patch wanted to kill me, he'd crafted the perfect murder, hadn't he? He was my guardian angel. He was charged with keeping me safe. No one would suspect him. . . .

But he'd already had his chance to kill me. And he hadn't taken it. He'd sacrificed the one thing he wanted most of all—a human body—to save my life. He wouldn't do that if he wanted me dead.

Would he?

I shook off my suspicions. Rixon was right. Suspecting Patch was ridiculous at this point.

"Is he happy with Marcie?" I clamped my mouth shut. I hadn't meant to ask the question in the first place. It had spilled out in the moment. A blush brushed my cheeks.

Rixon watched me, clearly giving his answer some thought. "Patch is the closest thing I've got to family, and I love the guy like a brother, but he's not right for you. I know it, he knows it, and deep down, I think you know it too. Maybe you don't want to hear this, but he and Marcie are alike. They're cut from the same cloth. Patch should be allowed to have a little fun. And he can—Marcie doesn't love him. Nothing she feels for him is going to tip off the archangels."

We sat in silence, and I struggled to stuff my emotions deep down. I'd tipped off the archangels, in other words. My feelings for Patch were what exposed us. It was nothing Patch had done or said. It was all me. According to Rixon's explanation, Patch had never loved me. He'd never reciprocated. I didn't want to accept it. I wanted Patch to have cared about me as much as I cared about him. I didn't want to think I'd been nothing more than entertainment, a way to pass the time.

There was one more question I desperately wanted to ask

Rixon. If Patch and I were still on good terms, I would have asked him, but that was a moot point now. Rixon was just as worldly as Patch, however. He knew things other people didn't—particularly when it came to fallen angels and Nephilim—and what he didn't know, he could find out. Right now, my best hope at finding the Black Hand was through Rixon.

I moistened my lips and decided to get the question over with. "Have you ever heard of the Black Hand?"

Rixon flinched. He studied me in silence a moment before his face blazed with amusement. "Is this a joke? I haven't heard that name in a long time. I thought Patch didn't like to be called it. Did he tell you about it, then?"

A slow freeze gripped my heart. I'd been on the brink of telling Rixon about the envelope with the iron ring and note claiming the Black Hand killed my father, but found myself grasping for a new response. "The Black Hand is Patch's nickname?"

"He hasn't gone by it in years. Not since I started calling him Patch. He never liked the Black Hand." He scratched his cheek. "Those were back in the days when we took jobs as mercenaries for the French king. Eighteenth-century black ops. Enjoyable stint. Good money."

I might as well have been slapped across the face. The whole moment felt unbalanced, tipped on its side. Rixon's words ran over me in a blur, as if he was speaking in a foreign language, and I couldn't keep up. I was immediately bombarded with doubts.

Not Patch. He hadn't killed my dad. Anyone else, but not him.

Slowly the doubts began to fall by the wayside, replaced by other thoughts. I found myself picking through facts, analyzing for evidence. The night I gave Patch my ring: The moment I'd said my dad had given it to me, he insisted he couldn't take it, almost adamantly so. And the mere name the Black Hand. It was fitting, almost too fitting. Forcing myself to hang on a few more moments, holding my emotions carefully in check, I selected my next words carefully.

"You know what I regret most?" I said, my tone as casual as I could make it. "It's the stupidest thing, and you'll probably laugh." To make my story convincing, I pulled a trivial laugh up from someplace deep inside me that I didn't even know existed. "I left my favorite sweatshirt at his house. It's from Oxford—my dream uni," I explained. "My dad picked it up for me when he went to England, so it means a lot."

"You were at Patch's place?" He sounded genuinely surprised.

"Just once. My mom was home, so we drove over to his place to watch a movie. I left my sweatshirt on the sofa." I knew I was walking a dangerous line—the more details I revealed about Patch's house, the higher the chance something wouldn't match up, and my cover would be blown. But along the same lines, if I was too vague, I was scared it would tip Rixon off that I was lying.

"I'm impressed. He likes to keep his home address off the radar."

And why was that? I wondered. What was he hiding? Why was

Rixon the only person allowed into Patch's inner sanctum? What could he share with Rixon, but no one else? Had he never allowed me inside because he knew something I'd see there would unravel the truth—that he was responsible for murdering my dad?

"Getting the sweatshirt back would mean a lot to me," I said. I felt somehow removed, as if I was watching myself converse with Rixon from several feet away. Someone stronger, more clever and contained was saying the words rolling from my mouth. I was not that person. I was the girl who felt herself crumbling into pieces as fine as the sand beneath her feet.

"Head over first thing in the morning. Patch leaves early, but if you're there by six thirty, you should catch him."

"I don't want to have to do it face-to-face."

"Want me to pick up the sweatshirt next time I'm over? I'm sure I'll be over there tomorrow night. This weekend at the latest."

"I'd like to get it sooner rather than later. My mom keeps asking about it. Patch gave me a key, and as long as he hasn't changed the locks, I could still get in. Trouble is, it was dark when we drove over, and I don't remember how to get to his place. I didn't pay attention, because I wasn't planning on having to drive back and get my sweatshirt, post-breakup."

"Swathmore. Near the industrial district."

My mind netted this information.

If his place was near the industrial district, I was betting he lived in one of the brick apartment buildings on the edge of Old

Town Coldwater. There wasn't much else to choose from, unless he'd taken up residence in one of the abandoned factories or vagabond shacks by the river, which seemed doubtful.

I smiled, hoping I appeared relaxed. "I knew it was over by the river somewhere. Top floor, right?" I said, taking a stab in the dark. It seemed to me Patch wouldn't want to hear his neighbors stomping around above him.

"Yeah," Rixon said. "Number thirty-four."

"Do you think Patch will be home tonight? I don't want to bump into him. Especially if he's there with Marcie. I just want to get the sweatshirt and get out."

Rixon coughed into his fist. "Uh, no, you should be good." He scratched his cheek and cast me a nervous, almost pitying, look. "Vee and I are actually meeting up with Patch and Marcie for a movie tonight."

I felt my spine stiffen. The air in my lungs seem to shatter ... and then, just when I felt all semblance of my carefully controlled emotions fleeing, I was speaking clearly again. I had to. "Does Vee know?"

"I'm still trying to figure out how to break the news."

"Break the news about what?"

Rixon and I both swung around as Vee plopped down with a cardboard crate of Cokes.

"Uh—a surprise," Rixon said. "I've got something planned for tonight."

Vee grinned. "A clue, a clue! Pleeeease?"

Rixon and I shared a quick glance, but I looked away. I didn't want any part of this. Besides, I'd already tuned out. My thoughts were robotically sifting through this new information: Tonight. Patch and Marcie. A date. Patch's apartment would be empty.

I had to get in.

CHAPTER

16

THREE HOURS LATER, THE FRONTS OF VEE'S THIGHS
were toasted red, the tops of her feet were blistered, and
her face was swollen with heat. Rixon had taken off an
hour ago, and Vee and I were lugging the umbrella and beach tote
up the alley branching off Old Orchard Street.

"I feel funny," Vee said. "Like I'm going to pass out. Maybe I
should have gone easy on the baby oil."

I was lightheaded and uncomfortably warm too, but it didn't

have anything to do with the weather. A headache sliced down the center of my skull. I kept trying to swallow the bad taste in my mouth, but the more I swallowed, the queasier my stomach grew. The name "the Black Hand" skipped around my mind like it was taunting me to give it my full attention, stabbing its nails into my headache every time I tried to ignore it. I couldn't think about it now, in front of Vee, having enough foresight to know I'd shatter the moment I did. I had to juggle the pain a little longer, tossing it up in the air every time it threatened to crash down. I clung to the safety of numb devastation, pushing the inevitable off as long as I could. Patch. The Black Hand. It couldn't be.

Vee came to a halt. "What is that?"

We were standing in the parking lot at the rear of the bookstore, a few feet from the Neon, and we were staring at the large piece of metal attached to the left rear tire.

"I think it's a wheel clamp," I said.

"I can see that. What's it doing on my car?"

"I guess when they say violators will be towed, they mean it."

"Don't get smart with me. What are we going to do now?"

"Call Rixon?" I suggested.

"He's not going to be very happy about having to drive all the way back out here. What about your mom? Is she back in town?"

"Not yet. How about your parents?"

Vee sat on the curb and buried her face in her hands. "It probably costs a fortune to get a clamp removed. This will be the last straw. My mom's going to ship me off to a monastery."

I took a seat beside her, and together we pondered our options.

"Don't we have any other friends?" Vee asked. "Someone we could call for a ride without feeling too guilty? I wouldn't feel guilty about making Marcie drive all the way out here, but I'm pretty sure she wouldn't do it. Not for us. Especially not for us. You're friends with Scott. Think he'd come get us? Hold on a minute . . . isn't that Patch's Jeep?"

I followed Vee's gaze down the opposite end of the alley. It fed into Imperial Street, and sure enough, parked on the far side of Imperial was a shiny black Jeep Commander. The windows were tinted, a glare of sun reflecting off them.

My heart accelerated. I couldn't run into Patch. Not here. Not yet. Not when the only thing keeping me from breaking down sobbing was a carefully constructed dam whose foundation cracked deeper with every passing second.

"He must be here somewhere," Vee said. "Text him and tell him we're stranded. I might not like him, but I'll use him if it gets me a ride home."

"I'd text Marcie before I'd text Patch." I hoped Vee didn't detect the strange, dull note of distress and loathing in my voice. The Black Hand . . . the Black Hand . . . not Patch . . . please, not Patch . . . a mistake, an explanation . . . The headache seared, as if my own body was warning me to stop this line of thinking for my own safety.

"Who else can we call?" Vee said.

We both knew who we could call. Absolutely no one. We were lame, friendless people. No one owed us a favor. The only person who would drop everything to come to my rescue was sitting beside me. And vice versa.

I directed my attention back to the Jeep. For no reason whatsoever, I stood. "I'm driving the Jeep home." I wasn't sure what kind of statement I intended to send to Patch. An eye for an eye? You hurt me, I'll hurt you? Or maybe, *This is only the start, if you had anything to do with my dad's death* . . .

"Is Patch going to be mad when he figures out you stole his Jeep?" Vee said.

"I don't care. I'm not going to sit here all evening."

"I have a bad feeling about this," Vee said. "I don't like Patch on a normal day, never mind when he's got his temper on."

"What happened to your sense of adventure?" A fierce desire had taken control of me, and I wanted nothing more than to take the Jeep and send Patch a message. I envisioned bumping the Jeep into a tree. Not hard enough to deploy the air bags, just hard enough to leave a dent. A little memento from me. A warning.

"My sense of adventure stops short of a kamikaze suicide mission," said Vee. "It's not going to be pretty when he figures out it was you."

The logical voice in my head might have instructed me to back away for a moment, but all logic had left me. If he'd hurt my family, if he'd destroyed my family, if he'd lied to me—

"Do you even know how to boost a car?" Vee asked.

"Patch taught me."

She didn't look convinced. "You mean you *saw* Patch steal a car, and now you think you'll give it a try?"

I strode down the alley toward Imperial Street, with Vee jogging close behind. I checked for traffic, then crossed to the Jeep. I tried the door latch. Locked.

"Nobody's home," Vee said, cupping her hands around her eyes to peer inside. "I think we should walk away. Come on, Nora. Back away from the Jeep."

"We need a ride. We're stranded."

"We still have two legs, leftie and rightie. Mine are in the mood for exercise. They feel like a nice long walk—Are *you crazy?*" she shrieked.

I was standing with the tip of the beach umbrella aimed at the driver's-side window. "What?" I said. "We have to get in."

"Put the umbrella down! You're going to draw a lot of negative attention if you smash out the window. What's gotten into you?" she said, watching me, wild-eyed.

A vision flashed across my mind. I saw Patch standing over my dad, gun in hand. The sound of a shot ripped the silence.

I braced my hands on my knees and leaned over, feeling tears sting behind my eyes. The ground lurched into a nauseating spin. Sweat curved trails down the sides of my face. I was being smothered, as if all oxygen had suddenly evaporated from the air. The more I tried to draw air, the more paralyzed my lungs became. Vee was shouting at me, but it came from far away, an underwater sound.

All of a sudden the ground halted. I took three sharp breaths. Vee was ordering me to sit, yelling something about heat exhaustion. I pulled free from her grip.

"I'm okay," I said, holding up a hand when she came for me again. "I'm okay."

To show her I was fine, I bent to pick up my tote, which I must have dropped, and it was then that I saw the spare key to the Jeep gleaming gold in the bottom. The one I'd stolen from Marcie's bedroom the night of her party.

"I have a key to the Jeep," I said, the words surprising even me.

A frown mark stretched across Vee's forehead. "Patch never asked for it back?"

"He never gave it to me. I found it in Marcie's room Tuesday night."

"Whoa."

I shoved the key in the lock, climbed in, and sat in the driver's seat. Then I adjusted the seat forward, cranked the ignition, and gripped the steering wheel with both hands. Despite the heat, my hands were cold and jittery.

"You're not thinking about doing more damage than just driving this thing home, are you?" Vee asked, buckling herself into shotgun. "Because the vein in your temple is throbbing, and the last time I saw it do that was right before you clipped Marcie in the jaw at the Devil's Handbag."

I licked my lips, which felt sandpapery and rubbery at the same time. "He gave Marcie a spare to the Jeep—I should park this thing in the ocean, twenty feet under."

"Maybe he had a really good reason," Vee said nervously.

I gave a high slight laugh. "I won't do anything to it until after I drop you off." I cranked the wheel to the left and peeled onto the street.

"You swear to add that disclaimer when you try explaining to Patch why you stole his Jeep?"

"I'm not stealing it. We're stranded. This is called borrowing."

"This is called you're crazy." I could feel Vee's bewilderment at my anger. I could see irrational in the way she stared at me. Maybe I was irrational. Maybe I'd pushed things over the edge. Two people can have the same nickname, I thought, trying to convince myself. They could. They could, they could, they could. I hoped the more I said it, the more I'd come to believe it, but the place that I reserved in my heart for trust felt hollow.

"Let's get out of here," Vee said, using a wary, frightened voice she never used with me. "We have lemonade at my place. After that we could watch TV. Maybe take a nap. Don't you have to work tonight?"

I was about to tell her that Roberta hadn't scheduled me tonight, when I tapped the brake. "What's that?"

Vee followed my gaze. She bent forward, pulling a scrap of pink fabric off the dash. She dangled the French bikini top between us.

We looked at each other, and we were both thinking the same thing.

Marcie.

No doubt about it, she was here with Patch. Right now. On the beach. Lying on the sand. Doing who knows what else.

A violent, traitorous surge of hate spiked through me. I hated him. And I hated myself for adding my name to the list of girls he'd seduced, then betrayed. A raw desire to rectify my ignorance gripped me. I wasn't going to be just another girl. He couldn't make me disappear. If he was the Black Hand, I would find out. And if he'd had anything to do with my dad's death, I would make him pay.

"He can find his own ride home," I said through a quivering jaw. I punched the gas, laying down a stretch of rubber on the street.

Hours later, I stood in front of the fridge, door open, surveying the contents, looking for something that could pass as dinner. When nothing popped out at me, I moved to the narrow pantry kitty-corner to the fridge and did the same thing. I settled on a box of bow-tie pasta and a jar of sausage spaghetti sauce.

When the stove timer beeped, I drained the pasta, poured myself a bowl, and stuck the sauce in the microwave. We were out of Parmesan, so I grated cheddar and called it good. The micro-wave chimed, and I spooned layers of sauce and cheese on top of the pasta. As I turned to carry everything to the table, I found Patch leaning against it. The bowl of pasta nearly slipped through my fingers.

"How did you get in?" I asked.

"Might want to keep the door locked. Especially when you're home alone."

His stance was relaxed, but his eyes were not. The color of black marble, they cut right through me. I had no doubt he knew I'd stolen the Jeep. Hard not to, since it was parked in the driveway. There were only so many places to hide a Jeep at a house surrounded by open fields on one side, and impenetrable woodlands on the other. I hadn't been thinking about hiding when I'd pulled the Jeep into the driveway; I'd been consumed by sickening abhorrence and shock. Everything had come into sharp focus: his smooth words, his black, glinting eyes, his broad experience with lies, seduction, women. I'd fallen in love with the devil.

"You took the Jeep," Patch said. Calm but not happy.

"Vee parked in an illegal zone and they put a clamp on her car. We had to get home, and that's when we saw the Jeep across the street." My palms touched with sweat, but I didn't dare wipe them dry. Not in front of Patch. He looked different tonight. More severe, hardened. The wan glow of the kitchen lights traced the cut of his cheekbones, and his black hair, tousled from a day at the beach, hung low across his forehead, nearly touching his obscenely long eyelashes. His mouth, which I'd always thought of as sensual, was turned up cynically on one side. It wasn't a warm smile.

"You couldn't call and give me a heads-up?" he asked.

"I didn't have my phone."

"And Vee?"

"She doesn't have your number on her phone. And I couldn't remember your new number anyway. We didn't have a way to reach you."

"You don't have a key to the Jeep. How'd you get in?"

It was all I could do not to give him a traitorous look. "Your spare."

I saw him trying to calculate where I was going with this. We both knew he'd never given me a spare. I watched him closely for any sign that he knew I was referring to Marcie's key, but the light of understanding never lit his eyes. Everything about him was controlled, impenetrable, unreadable.

"Which spare?" he asked.

This only made me angrier, because I'd expected him to know exactly which key I was talking about. How many spares did he have? How many other girls had a key to the Jeep stowed in their bags? "Your girlfriend," I said. "Or is that not enough of a clarification?"

"Let me see if I've got this. You stole the Jeep to get back at me for giving a spare to Marcie?"

"I stole the Jeep because Vee and I needed it," I said coolly. "There was a time when you were always there when I needed you.

I thought maybe that was still true, but apparently I was wrong."

Patch's eyes didn't waver from mine. "Want to tell me what this is really about?" When I didn't answer, he dragged out one of the kitchen chairs tucked under the table. He sat, arms crossed, legs stretched out languidly. "I've got time."

The Black Hand. That's what this was really about. But I was scared to confront him. Because of what I might learn, and how he might react. I felt sure that he had absolutely no idea how much I knew. If I accused him of being the Black Hand, there was no turning back. I would have to face the truth that held the power to break me down to my very soul.

Patch raised his eyebrows. "Silent treatment?"

"This is about telling the truth," I said. "Something you've never done." If he'd killed my dad, how could he have looked me in the eye all those times, telling me how sorry he was, and never told me the truth? How could he kiss me, caress me, hold me in his arms, and live with himself?

"Something I've never done? From the day we met, I never lied to you. You didn't always like what I had to say, but I was always up-front."

"You let me believe you loved me. A lie!"

"I'm sorry it felt like a lie." He wasn't sorry. There was a look of stony fury in his gaze. He hated that I was calling him out. He wanted me to be like all the other girls and disappear into his past without so much as a peep.

"If you felt anything for me, you wouldn't have moved on to Marcie in record time."

"And you didn't move on to Scott in record time? You'd rather have half a man than me?"

"Half a man? Scott is a person."

"He's Nephilim." He made a careless gesture in the direction of the front door. "The Jeep has more value."

"Maybe he feels the same way about angels."

He shrugged, lazy and arrogant. "I doubt it. If it weren't for us, his race wouldn't exist."

"Frankenstein's monster didn't love him."

"And?"

"The Nephilim race is already seeking revenge on angels. Maybe this is only the beginning."

Patch raised his ball cap and dragged a hand through his hair. From the look on his face, I got the impression that the situation was far more dangerous than I'd originally been led to believe. How close was the Nephilim race to overpowering fallen angels? Surely not by this Cheshvan. Patch couldn't mean that in less than five months, swarms of fallen angels would invade, and eventually kill, tens of thousands of humans. But everything in the way he held himself, down to the very look in his eye, told me that was exactly what was in store.

"What are you doing about it?" I asked, horrified.

He picked up the glass of water I'd poured for myself and left

699

on the table, and took a drink. "I've been told to stay out of it."

"By the archangels?"

"The Nephilim race is evil. They were never supposed to inhabit Earth. They exist because of the pride of fallen angels. The archangels want nothing to do with them. They're not going to step in where Nephilim are concerned."

"And all the humans who will die?"

"The archangels have their own plan. Sometimes bad things have to happen before good things can."

"Plan? What plan? To watch innocent people die?"

"The Nephilim are walking straight into a trap of their own making. If people have to die to annihilate the Nephilim race, the archangels will risk it."

The hairs on my scalp prickled. "And you agree with them?"

"I'm a guardian angel now. My allegiance is to the archangels." A blaze of killing hate rose in his eyes, and for one brief moment, I believed it was directed at me. As if he blamed me for what he'd become. In my defense, I felt a wash of anger. Had he forgotten everything from that night? I'd sacrificed my life for him, and he rejected it. If he wanted to blame someone for his circumstances, it wasn't me!

"How strong are the Nephilim?" I asked.

"Strong enough." His voice was disturbingly devoid of concern.

"They could hold off the fallen angels as early as this Cheshvan, couldn't they?"

He gave a nod.

I hugged myself to ward off a deep, sudden chill, but it was more psychological than physical. "You have to do something."

He shut his eyes.

"If fallen angels can't possess Nephilim, they'll move on to humans," I said, trying to break through his hands-off attitude and reach his conscience. "That's what you said. Tens of thousands of humans. Maybe Vee. My mom. Maybe me."

He still said nothing.

"Don't you even care?"

His eyes flicked to his watch, and he pushed up from the table. "I hate to rush out of here when we've got unfinished business, but I'm late." The spare key to the Jeep was lying in a dish on the sideboard, and he pocketed it. "Thanks for the key. I'll add borrowing the Jeep to your tab."

I parked myself between him and the door. "My tab?"

"I got you home from the Z, got you off Marcie's roof, and now I let you use my Jeep. I don't give out favors for free."

I was pretty sure he wasn't joking. In fact, I was pretty sure he was dead serious.

"We can work it so you pay me after each individual favor, but I figured a tab would be easier." His smile was a taunting curve. First-class-jerk smug.

I narrowed my eyes. "You're actually enjoying this, aren't you?"

"One of these days I'm going to come to collect on the favors, and then I'll really be enjoying it."

"You didn't loan me the Jeep," I argued. "I stole it. And it wasn't a favor—I commandeered it."

He gave his watch a second glance. "We're going to have to finish this later. I've got to run."

"That's right," I snapped. "A movie with Marcie. Go have fun while my world hangs in the balance." I told myself I wanted him to go. He deserved Marcie. I didn't care. I was tempted to hurl something after him; I thought about slamming the door at his back. But I wasn't going to let him go without asking the question that burned my every thought. I dug my teeth into the inside of my cheek to keep my voice from unraveling. "Do you know who killed my dad?" My voice was cold and controlled, and not my own. It was the voice of someone who was filled to the very tips of her fingers with hate, devastation, accusation.

Patch stopped with his back to me.

"What happened that night?" I didn't bother trying to hide the desperation in my voice.

After a moment of silence, he said, "You're asking me like you think I might know."

"I know you're the Black Hand." I shut my eyes briefly, feeling my whole body sway under a wave of nausea.

He looked over his shoulder. "Who told you that?"

"Then it's true?" I realized my hands were balled into fists at my sides, shaking violently. "You're the Black Hand." I watched his face, praying he'd somehow refute it.

The grandfather clock in the hall chimed the hour, a heavy, reverberating sound.

"Get out," I said. I wouldn't cry in front of him. I refused to. I wouldn't give him that satisfaction.

He stood in place, his face cold with shadow, mildly satanic.

The clock counted through the silence. One, two, three.

"I'll make you pay for it," I said, my voice still oddly foreign.

Four, five.

"I'll find a way. You deserve to go to hell. The only thing that could make me sorry is if the archangels beat me to it."

A flash of hot black crossed his eyes.

"You deserve everything that's coming to you," I told him. "Every time you kissed me and held me, knowing what you did to my dad—" I choked and turned away, falling apart when I could least afford it.

Six.

"Go away," I said, my voice quiet, but not steady.

I looked up, glaring, intending to make Patch leave with the intensity of hate and loathing in my eyes, but I was alone in the hall. I glanced around, expecting him to have stepped out of my view, but he wasn't there. A strange silence settled in between the shadows, and I realized the grandfather clock had stopped beating.

Its hands were frozen on the six and twelve, having stopped the moment Patch left for good.

CHAPTER

17

AFTER PATCH LEFT, I TRADED OUT MY BEACH cover-up for dark jeans and a tee, and zipped myself into a black Razorbills windbreaker I'd won at last year's eZine Christmas party. Even though the thought made my stomach swim uneasily, I had to look through Patch's apartment, and I had to do it tonight—before it was too late.

It had been stupid to tell Patch I knew he was the Black Hand. It had come out in a moment of hostile recklessness. I'd lost my advantage of surprise. I doubted he saw me as a real threat—he probably found my promise to send him to hell darkly amusing—but I had information he'd clearly worked very hard to keep concealed. Based on everything I knew about the all-knowing, ever-watchful archangels, it hadn't been easy keeping his involvement in my dad's murder from them. I couldn't send him to hell, but the archangels could. If I found a way to contact them, his carefully crafted secret would be blown open. The archangels were hunting for an excuse to banish him to hell. Well, I had a reason.

My eyes watered, and I blinked the tears hastily away. There was a time in my life when I never would have believed Patch capable of killing my dad. The idea would have been laughable, preposterous—offensive. But it only showed how cleverly and thoroughly he'd deceived me.

Everything told me the apartment on Swathmore was where he kept his secrets. It was his one vulnerability. Aside from Rixon, no one was allowed inside. Earlier today, when I'd mentioned to Rixon that I'd been there, he'd answered with genuine surprise. He likes to keep his home address off the radar, he'd said. Had Patch managed to keep it off the archangels' radar? It seemed highly unlikely, bordering on impossible, but Patch had proven that he was very good at finding a way around any obstacle placed in his path. If anyone was resourceful or clever enough to undermine the archangels, it was Patch. I shuddered unexpectedly as I wondered what he was keeping in his apartment. An ominous feeling that tickled my spine seemed to warn me not to go, but I owed it to my dad to bring his killer to justice.

I located a flashlight under my bed and zipped it inside the front pouch of the Windbreaker. As I was getting to my feet, Marcie's diary caught my eye. It was resting across a row of books on my bookshelf. I debated a moment, feeling a hole burn in my conscience. With a sigh, I tucked the diary alongside the flashlight, locked up behind me, and set out on foot.

I walked the mile stretch to Beech, then caught a bus to Herring Street. I walked three blocks to Keate, hopped on another bus to Clementine, then walked on foot up the winding, scenic hill leading into Marcie's neighborhood, which was about as close to posh as Coldwater came. The smell of fresh-cut grass and hydrangeas hung in the evening air, and traffic was nonexistent. Cars were kept neatly tucked away in the garages, making the streets seem wider, cleaner. The windows of the white colonial houses reflected the blaze of the slow-setting sun, and I imagined families sitting down together for a late dinner behind the shutters. I bit my lip, startled by a sudden rush of inconsolable regret. My family would never sit down together for a meal again. Three nights a week I ate dinner alone, or at Vee's. The other four nights, when my mom was home, we typically ate on trays in front of the TV.

Because of Patch.

I turned onto Brenchley, counting down houses to Marcie's. Her red Toyota 4-Runner was parked in the drive, but I knew she wasn't home. Patch would have picked her up for the movie in the Jeep. I was cutting across the lawn, thinking I would leave the diary on the porch, when the front door opened.

Marcie had her handbag slung over her shoulder, keys in hand, clearly on her way out. She froze in the doorway when she saw me. "What are you doing here?" she asked.

I opened my mouth, three full seconds ticking by before words came out. "I—I didn't think you'd be home."

She narrowed her eyes. "Well, I am."

"I thought you . . . and Patch . . ." I was barely speaking coherently. The diary was in my arms, in plain sight. Any minute Marcie would see it.

"He canceled," she snapped at me, like it was none of my business.

I hardly heard her. Any moment now she was going to see the diary. Like never before, I wanted to backpedal through time. I should have thought this through before coming. I should have counted on the chance that she'd be home. I glanced nervously behind me, staring at the street as if it could somehow come to my rescue.

Marcie gasped, a rush of air between her teeth. "What are you doing with my diary?"

I spun around, cheeks flaming.

She marched down the porch. She snatched the diary away and reflexively pinned it against her chest. "You—you took it?"

My hands fell uselessly to my sides. "I took it the night of your party." I shook my head. "It was a stupid thing to do. I'm so sorry—"

"Did you read it?" she demanded.

"No."

"You liar," she sneered. "You read it, didn't you? Who wouldn't? I hate you! Is your life so boring that you have to go snooping through mine? Did you read the whole thing, or just the parts about you?"

I was on the verge of adamantly denying even opening it, when Marcie's words caused my thoughts to catch and rewind. "Me? What did you write about me?"

She flung the diary onto the porch behind her, then straightened up, squaring her shoulders. "What do I care?" she said, crossing her arms and glaring at me. "Now you know the truth. How does it feel knowing your mom is screwing other people's husbands?"

I gave a disbelieving laugh that held more than its share of anger. "Excuse me?"

"You really think your mom is out of town all those nights? Ha!"

I adopted Marcie's posture. "Actually, I do." What was she insinuating?

"Then how do you explain why her car is parked down the street one night a week?"

"You have the wrong person," I said, feeling my rage boil up.

708

I was pretty sure I now knew exactly what Marcie was getting at. How dare she accuse my mom of having an affair. And with her dad, of all people. If he was the last man on the planet, my mom wouldn't be caught dead with him. I hated Marcie, and my mom knew it. She wasn't sleeping with Marcie's father. She would never do that to me. She would never do that to my dad. Never.

"Beige Taurus, license plate X4124?" Marcie's voice was arctic.

"So you know her license plate number," I said after a moment, trying to ignore the tightening sensation in my chest. "That doesn't prove anything."

"Wake up, Nora. Our parents knew each other in high school. Your mom and my dad. They were together."

I shook my head. "That's a lie. My mom has never said anything about your dad."

"Because she doesn't want you to know." Her eyes flashed. "Because she's still with him. He's her dirty little secret."

I shook my head harder, feeling like a broken doll. "Maybe my mom knew your dad in high school, but that was a long time ago, before she met my dad. You have the wrong person. You saw someone else's car parked down the street. When she's not home, she's out of town, working."

"I saw them together, Nora. It was your mom, so don't even try to make excuses for her. I went to school that day and spray-painted your locker with a message to your mom. Don't you get it?" Her voice was a revolted hiss. "They were sleeping together. All these years they've been doing it. Which means my dad could be your dad. And you could be my—sister."

Marcie's words dropped like a blade between us.

I hugged my arms around my middle and turned away, feeling like I might be sick. Tears choked up my throat, burning the back of my nose. Without a word, I walked stiffly down Marcie's walk. I thought she might shout something worse at my back, but there was nothing worse she could say.

I didn't go to Patch's.

I must have walked all the way back to Clementine, past the bus stop, the park, and the city swimming pool, because the next thing I remembered, I was sitting on a bench on the lawn in front of the public library. A cone of streetlight fell over me. It was a warm night, but I hugged my knees against my chest, my body wracked with tremors. My thoughts were a jumble of haunting theories.

I stared into the darkness settling around me. Headlights swung down the street, grew closer, moved on. Sporadic sitcom laughter carried out an open window across the street. Pockets of cool air flushed goose bumps across my arms. The heady smell of grass, musky and humid from the earlier sun, suffocated me.

I lay back on the bench, shutting my eyes against the dusting of stars. I laced my quivering hands on my stomach, my fingers feeling like frozen twigs. I wondered why life had to suck so hard sometimes, wondered why it was the people I loved the most who could disappoint me the hardest, wondered who I wanted to direct my hate at more—Marcie, her dad, or my mom.

Deep inside, I clung to the hope that Marcie was wrong. I hoped I'd get to fling this back in her face. But the sinking sensation that seemed to tug me inside out told me I was only setting myself up for disappointment.

I couldn't pinpoint the memory, but it was within the last year or so. Maybe shortly before my dad died . . . no. After. It had been a warm day—spring. The funeral was over, my grace period of grieving had ended, and I was back in school. Vee had talked me into ditching class, and in those days, I didn't offer much resistance to anything. I floated along. I got by. On the thought that my mom would be at work, we'd walked to my house. It must have taken us all of seventh hour to get there.

As the farmhouse came into view, Vee yanked me off the road.

"There's a car in your driveway," she said.

"Whose could it be? Looks like a Land Cruiser."

"Your mom doesn't drive one of those."

"Do you think it's a detective?" It wasn't likely that a detective would be driving a sixty- thousand-dollar SUV, but I was so used to detectives stopping by, it was the first thought that came to mind.

"Let's get closer."

We were almost to the driveway when the front door opened and voices carried out. My mom's . . . and a deeper voice. A man's.

Vee lugged me to the side of the house, out of sight.

We watched as Hank Millar climbed into the Land Cruiser and drove away.

"Holy freakshow," Vee said. "Normally I'd suspect foul play, but your mom is as straightlaced as they come. I bet he was trying to sell her a car."

"He came all this way for that?"

"Heck yeah, babe. Car salesmen don't know where to draw the line."

"She already has a car."

"A Ford. That's like Toyota's worst enemy. Marcie's dad won't be happy until the whole town is driving a Toyota. . . ."

I strayed out of the memory. But what if he hadn't been selling her a car? What if they'd—I swallowed involuntarily—been having an affair?

Where was I supposed to go now? Home? The farmhouse no longer felt like home. It no longer felt safe and secure. It felt like a box of lies. My parents had sold me a story about love, togetherness, and family. But if Marcie was telling the truth—and my greatest fear was that she was—my family was a joke. A big lie I'd never even seen coming. Shouldn't there have been warning signs? Shouldn't I have been hit with the realization that I'd secretly suspected this all along, but had chosen denial over the painful truth? This was my punishment for trusting others. This was my punishment for looking for the good in people. As much as I hated

Patch right now, I envied the cold detachment that separated him from everyone else. He suspected the worst in people; no matter how low they sank, he always saw it coming. He was hardened and worldly, but people respected him for it.

They respected him, and they lied to me.

I swung upright on the bench and punched my mom's number into my cell. I didn't know what I'd say when she answered; I'd let my anger and betrayal guide me. While her phone rang, hot tears tumbled down my cheeks. I slapped them away. My chin trembled, and every muscle in my body was drawn taut. Angry, spiteful words sprang to mind. I envisioned shouting them at her, cutting her off every time she tried to defend herself with more lies. And if she cried . . . I wouldn't feel sorry. She deserved to feel every last ounce of pain from the choices she'd made. Her voice mail picked up, and it was all I could do to keep from flinging the phone into the darkness.

I dialed Vee next.

"Yo, babe. Is this important? I'm with Rixon—"

"I'm leaving home," I said, not caring that my voice sounded thick from crying. "Can I stay at your house for a while? Until I figure out where I'm going."

Vee's breathing filled my ear. "Say what?"

"My mom gets home on Saturday. I want to be gone by then. Can I stay with you the rest of the week?"

"Um, can I ask—"

"No."

"Okay, sure," Vee said, trying to hide her shock. "You can stay, no problem. No problem at all. You'll tell me what's up when you're ready."

I felt fresh tears well up inside me. Right now, Vee was the only person I could count on. She could be obnoxious, annoying, and lazy, but she never lied to me.

I got to the farmhouse around nine, and slipped into a pair of cotton pj's. It wasn't a cold night, but the air was humid, and the moisture seemed to slip beneath my skin, chilling me to the bone. After making myself a cup of steamed milk, I sank into bed. It was too early for sleep, but I couldn't have slept if I'd tried; my thoughts were still dashing themselves to pieces. I stared at the ceiling, trying to erase the last sixteen years and start fresh. Hard as I might, I couldn't envision Hank Millar as my father.

I swung out of bed and marched down the hall to my mom's bedroom. I flung open her hope chest, searching for her high school yearbook. I didn't even know if she owned one, but if she did, the hope chest was the only place I could think to look. If she and Hank Millar went to school together, there would be pictures. If they'd been in love, he would have signed her yearbook in some special way that would signify it. Five minutes later, I'd thoroughly searched the chest and come up empty-handed.

I padded to the kitchen, looked through the cupboards for

something to eat, but found my appetite gone. I couldn't eat, thinking about the big lie my family had turned out to be. I found my
eyes traveling to the front door, but where would I go? I felt lost in
the house, restless to leave, but with nowhere to run. After standing
in the hallway for several minutes, I climbed back to my bedroom.
Lying in bed with the covers pulled up to my chin, I shut my eyes and
watched a reel of pictures slide across my mind. Pictures of Marcie;
of Hank Millar, whom I barely knew, and whose face I could conjure
up only with difficulty; of my parents. Faster and faster the images
came, until they blended together in a strange collage of madness.

The images seemed to lurch into reverse suddenly, traveling
backward through time. All color drained from the reel, until there
was nothing but fuzzy black and white. It was then that I knew I'd
slipped into the other realm.

I was dreaming.

I was standing in the front yard. A rowdy wind swept dead leaves
across the driveway, around my ankles. An odd funnel cloud swirled
in the sky overhead but made no move to touch down, as if it was
content to bide its time before striking. Patch was sitting on the
porch rail, head bowed, hands clasped loosely between his knees.

"Get out of my dream," I hollered at him over the wind.

He shook his head. "Not until I tell you what's going on."

I pulled my pajama top tighter. "I don't want to hear what you
have to say."

"The archangels can't hear us here."

I gave an accusatory laugh. "It wasn't enough manipulating me in real life—now you have to do it here, too?"

He lifted his head. "Manipulating? I'm trying to tell you what's going on."

"You're forcing your way inside my dreams," I challenged. "You did it after the Devil's Handbag, and you're doing it now."

A sudden gust of wind blew between us, causing me to take a step back. The tree branches creaked and moaned. I untangled my hair from my face.

Patch said, "After the Z, in the Jeep, you told me you'd had a dream about Marcie's dad. The night you had the dream, I was thinking about him. I was remembering the exact memory you dreamed about, wishing there was some way I could tell you the truth. I didn't know I was communicating with you."

"You made me have that dream?"

"Not a dream. A memory."

I tried to digest this. If the dream was real, Hank Millar had been living in England hundreds of years ago. My memory spun back to the dream. *Tell the barkeep to send help*, Hank had said. *Tell him there is no man. Tell him it is one of the devil's angels, come to possess my body and cast away my soul.*

Was Hank Millar—Nephilim?

"I don't know how I overlapped your dreams," Patch said, "but I've been trying to communicate with you the same way ever since.

I got through the night I kissed you after the Devil's Handbag, but now I keep hitting walls. I'm lucky I'm here now. I think it's you. You're not letting me in."

"Because I don't want you inside my head!"

He slid off the railing, coming down to meet me in the yard. "I need you to let me in."

I turned away.

"I was reassigned to Marcie," he said.

Five seconds passed before everything fell into place. The sick, hot feeling that had churned in my stomach since leaving Marcie's spread to my extremities. "You're Marcie's guardian angel?"

"It hasn't been a pleasure cruise."

"Did the archangels do this?"

"When they assigned me as your guardian, they made it clear I was supposed to have your best interests in mind. Getting involved with you wasn't in your best interest. I knew it, but I didn't like the idea of the archangels telling me what to do with my personal life. They were watching us the night you gave me your ring."

In the Jeep. The night before we broke up. I remembered.

"As soon as I realized they were watching us, I took off. But the damage was done. They told me I'd be out as soon as they found a replacement. Then they assigned me to Marcie. I went to her house that night to force myself to face what I'd done."

"Why Marcie?" I asked bitterly. "To punish me?"

He dragged a hand down over his mouth. "Marcie's dad is a

first-generation Nephilim, a purebred. Now that Marcie is sixteen, she's in danger of being sacrificed. Two months ago, when I tried to sacrifice you to get a human body, but ended up saving your life, there weren't many fallen angels who believed they could change what they were. I'm a guardian now. They all know it, and they all know it's because I saved you from dying. Suddenly a lot more of them believe they can cheat fate too. Either by saving a human and getting their wings back"—he exhaled—"or by killing their Nephil vassal and transforming their body from fallen angel to human."

I reviewed in my mind everything I knew about fallen angels and Nephilim. The Book of Enoch told of a fallen angel who became human after killing his Nephil vassal—by sacrificing one of the vassal's female descendants. Two months ago, Patch had attempted this very thing by intending to use me to kill Chauncey. Now, if the fallen angel who'd forced Hank Millar to swear fealty wanted to become human, well, he'd have to . . .

Sacrifice Marcie.

I said, "You mean it's your job to make sure the fallen angel who forced Hank Millar to swear fealty doesn't sacrifice Marcie to get a human body."

As if he thought he knew me well enough to guess my next question, he said, "Marcie doesn't know. She's completely in the dark."

I didn't want to talk about this. I didn't want Patch here. He'd killed my dad. He'd ripped away, forever, someone I loved. Patch was a monster. Nothing he could say could make me feel otherwise.

"Chauncey formed the Nephilim blood society," Patch said.

My attention snapped back. "What? How do you know?"

He looked reluctant to answer. "I've accessed a few memories. Other people's memories."

"Other people's memories?" I was shocked when I shouldn't have been. How could he justify all the horrible things he'd done? How could he come here and tell me he'd secretly examined people's most private and intimate thoughts, and expect me to admire him for it? Or even expect me to listen to him?

"A successor picked up where Chauncey left off. I haven't been able to get a name yet, but rumor has it he isn't happy about Chauncey's death, which doesn't make sense. He's in charge now—that alone should have wiped away any remorse he felt over Chauncey's death. Which makes me wonder if the successor was a close friend of Chauncey's, or a relative."

I shook my head. "I don't want to hear this."

"The successor has a contract out on Chauncey's killer." Any further protesting on my part died forming. Patch and I shared a look. "He wants the killer to pay."

"You mean he wants me to pay," I said, my voice barely pushing through.

"Nobody knows you killed Chauncey. He didn't know you were his female descendant until moments before he died, so there's little chance anyone else knew. Chauncey's successor might try to track down Chauncey's descendants, but I wish him luck. It took me a long time to find you." He took a step toward me, but I backed up. "When you wake up, I need you to say you want me as your guardian angel again. Say it like you mean it, so the archangels hear it, and hopefully grant your request. I'm doing everything I can to keep you safe, but I'm restricted. I need heightened access to the people around you, your emotions, everything in your world."

What was he saying? That the archangels had finally found my replacement guardian angel? Was this why he'd forced his way inside my dream tonight? Because he'd been cut off, and no longer had the access to me that he wanted?

I felt his hands slide to my hips, holding me protectively against him. "I'm not going to let anything happen to you."

I stiffened and shrugged free. My mind was in a tempest. *He wants the killer to pay.* I couldn't shake off the thought. The idea that someone out there wanted to kill me was numbing. I didn't want to be here. I didn't want to know these things. I wanted to feel safe again.

Realizing that Patch had no intention of leaving my dream, I made my own move. I fought against the invisible barriers of the dream by forcing myself awake. *Open your eyes,* I told myself. *Open them!*

Patch gripped my elbow. "What are you doing?"

I could feel myself becoming more lucid. I could feel the warmth of my sheets, my pillowcase soft against my cheek. All the familiar smells associated with my room comforted me.

"Don't wake up, Angel." He smoothed his hands against my hair, trapping my face, forcing me to look him in the eye. "There's more you need to know. There's a very important reason why you need to see these memories. I'm trying to tell you something that I can't tell you any other way. I need you to figure out what I'm trying to tell you. I need you to stop blocking me."

I jerked my face away. My feet seemed to rise up from the grass, drifting toward the stirring funnel cloud. Patch grabbed for me, swearing under his breath, but his hold on me was featherlight, imaginary.

Wake up, I ordered myself. Wake up.

I let the cloud consume me.

CHAPTER

18

I WOKE UP WITH A SHARP INTAKE OF AIR. MY ROOM was settled in shadow, the moon glowing like a crystal ball on the far side of the window. My sheets were hot and damp, tangled around my legs. The clock read nine thirty.

I flung myself out of bed and went to the bathroom, filling a cold glass of water. I gulped it down, then leaned against the wall. I couldn't fall back asleep. Whatever I did, I couldn't let Patch back in my dreams. I paced the upstairs hall, frantically trying to keep myself wide awake, but I was so worked up, I doubted I could have slept if I'd wanted to.

Several minutes later the throb of my pulse had died down, but my mind wasn't as easy to settle. The Black Hand. Those three words haunted me. They were elusive, menacing, taunting. I couldn't bring myself to look them straight on. Not without feeling my already flimsy world start to shatter. I knew I was avoiding finding a way to let the archangels know Patch was the Black Hand, and my father's killer, to protect myself from the shameful truth: I'd fallen in love with a killer. I'd let him kiss me, lie to me, betray me. When he touched me in my dreams, all my strength crumbled, and I felt myself being tangled up in his net all over again. He still held my heart in his hand, and that was the biggest betrayal of all. What kind of person was I, when I couldn't bring my own father's killer to justice?

Patch had said I could tell the archangels I wanted him as my guardian angel again through the simple act of saying it out loud. It seemed logical, then, that I could shout out, "Patch killed my dad!" and be done with it. Justice would be served. Patch would be sent to hell, and I could slowly start to rebuild my life. But I couldn't pull the words up, as if they were chained down someplace deep inside me.

Too many things weren't adding up. Why was Patch, an angel, mixed up with a Nephilim blood society? If he was the Black Hand, why was he branding Nephilim recruits? Why was he recruiting them in the first place? It wasn't just odd—it was illogical. The Nephilim race hated angels, and vice versa. And if the Black Hand was Chauncey's successor and the new leader of the society . . . how could that person possibly be Patch?

I squeezed the bridge of my nose, feeling like my head might crack from chasing the same questions over and over. Why was it that everything surrounding the Black Hand seemed to be an endless maze of trapdoor, after trapdoor, after trapdoor?

Right now Scott was my only reliable link left to the Black Hand. He knew more than he was letting on, I was sure of it, but he was too scared to talk. The tone of his voice when he'd spoken of the Black Hand carried sheer panic. I needed him to tell me what he knew, but he was running from his past, and nothing I said was going to make him turn back and face it. I pressed my forehead into the palms of my hands, trying to think clearly.

I called Vee.

"Good news," she said before I could get a word in edgewise. "I talked my dad into driving back to the beach with me and paying the fine to get the clamp off my car. I'm back in business."

"Good, because I need your help."

"Help is my middle name."

I was pretty sure she'd already told me bad was her middle name, but I kept my opinion to myself. "I need someone to help me look through Scott's bedroom." Chances were, Scott wasn't going to keep any evidence detailing his involvement with the Nephilim blood society out in the open, but what alternative did I have? He had done a terrific job of not giving me direct answers in the past, and after our last encounter, I knew he was wary of me. If I wanted to find out what he knew, I was going to have to do a little legwork.

"Apparently Patch canceled our double date, so my schedule is wide open," Vee said, a little too eagerly. I'd expected her to ask what we were snooping for in Scott's bedroom.

"Going through Scott's bedroom isn't going to be dangerous or exciting," I told her, just to make sure we were both on the same page. "All you're going to do is sit in the Neon outside his apartment and call me if you see him coming home. I'm the one who's going inside."

"Just because I'm not doing the spying doesn't mean it's not exciting. It'll be like watching a movie. Only, in the movies the good guy almost never gets caught. But this is real life, and there's a strong chance you'll get caught. See what I mean? The excitement factor is through the roof."

Personally, I thought Vee was a little overanxious to see me caught.

"You *are* going to warn me if Scott comes home, right?" I asked.

"Heck yeah, babe. I've got you covered."

My next call was to Scott's home line. Mrs. Parnell picked up.

"Nora, so good to hear your voice! Scott tells me things have been heating up between the two of you," she added in a conspirator's voice.

"Well, uh—"

"I always thought it would be real nice if Scott married a local girl. I don't much like the idea of him marrying into a family of strangers. What if his in-laws are nutcases? Your mom and I are such close friends, can you imagine the fun we'd have planning a wedding together? But I'm getting ahead of myself! All in good time, as they say."

Oh boy.

"Is Scott there, Mrs. Parnell? I have some news I think he'll be interested in."

I heard her cup a hand over the mouthpiece and shout, "Scott! Pick up the phone! It's Nora!"

A moment later Scott came on. "You can hang up now, Mom." His voice held a drop of wariness.

"Just making sure you got it, hon."

"I've got it."

"Nora has some interesting news," she said.

"Then hang up so she can tell me."

There was a sigh of disappointment, and a click.

"I thought I told you to stay away from me," Scott said.

"Have you found a band yet?" I asked, pushing forward, hoping to take control of the conversation and pique his interest before he hung up on me.

"No," he said with that same guarded skepticism.

"I mentioned to a friend that you play the guitar—"

"I play bass."

"—and he spread the word and found a band that wants to audition you. Tonight."

"What's the name of the band?"

I hadn't anticipated that question. "Uh—the Pigmen."

"Sounds like something out of 1960."

"Do you want the audition or not?"

"What time?"

"Ten. At the Devil's Handbag." If I'd known of a warehouse farther away, I would have mentioned it. As it was, I would have to make do with the twenty minutes it would take him to drive round trip.

"I'll need a contact name and number."

He definitely was not supposed to ask that.

I said, "I told my friend I'd pass the information along to you, but I didn't think to ask for names and numbers of the band members."

"I'm not going to blow my night on an audition without first getting an idea of who these guys are, what style they play, and where they've gigged. Are they punk, indie-pop, metal?"

"What are you?"

"Punk."

"I'll get their numbers and call you right back."

I disconnected from Scott and immediately dialed Vee. "I told Scott I got him an audition with a band tonight, but he wants to know what kind of music the band plays and where they've played. If I give him your number, would you pretend to be the girlfriend of someone from the band? Just say you always answer your boyfriend's phone when he's practicing. Don't elaborate further. Stick to the facts: They're a punk band, they're the next big thing, and he'd be stupid not to audition."

"I'm really starting to like all this spy work," Vee said. "When my normal life gets boring, all I have to do is sidle up next to you."

I was sitting on the front porch with my knees tucked against my chest when Vee cruised up.

"I think we should stop at Skippy's for hot dogs before we do this," she said when I swung in. "I don't know what it is about hot dogs, but they're like an instant shot of courage. I feel like I can do anything after I've had a hot dog."

"That's because you're high on all the toxins they pump inside those things."

"Like I said, I think we should stop by Skippy's."

"I already had pasta for dinner."

"Pasta isn't very filling."

"Pasta is *very* filling."

"Yeah, but not in the way mustard and relish are," Vee argued.

Fifteen minutes later, we were leaving the drive-through at Skippy's with two grilled hot dogs, one large carton of fries, and two strawberry milk shakes.

"I hate this kind of food," I said, feeling grease seep through the wax-paper-wrapped hot dog onto my hand. "It's unhealthy."

"So's a relationship with Patch, but that didn't stop you."

I didn't respond.

A quarter mile from Scott's complex, Vee steered to the side of the road. The biggest problem I foresaw was our location. Deacon Road dead-ended just past the complex. Vee and I were out in the open, and as soon as Scott drove past and saw Vee sitting in the Neon, he'd know something was up. I hadn't been worried that he'd recognize her voice on the phone, but I was worried he'd remember her face. He'd seen us together on more than one occasion, and had even seen us tailing him in the Neon once. She was guilty by association.

"You're going to have to drive off the road and park behind those bushes," I instructed Vee.

Vee leaned forward, peering into the darkness. "Is that a ditch between me and the bushes?"

"It's not very deep. Trust me, we'll clear it."

"Looks deep to me. This is a Neon we're talking about, not a Hummer."

"The Neon doesn't weigh very much. If we get stuck, I'll get out and push."

Vee put the car in drive and hopped the shoulder of the road, the sound of overgrown weeds dragging along the undercarriage.

"More g-gas!" I said, my teeth knocking together as we bounced over the rocky embankment. The car tipped forward and raced into the ditch, and the front tires slammed to a stop, hitting bottom.

"I don't think we're going to make it up," Vee said, feeding the Neon more gas. The tires spun but didn't find traction. "I need to approach this sucker from an angle." She cranked the wheel a hard left and punched the gas again. "That's more like it," she said as the Neon dug in and lurched forward.

"Watch out for the rock—," I began, but it was too late.

Vee drove the Neon straight over a large jutting rock half buried in the earth. She stomped on the brake and killed the engine. We got out and stared at the front left tire.

"Something doesn't look right," Vee said. "Is the tire supposed to look like that?"

I banged my head against the nearest tree trunk.

"So we've got a flat," Vee said. "What now?"

"We stick to the plan. I'll search Scott's room, and you'll keep a lookout. When I get back, you'll call Rixon."

"And tell him what?"

"That we saw a deer and you swerved to miss it. That's when you ran the Neon into the ditch and over a rock."

"I like that story," said Vee. "It makes me sound like an animal lover. Rixon will like that."

"Any questions?" I asked her.

"Nope, I've got it. Call you as soon as Scott leaves the premises. Call you again if he comes back and warn you to get the heck out of there." Vee dropped her eyes to my footwear. "Are you going to scale the building and climb in through a window? Because you might have wanted to wear tennis shoes for that. Your ballet flats are cute, but not practical."

"I'm going in through the front door."

"What are you going to say to Scott's mom?"

"It doesn't matter. She likes me. She'll let me walk right inside." I held out my hot dog, which had grown cold. "Do you want this?"

"No way. You're going to need it. If anything bad happens, just take a bite. Ten seconds later, you'll feel all warm and happy inside."

I jogged the rest of the way down Deacon, veering off into the shadows of the trees as soon as I could make out a human form moving back and forth across the lighted windows of Scott's third-story apartment. From what I could tell, Mrs. Parnell was in the kitchen, moving between the fridge and the sink, most likely baking dessert or throwing together a snack. The light in Scott's bedroom was on, but the shades were drawn. The light blinked out, and a moment later Scott entered the kitchen and brushed a kiss on his mom's cheek.

I stayed put, swatting mosquitoes for five minutes, before Scott walked out the front door carrying what looked like a guitar case. He stowed the case in the trunk of the Mustang and backed out of the parking space.

A minute later, Vee's ringtone sounded in my pocket.

"The eagle has flown the nest," she said.

"I know," I said. "Stay where you are. I'm going in."

I hiked up to the front door and rang the bell. The door opened, and as soon as Mrs. Parnell saw me, she broke into a wide smile.

"Nora!" she said, grasping me good-naturedly by the shoulders. "You just missed Scott. He left to audition with the band. I can't tell you how much it means to him that you went to the trouble to set this up. He's going to knock the socks off the other band members. Just you wait and see." She pinched my cheek affectionately.

"Actually, Scott just called me. He left some of his sheet music here and asked if I could pick it up. He would have come back for it himself, but he didn't want to show up late to the audition and make a bad impression."

"Oh! Yes, of course! Come right in. Did he say which music he wanted?"

"He texted me a couple of titles."

She drew the door all the way open. "I'll walk you back to his room. Scott will be so upset if the audition doesn't go just the way he wants. He's usually so particular about taking the right music, but it all happened on such short notice. I'm sure he's going out of his mind, poor thing."

"He sounded really upset," I agreed. "I'll hurry as fast as I can."

Mrs. Parnell led the way down the hall. As I stepped across the threshold into Scott's bedroom, I took in the complete change of scenery. The first thing I noticed was the black paint on the walls. They'd been white the last time I came over. The *Godfather* poster and the New England Patriots pennant had been ripped down. The air smelled heavily of paint and Febreze.

"You'll have to excuse the walls," Mrs. Parnell said. "Scott's been going through a bit of an emotional downturn. Moving can be hard. He needs to get out more." She looked meaningfully at me. I pretended to miss the hint.

"So that's the sheet music?" I asked, gesturing at a heap of paper on the floor.

Mrs. Parnell wiped her hands on her apron. "Do you want me to help you hunt down the titles?"

"It's no problem, really. I don't want to keep you. It'll just take me a second."

As soon as she left, I closed the door. I set my cell and the Skippy's hot dog on the desk opposite the bed, then moved to the closet.

A pair of white high-tops stuck out from a mound of jeans and T-shirts on the floor. Only three lumberjack shirts were left on hangers. I wondered if Mrs. Parnell had bought them, because I couldn't picture Scott in flannel.

Under the bed I found one aluminum bat, one baseball mitt, and one potted plant. I called Vee.

"What does marijuana look like?"

"Five leaves," Vee said.

"Scott is growing marijuana in here. Under his bed."

"Are you surprised?"

I wasn't, but it did explain the Febreze. I wasn't sure I could picture Scott smoking pot, but I wouldn't put him past selling it. He was desperate for cash.

"I'll call back if I find anything else," I said. I dropped my cell on Scott's bed and turned a slow circle around the room. There weren't many hiding places. The underside of the desk was clean. The heating vents were empty. Nothing was sewn into his blanket. I was about to give up when something high in the closet caught my eye. There was damage to the wall.

I dragged the desk chair over and stepped up. A medium-size square hole had been cut out of the wall, but the plaster had been replaced to make it appear as if the hole wasn't there. Using a wire hanger, I reached up as high as I could and knocked the square of plaster out. From what I could tell, an orange Nike shoe box was crammed into the space. I jabbed at it with the hanger, but ended up pushing it farther back.

A soft buzzing sound broke my concentration, and I realized my cell was ringing on vibrate, the blankets on Scott's bed muffling the sound.

I jumped down. "Vee?" I answered.

"Get out of there!" she hissed in a panicked undertone. "Scott called again and asked for directions to the warehouse, but I didn't know which warehouse you told him. I sort of stalled and said I was only the girlfriend, and I didn't know where the band held its auditions. He asked which warehouse they practiced at, and I said I didn't know that, either. The good news is, he hung up, so I didn't have to lie my way into a bigger hole. The bad news is, he's on his way home. Right now."

"How much time do I have?"

"Since he already flew past here at about a hundred miles per hour, I'd guess a minute. Or less."

"Vee!"

"Don't blame me—you're the one who wasn't answering your phone!"

"Chase him down and stall for time. I need two more minutes."

"Chase him down? How? The Neon has a flat."

"With your own two feet!"

"You mean exercise?"

Cradling the phone under my chin, I found a scrap of paper in my handbag and hunted through Scott's desk for a pen. "It's less than a fourth of a mile. That's one lap around the track. Go!"

"What do I say when I catch him?"

"This is what spies do—they improvise. You'll think of something. I have to go." I broke the connection.

Where were all the pens? How could Scott have a desk with no pens, no pencils? Finally I found one in my bag and scribbled a quick note on the scrap of paper. I slid the paper under the hot dog.

Outside, I heard the Mustang roar into the complex's parking lot.

I crossed to the closet and climbed up a second time. I was

stretched on my tiptoes, stabbing at the box with the hanger.

The front door slammed.

"Scott?" I heard Mrs. Parnell say from the kitchen. "What are you doing back so soon?"

I got the hook part of the hanger under the lip of the lid and coaxed it out of the compartment. Once I had it halfway out, gravity did the rest. The box dropped into my hands. I'd just shoved it inside my bag and one-armed the chair back to its place at the desk, when the bedroom door smacked open.

Scott's eyes found me in an instant. "What are you doing?" he demanded.

"I wasn't expecting you to come back so fast," I stammered.

"The audition was fake, wasn't it?"

"I—"

"You wanted me out of the apartment." He crossed to me in two steps and took my arm, giving me a rough shake. "You made a big mistake coming here."

Mrs. Parnell moved into the doorway. "What's the matter, Scott? For heaven's sake, let her go! She came by to pick up the sheet music you forgot."

"She's lying. I didn't forget any sheet music."

Mrs. Parnell looked at me. "Is that true?"

"I lied," I confessed shakily. I swallowed, trying to inject a measure of calm into my voice. "The thing is, I really wanted to ask Scott to the Summer Solstice party at Delphic, but I couldn't bring myself to do it in person. This is really awkward." I walked to the desk and offered him the hot dog along with the scrap of paper I'd scribbled the note on.

"'Don't be a wiener,'" Scott read. "'Go to Summer Solstice with me.'"

"Well? What do you think?" I tried to hold a smile. "Do you want to be a wiener or not?"

Scott looked from the note to the hot dog to me. "What?"

"Well, isn't that the cutest thing ever," Mrs. Parnell chimed in. "You don't want to be a wiener, do you, Scott?"

"Give us a minute, Mom?"

"Is Summer Solstice a dress-up party?" Mrs. Parnell asked. "Like a dance? I could make a reservation at Todd's Tuxes—"

"Mom."

"Oh. Right. I'll just be in the kitchen. Nora, I've got to hand it to you. I had no idea you were up here planting an invite to the party. I really thought you were picking up sheet music. Very clever." She winked, then backed out, pulling the door shut behind her.

I was left alone with Scott, and all my relief scattered.

"What are you really doing here?" Scott repeated, his voice significantly darker.

"I told you—"

"Not buying it." His eyes flicked beyond me, surveying the room. "What did you touch?"

"I came by to give you the hot dog, I swear. I looked in the desk for a pen to write the wiener note, but that's it."

Scott strode to the desk, pulled out each drawer, and sifted through the contents. "I know you're lying."

I backed toward the door. "You know what? Keep the hot dog, but forget about Summer Solstice. I was just trying to be nice. I was trying to make up for the other night, because I felt responsible for your face getting smashed. Forget I said anything."

He assessed me in silence. I had no idea if he'd bought my act, but I didn't care. The only thought running through my mind was of getting out.

"I've got my eye on you," he said at last, in a tone I found to be startlingly threatening. I'd never seen Scott so icily hostile. "Think about that. Every time you think you're alone, think again. I'm watching you. If I ever catch you in my room again, you're dead. We all clear?"

I swallowed. "Crystal."

On my way out, I passed Mrs. Parnell standing near the fireplace, drinking a glass of iced tea. She took a swig, set the glass on the mantel, and flagged me down.

"Scott is quite the boy, isn't he?" she said.

"That's one way of putting it."

"I bet you asked him to the party early because you knew all the other girls would race to get in line if you didn't act fast."

Summer Solstice was tomorrow night, and everyone going already had dates. Unable to tell this to Mrs. Parnell, I opted for a smile. She could interpret it however she wanted.

"Do I need to get him fitted for a tux?" she asked.

"Actually, the party is really casual. Jeans and a shirt are fine." I'd let Scott break the news to her that we were no longer going together.

Her face fell slightly. "Well, there's always homecoming. I don't suppose you're planning to ask him to homecoming?"

"I really haven't thought about it yet. And anyway, Scott might not want to go with me."

"Don't be silly! You and Scott go way back. He's crazy about you." Or crazy, period.

"I have to go, Mrs. Parnell. It was great seeing you again."

"Drive safely!" she called, giving me a finger wave.

I met Vee outside in the parking lot. She was hunched over, fists pressed into her knees, sucking air. A splotch of sweat stained the back of her shirt.

"Nice decoy work," I said.

She looked up, her face pink as a Christmas ham. "You ever try chasing down a car?" she gasped.

"I'll one-up you. I gave Scott my hot dog and asked if he'd go to Summer Solstice with me."

"What does the hot dog have to do with anything?"

"I said he'd be a wiener if he didn't go with me."

Vee wheezed laughter. "I'd have run harder had I known I'd get to see you call him a wiener."

Forty-five minutes later, Vee's dad had called AAA and had the Neon towed back onto the road and dropped me off in front of the farmhouse. I didn't waste any time clearing off the kitchen table and shaking Scott's shoe box out of my handbag. Multiple layers of duct tape were wrapped around the box, nearly a quarter of an inch thick. Whatever Scott was hiding, he didn't want the rest of the world finding it.

I sawed through the tape with a steak knife. I freed the lid, set it aside, and peered into the box. A plain white tube sock lay innocently at the bottom.

I stared at the sock, feeling my heart drop with disappointment. Then I frowned. I stretched the sock open just wide enough to look inside. My knees went soft.

Inside was a ring. One of the Black Hand's rings.

I STARED AT THE RING BLANKLY. I COULD HARDLY CONTAIN my thoughts. Two rings? I didn't know what it meant. Clearly the Black Hand had more than one ring, but why did Scott have one? And why had he gone to the trouble of hiding it in a secret compartment in his wall?

And why, if he was so ashamed of the branding on his chest, was he holding on to the ring that presumably had given it to him?

In my bedroom, I dug my cello out of the closet and stowed

Scott's ring in the zippered music pouch, right next to its twin, the ring I'd received by envelope last week. I didn't know how to make sense of it. I'd gone to Scott's looking for answers, and was left feeling more confused than ever. I would have dwelt on the rings longer, maybe pieced together a few theories, but I was at a complete and utter loss.

When the grandfather clock chimed midnight, I double-checked the door locks one last time and crawled into bed. I propped my pillows up, sat upright, and painted my fingernails midnight blue. After my fingernails, I moved on to my toenails. I turned on my iPod. I read several chapters in my chemistry text. I knew I couldn't go forever without sleep, but I was determined to put it off as long as possible. I was terrified Patch would be waiting for me on the other side if I did.

I hadn't realized I'd fallen asleep until I woke to a strange scraping sound. I lay in bed, frozen, straining to hear the sound again and place it. The drapes were drawn, the room shadowy. I slipped out of bed and dared a look through the drapes. The backyard was still. Undisturbed. Deceptively peaceful.

A low creak sounded downstairs. I grabbed my cell phone off the nightstand and opened my bedroom door just wide enough to peer out. The hall outside was clear, and I turned into it, my heart beating so hard against my ribs, I thought my chest might crack. I'd made it to the top of the stairs when the softest click alerted me that the knob on the front door was turning.

The door opened, and a figure stepped cautiously into the dark foyer. Scott was in my house, standing fifteen feet away, at the base of the stairs. I steadied my grip on the cell phone, which was slick with sweat.

"What are you doing here?" I called down to Scott.

He jerked his head up, startled. He raised his hands level with his shoulders, showing he was harmless. "We need to talk."

"The door was locked. How did you get in?" My voice was high, shaky.

He didn't answer, but he didn't need to. Scott was Nephilim— freakishly strong. I was almost positive that if I'd walked down to check the deadbolt, I would have found it damaged by the sheer strength of his hands.

"Breaking and entering is illegal," I said.

"So's theft. You stole something that belongs to me."

I moistened my lips. "You have one of the Black Hand's rings."

"It's not mine. I—I stole it." His slight hesitation told me he was lying. "Give me the ring back, Nora."

"Not until you tell me everything."

"We can do this the hard way, if you want." He climbed the first step.

"Don't move!" I ordered, scrambling to dial 911 on my cell. "If you come another step, I'll call the police."

"It will take the police twenty minutes to get out here."

"That's not true." But we both knew it was.

He advanced to the second step.

"Stop," I ordered. "I'll place the call, I swear I will."

"And tell them what? That you broke into my room? That you stole valuable jewelry?"

"Your mom let me inside," I said nervously.

"She wouldn't have, if she'd known you were going to steal from me." He took another step, the stairs creaking under his weight.

I racked my brain for a way to divert him from climbing higher. At the same time, I wanted to goad him into telling me the truth, once and for all. "You lied to me about the Black Hand. That night in your bedroom, wow, quite an act. The tears were almost convincing."

I could see his mind spinning, trying to figure out how much I knew. "I did lie," he said at last. "I was trying to keep you out of the middle of things. You don't want to get mixed up with the Black Hand."

"Too late. He killed my dad."

"Your dad isn't the only one the Black Hand wants dead. He wants me dead, Nora. I need the ring." Suddenly he was on the fifth step.

Dead? The Black Hand couldn't kill Scott. He was immortal. Did Scott think I didn't know? And why was he so intent on getting the ring back? I thought he despised his branding. A new piece of information rose to the surface of my mind. "The Black Hand didn't force you to get the branding mark, did he?" I said. "You wanted it. You wanted to join the society. You wanted to swear allegiance. That's why you kept the ring. It's a sacred token, isn't it? Did the Black Hand give it to you after he finished branding you?"

His hand flexed around the banister. "No. I was forced."

"I don't believe you."

His eyes narrowed. "Do you think I'd let some psychopath grind a burning hot ring into my chest? If I'm so proud of the branding, why am I always covering it up?"

"Because it's a secret society. I'm sure you thought a branding was a small price to pay for the benefits that come with being part of a powerful society."

"Benefits? You think the Black Hand has done a single thing for me?" His tone was cut with anger. "He's the Grim Reaper. I can't escape him, and trust me, I've tried. More times than I can count."

I absorbed this, catching Scott in another lie. "He came back," I said, speaking my thoughts aloud. "After he branded you. You lied when you said you never saw him again."

"Of course he came back!" Scott snapped. "He'd call late at night, or sneak up on me on my way home from work, wearing a ski mask. He was always there."

"What did he want?"

His eyes gauged me. "If I talk, will you give the ring back?"

"Depends if I think you're telling the truth."

Scott scrubbed his knuckles furiously over his head. "The first time I saw him was on my fourteenth birthday. He said I wasn't human. He said I was Nephilim, like him. He said I had to join this group he belonged to. He said all Nephilim had to band together. He said there was no other way we could free ourselves from the fallen angels." Scott glared up the stairs at me, defiant, but his eyes held a shadow of wariness, as if he thought I might think he was crazy. "I thought he'd lost it. I thought he was hallucinating. I kept dodging him, but he kept coming back. He started threatening me. He said the fallen angels would get me once I turned sixteen. He'd follow me around, after school and work. He said he was watching my back, and I should be grateful. Then he found out about my gambling debts. He paid them off, thinking I'd see it as a favor and want to join his group. He didn't get it—I wanted him to go away. When I told him I was going to get my dad to slap a restraining order on him, he hauled me into the warehouse, tied me down, and branded me. He said it was the only way he could keep me safe. He said that someday I'd understand and I'd thank him." The tone of Scott's voice told me that day was never going to come.

"Sounds like he's obsessed with you."

Scott shook his head. "He thinks I betrayed him. My mom and I moved here to get away from him. She doesn't know about the Nephilim stuff, or the branding, she just thinks he's a stalker. We moved, but he doesn't want me running off, and he especially doesn't want to risk having me open my mouth and blow the cover on his secret cult."

"Does he know you're in Coldwater?"

"I don't know. That's why I need the ring. When he finished

branding me, he gave me the ring. He said I had to keep it and find other members to recruit. He told me not to lose it. He said something bad would happen if I did." Scott's voice shook slightly. "He's crazy, Nora. He could do all kinds of things to me."

"You have to help me find him."

He advanced two more steps. "Forget it. I'm not going looking for him." He reached his hand out. "Now give me the ring. Stop stalling. I know it's here."

For no reason other than instinct, I turned and ran. I slammed the bathroom door shut behind me and punched the lock.

"This is getting old," Scott said through the door. "Open up." He waited. "You think this door is going to stop me?"

I didn't, but I didn't know what else to do. I was pressed against the back wall of the bathroom, and that was when I saw the paring knife on the counter. I kept it in the bathroom to open cosmetic packages and to easily remove tags from my clothes. I picked it up, pointing the blade out.

Scott rammed his body against the door, and it banged open, slamming back against the wall.

We were standing face-to-face, and I leveled the knife at him.

Scott walked up to me, yanked the knife out of my grasp, and redirected it at me. "Who's in charge now?" he sneered.

The hallway behind Scott was dark, light from the bathroom illuminating the faded flower wallpaper in the hall. The shadow moved so stealthily across the wallpaper, I almost missed it. Rixon appeared behind Scott, holding the base of the brass lamp my mom kept on the entryway table. He brought the lamp down on Scott's skull in a crushing blow.

"Oouf!" Scott blubbered, staggering around to see what had hit him. In what looked like a jerk of reflex, he yanked the knife up and sliced blindly.

The knife missed, and Rixon slammed the lamp down on Scott's arm, causing him to drop the knife at the same moment that he collapsed sideways into the wall. Rixon kicked the knife down the hall, out of reach. He rammed his fist into Scott's face. A spray of blood flecked the wall. Rixon threw a second punch, and Scott's back dragged down the wall until he sat slumped on the floor. Gripping Scott's collar, Rixon uprighted him long enough to deliver a third punch. Scott's eyes rolled back in his head.

"Rixon!"

I jerked away from the violence at the sound of Vee's hysterical voice. She hiked up the stairs, using the banister to pull herself faster. "Stop, Rixon! You're going to kill him!"

Rixon let go of Scott's collar and stepped away. "Patch would kill me if I didn't." He turned his attention to me. "You okay?"

Scott's face was splattered with blood, and it made my stomach roll. "I'm fine," I said numbly.

"You sure? You need something to drink? A blanket? You want to lie down?"

I looked between Rixon and Vee. "What are we going to do now?"

"I'm going to call Patch," Rixon said, flipping his cell open and pressing it to his ear. "He's going to want to be here for this."

I was too much in shock to argue otherwise.

"We should call the cops," Vee said. She stole a brief look at Scott's unconscious and battered body. "Should we tie him up? What if he wakes up and tries to get away?"

"I'll tie him in the back of the truck as soon as I finish this call," Rixon said.

"Come here, babe," said Vee, pulling me into her arms. She guided me down the stairs, her arm curled around my shoulder. "Are you okay?"

"Yes," I answered automatically, still in a daze. "How did you guys get here?"

"Rixon came over, and we were hanging out in my bedroom when I got one of those creepy feelings that we should check on you. When we pulled up, Scott's Mustang was parked in the driveway. I figured his being here couldn't be good, especially since we'd been snooping around his bedroom. I told Rixon something was wrong, and he told me to wait in the car while he went in. I'm just glad we made it before something worse happened. Holy freak show. What was he thinking, pulling a knife on you?"

Before I could tell her I'd pulled the knife first, Rixon jogged downstairs, joining us in the foyer. "I left a message for Patch," he said. "He should be here soon. I also called the cops."

Twenty minutes later, Detective Basso braked at the bottom of the driveway, a Kojak light flashing on the roof of his car. Scott was slowly regaining consciousness, stirring and groaning in the bed of Rixon's truck. His face was a swollen, blotchy mess, and his hands were roped at his lower back. Detective Basso hauled him out and swapped the rope for handcuffs.

"I didn't do anything," Scott protested, his lip a blubbery mess of blood and tissue.

"Breaking and entering is nothing?" Detective Basso echoed. "Funny, the law disagrees."

"She stole something from me." Scott jerked his chin in my direction. "Ask her. She was in my bedroom earlier tonight."

"What did she steal?"

"I—I can't talk about it."

Detective Basso looked to me for confirmation.

"She's been with us all night," Vee inserted quickly. "Right, Rixon?"

"Absolutely," Rixon said.

Scott nailed me with a look of betrayal. "Not so goody-two-shoes now, are you?"

Detective Basso ignored him. "Let's talk about this knife you pulled."

"She pulled it first!"

"You broke into my house," I said. "Self-defense."

"I want a lawyer," Scott said.

Detective Basso smiled, but there was no patience in it. "A lawyer? You sound guilty, Scott. Why'd you try to knife her?"

"I didn't try to knife her. I took the knife out of her hand. She was the one trying to knife me."

"He's a good liar, I'll give him that," Rixon said.

"You're under arrest, Scott Parnell," Detective Basso said, ducking Scott's head as he directed him into the backseat of the patrol car. "You have the right to remain silent. Anything you say can and will be used against you."

Scott kept his expression hostile, but beneath all the cuts and bruises, he seemed to pale. "You're making a big mistake," he said, only he was looking right at me. "If I go to jail, I'm like a rat in a cage. He'll find me and kill me. The Black Hand will."

He sounded genuinely terrified, and I was torn between silently congratulating him on a well-delivered act . . . and thinking maybe he really had no idea what he was capable of as Nephilim. But how could he be branded into a Nephilim blood society and have no clue that he was immortal? How could the society have failed to mention that?

Scott didn't move his eyes from mine. Adopting a pleading tone, he said, "This is it, Nora. If I leave here, I'm dead."

"Yeah, yeah," Detective Basso said, shutting the door hard. He turned to me. "Think you could stay out of trouble the rest of the night?"

I RAISED MY BEDROOM WINDOW AND SAT ON THE LEDGE, thinking. A refreshing breeze and a night chorus of insects kept me company. At the far end of the field, a light blinked on in one of the houses. It felt strangely reassuring to know I wasn't the only person still awake at this hour.

After Detective Basso had driven away with Scott, Vee and Rixon had examined the lock on the front door.

"Whoa," Vee had said, staring at the mangled door. "How did

Scott get the deadbolt to bend like that? A blowtorch?"

Rixon and I had merely looked at each other.

"I'll stop by tomorrow and install a new lock," he'd said.

That had been over two hours ago, and Rixon and Vee were long gone, leaving me alone with my own thoughts. I didn't want to think about Scott but found my mind straying there anyway. Was he overreacting, or was I going to find out tomorrow that he'd been mysteriously roughed up while in police custody? Either way, he wouldn't die. A few bruises, maybe, but not death. I didn't allow myself to think the Black Hand might take it further than that—if the Black Hand was even a threat. Scott wasn't even sure the Black Hand knew he was in Coldwater.

Instead I told myself there was nothing I could do at this point. Scott had broken into my house and pointed a knife at me. He was behind bars because of himself. He was locked up, and I was safe. The irony was, I wished I could be at the jail tonight. If Scott was bait for the Black Hand, I wanted to be there to face the Black Hand once and for all.

My concentration was dulled by the need for sleep, but I did my best to sort through the information I had. Scott was branded by the Black Hand, a Nephil. Rixon said Patch was the Black Hand, an angel. It almost seemed like I was looking for two different individuals sharing the same name. . . .

The hour had stretched long past midnight, but I didn't want to sleep. Not when it meant opening myself up to Patch, feeling his net close around me, seducing me with words and his silky touch, confusing me more than I already was. More than sleep, I wanted answers. I still hadn't been to Patch's apartment, and more than ever, I felt certain that was where the answers were.

I tugged on dark-wash matchstick jeans and a black fitted tee. Because the forecast called for rain, I opted for tennis shoes and my waterproof Windbreaker.

I took a taxi to the easternmost edge of Coldwater. The river shimmered like a wide black snake. The outline of factory chimneys beyond the river played tricks in the night, making me think of hulking monsters if I looked at them from the corner of my vision. When I'd walked to the five hundred block of the industrial district, I found two apartment buildings, both three stories high. I let myself into the lobby of the first building. All was quiet, and I assumed the tenants were tucked in their beds. I checked the mailboxes in the back, but there was no listing for Cipriano. Not that Patch would be careless enough to leave his name behind, if he really was going to great lengths to keep his place off the radar. I climbed the stairs to the top. Apartments 3A, B, and C. No apartment 34. I jogged down the steps, walked a half block down, and tried the second building.

Behind the main doors sat a cramped lobby with scuffed tiles and a thin coat of paint barely masking red and black graffiti. Just like the previous building, mailboxes stood in a line at the back. Near the front, the air conditioner rattled and buzzed while the door to an old cage elevator stood open like mesh jaws waiting to snap me up. I bypassed the elevator in favor of the stairs. The building had a lonely, derelict feel to it. A place where neighbors minded their own business. A place where nobody knew anyone else, and secrets were easy to keep.

The third floor was dead calm. I walked past apartments 31, 32, and 33. At the back of the hall I found apartment number 34. I suddenly wondered what I was going to do if Patch was home. At this point, I could only hope he wasn't. I knocked, but there was no answer. I tried the door handle. To my surprise, it gave.

I peeked inside at darkness. I stood motionless, listening for movement.

I flipped on the light switch just inside the door, but either the lightbulbs had burned out or the electricity had been shut off. Pulling the flashlight out of my jacket, I let myself in and shut the door.

The rancid smell of spoiled food overwhelmed me. I aimed the flashlight in the direction of the kitchen. A skillet with days-old scrambled eggs and a partially full gallon of milk that had soured to the point of bloating sat on the counter. It wasn't the kind of place I imagined Patch calling home, but this only proved there were many things I didn't know about him.

I set my keys and handbag on the counter and pulled my shirt up over my nose in an attempt to block out the stench. The walls were bare, the furniture sparse. One antiquated TV with rabbit ears, probably black and white, and a ratty sofa in the living room. Both were out of view of the window, which had butcher paper taped across it.

Keeping the flashlight beam low, I made my way down the hall to the bathroom. It was stark, other than a beige shower curtain that had probably started out white, and a dingy hotel towel draped over the rod. No soap, no razor, no shaving cream. The linoleum floor was peeling back at the edges, and the medicine cabinet over the sink was empty.

I continued down the hall to the bedroom. I turned the knob and pushed the door inward. The stale smell of sweat and unwashed bed clung to the air. Since the lights were off, I figured it was safe to raise the blinds, and I forced the window open, allowing fresh air inside. A streetlight's glow trickled in, casting a hazy gray around the room.

Dishes caked with dried food were stacked on the nightstand, and while the bed had sheets, they lacked the crisp look of freshly laundered linens. In fact, judging by the smell, they hadn't seen laundry soap in months. A small desk with a computer monitor sat in the back corner. The actual computer was gone, and it occurred to me that Patch had taken great care not to leave any trace of himself behind.

I crouched in front of the desk, opening and closing drawers. Nothing struck me as out of the ordinary: pencils, and a copy of the Yellow Pages. I was about to close the door when a small black jewelry box taped to the underside of the desk caught my eye. I ran my hand under the desk, blindly peeling the box free from the tape holding it in place. I lifted the lid. Every hair on my body stood on end.

The box held six of the Black Hand's rings.

At the far end of the hall, the front door creaked open.

I shot to my feet. Had Patch returned? I couldn't let him find me. Not now, not when I'd just discovered the Black Hand's rings in his apartment.

I looked around for somewhere to hide. The twin-size bed stood between me and the closet. If I tried to walk around the bed, I risked being seen from the doorway. If I climbed over the bed, I risked the bedsprings squeaking.

The front door closed with a soft click. Solid footsteps crossed the linoleum in the kitchen. Seeing no other choice, I boosted myself onto the windowsill, swung my legs out, and dropped as silently as possible onto the fire escape. I tried to pull the window shut behind me, but the sliders stuck, refusing to budge. I ducked all but my eyes below the window, keeping them trained inside the apartment.

A shadow appeared on the hall wall, stretching closer. I ducked out of sight.

I was scared that this was it—I was going to be caught—when the footsteps retreated. Less than a minute later, the front door opened, closed. An eerie silence once again settled over the apartment.

Slowly I brought myself back to standing. I stayed that way another minute, and when I was certain the apartment was in fact empty, I crawled back inside. Feeling suddenly conspicuous and vulnerable, I strode down the hall. I needed to go somewhere quiet, where I could sort through my thoughts. What was I missing? Patch was clearly the Black Hand, but how did he play into the Nephilim blood society? What was his role? What the hell was going on? I threw my handbag over my shoulder and headed for the exit.

I had my hand on the doorknob when a strange noise penetrated my thoughts. A clock. The soft, rhythmic tick of a clock. I frowned and turned back to the kitchen. The sound hadn't been there when I came in—at least, I didn't think it had. Listening intently, I followed the muffled tick across the room. I crouched down in front of the cabinet below the kitchen sink.

With growing alarm, I opened the cabinet. Through all the panic and confusion, I made sense of the contraption sitting inches from my knees. Sticks of dynamite. Duct tape. White, blue, and yellow wires.

I stumbled to my feet and ran out the front door. My feet clattered down the stairs so fast I had to hold the handrail to keep from falling. At the bottom, I shoved my way out to the street and kept running. Flipping my head back once, I saw a snap of light an instant before fire erupted from the windows of the third floor of the building. Smoke billowed up in the night. Debris of bricks and wood, glowing orange with heat, hailed down to the street.

The far-away sound of sirens ricocheted off the buildings, and I alternately speed-walked and ran to the next block, terrified of drawing attention, but too distraught not to flee the scene. When I rounded the corner, I broke into a wild sprint. I didn't know where I was going. My pulse was all over the place, my thoughts reeling. If I'd stayed in the apartment another few minutes, I'd be dead.

A shuddering sob escaped me. My nose was running, my stomach cramping. I wiped my eyes with the back of my hand and tried to focus on the shapes jumping out of the darkness ahead: street signs, parked cars, the curb—the deceptive shimmer of lamplight on windows. In a matter of seconds, the world had turned into a confusing labyrinth; the truth there and not there, shifting out beneath my feet, vanishing when I tried to look it head-on.

Had someone tried to blow up evidence left in the apartment? Like the Black Hand's rings? Was Patch responsible?

Ahead, a gas station came into view. I staggered around to the outside bathroom and locked myself inside. My legs were wobbly, and my fingers trembled so hard it was all I could do to coordinate turning on the faucet. I splashed frigid water on my face to startle me out of sliding into shock. Bracing my arms on the sink, I breathed in gulps and gasps.

CHAPTER

21

I HADN'T SLEPT IN OVER THIRTY-SIX HOURS, EXCEPT FOR
very briefly Thursday evening, when Patch had met me inside
my dream.

Staying awake through the night hadn't been a struggle; every
time I felt my eyes dipping closed, the explosion would blaze
across my mind, jolting me upright. Unable to sleep, I'd spent the
night thinking about Patch.

When Rixon had told me Patch was the Black Hand, he'd planted a seed of doubt inside me that had swollen and blossomed with the worst kind of violation of trust, but it hadn't choked me completely. Not yet. There was still a part of me that wanted to weep and shake my head adamantly at the idea that Patch could have killed my dad. I bit my lip hard, concentrating on the pain there, rather than remembering all the times he'd stroked my mouth with his finger, or kissed the curve of my ear. I couldn't think about those things.

I hadn't bothered crawling out of bed at seven for summer school. I'd left a series of phone messages for Detective Basso throughout the morning, then the afternoon, and on into the evening, one call every hour, none of which he'd returned. I told myself I was calling to check on Scott, but deep down, I suspected I just wanted to know the police were close. As much as I disliked Detective Basso, I felt a tiny bit safer believing he was only a phone call away. Because a small part of me was beginning to believe maybe last night wasn't about destroying evidence.

What if someone had tried to kill me?

In the middle of all the thinking I'd done last night, I'd shifted around the fragments of information I had, trying to make something fit. The one clear fragment I kept coming back to was the Nephilim blood society. Patch said Chauncey's successor wanted to avenge his death. Patch swore nobody could trace Chauncey's death back to me, but I was beginning to fear otherwise. If the successor knew about me, maybe last night had been his first stab at revenge.

It seemed unlikely that anyone had followed me to Patch's

apartment so late last night, but if there was one thing I knew about Nephilim, it was that they were very good at doing the unlikely.

My cell rang in my pocket and I whipped it out before the first ring had time to finish.

"Hello?"

"Let's go to Summer Solstice," Vee said. "We'll eat a little cotton candy, catch a few rides, maybe get hypnotized and do stuff that would make *Girls Gone Wild* look tame."

My heart, which had been up in my throat, slid back into place. Not Detective Basso, then. "Hey."

"What say you? You in the mood for some action? You in the mood for Delphic?"

Honestly, I wasn't. I'd planned on redialing Detective Basso at sixty-minute intervals until he picked up one of my calls.

"Earth to babe."

"I'm not feeling well," I said.

"Not feeling well how? Stomachache? Headache? Cramps? Food poisoning? Delphic is the cure for just about all those things."

"I'm going to pass, thanks anyway."

"Is this because of Scott? Because he's in jail. He can't get to you. Come have fun. Rixon and I won't kiss in front of you, if that's what's bothering you."

"I'm going to put on my pj's and watch a movie."

"Are you saying a movie is more fun than me?"

"Tonight it is."

"Huh. Movie this. You know I'm not going to stop harassing you until you come."

"I know."

"So make this easy and just say yes."

I blew out a sigh. I could sit home all night and wait for Detective Basso to get around to answering my calls, or I could take a small break and start up again when I got back. Besides, he had my cell phone number and could reach me anywhere.

"All right," I told Vee. "Give me ten."

In my bedroom, I squeezed into a pair of toothpick jeans, pulled on a graphic tee and cardigan, and finished the look with suede driving mocs. I smoothed my hair into a low ponytail, offsetting it so it hung over my right shoulder. Having not slept in more than a full day, my eyes were ringed by smoky circles. I brushed on mascara, silver eye shadow, and lip gloss, hoping I looked more pulled-together than I felt. I left a rather bland note on the kitchen counter for my mom, telling her I'd gone to Summer Solstice at Delphic. She wasn't due back until tomorrow morning, but she surprised me more often than not by coming home early. If she did make it home tonight, this was probably going to be one time when she wished she'd drawn out her trip. I'd been practicing what I was going to say to her. Whatever I did, I couldn't break eye contact when I told her I knew about her affair with Hank. And I couldn't let her get a word in before I told her I was moving out. As I'd practiced it, I planned to walk out at that point. I wanted to send her the message that it was too late to talk—if she'd wanted to tell me the truth, she'd had sixteen years to do it. Now it was too late.

I locked up and jogged down the drive to meet Vee.

An hour later, Vee squeezed the Neon into a parking spot between two oversize trucks that extended into our space on both sides. We rolled down the windows and boosted ourselves out backward to keep from scratching the paint by opening the doors. We crossed the parking lot and paid our way inside the gates. The park was more crowded than usual due to Summer Solstice—the longest day of the year. Right away I recognized a few faces from school, but for the most part, I felt like I was standing in a sea of strangers. Most of the crowd was wearing jewel-toned butterfly masks that concealed half their faces. One of the vendors must have been selling them at a discount.

"Where should we start?" Vee asked. "The arcade? The fun house? The food vendors? Personally, I think we should start with the food. That way, we'll eat less."

"Your logic?"

"If we stop by the vendors last, we'll have worked up our appetites. I always eat more when I've worked up an appetite."

I didn't care where we started. I was only here to distract myself for a couple of hours. I checked my cell, but there were no missed calls. How long did it take Detective Basso to return a call? Had something happened to him? I had a black cloud hanging at the back of my mind, and I didn't like how it made me feel ill at ease.

"You look all pasty," Vee said.

"I told you: I don't feel great."

"That's because you haven't eaten enough. Sit down. I'll go get us some cotton candy and hot dogs. Just think about all that relish and mustard. I don't know about you, but I can already feel my head clearing and my pulse slowing."

"I'm not hungry, Vee."

"Of course you're hungry. Everybody's hungry. That's why they've got all these vendors." Before I could stop her, she marched into the crowd.

I was pacing the walkway, waiting for Vee, when my cell phone chirped. Detective Basso's name showed on the screen.

"Finally," I breathed, flipping the cell open.

"Nora, where are you?" he said the moment I picked up. He was speaking fast, and I could tell he was upset. "Scott escaped. He got away. We've got the whole force looking for him, but I want you to stay the hell away from him. I'm coming to pick you up until this blows over. I'm on my way to your house right now."

My throat constricted, making it hard to force words out. "What? How did he get out?"

Detective Basso hesitated before answering. "He bent the bars in his cell."

Of course he did. He was Nephilim. Two months ago I'd watched Chauncey mangle my cell phone with a mere squeeze of his hand. It didn't seem too unrealistic to imagine Scott using his Nephilim strength to break out of jail.

"I'm not at home," I said. "I'm at Delphic amusement park." Without meaning to, I cast my eyes over the crowd, looking for Scott. But there was no way he could know I was here. After breaking out of jail, he'd probably gone directly to my house, expecting to find me there. I felt incredibly grateful to Vee for dragging me out tonight. Scott was probably at my house right this very minute—

The cell slipped a notch through my hand. The note. On the counter. The one I'd left for my mom, telling her I'd gone to Delphic.

"I think he knows where I am," I told Detective Basso, feeling the first licks of panic. "How soon can you get here?"

"Delphic? Thirty minutes. Go to security. Whatever you do, keep your phone on you. If you see Scott, call me immediately."

"They don't have security at Delphic," I said, my mouth gone to dust. It was widely known that the park didn't employ security, which was one of many reasons why my mom didn't like me coming here.

"Then get out of there," he barked. "Drive back to Coldwater and meet me at the station. Can you do that?"

Yes. I could do that. Vee would give me a ride. I was already walking in the direction she'd departed, eyes raking the crowd for her.

Detective Basso exhaled. "You're going to be fine. Just . . . hurry back here. I'll send the rest of the force to Delphic to go after Scott. We'll find him." The anxiety in his voice didn't console me.

I hung up. Scott was out. The police were on their way, and this was all going to end fine . . . as long as I got out now. I sketched a quick plan. First, I had to find Vee. I also had to get out of the open. If Scott came walking down the path right this moment, he would see me.

I was jogging toward the food vendors when my ribs were elbowed from behind. Something about the force of the elbowing told me this was more than an accident. I turned, and before I'd come full circle, my brain prickled as it registered a familiar face. The first thing I noticed was the flash from the silver hoop in his ear. The second thing I noticed was how beat-up his face was. His nose was broken—crooked and bruised deep red. The bruise spread below both eyes, turning a deep violet.

The next thing I knew, Scott had me by the elbow and was steering me down the walkway.

"Get your hands off me," I said, wrestling against him. But Scott was stronger, and his grip held.

"Sure, Nora, after you tell me where it is."

"Where what is?" I said, my voice passive-aggressive.

He laughed humorlessly.

I kept my expression as opaque as I could, but my thoughts were racing. If I told him the ring was at my home, he'd leave the park. He'd probably drag me with him. When the police arrived, they'd find us both gone. It wasn't like I could call Detective Basso and tell him we were headed to my place. Not with Scott standing over me. No, I had to keep him here, in the park.

"Did you give it to Vee's boyfriend? Did you think he could protect it from me? I know he's not—normal." Scott's eyes held that same terrified uncertainty. "I know he can do things other people can't."

"Like you?"

Scott glared down at me. "He's not like me. He's not the same. That much I can tell. I'm not going to hurt you, Nora. All I need is the ring. Give it to me, and you'll never see me again."

He was lying. He would hurt me. He was desperate enough to break out of jail. Nothing was too extreme at this point—he would get the ring back, no matter the cost. Adrenaline pumped through my legs and I couldn't think clearly. But somewhere in the back of my mind, my sense of survival told me I needed to take charge of the situation. I needed to find a way to separate myself from Scott. Blindly following my instincts, I said, "I have the ring."

"I know you have it," he said impatiently. "Where?"

"It's here. I brought it with me."

He considered me for a moment, then yanked my handbag off my arm and ripped it open, searching it.

I shook my head. "I threw it away."

He shoved the handbag back at me, and I caught it, clutching it against my chest. "Where?" he demanded.

"A trash can near the entrance," I said automatically. "Inside one of the women's restrooms."

"Show me."

As we made our way down the walkway, I ordered myself to stay calm long enough to figure out my next move. Could I run? No,

Scott would catch me. Could I hide out in one of the women's restrooms? Not indefinitely, no. Scott wasn't timid, and he wouldn't have a problem going in after me if it meant getting what he wanted. I still had my cell phone, however. In the women's room, I could call Detective Basso.

"This one," I said, pointing at one of the cinderblock shelters. The entrance to the women's room was straight ahead, down a sloping stretch of cement, with the men's room around the back.

Scott grabbed me by the shoulders and shook me. "Don't lie to me. They'll kill me if I lose it. If you're lying to me, I'll . . ." He caught himself, but I knew what he'd been about to say. *If you're lying to me, I'll kill you.*

"It's in the bathroom." I nodded, more to convince myself I could do this than to reassure him. "I'll go get it. And then you'll leave me alone, right?"

Instead of answering, Scott shoved out a hand, catching me in the navel. "Your cell."

My heart fumbled. Seeing no other choice, I retrieved my phone and held it out to him. My hand shook slightly, but I steadied it, refusing to let him know I'd had a plan, or that he'd just shattered it.

"You've got one minute. Don't try anything stupid."

Inside the restroom, I made a quick survey. Five sinks against one wall, and five stalls opposite them. Two college-age girls were at the sinks, a foam of bubbles covering their hands. There was a small window on the far wall, and it was cranked open. Without eating up any more time, I got my foot up on the last sink and pulled myself to standing. The window was level with my elbows now, and while there wasn't a screen to block me, it was going to be a tight fit to squeeze through. I could feel the eyes of everyone on me, but I ignored them and hoisted myself up on the ledge, hardly aware of the splattered bird poop or spiderwebs.

When I pushed on the open windowpane, it popped free and fell to the ground outside with a clatter. I sucked in a breath, thinking Scott had heard, but the crowds out on the walkways had stifled the sound. Propping my stomach on the windowsill, I lifted my left leg up, cramming it against my body until I was able to roll it through the window. I wiggled the rest of the way through, my right leg sliding out last. I hung from the windowsill by my fingers, then dropped to the sidewalk outside. I stayed in a crouch a moment, half expecting Scott to round the building.

Then I ran toward the park's main walkway and slipped inside the stream of the crowd.

ARKNESS WAS STRETCHING ACROSS THE SKY, eclipsing the pale streaks of light fanning out from the horizon. I walked in a hurry toward the park's exit. I could see the gates ahead. Almost there. I was pushing through the fringe of the crowd when I came up short. Less than two hundred feet away, Scott was pacing the gates, his eyes sweeping the crush of bodies pouring in and out of the gates. He'd figured out I'd escaped the bathroom and was blocking the only way out of the park. A high chain-link fence topped with barbed wire encircled the park, and the only way I was getting out was through the exit gates. I knew it, and Scott knew it.

I turned abruptly and melted back into the crowd, checking behind me every few seconds to make sure Scott hadn't spotted me.

I worked my way deeper into the park on the assumption that the last place I had seen Scott was at the gates, and it was in my best interest to get as far away from them as I could. I could hide in the darkness of the fun house until the police arrived, or I could take the sky ride above the park, where I might be able to see Scott below and keep an eye on him. As long as he didn't look up, I'd be fine. Of course, if he did see me, I had no doubt he'd be waiting for me at the end of the ride. I decided to keep moving, stay in the heaviest pockets of traffic, and wait this out.

The walkway split at the Ferris wheel, one path branching off toward the water rides, the other leading to the Archangel roller coaster. I'd just veered onto the latter when I saw Scott. He saw me, too. We were on parallel walkways, the chair lift to the sky ride separating us. A boy and girl took their seats on a chair as it swung around the conveyor, momentarily breaking our eye contact. I took that moment to run.

I shoved my way through the crowd, but the walkways were congested, making it hard to move faster than stop-and-go. Worse, the walkways in this section of the park were lined with high hedges, squeezing traffic through the labyrinth of twists and turns. I didn't dare look behind me, but I knew Scott couldn't be far behind. He wouldn't try anything in front of all these people, would he? I shook my head to flush out the thought, and concentrated instead on where I was going. I'd been to Delphic only three or four times before, always at night, and I didn't know the layout well. I could have kicked myself for not grabbing a map on my way in. I found it absurdly ironic that thirty seconds ago I'd been running away from the exit; now getting to it was the only thing on my mind.

"Hey! Watch out!"

"Excuse me," I said, breathless. "Which way to the exit?"

"Where's the fire, man?"

I fought my way past the crowd. "Excuse me. I have to get through . . . excuse me." Above the hedges, the lights of the rides blazed and glittered against the backdrop of night. I paused at an intersection, trying to orient myself. Left or right? Which would get me to the exit faster?

"There you are." Scott's breath warmed my ear. He laid his hand on my neck, sending a spike of chills ricocheting to the bone.

"Help!" I shouted on instinct. "*Someone help me!*"

"My girlfriend," Scott explained to the few people who'd paused long enough to direct their attention at us. "This is a game we play."

"I'm not his girlfriend!" I shouted in a panic. "Get your hands off me!"

"Come here, sweetheart." Scott wrestled me into his arms, pinning me against him. "I warned you not to lie to me," he murmured in my ear. "I need the ring. I don't want to hurt you, Nora, but I will, if you make me."

"Get him off me!" I shouted to anyone who would listen.

Scott wrenched my arm behind my back. I spoke through gritted teeth, trying to battle the pain. "Are you insane?" I said. "I don't have the ring. I gave it to the police. Last night. Go get it from them."

"Quit lying!" he growled.

"Call them yourself. It's the truth. I gave it to them. I don't have it." I shut my eyes, praying he believed me and released my arm.

"Then you're going to help me get it back."

"They aren't going to give it to me. It's evidence. I told them it was your ring."

"They'll give it back," he said slowly, as if he was forming a plan as he went. "If I trade you for the ring."

It all clicked into place. "You're going to hold me hostage? Trade me for the ring? Help!" I screamed. "Somebody get him off me!"

One of the people standing nearby laughed.

"This isn't a joke!" I yelled, feeling blood rise in my neck, terror and desperation scraping away at me. "Get him off—"

Scott sealed his hand over my mouth, but I got my foot up and kicked him in the shin. He gave a grunt of pain and buckled in half.

His arms loosened slightly in the surprise of the attack, and I shoved myself free. I fumbled back a step, watching agony twist on his face, then turned and bolted, seeing glimpses of the rides through the gaps in the crowd. All I had to do was make it out. The police had to be close. Then I'd be safe. *Safe.* I repeated the word frantically as motivation to keep my head and not succumb to panic. There was a wan light left in the western sky, and I used it to orient myself north. If I continued north, the pathway would eventually deliver me to the gates.

An explosion shattered my ear. It startled me so much, I tripped and went down on my knees. Or maybe I'd acted reflexively, because there were others around me who'd dropped to the pavement too. There was a moment of hair-raising quiet, and then everyone was screaming and scrambling in every direction.

"He's got a gun!" The words blurred together in my ears, sounding so very far away.

Even though not one part of me wanted to, I found myself turning back. Scott was clutching his side, bright red liquid flowering through his shirt. His mouth was open, his eyes wide with shock.

He went down on one knee, and I saw someone standing several yards behind him, holding a gun. Rixon. Vee was at his side, her hands clamped over her mouth, her face as white as a sheet.

There was a chaotic stampede of feet and limbs and panicked, chilling screams, and I scooted to the side of the path, trying to avoid getting trampled on.

"He's getting away!" I heard Vee shriek. "Someone get him!"

Rixon fired several shots, but this time nobody dropped. In fact, the rush to get out intensified. I pulled myself to standing and looked back to where I'd last seen Rixon and Vee. The echo of the shots still pealed in my ears, but I read the words as they fell from Rixon's lips. *Over here.* He flagged his free arm through the air. In what felt like slow motion, I fought the stream of traffic and ran to him.

"What the hell?!" Vee shrieked. "Why did you shoot him, Rixon?"

"Citizen's arrest," he said. "Well, that, and Patch told me to."

"You can't shoot people just because Patch says to!" Vee said, her eyes wild. "You're going to get arrested. What are we doing to do now?" she moaned.

"The police are on their way," I said. "They know about Scott."

"We have to get out of here!" said Vee, still hysterical, flapping her arms and pacing a few feet, only to spin back and come back to where she'd started. "I'll take Nora to the police station. Rixon, go get Scott, but don't shoot him again—tie him up like last time!"

"Nora can't use the gates," Rixon said. "That's what he'll expect. I know another way out. Vee, get the Neon and meet us at the south end of the parking lot, near the Dumpsters."

"How are you going to get out?" Vee wanted to know.

"Through the underground tunnels."

"There are tunnels under Delphic?" Vee asked.

Rixon kissed her forehead. "Hurry, love."

The crowd had scattered, leaving the pathway empty. I could still hear panicked shrieks and screams echoing down the walkway, but they sounded a world away. Vee hesitated a moment, then gave a resolute nod. "Just hurry, okay?"

"There's a mechanical room in the basement of the fun house," Rixon explained to me as we walked in a hurry down the opposite pathway. "It has a door leading into the tunnels under Delphic. Scott may have heard of the tunnels, but if he figures out where we've gone and follows us, there's no way he'll find us. It's like a maze down there, and it goes on for miles." He gave a nervous smile. "Don't worry, Delphic was built by fallen angels. Not me in particular, but a few of my mates helped. I know the routes by heart. Er, mostly."

A S WE DREW CLOSER TO THE GRINNING CLOWN'S head leading inside the fun house, the distant screams were replaced by creepy music-box carnival music, tinkling loudly from the bowels of the fun house. I stepped through the mouth, and the floor shifted. I reached out to steady myself, but the walls turned, rolling under my hands. As my eyes adjusted to the traces of light filtering through the mouth of the clown behind me, I saw that I was inside a revolving barrel that seemed to stretch on forever. The barrel was painted with alternating stripes of red and white, and they blurred together into a dizzying pink.

"Here," Rixon said, guiding me through the barrel.

I put one foot in front of the other, sliding and blundering forward. At the end, I stepped out to solid ground, only to have a jet of icy air shoot up from the floor. The cold licked my skin, and I jumped sideways with a startled gasp.

"It's not real," Rixon assured me. "We have to keep going. If Scott decides to search the tunnels, we have to beat him inside."

The air was stale and humid, and smelled of rust. The clown's head was a distant memory now. The only light came from red bulbs in the cavernous ceiling that blazed to life just long enough to spotlight a dangling skeleton, unraveling zombie, or vampire rising from a coffin.

"How much farther?" I asked Rixon over the distorted cacophony of hoots, cackles, and wails that echoed all around.

"The mechanical room is just ahead. After that, we'll be in the tunnels. Scott's bleeding pretty bad. He won't die—Patch has told you all about Nephilim, right?—but he could pass out from loss of blood. Chances are, he won't find an entrance to the tunnels before he does. We'll be back above ground before you know it." His confidence sounded slightly inflated, a little too optimistic.

We pushed on, and I felt the eerie sensation that we were being followed. I spun back, but the darkness was consuming. If someone was back there, I couldn't see.

"Do you think Scott could have followed us?" I asked Rixon, keeping my voice low.

Rixon stopped, turned back. Listened. After a moment, he said with certainty, "There's no one there."

We were continuing our hurried pace toward the mechanical room, when I once again felt a presence behind me. My scalp tingled, and I cut a look over my shoulder. This time, the outline of a face materialized through the darkness. I almost cried out, and then the outline solidified into a distinct and familiar face.

My dad.

His blond hair was bright against the darkness, his eyes shining, yet sad. *I love you.*

"Dad?" I whispered. But I took a cautionary step back. I reminded myself of the last times. He was a trick. A lie.

I'm sorry I had to leave you and your mom.

I willed him to disappear. He wasn't real. He was a threat. He wanted to hurt me. I remembered the way he'd yanked my arm through the townhouse window and tried to cut me. I remembered how he'd chased me through the library.

But his voice was the same gentle coaxing he'd used that very first time at the townhouse. Not the stern, sharp voice that had replaced it. It was his voice.

I love you, Nora. Whatever happens, promise me you'll remember that. I don't care how or why you came into my life, only that you did. I don't remember all the things I did wrong. I remember what I did right.

I remember you. You made my life meaningful. You made my life special.

I shook my head, trying to sweep out his voice, wondering why Rixon wasn't saying anything—couldn't he see my dad? Wasn't there anything we could do to make him go away? But the truth of the matter was, I didn't want his voice to stop. I didn't want him to leave. I wanted him to be real. I needed him to wrap his arms around me and tell me everything was going to be all right. Most of all, I longed for him to come home.

Promise you'll remember.

Tears dripped down my cheeks. I promise, I thought back, even though I knew he couldn't hear me.

An angel of death helped me come here to see you. She's holding time still for us, Nora. She's helping me speak to your mind. There's something important I need to tell you, but I don't have much time. I have to go back soon, and I need you to listen carefully.

"No," I choked, my voice coming out strangled. "I'm going with you. Don't leave me here. I'm going with you! You can't leave me again!"

I can't stay, baby. I belong somewhere else now.

"Please don't go," I sobbed, clutching my fists against my chest as if I could stop my heart from swelling. A certain desperate panic seized me when I thought of him leaving again. My sheer sense of abandonment outweighed everything else. He was going to leave me here. In the fun house. In the dark, with no one to help me but Rixon. "Why are you leaving me all over again? I need you!"

Touch Rixon's scars. The truth is there.

My dad's face receded into the darkness. I reached out to stop him, but his face turned into a ribbon of fog at my touch. The silvery white threads dissolved into the darkness.

"Nora?"

I started at the sound of Rixon's voice. "We have to hurry," he said, as if no more than a ripple of time had passed. "We don't want to meet up with Scott in the outer ring of the tunnels, where all the entrances feed."

My dad was gone. For reasons I couldn't explain, I knew I'd seen him for the last time. The pain and loss was unbearable. At the moment when I needed him most, when I was heading into the tunnels, scared and lost, he'd left me to face this alone.

"I can't see where I'm going," I gasped, swatting my eyes dry, struggling through the frustrating process of trying to focus my thoughts on one specific goal: getting to the tunnels and meeting Vee on the other side. "I need something to hold."

Rixon impatiently thrust the hem of his shirt out to me. "Hold the back of my shirt and follow me. Keep up. We haven't got a lot of time."

I squeezed the worn cotton between my fingers, my heart beating stronger. Inches away was the bare skin of his back. My dad had told me to touch his scars; it would be so easy now. All I had to do was slide my hand . . .

Succumb to the dark suction that would swallow me whole . . .

I thought back to the times I'd touched Patch's scars, and how I'd been briefly transported inside his memory. Without a shred of doubt, I knew touching Rixon's scars would do the same thing.

I didn't want to go. I wanted to keep my feet under me, get to the tunnels, and get out of Delphic.

But my dad had come back to tell me where to find the truth. Whatever I'd see in Rixon's past, it had to be important. As much as it hurt to know my dad had left me here, I had to trust him. I had to trust he'd risked everything to tell me.

I slid my hand up the back of Rixon's shirt. I felt smooth skin . . . then a bumpy ridge of scar tissue. I splayed my hand against the scar, waiting to be ripped into a strange, foreign world.

The street was quiet, dark. The houses framing both sides of it were derelict, ramshackle. Yards were small and fenced. Windows were boarded or barred. A heavy frost sank its teeth into my skin.

Two loud explosions ruptured the silence. I swung to face the house across the street. *Gunshots?* I thought in a panic. I immediately searched through my pockets for my cell phone, meaning to call 911, when I remembered I was trapped in Rixon's memory. Everything I was seeing had happened in the past. I couldn't change anything now.

The sound of running footsteps rang through the night, and I watched in shock as my dad let himself through the gate of the house across the street and disappeared around the side yard. Without waiting, I took off after him.

"Dad!" I screamed, unable to help myself. "Don't go back there!" He was wearing the same clothes he'd gone out in the night he'd been killed. I pushed through the gate and met him at the back corner of the house. Sobbing, I threw my arms around him. "We have to go back. We have to get out of here. Something horrible is going to happen."

My dad walked right through my arms, crossing to a small stone wall that ran alongside the property. He inched down the wall in a crouch, eyes trained on the back door of the house. I leaned into the siding, bowed my head against my arms, and cried. I didn't want to see this. Why had my dad told me to touch Rixon's scars? I didn't want this. Didn't he know how much pain I'd already suffered?

"Last chance." The words were spoken from inside the house, drifting out through the open back door.

"Go to hell."

Another explosion, and I slumped to my knees, pressing myself against the siding, willing the memory to end.

"Where is she?" The question was asked so quietly, so calmly, I almost couldn't hear it over my soft crying.

Out of the corner of my eye, I saw my dad move. He crept across the yard, moving toward the door. A gun was in his hand, and he raised it, taking aim. I ran at him, grabbing at his hands, trying to wrestle the gun away from him, trying to push him back into the shadows. But it was like moving a ghost—my hands passed right through him.

My dad pulled the trigger. The shot cut open the night, ripping the silence in half. Again and again he fired. Even though no part of me wanted to, I faced the house, seeing the lean build of the young man my dad was shooting from behind. Just beyond him, another man sat slumped on the floor, his back propped up by the sofa. He was bleeding, and his expression was twisted in agony and fear.

In a moment muddled with confusion, I realized it was Hank Millar.

"Run!" Hank shouted at my dad. "Leave me behind! Run and save yourself!"

My dad didn't run. He held the gun level, shooting over and over, sending bullets flying at the open door, where the young man in a blue ball cap seemed impervious to them. And then, very slowly, he turned to face my dad.

RIXON GRABBED MY WRIST, GIVING IT A FIRM squeeze. "Careful whose business you go sticking your nose in." His jaw was set in anger, his nostrils flaring slightly. "Maybe that's the way it is with Patch, but nobody touches my scars." He arched his eyebrows meaningfully.

My stomach was cinched with a knot so tight I almost doubled over. "I saw my dad die," I blurted, stricken with horror.

"Did you see the killer?" Rixon asked, shaking my wrist to pull me all the way back to the present.

"I saw Patch from behind," I gasped. "He was wearing his ball cap."

He nodded, as if accepting that what I'd seen couldn't be undone. "He didn't want to keep the truth from you, but he knew that if he told you, he'd lose you. It happened before he knew you."

"I don't care when it happened," I said, my voice shrill and shaking. "He needs to be brought to justice."

"You can't bring him to justice. He's Patch. If you report him, do you really think he's going to let the cops haul him off?"

No, I didn't. The police meant nothing to Patch. Only the archangels could stop him. "There's just one thing I don't understand. There were only three people in the memory. My dad, Patch, and Hank Millar. The three of them saw what happened. Then how am I seeing this in your memory?"

Rixon didn't say anything, but the lines around his mouth tightened.

A horrible new thought settled over me. All certainty in regard to my dad's killer evaporated. I'd seen the killer from the back and assumed it was Patch because of the ball cap. But the longer I dwelled on the memory, the more I was sure the killer was too lanky to be Patch, the cut of his shoulders too angular.

In fact, the killer looked a lot like . . .

"You killed him," I whispered. "It was you. You were wearing

Patch's hat." The shock of the moment was quickly being eaten up by abhorrence and ice-cold fear. "You killed my dad."

Any trace of kindness or sympathy vanished from Rixon's eyes. "Well, this is awkward."

"You were wearing Patch's hat that night. You borrowed it, didn't you? You couldn't kill my dad without assuming another identity. You couldn't do it unless you removed yourself from the situation," I said, drawing on everything I remembered from the psychology unit in my freshman health class. "No. Wait. That's not it. You pretended to be Patch because you wish you were him. You're jealous of him. That's it, isn't it? You'd rather be him—"

Rixon gripped my cheekbones, forcing me to stop. "*Shut up.*"

I recoiled, my jaw aching where he'd squeezed me. I wanted to fling myself at him, hitting him with everything I had, but knew I needed to stay calm. I needed to find out what I could. I was beginning to think Rixon hadn't brought me into the tunnels to help me escape. Worse, I was beginning to think he had no intention of ever taking me back up.

"Jealous of him?" he said cruelly. "Sure I'm jealous. He isn't the one on the fast track to hell. We were in this together, and now he's gone and gotten himself his wings back." His eyes raked over me in disgust. "Because of you."

I shook my head, not buying it. "You killed my dad before you even knew who I was."

He laughed, but it lacked humor. "I knew you were out there somewhere, and I was looking for you."

"Why?"

Rixon slipped the gun out from under his shirt and used it to motion deeper into the fun house. "Keep walking."

"Where are we going?"

He didn't answer.

"The police are on their way."

"Hang the police," Rixon said. "I'll be finished before they get here."

Finished?

Stay calm, I told myself. *Stall.* "You're going to kill me now that I know the truth? Now that I know you killed my dad?"

"Harrison Grey wasn't your dad."

I opened my mouth, but the argument I expected to come flying out didn't. The one image splayed across the forefront of my mind was of Marcie standing in her front yard, telling me Hank Millar could be my father. I felt my stomach heave. Did this mean Marcie was telling the truth? For sixteen years I'd been kept in the dark about the truth behind my family? I wondered if my dad had known—my real dad. Harrison Grey. The man who'd raised and loved me. Not my biological father, who'd abandoned me. Not Hank Millar, who could go to hell for all I cared.

"Your dad is a Nephil named Barnabas," Rixon said. "More recently, he goes by Hank Millar."

No.

I stepped sideways, dizzy with the truth. The dream. Patch's dream. It was a real memory. He hadn't been lying. Barnabas—Hank Millar—was Nephilim.

And he was my father.

My world threatened to crash down around me, but I forced myself to stay in the moment a little longer. In the far back of my mind, I shook my memory, frantically trying to remember where I'd heard the name Barnabas before. I couldn't place it, but I knew this wasn't the first time I'd heard it. It was too unusual to forget. Barnabas, Barnabas, Barnabas . . .

I grappled to fit two loose ends together. Why was Rixon telling me this? Why did he know about my biological father? Why did he care? And then it hit me. Once, when I'd touched Patch's scars and gone into his memory, I'd heard him talk about his Nephil vassal, Chauncey Langeais. He'd also talked about Rixon's vassal, Barnabas. . . .

"No," I whispered, the word slipping out.

"Aye."

I desperately wanted to run, but my legs were wooden, stiff as posts.

"When Hank got your mum pregnant, he'd heard enough rumors about the Book of Enoch to worry that I'd come looking for the baby, especially if it was a girl. So he did the only thing he could. He hid her. You. When Hank told his mate Harrison Grey that your mum was in trouble, he agreed to marry her and pretend you were his."

No, no, no. "But I'm descended from Chauncey. On my father's side. On Harrison Grey's side. I have a mark on my wrist that proves it."

"Aye, you do. Many centuries ago, Chauncey entertained a naive farm girl. She had a son. Nobody thought anything particular about the boy, or his sons, or their sons, and so on through the ages, until one of the sons slept with a woman outside of wedlock. He injected the noble Nephilim blood of his ancestor, the duke of Langeais, into another line. The line that eventually produced Barnabas, or Hank, as he seems to prefer recently." Rixon gestured impatiently for me to put two and two together. I already had.

"You're saying both Harrison and Hank have Chauncey's Nephilim blood," I said. And Hank, a purebred first-generation Nephil, was immortal, while my own dad's Nephilim blood, diluted over centuries just like mine, was not. Hank, a man I hardly knew and respected even less, could live forever.

While my dad was gone forever.

"I am, love."

"Don't call me love."

"You'd prefer Angel?"

He was making fun of me. Toying with me, because he had me right where he wanted. I'd been through this once before, with Patch, and I knew what was coming. Hank Millar was my biological father and Rixon's Nephil vassal. Rixon was going to sacrifice me to kill Hank Millar and get a human body.

"Do I get any last-minute answers?" I asked, my tone edging toward challenging, in spite of my fear.

He shrugged. "Why not?"

"I thought only first-generation purebred Nephilim could swear fealty. In order for Hank to be first-generation, he'd have to have a human and a fallen angel parent. But his father wasn't a fallen angel. He was one of Chauncey's male descendants."

"You're overlooking the fact that men can have affairs with female fallen angels."

I shook my head. "Fallen angels don't have human bodies. Females can't give birth. Patch told me."

"But a female fallen angel, possessing a female human body during Cheshvan, can produce a baby. The human may give birth to the baby long after Cheshvan, but the baby is tainted. It was conceived by a fallen angel."

"That's revolting."

He smiled faintly. "I agree."

"Out of morbid curiosity, when you sacrifice me, does your body just become human, or do you possess another human body for good?"

"I become human." His mouth curved slightly. "So if you come back to haunt me from the grave, just know you'll be looking for my same handsome mug."

"Patch could show up any minute now and stop you," I said, trying to be strong, but unable to stop the unbearable shaking in every limb of my body.

His eyes laughed at me. "I had my work cut out, but I'm confident I drove the wedge between the two of you about as deep as it could go. You got the ball rolling by breaking up with him—I couldn't have planned it better myself. Then there was the constant fighting, your jealousy over Marcie, and Patch's card—which I drugged to toss in just one more seed of distrust. When I stole the ring from Barnabas and had it delivered to you at the bakery, I had no doubt Patch was the last person you'd run to. Swallow your pride and ask for his help? When you thought he was hooked up with Marcie? Not a chance. You played right into my hands when you asked me if he was the Black Hand. I made the evidence against him overwhelming when I answered that yes, he was. Then I took advantage of the turn in our conversation to mention the address of one of Barnabas's Nephilim safe houses as Patch's, knowing full well you'd go snooping around and probably find memorabilia from the Black Hand. I canceled the movie plans last night, not Patch. I didn't want to be stuck inside a movie theater while you were all alone in the apartment. I needed to follow you. I planted the dynamite once you were inside, hoping to sacrifice you, but you got away."

"I'm touched, Rixon. A bomb. How elaborate. Why didn't you keep things simple and just march inside my bedroom one night and put a bullet between my eyes?"

He spread his hands in front of him. "This is a big moment for me, Nora. Can you blame me for wanting a little flourish? I tried posing as Harrison's ghost to lure you close, thinking how fantastic it would be to send you to the grave thinking your own father had killed you, but you didn't trust me. You kept running away." He frowned a little.

"You're a psychopath."

"I prefer creative."

"What else was a lie? At the beach, did you tell me Patch was still my guardian angel—"

"To lull you into a false sense of security? Yes."

"And the blood oath?"

"A spur-of-the-moment lie. Just to keep things interesting."

"So basically you're telling me nothing you've ever said to me was true."

"Except the part about sacrificing you. I was dead serious about that. Enough talking. Let's get on with this." Using the gun, he shoved me deeper into the fun house. The rough prod tipped me off balance, and I stepped sideways to catch my footing, landing on a section of floor that began undulating up and down. I felt Rixon grab for my wrist to steady me, only something went wrong. His hand slipped down over mine. I heard the soft thud of his body landing. The sound seemed to come from directly below. A thought brushed my mind—that he'd fallen down one of the many trapdoors rumored to be scattered throughout the fun house—but

I didn't stay around long enough to see if I'd guessed right.

I bolted back the way we'd come, searching for the clown head. A figure sprang out in front of me, a light flashing overhead to illuminate a blood-soaked ax wedged in a bearded pirate's head. He leered at me a moment before his eyes rolled back in his head and the light faded.

I drew several sharp breaths, telling myself it was pretend, but unable to steady myself as the floor quaked and shifted under my shoes. I went down on my knees, crawling over the grime and grit pressing into my palms, trying to calm my head, which seemed to tilt with the floors. I crawled for several feet, not wanting to stop moving long enough to let Rixon find a way out of the trapdoor.

"Nora!" Rixon's rough bark carried up behind me.

I pulled myself up, using the walls to support me, but the walls were coated in slime that oozed onto my hands. Somewhere overhead, laughter boomed, tapering off to a cackle. I shook my hands hard to slough off the slime. Then I fished my way into the sheer blackness that lay ahead. I was lost. Lost, lost, lost.

I jogged a few steps forward, rounded a turn, and squinted at the faint glow of orange light several yards down the path. It wasn't the clown's head, but I was drawn to the promise of light like a moth. When I reached the lantern, the tacky Halloweenish light illuminated the words TUNNEL OF DOOM. I was standing on a boat dock. Small plastic boats were parked nose-to-bumper, water from the canal lapping their sides.

I heard footsteps on the path behind me. With no time to

second-guess, I stepped into the boat closest to me. I'd just found my balance when the boat lurched into motion, jerking me down onto the slat of wood that served as a seat. The boats were moving in a single-file line, the tracks below clacking as they steered the boats into the tunnel ahead. A pair of saloon-style doors flung open, swallowing my boat into the tunnel.

Feeling my way to the front of the boat, I climbed over the safety bar and onto the bow. I stayed there a moment, one hand anchoring me to the boat, while my other hand reached ahead, trying to grab the rear bar of the boat one up. I was a few inches short. I would have to jump. I scooted up the bow as far as I dared. I tucked my legs under me, then leaped, managing to skid onto the back of the next boat up.

I allowed myself one moment of relief, then went back to work. Once again, I moved up the bow, with the intention of jumping boats all the way to the end of the ride. Rixon was bigger and faster, and he had a gun. My only hope of survival was to keep moving, to keep drawing out the time it took for him to catch me.

I was on the next bow, preparing to jump, when a siren blasted and the sudden illumination of a red light overhead blinded me. A skeleton dropped from the ceiling of the tunnel, smacking into me. I lost my footing and felt a wash of vertigo as I skidded sideways, overboard. Frigid water rushed through my clothes, closing over my head. Instantly I put my feet down, broke the water's surface, and waded through the chest-deep water back to the boat.

Gritting my teeth against the cold, I clamped my hands around the boat's safety bar and hauled myself back inside.

Several loud shots ricocheted through the tunnel, one of the bullets whizzing past my ear. I dropped low in the boat, while Rixon's laugh carried from a few boats back. "A matter of time," he called.

More lights were flashing overhead, and between the pulses of light, I could see Rixon making his way across the boats toward me.

A faint roar sounded somewhere ahead. My stomach slid out from beneath me. I felt my concentration peel away from Rixon and shift to the spray of moisture in the air. My heart stopped for a half moment, then started pounding much too hard.

Grabbing hold of the metal bar, I braced myself for the fall. The front of the boat tipped, then plunged over the waterfall. The boat splashed at the bottom, sending water spraying over the sides. The water might have felt cold, had I not already been drenched and shivering. I wiped my eyes dry, and that was when I saw a small maintenance platform carved out of the tunnel wall to my right. A door marked DANGER: HIGH VOLTAGE sat just back from the platform.

I looked back at the waterfall. Rixon's boat hadn't fallen yet, and with only seconds to spare, I made a risky decision. Jumping over the side of the boat, I waded as quickly as I could to the platform, hoisted myself up, and tried the door. It opened, letting out the loud hissing and clanking of machines, hundreds of gears churning and grinding. I'd found the mechanical heart of the fun house, and the entrance to the underground tunnels.

I closed the door most of the way behind me, leaving a thin crack to see out.

With one eye pressed to the crack, I watched the next boat fly down the waterfall. Rixon was in the boat. He was leaning over the metal sidebar, searching the water. Had he seen me jump out? Was he looking for me? His boat continued down the track, and he eased himself overboard, landing feetfirst in the water. Using his hands to hold his wet hair out of his face, he searched the murky surface of the water. It was then that I realized his hands were empty. He wasn't looking for me—he'd dropped the gun in the fall, and he was looking for it.

The tunnel was dark, and I found it impossible to believe Rixon could see all the way to the bottom of the canal. Which meant he was going to have to feel his way to the gun. That would take time. Of course, I needed more than time. I needed a stroke of impossible luck. The police had to be combing the park by now, but would they think to look in the underbelly of the fun house before it was too late?

I shut the door softly, hoping to find a lock on the inside, but there was none. Suddenly I wished I'd risked my chances making it out of the tunnel before Rixon, rather than circling back to hide. If Rixon came inside the service room, I was trapped.

Ragged breathing came from my left, behind an electrical box.

I swung around, eyes darting through the blackness. "Who's there?"

"Who do you think?"

I blinked against the shadows. "Scott?" I took several nervous steps backward.

"I got lost in the tunnels. I took a door, and came out in here."

"Are you still bleeding?"

"Yeah. Surprisingly, I'm not completely drained yet." His words were choppy, and I could tell it took a lot of energy for him to speak.

"You need a doctor."

He gave a spent laugh. "I need the ring."

At this point, I didn't know how serious Scott was about getting the ring back. He was exhausted with pain, and I was pretty sure we both knew he wasn't going to drag me out of here to hold as a hostage. He was weakened by the shot, but he was Nephilim. He would survive this. Working together, we had a chance at getting out. But before I could convince him to help me escape Rixon, I needed him to trust me.

I walked over to the electrical box and knelt down beside him. He had one hand pressed against his side, just below his rib cage, stopping the flow of blood. His face was the color of cornstarch, and the wasted look in his eyes proved what I already knew: He was in a lot of pain. "I don't believe you're going to use the ring to recruit new members," I said quietly. "You aren't going to force other people into the society."

Scott shook his head, agreeing with me. "There's something I need to tell you. Remember when I told you I was working the night your dad was shot?"

I vaguely remembered him telling me he'd been at work when he got the call about my dad's murder. "Where's this going?" I asked hesitantly.

"I worked at a convenience store called Quickies that was only a few blocks away." He paused, as if waiting for me to come to some grand conclusion. "I was supposed to follow your dad that night. The Black Hand told me to. He said your dad was on his way to a meeting, and I had to keep him safe."

"What are you saying?" I asked in a voice as dry as chalk.

"I didn't follow him." Scott bowed his face into his hands. "I wanted to show the Black Hand he couldn't order me around. I wanted to show him I wouldn't be part of his society. So I stayed at work. I didn't leave. I didn't follow your dad. And he died. He died because of me."

I slid my back down the wall until I was seated beside him. I couldn't speak. The right words weren't there.

"You hate me, don't you?" he asked.

"You didn't kill my dad," I said numbly. "It's not your fault."

"I knew he was in trouble. Why else would the Black Hand want to make sure he made it to the meeting safe? I should have gone. If I'd followed the Black Hand's orders, your dad would be alive."

"It's in the past," I whispered, trying not to let this information cause me to blame Scott. I needed his help. Together, we could get out of here. I couldn't allow myself to hate him. I had to work with him. I needed to trust him, and I needed him to trust me.

"Just because it's in the past doesn't mean it's easy to forget. Less than an hour after I was supposed to follow your dad, my dad called with the news."

Without meaning to, I made a small whimpering noise.

"Then the Black Hand came into the convenience store. He was wearing a mask, but I recognized his voice." Scott shuddered. "I'll never forget that voice. He gave me a gun and told me to make sure it never surfaced again. It was your dad's gun. He said he wanted the police report to say your dad died an innocent and unarmed man. He didn't want to put your family through the pain and confusion of knowing what really happened that night. He didn't want anyone to suspect your dad was involved with criminals like himself. He wanted it to look like a random mugging.

"I was supposed to toss the gun in the river, but I kept it. I wanted out of the society. The only way I saw that happening was if I had something I could use to blackmail the Black Hand. So I kept the gun. When my mom and I moved here, I left a message behind for the Black Hand. I told him if he came looking for me, I'd make sure the police got their hands on Harrison Grey's gun. I'd make sure the whole world knew he had ties to the Black Hand. I swore I'd drag your dad's name through the mud as many times as it took, if it meant I got my life back. I still have the gun." He opened his hands, and it dropped between his knees, clattering on the cement. "I still have it."

A dull and furious pain ricocheted through me.

"It was so hard to be around you," Scott said, his voice brittle. "I wanted to make you hate me. God knows I hated myself. Every time I saw you, all I could think about was that I chickened out. I could have saved your dad's life. I'm sorry," he said, his voice cracking.

"It's okay." I said it as much for myself as Scott. "Everything's going to be okay." But it felt like the worst lie yet.

Scott picked up the gun, fingering it. Before the whole moment made sense to me, I saw him raise it to his head. "I don't deserve to live," he said.

A veil of ice choked my heart. "Scott—," I began.

"Your family deserves this. I can't face you anymore. I can't face myself." His finger slid to the trigger.

There was no time to think. "You didn't kill my dad," I said. "Rixon did—Vee's boyfriend. He's a fallen angel. It's real, all of it. You're Nephilim, Scott. You can't kill yourself. Not this way. You're immortal. You're never going to die. If you want to make amends for any guilt you feel over my dad's death, help me get out of here. Rixon is on the other side of that door, and he's going to kill me. The only way I'm going to survive is if you help me."

Scott stared back wordlessly. Before he could answer, the service room door scraped open. Rixon appeared in the opening. He raked his hair off his forehead and cast his eyes around the small utility room. On an impulse of self-protection, I drew closer to Scott.

Rixon's gaze shifted from me to Scott.

"You're going to have to go through me before you get to her," Scott said, laying his left arm across me and shifting his weight to shield my body. He was breathing rapidly.

"No problem." Rixon raised his gun and fired several rounds into Scott. Scott slumped, his body lax against mine.

Tears streamed down my face. "Stop," I whispered.

"Don't cry, love. He's not dead. Make no mistake—he'll be in tremendous pain when he comes around, but that's the price you pay for a body. Get up and come here."

"Screw you." I didn't know where my courage was coming from, but if I was going to die, it wouldn't be without a fight. "You killed my dad. I'm not doing anything for you. If you want me, come and get me yourself."

Rixon brushed his thumb across his mouth. "I don't see why you're so worked up about it. Technically, Harrison wasn't your dad."

"You killed my *dad*," I repeated, meeting Rixon's eyes, feeling anger so sharp and slicing, it seemed to eat its way out of me.

"Harrison Grey killed himself. He should have stayed out of the picture."

"He was trying to save another man's life!"

"A man?" Rixon snorted, rolling his wet sleeves up to his

elbows. "I'd hardly call Hank Millar a man. He's Nephilim. An animal, more like it."

I laughed, actually laughed, but it seemed to swell like a bubble in my throat, choking me. "You know what? I almost feel sorry for you."

"Funny, I was just about to say the same thing to you."

"You're going to kill me now, aren't you?" I expected the realization to draw another measure of fear from deep inside me, but all my fear was spent. I felt a certain frozen calm. Time didn't slow down, and it didn't speed up. It looked me right in the eye, as cold and unemotional as the gun Rixon was now pointing at me.

"No, not kill. I'm going to sacrifice you." His mouth curled up on one side. "Makes a world of difference."

I tried to run, but the searing fire exploded, and my body was thrown back against the wall. The pain was everywhere, and I opened my mouth to scream, but it was too late. An invisible blanket suffocated me beneath its folds. I watched Rixon's smiling face swim in and out of focus while I clawed uselessly at the blanket. My lungs expanded, threatening to burst, and just when I thought I couldn't stand it any longer, my chest went soft. Over Rixon's shoulder, I saw Patch move into the doorway.

I tried to call out to him, but the desperate need to draw air dissolved.

It was over.

25

"Nora?"

I tried to open my eyes, but while my brain relayed the message, my body wasn't listening. A slur of voices drifted in and out. Somewhere in the back of my mind I knew the night was warm, but I felt bathed in cold sweat. And something else. Blood.

My blood.

"You're okay," Detective Basso said as I cried out, my voice sounding strangled. "I'm right here. I'm not going anywhere. Stay with me, Nora. Everything is going to be fine."

I tried to nod, but still felt as if I existed somewhere outside my body.

"Paramedics are taking you to the ER. They've got you on a gurney. We're on our way out of Delphic right now."

A few hot tears tumbled down my cheeks, and I blinked my eyes open. "Rixon." My tongue felt slippery, the words stumbling out. "Where's Rixon?"

Detective Basso's mouth pinched at the edges. "Shh. Don't talk. You took the bullet in the arm. Flesh wound. You got lucky. Everything's going to be fine."

"Scott?" I said, just now remembering. I tried to raise myself up, but found I was strapped down. "Did you get Scott out?"

"Scott was with you?"

"Behind the electrical box. He's hurt. Rixon shot him, too."

Detective Basso yelled at one of the uniformed officers standing off to the side of the ambulance, and he jumped to life, striding over. "Yes, sir, Detective?"

"She says Scott Parnell was in the mechanical room."

The officer shook his head. "We searched the room. Nobody else was in there."

"Well, search it again!" Detective Basso shouted, flinging his arm at Delphic's gates. He turned to me. "Who the hell is Rixon?"

Rixon. If the police had found no one else in the mechanical

room, it meant he'd escaped. He was out there somewhere, probably watching from a distance, waiting for his second chance at me.
I grappled for Detective Basso's hand, clutching it. "Don't leave me
alone."

"Nobody's leaving you alone. What can you tell me about
Rixon?"

The gurney bounced across the parking lot, and the paramedics hoisted me into the back of the ambulance. Detective
Basso pulled himself up, taking a seat beside me. I barely noticed;
my attention had run off in another direction. I had to talk to
Patch. I had to tell him about Rixon—

"What does he look like?"

The sound of Detective Basso's voice yanked me back. "He was
there. Last night. He tied Scott in the back of his truck."

"That guy shot you?" Detective Basso spoke into his radio. "Suspect's name is Rixon. Tall and skinny, black hair. Hawk nose. Age
twenty, give or take."

"How did you find me?" My memory was slowly sewing itself
back together, and I remembered seeing Patch step into the doorway to the mechanical room. It was only for a split second, but he
was there. I was sure of it. Where was he now? Where was Rixon?

"Anonymous tip. The caller told me I'd find you in the service
room at the bottom of the Tunnel of Doom. It seemed like a long
shot, but I couldn't ignore it. He also said he'd take care of the
guy who shot you. I thought he was referring to Scott, but you tell

me Rixon is responsible. Want to tell me what's going on? Starting with the name of this guy who's got your back, and where I can find him?"

Hours later, Detective Basso slowed against the curb in front of the farmhouse. It was edging up toward two in the morning, and the windows reflected the starless sky. I'd been released from the ER, cleaned and bandaged. While the hospital staff had spoken with my mom over the phone, I hadn't. I knew I was going to have to talk to her sooner or later, but the hustle and bustle of the hospital hadn't seemed like the right place, and I'd shaken my head no at the nurse when she'd held out the phone to me.

I'd also given my statement to the police. I was pretty sure Detective Basso thought I'd hallucinated seeing Scott in the mechanical room. I was pretty sure he thought I was withholding information on Rixon, too. He was right about the latter, but even if I told Detective Basso everything, he wasn't going to find Rixon. Patch clearly had, however—or at least had made it known that was his plan. But I knew nothing beyond that. I'd carried my heart in my throat since leaving Delphic, wondering where Patch was, and what had happened after I blacked out.

We swung out of the car, and Detective Basso walked me to the door.

"Thanks again," I told him. "For everything."

"Call if you need me."

Inside, I flicked on the lights. In the bathroom, I peeled out of my clothes, my progress hampered by the fact that the upper half of my left arm was swathed in bandages. The tang of fear and panic was fresh on my clothes, and I left them in a heap on the floor. After wrapping my bandages in plastic, I climbed into the steam of the shower.

As the hot water drummed down on me, scenes from earlier tonight replayed in bursts across my mind. I pretended the water could wash away all of it, carrying everything I'd been through down the drain. It was over. All of it. But there was one thing I couldn't wash away. The Black Hand.

If Patch wasn't the Black Hand, who was? And how did Rixon, a fallen angel, know so much about him?

Twenty minutes later, I toweled off and checked the home phone for messages. One call from Enzo's, seeing if I could take a shift tonight. An irate call from Vee demanding to know where I was. The police had kicked her out of the parking lot and closed down the amusement park—but not before telling her they could personally assure her that I was safe, and would she please drive home and stay there? She ended the call by shouting, "If I missed out on some really big action, I'm going to be royally pissed off!"

The third message was from an unknown caller, but I recognized Scott's voice the minute he started talking. "If you tell the police about this message, I'll be long gone before they track me down. Just wanted to say sorry one more time." He paused, and I heard a smile inch into his voice. "Since I know you're worried sick about me, I thought I'd let you know I'm healing, and I'll be good as new in no time. Thanks for the tip regarding my, uh, *health*."

A tiny smile broke inside me, and the weight of the unknown lifted. Scott was okay after all.

"It was nice knowing you, Nora Grey. Who knows. Maybe this isn't the last you'll hear of me. Maybe we'll cross paths in the future." Another pause. "One more thing. I sold the Mustang. Too conspicuous. Don't get too excited, but I bought you a little something with the extra cash. I heard you've had your eye on a Volkswagen. The owner is dropping it by tomorrow. I paid for a full tank of gas, so make sure she delivers."

The message ended, but I was still staring at the phone. The Volkswagen? For *me*? I was dazed with delight and baffled surprise. A car. Scott had bought me a car. In an attempt to return the favor, I deleted the message, erasing all evidence he'd ever called. If the police found Scott, it wouldn't be because of me. Somehow, I didn't think they'd find him anyway.

Phone in hand, I called my mom. I wasn't going to put this off any longer. I'd come too close to death tonight. I was amending my life, cleaning out and starting fresh, and I was doing it now. The only thing left standing in my way was this call.

"Nora?" she answered in a panicked voice. "I got the detective's message. I'm on my way home right now. Are you all right? Tell me you're all right!"

I drew a shaky breath. "I am now."

"Oh, baby, I love you so much. You know that, right?" she sobbed.

"I know the truth."

A pause.

"I know the truth about what really happened sixteen years ago," I said more clearly.

"What are you talking about? I'm almost home. I haven't been able to stop shaking since I hung up with the detective. I'm a wreck, an absolute wreck. Do they have any idea who this guy—this Rixon—is? What he wanted with you? I don't understand how you got dragged into this."

"Why couldn't you have just told me?" I whispered, tears brimming my eyes.

"Baby?"

"Nora." I'm not a little girl anymore. "All those years you lied to me. All those times I went off on Marcie. All those times we laughed at the Millars for being stupid and rich and tactless—" My voice caught.

I'd been brimming with anger earlier, but I didn't know how to feel now. Upset? Weary? Lost and all in a jumble? My parents had started out doing Hank Millar a favor, but obviously grew to love each other . . . and me. We'd made things work. We'd been happy. My dad was gone now, but he still thought about me. He still cared about me. He would want me to keep what was left of our family together instead of running away from my mom.

It's what I wanted too.

I sucked in some air. "When you get home, we need to talk. About Hank Millar."

I microwaved a mug of hot chocolate and carried it to my bedroom. My first reaction was to feel fear over being all alone in the farmhouse, knowing Rixon could be running free. My second reaction was a quiet calm. I couldn't say why, but somehow, I knew I was safe. I tried to remember what had happened in the mechanical room moments before I fell unconscious. Patch had walked into the room. . . .

And then I drew a blank. Which was frustrating, because I sensed more to the memory. It danced just out of reach, but I knew it was important.

After a while, I gave up trying to recapture the memory, and my thoughts took a sharp, alarming turn. My biological father was alive. Hank Millar had given me life, then given me up to protect me. Right now, I had no desire to contact him. It was too painful to even think about approaching him. It would be admitting he was my father, and I didn't want that. It was hard enough keeping my real dad's face in my memory; I didn't want to replace that picture or fade it any faster than it already would. No, I'd leave Hank Millar right where he was—at a distance. I wondered if someday I'd change my mind, and the possibility terrified me. Not only the fact that I had a whole other life hidden away, but the fact that once I uncovered it, the life I currently had would be altered forever.

I didn't have any desire to dwell on Hank further, but there was one thing still not adding up. Hank hid me away as a baby to protect me from Rixon because I was a girl. But what about Marcie? My—sister. She had as much of his blood as I did. Then why didn't he hide her? I tried reasoning it out in my head, but I didn't have an answer.

I'd just curled under the blankets when there was a knock at the door. I set the mug of hot chocolate on the nightstand. There weren't too many people who would be stopping by this late at night. I padded downstairs and peered into the peephole. But I didn't need the peephole to confirm who stood on the other side of the door. I knew it was Patch from the way my heart couldn't carry a steady rhythm.

I opened the door. "You told Detective Basso where to find me. You stopped Rixon from shooting me."

Patch's dark eyes assessed me. For half a moment, I saw a string of emotions play out inside them. Exhaustion, worry, relief. He smelled of rust, stale cotton candy, and dank water, and I knew he'd been close by when Detective Basso found me in the heart of the fun house. He'd been right there the whole time, making sure I was safe.

He wrapped his arms around me and held me tight, clutching me against him. "I thought I got there too late. I thought you were dead."

I curled my hands into the front of his shirt and bent my head against his chest. I didn't care that I was crying. I was safe, and Patch was here. Nothing else mattered.

"How did you find me?" I asked.

"I'd thought for a while it was Rixon," he said quietly. "But I had to make sure."

I looked up. "You knew Rixon wanted to kill me?"

"I kept picking up clues, but I didn't want to believe them. Rixon and I were friends—" Patch's voice cracked. "I didn't want to believe he'd cross me. When I was your guardian angel, I sensed someone was out to kill you. I didn't know who, because they were being careful. They weren't actively meditating on killing you, so I wasn't getting much of a picture. I knew a human wouldn't cover their thoughts that carefully. They wouldn't know their thoughts were transmitting all kinds of information to angels. Every now and then I'd get a flash of insight. Little things that made me look at Rixon, even though I didn't want to. I set him up with Vee so I could keep a closer watch on him. Also because I didn't want to give him any reason to think I was onto him. I knew the only reason he'd kill you was for a human body, so I started digging into Barnabas's past. That's when I figured out the truth. Rixon was two steps ahead of me, but he must have found out after I tracked you down and enrolled in school last year. He wanted to sacrifice you as much as I did. He did everything he could to convince me to give up on the Book of Enoch so I wouldn't kill you and he could."

"Why didn't you tell me he was trying to kill me?"

"I couldn't. You fired me as your guardian angel. I physically couldn't intervene in your life when it came to your safety. The archangels blocked me every time I tried. But I found a way around them. I figured out I could make you see my memories while you were sleeping. I tried to give you the information you'd need to figure out Hank Millar was your biological dad, and Rixon's Nephilim vassal. I know you think I abandoned you when you needed me most, but I never gave up searching for a way to warn you about Rixon." His mouth tugged up on one side, but it was a tired gesture. "Even when you kept blocking me."

I realized I was holding my breath and slowly released it. "Where is Rixon now?"

"I sent him to hell. He's never coming back." Patch stared straight ahead, his eyes hard, but not angry. Disappointed, maybe. Wishing for a different outcome. But underneath it all, I suspected he was suffering more than he let on. He'd sent his closest friend, and the one person who'd been at his side through everything, to face an eternity of darkness.

"I'm so sorry," I whispered.

We stood in silence a moment, both of us replaying our own image of Rixon's fate in our heads. I hadn't seen it firsthand, but the image I conjured up was gruesome enough to send a shudder right through me.

Finally Patch said in my thoughts, *I've gone rogue, Nora. As soon* as the archangels figure it out, they'll come looking for me. You were right. I don't really care about breaking rules.

I felt the mad impulse to push Patch out the door. His words drummed in my head. Rogue? The first place the archangels would look was here. Was he being deliberately careless? "Are you crazy?" I said.

"Crazy about you."

"Patch!"

"Don't worry, we've got time."

"How do you know?"

He staggered back a step, with his hand over his heart. "Your lack of faith hurts."

I only looked more sternly at him. "When did you do it? When did you go rogue?"

Earlier tonight. I dropped by here to make sure you were safe. I knew Rixon was at Delphic, and when I saw the note on your counter saying that's where you'd gone, I knew he was going to make his move. I broke with the archangels and went after you. If I hadn't broken with them, Angel, I physically couldn't have stepped in. Rixon would have won.

"Thank you," I whispered.

Patch held me tighter. I wanted to stay in his embrace and ignore everything but the feel of his strong, solid body, yet there were questions that couldn't wait.

"Does this mean you'll no longer be Marcie's guardian angel?" I asked.

I felt Patch smile. "I'm a private contractor now. I choose my clients, not the other way around."

"Why did Hank hide me but not Marcie?" I turned my face into his shirt so he wouldn't see my eyes. I didn't care about Hank. Not at all. He was nothing to me, and yet, in a secret place in my heart, I wanted him to love me as much as Marcie. I was his daughter too. But all I saw was that he'd chosen Marcie over me. He'd sent me away and doted on her.

"I don't know." It was so quiet I could hear him breathing. "Marcie doesn't have your mark. Hank does, and Chauncey did. I don't think it's a coincidence, Angel."

My eyes traveled to the inside of my right wrist, to the dark slash that people often mistook as a scar. I'd always thought the birthmark was unique. Until I met Chauncey. And now Hank. I had a feeling the meaning behind the mark went deeper than linking me biologically to Chauncey's bloodline, and it was a frightening thought.

"You're safe with me," Patch murmured, caressing my arms.

After a beat of silence, I said, "Where does this leave us?"

"Together." He lifted his eyebrows in question and crossed his fingers, as if begging for luck.

"We fight a lot," I said.

"We also make up a lot." Patch reached for my hand and pushed my dad's ring off the tip of his finger and into my palm, curling my fingers around it. He kissed my knuckles. "I was going to give this back earlier, but it wasn't finished."

I opened my palm and held the ring up. The same heart was engraved on the underside, but now there were two names carved on either side of it: NORA and JEV.

I looked up. "Jev? That's your real name?"

"Nobody's called me that in a long time." He stroked his finger across my lip, assessing me with his soft black eyes.

Desire melted through me, hot and urgent.

Apparently feeling the same way, Patch shut the door and turned the lock. He flipped the main light off, and the room settled into darkness, lit only by the moonlight sifting through the drapes. At the same time, our eyes shifted to the sofa.

"My mom's coming home soon," I said. "We should go to your place."

Patch ran a hand across the shadow of stubble along his jaw. "I have rules about who I take there."

I was getting really tired of that answer.

"If you showed me, you'd have to kill me?" I guessed, fighting the urge to feel irritated. "Once I'm inside, I can never leave?"

Patch studied me a moment. Then he reached into his pocket, twisted a key off his key chain, and slipped it into the front pocket of my pajama top.

"Once you've gone inside, you have to keep coming back."

Forty minutes later, I discovered which door the key unlocked. Patch pulled the Jeep into Delphic amusement park's vacant parking lot. We crossed the lot hand in hand, a cool summer breeze tangling my hair in my face. Patch creaked the gate open, holding it while I passed through.

Delphic had a completely different feel without the barrage of noise and carnival lights. A quiet, haunted, magical place. A discarded soda can scraped the pavement as the breeze pushed it along. Sticking to the walkway, I kept my eyes fastened on the dark skeleton of the Archangel rising up against the black sky. The air smelled like rain. A distant grumble of thunder reeled overhead.

Just north of the Archangel, Patch pulled me off the walkway. We climbed the steps to a utility shed. He unlocked the door just as a pattering of rain spilled from the sky, dancing on the pavement. The door swung shut behind me, shrouding us in stormy darkness. The park was eerily quiet, except for the steady rat-a-tat of rain splattering the roof. I felt Patch move behind me, his hands on my waist, his voice soft in my ear.

"Delphic was built by fallen angels, and is the one place the archangels won't go near. It's just you and me tonight, Angel."

I turned, absorbing the heat of his body. Patch tipped my chin up and kissed me. The kiss was warm and sent a shiver of pleasure through me. His hair was damp from rain, and I could smell a faint trace of soap. Our mouths slipped over each other, our skin slick with rain that dripped through the low ceiling, sprinkling us with little pricks of cold. Patch's arms enveloped me, holding me with an intensity that only made me want to sink deeper into him.

He sucked some of the rain from my bottom lip, and I felt his mouth smile against mine. He swept my hair aside and kissed me just above the collarbone. He nibbled at my ear, then sank his teeth into my shoulder.

I hung my fingertips on his waistband, tugging him closer.

Patch buried his face in the curve of my shoulder, his hands flexing over my back. He gave a low groan. "I love you," he murmured into my hair. "I'm happier right now than I ever remember being."

"How very touching." A deep voice carried out of the darkest part of the shed, along the back wall. "Seize the angel."

A handful of overly tall young men, undoubtedly Nephilim, came out of the shadows and surrounded Patch, twisting his arms behind his back. To my confusion, Patch let them do it without resistance.

When I start fighting, run, Patch spoke to my thoughts, and I realized he'd stalled fighting to speak to me, to help me find a way out. *I'll distract them. You run. Take the Jeep. Do you remember how to hot-wire it? Don't go home. Stay in the Jeep until I find you—*

The man who lingered at the back of the shed, commanding the others, stepped forward into a hazy ray of light slicing through one of the shed's many cracks. He was tall, lean, handsome, unnaturally young-looking for his age, and dressed impeccably in a white country-club polo and cotton twill trousers.

"Mr. Millar," I whispered. I couldn't think of anything else to call him. Hank seemed too informal; Dad seemed revoltingly intimate.

"Let me introduce myself properly," he said. "I'm the Black Hand. I knew your father Harrison well. I'm glad he's not here now to see you debasing yourself with one of the devil's brood." He wagged his head. "You're not the girl I thought you'd grow up to be, Nora. Fraternizing with the enemy, making a mockery of your heritage. I believe you even blew up one of my Nephilim safe houses last night. But no matter. I can forgive that." He paused with significance. "Tell me, Nora. Was it you who killed my dear friend Chauncey Langeais?"

Read on for a sneak peek at Becca Fitzpatrick's brand new and chilling thriller . . .

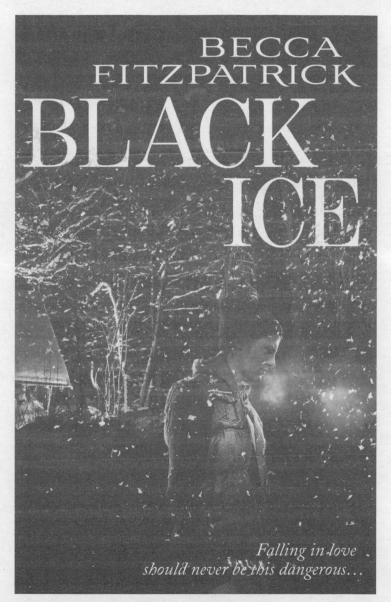

BECCA
FITZPATRICK

BLACK ICE

*Falling in love
should never be this dangerous . . .*

Hot. Cold. Deadly.

Released October 2014

The door chimed and my fake boyfriend strolled inside. He was even better-looking up close. And his eyes were most definitely brown—a weathered brown that reminded me of driftwood. He reached into his back pocket for his wallet, and I grabbed Calvin's arm and hauled him behind a shelf stacked with Fig Newtons and Oreos.

"What are we doing?" Calvin asked, staring at me like I'd sprouted two heads.

"I don't want him to see me," I whispered.

"Because he's not really your boyfriend, right?"

"That's not it. It's—"

Where was a third lie when I needed it?

Cal smiled devilishly, and the next thing I knew, he had shaken off my hand and was ambling toward the front counter. I trapped a groan between my teeth and watched, peering between the two top shelves.

"Hey," Calvin said affably to the guy, who wore a buffalo-check flannel shirt, jeans, and hiking boots.

With barely a glance up, the guy tipped his head in acknowledgment.

"I hear you're dating my ex," Calvin said, and there was something undeniably smug in his tone. He was giving me a taste of my own medicine, and he knew it.

Calvin's remark drew the full attention of the guy. He studied Calvin curiously, and I felt my cheeks grow even hotter.

"You know, *your girlfriend*," Calvin prodded. "Hiding behind the cookies over there."

He was pointing at me.

I straightened, my head surfacing above the top shelf. I smoothed my shirt and opened my mouth, but there were no words. No words at all.

The guy looked beyond Calvin to me. Our gazes locked briefly, and I mouthed a humiliated I *can explain* . . . But I couldn't.

Then something unexpected happened. The guy looked squarely at Calvin, and said in an easy, unruffled voice, "Yeah. My girlfriend. Britt."

I flinched. *He knew my name?*

Calvin appeared similarly startled. "Oh. Hey. Sorry, man. I thought—" He stuck out his hand. "I'm Calvin Versteeg," he stammered awkwardly. "Britt's . . . ex."

"Mason."

Mason eyed Calvin's outstretched hand but didn't take it. He placed three twenties on the counter for Willie Hennessey. Then he crossed to me and kissed my cheek. It was a no-frills kiss, but my pulse thrummed just the same.